THE COLLECTED
SHORT STORIES
OF LOUIS L'AMOUR

Bantam Books by Louis L'Amour

NOVELS
Bendigo Shafter
Borden Chantry
Brionne
The Broken Gun
The Burning Hills
The Californios
Callaghen
Catlow
Chancy
The Cherokee Trail
Comstock Lode
Conagher
Crossfire Trail
Dark Canyon
Down the Long Hills
The Empty Land
Fair Blows the Wind
Fallon
The Ferguson Rifle
The First Fast Draw
Flint
Guns of the Timberlands
Hanging Woman Creek
The Haunted Mesa
Heller with a Gun
The High Graders
High Lonesome
Hondo
How the West Was Won
The Iron Marshal
The Key-Lock Man
Kid Rodelo
Kilkenny
Killoe
Kilrone
Kiowa Trail
Last of the Breed
Last Stand at Papago Wells
The Lonesome Gods
The Man Called Noon
The Man from Skibbereen
The Man from the Broken
    Hills
Matagorda
Milo Talon
The Mountain Valley War
North to the Rails
Over on the Dry Side
Passin' Through
The Proving Trail

The Quick and the Dead
Radigan
Reilly's Luck
The Rider of Lost Creek
Rivers West
The Shadow Riders
Shalako
Showdown at Yellow
    Butte
Silver Canyon
Sitka
Son of a Wanted Man
Taggart
The Tall Stranger
To Tame a Land
Tucker
Under the Sweetwater Rim
Utah Blaine
The Walking Drum
Westward the Tide
Where the Long Grass
    Blows

SHORT STORY
    COLLECTIONS
Beyond the Great Snow
    Mountains
Bowdrie
Bowdrie's Law
Buckskin Run
The Collected Short Stories
    of Louis L'Amour
    (vols. 1–7)
Dutchman's Flat
End of the Drive
From the Listening Hills
The Hills of Homicide
Law of the Desert Born
Long Ride Home
Lonigan
May There Be a Road
Monument Rock
Night over the Solomons
Off the Mangrove Coast
The Outlaws of Mesquite
The Rider of the Ruby
    Hills
Riding for the Brand
The Strong Shall Live
The Trail to Crazy Man
Valley of the Sun
War Party

West from Singapore
West of Dodge
With These Hands
Yondering

SACKETT TITLES
Sackett's Land
To the Far Blue
    Mountains
The Warrior's Path
Jubal Sackett
Ride the River
The Daybreakers
Sackett
Lando
Mojave Crossing
Mustang Man
The Lonely Men
Galloway
Treasure Mountain
Lonely on the Mountain
Ride the Dark Trail
The Sackett Brand
The Sky-Liners

THE HOPALONG CASSIDY
    NOVELS
The Riders of High Rock
The Rustlers of West Fork
The Trail to Seven Pines
Trouble Shooter

NONFICTION
Education of a
    Wandering Man
Frontier
THE SACKETT COMPANION:
    A Personal Guide to the
    Sackett Novels
A TRAIL OF MEMORIES:
    The Quotations of
    Louis L'Amour,
    compiled by
    Angelique L'Amour

POETRY
Smoke from This Altar

LOST TREASURES
Louis L'Amour's Lost
    Treasures: Volume 1
No Traveller Returns

THE
COLLECTED
SHORT STORIES
OF
LOUIS L'AMOUR

FRONTIER STORIES
Volume 3

Louis L'Amour

BANTAM BOOKS
NEW YORK

2015 Bantam Books Mass Market Edition

Copyright © 2005 by Louis & Katherine L'Amour Trust

Excerpt from *Law of the Desert Born, A Graphic Novel,* by Louis L'Amour copyright © 2013 by Beau L'Amour and Louis L'Amour Enterprises, Inc.

All rights reserved.

Published in the United States by Bantam Books, an imprint of Random House, a division of Random House LLC, a Penguin Random House Company, New York.

BANTAM BOOKS and the HOUSE colophon are registered trademarks of Random House LLC.

Originally published in hardcover in the United States by Bantam Books, an imprint of Random House, a division of Random House LLC, in 2005.

ISBN 978-0-8041-7973-7
eBook ISBN 978-0-553-90078-1

Cover design: Scott Biel
Cover art: *Carson's Men* by Charles Russel /
Gilcrease Museum, Tulsa, OK

Photograph of Louis L'Amour by John Hamilton—Globe Photos, Inc.

Printed in the United States of America

www.bantamdell.com

16 18 19 17 15

Bantam Books mass market edition: January 2015

CONTENTS

Riding for the Brand   1
Four-Card Draw   31
One Last Gun Notch   53
Shandy Takes the Hook   63
A Night at Wagon Camp   76
Six-Gun Stampede   94
Valley of the Sun   105
Fork Your Own Broncs   122
Pardner from the Rio   138
The Guns Talk Loud   157
Squatters on the Lonetree   170
That Slash Seven Kid   188
Home in the Valley   206
Red Butte Showdown   224
Jackson of Horntown   238
Ride or Start Shootin'   255
Regan of the Slash B   280
Lonigan   298
Lit a Shuck for Texas   320
West of Dry Creek   339
There's Always a Trail   356
We Shaped the Land with Our Guns   374
To Hang Me High   396
West of Dodge   410
Monument Rock   428
A Gun for Kilkenny   519
In Victorio's Country   526
That Packsaddle Affair   543
About Louis L'Amour   559

THE COLLECTED
SHORT STORIES OF
LOUIS L'AMOUR

RIDING FOR THE BRAND

H E HAD BEEN watching the covered wagon for more than an hour. There had been no movement, no sound. The bodies of the two animals that had drawn the wagon lay in the grass, plainly visible. Farther away, almost a mile away, stood a lone buffalo bull, black against the gray distance.

Nothing moved near the wagon, but Jed Asbury had lived too long in Indian country to risk his scalp on appearances, and he knew an Indian could lie ghost-still for hours on end. He had no intention of taking such a chance, stark naked and without weapons.

Two days before, he had been stripped to the hide by Indians and forced to run the gauntlet, but he had run better than they had expected and had escaped with only a few minor wounds.

Now, miles away, he had reached the limit of his endurance. Despite little water and less food he was still in traveling condition except for his feet. They were lacerated and swollen, caked with dried blood.

Warily, he started forward, taking advantage of every bit of cover and moving steadily toward the wagon. When he was within fifty feet he settled down in the grass to study the situation.

This was the scene of an attack. Evidently the wagon had been alone, and the bodies of two men and a woman lay stretched on the grass.

Clothing, papers, and cooking utensils were scattered, evidence of a hasty looting. Whatever had been the dreams of these people they were ended now, another sacrifice to the westward march of empire. And the dead would not begrudge him what he needed.

Rising from the grass he went cautiously to the wagon, a tall, powerfully muscled young man, unshaven and untrimmed.

He avoided the bodies. Oddly, they were not mutilated, which was unusual, and the men still wore their boots. As a last resort he would take a pair for himself. First, he must examine the wagon.

If Indians had looted the wagon they had done so hurriedly, for the interior of the wagon was in the wildest state of confusion. In the bottom of a trunk he found a fine black broadcloth suit as well as a new pair of hand-tooled leather boots, a woolen shirt, and several white shirts.

"Somebody's Sunday-go-to-meetin' outfit," he muttered. "Hadn't better try the boots on, the way my feet are swollen."

He found clean underwear and dressed, putting on some rougher clothes that he found in the same chest. When he was dressed enough to protect him from the sun he took water from a half-empty barrel on the side of the wagon and bathed his feet; then he bandaged them with strips of white cloth torn from a dress.

His feet felt much better, and as the boots were a size larger than he usually wore, he tried them. There was some discomfort, but he could wear them.

With a shovel tied to the wagon's side he dug a grave and buried the three side by side, covered them with quilts from the wagon, filled in the earth, and piled stones over the grave. Then, hat in hand, he recited the Twenty-third Psalm.

The savages or whoever had killed them had made only a hasty search, so now he went to the wagon to find whatever might be useful to him or might inform him as to the identity of the dead.

There were some legal papers, a will, and a handful of letters. Putting these to one side with a poncho he found, he spotted a sewing basket. Remembering his grandmother's habits he emptied out the needles and thread, and under the padded bottom of the basket he found a large sealed envelope.

Ripping it open he grunted with satisfaction. Wrapped in carefully folded tissue paper were twenty twenty-dollar gold pieces. Pocketing them, he delved deeper into the trunk. He found more carefully folded clothes. Several times he broke off his searching of the wagon to survey the country about, but saw nothing. The wagon was in a concealed situation where a rider might have passed within a few yards and not seen it. He seemed to have approached from the only angle from which it was visible.

In the very bottom of the trunk he struck paydirt. He found a steel box. With a pick he forced it open. Inside, on folded velvet, lay a magnificent set of pistols, silver plated and beautifully engraved, with pearl handles. Wrapped in a towel nearby he found a pair of black leather cartridge belts and twin holsters. With them was a sack of .44 cartridges. Promptly, he loaded the guns and then stuffed the loops of both cartridge belts. After that he tried the balance of the guns. The rest of the cartridges he dropped into his pockets.

In another fold of the cloth he found a pearl-handled knife of beautifully tempered steel, a Spanish fighting knife and a beautiful piece of work. He slung the scabbard around his neck with the haft just below his collar.

Getting his new possessions together he made a pack of the clothing inside the poncho and used string to make a backpack of it. In the inside pocket of the coat he stowed the legal papers and the letters. In his hip pocket he stuffed a small leather-bound book he found among the scattered contents of the wagon. He read little, but knew the value of a good book.

He had had three years of intermittent schooling, learning to read, write, and cipher a little.

There was a canteen and he filled it. Rummaging in the wagon he found the grub box almost empty, a little coffee, some moldy bread, and nothing else useful. He took the coffee, a small pot, and a tin cup. Then he glanced at the sun and started away.

Jed Asbury was accustomed to fending for himself. That there could be anything wrong in appropriating what he had found never entered his head, nor would it have entered the head of any other man at the time. Life was hard, and one lived as best one might. If the dead had any heirs, there would be a clue in the letters or the will. He would pay them when he could. No man would begrudge him taking what was needed to survive, but to repay the debt incurred was a foregone conclusion.

Jed had been born on an Ohio farm, his parents dying when he was ten years old. He had been sent to a crabbed uncle living in a Maine fishing village. For three years his uncle worked him like a slave, sending him out on the Banks with a fishing boat. Finally, Jed had abandoned the boat, deep-sea fishing, and his uncle.

He walked to Boston and by devious methods reached Philadelphia. He had run errands, worked in a mill, and then gotten a job as a printer's devil. He had grown to like a man who came often to the shop, a quiet man with dark hair and large gray eyes, his head curiously wide across the temples. The man wrote stories and literary criticism and occasionally loaned Jed books to read. His name was Edgar Poe and he was reported to be the foster son of John Allan, said to be the richest man in Virginia.

When Jed left the print shop it was to ship on a windjammer for a voyage around the Horn. From San Francisco he had gone to Australia for a year in the goldfields, and then to South Africa and back to New York. He was twenty then and a big, well-made young man hardened by the life he had lived. He had gone west on a riverboat and then down the Mississippi to Natchez and New Orleans.

In New Orleans Jem Mace had taught him to box. Until then all he had known about fighting had been acquired by applying it that way. From New Orleans he had gone to Havana, to Brazil, and then back to the States. In Natchez he had caught a cardsharp cheating. Jed Asbury had proved a bit quicker, and the gambler died, a victim of six-shooter justice. Jed left town just ahead of several of the gambler's irate companions.

On a Missouri River steamboat he had gone up to Fort Benton and then overland to Bannock. He had traveled with wagon freighters to Laramie and then to Dodge.

In Tascosa he had encountered a brother of the dead

Natchez gambler accompanied by two of the irate companions. He had killed two of his enemies and wounded the other, coming out of the fracas with a bullet in his leg. He traveled on to Santa Fe.

At twenty-four he was footloose and looking for a destination. Working as a bullwhacker he made a round-trip to Council Bluffs and then joined a wagon train for Cheyenne. The Comanches, raiding north, had interfered, and he had been the sole survivor.

He knew about where he was now, somewhere south and west of Dodge, but probably closer to Santa Fe than to the trail town. He should not be far from the cattle trail leading past Tascosa, so he headed that way. Along the river bottoms there should be strays lost from previous herds, so he could eat until a trail herd came along.

Walking a dusty trail in the heat, he shifted his small pack constantly and kept turning to scan the country over which he had come. He was in the heart of Indian country.

On the morning of the third day he sighted a trail herd, headed for Kansas. As he walked toward the herd, two of the three horsemen riding point turned toward him.

One was a lean, red-faced man with a yellowed mustache and a gleam of quizzical humor around his eyes. The other was a stocky, friendly rider on a paint horse.

"Howdy!" The older man's voice was amused. "Out for a mornin' stroll?"

"By courtesy of a bunch of Comanches. I was bullwhackin' with a wagon train out of Santa Fe for Cheyenne an' we had a little Winchester arbitration. They held the high cards." Briefly, he explained.

"You'll want a hoss. Ever work cattle?"

"Here and there. D'you need a hand?"

"Forty a month and all you can eat."

"The coffee's a fright," the other rider said. "That dough wrangler never learned to make coffee that didn't taste like strong lye!"

That night in camp Jed Asbury got out the papers he had found in the wagon. He read the first letter he opened.

Dear Michael,

When you get this you will know George is dead. He was thrown from a horse near Willow Springs, dying the following day. The home ranch comprises 60,000 acres and the other ranches twice that. This is to be yours or your heirs' if you have married since we last heard from you, if you or the heirs reach the place within one year of George's death. If you do not claim your estate within that time the property will be inherited by next of kin. You may remember what Walt is like, from the letters.

Naturally, we hope you will come at once for we all know what it would be like if Walt took over. You should be around twenty-six now and able to handle Walt, but be careful. He is dangerous and has killed several men.

Things are in good shape now but trouble is impending with Besovi, a neighbor of ours. If Walt takes over that will certainly happen. Also, those of us who have worked and lived here so long will be thrown out.

Tony Costa

The letter had been addressed to Michael Latch, St. Louis, Missouri. Thoughtfully, Jed folded the letter and then glanced through the others. He learned much, yet not enough.

Michael Latch had been the nephew of George Baca, a half-American, half-Spanish rancher who owned a huge hacienda in California. Neither Baca nor Tony Costa had ever seen Michael. Nor had the man named Walt, who apparently was the son of George's half brother.

The will was that of Michael's father, Thomas Latch, and conveyed to Michael the deed to a small California ranch.

From other papers and an unmailed letter, Jed discovered that the younger of the two men he had buried had been Michael Latch. The other dead man and the woman had been Randy and May Kenner. There was mention in a letter of a girl named Arden who had accompanied them.

"The Indians must have taken her with them," Jed muttered.

He considered trying to find her, but dismissed the idea as impractical. Looking for a needle in a haystack would at least be a local job, but trying to find one of many roving bands of Comanches would be well-nigh impossible. Nevertheless, he would inform the Army and the trading posts. Often, negotiations could be started, and for an appropriate trade in goods she might be recovered, if still living.

Then he had another idea.

Michael Latch was dead. A vast estate awaited him, a fine, comfortable, constructive life, which young Latch would have loved. Now the estate would fall to Walt, whoever he was, unless he, Jed Asbury, took the name of Michael Latch and claimed the estate.

The man who was his new boss rode in from a ride around the herd. He glanced at Jed, who was putting the letters away. "What did you say your name was?"

Only for an instant did Jed hesitate. "Latch," he replied, "Michael Latch."

————

WARM SUNLIGHT LAY upon the hacienda called Casa Grande. The hounds sprawling in drowsy peace under the smoke trees scarcely opened their eyes when the tall stranger turned his horse through the gate. Many strangers came to Casa Grande, and the uncertainty that hung over the vast ranch had not reached the dogs.

Tony Costa straightened his lean frame from the doorway and studied the stranger from under an eye-shielding hand.

"Señorita, someone comes!"

"Is it Walt?" Sharp, quick heels sounded on the flat-stoned floor. "What will we do? Oh, if Michael were only here!"

"Today is the last day," Costa said gloomily.

"Look!" The girl touched his arm. "Right behind him! That's Walt Seever!"

"Two men with him. We will have trouble if we try to stop him, señorita. He would not lose the ranch to a woman."

The stranger on the black horse swung down at the steps. He wore a flat-crowned black hat and a black broadcloth suit. His boots were almost new and hand tooled, but when her eyes dropped to the guns, she gasped.

"*Tony!* The guns!"

The young man came up the steps, swept off his hat, and bowed. "You are Tony Costa? The foreman of Casa Grande?"

The other riders clattered into the court, and their leader, a big man with bold, hard eyes, swung down. He brushed past the stranger and confronted the foreman.

"Well, Costa, today this ranch becomes mine, and you're fired!"

"I think not."

All eyes turned to the stranger. The girl's eyes were startled, suddenly cautious. This man was strong, she thought suddenly, and he was not afraid. He had a clean-cut face, pleasant gray eyes, and a certain assurance born of experience.

"If you are Walt," the stranger said, "you can ride back where you came from. This ranch is mine. I am Michael Latch."

Fury struggled with shocked disbelief in the expression on Walt Seever's face. "*You?* Michael Latch? You couldn't be!"

"Why not?" Jed was calm. Eyes on Seever, he could not see the effect of his words on Costa or the girl. "George sent for me. Here I am."

Mingled with the baffled rage, there was something else in Walt's face, some ugly suspicion or knowledge. Suddenly Jed suspected that Walt knew he was not Michael Latch. Or doubted it vehemently.

Tony Costa had moved up beside him. "Why not? We have expected him. His uncle wrote for him, and after Baca's death, I wrote to him. If you doubt it, look at the guns. Are there two such pairs of guns in the world? Are there two men in the world who could make such guns?"

Seever's eyes went to the guns, and Jed saw doubt and puzzlement replace the angry certainty.

"I'll have to have more proof than a pair of guns!"

Jed took the letter from his pocket and passed it over. "From Tony. I also have my father's will and other letters."

Walt Seever glanced at the letter and then hurled it into the dust. "Let's get out of here!" He started for his horse.

Jed Asbury watched them go, puzzling over that odd reaction of Walt's. Until Seever saw that letter he had been positive Jed was not Michael Latch. Now he was no longer sure. But what could have made him so positive in the beginning? What could he know?

The girl was whispering something to Costa. Jed turned, smiling at her. "I don't believe Walt was too happy at my being here," he said.

"No," Costa's expression was unrevealing, "he isn't. He expected to have this ranch for himself." Costa turned toward the girl. "Señor Latch? I would introduce to you Señorita Carol James, a—a ward of Señor Baca's and his good friend."

Jed acknowledged the introduction.

"You must bring me up to date. I want to know all you can tell me about Walt Seever."

Costa exchanged a glance with Carol. "Of course, señor. Walt Seever is a *malo hombre,* señor. He has killed several men, is most violent. The men with him were Harry Strykes and Gin Feeley. They are gunmen and believed to be thieves."

Jed Asbury listened attentively, yet wondered about Carol's reaction. Did she suspect he was not Michael Latch? Did she *know* he was not Latch? If so, why didn't she say something?

He was surprised they had accepted him so readily, for even after he had decided to take the dead man's place he had not been sure he could go through with it. He had a feeling of guilt and some shame, yet the real Michael Latch was dead, and the only man he was depriving seemed to be a thoroughly bad one whose first action would have been to fire the ranch's foreman, a man whose home had always been this hacienda.

He had made a wild ride over rough country to get here in time, but over all that distance he had debated with himself about the rights and the wrongs of his action.

He was nobody, a drifter, worker at whatever came to hand, an adventurer, if you will, but not unlike hundreds of others who came and went across the West and more often than not left their bones in the wilderness, their flesh to feed the ancient soil.

He had not known Michael Latch, or what kind of man he had been, but he suspected he had been a good man and a trusted one. Why could he not save the ranch from Walt Seever, find a home for himself at last, and be the kind of man Michael Latch would have been?

All through that wild ride west he had struggled with his conscience, trying to convince himself that what he did was the right thing. He could do Latch no harm, and Costa and Carol seemed pleased to have him here, now that he had arrived. The expression on Seever's face had been worth the ride, if nothing more.

There was something else that disturbed him. That was Walt Seever's odd reaction when he had said he was Michael Latch.

"You say," Jed turned to Carol, "that Seever was sure he would inherit?"

She nodded. "Yes, though until about three months ago he was hating George Baca for leaving the ranch to you. Then suddenly he changed his mind and seemed sure he would inherit, that you would never come to claim your inheritance."

It had been about three months ago that Jed Asbury had come upon the lone wagon and the murdered people, a murder he had laid to Indians. But leaving the corpses with their clothing and the wagon unlooted did not seem like any raiding parties of which he had known.

Three people murdered—could Seever have known of that? Was that why he had suddenly been sure he would inherit?

The idea took root. Seever must have known of the killings. If that was so, then the three had not been killed by Indians, and a lot remained to be explained. How did the wagon happen to be alone, so far from anywhere? And what had become of the girl, Arden?

If Indians had not made the attack and carried Arden off, then somebody else had captured her, and wherever she was she would know he was not the real Michael Latch. She would know Jed Asbury for an imposter, but she might also know who the killers were.

Walking out on the wide terrace overlooking the green valley beyond the ranch house, Jed stared down the valley, his mind filled with doubts and apprehensions.

It was a lovely land, well watered and rich. Here, with what he knew of land and cattle, he could carry on the work George Baca had begun. He would do what Michael Latch would have done, and he might even do it better.

There was danger, but when had he not known danger? And these people at the ranch were good people, honest people. If he did not do more than save the ranch from Seever and his lawless crowd he would have adequate reason for taking the place of the dead man. Yet he was merely finding excuses for his conduct.

The guns he wore meant something, too. Carol had recognized them, and so had Seever. What was their significance?

He was in deep water here. Every remark he made must be guarded. Even if they had not seen him before, there must be family stories and family tradition of which he knew nothing. There was a movement behind him, and Jed Asbury turned. In the gathering dusk he saw Carol.

"Do you like it?" She gestured toward the valley.

"It's splendid! I have never seen anything prettier. A man could do a lot with land like that. It could be a paradise."

"Somehow you are different than I expected."

"I am?" He was careful, waiting for her to say more.

"You're much more assured than I expected you to be. Mike was quiet, Uncle George used to say. Read a lot, but did not get around much. You startled me by the way you handled Walt Seever."

He shrugged. "A man changes. He grows older, and coming west to a new life makes a man more sure of himself."

She noticed the book in his pocket. "What book do you have?" she asked curiously.

It was a battered copy of Plutarch. He was on safe ground here, for on the flyleaf was written, *To Michael, from Uncle George.*

He showed it to her and she said, "It was a favorite of Uncle George. He used to say that next to the Bible more great men had read Plutarch than any other book."

"I like it. I've been reading it nights." He turned to face her. "Carol, what do you think Walt Seever will do?"

"Try to kill you or have you killed," she replied. She gestured toward the guns. "You had better learn to use those."

"I can, a little."

He dared not admit how well he could use them, for a man does not come by such skill overnight, nor the cool nerve it takes to use them facing an armed enemy. "Seever has counted on this place, has he?"

"He has made a lot of talk." She glanced up at him. "You know, Walt was no blood relation to Uncle George. He was the son of a woman of the gold camps who married George Baca's half brother."

"I see." Actually, Walt Seever's claim was scarcely better than his own. "I know from the letters that Uncle George wanted me to have the estate, but I feel like an outsider. I am afraid I may be doing wrong to take a ranch built by the work of other people. Walt may have more right to it than I. I may be doing wrong to assert my claim."

He was aware of her searching gaze. When she spoke it was deliberately and as if she had reached some decision.

"Michael, I don't know you, but you would have to be very bad, indeed, to be as dangerous and evil as Walt Seever. I would say that no matter what the circumstances, you should stay and see this through."

Was there a hint that she might know more than she admitted? Yet it was natural that he should be looking for suspicion behind every phrase. Yet he must do that or be trapped.

"However, it is only fair to warn you that you have let yourself in for more than you could expect. Uncle George knew very well what you would be facing. He knew the viciousness of Walt Seever. He doubted you would be clever or bold enough to defeat Seever. So I must warn you, Michael Latch, that if you do stay, and I believe you should, you will probably be killed."

He smiled into the darkness. Since boyhood he had lived in proximity to death. He was not foolhardy or reckless, for a truly brave man was never reckless. He knew he could skirt the ragged edge of death if need be. He had been there before.

He was an interloper here, yet the man whose place he had

taken was dead, and perhaps he could carry on in his place, making the ranch safe for those who loved it. Then he could move on and leave this ranch to Carol and to the care of Tony Costa.

He turned. "I am tired," he said. "I have ridden long and hard to get here. Now I'd like to rest." He paused. "But I shall stay, at least—"

Jed Asbury was already fast asleep when Carol went into the dining room where Tony Costa sat at the long table. Without him, what would she have done? What could she have done? He had worked with her father for thirty years and had lived on the hacienda all his life, and he was past sixty now. He still stood as erect and slender as he had when a young man. And he was shrewd.

Costa looked up. He was drinking coffee by the light of a candle. "For better or worse, señorita, it has begun. What do you think now?"

"He told me, after I warned him, that he would stay."

Costa studied the coffee in his cup. "You are not afraid?"

"No. He faced Walt Seever and that was enough for me. Anything is to be preferred to Walt Seever."

"Sí." Costa's agreement was definite. "Señorita, did you notice his hands when he faced Seever. They were ready, Carolita, ready to draw. This man has used a gun before. He is a strong man, Carolita!"

"Yes, I think you are right. He is a strong man."

For two days nothing happened from the direction of town. Walt Seever and his hard-bitten companions might have vanished from the earth, but on the Rancho Casa Grande much was happening, and Tony Costa was whistling most of the time.

Jed Asbury's formal education was slight, but he knew men, how to lead them and how best to get results. Above all he had practical knowledge of handling cattle and of range conditions.

He was up at five the morning after his discussion with Carol, and when she awakened, old Maria, the cook, told her the señor was hard at work in his office. The door was open a crack, and as she passed by she glimpsed him deep in the accounts of the ranch. Pinned up before him was a map of the Casa Grande holdings, and as he checked the disposition of the cattle, he studied the map.

He ate a hurried breakfast and at eight o'clock was in the saddle. He ate his next meal at a line camp and rode in long after dark. In two days he spent twenty hours in the saddle.

On the third day he called Costa to the office and sent Maria to request the presence of Carol. Puzzled and curious, she joined them.

Jed wore a white shirt, black trousers, and the silver guns. His face seemed to have thinned down in just the two days, but when he glanced at her, he smiled.

"You have been here longer than I and are, in a sense, a partner." Before she could interrupt he turned to Costa. "I want you to remain as foreman. However, I have asked you both to be here as I plan some changes."

He indicated a point on the map. "That narrow passage leads into open country and then desert. I found cattle tracks there, going out. It might be rustlers. A little blasting up in the rocks will close that gap."

"It is a good move," Costa agreed.

"This field—" Jed indicated a large area in a field not far from the house, "must be fenced off. We will plant it to flax."

"Flax, señor?"

"There will be a good market for it." He indicated a smaller area. "This piece we will plant to grapes, and all that hillside will support them. There will be times when we cannot depend on cattle or horses, so there must be other sources of income."

Carol watched in wonderment. He was moving fast, this new Michael Latch. He had grasped the situation at once and was moving to make changes that Uncle George had only thought about.

"Also, Costa, we must have a roundup. Gather the cattle and cut out all those over four years old, and we'll sell them. I saw a lot of cattle from five to eight years old back there in the brush."

After he had ridden away to study another quarter of the ranch, Carol walked to the blacksmith shop to talk to Pat

Flood. He was an old seafaring man with a pegleg whom Uncle George had found broke and on the beach in San Francisco and who had proved to be a marvel with tools.

He looked up from under his bushy brows as she stopped at the shop. He was cobbling a pair of boots. Before she could speak he said, "This here new boss, Latch? Been to sea, ain't he?"

Surprised, she said, "What gave you that idea?"

"Seen him throw a bowline on a bight yesterday. Purtiest job I seen since comin' ashore. He made that rope fast like he'd been doin' it for years."

"I expect many men handle ropes well," she commented.

"Not sailor fashion. He called it a line, too. 'Hand me that line!' he says. Me, I been ashore so long I'm callin' them ropes m'self, but not him. I'd stake my supper that he's walked a deck."

Jed Asbury was riding to town. He wanted to assay the feeling of the townspeople toward the ranch, toward George Baca and Walt Seever. There was a chance he might talk to a few people before they discovered his connection. Also, he was irritated at the delay in the showdown with Seever. His appearance in town might force that showdown or allow Seever an opportunity if he felt he needed one. If there was to be a meeting he wanted it over with so he could get on with work at the ranch.

He had never avoided trouble. It was his nature to go right to the heart of it, and for this trip he was wearing worn gray trousers, boots, his silver guns, and a battered black hat. He hoped they would accept him as a drifting puncher.

Already, in riding around the ranch and in casual talk with the hands, he had learned a good deal. He knew the place to go in town was the Golden Strike. He tied his horse to the hitching rail and went inside.

Three men loafed at the bar. The big man with the scar on his lip was Harry Strykes, who had ridden with Seever. As Jed stepped to the bar and ordered his drink, a man seated at a table got up and went to Strykes. "Never saw him before," he said.

Strykes went around the man and faced Jed. "So? Cuttin'

in for yourself, are you? Well, nobody gets in the way of my boss. Go for your gun or go back to Texas. You got a choice!"

"I'm not going to kill you," Jed said. "I don't like your manner, but if you touch that gun I'll have to blow your guts out. Instead, I'd rather teach you a lesson."

His left hand grabbed Strykes by the belt. He shoved back and then lifted, and his left toe kicked Strykes's foot from under him as Jed lifted on the belt and then let go.

The move caught Strykes unaware, and he hit the floor hard. For an instant he was shaken, but then he came off the floor with a curse.

Jed Asbury had taken up his drink with his left hand, leaning carelessly against the bar. Jed's left foot was on the brass rail, and as Strykes swung his right fist, Jed straightened his leg, moving himself out from the bar so that the punch missed, throwing Strykes against the bar. As his chest hit the bar Jed flipped the remainder of his drink into Strykes's eyes.

Moving away from the bar he made no attempt to hit Strykes, just letting the man paw at the stinging whiskey in his eyes. When he seemed about to get his vision cleared, Jed leaned forward and jerked open Strykes's belt. Strykes's pants slid toward his knees, and he grabbed at them. Jed pushed him with the tips of his fingers. With his pants around his knees Strykes could not stagger, so he fell.

Jed turned to the others in the room. "Sorry to have disturbed you, gentlemen! The name is Mike Latch. If you are ever out to the Casa Grande, please feel free to call."

He walked out of the saloon, leaving laughter behind him as Strykes struggled to get up and pull his pants into place.

Yet he was remembering the man who had stepped up to Strykes saying he had never seen Jed before. Had that man known the real Mike Latch? If Walt Seever knew of the covered wagon with its three murdered people, he would know Jed Asbury was an impostor and would be searching for a way to prove it. The vast and beautiful acres of Rancho Casa Grande were reason enough.

Riding homeward he mulled over the problem. There was, of course, a chance of exposure, yet no one might ever come near who could actually identify him.

His brief altercation with Strykes had gotten him nowhere. He had undoubtedly been observed when riding into town, and the stranger must have known the real Latch. Nevertheless, the fight, if such it could be called, might have won a few friends. In the first place he could not imagine a man of Seever's stamp was well liked; in the second he had shown he was not anxious to get into a gun battle. Friends could be valuable in the months to come, and he was not catering to the rowdy element who would be Seever's friends.

Seever, however, would now be spoiling for a fight, and Jed might be killed. He must find a way to give Carol a strong claim on the ranch. Failing in that, he must kill Walt Seever.

Jed Asbury had never killed a man except to protect his own life or those close to him. Deliberately to hunt down and shoot a man was something he had never dreamed of doing, yet it might prove the only way he could protect Carol and Tony Costa. With a shock he realized he was thinking more of Carol than of himself, and he hardly knew her.

Apparently the stranger had known he was not Mike Latch. The next time it might be a direct accusation before witnesses. Jed considered the problem all the way home.

Unknown to Jed, Jim Pardo, one of the toughest hands on the ranch, had followed him into town. On his return, Pardo drew up before the blacksmith shop and looked down at Pat Flood. The gigantic old blacksmith would have weighed well over three hundred pounds with two good legs, and he stood five inches over six feet. He rarely left the shop, as his wooden leg was always giving him trouble.

"He'll do," Pardo said, swinging down.

Flood lit his corncob pipe and waited.

"Had a run-in with Harry Strykes."

Flood drew on the pipe, knowing the story would come.

"Made a fool of Harry."

"Whup him?"

"Not like he should of, but maybe this was worse. He got him laughed at."

"Strykes will kill him for that."

Pardo rolled a cigarette and explained. "If Strykes is smart he will leave him alone. This here Latch is no greenhorn. He's a man knows what he can do. No other would have handled it like he did. Never turned a hair when Strykes braced him. He's got sand in his gizzard, an' I'm placin' my bets that he'll prove a first-class hand with a shootin' iron. This one's had trouble before."

"He's deep," Flood said, chewing on his pipe stem.

"Old George always said Latch was a book reader, an' quiet-like."

"Well," Flood was thoughtful, "he's quiet enough, an' he reads books."

Tony Costa learned of the incident from Pardo, and Maria related the story to Carol. Jed made no reference to it at supper.

Costa hesitated after arising from the table. "Señor, since Señor Baca's death the señorita has permitted me to eat in the ranch house. There was often business to discuss. If you wish, I can—"

"Forget it, and unless you're in a hurry, sit down. Your years on the ranch have earned you your place at the table."

Jed took up the pot and filled their cups. "Yesterday I was over in Fall Valley and I saw a lot of cattle with a Bar O brand."

"Bar O? Ah, they try it again! This brand, señor, belongs to a very big outfit! Frank Besovi's ranch. He is a big man, señor, a very troublesome man. Always he tries to move in on that valley, but if he takes that he will want more. He has taken many ranches, so."

"Take some of the boys up there and throw those cattle off our range."

"There will be trouble, señor."

"Are you afraid of trouble, Costa?"

The foreman's face tightened. "No, señor!"

"Neither am I. Throw them off."

When the punchers moved out in the morning, Jed mounted a horse and rode along. And there would be trouble. Jed saw that when they entered the valley.

Several riders were grouped near a big man with a black beard. Their horses all carried the Bar O brand.

"I'll talk to him, Costa. I want to hear what Besovi has to say."

"Very bad man," Costa warned.

Jed Asbury knew trouble when he saw it. Besovi and his men had come prepared for a showdown. Jed did not speak, he simply pushed his black against Besovi's gray. Anger flared in the big man's eyes. "What the hell are you tryin' to do?" he roared.

"Tell your boys to round up your Bar O cattle and run them back over your line. If you don't, I'll make you run 'em back, afoot!"

"What?" Besovi was incredulous. "You say that to *me?*"

"You heard me. Give the order!"

"I'll see you in hell first!" Besovi shouted.

Jed Asbury knew this could be settled in two ways. If he went for a gun there would be shooting and men would be killed. He chose the other way.

Acting so suddenly the move was unexpected, he grabbed Besovi by the beard and jerked the rancher sharply toward him, at the same time he kicked the rancher's foot loose from his stirrup and then shoved hard. Besovi, caught unawares by the sheer unexpectedness of the attack, fell off his horse, and Jed hit the ground beside him.

Besovi came to his feet, clawing for his gun. "Afraid to fight with your hands?" Jed taunted.

Besovi glared and then unbuckled his gun belts and handed them to the nearest horseman. Jed stripped off his own gun belts and handed them to Costa.

Besovi started toward him with a crablike movement that made Jed's eyes sharpen. He circled warily, looking the big man over.

Jed was at least thirty pounds lighter than Besovi, and it was obvious the big man had power in those mighty shoulders. But it would take more than power to win this kind of a fight. Jed moved in, feinting to get Besovi to reveal his fighting style. Besovi grabbed at his left wrist, and Jed brushed the hand aside and stiffened a left into his face.

Blood showed, and the Casa Grande men yelled. Pardo, rolling his quid of tobacco in his jaws, watched. He had seen Besovi fight before. The big man kept moving in, and Jed circled, wary. Besovi had some plan of action. He was no wild-swinging, hit-or-miss fighter.

Jed feinted again and then stabbed two lefts to Besovi's face, so fast one punch had barely landed before the other smacked home. Pardo was surprised to see how Besovi's head jerked under the impact.

Besovi moved in, and when Jed led with another blow, the bigger man went under the punch and leaping close encircled Jed with his mighty arms. Jed's leap back had been too slow, and he sensed the power in that grasping clutch. If those huge arms closed around him he would be in serious trouble, so he kicked up his feet and fell.

The unexpected fall caught Besovi off balance and he lunged over him, losing his grip. Quickly, he spun, but Jed was already on his feet. Besovi swung and the blow caught Jed on the cheekbone. Jed took the punch standing and Pardo's mouth dropped open in surprise. Nobody had ever stood up under a Besovi punch before.

Jed struck then, a left and right that landed solidly. The left opened the gash over Besovi's eye a little wider, and the right caught him on the chin, staggering him. Jed moved in, landing both fists to the face. The big man's hands came up to protect his face and Jed slugged him in the stomach.

Besovi got an arm around Jed and hooked him twice in the face with wicked, short punches. Jed butted him in the face with his head, breaking free.

Yet he did not step back but caught the rancher behind the head with his left hand and jerked his head down to meet a smashing right uppercut that broke Besovi's nose.

Jed pushed him away quickly and hit him seven fast punches before Besovi could get set. Like a huge, blind bear Besovi tried to swing, but Jed ducked the punch and slammed both fists to the body.

Besovi staggered, almost falling, and Jed stepped back. "You've had plenty, Besovi, and you're too good a fighter to kill. I could kill you with my fists, but I'd probably ruin my hands in doing it. Will you take those cattle and get out of here?"

Besovi, unsteady on his feet, wiped the blood from his eyes. "Well, I'll be damned! I never thought the man lived—! Will you shake hands?"

"I'd never shake with a tougher man or a better one!"

Their hands gripped, and suddenly Besovi began to laugh. "Come over to supper some night, will you? Ma's been tellin' me this would happen. She'll be pleased to meet you!"

He turned to his riders. "The fun's over, boys! Round up our stock an' let's go home."

The big rancher's lips were split; there was a cut over his right eye and another under it. The other eye was swelling shut. There was one bruise on Jed's cheekbone that would be bigger tomorrow, but it wasn't enough to show he had been in a fight.

"Can't figure him," Pardo told Flood, later. "Is he scared to use his guns? Or does he just like to fight with his hands?"

"He's smart," Flood suggested. "Look, he's made a friend of Besovi. If he'd beaten him to the ground, Besovi might never have forgiven him. He was savin' face for Besovi just like they do it over China way. And what if he'd gone for his guns?"

"Likely four or five of us might not have made it home tonight."

"That's it. He's usin' his head for something more than a place to hang a hat. Look at it. He's made a friend of Besovi and nobody is shot up."

Jed, soaking his battered hands, was not so sure. Besovi might have gone for a gun, or one of his hands might have. He had taken a long gamble and won; next time he might not be so lucky.

At least Rancho Casa Grande had one less enemy and one more friend.

If anything happened to him Carol would need friends. Walt Seever was ominously quiet, and Jed was sure the man was waiting for proof that he was not Michael Latch.

And that gave Jed an idea. It was a game at which two could play.

Carol was saddling her horse when he walked out in the morning. She glanced at him, her eyes hesitating on the bruise. "You seem to have a faculty for getting into trouble!" she said, smiling.

He led the black gelding out. "I don't believe in ducking troubles. They just pile up on you. Sometimes they get too big to handle."

"You seem to have made a friend of Besovi."

"Why not? He's a good man, just used to taking in all he can put his hands on, but he'll prove a good neighbor." He hesitated and then glanced off, afraid his eyes would give him away. "If anything happens to me, you'll need friends. I think Besovi would help you."

Her eyes softened. "Thank you, Mike." She hesitated just a little over the name. "You have already done much of what Uncle George just talked of doing."

Costa was gathering the herd Jed wanted to sell, and Pardo was riding with him. Jed did not ask Carol where she was going, but watched her ride away toward the valley. He threw a saddle on his own horse and cinched up. At the sound of horses' hoofs he turned.

Walt Seever was riding into the yard. With him were Harry Strykes and Gin Feeley. The fourth man was the one he had seen in the saloon who had told Walt he was not Michael Latch. Realizing he wore no guns, Jed felt naked and helpless. There was no one around the ranch house of whom he knew.

Seever drew rein and rested his hands on the pommel of his saddle. "Howdy! Howdy, Jed!"

No muscle changed on Jed Asbury's face. If trouble came he was going right at Walt Seever.

"Smart play," Seever said, savoring his triumph. "If it hadn't been for me doubtin' you, you might have pulled it off."

Jed waited, watching.

"Now," Seever said, "your game is up. I suppose I should let you get on your horse an' ride, but we ain't about to."

"You mean to kill me like you did Latch and his friends?"

"Think you're smart, do you? Well, when you said that you dug your own grave."

"I suppose your sour-faced friend here was one of those you sent to kill Latch," Jed commented. "He looks to be the kind."

"Let me kill him, Walt!" The man with the sour face had his hand on his gun. "Just let me kill him!"

"What I want to know," Seever said, holding up a hand to stop the other man, "is where you got them guns."

"Out of the wagon, of course! The men you sent to stop Latch before he got here messed up. I'd just gotten away from a passel of Indians and was stark naked. I found clothes in the wagon. I also found the guns."

"About like I figured. Now we'll get rid of you, an' I'll have Casa Grande."

Jed was poised for a break, any kind of a break, and stalling for time. "Thieves like you always overlook important things. The men you sent messed up badly. They were in too much of a hurry and didn't burn the wagon. And what about Arden?"

"Arden? Who the devil is Arden?"

Jed had come a step nearer. They would get him, but he was going to kill Walt Seever.

He chuckled. "They missed her, Walt! Arden is a girl. She was with Latch when he was killed."

"A girl?" Seever turned on the other man. "Clark, you never said anything about a girl!"

"There wasn't any girl," Clark protested.

"He killed three of them, but she was out on the prairie to gather wild onions or something."

"That's a lie! There was only the three of them!" Clark shouted.

"What about those fancy clothes you threw around in the wagon? Think they were old woman's clothes?"

Walt was furious. "Damn you, Clark! You said you got all of them!"

"There wasn't no girl," Clark protested. "Anyway, I didn't see one!"

"There was a girl, Walt, and she's safe. If something goes wrong here you will have to answer for it, Walt. You haven't a chance!"

Seever's face was ugly with anger. "Anyway, we've got you! We've got you dead to rights!" His hand moved toward his gun, but before Jed Asbury could move a muscle, there was a shot.

From behind Jed came Pat Flood's voice. "Keep your hands away from those guns, Walt. I can shoot the buttons off your shirt with this here rifle, and in case that ain't enough I got me a scattergun right beside me. Now you gents just unbuckle your belts, real easy now! You first, Seever!"

Jed dropped back swiftly and picked up the shotgun.

The men shed their guns. "Now get off your hosses!" Flood ordered.

They dismounted and Flood asked, "What you want done with 'em, boss? Should we bury them here or give them a runnin' chance?"

"Let them walk back to town," Jed suggested. "All but Clark. I want to talk to Clark."

Seever started to speak, but the buffalo gun and the shotgun were persuasive. He led the way.

"Let me go!" Clark begged. "They'll kill me!"

Jed gathered the gun belts and walked to the blacksmith shop, behind Clark.

"How much did you hear?" he asked Flood.

"All of it," the big blacksmith replied bluntly, "but my memory can be mighty poor. I judge a man by the way he handles himself, and you've been ridin' for the brand. I ain't interested in anything else."

Jed turned on Clark. "Get this straight. You've one chance to live, and you shouldn't have that. Tell us what happened, who sent you and what you did." He glanced at Flood. "Take this down, every word."

"I got paper and pencil," Flood said. "I always keep a log."

"All right, Clark, a complete confession and you get your horse and a running start."

"Seever will kill me."

"Make your choice. You sign a confession or you can die right here at the end of a rope behind a runaway horse. Seever's not going to kill anybody, ever again."

Clark hesitated, and then he said, "I was broke in Ogden when Seever found me. I'd knowed him before. He told me I was to find this here wagon that was startin' west from St. Louis. He said I was to make sure they never got there. I never knew there was a woman along."

"Who was with you?"

"Feller named Quinby and a friend of his'n named Buck Stanton. I met up with 'em in Laramie."

At Jed's exclamation, Flood glanced at him. "You know them?"

"I killed Buck's brother Cal. They were crooked gamblers."

"Then you were the man they were huntin'!" Clark exclaimed.

"Where are they now?"

"Comin' this way, I suppose. Seever sent for 'em for some reason. Guess he figured they could come in here and prove you was somebody different than you said."

"Seever ordered the killing?"

"Yes, sir. He surely did."

A few more questions and the confession was signed.

"Now get on that horse and get out of here before we change our minds and hang you."

"Do I get my guns?"

"You do not. Get going!"

Clark fairly threw himself into the saddle and left at a dead run.

Flood handed the confession to Jed. "Are you going to use it?"

"Not right now. I'll put it in the safe in the house. If Carol ever needs it, she can use it. If I brought it out now it would prove that I am not Michael Latch."

"I knew you weren't him," Flood said. "Old George told me a good bit about him, but just seein' you around told me you'd covered a lot more country than he ever did."

"Does Carol know?"

"Don't reckon she does, but then she's a right canny lass."

If Stanton and Quinby were headed west, then Seever must have telegraphed for them to come, and they would certainly ally themselves with Seever against him. As if he did not have trouble enough!

Costa and Jim Pardo rode into the yard, and Costa trotted his horse over to Jed, who was wearing the silver guns now.

"There were many cattle! More than expected! We came to see if the Willow Springs boys can help us."

"Later. Was Miss Carol out with you?"

"No, señor. She went to town."

Jed swore. "Flood, you take care of things here. We're riding into town!"

Seever would stop at nothing now, and if Quinby and Stanton had arrived in town Jed's work would be cut out for him. No doubt Seever had known how to reach them, and it must have been from Stanton that Seever learned his name. A description from Seever would have been enough for Stanton to recognize who he was.

The town lay basking in a warm sun. In the distance the Sierras lifted snowcapped peaks against the blue sky. A man loitering in front of the Golden Strike stepped through the doors as Jed appeared in the street with his Casa Grande cowboys. Walt Seever stepped into the doorway, nonchalant, confident.

"Figured you'd be in. We sort of detained the lady, knowin' that would bring you. She can go loose now that you're where we want you."

Jed stepped down from the saddle. This was a trap, and they had ridden right into it.

"There's a gent in front of the express office, boss," Pardo said.

"Thanks, and watch the windows," Jed suggested. "Upstairs windows."

Jed was watching Seever. Trouble would begin with him. He moved away from his horse. No sense in getting a good animal killed. He did not look to see what Costa and Pardo were doing. They would be doing what was best for them and for what was coming.

"Glad you saved me the trouble of hunting you, Seever," he said.

Seever was on the edge of the boardwalk, a big man looking granite hard and tough. "Save us both trouble. Folks here don't take to outsiders. They'd sooner have somebody like me runnin' the outfit than a stranger. Shuck your guns, get on your horses, and you can ride out of town."

"Don't do it, boss!" Pardo warned. "He'll shoot you as soon as your back is turned."

"The ranch goes to Miss Carol, Seever. You might get me, but I promise you, you will die."

"Like hell!" Seever's hand swept for his gun. "I'll kill—!"

"Look out!" Pardo yelled.

Jed stepped aside as the rifle roared from the window over the livery barn, and his guns lifted. His first bullet took Walt Seever in the chest; his second went into the shadows behind a rifle muzzle in the barn loft.

Seever staggered into the street, his guns pounding lead into the street. Oblivious of the pounding guns around him, Jed centered his attention on Seever, and when the man fell, the pistol dribbling from his fingers, Jed looked around, keeping his eyes from this man he had killed, hating the sight of what he had done.

Costa was down on one knee, blood staining the left sleeve of his shirt, but his face was expressionless, his pistol ready.

A dead man sprawled over the windowsill above the barn. A soft wind stirred his sandy hair. That would be Stanton. Pardo was holstering his gun. There was no sign of Stryker or Feeley.

"You all right, boss?" Pardo asked.

"All right. How about you?"

Tony Costa was getting to his feet. "Caught one in the shoulder," he said. "It's not bad."

Heads were appearing in doors and windows, but nobody showed any desire to come outside. Then a door slammed down the street, and Carol was running to them.

"Are you hurt?" She caught his arm. "Were you shot?"

He slid an arm around her as she came up to him, and it was so natural that neither of them noticed. "Better get that shoulder fixed up, Costa." He glanced down at Carol. "Where did they have you?"

"Strykes and Feeley were holding me in a house across the street. When Feeley saw you were not alone he wanted Harry Strykes to leave. Feeley looked out the door and Pat Flood saw him."

"Flood?"

"He followed you in, knowing there'd be trouble. He came in behind them and had me take their guns. He was just going out to help you when the shooting started."

"Carol," he hesitated. "I've got a confession to make. I am not Michael Latch."

"Oh? Is that all? I've known that all the time. You see, I was Michael Latch's wife."

"His what?"

"Before I married him I was Carol Arden James. He was the only one who ever called me Arden. During the time we were coming west I was quite ill, so I stayed in the wagon and Clark never saw me at all.

"He convinced Michael there was a wagon train going by way of Santa Fe that would take us through sooner, and if we could catch them it would help. It was all a lie to get us away from the rest of the wagons, but Michael listened, as the train we were with was going only as far as Laramie.

"After we were on the trail, Clark left us to locate the wagon train, as he said. Randy Kenner and Mike decided to camp, and I went over the hill to a small pool to bathe. When I was dressing I heard shooting, and believing it was Indians, I crept to the top of a hill so I could see our wagon.

"It was all over. Clark had ridden up with two men and opened fire at once. They'd had no warning, no chance.

"Randy was not dead when I saw them. One of the men kicked a gun out of his hand—he was already wounded—and shot him again. There was nothing I could do, so I simply hid."

"But how did you get here?"

"When they left I did not go back to the wagon. I simply *couldn't,* and I was afraid they might return. So I started walking back to the wagon train we had left. I hadn't gone far when I found Old Nellie, our saddle mare. She knew me and came right up to me, so I rode her back to the wagon train. I came from Laramie by stage."

"Then you knew all the time that I was faking?"

"Yes, but when you stopped Walt I whispered to Costa not to say anything."

"He knew as well?"

"Yes. I'd showed him my marriage license, which I always carried with me, along with a little money."

"Why didn't you say something? I was having a battle with my conscience, trying to decide what was right, always knowing I'd have to explain sooner or later."

"You were doing much better with the ranch than Michael could have. Michael and I grew up together and were much more like brother and sister than husband and wife. When he heard from his uncle George, we were married, and we liked each other."

Suddenly it dawned on Jed that they were standing in the middle of the street and he had his arm around Carol. Hastily he withdrew it.

"Why didn't you just claim the estate as Michael's wife?"

"Costa was afraid Seever would kill me. We had not decided what to do when you appeared."

"What about these guns?"

"My father made them. He was a gunsmith and he had made guns for Uncle George. These were a present to Mike when he started west."

His eyes avoided hers. "Carol, I'll get my gear and move on. The ranch is yours, and with Seever gone you will be all right."

"I don't want you to go."

He thought his ears deceived him. "You—what?"

"Don't go, Jed. Stay with us. I can't manage the ranch alone, and Costa has been happy since you've been here. We need you, Jed. I—I need you."

"Well," he spoke hesitantly, "there are things to be done

and cattle to be sold, and that quarter section near Willow Springs could be irrigated."

Pardo, watching, glanced at Flood. "I think he's going to stay, Pat."

"Sure," Flood said. "Ships an' women, they all need a handy man around the place!"

Carol caught Jed's sleeve. "Then you'll stay?"

He smiled. "What would Costa do without me?"

FOUR-CARD DRAW

WHEN A MAN drew four cards he could expect something like this to happen. Ben Taylor had probably been right when he told him his luck had run out. Despite that, he had a place of his own, and come what may, he was going to keep it.

Nor was there any fault to find with the place. From the moment Allen Ring rode his claybank into the valley he knew he was coming home. This was it; this was the place. Here he would stop. He'd been tumbleweeding all over the West now for ten years, and it was time he stopped if he ever did, and this looked like his fence corner.

Even the cabin looked good, although Taylor told him the place had been empty for three years. It looked solid and fit, and while the grass was waist high all over the valley and up around the house, he could see trails through it, some of them made by unshod ponies, which meant wild horses, and some by deer. Then there were the tracks of a single shod horse, always the same one.

Those tracks always led right up to the door, and they stopped there, yet he could see that somebody with mighty small feet had been walking up to peer into the windows. Why would a person want to look into a window more than once? The window of an empty cabin? He had gone up and looked in himself, and all he saw was a dusty, dark interior with a ray of light from the opposite window, a table, a couple of chairs, and a fine old fireplace that had been built by skilled hands.

"You never built that fireplace, Ben Taylor," Ring had muttered, "you who never could handle anything but a running iron or a deck of cards. You never built anything in your life as fine and useful as that."

The cabin sat on a low ledge of grass backed up against the towering cliff of red rock, and the spring was not more than fifty feet away, a stream that came out of the rock and trickled pleasantly into a small basin before spilling out and winding thoughtfully down the valley to join a larger stream, a quarter of a mile away.

There were some tall spruces around the cabin, and a couple of sycamores and a cottonwood near the spring. Some gooseberry bushes, too, and a couple of apple trees. The trees had been pruned.

"And you never did that, either, Ben Taylor!" Allen Ring said soberly. "I wish I knew more about this place."

Time had fled like a scared antelope, and with the scythe he found in the pole barn he cut off the tall grass around the house, patched up the holes in the cabin where the packrats had got in, and even thinned out the bushes—it had been several years since they had been touched—and repaired the pole barn.

———

THE DAY HE picked to clean out the spring was the day Gail Truman rode up to the house. He had been putting the finishing touches on a chair bottom he was making when he heard a horse's hoof strike stone, and he straightened up to see the girl sitting on the red pony. She was staring openmouthed at the stacked hay from the grass he had cut and the washed windows of the house. He saw her swing down and run up to the window, and dropping his tools he strolled up.

"Huntin' somebody, ma'am?"

She wheeled and stared at him, her wide blue eyes accusing. "What are you doing here?" she demanded. "What do you mean by moving in like this?"

He smiled, but he was puzzled, too. Ben Taylor had said nothing about a girl, especially a girl like this. "Why, I own the place!" he said. "I'm fixin' it up so's I can live here."

"You own it?" Her voice was incredulous, agonized. "You couldn't own it! You couldn't. The man who owns this place is gone, and he would never sell it! Never!"

"He didn't exactly sell it, ma'am," Ring said gently. "He lost it to me in a poker game. That was down Texas way."

She was horrified. "In a poker game? Whit Bayly in a poker game? I don't believe it!"

"The man I won it from was called Ben Taylor, ma'am." Ring took the deed from his pocket and opened it. "Come to think of it, Ben did say that if anybody asked about Whit Bayly to say that he died down in the Guadalupes—of lead poisoning."

"Whit Bayly is dead?" The girl looked stunned. "You're sure? Oh!"

Her face went white and still and something in it seemed to die. She turned with a little gesture of despair and stared out across the valley, and his eyes followed hers. It was strange, Allen Ring told himself, that it was the first time he had looked just that way, and he stood there, caught up by something nameless, some haunting sense of the familiar.

Before him lay the tall grass of the valley, turning slightly now with the brown of autumn, and to his right a dark stand of spruce, standing stiffly, like soldiers on parade, and beyond them the swell of the hill, and farther to the right the hill rolled up and stopped, and beyond lay a wider valley fading away into the vast purple and mauve of distance and here and there spotted with the golden candles of cottonwoods, their leaves bright yellow with nearing cold.

There was no word for this; it was a picture, yet a picture of which a man could only dream and never reproduce.

"It—it's beautiful, isn't it?" he said.

She turned on him, and for the first time she seemed really to look at him, a tall young man with a shock of rust-brown hair and somber gray eyes, having about him the look of a rider and the look of a lonely man.

"Yes, it is beautiful. Oh, I've come here so many times to see it, the cabin, too. I think this is the most lovely place I have ever seen. I used to dream about—" She stopped, suddenly confused. "Oh, I'm sorry. I shouldn't talk so."

She looked at him soberly. "I'd better go. I guess this is yours now."

He hesitated. "Ma'am," he said sincerely, "the place is

mine, and sure enough, I love it. I wouldn't swap this place for anything. But that view, that belongs to no man. It belongs to whoever looks at it with eyes to see it, so you come anytime you like, and look all you please."

Ring grinned. "Fact is," he said, "I'm aimin' to fix the place up inside, an' I'm sure no hand at such things. Maybe you could sort of help me. I'd like it kind of homey-like." He flushed. "You see, I sort of lived in bunkhouses all my life an' never had no such place."

S HE SMILED WITH a quick understanding and sympathy. "Of course! I'd love to, only"—her face sobered—"you won't be able to stay here. You haven't seen Ross Bilton yet, have you?"

"Who's he?" Ring asked curiously. He nodded toward the horsemen he saw approaching. "Is this the one?"

She turned quickly and nodded. "Be careful! He's the town marshal. The men with him are Ben Hagen and Stan Brule."

Brule he remembered—but would Brule remember him?

"By the way, my name is Allen Ring," he said, low voiced.

"I'm Gail Truman. My father owns the Tall T brand."

Bilton was a big man with a white hat. Ring decided he didn't like him and that the feeling was going to be mutual. Brule he knew, so the stocky man was Ben Hagen. Brule had changed but little, some thinner, maybe, but his hatchet face as lean and poisonous as always.

"How are you, Gail?" Bilton said briefly. "Is this a friend of yours?"

Allen Ring liked to get his cards on the table. "Yes, a friend of hers, but also the owner of the place."

"You own Red Rock?" Bilton was incredulous. "That will be very hard to prove, my friend. Also, this place is under the custody of the law."

"Whose law?" Ring wanted to know. He was aware that Brule was watching him, wary but uncertain as yet.

"Mine. I'm the town marshal. There was a murder committed here, and until that murder is solved and the killer brought to justice this place will not be touched. You have already seen fit to make changes, but perhaps the court will be lenient."

"You're the town marshal?" Allen Ring shoved his hat back on his head and reached for his tobacco. "That's mighty interestin'. Howsoever, let me remind you that you're out of town right now."

"That makes no difference!" Bilton's voice was sharp. Ring could see that he was not accustomed to being told off, that his orders were usually obeyed. "You will get off this place before nightfall!"

"It makes a sight of difference to me," Allen replied calmly. "I bought this place by stakin' everything I had against it in a poker game. I drew four cards to win, a nine to match one I had and three aces. It was a fool play that paid off. I registered the deed. She's mine legal. I know of no law that allows a place to be kept idle because there was a murder committed on it. If after three years it hasn't been solved, I suggest the town get a new marshal."

Ross Bilton was angry, but he kept himself under control. "I've warned you, and you've been told to leave. If you do not leave, I'll use my authority to move you."

Ring smiled. "Now listen, Bilton! You might pull that stuff on some folks that don't like trouble! You might bluff somebody into believin' you had the authority to do this. You don't bluff me, an' I simply don't scare—do I, Brule?"

He turned on Brule so sharply that the man stiffened in his saddle, his hand poised as though to grab for a gun. The breed's face stiffened with irritation, and then recognition came to him. "Allen Ring!" he said. "You again!"

"That's right, Brule. Only this time I'm not takin' cattle through the Indian Nation. Not pushin' them by that ratty bunch of rustlers an' highbinders you rode with." Ring turned his eyes toward Bilton. "You're the law? An' you ride with *him*? Why, the man's wanted in ever' county in Texas for everythin' from murder to horse thievin'."

Ross Bilton stared at Ring for a long minute. "You've been warned," he said.

"An' I'm stayin'," Ring replied sharply. "And keep your coyotes away if you come again. I don't like 'em!"

BRULE'S FINGERS SPREAD and his lips stiffened with cold fury. Ring watched him calmly. "You know better than that, Brule. Wait until my back is turned. If you reach for a gun I'll blow you out of your saddle."

Stan Brule slowly relaxed his hand, and then, wordless, he turned to follow Bilton and Hagen, who had watched with hard eyes.

Gail Truman was looking at him curiously. "Why, Brule was afraid of you!" she exclaimed. "Who are you, anyway?"

"Nobody, ma'am," he said simply. "I'm no gunfighter, just an hombre who ain't got brains enough to scare proper. Brule knows it. He knows he might beat me, but he knows I'd kill him. He was there when I killed a friend of his, Blaze Garden."

"But—but then you must be a gunman. Blaze Garden was a killer! I've heard Dad and the boys talk about him!"

"No, I'm no gunman. Blaze beat me to the draw. In fact, he got off his first shot before my gun cleared the holster, only he shot too quick and missed. His second and third shots hit me while I was walkin' into him. The third shot wasn't so bad because I was holdin' my fire and gettin' close. He got scared an' stepped back, and the fourth shot was too high. Then I shot and I was close up to him then. One was enough. One is always enough if you place it right."

He gestured at the place. "What's this all about? Mind tellin' me?"

"It's very simple, really. Nothing out here is very involved when you come to that. It seems that there's something out here that brings men to using guns much faster than in other places, and one thing stems from another.

"Whit Bayly owned this place. He was a fixing man, always tinkering and fixing things up. He was a tall, handsome man whom all the girls loved—"

"You, too?" he asked quizzically.

She flushed. "Yes, I guess so, only I'm only eighteen now, and that was three, almost four years ago. I wasn't very pretty or very noticeable and much too young.

"Sam Hazlitt was one of the richest men in the country

around here, and Whit had a run-in with him over a horse. There had been a lot of stealing going on around, and Hazlitt traced some stock of his to this ranch, or so he claimed. Anyway, he accused Bayly of it, and Whit told him not to talk foolish. Furthermore, he told Hazlitt to stay off of his ranch. Well, folks were divided over who was in the right, but Whit had a lot of friends and Hazlitt had four brothers, clannish as all get-out.

"Not long after, some riders from Buck Hazlitt's ranch came by that way and saw a body lying in the yard, right over near the spring. When they came down to have a look, thinking Whit was hurt, they found Sam Hazlitt, and he'd been shot dead—in the back.

"They headed right for town, hunting Whit, and they found him. He denied it, and they were goin' to hang him, had a rope around his neck, and then I—I—well, I swore he wasn't anywhere near his ranch all day."

"It wasn't true?" Ring asked keenly, his eyes searching the girl's face. She avoided his eyes, flushing even more.

"Not—not exactly. But I knew he wasn't guilty! I just knew he wouldn't shoot a man in the back! I told them he was over to our place, talking with me, and he hadn't time to get back there and kill Sam.

"Folks didn't like it much. Some of them still believed he killed Sam, and some didn't like it because despite the way I said it, they figured he was sparking a girl too young for him. I always said it wasn't that. As a matter of fact, I did see Whit over our way, but the rest of it was lies. Anyway, after a few weeks Whit up and left the country."

"I see—and nobody knows yet who killed Sam Hazlitt?"

"Nobody. One thing that was never understood was what became of Sam's account book—sort of a tally book, but more than that. It was a sort of record he kept of a lot of things, and it was gone out of his pocket. Nobody ever found it, but they did find the pencil Sam used on the sand nearby. Dad always figured Sam lived long enough to write something, but that the killer stole the book and destroyed it."

"How about the hands? Could they have picked it up? Did Bilton question them about that?"

"Oh, Bilton wasn't marshal then! In fact, he was riding for Buck Hazlitt then! He was one of the hands who found Sam's body!"

————

AFTER THE GIRL had gone Allen Ring walked back to the house and thought the matter over. He had no intention of leaving. This was just the ranch he wanted, and he intended to live right here, yet the problem fascinated him.

Living in the house and looking around the place had taught him a good deal about Whit Bayly. He was, as Gail had said, "a fixin' man," for there were many marks of his handiwork aside from the beautifully made fireplace and the pruned apple trees. He was, Ring was willing to gamble, no murderer.

Taylor had said he died of lead poisoning. Who had killed Bayly? Why? Was it a casual shooting over some rangeland argument, or had he been followed from here by someone bent on vengeance? Or someone who thought he might know too much?

"You'll like the place," Taylor had said—that was an angle he hadn't considered before. Ben Taylor had actually seen this place himself! The more sign he read, the more tricky the trail became, and Allen walked outside and sat down against the cabin wall when his supper was finished, and lighted a smoke.

Stock had been followed to the ranch by Sam Hazlitt. If Whit was not the thief, then who was? Where had the stock been driven? He turned his eyes almost automatically toward the Mogollons, the logical place. His eyes narrowed, and he recalled that one night while playing cards they had been talking of springs and waterholes, and Ben Taylor had talked about Fossil Springs, a huge spring that roared thousands of gallons of water out of the earth.

"Place a man could run plenty of stock," he had said and winked, "and nobody the wiser!"

Those words had been spoken far away and long ago, and the Red Rock ranch had not yet been put on the table; that was months later. There was, he recalled, a Fossil Creek somewhere north of here. And Fossil Creek might flow from Fossil Springs—perhaps Ben Taylor had talked more to effect than he knew. That had been Texas, and this was Arizona, and a casual bunkhouse conversation probably seemed harmless enough.

"We'll see, Ben!" Ring muttered grimly. "We'll see!"

Ross Bilton had been one of the Hazlitt hands at the time of the killing, one of the first on the scene. Now he was town marshal but interested in keeping the ranch unoccupied— why?

None of it made sense, yet actually it was no business of his. Allen Ring thought that over and decided it was his business in a sense. He now owned the place and lived on it. If an old murder was to interfere with his living there, it behooved him to know the facts. It was a slight excuse for his curiosity.

Morning came and the day drew on toward noon, and there was no sign of Bilton or Brule. Ring had loaded his rifle and kept it close to hand, and he was wearing two guns, thinking he might need a loaded spare, although he rarely wore more than one. Also, inside the cabin door he had his double-barreled shotgun.

The spring drew his attention. At the moment he did not wish to leave the vicinity of the cabin, and that meant it was a good time to clean out the spring. Not that it needed it, but there were loose stones in the bottom of the basin and some moss. With this removed he would have more water and clearer water. With a wary eye toward the canyon mouth, he began his work.

———

THE SOUND OF an approaching horse drew him erect. His rifle stood against the rocks at hand, and his guns were ready, yet as the rider came into sight, he saw there was only one man, a stranger.

He rode a fine bay gelding and he was not a young man, but thick and heavy with drooping mustache and kind blue eyes. He drew up.

"Howdy!" he said affably, yet taking a quick glance around

before looking again at Ring. "I'm Rolly Truman, Gail's father."

"It's a pleasure," Ring said, wiping his wet hands on a red bandanna. "Nice to know the neighbors." He nodded at the spring. "I picked me a job. That hole's deeper than it looks!"

"Good flow of water," Truman agreed. He chewed his mustache thoughtfully. "I like to see a young man with get-up about him, startin' his own spread, willin' to work."

Allen Ring waited. The man was building up to something; what, he knew not. It came then, carefully at first, yet shaping a loop as it drew near.

"Not much range here, of course," Truman added. "You should have more graze. Ever been over in Cedar Basin? Or up along the East Verde bottom? Wonderful land up there, still some wild, but a country where a man could really do something with a few whiteface cattle."

"No, I haven't seen it," Ring replied, "but I'm satisfied. I'm not land hungry. All I want is a small piece, an' this suits me fine."

Truman shifted in his saddle and looked uncomfortable. "Fact is, son, you're upsettin' a lot of folks by bein' here. What you should do is to move."

"I'm sorry," Ring said flatly. "I don't want to make enemies, but I won this place on a four-card draw. Maybe I'm a fatalist, but somehow or other, I think I should stick here. No man's got a right to think he can draw four cards and win anythin', but I did, an' in a plenty rough game. I had everythin' I owned in that pot. Now I got the place."

The rancher sat his horse uneasily, and then he shook his head. "Son, you've sure got to move! There's no trouble here now, and if you stay she's liable to open old sores, start more trouble than any of us can stop. Besides, how did Ben Taylor get title to this place? Bayly had no love for him. I doubt if your title will stand up in court."

"As to that I don't know," Ring persisted stubbornly. "I have a deed that's legal enough, and I've registered that deed an' my brand along with it. I did find out that Bayly had no heirs. So I reckon I'll sit tight until somebody comes along with a better legal claim than mine."

Truman ran his hand over his brow. "Well, I guess I don't blame you much, son. Maybe I shouldn't have come over, but I know Ross Bilton and his crowd, and I reckon I wanted to save myself some trouble as well as you. Gail, she thinks you're a fine young man. In fact, you're the first man she's ever showed interest in since Whit left, and she was a youngster then. It was a sort of hero worship she had for him. I don't want trouble."

Allen Ring leaned on the shovel and looked up at the older man. "Truman," he said, "are you sure you aren't buyin' trouble by tryin' to avoid it? Just what's your stake in this?"

The rancher sat very still, his face drawn and pale. Then he got down from his horse and sat on a rock. Removing his hat, he mopped his brow.

"Son," he said slowly, "I reckon I got to trust you. You've heard of the Hazlitts. They are a hard, clannish bunch, men who lived by the gun most of their lives. Sam was murdered. Folks all know that when they find out who murdered him and why, there's goin' to be plenty of trouble around here. Plenty."

"Did you kill him?"

Truman jerked his head up. "No! No, you mustn't get that idea, but—well, you know how small ranchers are. There was a sight of rustlin' them days, and the Hazlitts were the big outfit. They lost cows."

"And some of them got your brand?" Ring asked shrewdly.

Truman nodded. "I reckon. Not so many, though. And not only me. Don't get me wrong, I'm not beggin' off the blame. Part of it is mine, all right, but I didn't get many. Eight or ten of us hereabouts slapped brands on Hazlitt stock—and at least five of us have the biggest brands around here now, some as big almost as the Hazlitts."

ALLEN RING STUDIED the skyline thoughtfully. It was an old story and one often repeated in the West. When the

War Between the States ended, men came home to Texas and the Southwest to find cattle running in thousands, unbranded and unowned. The first man to slap on a brand was the owner, with no way he could be contested.

Many men grew rich with nothing more than a wide loop and a running iron. Then the unbranded cattle were gone, the ranches had settled into going concerns, and the great days of casual branding had ended, yet there was still free range, and a man with that same loop and running iron could still build a herd fast.

More than one of the biggest ranchers had begun that way, and many of them continued to brand loose stock wherever found. No doubt that had been true here, and these men like Rolly Truman, good, able men who had fought Indians and built their homes to last, had begun just that way. Now the range was mostly fenced, and ranches had narrowed somewhat, but Ring could see what it might mean to open an old sore.

Sam Hazlitt had been trailing rustlers—he had found out who they were and where the herds were taken, and he had been shot down from behind. The catch was that the tally book, with his records, was still missing. That tally book might contain evidence as to the rustling done by men who were now pillars of the community and open them to the vengeance of the Hazlitt outfit.

Often western men threw a blanket over a situation. If a rustler had killed Sam, then all the rustlers involved would be equally guilty. Anyone who lived on this ranch might stumble on that tally book and throw the range into a bloody gun war in which many men now beyond the errors of their youth, with homes, families, and different customs, would die.

It could serve no purpose to blow the lid off the trouble now, yet Allen Ring had a hunch. In their fear of trouble for themselves they might be concealing an even greater crime, aiding a murderer in his escape. There were lines of care in the face of Rolly Truman that a settled, established rancher should not have.

"Sorry," Ring said, "I'm stayin'. I like this place."

ALL THROUGH THE noon hour the tension was building. The air was warm and sultry, and there was a thickening haze over the mountains. There was that hot thickness in the air that presaged a storm. When he left his coffee to return to work, Ring saw three horsemen coming into the canyon mouth at a running walk. He stopped in the door and touched his lips with his tongue.

They reined up at the door, three hard-bitten, hard-eyed men with rifles across their saddlebows. Men with guns in their holsters and men of a kind that would never turn from trouble. These were men with the bark on, lean fanatics with lips thinned with old bitterness.

The older man spoke first. "Ring, I've heard about you. I'm Buck Hazlitt. These are my brothers, Joe and Dolph. There's talk around that you aim to stay on this place. There's been talk for years that Sam hid his tally book here. We figure the killer got that book and burned it. Maybe he did, and again, maybe not. We want that book. If you want to stay on this place, you stay. But if you find that book, you bring it to us."

Ring looked from one to the other, and he could see the picture clearly. With men like these, hard and unforgiving, it was no wonder Rolly Truman and the other ranchers were worried. The years and prosperity had eased Rolly and his like into comfort and softness, but not these. The Hazlitts were of feudal blood and background.

"Hazlitt," Ring said, "I know how you feel. You lost a brother, and that means somethin', but if that book is still around, which I doubt, and I find it, I'll decide what to do with it all by myself. I don't aim to start a range war. Maybe there's some things best forgotten. The man who murdered Sam Hazlitt ought to pay."

"We'll handle that," Dolph put in grimly. "You find that book, you bring it to us. If you don't—" His eyes hardened. "Well, we'd have to class you with the crooks."

Ring's eyes shifted to Dolph. "Class if you want," he flared. "I'll do what seems best to me with that book. But all of you folks are plumb proddy over that tally book. Chances are nine out of ten the killer found it and destroyed it."

"I don't reckon he did," Buck said coldly, "because we know he's been back here, a-huntin' it. Him an' his girl."

Ring stiffened. "You mean—?"

"What we mean is our figger, not yours." Buck Hazlitt reined his horse around. "You been told. You bring that book to us. You try to buck the Hazlitts and you won't stay in this country."

Ring had his back up. Despite himself he felt cold anger mounting within him. "Put this in your pipe, friend," he said harshly. "I came here to stay. No Hazlitt will change that. I ain't huntin' trouble, but if you bring trouble to me, I'll handle it. I can bury a Hazlitt as easy as any other man!"

Not one of them condescended to notice the remark. Turning their horses they walked them down the canyon and out of it into the sultry afternoon. Allen Ring mopped the sweat from his face and listened to the deep rumbling of far-off thunder, growling among the canyons like a grizzly with a toothache. It was going to rain. Sure as shootin', it was going to rain—a regular gully washer.

There was yet time to finish the job on the spring, so he picked up his shovel and started back for the job. The rock basin was nearly cleaned and he finished removing the few rocks and the moss that had gathered. Then he opened the escape channel a little more to ensure a more rapid emptying and filling process in the basin into which the trickle of water fell.

The water emerged from a crack in the rocks and trickled into the basin, and finishing his job, Ring glanced thoughtfully to see if anything remained undone. There was still some moss on the rocks from which the water flowed and, kneeling down, he leaned over to scrape it away, and pulling away the last shreds, he noticed a space from which a rock had recently fallen. Pulling more moss away, he dislodged another rock, and there, pushed into a niche, was a small black book!

Sam Hazlitt, dying, had evidently managed to shove it

back in this crack in the rocks, hoping it would be found by someone not the killer.

Sitting back on his haunches, Ring opened the faded, canvas-bound book. A flap crossed over the page ends, and the book had been closed by a small tongue that slid into a loop of the canvas cover. Opening the book, he saw the pages were stained, but still legible.

The next instant he was struck by lightning. At least, that was what seemed to happen. Thunder crashed, and something struck him on the skull and he tried to rise and something struck again. He felt a drop of rain on his face and his eyes opened wide and then another blow caught him and he faded out into darkness, his fingers clawing at the grass to keep from slipping down into that velvety, smothering blackness.

———

HE WAS WET. He turned a little, lying there, thinking he must have left a window open and the rain was—his eyes opened and he felt rain pounding on his face and he stared, not at a boot with a California spur, but at dead brown grass, soaked with rain now, and the glistening smoothness of waterworn stones. He was soaked to the hide.

Struggling to his knees, he looked around, his head heavy, his lips and tongue thick. He blinked at a gray, rain-slanted world and at low gray clouds and a distant rumble of thunder following a streak of lightning along the mountaintops.

Lurching to his feet, he stumbled toward the cabin and pitched over the doorsill to the floor. Struggling again to his feet he got the door closed, and in a vague, misty half world of consciousness he struggled out of his clothes and got his hands on a rough towel and fumblingly dried himself.

He did not think. He was acting purely from vague instinctive realization of what he must do. He dressed again, in dry clothes, and dropped at the table. After a while he sat up and it was dark, and he knew he had blacked out again. He lighted a light and nearly dropped it to the floor. Then he stumbled to the washbasin and splashed his face with cold water. Then he bathed his scalp, feeling tenderly of the lacerations there.

A boot with a California spur.

That was all he had seen. The tally book was gone, and a man wearing a new boot with a California-type spur, a large rowel, had taken it. He got coffee on, and while he waited for it he took his guns out and dried them painstakingly, wiping off each shell, and then replacing them in his belt with other shells from a box on a shelf.

He reloaded the guns, and then slipping into his slicker he went outside for his rifle. Between sips of coffee, he worked over his rifle until he was satisfied. Then he threw a small pack together and stuffed his slicker pockets with shotgun shells.

The shotgun was an express gun and short barreled. He slung it from a loop under the slicker. Then he took a lantern and went to the stable and saddled the claybank. Leading the horse outside into the driving rain, he swung into the saddle and turned along the road toward Basin.

There was no letup in the rain. It fell steadily and heavily, yet the claybank slogged along, alternating between a shambling trot and a fast walk. Allen Ring, his chin sunk in the upturned collar of his slicker, watched the drops fall from the brim of his Stetson and felt the bump of the shotgun under his coat.

He had seen little of the tally book, but sufficient to know that it would blow the lid off the very range war they were fearing. Knowing the Hazlitts, he knew they would bring fire and gunplay to every home even remotely connected with the death of their brother.

———

THE HORSE SLID down a steep bank and shambled across the wide wash. Suddenly, the distant roar that had been in his ears for some time sprang into consciousness and he jerked his head up. His horse snorted in alarm, and Ring stared, openmouthed, at the wall of water, towering all of ten feet high, that was rolling down the wash toward him.

With a shrill rebel yell he slapped the spurs to the claybank, and the startled horse turned loose with an astounded leap and hit the ground in a dead run. There was no time to slow for the bank of the wash, and the horse went up, slipped at the very brink, and started to fall back.

Ring hit the ground with both boots and scrambled over the brink, and even as the flood roared down upon them, he heaved on the bridle and the horse cleared the edge and stood trembling. Swearing softly, Ring kicked the mud from his boots and mounted again. Leaving the raging torrent behind him, he rode on.

Thick blackness of night and heavy clouds lay upon the town when he loped down the main street and headed the horse toward the barn. He swung down and handed the bridle to the handyman.

"Rub him down," he said. "I'll be back."

He started for the doors and then stopped, staring at the three horses in neighboring stalls. The liveryman noticed his glance and looked at him.

"The Hazlitts. They come in about an hour ago, ugly as sin."

Allen Ring stood wide legged, staring grimly out the door. There was a coolness inside him now that he recognized. He dried his hands carefully.

"Bilton in town?" he asked.

"Sure is. Playin' cards over to the Mazatzal Saloon."

"He wear Mex spurs? Big rowels?"

The man rubbed his jaw. "I don't remember. I don't know at all. You watch out," he warned. "Folks are on the prod."

Ring stepped out into the street and slogged through the mud to the edge of the boardwalk before the darkened general store. He kicked the mud from his boots and dried his hands again, after carefully unbuttoning his slicker.

Nobody would have a second chance after this. He knew well enough that his walking into the Mazatzal would precipitate an explosion. Only, he wanted to light the fuse himself, in his own way.

He stood there in the darkness alone, thinking it over. They would all be there. It would be like tossing a match into a lot of fused dynamite. He wished then that he was a better man with a gun than he was or that he had someone to side him in this, but he had always acted alone and would scarcely know how to act with anyone else.

He walked along the boardwalk with long strides, his boots making hard sounds under the steady roar of the rain. He couldn't place that spur, that boot. Yet he had to. He had to get his hands on that book.

Four horses stood, heads down in the rain, saddles covered with slickers. He looked at them and saw they were of three different brands. The window of the Mazatzal was rain wet, yet standing at one side he glanced within.

The long room was crowded and smoky. Men lined the bar, feet on the brass rail. A dozen tables were crowded with cardplayers. Everyone seemed to have taken refuge here from the rain. Picking out the Hazlitt boys, Allen saw them gathered together at the back end of the room. Then he got Ross Bilton pegged. He was at a table playing cards, facing the door. Stan Brule was at this end of the bar, and Hagen was at a table against the wall, the three of them making three points of a flat triangle whose base was the door.

———

IT WAS NO accident. Bilton, then, expected trouble, and he was not looking toward the Hazlitts. Yet, on reflection, Ring could see the triangle could center fire from three directions on the Hazlitts as well. There was a man with his back to the door who sat in the game with Bilton. And not far from Hagen, Rolly Truman was at the bar.

Truman was toying with his drink, just killing time. Everybody seemed to be waiting for something.

Could it be him they waited upon? No, that was scarcely to be considered. They could not know he had found the book, although it was certain at least one man in the room knew, and possibly others. Maybe it was just the tension, the building up of feeling over his taking over of the place at Red Rock. Allen Ring carefully turned down the collar of his slicker and wiped his hands dry again.

He felt jumpy and could feel that dryness in his mouth that always came on him at times like this. He touched his gun butts and then stepped over and opened the door.

Everyone looked up or around at once. Ross Bilton held a card aloft, and his hand froze at the act of dealing, holding still for a full ten seconds while Ring closed the door. He surveyed the room again and saw Ross play the card and say something in an undertone to the man opposite him. The man turned his head slightly and it was Ben Taylor!

The gambler looked around, his face coldly curious, and for an instant their eyes met across the room, and then Allen Ring started toward him.

There was no other sound in the room, although they could all hear the unceasing roar of the rain on the roof. Ring saw something leap up in Taylor's eyes, and his own took on a sardonic glint.

"That was a good hand you dealt me down Texas way," Ring said. "A good hand!"

"You'd better draw more cards," Taylor said. "You're holdin' a small pair!"

Ring's eyes shifted as the man turned slightly. It was the jingle of his spurs that drew his eyes, and there they were, the large-roweled California-style spurs, not common here. He stopped beside Taylor so the man had to tilt his head back to look up. Ring was acutely conscious that he was now centered between the fire of Brule and Hagen. The Hazlitts looked on curiously, uncertain as to what was happening.

"Give it to me, Taylor," Ring said quietly. "Give it to me now."

There was ice in his voice, and Taylor, aware of the awkwardness of his position, got to his feet, inches away from Ring.

"I don't know what you're talking about," he flared.

"No?"

Ring was standing with his feet apart a little, and his hands were breast high, one of them clutching the edge of his raincoat. He hooked with his left from that position, and the blow was too short, too sudden, and too fast for Ben Taylor.

The crack of it on the angle of his jaw was audible, and then Ring's right came up in the gambler's solar plexus and the man's knees sagged. Spinning him around, Ring ripped open his coat with a jerk that scattered buttons across the room. Then from an inside pocket he jerked the tally book.

He saw the Hazlitts start at the same instant that Bilton sprang back from the chair, upsetting it.

"Get him!" Bilton roared. "Get him!"

Ring shoved Taylor hard into the table, upsetting it and causing Bilton to spring back to keep his balance, and at the same instant, Ring dropped to a half crouch and turning left he drew with a flash of speed and saw Brule's gun come up at almost the same instant, and then he fired!

————

STAN BRULE WAS caught with his gun just level, and the bullet smashed him on the jaw. The tall man staggered, his face a mask of hatred and astonishment mingled, and then Ring fired again, doing a quick spring around with his knees bent, turning completely around in one leap, and firing as his feet hit the floor. He felt Hagen's bullet smash into him, and he tottered. Then he fired coolly, and swinging as he fired, he caught Bilton right over the belt buckle.

It was fast action, snapping, quick, yet deliberate. The four fired shots had taken less than three seconds.

Stepping back, he scooped the tally book from the floor where it had dropped and then pocketed it. Bilton was on the floor, coughing blood. Hagen had a broken right arm and was swearing in a thick, stunned voice.

Stan Brule had drawn his last gun. He had been dead before he hit the floor. The Hazlitts started forward with a lunge, and Allen Ring took another step backward, dropping his pistol and swinging the shotgun, still hanging from his shoulder, into firing position.

"Get back!" he said thickly. "Get back or I'll kill the three of you! Back—back to where you stood!"

Their faces wolfish, the three stood lean and dangerous, yet the shotgun brooked no refusal, and slowly, bitterly and reluctantly, the three moved back, step by step.

Ring motioned with the shotgun. "All of you—along the wall!"

The men rose and moved back, their eyes on him, uncertain, wary, some of them frightened.

Allen Ring watched them go, feeling curiously lightheaded and uncertain. He tried to frown away the pain from his throbbing skull, yet there was a pervading weakness from somewhere else.

"My gosh!" Rolly Truman said. "The man's been shot! He's bleeding!"

"Get back!" Ring said thickly.

His eyes shifted to the glowing potbellied stove, and he moved forward, the shotgun waist high, his eyes on the men who stared at him, awed.

The sling held the gun level, his hand partly supporting it, a finger on the trigger. With his left hand he opened the stove and then fumbled in his pocket.

Buck Hazlitt's eyes bulged. "No!" he roared. "No you don't!"

He lunged forward, and Ring tipped the shotgun and fired a blast into the floor, inches ahead of Hazlitt's feet. The rancher stopped so suddenly he almost fell, and the shotgun tipped to cover him.

"Back!" Ring said. He swayed on his feet. "Back!" He fished out the tally book and threw it into the flames.

Something like a sigh went through the crowd. They stared, awed as the flames seized hungrily at the opened book, curling around the leaves with hot fingers, turning them brown and then black and to ashes.

Half hypnotized the crowd watched. Then Ring's eyes swung to Hazlitt. "It was Ben Taylor killed him," he muttered. "Taylor, an' Bilton was with him. He—he seen it."

"We take your word for it?" Buck Hazlitt demanded furiously.

Allen Ring's eyes widened and he seemed to gather himself. "You want to question it? You want to call me a liar?"

Hazlitt looked at him, touching his tongue to his lips. "No," he said. "I figured it was them."

"I told you true," Ring said, and then his legs seemed to fold up under him and he went to the floor.

The crowd surged forward and Rolly Truman stared at

Buck as Hazlitt neared the stove. The big man stared into the flames for a minute. Then he closed the door.

"Good!" he said. "Good thing! It's been a torment, that book, like a cloud hangin' over us all!"

———

THE SUN WAS shining through the window when Gail Truman came to see him. He was sitting up in bed and feeling better. It would be good to be back on the place again, for there was much to do. She came in, slapping her boots with her quirt and smiling.

"Feel better?" she asked brightly. "You certainly look better. You've shaved."

He grinned and rubbed his jaw. "I needed it. Almost two weeks in this bed. I must have been hit bad."

"You lost a lot of blood. It's lucky you've a strong heart."

"It ain't—isn't so strong anymore," he said, "I think it's grown mighty shaky here lately."

Gail blushed. "Oh? It has? Your nurse, I suppose?"

"She is pretty, isn't she?"

Gail looked up, alarmed. "You mean, you—"

"No, honey," he said, "you!"

"Oh." She looked at him and then looked down. "Well, I guess—"

"All right?"

She smiled then, suddenly and warmly. "All right."

"I had to ask you," he said. "We had to marry."

"Had to? Why?"

"People would talk, a young, lovely girl like you over at my place all the time—would they think you were looking at the view?"

"If they did," she replied quickly, "they'd be wrong!"

"You're telling me?" he asked.

ONE LAST GUN NOTCH

MORGAN CLYDE STUDIED his face in the mirror. It was an even-featured, pleasant face. Neither the nose nor jaw was too blunt or too long. Now, after his morning shave, his jaw was still faintly blue through the deep tan, and the bronze curls above his face made him look several years younger than his thirty-five.

Carefully, he knotted the black string tie on the soft gray shirt and then slipped on his coat. When he donned the black, flat-crowned hat, he was ready. His appearance was perfect, with just a shade of studied carelessness. For ten years now, Morgan Clyde's morning shave and dressing had been a ritual from which he never deviated.

He slid the two guns from their holsters and checked them carefully. First the right, then the left. On the butt of the right-hand gun there were nine filed notches. On the left, three. He glanced at them thoughtfully, remembering.

That first notch had been for Red Bridges. That was the year they had run his cattle off. Bridges had come out to the claim when Clyde was away, cut his fence down, run his cattle off, and shot his wife down in cold blood.

Thoughtfully, Morgan Clyde looked back into the mirror. He had changed. In his mind's eye he could see that tall, loose-limbed young man with the bronze hair and boyish face. He had been quiet, peace loving, content with his wife, his homestead, and his few cattle. He had a gift for gun handling, but never thought of it. That is, not until that visit by Bridges.

Returning home with a haunch of antelope across his saddle, he had found his wife and the smoking ruins of his home. He did not have to be told. Bridges had warned him to move, or else. Within him something had burst, and for an instant his eyes were blind with blood. When the moment had passed, he had changed.

He had known, then, what to do. He should have gone to the governor with his story, or to the U.S. marshal. And he could have gone. But there was something red and ugly inside him that had not been there before. He had swung aboard a little paint pony and headed for Peavey's Mill.

The town's one street had been quiet, dusty. The townspeople knew what had happened, because it had been happening to all homesteaders. Never for a moment did they expect any reaction. Red Bridges was too well known. He had killed too many times.

Then Morgan Clyde rode down the street on his paint pony, saw Bridges, and slid to the ground. Somebody yelled, and Bridges turned. He looked at Morgan Clyde's young, awkward length and laughed. But his hand dropped swiftly for his gun.

But something happened. Morgan Clyde's gun swung up first, spouting fire, and his two shots centered over Bridges's heart. The big man's fingers loosened, and the gun slid into the dust. Little whorls rose slowly from where it landed. Then, his face puzzled, his left hand fumbling at his breast, Red Bridges wilted.

He could have stopped there. Now, Morgan Clyde knew that. He could have stopped there, and *should* have stopped. He could have ridden from town and been left alone. But he knew Bridges was a tool, and the man who used the tool was Erik Pendleton, in the bank. Bridges had been a gunman; Pendleton was not.

The banker looked up from his desk and saw death. It was no mistake. Clyde had walked up the steps, around the teller's cage, and opened the door of Pendleton's office.

The banker opened his mouth to talk, and Morgan Clyde shot him. He had deserved it.

The posse lost him west of the Brazos, and he rode on west into a cattle war. He was wanted then and no longer cared. The banker hadn't rated a notch, but the three men he killed in the streets of Fort Sumner he counted, and the man he shot west of Gallup.

There had been trouble in St. George, and then in Virginia City. After that, he had a reputation.

Morgan Clyde turned and stared at the huge old grandfather's clock. It remained his only permanent possession. It had come over from Scotland years ago, and his family had carried it westward when they went to Ohio, and later to Illinois; and then to Texas. He had intended sending for it when the homestead was going right, and everything was settled. To Diana and himself it had been a symbol of home, of stability.

What could have started him remembering all that? The past, he had decided long ago, was best forgotten.

———

HE RODE THE big black down the street toward Sherman's office. He knew what was coming. He had been taking money for a long time from men of Sherman's stripe. Men who needed what force could give them but had nothing of force in themselves.

Sherman had several gunmen on his payroll. He kept them hating one another and grew fat on their hatred. Tom Cool was there, and the Earle brothers. Tough and vicious, all of them.

Perhaps it was this case this morning that had started him thinking. Well, that damned fool nester should have known better than to settle on that Red Basin land. It was Sherman's best grazing land, even if he didn't own it. But a kid like that couldn't buck Sherman. The man was a fool to think he could.

The thought of that other young nester came into his mind. He dismissed it with an impatient jerk of his head.

The Earle brothers, Vic and Will, were sitting in the bar as he passed through. The two big men looked up, hate in their eyes.

Sherman was sitting behind the desk in his office and he looked up, smiling, when Morgan Clyde came in. "Sit down, Morg," he said cheerfully. He leaned back in his chair and put his fingertips together. "Well, this is it. When we get this Hallam taken care of, the rest of the nesters will see we mean business. We can have that range clean by spring, an' that means I'll be running the biggest herd west of the Staked Plains."

Tom Cool was sitting in a chair tilted against the wall. He had a thin, hatchet face and narrow eyes. He was rolling a smoke now, and he glanced up as his tongue touched the edge of the yellow paper.

"You got the stomach for it, Morg?" he asked dryly. "Or would you rather I handle this one? I hear you was a nester once yourself."

Morgan Clyde glanced around casually, one brow lifting. "You handle my work?" He looked his contempt. "Cool, you might handle this job. It's just a cold-blooded killing, and more in your line. I'm used to men with guns in their hands."

Cool's eyes narrowed dangerously. "Yeah?" His voice was a hoarse whisper. "I can fill mine fast enough, Clyde, anytime you want to unlimber."

"I don't shoot sitting pigeons," Morgan said quietly.

"Why, you—" Tom Cool's eyes flared with hatred, and his hand dropped away from the cigarette in a streak for his gun.

Morgan Clyde filled his hand without more than a hint of movement. Before a shot could crash, Sherman's voice cut through the hot intensity of the moment with an edge that turned both their heads toward the leader. There was a gun in his hand.

Queerly, Morgan was shocked. He had never thought of Sherman as a fast man with a gun, and he knew that Cool felt the same. Sherman a gunman! It put a new complexion on a lot of things. Clyde glanced at Tom Cool and saw the man's hand coming away from his gun. There had been an instant when both of them could have died. If not by their own guns, by Sherman's. Neither had been watching him.

"You boys better settle down," Sherman said, leaning back in his swivel chair. "Any shooting that's done in my outfit will be done by me."

He looked up at Clyde, and there was something very much like triumph in his eyes. "You're getting slow, Morg," Sherman said. "I could have killed you before you got your gun out."

"Maybe."

Sherman shrugged. "You go see this Hallam, Clyde. I want him killed, see? An' the house burned. What happens to his wife is no business of yours. I got other plans." He grinned, revealing broken teeth. "Yeah, I got other plans for her."

Clyde spun on his heel and walked outside. He was just about to swing into the saddle when Tom Cool drifted up. Cool spoke low and out the corner of his mouth. "Did you see that, Morg? Did you see the way he got that gun into action? That gent's poison. Why's he been keepin' that from us? Somethin' around here smells to high heaven."

He took his belt up a notch. "Morg, let's move in on him together. Let's take this over. There's goin' to be a fortune out there in that valley. You got a head on you. You take care of the business, an' I'll handle the rough stuff. Let's take Sherman out of there. He's framin' to queer both of us."

Morgan Clyde swung into the saddle. "No sale, Tom," he said quietly. "Riding our trail, we ride alone. Anyway, I'm not the type to sell out or double-deal. When I'm through with Sherman I'll tell him so to his face."

"He'll kill you!"

Clyde smiled wearily. "Maybe."

———

He TURNED HIS horse and rode away. So Sherman was a gunman.

Tom Cool was right, there was something very wrong about that. The man hired his fighting done, rarely carried a weapon, and no one had ever suspected he might be fast. That was a powerful weapon in the hands of a double-crosser. A man who was lightning with a gun and unsuspected—

After all, where did he and Cool stand? Sherman owed him ten thousand dollars for dirty work done, for cattle run off, for forcing men to leave, for a couple of shootings. Tom Cool was in the same position. Now, with Hallam out of the way and the nesters gone, he would no longer need either Cool or himself.

Suddenly, Morgan Clyde remembered Sherman's broken teeth, his sly smile, his insinuating manner when he spoke of

Hallam's wife. Oddly, for the first time, he began to see himself in a clear light. A hired gun for a man with the instincts of a rat! It wasn't a nice thought. He shook himself angrily, forcing himself to concentrate on the business at hand.

Vic Hallam was young, and he was green. He was, they said, a fine shot with a rifle, and a fair man with a gun when he got it out, but by western standards he was pitifully slow. He was about twenty-six, his wife a mere girl of nineteen, and pretty. Despite his youth, Hallam was outspoken. He had led the resistance against Sherman, and had sworn to stay in Red Basin as long as he wished. He had every legal right to the land, and Sherman had none.

But Morgan Clyde had long ago shelved any regard for the law. The man with the fastest gun was the law along the frontier, and so far he had been fastest. If Sherman wanted the Red Basin, he'd get it. If it was over Hallam's dead body, then that's how it would be.

He had never backed out on a job yet, and never would. Hallam would be taken care of.

Morgan rode at a rapid trot, knowing very well what he had to do. Hallam was a man of a fiery temper, and it would be easy to goad him into grabbing for a gun.

Clyde shook his head, striving to clear it of upsetting thoughts. With the ten thousand he had coming, he could go away. He could find a new country, buy a ranch, and live quietly somewhere beyond the reach of his reputation. Yet even as he told himself that, he knew it was not true. A few years ago he might have done just that, but now it was too late. Wherever he went there would be smoking guns, split seconds of blasting fire and the thunder of shooting. And wherever he went he would be pointed out as a killer.

The heat waves danced along the valley floor, and he reined in his horse, moving at a walk. In his mind he seemed to be back again in the house he had built with Diana, and he remembered how they had talked of having the clock.

Then he was riding around the cluster of rocks and into the ranchyard at Red Basin. Sitting warily, with his hands loose and ready, he rode toward the house. A young woman came to the door and threw out some water. When she looked up, she saw him.

He was close enough then, and her face went deathly pale. Her eyes widened a little. Something inside of him shrank. He knew she recognized him.

"What—what do you want?" she asked.

He looked down at her wide eyes. She was pretty, he decided.

"I wanted to see Mr. Hallam, ma'am."

She hesitated. "Won't you get down and sit on the porch? He's gone out now, but he'll be back soon. He—he saw some antelope over by the Rim Rocks."

Antelope! Morgan Clyde stiffened a little, then relaxed. He had hard work to make believe this was real. The girl—why, she was almost the size of Diana and almost, he admitted, as pretty. And the house—there was the wash bench, the homemade furniture, just like their own place. And now Hallam was after antelope.

It was all the same, even the rifle in the corner. . . . Something in him leaped. The rifle! A moment ago it had stood in the corner, and now it was gone! Instinctively, he threw himself from his chair—a split second before the shot blasted past his head.

Catlike, he came to his feet. He had twisted the rifle from the girl's hands before she could shoot again. Coolly, he ejected the shells from the rifle and dropped them on the table. He looked at the girl, smiling with an odd light of respect in his eyes. He noted there wasn't a sign of fright or tears in hers.

"Nice try," he said quietly.

"You came here to kill my husband," she said. It wasn't an accusation; it was a flat statement.

"Maybe." He shrugged. "Maybe so."

"Why do you want to kill him?" she demanded fiercely. "What did he ever do to you?"

Morgan Clyde looked at her thoughtfully. "Nothing, of course. But this land is needed by someone else. Perhaps you should move off."

"We like it here!" she retorted.

He looked around. "It's nice. I like it, too." He pointed to the corner across the room. "There should be a clock over there, a grandfather's clock."

She looked at him, surprised. "We—we're going to have one. Someday."

He got up and walked over to the newly made shelves and looked at the china. It had blue figures running around the edges, Dutch boys and girls and mills.

He turned toward the window. "I should think you'd have it open on such a nice morning," he said. "More air. And I like to see a curtain stir in a light wind. Don't you?"

"Yes, but the window sticks. Vic was going to fix it, but he's been so busy."

Morgan Clyde picked up the hammer and drew the strips of molding from around the window, then lifted it out. Resting one corner on the table, he slipped his knife from his pocket and carefully shaved the edges. He tried the window twice before it moved easily. Then he replaced it and nailed the molding back in position. He tried it again, sliding the window up. A light breeze stirred the curtain, and the girl laughed. He turned, smiling gravely.

The sunlight fell across the rough-hewn floor, and when he raised his eyes, he could see a man riding down the trail.

Morgan Clyde turned slowly, and looked at the girl. Her eyes widened.

"No!" she gasped. "Please! Not that!"

Morgan Clyde didn't look back. He walked out to the porch and swung into the saddle. He reined the black around and started toward the approaching homesteader.

Before Hallam could speak, Clyde said, "Bad way to carry your rifle. Never can tell when you might need it!"

"Clyde!" Hallam exclaimed sharply. "What—"

"Good morning, Mr. Hallam," Morgan Clyde said, smiling a little. "Nice place you've got here."

He touched his heels to the black and rode away at a canter. Behind him, the man stared, frowning. . . .

It wasn't until Clyde was riding down the street of the town that he thought of what was coming. *This is it,* he said to himself. *You knew there would have to be an end to this sort of thing, and this is it.*

The Earle brothers were still in the bar. They looked up at him as he passed, their eyes hard. He stepped to the door of the office and opened it. Sherman was seated at the desk, and Tom Cool was tilted back on his chair against the wall. Nothing, apparently, had changed—except himself.

"I'm quitting, Sherman," he said quietly. "You owe me ten thousand dollars. I want it—*now.*"

Sherman's eyes narrowed. "Hallam? What about him?" he demanded.

Morgan Clyde smiled thinly, with amusement in his eyes. "He's taken care of. Very nicely, I think."

"What's this nonsense about quitting?" Sherman demanded.

"That's it, I'm quitting."

"You don't quit until I'm ready," Sherman snapped harshly. "I want to know what happened out there."

Clyde stepped carelessly to one side so that he could face Tom Cool, too. "Nothing happened," he said quietly. "They had a nice place there. A nice couple. I envied them, so I decided to let them stay."

"*You* decided?"

He's faster than I am, Clyde's brain told him, even as he moved. *He'll shoot first, anyway, so—*

Morgan Clyde's gun roared, and the shot caught Tom Cool in the chest, even as the gunman's weapon started to swing up to shoot him. Clyde felt a bullet fan past his own face, but he shot Cool again before he turned. Something struck him hard in the body, and then in one leg. He went down, then staggered up and emptied his gun into Sherman.

Sherman's body sagged, and a slow trickle of blood came from the corner of his mouth.

Turning, Clyde got to the office door, walking very straight. His brain felt light, even a little giddy. He opened the door precisely and stepped out into the barroom. Across the room, the Earles, staring wide-eyed, jerked out their guns.

Through the door behind him they could see Sherman's

body sagging in death. They moved as one man. Gritting his teeth, Morgan Clyde triggered his gun. He shot them both. . . .

Morgan Clyde almost made it to his horse before he fell, sprawling his length in the dust. Vaguely he heard a roar of horse's hoofs, and then he felt himself turned over onto his back. Vic Hallam was staring at him.

Morgan Clyde's breath came hoarsely. He looked up, remembering. "My place," he muttered thickly through the blood that frothed his lips. "There's a clock. Put—put it—in the corner."

There was sympathy and a deep understanding in Hallam's face. "Sure, that'd be fine. When you get well, we'll move it over together—on condition that you'll go partners on the homestead. . . . But why didn't you wait, man? I'd have come with you."

"Partners," Morgan Clyde said, and it seemed good to be able to smile. "That'd be fine. Just fine."

SHANDY TAKES THE HOOK

F OR THREE DAYS Shandy Gamble had been lying on his back in the Perigord House awaiting the stranger in the black mustache. Nichols, his name was, and if they were ever going to start cattle buying they had better be moving. The season was already late.

Shandy Gamble was seventeen years old and tall for his age. In fact, he was tall for any age. Four inches over six feet, he was all feet, hands, and shoulders. With his shirt off you could count every rib in his lean body.

Perigord was the biggest town Shandy had ever seen. In fact, it was only the third town he had seen in his life. With the cattle buyers in town there was 'most a thousand head of folks, and on the street Shandy felt uncomfortable and mighty crowded. Most of his time he spent down at the horse corrals or lying on his bed waiting for Nichols.

He had come to town to buy himself a new saddle and bridle. Maybe a new hat and shirt. He was a saving man, Shandy Gamble was, despite his youth. Now he not only was holding his own money but five hundred dollars belonging to Nichols. Had it not been for that he wouldn't have waited, for by now he was homesick for the KT outfit.

Nichols was a big, powerful man with a smooth-shaved face and black, prominent eyes. He also had black hair and a black mustache. Shandy had been leaning on the corral gate when Nichols approached him.

"Good afternoon, sir!" Nichols thrust out a huge hand. "I understand you're a cattleman?"

Shandy Gamble blinked. Nobody had ever called him a cattleman before and his chest swelled appreciably. He was a forty-dollar-a-month cowhand, although at the moment he did have five hundred and fifty-two dollars in his pocket.

Fifty-two dollars was saved from his wages, and the five hundred was half the reward money for nailing two horse thieves back in the cedar country. Shandy had tracked them back there for Deputy Sheriff Holloway, and then when they killed Holloway he got mad and went in after them. He brought one out dead and one so badly mauled he wished he was dead. There was a thousand dollars on their heads and Shandy tried to give it to Mrs. Holloway, but she would accept only half.

Shandy shifted uneasily on the bed. It was time Nichols got back. The proposition had sounded good, no question about that. "You can't beat it, Gamble," Nichols had said. "You know cattle and I've the connections in Kansas City and Chicago. We can ride over the country buying cattle, then ship and sell them. A nice profit for both of us."

"That would take money, and I ain't got much," Shandy had said.

Nichols eyed him thoughtfully. No use telling the boy he had seen that roll when Shandy paid for his room in advance. "It won't take much to start." Nichols scowled as he considered the size of Shandy's roll. "Say a thousand dollars."

"Shucks." Shandy was regretful. "I ain't got but five hundred."

"Fine!" Nichols clapped him on the shoulder. "We're partners, then! You put up five hundred and I'll put up five hundred! We'll bank that here, and then start buying. I've got unlimited credit east of here, and when the thousand is gone, we'll draw on that. At this stage you'll be the one doing most of the thinking, so you won't need to put as much cash into it as I do."

"Well—" Shandy was not sure. It sounded like a good deal, and who knew cows better than he did? He had been practically raised with cows. "Maybe it would be a good deal. Old Ed France has a herd nobody's looked at, nice, fat stock, too."

"Good!" Nichols clapped him on the shoulder again. From his pocket he took a long brown envelope and a sheaf of bills. Very carefully he counted off five hundred dollars and stuck it into the envelope. "Now your five hundred."

Shandy dug down and hauled out his bills and counted off the five hundred dollars and tucked it into the envelope.

"Now," Nichols started to put the envelope in his pocket, "we'll go to the bank, and—"

He stopped, then withdrew the envelope. "No, you just keep this on you. We'll bank it later."

Shandy Gamble accepted the fat envelope and stuck it into his shirt. Nichols glanced at his watch, then rubbed his jaw. "Tell you what," Nichols said, "I've got to catch the stage for Holbrook. I'll be back tomorrow night. You stick around and don't let this money out of your hands, whatever you do. I'll see you at the hotel."

Shandy watched him go, shrugged, and went back to watching the horses. There was a fine black gelding there. Now, if he was a cattle buyer, he would own that gelding, buy the new saddle and bridle, and some fancy clothes like Jim Finnegan wore, and would he show that outfit back on the KT!

The wait had dampened his enthusiasm. Truth was, he liked the KT and liked working with the boys. They were a good outfit. He rolled over on the bed and swung his feet to the floor. Reaching for his boots he shoved his big feet into them and stood up.

To blazes with it! He'd open the envelope, leave the money in the bank for Nichols, and go back to the outfit. He was no cattle buyer, anyway. He was a cowhand.

Taking out the brown envelope, he ripped it open. Slowly he turned cold and empty inside, and stood there, his jaw slack, his shock of corn-silk hair hanging over his face. The envelope was stuffed with old newspapers.

———

THE SPRING GRASS faded from green to brown and dust gathered in the trails. Water holes shrank and the dried earth cracked around them and the cattle grew gaunt. It was a hard year on the caprock and that meant work for the hands.

Shandy Gamble was in the saddle eighteen to twenty hours most days, rounding up strays and pushing them south to the gullies and remaining water holes. When he had returned without his saddle there was a lot of jawing about it, and the boys all poked fun at Shandy, but he grinned widely and took it, letting them believe he had drunk it up or spent it on women.

Jim Finnegan rode out one day on a gray horse. He was looking the situation over and making estimates on the beef to be had after the fall roundup. Shandy was drifting south with three head of gaunted stock when they met. Gamble drew up and Finnegan joined him. "Howdy, son! Stock looks poor."

"Yeah," Shandy dug for the makings, "we need rain plumb bad." He rolled his smoke, then asked quietly, "You ever hear of a buyer name of Nichols? Big, black-eyed man?"

Shandy's description was accurate and painstaking, the sort of description a man might give who was used to reading sign and who thirty seconds after a glimpse of a horse or cow could describe its every hair and ailment.

"Nichols? You've forgotten the name, son. No, the hombre you describe is Abel Kotch. He's a card slick an' confidence man. Brute of a fighter, too. Brags he never saw the man could stand up to him in a fistfight."

"Seen him around?"

"Yeah, he was around Fort Worth earlier this year. He rousts around with the June boys."

The June boys. There were five of the Junes—the old man, Pete June, and the four outlaw sons: Alec, Tom, Buck, and Windy. All were gun slicks, bad men, dirty, unkempt drifters, known to be killers, believed to be horse and cow thieves, and suspected of some out-and-out murders.

Two nights later, back at the bunkhouse, Johnny Smith rode in with the mail, riding down from Tuckup way where he had stopped to ask after some iron work being done for the ranch by the Tuckup blacksmith. Tuckup was mostly an outlaw town, but the blacksmith there was the best around. Cowhands do most of their own work, but the man at Tuckup could make anything with iron, and the KT boss had been getting some fancy andirons for his fireplace.

"Killin' over to Tuckup," Johnny said, as he swung down.

"That Sullivan from Brady Canyon tangled with Windy June. Windy bored him plenty."

Shandy Gamble's head came up. "June? The rest of that outfit there?"

"Sure, the whole shootin' match o' Junes!"

"Big, black-eyed fellow with 'em? Black mustache?"

"Kotch? Sure as you know he is. He whupped the black-smith. Beat him so bad he couldn't finish the old man's and-irons. That's a rough outfit."

The boss of the KT was talking to Jim Finnegan when Shandy strolled up. "Boss, anything you want done over Tuckup way? I got to ride over there."

The boss glanced at him sharply. It was unlike Gamble to ask permission to be away from his work. He was a good hand and worked like two men. If he wanted to go to Tuckup there was a reason.

"Yeah. Ask about my irons. Too, you might have a look up around the water pocket. We're missin' some cows. If you find them, or see any suspicious tracks, come a-hootin' an' we'll ride up that way."

———

SHANDY GAMBLE WAS astride a buckskin that belonged to the KT. He was a short-coupled horse with a wide head, good at cutting or roping, but a good trail horse, too. Johnny Smith, who was mending a bridle, glanced up in time to see Gamble going out of the door with his rifle in his hand. That was not too unusual, with plenty of wolves and lions around, but Shandy was wearing two guns, something that hadn't happened for a long time. Johnny's brow puckered, then he shrugged and went back to work on the bridle.

The Tuckup Trail was a scar across the face of the desert. It was a gash in the plateau, and everywhere was rock, red rock, pink rock, white, yellow, and buff rock, twisted and gnarled into weird shapes. By night it was a ghost land where a wide moon floated over the blasted remains of ancient mountains, and by day it was an oven blazing with heat and dancing with dust devils and heat-waved distance.

Tuckup was a cluster of shabby down-at-heel buildings

tucked back into a hollow among the rocks. It boasted that there was a grave in Boot Hill for every living person in town, and they always had two empty graves waiting to receive the next customers.

Tuckup was high, and despite the blazing heat of the day, a fire was usually welcome at night. The King High Saloon was the town's resort, meeting place, and hang-out. Second only to it was the stable, a rambling, gloomy building full of stalls for sixty horses and a loft full of hay.

Shandy Gamble stabled his horse and gave it a good rubdown. It had a hard ride ahead of it, for he knew that there would be no remaining in town after he had done what he had to do.

Lean, gangling, and slightly stooped, he stood in the stable door and rolled a smoke. His shoulders seemed excessively broad above the narrow hips, and the two .44s hung with their butts wide and easy to his big hands. He wore jeans and a faded checkered shirt. His hat was gray, dusty and battered. There was a hole through the crown that one of the horse thieves had put there.

There was the saloon, a general store, the blacksmith shop, and livery stable. Beyond and around was a scattering of a dozen or so houses, mostly mere shacks. Then there were two bunkhouses that called themselves hotels.

Shandy Gamble walked slowly across to the blacksmith shop. The smith was a burly man, and when he looked up, Shandy saw a deep half-healed cut on his cheekbone and an eye still swollen and dark. "KT irons ready?" Shandy asked, to identify himself.

"Will be." The smith stared at him. "Rider from there just here yestiddy. Your boss must be in a mighty hurry."

"Ain't that. I had some business over here. Know an hombre name of Kotch?"

The smith glared. "You bein' funny?"

"No. I got business with him."

"Trouble?"

"Uh-huh. I'm goin' to beat his head in."

The smith shrugged. "Try it if you want. I done tried but not no more. He durned near kilt me."

"He won't kill me."

"Your funeral. He's up at the King High." The smith looked at him. "You be keerful. Them Junes is up there, too." He wiped his mustache. "KT, you better think again. You're only a kid."

"My feet make as big tracks as his'n."

"Goin' in, they may. Comin' out they may be a sight smaller."

Shandy Gamble's eyes were chill. "Like you said, it's my funeral."

He hitched his guns in place and started across the street. He was almost to the hitch rail in front of the King High when he saw a fresh hide hung over the fence. It was still bloody. Curious, he walked back. The brand had been cut away from the rest of the hide. Poking around in a pile of refuse ready for burning, he found it, scraped it clean, and tucked it into his pocket. He was turning when he looked up to see a man standing near him.

He was several inches shorter than Shandy, but he was wide and blocky. He wore his gun tied down and he looked mean. His cheeks were hollow and his eyes small. "What you doin', pokin' around here?"

"Just lookin'." Shandy straightened to his full height. "Sort of proddin' around."

"Whar you from?"

"Ridin' for the KT."

The man's lips tightened. "Git out of here!"

"Don't aim to be in no hurry."

"You know who I am? I'm Tom June, an' when I say travel, I mean it!"

Shandy stood looking at him, his eyes mild. "Well, now. Tom June, I've heard o' you. Heard you was a cow thief an' a rustler."

"Why, you—!" His hand swept for his gun, but Shandy had no idea to start a shooting now. His long left slammed out, his fist balled and rock hard. It caught Tom June flush on the mouth as his hand swept back for his gun and his head came forward. At the same time, Shandy's right swung into the pit of the man's stomach and his left dropped to the gun wrist.

The struggle was brief, desperate, and final. Shandy clubbed a big fist to the man's temple and he folded. Hurriedly, Shandy dragged him into a shed, disarmed and tied him. The last job he did well. Then he straightened and walked back to the street.

A quick glance up and down, and then he went up the steps to the porch in front of the King High Saloon, and through the batwing doors.

Five men sat around a poker game. Shandy recognized the broad back instantly as that of Nichols, who he now knew was Abel Kotch. At least two of the others were Junes, as he could tell from their faces.

Shoving his hat back on his head he stood behind Kotch and glanced down at his cards. Kotch had a good hand. The stack of money before him would come to at least two hundred dollars.

"Bet 'em," Shandy said.

Kotch stirred irritably in his chair. "Shut up!" he said harshly.

Shandy's gun was in his hand, the muzzle against Kotch's ear. "Bet 'em, I said. Bet 'em strong."

Kotch's hands froze. The Junes looked up, staring at the gangling, towheaded youth. "Beat it, kid!" one said sharply.

"You stay out of this, June!" Shandy Gamble's voice was even. "My argyment's with this coyote. I'd as soon blow his head off as not, but if'n he does what he's told the worst he'll get is a beatin'!"

Kotch shoved chips into the center of the table. The Junes looked at their cards and raised. Kotch bet them higher. He won. Carefully, he raked in the coin.

"This is Shandy Gamble, Kotch. You owe me five hundred. Count it out before I forget myself an' shoot you anyway."

"There ain't five hundred here!" Kotch protested.

"There's better'n four. Count it!"

"Well, what do you know, Windy?" The thin man grinned across the table. "Ole Kotch run into the wrong hombre for once! Wished Buck was here to see this!"

Reluctantly, Kotch counted the money. It came to four hundred and ten dollars. Coolly, Shandy Gamble pocketed the money. "All right," he said, "stand up mighty careful an' unload your pockets."

"What?" Kotch's face was red with fury. "I'll kill you for this!"

"Empty 'em. I want more money. I want a hundred an' twenty dollars more."

"You ain't got it comin'!" Kotch glared at him.

"Five hundred an' interest for one year at six percent. You get it for me or I'll be forced to take your horse an' saddle."

"Why, you—!"

The gun lifted slightly and Abel Kotch shut up. His eyes searched the boy's face and what he read there wasn't pleasant. Kotch decided suddenly that this youngster would shoot, and shoot fast.

Carefully, he opened a money belt and counted out the hundred and twenty dollars, which Gamble quietly stowed in his pockets. Then he holstered his gun and hitched the belts into place. "Now, just for luck, Mr. Cattle Buyer, I'm goin' to give you a lickin'!"

Kotch stared. "Why, you fool! You—!" He saw the fist coming and charged, his weight slamming Shandy back against the wall, almost knocking the wind from him. Kotch jerked a knee up to Gamble's groin, but the boy had grown up in cow camps and cattle towns, cutting his fighting teeth on the bone-hard, rawhide-tough teamsters of the freight outfits. Gamble twisted and threw Kotch off balance, then hit him with a looping right that staggered the heavier man.

Kotch was no flash in the pan. He could fight and he knew it. He set himself, feinted, and then threw a hard right that caught the boy flush on the chin. Shandy staggered but recovered as Kotch rushed, and dropping his head, butted the heavier man under the chin. Kotch staggered, swinging both hands; and straightening, Shandy walked into him slugging.

They stood there wide legged and slugged like madmen, their ponderous blows slamming and battering at head and body. Shandy's head sang with the power of those punches and his breath came in gasps, but he was lean and hard from years of work on the range, and he fell into a rhythm of punching. His huge fists smashed at the gambler like batter-ing rams.

Kotch was triumphant, then determined, then doubtful. His punches seemed to be soaked up by the boy's abundant vitality, while every time one of those big fists landed it jarred him to the toes. Suddenly he gave ground and swung a boot toe for Shandy's groin.

Turning, Gamble caught it on his leg, high up, then grabbed the boot and jerked. Kotch's other foot lost the ground and he hit the floor hard. Gamble grabbed him by the shirt front and smashed him in the face, a free swing that flattened the bone in Kotch's nose. Then, jerking him erect, Shandy gripped him with his left hand and swung a looping blow to the wind. Kotch's knees buckled, and Shandy smashed him in the face again and again. Then he shoved him hard. Kotch staggered, brought up against the back wall, and slid to a sitting posi-tion, his face bloody, his head loose on its neck.

Shandy Gamble drew back and hitched his belts into place again. He mopped his face with a handkerchief while he got his breath back. There were five men in the room now, all enemies without doubt. Two of them were Junes—obviously from the earlier conversation they were Windy and Alec.

Shandy hitched his gun belts again and left his thumbs tucked in them. He looked at Windy June. "Found a cowhide out back," he said, casually, "carried a KT brand."

Instantly, the room was still. Windy June was staring at him, his eyes ugly. Alec was standing with his right hand on the edge of the bar; the others spread suddenly, getting out of the way. This, then, was between himself and the Junes.

"What then?" Windy asked, low voiced.

"Your brother Tom didn't like it. I called him a rustler, and he didn't like that."

"You called Tom June a rustler?" Windy's voice was low with amazement. "And you're alive?"

"I took his gun away an' tied him up. I'm takin' him to the sheriff."

"You're takin'—why, you fool kid!"

"I'm takin' him, an' as you Junes ride together, I reckon you an' Alec better come along, too."

Windy June was astonished. Never in his life had he been called like this, and here, in his own bailiwick, by a kid. But then he remembered the job this kid had done on Abel Kotch and his lips grew close and tight.

"You better git," he said, "while you're all in one piece!"

The bartender spoke. "Watch yourself, Windy. I know this kid. He's the one that brought the boys in from Cottonwood, one dead an' one almost."

Windy June smiled thinly. "Look, kid. We don't want to kill you. There's two of us. If you get by us, there's still Buck an' Pop. You ain't got a chance with me alone, let alone the rest of them."

Shandy Gamble stood tall in the middle of the floor. His long face was sober. "You better come along then, Windy, because I aim to take you in, dead or alive!"

Windy June's hand was a blur of speed. Guns thundered and the walls echoed their thunder. In the close confines of the saloon a man screamed. There was the acrid smell of gunpowder and Shandy Gamble weaving in the floor's middle, his guns stabbing flame. He fired, then moved forward. He saw Alec double over and sprawl across Windy's feet, his gun sliding across the floor.

Windy, like a weaving blade of steel, faced Shandy and fired. Gamble saw Windy June's body jerk with the slam of a .44, saw it jerk again and twist, saw him going to his knees with blood gushing from his mouth, his eyes bitterly, wickedly alive, and the guns in his big fists hammering their futile bullets into the floor. Then Shandy fired again, and Windy June sprawled across Alec and lay still. In the moment of silence that followed the cannonading of the guns, Windy's foot twitched and his spur jingled.

Shandy Gamble faced the room, his eyes searching the faces of the other men. "I don't want no trouble from you. Two of you load the bodies on their horses. I'm taking 'em with me, like I said."

Abel Kotch sat on the floor, his shocked and bloody face stunned with amazement at the bodies that lay there. He had taken milk from a kitten and had it turn into a raging mountain lion before his eyes. He sat very still. He was out of this.

He wanted to stay out. He was going to make no move that could be misinterpreted.

Slowly, they took the bodies out and tied them on the horses of the two June boys. Shandy watched them, then walked across to the stable to get his own horse, his eyes alert for the other Junes.

When he had the horse he walked back to the shed and saw Tom June staring up at him.

"What happened? I heard shootin'?"

"Yeah."

Shandy reached down and caught him by his jacket collar with his left hand and coolly dragged him out of the shed, his feet dragging. He took him to the front of the saloon and threw him bodily across his horse. The bound man saw the two bodies, dripping and bloody. He cried out, then began to swear, viciously and violently.

"Look out, kid."

Who spoke, he did not know, but Shandy Gamble glanced up and saw two other men who wore the brand of the June clan—Pop and Buck June—wide apart in the street. Their faces were set and ready.

Shandy Gamble stepped away from the horses into the street's center. "You can drop your guns an' come with me!" he called.

Neither man spoke. They came on, steadily and inexorably. And then something else happened. Up the street behind them appeared a cavalcade of riders, and Shandy recognized his boss, leading them. Beside him rode Johnny Smith and Jim Finnegan and behind them the riders from the KT.

"Drop 'em, June!" The boss's voice rang out sharp and clear. "There's nine of us here. No use to die!"

The Junes stopped. "No use, Buck," Pop June said, "the deck's stacked agin us."

———

THE BOSS RODE on past and stopped. He stared at the dead Junes and the bound body of Tom. He looked at Shandy as if he had never seen him before.

"What got into you, Shandy?" he asked. "We'd never have

known, but Johnny told us when you heard the Junes were here you got your guns and left. Then Jim remembered you'd been askin' him about this here Kotch, who trailed with 'em."

Shandy shrugged, building a smoke. "Nothin'. We'd had trouble, Kotch an' me." He drew the patch of hide from his pocket. "Then there was this, out back. Tom started a ruction when he seen me find it."

Shandy Gamble swung into his saddle. "I reckon the Junes'll talk, an' they'll tell you where the cows are. An', boss," Shandy puckered his brow, "could I ride into Perigord? I want to git me a new saddle."

"You got the money?" The boss reached for his pocket.

"Yeah," Shandy smiled, "I got it from Kotch. He'd been holdin' it for me."

"Holdin' it for him!" Finnegan exploded. "He trusted Kotch—with money?"

Kotch had come to the door and was staring out at them. The boss chuckled. "Well, trust or not, looks like he collected!"

A NIGHT AT WAGON CAMP

N O HORSES STOOD in the corral, no smoke rose from the chimney. Jake Molina slid his rifle from the boot and rode with it across his saddle.

The squat, unpainted shack, the open-faced shed, the pole corral, the stock tank filled with water piped from the spring . . . nothing had changed. It was bleak, lonely, and drought-stricken as always. . . .

Molina dismounted, careful to keep his horse between himself and the house. Pike should have been here to meet him but there was no sign of life anywhere. The ranch had been abandoned ten years before, and looked it.

Rifle in hand he crossed to the house, pausing on the step to turn for one more careful yet uneasy glance.

The kitchen was empty but for a bare table and a broken chair that lay on its side. Crossing to the fireplace he turned a charred stick with the muzzle of his rifle, then knelt and put his fingers upon it for an instant. It was cold and dead.

There were two more rooms. Using his rifle like an extension of his arm he pushed open the doors, but there was nothing but a dried-out, sunbaked boot and a coat that had been dropped on the floor. There was no dust on the coat, however, and it lay in a scuffle of recent footprints . . . in this abandoned place here was something that did not fit, something important to his quest.

Crossing to the coat he touched it with gentle fingers, and found a piece of board shoved down in the inside pocket. On it something had been scratched with a nail:

> Just rode in, Lew Stebbins—
> Monty Short—a stranger.

It was signed by Pike.

He stepped outside and looked slowly around. By now they would be miles from here, for they had not known he was coming. In growing fear he realized what they must have left behind. Grimly, he dropped the coat to his feet and slipped the thong off of his right-hand gun. He listened, and heard only the trickle of water, the wind, and an aimless tapping that came at intervals. The tapping drew him and he walked around the end of the corral toward the shed.

———

PIKE WAS SUSPENDED by his wrists, arms spread wide and tied to poles of the shed wall. His chin hung down on his chest, and his toes just barely touched the earth. His shirt had been ripped from his body and his body had been beaten by a length of trace chain which now hung over the top bar of the corral. It was the wind, moving that chain in the hard gusts, that caused the tapping he had heard.

Pike had been dead for several hours, yet he had lived long enough. . . . With one toe he had scratched an arrow, pointing west.

———

UNTIL HE HAD met Pike, the trails Jake Molina had ridden were ridden alone, for it was his nature to ride alone, to ask nothing of any man but to be let alone. With Pike he had gone up the trail to Kansas, and he knew what Pike would have done for him, and what he must do for Pike. Above all there was Tom Gore's family to think of, and those neighbors who had trusted him with their cattle.

He buried Pike where the shack cast a shadow, and put a marker over the grave. Once, straightening up suddenly, he caught a flash of light from a hillside, and then he worked on and finished his job, sure he was being watched.

He rode out of the ranch yard at a lope and went up to the crest of the ridge, then went west holding to the skyline. Usually a bad thing to do, he did it now because the country lay wide and he'd rather see than worry about being seen. He headed due west, following the trail of the three riders until it broke off and went into the badlands to the south.

———

ON THE THIRD morning he started early and when well down the trail he turned off and doubled back parallel to the route he had followed. He was back behind a clump of mesquite but had the trail fairly covered, and he waited no more than an hour.

Through the leaves he saw a man in a black suit coat and a black hat of more expensive make than a cowhand could afford. The man's face was wide and strongly boned, and although his saddle was worn from use, the boots had been well polished before the dust fell on them.

When the man had gone by Molina stepped into the trail. "You'd better have a good reason for following me, mister, and I'd better like the reason."

"I believe we should talk," the man said. "I think we're doing the same job."

Molina waited, never taking his eyes off the stranger.

"You buried a man back yonder, and you're trailing the three men who killed him. I want those men, too," the man continued.

"If you're the law you're not needed. If you're an outlaw you're trailing men who don't want company."

"I'm a Pinkerton man."

"Most places that would get you killed."

"My name is Hale. Do you know who you're following?"

"Pike told me."

Hale looked at him carefully. "Now, that's interesting. Pike was dead before you got there because I was there before you were. He couldn't tell you anything."

Molina took the piece of shingle from his pocket, and explained how he found it.

"Pike was a shrewd man. He also knew me, and he knew how I think. He also knew that I know what they want, and somehow he thought things out so that when they lead me to the place, I'll be the one who finds it."

"Money?"

"Yes . . . it belongs to friends of ours."

Hale lit a cigar. "My job is to get those men and I can use help just as much as you can. Monty Short is a gunman, and Stebbins was a buffalo hunter and is one of the best rifle shots around. I don't know the other man, but I've an idea. Why don't we ride together?"

"Up to you . . . I'm riding west. Come along if you've a mind to."

———

THE COUNTRY WAS broken into canyons now, the slopes covered with scattered juniper. Nor was the trail difficult to follow, for at no time had there been an effort to conceal it; the men had no reason to believe themselves followed.

"Nobody ever comes into this country," Molina said, "too dry for ranching these years, no more buffalo, so the Comanches rarely come. It's an empty land."

"Want to tell me about the money?"

"Tom Gore drove cattle belonging to some friends and himself to Dodge. He sold out for thirty thousand in gold and started home, and then he got the idea that some of his hands were going to rob him, so he gave a message to Pike telling him to take it to the ranch, and telling where the gold was, then he slipped out one night and hid the gold. When they murdered him for it a few nights later, they found nothing."

"And you know where it is?"

"Only Pike knew, so Pike had to tell them when he saw they were going to kill him anyway. Otherwise nobody would ever know where it was . . . he's relying on me to trail them and find it before they do, failing that, to take it from them."

"A large order."

It was cold, with a chill wind blowing over the country and moaning in the canyons. The trail of the three riders had vanished. Hale studied the earth, but saw nothing. Molina did not slow his pace, nor did he pause to look around.

"You know where you're going?" Hale asked mildly.

"Sure . . . only three ways they can go from out here. Everything in the desert that moves has to move toward a water hole. Over there," he pointed southeast, "are the Comanche Wells . . . seventy miles as the crow flies, and out of the way for Tom Gore, who was heading home.

"Gore was coming from the northwest, but he never got this far. So the Wells are out. That leaves Lost Lake and the Wagon Camp. They found Gore's body at Lost Lake, so my guess would be Wagon Camp or some dry camp near there."

"I see." Hale considered the subject. "What if they don't think the same way?"

"They will. They've got to. All life is tied to water holes here, and they know every camp because two of them, at least, rode with Gore when he was killed."

Molina drew up, studying the ground. He walked his horse forward a little, then drew up again. "That's funny. They're going to Lost Lake."

Hale lit a cigar and waited. He was out of his depth and realized it. He had believed himself a good tracker, yet he could see nothing here, no sign of passage more than a crow might have left. Molina rode on a few steps farther, then returned.

"They're going to Lost Lake, so we'll cut across country to Wagon Camp."

"What if we lose them?"

"We won't."

———

THEY CAME UP to Wagon Camp in the cool of the evening, and watered their horses at the seep and stood in the stillness, looking around them. The wind ruffled the water in the pool, and Molina looked around carefully. A quail called in the shadows.

"We're here," Hale said, "or were you just guessing?"

"The gold will be here," Molina said. "I'm sure of it."

Squatting over a small fire built from gathered sticks and buffalo chips, Hale began to prepare their food. He was a big man and in his shirtsleeves the bulging muscles in his arms stretched his shirt. He wore suspenders and sleeve garters. Jake dipped water for coffee and gathered more fuel.

The Wagon Camp was only slightly less barren than the

country around. Here where the water from the seep irrigated a small meadow and some bordering trees, there were two dozen scattered cottonwoods, several of them huge and ancient; there were some vines, willow brush, and farther away, low-growing mesquite and prickly pear.

"We've got a day for sure," Molina said, "another day for possible. Then we can get set for trouble, because they'll be along."

Hale looked around doubtfully. "The gold could be buried anywhere," he said, "how would a man know? A few days of the blowing this country gets and it would look like any other place."

"He didn't bury it." Molina squatted on his heels and fed sticks into the fire. "He would have been afraid of the noise. He hid it someplace that was ready for him."

"Noise?"

"Digging . . . at night it would have awakened everybody. Even if he dug it out with his hands it would have to be a pretty fair-sized hole, and men on the trail sleep mighty light."

––––––––––

YET BY SUNDOWN the following day they were no closer to the solution. Every hole in the rocks behind the pool, and there were not many, had been examined. Trees, brush piles, everywhere either of them could imagine had been carefully checked. It could not have been far from camp, yet they looked and looked without luck.

Hale was irritable. "Molina, you've had it your way. Now we're here, and for all we know they've got your gold and have ridden out of the country. I say we mount up and ride out of here."

Molina glanced up. "You ride out. That gold is here, and sooner or later they'll come. Maybe tonight."

Hale got up and walked to his horse. He picked up his saddle to swing to his horse's back but when he looked across the saddle blanket he froze. "I see them," he said. "They're coming now, and they've seen our fire."

"Sit tight then, and be ready."

They came riding, spread out and ready for trouble. They drew up and Molina looked up and said, "Light and set. The coffee's hot."

"Where'd you come from?" Stebbins was doing the talking. Short was beside him, the stranger a little behind. He was a thin, narrow-faced man with empty eyes.

"Fort Griffin," Molina lied coolly, holding his cup in his left hand.

They did not like it, that was obvious enough. They didn't like Hale sitting there with a shotgun across his lap, either.

These were the men who had tortured and killed Pike. Molina thought of that and grew hard and cold inside.

"You're off the trail, aren't you?" he asked. "This is one of the loneliest water holes in creation."

Monty Short got down from his horse. "I'll try that coffee," he said, and held out a cup for it.

Molina smiled at him. "There's the pot. Pour it for yourself."

Molina's words had apparently aroused the stranger's curiosity, and he sized Molina up with attentive eyes.

"You might be off the trail yourself," the stranger suggested. "This is, as you say, a lonely water hole."

"Used to be good country," Molina agreed, conversationally, "there was good grass all through here." He indicated Hale. "This man is Bob Hale; he's a cattle buyer, and finances some ranching operations. We figured to start us a place right here if the grass is good."

Stebbins chuckled without humor. "A man's lucky to find feed for his horse. You couldn't run ten head on ten square miles of it now."

The stranger was still watching Molina and suddenly he said, "I don't like him, Lew," he indicated Molina, "this one is smart."

All three looked at Molina, and ever so gently Hale's shotgun moved so it was still on his lap but pointed casually at the group. The movement went unobserved with all attention centered on Molina.

Molina lifted his coffee cup and sipped a swallow of coffee, and then said quietly, "So you don't like it. We got here first. We're staying. If you boys want to use the water, you're welcome."

"We think you're the ones who should leave," Short spoke suddenly. "We think you should mount up and ride out."

Molina smiled wryly. "Now, that's foolish talk, Monty. You might get us but we'd take a couple of you with us, and probably all three. You and Lew aren't going to buy trouble you don't need."

Molina merely looked at them. "I told you . . . I came here from Fort Griffin, but I've also been in Mobeetie. What you do is your own business, but I wouldn't go back that way with posters on both of you."

Stebbins turned abruptly away, and as he did so, he saw the shotgun in Hale's hands. "Let's build a fire, Monty," he said, and he walked away. After an instant's hesitation, the others followed, the stranger lingering to take a last, careful look at Molina.

When they had gone, Molina sat down and filled his cup. "If I could only think!" he said angrily. "I know the stuff is here." Then he looked across his cup at Hale. "Which one are you after?"

"Short and Stebbins . . . train holdup. They didn't get much, but that doesn't matter to us. That other one . . . he should be wanted somewhere."

———

IT WAS AFTER midnight, and Hale was on guard when they heard the wagon. Hale had been watching the other fire. He wanted his prisoners and expected to take them when they fell asleep, but they had a man on watch also, and there was small chance to even make a move without being seen. Then he heard the sound of wheels.

Hale did not believe what he heard, and neither did Stebbins, who was on watch in the other camp. Stebbins got to his feet and drew back from the fire, and Hale did likewise. Somehow the sound got through to Molina and he sat up.

The wagon rolled in from the darkness, drawn by two mules, and stopped on the edge of the firelight. There was a bearded man on the seat, and beside him a girl.

She was young; Molina saw that quickly . . . and her eyes found his across the intervening space with what seemed to be a plea for help. Yet that was foolish . . . he could not read a glance at that distance . . . but of one thing he was sure; she did not belong with the man on the wagon seat beside her.

When he got down and the firelight fell on his face, Molina saw the man was old, but still strong and wiry, and there was a sly, suspicious way about him that Molina distrusted.

"Quite a settlement," the old man looked around inquisitively, "somethin' goin' on?"

"Just passing through," Molina said. "How about you?"

The old man chuckled. "Might say we're passin' through, ourselves. My name's Barnes . . . that there's my niece, name of Ruth Crandall." He looked around carefully, his eyes remaining on the other fire for the longest time.

"Now, there," he said, his eyes on the stranger, "is a man to remember."

"You know him?"

"Why, sure. I'd say I know him . . . but he don't know me. Not yet, he don't." He threw a shrewd glance at Molina. "Name of Van Hagan . . . a man well known in Montana and Wyoming."

He peered around. "Been some time since folks camped around here, I expect." He paused. "Can't see how anybody would drive cattle through here."

"Nobody has," Molina told him, "lately."

"Now, that's odd," Barnes spat, "for I did hear about a man named Gore driving through this country."

Molina took out the makings and began to build a smoke. Was everybody in Texas thinking about that gold? "Tom Gore," he said, "made his drive away east of here. He was driving for Wichita, then changed his mind and went to Dodge."

Barnes nodded. "Now, that sounds right. It surely does. Maybe it was when he was coming back that Gore went through here, and a passel of hands with him." He turned his head on his thin, buzzardlike neck. "Might you be one of them?"

"I worked for Tom on the home ranch," Molina said. "He was a friend of mine."

Ruth had gotten down from the wagon and walked nearer, and as they talked, she listened, looking from time to time at Molina, but trying to keep out of Barnes's line of sight. There was more here, Molina decided, than was apparent at first glance. One thing was obvious: here was another man on the trail of the Gore money.

It seemed impossible for anything to be hidden here, of all places. And he had looked around and examined the ground pretty thoroughly on the basis of earlier familiarity. However, Tom Gore had known this place, and so had Pike. Gore had planned to have Pike locate the gold and there might have been something each knew that was unknown to anyone else.

Obviously, the three outlaws did not know the exact location or they would have made a move toward it . . . or were they worried by Molina and Hale?

They had murdered once for this gold, and they would not hesitate again.

———

HALE STOOD GUARD and Molina slept while the camp quieted down, and in the early hours before dawn, he awakened Molina.

"All quiet . . . But I don't believe those boys will wait much longer."

Molina slid out of his bed roll and pulled on his boots. The night was cold, the coals of the fire glowed red with a few thin tendrils of flame licking the length of sticks just placed in the fire. Across the way the other fire was only a faint glow, and the wagon was silent. Molina could see Barnes bedded down beneath the wagon.

Moving back from the fire he saw Hale turn in and then he moved back still farther until only his boots showed in the edge of light. Beyond that his figure was shrouded by the dead black of the shadow under a huge cottonwood. Carefully, he slid out of his boots and donned the moccasins he always carried folded in a pocket. Leaving the boots where they could be seen, the upper part of them in the shadow, he moved back away from the fire, and from among the trees he studied the camp with infinite care.

There were no hollow trees, no box concealed in a fork of the branches, and it had not been sunk in the pool at the seep. The water was shallow and perfectly clear. Nor were there any signs of digging . . . blown dust would have concealed it long since.

A thought caught at his attention, and he scowled, trying to grasp what it was he had almost thought of but which had slipped his attention. And then he saw movement at the back of the wagon.

Ruth Crandall was getting out, ever so carefully, of the covered wagon.

He watched her get down from the wagon and fade back into the darkness. When he located her again it was by the faintest of sounds, and near him. He spoke in a whisper. "Late to go hunting."

She came up to him in the darkness. "Take me away from here, Mr. Molina. Just take me away."

"What's wrong? There is a problem with your uncle?"

"He's not my uncle! Not really. He married my aunt after my uncle died. Neither of them were related to me by blood. Then a few weeks ago she died and he started over here."

"Why did he come?"

"It was Art. You remember Art Tomkins? He worked with you at Gore's? He returned with the bunch after the drive, and he was one of those who planned to kill Mr. Gore. Well, he did help kill him, and then Monty, Stebbins, and Van Hagan killed the others. Then they tried to kill Art. After they left, he was hurt and he stole a horse from a ranch and came to us. He remembered hearing some movement at night while at Wagon Camp, so he was sure the gold was hidden here. He died a few days after he got to us, and here we are."

Molina remembered Art. A lazy, down-on-his-luck cow-hand who was always talking about the James boys.

"You've got to get me away from him," Ruth insisted. "If you don't . . . he's been telling me how much money I could make in Dodge or Fort Worth. How we could live real easy on the money I'd make." She caught his arm. "I don't want that kind of money, Mr. Molina."

"All right," he said, "but stay shy of us until this is settled."

She disappeared as quietly as she had come. She moved, he reflected, like an Indian . . . and fortunately, for that old man would be a light sleeper.

Sharply, he was aware of something else. He had watched the camp while Ruth talked to him, but there had been a time or two when his eyes were averted, and something had changed at the camp over there. One of the beds looked mighty slack.

Gray light was showing in the east, and he shifted position suddenly, nervously, realizing he had been still too long. And as he changed position he heard a voice behind him say, "Right there, Molina. Hold it right there."

With what had happened to Pike fresh in his mind, he threw himself to the side and rolled over in the darkness and came up, firing at the dart of flame before he heard the sound of the shot. He heard the hard impact of a bullet on flesh and dove forward as a bullet struck where he had been.

Farther off there was a sudden drum of gunshots. He held his fire, and glanced swiftly toward his camp.

Hale was gone.

The wagon was dark, but there was nobody under the wagon where reflected light had shown the long dark bundle of Barnes, sleeping.

Nearby Molina could hear the slow, heavy breathing of an injured man, but the fellow might be waiting for a shot and he dared not move. There were leaves and brush under the trees, and while he had not made any sound moving, the next step might not be so fortunate. Yet he had moccasins on . . . he put a foot out carefully as he straightened up, testing the ground. It was soft earth. Carefully, he let his weight down.

Then he saw the man who had tried to take him. He was down on the ground but he was still gripping a gun.

Squatting, he felt around on the ground and found a dead branch, fallen from one of the trees above. He straightened up but did not throw it. Instead, reaching off to one side with the branch, he made faint rustling sounds in the brush. Instantly the shot came and he fired in reply.

The camp was very still. Carefully, he worked his way to the man he had shot and picked up his pistol, then stripped the gun belt from the body and looped it over his shoulder after loading the extra pistol and tucking it in his belt.

Hale had vanished; so had Barnes. Nowhere was there a sign of anyone. It was so still he could hear the horses cropping grass.

It would soon be light, and what happened after that would settle things here. He had not found the gold, and he had no intention of leaving without it. One of the outlaws was down, but the other shooting he had dimly heard while he was fighting his own battle might mean anything or nothing.

Hale had vanished at the first shot, but was he alive? Or injured and lying hidden?

Molina moved to the shelter of a large tree, then lowered himself to the ground. His rifle was in camp and he would need it. Crawling, keeping to the shelter of the brush, which was sparse but in the darkness sufficient cover, he got back to a place close to their own fire. Only gray coals remained, a slow thread of smoke rising in the still air of the hour before dawn.

The sky in the east was gray with a shading of lemon near the horizon.

Nothing moved.

And then there was movement, the slightest stirring in the darkness near the rear wheel of the wagon, and a faint glint of light on a rifle barrel. Barnes was lying there with a rifle, probably the buffalo gun Molina had seen him with earlier. And on whose side was Barnes?

Neutral, Molina decided, neutral and protecting himself while the others fought it out, and then he would do his part. So there was that to consider during whatever took place now, and whoever won must be prepared to handle Barnes.

Dawn came slowly on the high plains, the sun rising behind far gray clouds. Barnes was discernible now, sitting at the rear wheel of the big wagon, his rifle ready for use, an armed spectator.

Ruth got down from the wagon and went to the fire. Adding fuel she built up the fire and put on a coffeepot. Then she went quietly about the business of preparing breakfast. Molina glanced at her from time to time, astonished at her coolness in the midst of a situation where shooting might break out again at any moment.

From where he lay he could cover the area at Wagon Camp. His only danger was if someone got behind a big clump of prickly pear off on his left and outside the grove of trees and brush. Some of that pear was tall as a man, and it was a big clump, banked with drifted sand. It made him uneasy, and he wanted to move, but there was no chance.

Desperately, he wanted his rifle, and he could see the stock from where he lay. Beyond it he could see a man's shoulder and hand. It was Hale.

The Pinkerton man lay in the slight hollow at the seep, a hollow just deep enough to give him the slightest cover, but whether he was alive or dead, Molina could not see.

Windblown sand had heaped up around some of the trees, but elsewhere the wind had scooped hollows, exposing the roots. No one of these places seemed adequate cover, and it was unbelievable that within this small area there should be four men hidden from each other.

Four men who waited for the slightest move, four men ready to shoot and to kill . . . and at one side, an old man with a rifle, taking no part, but also ready to kill. And a girl who prepared a meal in the midst of it, who went about her task as though the scene were as peaceful as it actually appeared.

An hour went by, and the wind skittered a few leaves along the ground, stirred the green hands of the cottonwoods.

A storm was coming. . . .

Immediately, Jake Molina began to think of how he could turn the storm to advantage. He had been waiting for the others to move . . . he would wait no longer.

Hale had to have his prisoners, but all Molina had to have was the gold. Too many people needed that money, and although it would make none of them rich, it would help them through the bad times . . . especially the Gore family, who would have no husband now, and no father.

And Hale might be dead . . . there had been no move from the shoulder he could see, or no move that he had observed.

Taking his Colt from its holster, Molina touched his tongue to dry lips and stood up. He might outflank and drive them into the open, for where they were hidden there was no more shelter than either he or Hale had.

He moved swiftly, dodging into a position behind another tree, and the shot that came was much too late . . . next time they would be prepared for him.

Ruth had merely glanced up from her fire. Barnes had shifted position enough so that he was on one knee ready for the final shot, when his chance came.

There was a big tree in the direction he was headed, not over fifteen feet away, but that was where they would expect him to go. Straight ahead of him was another cottonwood, almost in line with his present hiding place. He ducked around his tree and ran and as a head and a rifle came up he fired—fired as his right foot hit ground. He saw the man jerk and drop his rifle, drop from sight, and then a hand came swiftly up to grab the rifle.

He was closer now, and he was out of the trees except to his right or left.

He was sure the man in the hole had not been wounded badly, probably only a burn, or even more likely, just a bullet past his ear. But enough to make him cautious about lifting his head.

No move from Hale, and none from the second of the murderers, but Molina was not fooled . . . the other man was there, waiting.

It was point-blank range now, and no chance to get to one of those trees to right or left, but it was no more than sixty feet to where the one man lay waiting. He swung his eyes, peering past the tree, trying to find the second man.

Suddenly a voice called out, "Barnes! We'll split even if you get Molina!"

Barnes hesitated, and in that instant, Hale came up out of the basin by the pool, gun in hand. He took one quick step to the right and fired across the rocks behind the pool.

The man opposite Molina started to rise and Molina sprang from behind his tree and ran three quick steps toward him, slid to a halt and fired. The gunman had leaped up, but the bullet caught him in the shoulder and spun him halfway around.

Barnes lifted his rifle to fire and Ruth threw the coffeepot at him. It struck him alongside the head and ruined his aim. The buffalo gun went off into the air and Molina sprang into position half behind Monty Short, where he could cover both the wounded Short and Barnes.

And that was the end of it.

Hale was walking toward them. "Van Hagan's out of it," he said. "Short, you're wanted for robbery. I'm a Pinkerton man."

Barnes got up slowly, holding the side of his head and moaning between agonized curses. The full coffeepot had not only scalded his face and shoulder, but the edge of the pot had cut his scalp and a thin trickle of blood ran down his face.

Ruth calmly picked up her coffeepot, refilled it and put it on the fire. Her face was white and her eyes large with fright, and she avoided looking toward Van Hagan, who was sprawled on the ground near the pool.

Molina walked over and picked up Barnes's rifle, then held out his hand for his six-shooter. Barnes hesitated, but Molina merely looked at him and, reluctantly, the old man drew his gun and extended it carefully.

"Drop it," Molina said, "I'll pick it up."

Hale was working to stop the blood in Short's shoulder. He glanced over at Molina. "Where's Stebbins?"

"Over there," Molina said, "but he isn't going anyplace."

Barnes got up slowly. "All right," he said, "we'll be pullin' out. You've no reason to hold me."

"You can go," Molina said. "Ruth stays with us."

Barnes's eyes flashed with anger. "She's comin' with me. She's my own niece. You got no call—"

"I am not your niece," Ruth said, "and I am going with them."

"You give us any trouble," Hale interrupted, "and we'll

take you in for aiding and abetting. We might not make the charge stick but she'll go her own way nonetheless."

Barnes glared at them, then abruptly turned his back and went to get his mules.

Hagan and Stebbins were both dead. With Monty Short handcuffed and Ruth ready to ride in on Stebbins's horse, Hale looked at Molina. "Looks like I've scored . . . what about the gold?"

Molina took the shovel from the wagon. "Why, I'm going to get it now. Seems a man can be mighty slow to get things, sometimes. . . . Stands to reason, a man hiding something at night would have to drop it in a hole or cover it up. He couldn't be sure at night whether or not it could be seen, otherwise. Now, there aren't any holes around, and if he did any digging the fresh dirt would be noticed even if the sound of digging wasn't. So what's the answer?"

"You tell me," Hale said.

"Why, someplace where he could dig with his hands and where it wouldn't be noticed. That means drifted sand to me."

Taking a shovel from the wagon he walked to the huge stand of prickly pear he had noticed before and walked around it until he found a place with an opening among the pear leaves and thorns that was large enough for a man to get a hand in without being badly scratched. The second shovel of sand disclosed the first of the sacks. In a few minutes he had them all.

Molina put the gold in his saddlebags and then saddled his horse. As he mounted up, Barnes walked toward them.

"What about my guns?" he protested.

"Tell you what," Molina said, "I'll leave them with the marshal in Fort Griffin. Anytime you want them you just ride in and explain to him how you lost them. You do that and you can have them back."

———

TEN MILES AND more than two hours later, Hale glanced over at Molina. "You should be a Pinkerton man. We could use you."

"Once I get this gold to Mrs. Gore," Molina replied, "I'll be hunting a job."

He glanced at Ruth. "Helen Gore," he said, "is a mighty fine woman. She could use a friend right now, and some help."

Where the trails forked at a clump of mesquite they drew up. "We'll be leaving you," Molina said. "Good luck."

Hale lifted a hand. "Come and see us," he said. "And thanks."

Monty Short, handcuffed, threw him a hard stare. "You get no thanks from me."

"You should," Molina said, "you're alive."

SIX-GUN STAMPEDE

"**I**T'S NO USE, Tom," Ginnie Rollins said. "Dad just won't listen. He says you're no good. That you've no sense of responsibility. He says you haven't anything and you never will have."

"Do you think that, Ginnie?" Tom Brandon asked. "Do you?"

"You know I don't, Tom. You shouldn't even ask. But you can't blame Dad. He only wants what is best for me, and every time I mention you, he brings up the fact that you are always racing horses and fighting. He says he'll have no saloon brawler for a son-in-law."

"It isn't only that," Tom said, discouragement heavy in his voice, "it's that herd I lost. Every time I try to get a job, they bring that up. I reckon half of 'em think I was plumb careless an' the other half think I'm a thief." They both sat silent. Despite the cold wind neither felt like moving. It was not often anymore that they had a chance to talk, and this meeting had been an accident—but an accident each of them had been hoping would happen.

Whether they would see each other again was doubtful. Jim Rollins was a hard-bitten old cattleman with one of the biggest ranches in the country, and he had refused Tom Brandon the right to come on his spread. Not only refused him the premises, but had ordered his hands to enforce it. Though several of them were old friends of Tom's, the foreman was Lon Huffman, with whom Tom had two disastrous fistfights, both of which Huffman had won.

Lon was a good deal the bigger man, and skilled in rough-and-tumble fighting, but each time he had a bad time in beating Brandon, who was tough, willing, and wiry. His dislike for Tom was no secret, and it extended to his particular cronies, Eason and Bensch.

"I'll always think somebody deliberately stampeded that herd on me," Brandon said. "The whole thing was too pat. There it was, the herd close to the border an' well bedded down. All of a sudden, they busted loose an' started to run—right over into Mexico. An' when I started after 'em, there was the Rurales lined up on the border sayin' no. It looked like a rigged deal."

"But who would do such a thing, Tom?" Ginnie protested. "I know you've said that, but Dad claims it's just an excuse. Who would do anything of the sort? There's no rustling here, and there haven't been any bandits for years."

"Just the same," Tom insisted, "if a man made a deal with old Juan Morales over at Los Molinos, he could get a good price for those cattle. Those Rurales were too much Johnny-on-the-spot."

Finally, they said a hopeless good-bye and Tom Brandon turned his grulla and started for Animas. He was broke, out of a job, and had nothing in sight. The wind was blowing cold from the north, but it seemed to be falling off a little. If the weather got warmer it would help some. It began to look like he would be camping out all winter, he reflected grimly, or riding the chuck line.

Animas was a quiet town. There had been but one killing all year, and that because of a misguided attempt by a half-breed to draw a gun on Lon Huffman. What had started the altercation was not known aside from what Huffman himself had said and Eason had verified. The half-breed, a man with a reputation as a hard character in Sonora, had come into town hunting Huffman. He had found him, there had been angry words, and Huffman had killed the breed. "Just a trouble hunter," Huffman said gruffly. "Came into town aimin' to kill somebody, an' picked me."

———

THERE WERE FOUR general stores in Animas and but three saloons. The only gambling done was a few games of draw or stud between friends or casual acquaintances.

Tom Brandon swung down from his grulla and led the horse into the stable. Old Man Hubbell looked up at him. "Sorry to bother you, Tom, but you better have some money soon. The boss is gettin' riled."

"Sure, Hub. An' thanks." He turned and walked toward the Animas Saloon, reflecting grimly that if he had any friends left, they would be there. It was remarkable how a man's friends fell away when he was out of a job and broke. Luckily, he had always been considerate to old Hub, which was more than most of the riders were. Hub remembered, and his brother, Neil Hubbell, who owned the Animas, was also friendly.

It was warm inside and the potbellied stove was glowing with heat. Neil nodded from a table as he came in, and indicated a bottle that stood on the bar. "Help yourself, Tom. I'm about to take some money away from Jim."

Jim Rollins glanced up briefly, his hard old eyes showing his disapproval, but he said nothing. Lon Huffman, who was sitting by the stove, tipped back in his chair and grinned maliciously. "You goin' to be that good to me if I become a pauper, Neil?"

The room was suddenly dead still and Tom Brandon jerked his hand away from the bottle as if stung. He turned slowly, his face white. Why he said it, he would never know, but somehow the words just came of their own free will. "I'd rather be an honest pauper," he said, "than a rich thief."

Lon Huffman's face turned dark and his chair legs slammed down. "I reckon," he said, getting to his feet, "I'm goin' to have to beat some more sense into that thick skull o' your'n."

"That's good because I'm not wearin' a gun, Lon," Brandon said coolly, "so you've no excuse to murder me."

Rollins turned sharply. "Brandon, that's uncalled for!" he declared angrily. "You got no cause to call Lon a murderer because some breed hunted him for trouble!"

Tom Brandon was raging inside. He had nothing on which to base his accusation but suspicion, and that, he admitted to himself, might stem from his own dislike of Huffman, but he spoke again regardless. "Nobody knows he came huntin' for trouble. Lon says so. Eason says so. But when didn't Eason say what Lon wanted him to?"

Lon Huffman's mouth was an ugly line. He was a big, hard man but he moved fast. Also, this talk was not doing him any good. The sooner it was stopped, the better. "You said enough," he said. "You done called me a liar! You called Eason a liar." He grabbed at Tom, and Brandon stepped back and hit him.

The punch caught Lon on the chin but lacked force, as Tom was stepping back. Huffman ducked his head a little and struck swiftly. The first punch caught Tom on the jaw and smashed his head back. The second hit him on the temple and he started to fall. Huffman lunged close, trying with his knee, but Tom grabbed both hands around the underside of the knee and jerked up. Lon Huffman lost balance and fell hard. Tom stepped back, wiping blood from his lips. He was still stunned by those first blows.

Huffman got up, then rushed. Tom struck out wickedly and the two fought savagely while the men in the room sat silent, watching.

Most of them had seen the two other fights and there was no doubt about what would happen now. And inevitably, it did happen. They had been fighting several minutes when Huffman's superior weight and strength began to tell. Tom fought back gamely but he was beaten to the floor. He struggled up, was knocked down again, and fell over against the bar. Huffman was only stopped from putting the boots to him by the other men in the room.

Bloody and battered, Tom Brandon staggered from the room. Outside, the wind was cold and his face was left numb. Grimly he looked at his battered hands, and then he turned and half walked and half staggered to the livery stable, where he crawled into the hay and wrapped himself in his blanket.

Before daybreak he was in the saddle and heading out of town. He was through here, of that there could be no question now. He was being kicked around by everybody, and just a few months before he had been liked and respected. It had started with his first fight with Huffman, then the loss of the herd and the talk about it. After that, things had unraveled rapidly. There was nothing to do but drift.

By noon he was miles to the east and riding huddled in the

saddle, cold and hungry. Suddenly, he saw several cattle drifting sullenly along the trail toward him. As he came up to them, he saw they wore a Rafter H brand. The Rafter H, he recalled, was a small spread some seven or eight miles farther east. These cattle were rapidly drifting away and might never get home in this cold. Turning them, he started them back toward their home ranch, and through the next hour and a half, he kept them moving. When he sighted the cabin and the gate, he hallooed loudly.

The door opened and a stocky, powerful man stepped to the door and at Brandon's hail, opened the gate. Brandon herded the cattle inside and drew up.

"Thanks." The cattleman strode toward him. "Where'd you find 'em?"

Brandon explained, and the man looked at his face, then said, "My name's Jeff Hardin. Get down and come in, you look about beat. Anyway, I'm just fixin' supper."

Hours later they sat together in front of the fireplace. Hardin had proved an interested listener, and Brandon had been warmed by coffee and companionship into telling his troubles. Hardin chuckled softly. "Friend," he said, "you've had it rough. What you doin' now? Lightin' a shuck?"

"What else can I do? Nobody would give me a job there, an' I can't lick Huffman. He's whipped me three times runnin' an' a man ought to know when he's whipped."

Hardin shrugged. "How do you feel about it? Do you feel like you'd been licked?"

Brandon looked rueful. "That's the worst of it," he said. "I don't. I'd like to tackle him again, but he's just too all-fired big for me."

Hardin got to his feet and stretched. "Well, if you ain't headed anywhere in particular, why not spend a month or so here? I could use the help, an' she gets mighty lonesome by myself. I'm a good cook," he added, "but a feller don't feel like it much when he's by himself."

For three days, Brandon worked cattle, cut wood, and fed stock and then one morning, Jeff Hardin came from the house carrying a set of boxing gloves.

"Ever have these on?" he asked.

"Never saw any before," Tom admitted, "although I heard somebody invented something of the kind. What's the idea?"

"Why," Hardin said quietly, "I figure any man who will tackle a bigger, stronger man three times in a row an' is still willin' to try it again should have his chance. Now, I used to take beef to New Orleans an' Kansas City, an' I used to know a few prizefighters. They taught me some things. I also know some Cornish-style wrestlin'. I figure you should go back to Animas in a couple of months and whip the socks off Huffman. You want to try learnin'?"

Tom Brandon grinned. "You've got yourself a pupil!" he said. "Let's have those mitts."

————

A MONTH LATER, Hardin ended a hot session with Tom and grinned as he wiped sweat off of his forehead. "You're good, Tom," he admitted, "an' a sight younger than I am. You've got a good left an' you've got that short right to the body in good shape. I reckon you'll be ready in a little while."

Several weeks passed and the weather settled down into day after day of cold. "You know," Hardin said one evening, "this here breed you were sayin' was killed by that Lon Huffman—he reminds me of a feller used to ride with: Juan Morales."

That brought Tom up straight. "Are you sure?"

"Sounds like him. One time I was way down south an' I seen someone who looked like that. Folks said he was mixed up in some shady cattle deals with Morales, and how he buys ever' stolen cow he can get." He puffed for a few minutes on his pipe. "Tom, d'you s'pose that Huffman could have suddenly decided to drive off that herd o' yours?"

Tom Brandon was dubious. "I practically accused him of it when we had that last fight," he admitted, "but it was temper talkin'. I never should have said it. Only something about that killin' didn't smell right."

"Pay you to look into it," Hardin advised, "when I get back."

"Back?" Brandon looked up in surprise. "Where you goin'?"

"Got a letter," he said, carelessly. "I'll have to leave you here alone. Look after the place, will you? I want to buy some stock. I'll be back in a couple of weeks."

———

ALONE ON THE place, it surprised Brandon that he could find so much to keep him busy. There was the stable door that needed fixing, a couple of water holes that needed cleaning out, then a dam to stop a wash that had started. Day after day he was up with the sun, riding over the range, working, losing himself in the many tasks to be done. In all that time, he never went near town. He thought of faraway Animas, but that was behind him. Only at times, when he thought of Ginnie Rollins, it was almost all he could do not to saddle up and start back.

There was no word from Jeff for almost a month, and then a letter did come, from El Paso.

Been busy. Just returned from Mexico. Will see you next month. Met a mighty pretty girl.

Tom read the note and grinned. Met a pretty girl! At his age! He chuckled, and returned to work. That was the good thing about a ranch, he reflected, a man was never out of work. He could always find something to do. He branded a few strays, moved some of the younger stock down nearer the ranch, hunted down a cougar who had been giving them trouble, and killed two wolves, both with his Winchester at more than three hundred yards.

The days drifted into weeks, and alone on the ranch, Tom Brandon worked hard. Jeff Hardin had been a friend to him when he needed a friend, and he wanted to surprise him, but it was a pleasure just to do what he knew needed to be done. He broke horses, built and repaired fence, cleaned up a patch for a garden, and when Jeff had been gone two months, the place had changed beyond belief.

Then, suddenly, a package was delivered to him at the

gate. Ripping it open, he found a letter from Jeff on top. Beneath the letter were several legal-looking papers.

These will explain the delay in returning. When you get this stuff, better high-tail it for Animas.

Stunned, he stared at the papers. On top was a statement, sworn to before a notary, that the signer had seen Juan Morales pay money to Lon Huffman for cattle. The second was a statement by a Mexican that Morales had given him orders to be at the border to receive a bunch of stampeding cattle, and that the letter informing Morales about the cattle had been in English. The Mexican also testified that Lon Huffman had been with the stampeding cattle, which had all worn the Rollins R brand.

Staying only long enough to get an old man who lived nearby to feed the stock, Brandon threw a saddle on his horse and headed back for Animas.

———

MONTHS HAD GONE by since he had seen the town, and he came up the street at a canter and drew up before the saloon. Swinging down, he pushed through the doors and walked at once to the bar.

Neil Hubbell broke into a smile when he saw him, then glanced hastily at the door. "Tom, you be careful! Lon Huffman's been sayin' he drove you out of town an' that if you ever show your face around, he'll kill you."

"Neil," Tom requested, "come around here and search me. I'm not heeled except with this gun that I'm leavin' with you." He stripped off his pistol and belt, handing them over the bar. "I want to see Lon, but I want to fight him bare-handed."

"Ain't you had enough of that?" Hubbell demanded. "Tom, I think—" He broke off as the door opened and Lon Huffman came in with Eason and Bensch. Huffman stopped abruptly when he saw Tom.

"You?" he said. "Well, I ran you off once an' I'll do it again!" He spread his hands over his guns.

"Hold it, Lon!" Hubbell's voice was stern. "Brandon just turned his gun over to me. He ain't heeled."

"Then give it back to him!"

Tom Brandon took an easy step forward, his heart pounding and his mouth dry. Here it was, the fourth time—would this be another beating? Or were the things that Jeff had taught him the answer? "Unless you're dead set on gettin' killed, Lon," he said quietly, "I'd like to beat your ears in with my fists."

Huffman stared, then he took a fast step forward and swung.

Tom's move was automatic, and it was so easy that it astonished him. He threw up his left forearm to catch the swing, then smashed his own right fist to the ribs. Huffman stopped in his tracks, jolted to the heels. Before he could get set, Tom chopped a short left to the cheek that cut deep and started blood coming down Huffman's face.

Huffman lunged close, swinging with both hands, and Tom stepped inside of a left and, grabbing the sleeve of Huffman's right arm with his own left, he threw his hip into Huffman and jerked hard on the left. Huffman hit the floor hard, and his face went dark with blood. With a lunge, he came off the floor, and Tom Brandon waited for him. This was easy, almost too easy!

Tom stiffened his left into Lon's face, then hit him with a short right to the wind. Huffman backed up, looking sick, and Tom closed in, then struck twice, left and right to the face. Blood was over Huffman's eye and cheek now, and he was staggering.

Brandon moved in, feinted, then whipped that right to the wind. Huffman stopped in his tracks and Tom hit him with a left three times before Huffman could get sorted out. He lunged forward and Brandon stepped in with a short right that dropped Huffman to his knees, his nose welling blood.

He looked up then and was amazed to see Jeff Hardin standing in the door with Jim and Ginnie Rollins beside him.

"Nice work, boy!" Hardin stepped forward grinning. "Very nice work!" Then his face became stern. "Have you got those papers?"

Tom Brandon reached into his shirt for the papers and Hardin handed them to the older man. As Rollins looked at them, his face became hard and cold. Lon Huffman was on his feet, helped there by Bensch.

"An' I trusted you!" Jim Rollins growled. "You dirty . . . no-good . . ."

Huffman wiped blood from his face and stared at them sullenly. "What's the matter?" he demanded. "You gone crazy?"

"Just a matter of a stampeded herd, Lon," Brandon said quietly. "Just a matter of a herd stampeded over the border so Juan could get his brother-in-law up there with the Rurales and prevent our recovering them. They call that stealing, Lon."

Huffman tried to bluff it through. "Didn't do no such thing!" he said. "An' there ain't nobody can say I did!"

Brandon smiled. "Those papers Jim has say so. We've got proof. Even Juan Morales hasn't any respect for a man who would double-cross his employer—or shoot a rider of his because he was afraid the fellow would talk too much while he was drunk!"

Awareness cleared Huffman's brain. He hesitated, then half-turned, throwing a meaningful glance at Eason. He was trapped.

He ran a hand over his face. "Guess there ain't nothin' but to give up—"

Eason had edged to the door and now he suddenly whipped it open, and at the same instant, Huffman went for his gun. Bensch plunged out the door, hit the saddle, and shucked his Winchester, but as Huffman's gun came up, both Rollins and Hardin fired. Struck with two bullets, Lon pitched over on his face.

Eason had frozen where he was, his fingers pulling away from the gun butt.

Bensch took one look, then wheeled his horse. Rollins lifted his gun, but Hardin brushed it aside. "Let him go. He won't do us any harm."

Hardin smiled then. "This here's that pretty girl I spoke of meetin', son. You told me so much about her an' about all that happened here that it decided me. I used to be a Pinkerton man. Well, you were in a bad position and it seemed to me the right man might get you out of it. It was small pay for the way you were fixin' up my ranch. Actually, I've been settin' around too long. Needed a vacation."

"You got here just in time," Tom admitted, smiling.

"Tom," Rollins thrust out a hand, "I reckon I'm an old fool. I'm sorry."

Tom took the hand and when he released it he took Ginnie's arm. "Why don't you two go get yourselves a drink? Because Ginnie and I have things to talk about."

VALLEY OF THE SUN

SPRAWLED ON HIS face beside the cholla, the man was not dead. The gun that lay near his hand had not been fired. He lay now as he had fallen six hours earlier when the two bullets struck him. But the dark stain on the back of his sun-faded shirt was from blood that had caked hard, dried in the blasting sun.

Above him, like the tower of a feudal castle, was the soaring height of Rattlesnake Butte. It loomed like a sentinel above the sun-tortured waste of the valley.

Near the wounded man's hand a tiny lizard stopped. Its heart throbbed noticeably through the skin as it stared in mingled amazement and alarm at the sprawled figure of the man. It sensed the warning of danger in the stale smell of sweat and blood.

Under the baking heat of the sun, the man's back muscles stirred. The lizard darted away, losing itself in a tiny maze of rocks and ruined mesquite. But the muscles of the wounded man, having stirred themselves, relaxed once more and he lay still. Yet the tiny movement, slight as it had been, seemed to start the life processes functioning again. Little by little, as water finds its way through rocks, consciousness began to trickle back into his brain.

His eyes were open a long time before he became aware of his position. At first, he merely lay there, his mind a complete blank, until finally the incongruity of his stillness filtered into his mind and stirred him to wonder as to the cause.

Then memory broke the dam caused by bullet shock and flooded him suddenly.

He knew then that he had been shot. Understanding the manner of men who fired upon him, he knew also that they had left him for dead. He was immediately aware of the advantage this gave him.

Mentally, he explored his body. He was wounded, but where and how he did not know. From the dull throb in his skull he suspected at least one bullet must have hit him in the head. There was, he discovered, a stiffness low down on his left side.

He could remain here no longer. He must first get out of the sun. Then he must take stock of his position and decide what was to be done. Being a desert man, he was acutely aware of the danger of lying in the sun and having all the water drawn from his body. There was a greater danger from heat and thirst than from men determined to kill him.

———

BRETT LARANE GOT his hands under him and very carefully pushed himself up. He flexed his knees with great caution. His arms and legs functioned normally, which was a good sign. To be helpless now would mean sure death.

When he was on his knees he lifted a hand to the scalp wound in his head. It was just that, no more nor less. No doubt there had been a mild concussion also. The wound in his lower left side was worse, and from the caked condition of his shirt and pants, he knew he must have lost a great deal of blood.

Bleeding, he knew, would make a man thirsty, and this was an added danger.

He retrieved his gun and returned it to his holster. The shot that struck him down had come utterly without warning. The drawing of the gun had been one of those purely instinctive actions, natural to a man who is much dependent upon a weapon. It had been due to conditioning rather than intelligence.

Shakily, he got to his feet and glanced around for his horse, but it was nowhere in sight.

They had taken his outfit, then. He was a man afoot in the desert, miles from possible aid, a man who had lost his saddle. In this country, that alone was tantamount to a death sentence.

There was shade under the overhang of the butte and he moved toward it, walking carefully. Once there, he lowered himself gingerly to a sitting position. He was afraid of opening the wound and starting the bleeding again. Weakness flooded him, and he sat there, gasping and half-sick with fear. Nausea swept over him and came up in his throat.

He wanted to live, he wanted desperately to live.

He wanted to see Marta once more, to finish the job he had begun for her. He wanted to repay those who had shot him down from ambush. He wanted all these things, and not to die here alone in the shadow of a lost butte on a sun-parched desert.

Realist that he was, he knew his chances of survival were slight. On this desert without a horse, a strong man might figure the odds as at least fifty to one against him. For a wounded man, the odds went to such figures that they were beyond the grasp of any run-of-the-herd cowhand.

Horse Springs, the last settlement, lay sixty miles behind him. And in this heat and without water, that distance made the town as remote as a distant planet. Willow Valley lay some forty or fifty miles ahead, somewhere over yonder in the blue haze that shrouded the mountains along the horizon.

No doubt there was water not too far distant, but in what direction and how far?

There are few stretches of desert without some sort of spring or water hole. But unless one knew their location they were of no use, for no man could wander about at random hoping to find one. One might be within a dozen yards of one and never know it.

All the while he thought of this he knew he dared not look. He would have no direction, no indication, and in his condition there was but one thing, to head for Willow Valley and hope someone found him before he died.

Nor was the trail one often traveled. Outlaws like those who shot him infested this country. Few people wanted to go to Horse Springs, so the desert was avoided. He had taken this road for that purpose, never dreaming that Joe Creet would guess the route he had chosen.

It had been Creet, of course, who shot him. Larane had

heard his jeering voice in the momentary space that separated the shots.

He had seen the three riders from the Saxon Hills in one fleeting glimpse as he tumbled from the saddle, and he would not soon forget their faces. Joe Creet, Indian Frank, and Gay Tomason.

Trouble had been building for some time between Creet and himself, but it was Tomason's presence there that surprised him. An expression of cold triumph was on the man's face as he lifted his gun.

Joe Creet's motive was obvious enough. The outlaw had always hated him. Only six weeks ago he had given Creet a beating that left marks still visible on the man's face. Moreover, Creet must have learned about Marta Malone's money, which he had been carrying.

But Tomason?

Gay had been his friend, they had ridden together, worked together, come west together.

The answer to that was Marta. With him out of the running, Gay would have the inside track with her. With no other eligible men around, Gay would probably win her. For a long time Brett Larane had been aware of Gay's interest in the girl, but he had never believed it would go this far.

———

LARANE WAS A quiet man, tall and strong, and given to deep, abiding loyalties and lasting friendships.

It would have been Gay who told Creet what trail he was to take. Creet could have trailed him, but could not have been lying in wait for him as he had been, so Tomason must have told Creet or even led him to the spot. Yet with both men, and with Indian Frank, who followed wherever Creet led, the motive lay deeper than these more obvious things.

No one needed to tell Brett Larane of the seriousness of his position. In this heat a man without water, by resting in the shade at all times, might live from two to five days. Traveling by night and resting in the shade by day, he might live from one to three days, and might make twenty miles. And twenty miles would leave him exactly nowhere.

Yet if he was to survive, he must make an effort. Here in the shade of Rattlesnake Butte he could not afford to wait. Time was precious, and he must move on. And well he knew that all of those calculations on time and distance concerned a man in the full flower of health, and he was wounded and weak.

For the time at least, he must wait. To start in the sun would finish him within a few miles at most.

Sweat trickled down his face, and he fanned himself weakly with his hat. He felt faint and sick now, all his rugged strength seeming to drain away. He tried not to think of the thirst that was already drying his throat and cracking his parched lips. He thought of Marta Malone, and the Hidden Valley Ranch.

It was a small ranch, lonely and yet beautiful, nestling in the shoulder of the mountains that somebody had named Hidden Valley. A pleasant place, a place where he had thought to live out his life with Marta.

That had been his one thought, ever since he drifted into the Valley of the Sun and went to work for her, first as a puncher, and then when they all quit, as foreman of a ranch without hands. But he had worked on. He had dammed the spring and formed a pool, he had repaired the house and built an adobe barn. He had broken fifteen wild horses, branded cattle, and kept at it, doing everything possible without thought of reward.

Hiring some drifting cowhands, he had taken her herd to the stock pens at Horse Springs and sold them to a stock buyer for a good price, the first returns that Marta had won from the ranch since her father died. And then he had been robbed.

The worst of it was, they would probably tell her he had run off with her money, and she would have little choice but to believe them.

His head throbbed with dull pain, and the angry teeth of a more raw and bitter pain gnawed at his wounded side. He knew that his wounds should be washed and cleansed, but he had no water, and there was nothing he could do.

The day drew on and the band of shadow in which he sat narrowed. The stifling heat danced upon the far length of the desert. Dust devils moved in a queer rigadoon across the levels. Heat beat down upon him, but at last his eyes closed and he slept, his face greasy with sweat, his body stiff with the torture from his wounds.

A buzzard circled in the sky, and then another came near, and a long time later Brett opened his eyes. Weakly, he pushed himself erect, staring with dazed eyes over the gathering of shadows around him, and the red-and-gold-tipped peaks of the far-off mountains. It would soon be time to move.

Automatically, he felt for his gun. One shot, and then he would need to worry no more. Just one, and then no more pain, no more trouble. Yet even as he thought of it he remembered the beauty of Marta, awaiting him in the doorway at Hidden Valley, her hand shading her eyes, then a smile, and she would come running down the steps. In these past months they had drawn very close to one another.

He looked down at the gun. They had left him that, never guessing he would have the chance to use it again, and he might not.

Marta needed that money. Her whole existence at Hidden Valley depended on it. Only his efforts had enabled her to gather the cattle and get them on the road to market. Without him and the money she could do nothing. And because he had trusted Gay, she would trust him.

Brett Larane felt with a thick and fumbling tongue for the parched and cracked lips. Then he got a fingerhold in a crevice of the rock and looked out at the desert. The sun was gone now, and a vague coolness seemed to drift over the desert. He turned and braced himself, gathering his strength. Then he pushed away from the cliff and began to walk.

He was weak, but he kept his eyes on the mountains and moved along steadily. When he had walked a half mile he paused and seated himself carefully on a rock, resting. Nearby there was a mesquite root that would do for a cane. After ten minutes he got up and started on.

DARKNESS CLOSED AROUND him and he kept moving. Once, far off over the desert, he heard a coyote howl, and once a rabbit scurried by him, dodging away through the rocks and cholla.

He walked on and on, resting at intervals, but continuing to push on. Once, he stumbled and was too weak to rise for a long time. So he lay sprawled out on the desert, his body deliciously cool and relaxed even while his throat burned with thirst.

When he opened his eyes the sky was faintly gray in the east. He struggled to his feet and started on.

Now he must find shelter from the sun. He must find something, somehow, nearby. He would make no more than a couple of miles at his present pace before the sun was up. Yet there was nothing in sight and he pushed on. Suddenly the face of the desert was broken by the sandy scar of a wash. It came down from low hills, and he followed along the lip, walking away from his trail, for often along a wash one might find water.

The sun was looking over the horizon when he glimpsed the green of a cottonwood. His tongue was swollen, but felt thick and dry. He pushed on, then hearing a noise in the brush close to the base of the slim young cottonwood, he halted and, creeping closer, peered through.

Two porcupines were digging industriously into the sand, and he waited for a minute, watching, and then seeing damp sand being scraped from the hole they were digging, he moved up and drove them away.

Water!

He fell on his knees and dug eagerly into the damp sand at the bottom of the hole, and soon it grew sloppy and muddy, and then he sat back, letting the water seep through into the hole. It was still muddy when he cupped his hand into it and lifted it to his lips. He managed to get a swallow, then moistened his lips and tongue with his damp hand.

All day he waited beside the hole, drinking from time to time, and resting in the flimsy shade of the cottonwood. Toward dusk he bathed his head and face. Then he bathed the raw wound in his side. Having nothing with which to bandage it, he took some green leaves, dipped them in water, and bound them on, using his handkerchief for a compress and a pigging string from his hip pocket to secure the makeshift dressing.

He was picking up his cane to go when he heard a movement in the brush. He froze, and his gun slid into his hand. There was the sound of a horse's hoof striking stone, and then the brush was thrust apart and a horse walked through, a horse with an empty saddle!

His heart gave a leap. "Buck!" he gasped joyfully. "Well, I'll be darned!"

The horse jerked his head up and stopped. He spoke again, and the animal thrust a wary nose out toward him, sniffing curiously of his hand, but not liking the smell of blood that lingered in the air. Brett got his hand on the bridle and led the horse to the small spring, scarcely more than a bucket of water in sight.

Obviously, the horse had escaped, running away when Brett was fired upon, and then the animal, probably headed toward home and browsing along the way, had smelled water. When the horse had drunk, Brett Larane pulled himself into the saddle and started for the trail.

As he rode he studied his situation. He was very weak, and the distance he had to go was great. Yet by resting from time to time he believed he could make it if the wound in his side did not again begin to bleed.

It was not only essential that he arrive at the ranch but that he reach it in condition to act. He had no doubt that if Gay Tomason and Creet were not already there, they soon would be. There was no aid anywhere near for Marta, even if she wished to protest whatever steps they might take. But the chances were that Tomason would go to her as a friend. And even if she knew much of what Joe Creet and Indian Frank were, she had believed that Tomason was a friend.

Darkness was falling when Brett rode the buckskin off the trail into the piñons along the mountainside. Buck pulled against his guiding hand, wanting the home corral and the feed that awaited him there. But Brett rode him up through the trees, skirting along a dim cattle trail until he could come down upon the Hidden Valley Ranch from behind, riding down through the aspens.

A light shone from the window of the small ranch house, and his eyes narrowed with thought as he saw another light come on in his own cabin, which had formerly served as the bunkhouse. They were there, then. Tomason was there, and probably Creet.

They had Marta's money, and now they wanted her ranch, and probably her.

He wondered if Tomason had thought of Creet and the girl. With his shrewd eyes, Brett had long been aware of Creet's desire for the girl, and he had watched the man speculatively appraising Marta on more than one occasion. Tomason, for all his gun skill, was no match for Creet.

The outlaw was a cold-blooded killer, and he was a deadly hand with a six-gun. Only Brett Larane might match him in gunplay, and of that fact only two men were aware—Larane himself, and Joe Creet.

———

CREET KNEW THAT Larane had a reputation in Hays and Tascosa, a fact unknown to Tomason or to any of the others in the Valley of the Sun country or the Saxon Hills. Larane had backed down the Catfish Kid on two occasions, and Jesse Evans, Billy the Kid's former pal and later enemy, had backed down for him. In that tough and hard-bitten crowd that included Hendry Brown, Frank Valley, and Dave Rudabaugh, Brett Larane had been left strictly alone.

Two things he must do now. He must at all costs recover the money for Marta, and he must kill Joe Creet and Gay Tomason.

Had he been a well man, he might have handled the situation without gunfire. But in his present shape, with no knowledge of how long he would be around, he dared take no chances. If he did not live, he must be sure that the others died. And he must be sure that if he was to be sick or crippled, none of the three were around to take advantage of his and the girl's helplessness.

He knew the risk he was taking, but at all costs he had to have water. He had ridden for hours now without a drink, and the water earlier had scarcely been sufficient to refresh him after his long thirst. Moreover, he must know who was at the ranch, and what was happening there.

Leaving the buckskin tethered in the aspens, he moved carefully toward the ranch house.

At the spring he lowered himself to the ground and drank long and deeply. Lifting his head, he studied the situation with care, then turned toward the bunkhouse. He must first know who was on the grounds. At a window, flattened against the side of the building, he glanced within.

Joe Creet was hunched over the table, and Indian Frank sat on the edge of a bunk. Gay Tomason was tipped back against the wall in a chair. "What I say"—Tomason was speaking—"is we split the money now. Then you hombres take a good-sized herd and leave me here. That's fair enough."

Creet's dry chuckle was a warning to Brett Larane, who knew his man, but Gay saw nothing in it. "Sure, that's fair enough," Joe agreed, "in fact, that's more than fair. But who wants to be fair?"

Tomason's smile faded. "Well, let's have your idea, then!" he demanded sharply. "I've stated my case."

"My idea?" Creet chuckled again, and his small black eyes were pinned on Tomason with contempt. "I want the money, and the girl."

Tomason's chair legs hit the floor, his face was dark with angry blood. "She's mine!" he said furiously. "She's in love with me, and she wants me! She doesn't enter into this!"

"Doesn't she?" Creet sneered. "I say she does. I'd kill"—he stared at Tomason—"for a woman like that as quick as for money. I'd even kill you, Gay."

Their eyes held, and Brett watched, fascinated. He saw what was in Creet's mind, and he could sense the evil triumph within the man at this moment. Joe Creet liked nothing and hated everything. He was a man eaten by a cancer of jealousy and hatred, and now he was savoring his triumph over the handsome Gay Tomason.

"So? That's the way it is?" Larane knew what Tomason

was going to do. The man did have courage, of a kind, and now he laughed suddenly. "Why, I might have guessed you'd never play fair with any man, Joe! I might have known that as soon as I helped you put Brett out of the way, I would come next.

"I see things different, myself. I wouldn't kill for any woman. You can have her. Now, if you like."

Tomason chuckled as he finished speaking, and leaned his elbows on his knees. "Let's forget her and split the money. If you insist on Marta, there's no reason for me staying around."

"Sure." Joe Creet got up slowly, smiling with hard eyes. "I think that's just what I'll do. Go up an' see her now." He turned on his heel with a last sneering glance at Gay, and stepped toward the door.

It was a trap, but Tomason was too intent on his own subterfuge, for as Creet's back turned to him Gay Tomason went for his gun and started to his feet in the same moment. And then Indian Frank buried his knife to the haft in the back of Tomason's neck!

The big cowhand gasped, his mouth opening and closing. He tried to lift his gun. But at the grunt of Indian Frank as he drove home the knife, Creet wheeled like a cat and shattered Gay's wrist with a sweeping blow of his gun barrel. Tomason's gun crashed to the floor, and the cowhand stood swaying, then his knees buckled under him, and he went down. Deliberately, Creet kicked him in the stomach, then the face.

––––––––––

"GOOD JOB," CREET said, grinning at his crony. "Now we'll have the money, and the girl." He looked up at the Indian. "And I mean both of us. Let's eat, and then we'll go up."

Carefully, Brett Larane eased away from the cabin wall. On cat feet he started for the house, and when he got to the door, he tried the knob. It was not locked. Opening it, he stepped in.

Marta heard the creak of the door and looked up. Her eyes went wide in startled horror. He lifted his finger to his lips. Then he got to the table and dropped into a chair. In gasping words, he told her of the shooting on the trail, of his own wounds, and of the murder of Gay Tomason.

His face was deathly pale, and he felt sick and empty. He tried holding his hands steady, and his lips stiffened as he felt them tremble. He could never hope to shoot accurately enough to kill both men before they got him. He needed time—time. And there was no time. They were coming now, in just a few minutes.

Yet there was a chance. If he could keep them in the cabin, prevent them from getting out . . . He looked up. "Where's my rifle?" he asked hoarsely. With the rifle he could pin them down, hold them back, possibly kill them at a distance. Away from Marta.

"They took it, Brett. Creet came in with Gay, said there was a coyote he wanted to kill. There isn't a gun in the house except the one you're wearing."

For money and a girl . . . they believed they had killed him, they knew they had killed Gay. They would stop at nothing, and they had been sure Marta had no weapons. The minutes fled, and he stared wildly from the girl to the window, trying desperately to think. Some way to stop them! There had to be a way! There just had to be!

His dwindling strength had mostly been dissipated on the long ride home. He knew, with an awful fear for Marta, that he could never get to the bunkhouse again. He doubted if he could cross the room. The sweat stood out on his face, and in the pale light he looked ghastly.

Slumped in the chair, his breath came in long gasps. His head throbbed, and the rat's teeth of agony bit into his side. He tried to force his fevered mind to function, to wrest from it one idea, anything, that might help.

When Creet saw him there, he was going to shoot. The outlaw would give him no chance to plan, to think. Nor would he hesitate. Creet knew him too well. He would, at first glimpse, realize Brett Larane's tragic weakness. There would be no second chance. Joe Creet must die before he cleared the doorstep, while he was stepping across it. Brett frowned against the pain, and his thoughts struggled with the problem.

He had no strength to lift a gun, no strength to hold a gun even, nor did he dare risk Marta's life by allowing her to use his gun. There was in his mind no thought of fair play, for there was nothing fair about any of this. It was murder, ugly and brutal, that they planned.

They had not thought of fair play when they ambushed him. Creet hadn't thought of fair play when he lured Gay Tomason into a chance at his back while Indian Frank sneaked up with his knife. If he was to save Marta and the ranch he had worked for, it must be now, and by any means.

Then he saw the box. It was a narrow wooden box, quite heavy, with rope handles. He had seen such boxes often used for carrying bar gold. The handles were inch-thick rope in this case, the ends run through holes and held on the inside by knots.

"Marta," he whispered hoarsely, "break the near end out of that box. Force the nails without noise, if you can."

He sat at the table and stared as she worked, and in a few minutes she had the end removed. "Now, from the other end," he whispered. "Cut the rope handle out and put the box on the table!"

Wondering, she did so, and looked at him curiously as he fumbled with the box to move it, the long way toward the door, the open end toward him. "Now," he said softly, "my gun."

Drawing it carefully from its worn holster, Marta placed it on the table beside him. Lifting the gun, he gripped the butt and pushed his arm and hand into the box, which was open on top. Marta, her eyes suddenly bright, caught his intention, and guided the muzzle of the barrel to one of the holes from which the rope had been taken. It was just large enough to take the muzzle of the six-gun.

"Now," he said, looking up at her, "throw a cloth over it, like it was food or something, covered on the table."

———

HIS HAND GRIPPING the butt on the gun, and the box covered by the cloth, Brett Larane sat facing the door, waiting. They would come, and they would come soon, and he had the gun fixed now, in position, pointed directly at the door. And he needed no strength to hold it ready for firing . . . but he had to get that first shot, while Joe Creet was in range, and he had to kill with that first shot. Afterward, Indian Frank might run off, or he might try to come through the door. If he came through the door, he, too, would die.

"Will you be all right, Brett?" Marta asked him gently.

He nodded, liking the feel of her hand on his shoulder. "Only, I hope they come . . . soon."

She left him to put coffee on the stove, and his eyes strayed toward the door, knowing as well as she what little chance they had. He must make desperately sure of that first shot. Indian Frank was not dangerous without Creet, but the outlaw would be dangerous at any time.

She glanced from the window, but shook her head, and Brett sipped the coffee she offered him, a little at a time. His left hand trembled so, she had to hold the cup to his lips. He drank, then managed a few swallows of food.

They came silently and were scarcely heard. A quick grasp on his shoulder and Brett opened his eyes, aware for the first time that he had fallen asleep. His heart pounding, he gripped the gun butt and his finger slid through the trigger guard. And then the door opened.

It was Creet, but even as Brett Larane's finger tightened on the trigger, Joe turned sidewise and motioned to Indian Frank. "Come in!" he said, and then his head swung toward the room.

For the first time he saw the man sitting across the table beyond the coal-oil lamp. He jumped as if shot, and his hand swept down for his gun, but at that instant, Indian Frank stepped into the doorway. Brett squeezed the trigger, and the concealed gun bellowed loud in the silent room.

Frank, caught in midstep, stopped dead still, then sprawled facedown in the doorway, and Joe Creet leaped aside. Brett's second shot, booming hollowly, lost itself through the open door.

Creet, gun in hand, stared at him. "Well, I'm forever damned!" he said softly. "You're a hard one to kill, Larane! A hard one! I'd have sworn you were dead back there, with blood all over you! And now you've got Frank . . . well, that saves me the trouble. I never figured on him sharing the money. I had plans for him."

He looked at the table and the cloth-covered box. "Whatever you've got there, I don't know," he said, his eyes wary, "but you'd never be settin' that way, your hand covered an' all, if you could hold a gun. You'd never have missed the second shot you fired. Nor would you be settin' there now. You'd have turned that gun on me.

"No, I reckon you're not dead, but you're not quite alive, either. You're hurt bad."

The outlaw's face was saturnine, and his eyes were wicked with triumph. "Well, well! I'm glad to see you, Larane! Always did sort of spoil my fun, thinkin' you wouldn't be here to watch."

Brett's fingers tightened on the gun butt, trying to ease it out of the hole in the box, but it would not come loose, or his strength was too little to exert the necessary pull.

"Come over here!" Creet looked up at Marta. "Come over here and do what I tell you, or I'll drill him right through the head."

Marta Malone, transfixed with horror, stared from Creet's tense, evil features to the poised gun in his hand. Then, as if walking in her sleep, she started to move toward him.

Brett Larane stared at Creet, too weak to lift a hand, helpless to prevent the outlaw from doing as he wished.

Suddenly, something clicked in his brain. It was a wild, desperate, impossible chance—but there was no other choice.

"Marta—!" he said, speaking as loudly as he could. *"Think!"*

"Shut up!" Creet snarled at him. "Shut up or I'll brain you!"

"Think, Marta!" Brett begged. "Please think! Marta . . . !" His voice lifted as she drew near Creet. *Think—the door!*

As if he had spoken his thought, Marta understood, and with all her strength she hurled herself at the side of the gunman! Her weight hit him, and he staggered. His gun blasted a stab of flame, and a dish across the room crashed into bits as Joe Creet went staggering into the open doorway!

As HE HIT the doorpost with his shoulder he ripped his next shot out, and the lamp beside Brett shattered into bits, splashing him with oil, and then his own gun bellowed, and the dark figure in the doorway jerked spasmodically. Brett triggered the gun again, and the outlaw screamed . . . then broke his scream off in a choking, rattling sound, drowned by Brett Larane's last shot.

Joe Creet, hit three times, toppled forward and sprawled on his face outside the door. For a moment, in a deathly silence, they could hear the scratching of his fingers on the hard-packed earth beyond the step. Scratching, and then silence, a lonely shuddering silence in which Marta Malone clasped Brett Larane's head against her breast and sobbed brokenly in relief and shock.

There was sunlight in his face when he opened his eyes, sunlight, but he liked it, enjoyed it.

He looked around, remembering Marta's room, and seeing the sharp, bright cleanliness of it, and the look of home about it.

The door opened as he lay there, enjoying the warmth and peace of it, and knowing it was early morning, and that he felt good.

The door opened, and Marta came in, her face bright when she saw he was awake. "Oh, Brett! You're up at last! I thought you would never awaken! How do you feel?" She put her hand on his face. He caught it and held it, looking up at her. "Like I never wanted to leave!" he said, smiling. "But what happened?"

"Nothing, until the next morning. Then a man came out from Willow Springs to get some money I owed him, and he buried the bodies and then he went in and sent the doctor out. I found the money they had stolen in Joe Creet's saddlebags in the bunkhouse."

"Better not think about it," he said quietly. "Tomorrow it will be an old story."

"Tomorrow, Brett? Why, it's already been more than two weeks! You've been awfully sick! Your side . . . the doctor said if it hadn't had care right away, you would have died!"

"Well, I didn't. Now we've got work to do. I'll have to find a crew, and—"

"We've got a bunch of boys, Brett. The doctor hired them for me, four of them, Texas men who were heading back after a cattle drive. You'll have a crew to boss when you can get around again!"

"And I suppose they are all flirting with you!" he said darkly. "I reckon it is time I got around!"

"No, they haven't flirted—much. The doctor told them we were going to be married."

"Oh, he did, did he? And what did you say?"

"Why, what could I say? He was such a nice man, and had been so helpful, I just couldn't have all those cowhands thinking he lied, could I?"

Brett Larane sank back against the pillow and grinned weakly. "You sure couldn't!" he said. "You sure couldn't!"

FORK YOUR OWN BRONCS

MAC MARCY TURNED in the saddle and, resting his left hand on the cantle, glanced back up the arroyo. His lean, brown face was troubled. There were cattle here, all right, but too few.

At this time of day, late afternoon and very hot, there should have been a steady drift of cattle toward the water hole.

Ahead of him he heard a steer bawl and then another. Now what? Above the bawling of the cattle he heard another sound, a sound that turned his face gray with worry. It was the sound of hammers.

He needed nothing more to tell him what was happening. Jingle Bob Kenyon was fencing the water hole!

As he rounded the bend in the wash, the sound of hammers ceased for an instant, but only for an instant. Then they continued with their work.

Two strands of barbed wire had already been stretched tight and hard across the mouth of the wash. Several cowhands were stretching the third wire of what was obviously to be a four-wire fence.

Already Marcy's cattle were bunching near the fence, bawling for water.

As he rode nearer, two men dropped their hammers and lounged up to the fence. Marcy's eyes narrowed and his gaze shifted to the big man on the roan horse. Jingle Bob Kenyon was watching him with grim humor.

Marcy avoided the eyes of the two other men by the fence, Vin Ricker and John Soley, who could mean only one thing for him—trouble, bad trouble. Vin Ricker was a gunhand and a killer. John Soley was anything Vin told him to be.

"This is a rotten trick, Kenyon," Marcy declared angrily. "In this heat my herd will be wiped out."

Kenyon's eyes were unrelenting. "That's just tough," he stated flatly. "I warned yuh when yuh fust come in here to git out while the gittin' was good. Yuh stayed on. Yuh asked for it. Now yuh take it or git out."

———

TEMPER FLARING WITHIN him like a burst of flame, Marcy glared. But deliberately he throttled his fury. He would have no chance here. Ricker and Soley were too much for him, let alone the other hands and Kenyon himself.

"If you don't like it," Ricker sneered, "why don't yuh stop us? I hear tell yuh're a plumb salty hombre."

"You'd like me to give you a chance to kill me, wouldn't you?" Marcy asked harshly. "Someday I'll get you without your guns, Ricker, an' I'll tear down your meat house."

Ricker laughed. "I don't want to dirty my hands on yuh, or I'd come over an' make yuh eat those words. If yuh ever catch me without these guns, yuh'll wish to old Harry I still had 'em."

Marcy turned his eyes away from the gunman and looked at Kenyon.

"Kenyon, I didn't think this of you. Without water, my cows won't last three days, an' you know it. You'll bust me flat."

Kenyon was unrelenting. "This is a man's country, Marcy," he said dryly. "Yuh fork your own broncs an' yuh git your own water. Don't come whinin' to me. Yuh moved in on me, an' if yuh git along, it'll be on your own."

Kenyon turned his horse and rode away. For an instant Marcy stared after him, seething with rage. Then, abruptly, he wheeled his grayish-black horse—a moro—and started back up the arroyo. Even as he turned, he became aware that only six lean steers faced the barbed wire.

He had ridden but a few yards beyond the bend when that thought struck him like a blow. Six head of all the hundreds he had herded in here! By rights they should all be at the water hole or heading that way. Puzzled, he started back up the trail.

By rights there should be a big herd here. Where could

they be? As he rode back toward his claim shack, he stared about him. No cattle were in sight. His range was stripped.

Rustlers? He scowled. But there had been no rustling activity of which he had heard. Ricker and Soley were certainly the type to rustle cattle, but Marcy knew Kenyon had been keeping them busy on the home range.

He rode back toward the shack, his heart heavy.

He had saved for seven years, riding cattle trails to Dodge, Abilene, and Ellsworth to get the money to buy his herd. It was his big chance to have a spread of his own, a chance for some independence and a home.

A home! He stared bitterly at the looming rimrock behind his outfit. A home meant a wife, and there was only one girl in the world for him. There would never be another who could make him feel as Sally Kenyon did. But she *would* have to be old Jingle Bob's daughter!

Not that she had ever noticed him. But in those first months before the fight with Jingle Bob became a dog-eat-dog fight, Marcy had seen her around, watched her, been in love with her from a distance. He had always hoped that when his place had proved up and he was settled, he might know her better. He might even ask her to marry him.

It had been a foolish dream. Yet day by day it became even more absurd. He was not only in a fight with her father, but he was closer than ever to being broke.

Grimly, his mind fraught with worry, he cooked his meager supper, crouching before the fireplace. Again and again the thought kept recurring—where were his cattle? If they had been stolen, they would have to be taken down past the water hole and across Jingle Bob's range. There was no other route from Marcy's corner of range against the rim. For a horseman, yes. But not for cattle.

The sound of a walking horse startled him. He straightened and then stepped away from the fire and put the bacon upon the plate, listening to the horse as it drew nearer. Then he put down his food, and loosening his gun, he stepped to the door.

The sun had set long since, but it was not yet dark. He

watched a gray horse coming down from the trees leading up to the rim. Suddenly he gulped in surprise.

———

IT WAS SALLY Kenyon! He stepped outside and walked into the open. The girl saw him and waved a casual hand and then reined in.

"Have you a drink of water?" she asked, smiling. "It's hot, riding."

"Sure," he said, trying to smile. "Coffee, if you want. I was just fixin' to eat a mite. Want to join me? Of course," he said sheepishly, "I ain't no hand with grub."

"I might take some coffee."

Sally swung down, drawing off her gauntlets. She had always seemed a tall girl, but on the ground she came just to his shoulder. Her hair was honey-colored, her eyes gray.

He caught the quick glance of her eyes as she looked around. He saw them hesitate with surprise at the spectacle of flowers blooming near the door. She looked up, and their eyes met.

"Ain't much time to work around," he confessed. "I sort of been tryin' to make it look like a home."

"Did you plant the flowers?" she asked curiously.

"Yes, ma'am. My mother was always a great hand for flowers. I like 'em, too, so when I built this cabin, I set some out. The wildflowers I transplanted."

He poured coffee into a cup and handed it to her. She sipped the hot liquid and looked at him.

"I've been hearing about you," she said.

"From Jingle Bob?"

She nodded. "And some others. Vin Ricker, for one. He hates you."

"Who else?"

"Chen Lee."

"Lee?" Marcy shook his head. "I don't place him."

"He's Chinese, our cook. He seems to know a great deal about you. He thinks you're a fine man. A great fighter, too. He's always talking about some Mullen gang you had trouble with."

"Mullen gang?" He stared. "Why, that was in—" He caught himself. "No, ma'am, I reckon he's mistook. I don't know any Chinese an' there ain't no Mullen gang around I know of."

That, he reflected, was no falsehood. The Mullen gang had all fitted very neatly into the boot hill he had prepared for them back in Bentown. They definitely weren't around.

"Going to stay here?" she asked, looking at him over her coffee cup, her gray eyes level.

His eyes flashed. "I was fixin' to, but I reckon your old man has stopped me by fencin' that water hole. He's a hard man, your father."

"It's a hard country." She did not smile. "He's got ideas about it. He drove the Mescaleros out. He wiped out the rustlers; he took this range. He doesn't like the idea of any soft-going, second-run cowhand coming in and taking over."

His head jerked up.

"Soft-going?" he flared. "Second-run? Why, that old billy goat!"

Sally turned toward her horse. "Don't tell me. Tell him. If you've nerve enough!"

He got up and took the bridle of her horse. His eyes were hard.

"Ma'am," he said, striving to make his voice gentle, "I think you're a mighty fine person, an' sure enough purty, but that father of yours is a rough-ridin' old buzzard. If it wasn't for that Ricker hombre—"

"Afraid?" she taunted, looking down at him.

"No, ma'am," he said quietly. "Only I ain't a killin' man. I was raised a Quaker. I don't aim to do no fightin'."

"You're in a fighting man's country," she warned him. "And you are cutting in on a fighting man's range."

She turned her gray and started to ride away. Suddenly she reined in and looked back over her shoulder.

"By the way," she said, "there's water up on the rim."

WATER UP ON the rim? What did she mean? He turned his head and stared up at the top of the great cliff, which loomed high overhead into the night. It was fully a mile away, but it seemed almost behind his house.

How could he get up to the rim? Sally had come from that direction. In the morning he would try. In the distance, carried by the still air of night, he heard a cow bawling. It was shut off from the water hole. His six head, starving for water!

Marcy walked out to the corral and threw a saddle on the moro. He swung into the saddle and rode at a canter toward the water hole.

They heard him coming, and he saw a movement in the shadows by the cottonwoods.

"Hold it!" a voice called. "What do you want?"

"Let that fence down an' put them cows through!" Marcy yelled.

There was a harsh laugh. "Sorry, amigo. No can do. Only Kenyon cows drink here."

"All right," Marcy snapped. "They are Kenyon cows. I'm givin' 'em to him. Let the fence down an' let 'em drink. I ain't seein' no animal die just to please an old plughead. Let 'em through."

Then he heard Sally's voice. He saw her sitting her horse beside old Joe Linger, who was her bodyguard, teacher, and friend. An old man who had taught her to ride and to shoot and who had been a scout for the Army at some time in the past.

Sally was speaking, and he heard her say, "Let them through, Texas. If they are our cows, we don't want to have them die on us."

Marcy turned the moro and rode back toward his cabin, a sense of defeat heavy upon him. . . .

He rolled out of his blankets with the sun and after a quick breakfast, saddled the grayish-black horse and started back toward the rim. He kept remembering Sally's words, "There is water on the rim." Why had she told him that? What good would water do him if it was way up on the rim?

There must be a way up. By backtracking the girl, he could find it. He was worried about the cattle. The problem of their disappearance kept working into his thoughts. That was another reason for his ride, the major reason. If the cattle were still on his ranch, they were back in the breaks at the foot of the rim.

As he backtracked the girl's horse, he saw cow tracks, more and more of them. Obviously, some of his cattle had drifted this way. It puzzled him, yet he had to admit that he knew little of this country.

Scarcely a year before, he had come into this range, and when he arrived, the grass in the lower reaches of the valley was good, and there were mesquite beans. The cattle grew fat. With hotter and dryer weather, they had shown more and more of a tendency to keep to shady hillsides and to the canyons.

The cow tracks scattered out and disappeared. He continued on the girl's trail. He was growing more and more puzzled, for he was in the shadow of the great cliff now, and any trail that mounted it must be frightfully steep. Sally, of course, had grown up in this country on horseback. With her always had been Joe Linger. Old Joe had been one of the first white men to settle in the rim country.

Marcy skirted a clump of piñon and emerged on a little sandy level at the foot of the cliff. This, at one distant time, had been a streambed, a steep stream that originated somewhere back up in the rimrock and flowed down here and deeper into his range.

Then he saw the trail. It was a narrow catwalk of rock that clung to the cliff's edge in a way that made him swallow as he looked at it. The catwalk led up the face of the cliff and back into a deep gash in the face of the rim, a gash invisible from below.

The moro snorted a few times, but true to its mountain blood, it took the trail on dainty feet. In an hour Marcy rode out on the rim itself. All was green here, green grass. The foliage on the trees was greener than below. There was every indication of water, but no sign of a cow. Not even a range-bred cow would go up such a trail as Marcy had just ridden.

———

FOLLOWING THE TRACKS of the gray, Marcy worked back through the cedar and piñon until he began to hear a muffled roar. Then he rode through the trees and reined in at the edge of a pool that was some twenty feet across. Water flowed into it from a fair-sized stream, bubbling over rocks and falling into the pool. There were a number of springs here, and undoubtedly the supply of water was limitless. But where did it go?

Dismounting, Marcy walked down to the edge of the water and knelt on a flat rock and leaned far out.

Brush hung far out over the water at the end of the pool, brush that grew on a rocky ledge no more than three feet above the surface of the water. But beneath that ledge was a black hole at least eight feet long. Water from the pool was pouring into that black hole.

Mac Marcy got up and walked around the pool to the ledge. The brush was very thick, and he had to force his way through. Clinging precariously to a clump of manzanita, he leaned out over the rim of the ledge and tried to peer into the hole. He could see nothing except a black slope of water and that the water fell steeply beyond that slope.

He leaned farther out, felt the manzanita give way slowly, and made a wild clutch at the neighboring brush. Then he plunged into the icy waters of the pool.

He felt himself going down, down, down! He struck out, trying to swim, but the current caught him and swept him into the gaping mouth of the wide black hole under the ledge.

Darkness closed over his head. He felt himself shooting downward. He struck something and felt it give beneath him, and then something hit him a powerful blow on the head. Blackness and icy water closed over him.

Chattering teeth awakened him. He was chilled to the bone and soaking wet. For a moment he lay on hard, smooth rock in darkness, head throbbing, trying to realize what had happened. His feet felt cold. He pulled them up and turned over to a sitting position in a large cave. Only then did he realize his feet had been lying in a pool of water.

Far above he could see a faint glimmer of light, a glimmer feebly reflecting from the black, glistening roar of a fall. He tilted his head back and stared upward through the gloom.

That dim light, the hole through which he had come, was at least sixty feet above him!

In falling he had struck some obstruction in the narrow chimney of the water's course, some piece of driftwood or brush insecurely wedged across the hole. It had broken his descent and had saved him.

His matches would be useless. Feeling around the cave floor in the dark, he found some dry tinder that had been lying there for years. He still had his guns, since they had been tied in place with rawhide thongs. He drew one of them, extracted a cartridge, and went to work on it with his hunting knife.

When it was open, he placed it carefully on the rock beside him. Then he cut shavings and crushed dried bark in his hand. Atop this he placed the powder from the open cartridge.

Then he went to work to strike a spark from a rock with the steel back of his knife. There was not the slightest wind here. Despite that, he worked for the better part of an hour before a spark sprang into the powder.

There was a bright burst of flame and the shavings crackled. He added fuel and then straightened up and stepped back to look around.

He stood on a wide ledge in the gloomy, closed cavern at the foot of the fall's first drop, down which he had fallen. The water struck the rock not ten feet away from him. Then it took another steep drop off to the left. He could see by the driftwood that had fallen clear that it was the usual thing for the rushing water to cast all water-borne objects onto this ledge.

The ledge had at one time been deeply gouged and worn by running water. Picking up a torch, Marcy turned and glanced away into the darkness. There lay the old dry channel, deeply worn and polished by former running water.

At some time in the past, this had been the route of the stream underground. In an earthquake or some breakthrough of the rock, the water had taken the new course.

Thoughtfully, Marcy calculated his situation.

HE WAS FEARFUL of his predicament. From the first moment of consciousness in that utter darkness, he had been so. There is no fear more universal than the fear of entombment alive, the fear of choking, strangling in utter darkness beyond the reach of help.

Mac Marcy was no fool. He was, he knew, beyond the reach of help. The moro was ground-hitched in a spot where there was plenty of grass and water. The grayish-black horse would stay right there.

No one, with the exception of Sally, ever went to the top of the rim. It was highly improbable that she would go again soon. In many cases, weeks would go by without anyone stopping by Marcy's lonely cabin. If he was going to get out of this hole, he would have to do it by his own efforts.

One glance up that fall showed him there was no chance of going back up the way he had come down. Working his way over to the next step downward of the fall, he held out his torch and peered below. All was utter blackness, with only the cold damp of falling water in the air.

Fear was mounting within him now, but he fought it back, forcing himself to be calm and to think carefully. The old dry channel remained a vague hope. But to all appearances it went deeper and deeper into the stygian blackness of the earth. He put more fuel on his fire and started exploring again. Fortunately, the wood he was burning was bone dry and made almost no smoke.

Torch in hand he started down the old dry channel. This had been a watercourse for many, many years. The rock was worn and polished. He had gone no more than sixty feet when the channel divided.

On the left was a black, forbidding hole, scarcely waist high. Down that route most of the water seemed to have gone, as it was worn the deepest.

On the right was an opening almost like a doorway. Marcy stepped over to it and held his torch out. It also was a black hole. He had a sensation of awful depth. Stepping back, he picked up a rock. Leaning out, he dropped it into the hole on the right.

For a long time he listened. Then, somewhere far below, there was a splash. This hole was literally hundreds of feet deep. It would end far below the level of the land on which his cabin stood.

He drew back. Sweat stood out on his forehead, and when he put his hand to it, his brow felt cold and clammy. He looked at the black waist-high hole on the left and felt fear rise within him as he had never felt it before. He drew back and wet his lips.

His torch was almost burned out. Turning with the last of its light, he retraced his steps to the ledge by the fall.

How long he had been belowground, he didn't know. He looked up, and there was still a feeble light from above. But it seemed to have grown less. Had night almost come?

Slowly he built a new torch. This was his last chance of escape. It was a chance he had already begun to give up. Of them all, that black hole on the left was least promising, but he must explore it.

He pulled his hat down a little tighter and started back to where the tunnel divided into two holes. His jaw was set grimly. He got down on his hands and knees and edged into the black hole on the left.

Once inside, he found it fell away steeply in a mass of loose boulders. Scrambling over them, he came to a straight, steep fall of at least ten feet. Glancing at the sheer drop, he knew one thing—once down there, he would never get back up!

Holding his torch high, he looked beyond. Nothing but darkness. Behind him there was no hope. He hesitated and then got down on his hands and knees, lowered himself over the edge, and dropped ten feet.

This time he had to be right, for there was no going back. He walked down a slanting tunnel. It seemed to be growing darker. Glancing up at his torch, he saw it was burning out. In a matter of minutes he would be in total darkness.

He walked faster and faster. Then he broke into a stumbling run, fear rising within him. Something brought him up short, and for a moment he did not see what had caused him to halt in his blind rush. Then hope broke over him like a cold shower of rain.

———

THERE ON THE sand beneath his feet were tiny tracks! He bent over them. A pack rat or some other tiny creature. Getting up, he hurried on, and seeing a faint glow ahead, he rushed around a bend. There before him was the feeble glow of the fading day. His torch guttered and went out.

He walked on to the cave mouth, trembling in every limb. Mac Marcy was standing in an old watercourse that came out from behind some boulders not two miles from his cabin.

He stumbled home and fell into his bunk, almost too tired to undress. . . .

Marcy awakened to a frantic pounding on his door. Staggering erect, he pulled on his boots, yelling out as he did so. Then he drew on his Levi's and shirt and opened the door, buttoning his shirt with one hand.

Sally, her face deathly pale, was standing outside. Beyond her gray mare stood Marcy's moro. At the sight of him the grayish-black horse lifted his head and pricked up his ears.

"Oh!" Sally gasped. "I thought you were dead—drowned!"

He stepped over beside her.

"No," he said, "I guess I'm still here. You're purty scared, ma'am. What's there for you to be scared about?"

"Why," she burst out impatiently, "if you—" She caught herself and stopped abruptly. "After all," she continued coolly, "no one wants to find a friend drowned."

"Ma'am," he said sincerely, "if you get that wrought up, I'll get myself almost drowned every day."

She stared at him and then smiled. "I think you're a fool," she said. She mounted and turned. "But a nice fool."

Marcy stared after her thoughtfully. Well now, maybe—

He glanced down at his boots. Where they had lain in the pool, there was water stain on them. Also, there was a small green leaf clinging to the rough leather. He stooped and picked it off, wadded it up, and started to throw it away when he was struck by an idea. He unfolded the leaf and studied the veins. Suddenly his face broke into a grin.

"Boy," he said to the moro, "we got us a job to do, even if you do need a rest." He swung into the saddle and rode back toward the watercourse, still grinning.

It was midafternoon when he returned to the cabin and ate a leisurely lunch, still chuckling. Then he mounted again and started for the old water hole that had been fenced by Jingle Bob Kenyon.

When Marcy rounded the bend, he could see that something was wrong. A dozen men were gathered around the water hole. Nearby and astride her gray was Sally.

The men were in serious conference, and they did not notice Marcy's approach. He rode up, leaning on the horn of the saddle, and watched them, smiling.

Suddenly Vin Ricker looked up. His face went hard.

Mac Marcy swung down and strolled up to the fence, leaning casually on a post.

"What's up?"

"The water hole's gone dry!" Kenyon exploded. "Not a drop o' water in it."

Smothering a grin, Marcy rolled a smoke.

"Well," he said philosophically, "the Lord giveth an' He taketh away. No doubt it's the curse of the Lord for your greed, Jingle Bob."

Kenyon glared at him suspiciously. "Yuh know somethin' about this?" he demanded. "Man, in this hot weather my cattle will die by the hundreds. Somethin's got to be done."

"Seems to me," Marcy said dryly, "I have heard them words before."

Sally was looking at him over her father's head, her face grave and questioning. But she said nothing, gave no sign of approval or disapproval.

"This here's a man's country," Marcy said seriously. "Yuh fork your own broncs an' you get your own water."

Kenyon flushed. "Marcy, if you know anythin' about this, for goodness' sake spill it. My cows will die. Maybe I was too stiff about this, but there's somethin' mighty funny goin' on here. This water hole ain't failed in twenty years."

"Let me handle him," Riker snarled. "I'm just achin' to git my hands on him."

"Don't ache too hard, or you'll git your wish," Marcy drawled, and he crawled through the fence. "All right, Kenyon, we'll talk business," Marcy said to the rancher. "You had me stuck yesterday with my tail in a crack. Now you got yours in one. I cut off your water to teach you a lesson. You're a blamed old highbinder, an' it's high time you had some teeth pulled.

"Nobody but me knows how that water's cut off and where. If I don't change it, nobody can. So listen to what I'm sayin.' I'm goin' to have all the water I need after this on my own place, but this here hole stays open. No fences.

"This mornin' when I went up to cut your water off, I saw some cow tracks. I'm missin' a powerful lot of cows. I follered the tracks into a hidden draw an' found three hundred of my cattle an' about a hundred head of yours, all nicely corraled an' ready to be herded across the border.

"While I was lookin' over the hideout, I spied Ricker there. John Soley then come ridin' up with about thirty head of your cattle, an' they run 'em in with the rest."

"You're a liar!" Ricker burst out, his face tense, and he dropped into a crouch, his fingers spread.

Marcy was unmoved. "No, I ain't bluffing. You try to prove where you were about nine this mornin'. An' don't go tryin' to git me into a gunfight. I ain't a-goin' to draw, an' you don't dare shoot me down in front of witnesses. But you take off those guns, an' I'll—"

Ricker's face was ugly. "Yuh bet I'll take 'em off! I allus did want a crack at that purty face o' yours."

He stripped off his guns and swung them to Soley in one movement. Then he rushed.

A wicked right swing caught Marcy before he dropped his gun belt and got his hands up, and it knocked him reeling into the dirt.

Ricker charged, his face livid, trying to kick Marcy with his boots, but Marcy rolled over and got on his feet. He lunged and swung a right that clipped Ricker on the temple. Then Marcy stabbed the rustler with a long left. They started to slug.

Neither had any knowledge of science. Both were raw and

tough and hard-bitten. Toe to toe, bloody and bitter, they slugged it out. Ricker, confident and the larger of the two men, rushed in swinging. One of his swings cut Marcy's eye; another started blood gushing from Marcy's nose. Ricker set himself and threw a hard right for Marcy's chin, but the punch missed as Marcy swung one to the body that staggered Ricker.

They came in again, and Marcy's big fist pulped the rustler's lips, smashing him back on his heels. Then Marcy followed it in, swinging with both hands. His breath came in great gasps, but his eyes were blazing. He charged in, following Ricker relentlessly.

Suddenly Marcy's right caught the gunman and knocked him to his knees. Marcy stepped back and let him get up and then knocked him sliding on his face in the sand. Ricker tried to get up, but he fell back, bloody and beaten.

Swiftly, before the slow-thinking Soley realized what was happening, Marcy spun and grabbed one of his own guns and turned it on this rustler.

"Drop 'em!" he snapped. "Unbuckle your belt an' step back!"

Jingle Bob Kenyon leaned on his saddle horn, chewing his pipestem thoughtfully.

"What," he drawled, "would yuh of done if he drawed his gun?"

Marcy looked up, surprised. "Why, I'd have killed him, of course." He glanced over at Sally, and then looked back at Kenyon. "Afore we git off the subject," he said, "we finish our deal. I'll turn your water back into this hole—I got it stopped up away back inside the mountain—but as I said, the hole stays open to anybody. Also"—Marcy's face colored a little—"I'm marryin' Sally."

"You're *what*?" Kenyon glared and then jerked around to look at his daughter.

Sally's eyes were bright. "You heard him, Father," she replied coolly. "I'm taking back with me those six steers he gave you so he could get them to water."

Marcy was looking at Kenyon when suddenly Marcy grinned.

"I reckon," he said, "you had your lesson. Sally an' me have got a lot of talkin' to do."

Marcy swung aboard the moro, and he and Sally started off together.

Jingle Bob Kenyon stared after them, grim humor in his eyes.

"I wonder," he said, "what he would have done if Ricker had drawed?"

Old Joe Linger grinned and looked over at Kenyon from under his bushy brows. "Jest what he said. He'd of kilt him. That's Quaker John McMarcy, the hombre that wiped out the Mullen gang single-handed. He jest don't like to fight, that's all."

"It sure does beat all," Kenyon said thoughtfully. "The trouble a man has to go to to git him a good son-in-law these days!"

PARDNER FROM THE RIO

T ANDY THAYER RODE up the river trail in the late afternoon, a tall young man with sand-colored hair, astride a gray horse. He drew rein before he reached the water hole, and looked carefully around as though searching for something missing from the terrain.

Tandy Thayer was slightly stooped as a man often becomes after long hours and years in the saddle, and his eyes had that steady, slow look of a man who knows his own mind and his own strength.

Turning in the saddle he studied the bare, burned red rock with a little frown gathering between his eyes. Here was where old man Drew's ranch should be, right on this spot. There was the water hole, and to the right, and not far distant, was the roar of the river. High upon the mountain to his left was that jagged streak of white rock pointing like an arrow to this place.

All the signs were right. The painstaking description had accounted for every foot of the trail until now. It had even accounted for every natural landmark here. Only there was no barn, no corral, no ranch house, and no Jim Drew. Nor was there any evidence that any of those things had existed upon this spot.

Tandy swung down from the saddle and trailed the bridle reins. The gray started purposefully but not too anxiously toward the water hole and sank his muzzle into the limpid pool. Thayer was thirsty himself, but his mind was occupied now with a puzzle. He shoved his hat back from his homely, weather-worn face with a quick, characteristic gesture and began to look around.

He heard the horse approaching before it arrived, so he

faced about, turning himself squarely toward the trail up which he had just ridden. Another rider. From where?

———

THE MAN WAS burly, a big man astride a powerful sorrel with a blazed face and three white stockings. His face was flat and swarthy, his eyes blue steel. He rode lopsided in the saddle with a careless cockiness that showed itself as well in the slant of his narrow-brimmed, flat-crowned hat.

"Howdy," he said, and inspected Tandy with a wary, casual interest. "Ridin' through?"

"I reckon. Huntin' an hombre name of Jim Drew. Know him?"

"Guess not. Was he comin' through here?"

"He lived here. Right on this spot if I figure right."

"Here?" The rider's voice was incredulous, but then he chuckled with a dry sound and his eyes glinted with what might have been malice. "Nobody ever lived here. You can see for yourself. Anyways, this here is Block T range, and they are mighty touchy folks. Me, I'd not ride it myself, only they know me." He dug into his shirt pocket for the makings. "How'd you happen to pick this spot?"

"Drew gave me directions, and mighty near drew me a map. He mentioned the river, the water hole, that streak on the mountain, and a few other things."

"Yeah?" The rider touched his tongue to the edge of the paper. "Must have slipped up somewheres along the trail. Nobody ever lived here in my time, and I've been around here more'n ten years. Closest house is the Block T, and that's six miles north of here. I live back down the country, myself." He struck a match and lighted his cigarette. "I'll be riding on. Gettin' hungry."

"You ride for the Block T?"

"No, I'm Kleinback. I own the K Bar. If you're over that-away drop by and set awhile. I'm headed to see Bill Hofer, the hombre who ramrods the Block T."

Tandy Thayer was a stubborn man, and it had been a long ride from Texas. Moreover, he had known Jim Drew long enough to know that Drew would never give wrong directions or invite him on a wild-goose chase.

"That trail was plain as if he'd blazed it," he muttered. "I'll just have a look around."

He had his look around, for his pains, and over his fire as dusk gathered, he considered the problem. His eyes had already told him there was nothing to see. The cabin, corrals, and stable so painstakingly described were nowhere to be seen, nor was there any stock.

Hesitant as he was to pull out without finding Drew, he felt that his best bet would be to try to land a job as a rider for the Block T. He couldn't live on desert grass.

Thayer organized the shadow of a meal from what he carried in his saddlebags, then lighted a cigarette and leaned back against a boulder to study things out. Jim Drew was weatherbeaten and cantankerous, but he was also sure-moving and painstaking. Despite Kleinback's statement, Tandy was sure Drew must be around somewhere.

Picking up another piece of mesquite, he tossed it on the fire. In the morning he would take a last look around. If this was the place Drew had meant, there would be some sign, surely.

Tandy had put out his hand for a stick and started to toss it, when he caught the motion in midair. Along the underside of that stick, his fingers had found a row of notches. Holding the mesquite close to the fire, he studied it.

Two notches, and then a space followed by another notch. As he stared at those notches, with the cuts still unweathered, his mind skipped back to a camp alongside the Rio Grande below San Marcial where he once had sat across a campfire and watched Jim Drew cutting just such notches as he talked. It had been a habit of the old rancher's, just as some men whittle and others doodle with pen or pencil.

So, then. He was not wrong, and Jim Drew *had* been here. But if he had been here, where was he now? And where were the ranch buildings? Why had Kleinback not known about him? Or had he known?

Tandy got swiftly to his feet, recalling something he had observed as he had ridden up, but which had made no impression at the time. It was the position of three clumps of mesquite. He strode to the nearest one and, grasping a branch, gave it a jerk. It came loose so suddenly he all but fell.

Bending over, he felt with his hand for the place from which the roots had come. There was loose dirt, but when he brushed it aside, his fingers found the round outline of a posthole!

———

GRIMLY HE GOT to his feet and replaced the mesquite, tamping the dirt around it. There was something wrong here, mighty wrong. He picked up a few loose sticks and walked slowly back to the fire.

He was feeding the sticks into the blaze when he heard another horse.

Busy little place, he mentally commented, straightening up.

He stepped back from the fire, then heard a hoof strike stone, and saddle leather creak as of someone dismounting.

"Come on up to the fire," he said. "We're all friends here."

A spur jingled, feet crunched on gravel, and then he was looking across the fire into the eyes of a girl, a tall girl with a slim, willowy body.

She wore blue jeans and a man's battered hat. Her shirt, with a buckskin vest worn over it, was gray. She wore a gun, Tandy observed.

"By jiminy!" he exclaimed. "A woman! Sure never figured to see a woman in these hills, ma'am. Will you join me in some coffee?"

Her eyes showed no friendliness. "Who are you?" she demanded. "What do you want here?"

"Me?" Tandy shrugged. "Just a driftin' cowhand, ma'am. This water hole figgered to be a good camp for the night."

"Here?" Her voice was dry, skeptical. "When it is only six miles to the Block T?"

"Well, now. I'd started my camp before I knowed that, ma'am. Hombre name of Kleinback told me about the Block T."

Tandy was watching her when he said the name, Klein-back, and he saw her face stiffen a little.

"Oh?" she said. "So you've seen Roy? Are you working for him?"

"Huntin' work, ma'am. I'm a top hand. You know the Block T? Mebbe they could use me?"

"I'm Clarabel Jornal," she told him. "My uncle ramrods the Block T. He won't need you."

"Mebbe I'd better talk to him," Tandy said, smiling.

Her eyes blazed, and she took a step nearer the fire.

"Listen, rider!" she said sharply. "You'd best keep right on drifting! There's nothing in this country for anybody as nosy as you! Get going! If you don't, I'll send Pipal down to see you in the morning!"

"Who's he? The local watchdog? Sorry, ma'am, but I don't scare easy, so maybe you'd better send him. I ain't a right tough hombre, but I get along. As for being nosy, if you think I'm nosy you must be right sort of nosy yourself, comin' down here advising me to move on. I like it here, ma'am. In fact"—he paused to give emphasis to his words—"I may set up a ranch right here."

"Here?" Consternation struggled with anger in her voice. "Why here, of all places? Anyway, this is Block T range."

"Not filed on by Block T. Just claimed." Thayer grinned. "Ma'am, you might's well have some coffee."

"No!" she flared. "You be out of here by daylight or I'll send Pipal after you! He's killed four men!"

Tandy Thayer smiled, but his lips were thin and his eyes cold.

"Has he now? Suppose you just keep him at home in the mornin', ma'am. I'll come right up to the Block T, and if he's in a sweat to make it five, he can have his chance!"

When the girl swung into the saddle, her face angry, Thayer leaned back against the boulder once more. She was from the Block T, and the Block T claimed this range. Perhaps they had objected to Jim Drew's ranching here. And Pipal, whoever he was, might have done the objecting with lead. . . .

By daylight the setup looked no different than it had the

previous night except that now Tandy Thayer studied the terrain with a new eye. Some changes, indicated by the mesquite bush planted in the posthole, had been made. With that in mind, he found the location of more postholes, found where the house had been and the barn.

Whoever had removed the traces of Drew and his ranch had removed them with extraordinary care. Evidently they had expected someone to come looking and had believed they could fool whoever it would be. Only they had not known of the painstaking care with which old Jim gave directions, nor his habit of doodling with a knife.

Saddling up, Tandy Thayer headed up the trail between the river and the mountains for the Block T.

The place was nothing to look at: a long L-shaped adobe house shaded by giant cottonwoods, three pole corrals, a combination stable and blacksmith shop, the corner of the shop shielded from the sun by still another huge cottonwood, and a long bunkhouse.

Two horses were standing near the corral when Tandy rode into the ranch yard, and a short, square man with a dark face and a thin mustache came to the bunkhouse door and shaded his eyes to look at him.

——

At ALMOST THE same moment, a tall man in a faded checked shirt and vest came from the house. Thayer reined in before him.

"Howdy!" he said. "You Bill Hofer?"

"That's right." The man had keen, slightly worried blue eyes with a guarded look in their depths. He wore a six-gun tied too high to be of much use.

"Hunting a riding job," Tandy said. "Top hand, horse wrangler."

Hofer hesitated. "I can use you, all right," he said then. "We're shorthanded here. Throw your gear in the bunkhouse and get some grub."

The man with the thin mustache was nowhere in sight when Tandy shoved through the bunkhouse door and dropped his saddlebags on the first empty bunk he saw. He glanced around, and a frown gathered between his eyes. The bunk-house had been built to accommodate at least twenty men, but only five bunks gave signs of occupancy.

As he was looking around, a redheaded hand came in, glancing at him.

"New, eh?" the redhead said. "Better throw your duffle back on your horse and ramble, pardner. This ain't a healthy place, noway."

Tandy turned, and his eyes swept the redhead. "That warning friendly, or not? Too many folks seem aimin' for me to move on."

Red shrugged. "Plumb friendly." He waved a hand at the empty bunks. "That look good? You ain't no pilgrim. What about a spread that ordinarily uses twenty hands, and could use thirty, but only has four workin' hands and a cook? Does that look good?"

"What's the trouble?" asked Tandy.

"Maybe one thing, and maybe another. The trouble is, the boss hires 'em and Pipal fires 'em."

"Who's Pipal?"

A foot grated in the doorway and Red turned, his face turning a shade lighter under the freckles. The man with the thin mustache above cruel lips, and black eyes that bored into Thayer, stood there. He wore two guns, tied low, and was plainly a half-breed.

Warning signals sounded in Tandy's brain. Four men killed. Had one of them been Jim Drew? The thought stirred something deep within him, something primeval and ugly, something he had forgotten was there. He met the black eyes with his own steady, unblinking gaze.

"I am Pipal," the swarthy man said, his voice flat and level. "We do not need another hand. You will mount and ride."

Thayer smiled suddenly. This was trouble, and he wasn't backing away from it. He was no gunslinger, but he had put in more than a few years fighting Comanches and rustlers.

"The boss hired me," he said coldly. "The boss can fire me."

"I said—*go!*" Pipal cracked the word like a man cracks a

bullwhip, and as he spoke, he stepped nearer, his hand dropping to his gun.

Tandy's left fist was at his belt where the thumb had been hooked a moment before. He drove it into the pit of Pipal's stomach with a snapping jolt, shooting it right from where it was. Pipal's wind left him with a grunt, and he doubled up in agony. Thayer promptly jerked his knee up into Pipal's face, knocking the man's head back. With Pipal's chin wide open and blood streaming from a smashed nose, Tandy set himself and swung left and right from his hip. Pipal went down in a heap.

Coolly, Tandy stepped over to him, jerked his guns from their holsters and shucked the shells into the palm of his hand. He dropped them into his pocket.

Pipal lay on the floor, blood dripping from his nose and his breath coming in racking gasps.

"You better hightail," Red suggested. "He's a ringtailed terror with them guns."

Thayer grinned at Red and drew a smiling response. "I like it here," he said. "I'm stayin'!"

Pipal started to get up, and Thayer looked around at him.

"You get out!" he said harshly. "I don't know who you're runnin' errands for, but I mean to find out."

The half-breed's eyes glared at him, hatred a burning light in their black depths.

"I kill you!" he said.

Tandy seized the man by the collar and, jerking him erect, hit him two fast punches in the wind, then slapped him across the face. With a shove, he drove the gunman through the door, where he tripped and sprawled on his face.

"Look!" Tandy yelled.

He whipped a playing card from his pocket and spun it high into the air. In almost the same motion, he drew and fired. The card fluttered to the earth, and he calmly walked over to it and picked it up, thrusting it before Pipal's eyes and the startled eyes of Red and Hofer, who had come from the house. It was an ace of spades—with the ace shot neatly through the center!

PIPAL GULPED AND slowly climbed to his feet. His nose still bled, and he backed away, wiping it with the back of his hand, an awed expression on his face. Calmly Tandy thrust the playing card into his shirt pocket and fed another shell into his six-gun.

"I don't like trouble," he remarked, "but I can handle it. . . ."

Three days passed quietly. There was plenty to do on the Block T, and Tandy Thayer had little time for looking around on his own, but he was learning things. The Block T was overrun with unbranded stock, and no effort was being made to brand any of it. Much of this stock was ranging far to the south around the Opal Mountains, where there was rich grass in the draws and plenty of water for that type of range.

Red Ringo was a mine of information. Red had been a rider for the Block T when he was sixteen, and had ridden for it four years. He then had drifted to Wyoming, Kansas, and Indian Territory, but finally headed back home. Three months before he had hired on at the Block T again, finding it vastly changed.

"Funny how a spread can go to pot in a short while," he commented to Tandy Thayer. "Even Bill Hofer's changed. He's thinner, cranky like he never used to be, and he packs a gun, something he never did in the old days. All the old hands are gone, and the last two was drove off by this Pipal. Why don't Hofer fire him?"

"Maybe he's afraid of him, too," Tandy suggested.

"Could be," Red agreed dubiously. "But he never used to be afraid of anything."

"When did all this trouble start?" asked Tandy.

"Well," Ringo said thoughtfully, "near as I know from what the old hands told me before they left, it started about the time the owner came out from Chicago. He came out and stayed on the ranch for a couple of weeks and then left, but whatever happened then, Hofer's never been the same since." Ringo leaned on the shovel with which he had been cleaning a water hole. "Another thing, Bill Hofer never had no use for

Roy Kleinback before, but he sees a lot of him now. So does Miss Clarabel."

"What about Kleinback? He owns the K Bar, don't he?"

"Sure does. Rawhider, or was. Lately he's been doing better. Pretty slick with a gun, and a hand with his fists, too. He has three or four hands down there with him, but they don't amount to much aside from bein' crooked enough to do anything they are told if there's money in it."

Tandy Thayer hesitated and then with his eyes on Red Ringo, asked casually, "Ever hear of an old-timer around here named Jim Drew?"

"Drew? Can't say as I have. You mean an old man, or old in the country?"

"An old man. Cantankerous old cuss. Makes the best coffee in the world and the best biscuits. He was a friend of mine, a mighty good friend, and he's how come I'm here at all."

Briefly, Thayer explained about the letters that brought him here, and about finding the ranch site. Ringo listened with attention, and when Tandy stopped talking, he bit off a healthy chew.

"Listen," he said. "I come back here about three months ago. That was a month or maybe less after the big boss was here. I hired on, but the very day I started work, Hofer told me I was to work away from the river, and on no account to go near Moss Springs. He said there'd been some trouble over it and 'til it was straightened out, we'd stay away. Moss Springs is the water hole you mentioned. . . ."

Back at the ranch, Tandy sat under a huge cottonwood near the blacksmith shop and studied the situation through the smoke of a half dozen cigarettes. No way could it make sense, so there must be something he didn't know.

Where was Jim Drew? What had caused the change in Bill Hofer and the Block T? Why was Pipal kept on? Did Hofer's new friendship for Kleinback have anything to do with all this?

In the three days Tandy had been on the ranch he had spent most of his time at work, and at no time had he seen Clarabel. Nor had he seen Kleinback. Pipal was around, but he remained strictly away from Tandy and never met his eyes if he could avoid it.

Obviously, the Drew ranch had been cleaned out because somebody did not want Tandy Thayer, the expected visitor, to find it. And they must have done away with Jim Drew at the same time. But why? What did they have to conceal?

Studied from every angle, the trouble seemed to have started with the leaving of the big boss, the owner—J. T. Martin. It was after that when Pipal came to the Block T, and after he came that the old hands started to drift away. It would almost appear that someone wanted the old hands driven off.

———

IF THERE HAD been such an attempt, and if Drew had been killed or run off in connection with it, then there had to be profit somewhere for the instigators of the plot. What was profitable in this ranch? Cattle? And the range now covered with thousands of unbranded cattle, ready for the taking?

"So? It's you?"

At the sound of the girl's voice, Tandy glanced up and then got slowly to his feet.

"I reckon it is, ma'am. Like a bad penny, always turnin' up."

She stepped near him in the dappling shadows of moonlight through the leaves.

"Go away—please! You don't know what you're doing here! Tonight Kleinback is coming, and if he finds you, there will be trouble!"

"Sorry, ma'am," Tandy said easily. "I'm stayin' 'til I'm ordered off. I've got work to do. Mebbe Kleinback is the man I'd better talk to."

"No!" There was sheer panic in Clarabel Jornal's voice. "You mustn't! Please go! I don't know what happened to your friend. I have no idea! I think he just pulled out and left!"

"You admit he was here, then?" Thayer shrugged. "Ma'am, Jim Drew sent for me to come, so he never pulled out. He wouldn't be driven, either! Ma'am, old Jim was killed, and I aim to find out who did it!"

She was silent for a minute, her hand still on his arm.

"Please!" she pleaded then. "You like me, I know you do! I've seen it in your eyes tonight, and I saw it the other day. If you'll go away, I'll go with you."

He shook his head. "That's a tempting offer, ma'am, but I can't do it. I sure do like you. You're pretty much of a woman, and a man could be proud of you, but I wouldn't take you that way. I wouldn't take any woman unless she loved me— and I reckon it would be pretty hard to love a man like me. I ain't no hand with womenfolks, and I sure ain't much for looks."

In the silence they heard the sound of a horse cantering up to the house. Clarabel looked up at Tandy.

"It's Roy Kleinback!" she said, and there was stark fear in her eyes.

Tandy caught her by the shoulders. "What's behind all this!" he demanded. "What's Kleinback to you? Who is he?"

"He's nothing to me! I—"

"Hofer," Kleinback's harsh voice interrupted. "Who's that hombre out there with Clarabel?"

The two men were walking toward the cottonwood. Clarabel stepped back, and her eyes looked like dark, haunted pools in the whiteness of her face. Kleinback walked up to her and Tandy, glancing from one to the other.

"Hofer," he said as his eyes fastened on Thayer, "you'd better fire this man. He's got some bad ideas. Thinks there used to be an hombre name of Jim Drew down at Moss Springs."

Thayer glimpsed a vague movement in the shadows and knew it was Pipal. He was boxed. If he started a fight now, he was finished.

"All right with me, if Hofer fires me," he drawled. "What about it, boss?"

"Maybe you'd better go," Hofer said. "Here's twenty dollars. That's more'n you got comin', but you've done a sight of work."

Kleinback was smiling. "Now, slope!" he said. "And once you start movin', keep goin'!"

Tandy Thayer offered no reply. He walked to the bunkhouse, threw his gear together, and saddled his horse. It was when he was saddling the horse that he brushed against Kleinback's mount near him, and against the coat that hung over the saddle horn. Something rustled in the pocket. On a hunch he turned and felt for the paper. It was an envelope. . . . No, there were three envelopes.

Shielding the match with his coat, he struck a light, and his heart gave a bound. All three were addressed to J. T. Martin at Nelson! Stuffing the letters back into the pocket he swung into the saddle and headed the gray toward the river.

The letters had been from Chicago, so in Chicago they believed Martin was here. And if Martin was neither here nor in Chicago, where was he?

Turning right near the river, Tandy Thayer headed south for Moss Springs. He did not ride fast, for he was in no hurry. The night stretched before him and he had only a few miles to go. In the meanwhile there was much to consider.

Martin had come to the Block T ranch and had probably received a report on the number of cattle there, but if he had known about all the unbranded cattle, obviously he would have been displeased. Suddenly, Tandy began to see more clearly, and the pieces of the plot began to fall into place.

Reaching Moss Springs he dismounted and made camp. Yet he was scarcely asleep before he heard the pounding of hoofs. Rolling out of his soogan he grabbed his Winchester and took shelter behind some rocks.

———

THE RACING HORSE came to a sliding stop, and he heard a girl gasping for breath.

"Tandy," she called softly. "Tandy Thayer! Where are you!"

"Here," he answered. "What's the trouble?"

She ran to him. "Oh, be careful! They've sent that man after you—Pipal!"

"They sent him? Who did?"

"Kleinback did. I heard him talking to Pipal. He told him to kill you, that you must never get to Nelson!"

"So?" Thayer went all quiet and still within, his mind examining the situation coolly. "Then he's guessed that I know what this is all about, or he is afraid I know." He looked around toward the dim outline of the girl's face. "Bel, what happened to Martin?"

Her breath caught. "I—I don't know."

"Bel, there's something plumb wrong going on here, and I think I know exactly what it is. Martin never went back to Chicago, Bel. Mail is still being addressed to him at Nelson, in care of the Block T. I found some letters to him in the pocket of Kleinback's coat. I think Martin was killed because of what he found at the ranch, or because somebody at the ranch was afraid of what he might do or know."

Clarabel was silent and he put his hand on her arm.

"Bel, did your uncle kill Martin?"

She jerked her arm away. "No!" she flared, and he could hear the anguish and tears in her voice. "No, he didn't! He couldn't have! He's always been good. Kind! He simply couldn't have!"

There was an answer here somewhere. All Tandy could see now was the vague, underlying plot, or what he believed was the plot. It would explain everything, and there was no other way that he could see for it to have been.

"Bel," he persisted, "what's Bill Hofer's tie-up with Kleinback?"

"I don't know." He could sense the honest doubt in her voice. "Uncle Bill used to dislike him very much, and I think he still does, but now Kleinback's around the ranch a lot and gives orders as much as my uncle does."

"Did it begin about the time that Martin left?"

She hesitated. "Yes, about then."

"Bel," Tandy suggested cautiously, "you think your uncle killed Martin, don't you?"

"I don't know, I tell you! But he couldn't have!"

"Bel, if your uncle killed Martin he's as guilty as any man, and deserves punishment if any man does. Now, we've got to get at the truth of this, and I don't think your uncle did kill him."

Tandy hesitated, listening for sounds in the night. If Pipal was coming, there was little time.

"Was Kleinback at the ranch the night Martin left?" he asked after a moment.

"No. He was there in the afternoon. He and Uncle Bill had a fearful argument about something; then he left. I heard Martin and Uncle Bill talking for a long time after supper. Martin brought some liquor out, and they both had a few drinks."

That could be it. Had Hofer been drunk? He asked the question. "I—I don't know," Clarabel said, and Tandy could sense that this was what was responsible for the girl's worry. "I don't think he was. He rode down the trail with Martin to get him started right, and I don't know when he got back. He didn't get up until almost noon, I know, and he looked a sight. I think he slept in his clothes."

Tandy gripped her arm in a signal for silence, for he had heard a faint sound in the darkness, a faint dragging, as of a heavy body along the mountainside. Drawing the girl back into the deep shadows of some mesquite, he listened. After a minute, both of them heard it again, a dragging sound, and what seemed like a grunt or a gasping breath.

Thayer stepped out into the moonlight, his brow furrowed. It was strange.

"So? We come together again, my friend!" Pipal's voice. "Make one move for your gun, and you die!" The renegade stepped forward into the moonlight. "Also the señorita will come from the darkness, or I shall have to shoot both of you!"

Clarabel, her face pale, stepped into sight and stood beside him. Pipal circled behind them and stripped them of their guns.

"Now," he said, moving away from them, "you will turn and walk toward the river. Bodies are so heavy to carry!"

"You're a fool, Pipal!" Thayer said.

His mouth felt dry, and he was weak in the knees. The half-breed was going to shoot, and any chance he took was a chance for the girl, too. If only she wasn't so close! Still, if he could get a hand on one of those guns, there might be a chance.

"Do you think Kleinback will let you go now, Pipal?" he

taunted. "You'll be the only one who knows. You're doing his killing for him, and what will you get out of it?"

Pipal shrugged. "Plenty. Leave that to me, señor. I shall not forget Pipal. I never forget Pipal!"

————

IN THE SILENCE, there was another sound, that faint dragging again. Pipal heard it also, and he started. He seemed to crouch a little, listening. His eyes dropped to the guns at Thayer's feet; then as the sound came again, he jerked his head around and Tandy's right hand dropped a little.

"Don't try it, son!" a voice roared out of the darkness. "I got him! Shoot me, will you? You dry-gulching—" The voice was drowned in the roar of a heavy rifle as Pipal swung his gun toward the darkness.

Pipal jerked sharply, then took two steps forward and fell on his face.

"Jim!" Tandy Thayer could not believe it. "Is that you out there?"

"Who did you reckon it was? Sandy Claws?" The old man's voice was testy. "Come out here and fetch me in. I can't walk!"

In a few running steps, Tandy had reached the old man. His eyes sharpened as he picked him up and carried him back into the moonlight.

"Build a fire!" he told Clarabel. "He's been hurt!"

"Hurt, your Aunt Mariar!" The old man was exasperated. "I'm nigh starved, that's all! I was hurt, all right. Shot by that durned breed. He got me twice, once in the shoulder and the other time in the leg. I fell in the river, yonder, but caught me some brush and hauled myself out of the water. Takes more'n a couple of slugs to kill an old sidewinder like me! I crawled back up yonder in an old prospect hole with what grub I could get out of the house before they got back.

"Boy, they tore that ranch of our'n right down! Every pole and log of her. Then they dropped 'em in the river and cleared up the ground so's nobody but somebody like you would ever guess what happened. Me, I laid up there in that hole, trying to get my leg mended, me with nothin' but a mite of grub and my old Sharps. I caught me a rabbit or two and et them down to the hair, then tonight I heard your voice a-talking to this here girl. I been a-draggin' down that mountain ever since."

"Why did Pipal shoot you?" Tandy demanded.

"Why? Because I seen Kleinback and Hofer coming down the trail with that city feller. Hofer, he was riding with him, drunk as a hoot owl, but Kleinback was a-ridin' back behind 'em a ways, following 'em, like."

Old Jim Drew told them quietly what had occurred, told them all he had seen, and Tandy nodded.

"I'd guessed most of it," he said, and swung into the saddle. "Jim, we're goin' to leave you here. We'll go back to the ranch and get a buckboard. Kleinback is still there, and I want to talk with him!"

The ranch was bathed in white moonlight when they rode up and swung down at the door. They halted at the sound of voices.

"Now is the time we'll sell, Hofer!" Kleinback was saying. "I'll start roundin' up tomorrow, and I'll get shut of them cows right away."

"I'll have no part of it!" Hofer said. "You got me into this, but I'll not get in any deeper."

"I got you into it?" Kleinback sneered. "Who killed young Martin? You did! What was your reason? Tryin' to rustle his cattle! There's a bad case against you, Hofer, but there's not a thing against me. I've got a clear trail behind me, and when I get the money for the cattle, I'll be free! I'll have plenty of money then, and not be tied to no two-by-four desert ranch!"

"You and Pipal," Hofer said, "between you, you ruined me. Between you two you ran my hands out of the country, and then after Martin was killed, you forced me to take Pipal on as a hand, so's he could spy on me and finish drivin' off the rest of 'em."

Roy Kleinback chuckled. "Sure. I've been running Block T stock back in the canyons of the Opals for the last couple of years. Holding 'em back there with no brands on 'em, so no evidence against me if somebody smartened up. Then when Martin came in and checked them draws and raised hob with you, I saw my only chance was to act fast. Then you up and killed him and saved my bacon."

"No, he didn't, Kleinback!"

The two men sprang to their feet, Bill Hofer startled and staring, Kleinback with a sudden wariness in his eyes.

Keeping his eyes on Kleinback, Tandy Thayer went on coolly: "Hofer, you never killed Martin! You were drunk and didn't know any better, but old Jim Drew saw it! Kleinback killed Martin, then shoved the gun in your hand. He'd killed him with one of your guns that he lifted as he came alongside, and you too drunk to know better!"

———

KLEINBACK HOOKED HIS thumbs in his belt.

"That's a foolish notion!" he said. "You couldn't prove no such thing!"

"Jim Drew is alive, Kleinback," Tandy said. "He saw it all, as you know. Pipal shot him and dropped him in the river, but he caught some brush and got ashore. He's alive and able to testify to all he saw. You're through!"

Kleinback's elbow jerked back and his palm slapped the walnut gun stock, but even as the gun started to lift, Tandy Thayer shot him.

The big rancher sagged back, struggling to get his gun up while his eyes slowly glazed over and the gun fell from his fingers to the floor. Then Kleinback fell across it. For an instant there was utter stillness while the wheel on one of Kleinback's spurs did a slow turn.

"It wasn't me!" Hofer gasped. "Man, I—"

Clarabel was around the table and had him in her arms.

"It's all right, Uncle Bill! Everything is all right." She looked over at Tandy, and there was a smile for him in her eyes. "You were going to stay with old Jim?" she asked. "Why don't you? It would be nice to have you for a neighbor. . . ."

In the morning, Red Ringo grinned at Tandy. "He should have knowed better than to draw against an hombre slick with a gun as you," he said. "That was plumb suicide!"

"Luck," Thayer said honestly. "Pure luck!"

"Huh!" Ringo was disgusted. "After that card I saw you shoot a hole into?"

Thayer reached in his pocket and took out another card.

"Look!" he said. Spinning it into the air, he drew and fired. "Now take a look at it."

Ringo walked over and picked up the card. It was a trey, and all the pips were shot out. He stared at it.

"But you only shot once!" he protested.

"Sure." Tandy Thayer reached in his pocket and pulled out a deck of cards with all the pips shot out. "I shoot 'em out first, then always have one around. You ain't got any idea how many arguments they stop!"

THE GUNS TALK LOUD

H E RODE INTO town on a brown mule and swung down from the saddle in front of the Chuck Wagon. He wore a high Mexican hat and a pair of tight Mex pants that flared over his boots. Shorty Duval started to open his mouth to hurrah this stranger when the hombre turned around.

Shorty Duval's mouth snapped shut like a steel trap, and you could almost see the sweat break out on his forehead.

One look was all anybody needed. Shorty was tough, but nobody was buying any trouble from the drifter in the high-crowned hat.

He had a lean brown face and a beak of a nose that had been broken sometime or other. There was a scar along his cheekbone that showed white against the leather brown of his face. But it was his eyes that gave you the chills. They were green and brown, but there was something in the way they looked at you that would make a strong man back up and think it over.

He was wearing two guns and crossed belts. They were not Peacemakers, but the older Colt, the baby cannon known as the Walker Colt. Too heavy for most men, they would shoot pretty accurate for well over a hundred yards, which wasn't bad for a rifle.

He wore one of them short Mex jackets, too, and when we looked from his queer getup to that brown mule that was all legs we couldn't figure him one little bit.

Not many strangers rode into White Hills. I'd been there all of two months, and I was the last one to come. This hombre showed he knowed the kind of a town he was in when he didn't look too long at anybody. In fact, he didn't even seem to notice us. He just pushed through the doors and bellied up to the bar.

Bill Riding was in there, and some four or five others. Being a right curious hombre, I walked in myself. If this gent did any talkin', I aimed to be where I could listen. I saw Riding look around when I come in. His eyes got mean. From the first day I hit town, we'd no use for each other.

Partly it was because of Jackie Belton's cur dog. Belton was a kid of fourteen who lived with his sister, Ruth, on a nice cattle spread six or seven miles out of White Hills. That dog ran across in front of Riding one day and come durned near trippin' him. He was a hot-tempered hombre, and when he drawed iron, I did, too.

Before he could shoot, I said, and I was standin' behind him, "You kill that dog, Riding, and I'll kill you!"

His face got red, and then white. His back was half toward me, and he knowed he didn't have a chance. "Someday," he said, his voice ugly, "you'll butt in at the wrong time!"

Jackie saw me, and so did his sister, and after the way they thanked me, I figgered it would have been cheap even if I'd had to kill Riding.

White Hills was an outlaw town. Most of the men in town were wanted somewheres, and while it wasn't doin' any deputy much good to come in here, the town was restless now. That was because the bank over to Pierce had been stuck up and ever'body in White Hills figgered the rangers would come here lookin' for him. That was why they'd looked so suspicious when I rode into town.

It didn't take no fortune-teller to guess that Harvey Kinsella had put Bill Riding to watchin' me. Kinsella was the boss o' that town, and he knowed everythin' that went on around.

Riding wasn't the only one had an eye on me, I knowed that. Kinsella had posted two or three other hombres for the same reason. Still, I stuck around. And part of the reason I stayed was Ruthie Belton.

The hombre with the high-crowned sombrero leaned against the bar and let those slow green eyes of his take in the place. They settled on Riding, swung past Shorty Duval, and finally settled on me.

They stayed there the longest, and I wasn't surprised none. We were the two biggest men in the place, me and him. Maybe I was a mite the bigger, but that hat made him look just as tall. His eyes didn't show what he was thinkin', but knowin' how a man on the dodge feels, I knowed what it was.

He had me sized up like I had him. Me, I growed up under the Tonto Rim, and when I wanted to ride the cattle trails, I had to ride east to git to 'em. I'd punched cows and dealt monte in Sonora, and I ain't braggin' none when I say that when I rode through New Mexico and hung around Lincoln and Fort Sumner and Sante Fe, not Billy the Kid nor Jesse Evans wanted any part of what I had to give. Not that I wanted them, either.

There wasn't no high Mex hat on me. Mine was flat-crowned and flat-brimmed, but my guns was tied down, and had been for more than a little while. My boots was some down at the heel, and I needed a shave, but no man in that place had the power in his shoulders I had, and no man there but me could bust a leather belt with his chest expansion.

He didn't need no second sight to tell him I was ridin' a lone trail, either. They never cut my hide to fit no Kinsella frame. Anyway, he looked at me, and then he says, "I'll buy you a drink!" An' the way he laid that "you" in there was like layin' a whip across the face of ever' other man in the saloon.

Bill Riding jerked like he'd been bee-stung, but Kinsella wasn't there, and Bill sat tight.

Me, I walks over to the bar and bellies up to it. Amigo, it done me good to look in that long mirror and see the two of us standin' there. Y' can ride for miles and never find two such big men together. Maybe I was a mite thicker'n him through the chest, but he was big, amigo, and he was mean.

"They call me Sonora," he said, lookin' at the rye in his glass.

"Me, I'm Dan Ketrel," I said, but I was thinkin' of what the descriptions of the bandit who robbed the bank at Pierce said. A big man, the descriptions said, a very big man, wearin' two guns.

Sonora was a big man, and he wore two guns. For that matter, I did, too. There was even another big man in town who wore two guns. The boss, it was, Harvey Kinsella.

We looked at each other right then, and neither of us was fooled a mite. He knowed what I was here for, and I knowed what he was here for, and neither of us was in friendly country.

Bill Riding didn't like me bein' here. It was chokin' up in him like a thunderstorm chokin' up a canyon with cloud. It was gittin' in his throat, the meanness of him, and I could see trouble was headin' our way.

For that matter, I'd knowed it was comin', soon or late. I knowed it was comin' because I knowed I was goin' to butt into somethin' that wasn't rightly my business. It had been buildin' for days, ever since I got the lay of the land, hereabouts.

I was goin' to tear down the fence that kept Ruth Belton's cows from grazin' in Reefer Canyon, where the good grass was.

You'd think, maybe, that tearin' down one fence wouldn't do no good. You'd think maybe they'd put it right up again. You'd be wrong.

If'n I tore down that fence once, it was goin' to stay down, because after I tore it down, I'd have to kill Harvey Kinsella and Bill Riding.

They was the ones out to break Ruthie Belton. When her old man was alive, they left him strictly alone. He was old, but he was a ring-tailed wolf on the prowl, and they knowed it. Then he got throwed from a bad hoss, and they started to move in on the Bar B.

It wasn't none of my business. Me, I was up here for a purpose, and rightly I shouldn't think of anythin' else, but sometimes a man stumbles into a place where, if he's a man, he's got to show it. And me, I was a-fixin' to tear down that fence.

It would mean shootin', and Kinsella was poison mean, and Riding damn near as bad. That was sayin' nothin' o' the rest of that outfit. But I had me a plan now, and that plan was buildin' around a certain tall hombre in a high-crowned hat, a man that rode a brown-legged mule and packed two Walker Colts.

Bill Riding got up and walked over to the bar. He was spoilin' for trouble. As big a man as Kinsella in weight, he was a mite shorter than either of us, but nearly as broad as me. A big-handed man, and a dirty fighter in a rough-and-tumble.

"Stranger," he says, starin' at Sonora, "y' seem kind of limitin' in your offer of a drink. Maybe y' think you're too durned good to drink with us!"

Sonora had his elbows on the bar right then, and he didn't straighten; he just turned his head and let those cold eyes take in Riding, head to foot; then he looked back at his drink.

Riding's face flamed up, and I saw his lips tighten. His hand shot out, and he grabbed Sonora by the shoulder. Bill just had to be top dog, he just had to have ever'body believin' he was a bad hombre, but he done the wrong thing when he laid a hand on Sonora.

The man in the high-crowned hat back-handed his fist into Bill's unprotected midsection. It caught Bill unsuspectin', and he staggered, gaspin' for breath. Then Sonora turned and slugged him. Bill went back into a table, upset it, and then he crawled out of the poker chips with a grunt and started for Sonora.

Just then Harvey Kinsella stepped into the room, and me, I slid back two quick steps and palmed a six-gun. "Hold it!" I said, hard-like. "Anybody butts into this scrap gets a belly-ful of lead!"

Kinsella looked at me then, the first time he ever seemed to see me. "If you didn't have that gun out," he said, "I'd kill you!"

Me, I laughed. If'n it hadn't been for Sonora, who was goin' to town on Riding, I'd have called him.

Bein' around like I have, I've seen some men take a whippin', but I never saw any man get a more artistic shellackin' than Sonora give Bill Riding. He started in on him, and he used both hands. He cut him like you'd chop beef. He sliced his face like he had a knife edge across his knuckles.

Me, Dan Ketrel, I slug 'em, and Pap always said I had the biggest fists he ever seen on a man, but Sonora, he went to work like a doc. He raised bumps all over Riding and then lanced ever' one o' them with his knuckles. Riding wanted to drop, but Sonora wouldn't let him fall. He just kept him on his feet until he got so bloody, even I couldn't take it. Then Sonora hooked one, high and hard, and Bill Riding went down into the sawdust.

Sonora looked over at me, standin' with a gun in my fist. "Thanks," he said, grinnin' a little. We understood each other, him and me.

Harvey Kinsella looked at Riding lying on the floor; then he looked from Sonora to me. "I'll give you until sundown," he said. Then he turned to go.

"I like it here," I said.

"I've told you," he replied.

Sonora and me walked outside. Me, I figgered it was time to talk. "There's been talk," I said, "of a ranger comin' in here after that hombre what done that Pierce bank job. Don't let it worry you none. Not for right now.

"Down the road a piece there's a girl, name of Ruth Belton. Her old man was a he-wolf. He's dead. This here Kinsella, he's tryin' to run her off her range. Scared to tackle it when the old man was alive. He's done put up a fence to keep her cows from the good grass. I aim to cut that fence."

He stood there, his big thumbs in his belt, listenin'. Me, I finished rollin' my smoke. "When I cut that fence, there's goin' to be some shootin', but I aim to cut it and aim to kill Harvey Kinsella. He's got word out that ary a hand on that fence and his guns talk loud.

"I aim to cut it. I aim to kill him so's he won't never put it up again. But he's got a sight of boys ridin' for him. One or two, I might git, but I don't want nothin' botherin' me when I go after Kinsella."

"Where's the fence?" he asked quietly.

"Down the road a piece." I struck a match on my pants. "I reckon if'n we was to ride that way, Ruthie would fix us a bait o' grub. She's quite some shakes with a skillet."

Me, I walked out and swung onto the hurricane deck of that big blue horse o' mine. Sonora lit his own shuck and then boarded his mule. He went down the street and took the trail for Ruthie Belton's place.

Neither of us said no words all the way until we got up to Ruthie's place and could see the flowers around her door, and Ruthie waterin' 'em down.

"I reckon," Sonora said then, "that ranger could hold off doin' what he has to do 'til a job like this was over. Don't reckon he'd wait much longer, though, would he?"

"Don't reckon so," I said grimly. "A man's got his duty. Still," I added, "maybe this ranger never seen the hombre he's lookin' for. Maybe he ain't sure when he does see him, so maybe he rides back without him?"

"Wouldn't do no good," Sonora objected. "Too many others lookin', and he'd be follered wherever he'd go."

Ruth looked up when she heard our horses and then turned to face us, smiling. She looked up at me, and when I looked down into those blue eyes, I figgered what a fool a man was to go lookin' into guns when there was eyes, soft like that.

"You're the man," she declared, "who protected Shep!"

Me, I got red around the gills. I ain't used to palaverin' with no womenfolk. "I reckon," I said.

"Won't you get down and come in? We were just about to eat."

We got down, and Sonora sweeps off that high-crowned hat and smiles. "I've heard some powerful nice things about the food you cook, ma'am," he said, "and thank you for a chance to try it."

We went inside, and pretty soon Jack come in. He smiled, but I could see he was plumb worried. It didn't take no mind reader to figger why. Those cows we'd seen was lookin' mighty poor. It wouldn't take much time for them to start dyin' off, eatin' only the skimpy dry, brown grass.

When she had the food on the table, Ruthie looked at me, and I could feel my thick neck gettin' red again. "You boys just riding, or are you going some particular place?"

Sonora looked over a forkful of fried spuds. "Dan here, he figgered there was a fence up here needed cuttin', and he 'lows as how he'll cut it. I'm just sort of ridin' along, in case."

Her face whitened. "Oh no! You mustn't! Harvey Kinsella will kill anybody who touches that fence—he warned us!"

"Uh-huh." I picked up my coffee cup. "We ain't got much time here, ma'am. I got a little job to do, and I reckon Sonora has, too. We sort of figgered we'd take care o' this and Kinsella, too. Then when we rode off up the trail, you'd be all right."

When we finished, I tipped back in my chair. It was right homey feelin', the sort of feelin' I ain't had since I was a kid, me bein' a roamin' man and all. I got up after a bit and saw Sonora look at me. That mule-ridin' man never had a hand far from a gun when we were together. For that matter, neither did I.

It wasn't that we didn't trust each other. We both had a job to do, him and me, but we were the cautious type.

I walked over and picked up the water bucket, then went to the spring and filled it. When I come back, I split a couple of armfuls of wood and packed it inside. Sonora, he sat there on the porch, sleepy-like, just a-watchin' me.

The door had a loose hinge, and I got me a hammer and fixed it, sort of like I used to when I was a kid, and like my pa used to do. It gives a man a sort of homey feelin', to be fixin' around. Once I looked up and saw Ruthie lookin' at me, a sort of funny look in her eyes.

Then I picked up my hat. "Reckon," I said, "we better be ridin' up to that fence. It's 'most two miles from here."

Ruthie, she come to the door, her eyes wide and her face pale. "Stop by," she said, "on your way back. I'll be takin' a cake out of the oven."

"Sure thing," Sonora said, grinning. "I always did like fresh cake."

That was a real woman. Not tellin' y' to be careful, not tellin' us we shouldn't. That was her, standin' there shadin' her eyes again' the sun as we rode off up the trail, me loungin' sideways in the saddle, a six-gun under my hand.

"You'd make a family man," Sonora said half a mile farther along. "Y' sure would. Ought to have a little spread o' your own."

That made me look up, it cut so close to the trail o' my own thoughts. "That's what I always figgered on," I told him. "Me, I'm through ridin' rough country."

We rode on quiet-like. Both of us knowed what was comin'. If'n we came out of this with a whole skin, there was still the main show. I should say, the big showdown. We both knowed it, and neither of us liked it.

In those few hours we'd come to find we was the same kind of hombre, the same kind of man, and we fought the same way. We were two big men, and when we rode that last mile up there to the fence, I was thinkin' that here, at last, was a man to ride through hell with. And then I had to do to him what I had to do because it was the job I had.

———

THE FENCE WAS there, tight and strong. "Give me some cover," I suggested to Sonora. "I'm goin' to ride up and cut her—but good!"

The air was clear, and my voice carried, and then I saw Bill Riding step down from the junipers, a rifle holdin' easy in his hands. His voice rang loud in the draw. "Y' ain't cuttin' nothin', neither of you!"

Me, I sat there with my hands down. My rifle was in my saddle boot, and he was out of six-gun range. I could see the slow smile on his face as that rifle came up.

That moro o' mine never lost a rider no quicker in his life. I went off, feet first, and hit the ground gun in hand. I'd no more than hit it before somethin' bellowed like a young cannon, and out of the tail o' my eye I saw Sonora had unlimbered those big Walker Colts.

My six-shooter was out, but I wasn't lookin' at Riding. He was beyond my reach, but there was a movement in the junipers close down, on our side of the fence, and I turned and saw Harvey Kinsella there behind us. He had a smile on his face, and I could almost see his lips tighten as he squeezed off his first shot.

When I started burnin' powder I don't know. Somethin' hit Kinsella, and he went back on his heels, his face lookin' sick, and then I started walkin' in on him. It helped me keep my mind on business to walk into a man while I was shootin'.

Somebody blazed at me from the brush, and when I tried a snapshot that way, I heard a whinin' cry and a rifle rattled on the rocks. But I was walkin' right at Kinsella, and his guns were goin'. I could see flame stabbin' at me from their muzzles, but when I figgered I had four shots left, I kept walkin' in and holdin' my fire.

Behind me them Walkers was blastin' like a couple of cannon from the War Atween the States. I wasn't worried about Sonora takin' out on me. He was an hombre to ride the river with. Besides, we each had us a job to do.

Then Kinsella was down on his face, the back o' his fancy coat stainin' red. Two other hombres were down, too, and I could hear the rattle of racin' hoofs as some others took off through the brush.

Then I turned, thumbin' shells into my guns, and Sonora was there, leanin' on a fence post, one o' those big guns danglin' from his fist.

Me, I walked over to the fence, haulin' the wire cutters from my belt, the pair I picked up at the girl's ranch. My head was drummin' somethin' awful, like maybe there was still more shootin'. But it wasn't that—it was deathly still. Y' couldn't hear a sound but the loud click o' my cutters.

When I finished, I turned toward Sonora. He was slumped over the fence then, and there was blood comin' from somewhere high up on his chest. I took the gun out of his fingers and stuck it in his holster. Then I hoisted him on my shoulder and started for his mule.

That mule wasn't noways skittish. I got Sonora aboard and then crawled up on the moro. When I was in the saddle again, I looked around.

Riding was dead, anybody could see that. He'd been hit more than once, and half his head was blowed off. There was another hombre close beside him, and he was dead, too.

As for Kinsella, I didn't have to look at him. I knowed when I was shootin' that I was killin' him, but I walked over to him.

Three times on my way back to Ruthie's I had to stop and straighten Sonora in the saddle, even with his wrists tied to the horn.

Before I got through the gate, Ruthie was runnin' down toward us, and Jack, too. Then I must've passed out.

When my eyes cracked to light again, it was lamplight, and the room wasn't very bright. Ruthie was sittin' by my bed, sewin'.

"Sonora?" I asked.

"He'll be all right. He'd been shot twice. You men! You're both so *big*! I don't see how any bullet could ever kill you!"

Me, I was thinkin' it might not take a bullet, but a rope.

Kinsella got me once, low down on the side. Just a flesh wound, but from what Jack told me, it must've bled like all get-out.

When it was later, Ruthie got up and put her sewin' away; then she went into another room and to sleep. I give her an hour, as close as I could figger. Then I rolled back the blanket and got my feet under me. I was some weak, but it takes a lot of lead to ballast down an hombre big as me.

Softly, I opened the door. Ruthie was lyin' on a pallet, asleep. Me, I blushes, seein' her that way, her hair all over the pillow like a lot of golden web caught in the moonlight.

Easy as could be, I slipped by. Sonora's door was open, and he was lyin' in Jack's bed, a chair under his feet to make it long enough.

Well, there he was, the hombre that meant my ranch to me. I'd strapped on my guns, but as I stood there lookin' down, I figgered it was a wonder he hadn't shot it out already. That reward was dead or alive.

Suddenly, I almost jumped out of my skin. Only one o' them big Walker Colts was in its holster! Why, that durned coyote! Lyin' there with a gun under the blanket, and the chances was he was awake that minute.

Hell! I'd go back to bed! It never did a man no good to run from the law, not even in the wild country! Soon or late, she always caught up with him.

———

IN THE MORNIN', I'd just finished splashin' water on my face when I looked up and he was leanin' again' the door post. "Howdy," he said, grinnin'. "Sleep well?"

My face burned. "Well as you did, y' durned possum-playin' maverick!"

He grinned. "Man in my place can't be too careful." He looked at me. "Ready to ride, or is it a showdown?"

Sonora had his guns on, and there was a quizzical light in those funny eyes o' his'n.

He was a big man, big as me, and the only man I ever saw I'd ride with. "Hell," I said, "ain't y' goin' to eat breaf'st? I'll ride with you because you're too good a man to kill!"

Ruthie was puttin' food on the table, and she looked at us queerly. "What's between you two?" she asked quick-like.

"Why, Ruthie," I said, "this here hombre's a Texas Ranger. He figgers I'm the hombre what robbed that bank over to Pierce!"

She stared at me. "Then—you're a prisoner?"

"Ma'am," Sonora said, gulpin' a big swaller o' hot coffee, "don't you fret none. I reckon he ain't no crook. Just had a minute or two o' bein' a durned fool! I reckon that bank's plumb anxious to git their money back, and I know this hombre's got it on him because last night"—he grinned—"when he was asleep, I had me a look at his money belt!"

Before I could bust out and say anythin', he adds, "I figger that bank's goin' to be so durned anxious to git their money back, they won't fret too much when I suggest this hombre be sent back here, sort of on good behavior. I'd say he'd make a good hand around a layout like this."

Then I bust in. "Y' got this all wrong, Sonora," I told him. "Y' been trailin' the wrong man! Rather, y' trailed the right man, and then when y' walked into the Chuck Wagon, y' took too much for granted.

"I didn't rob no bank. I'll admit I got to thinkin' about ownin' a ranch, and I rode into town with the money in mind. Then I heard the shootin' and lit out. The man who robbed the bank," I said, "was Harvey Kinsella. I took the money belt off him. His name's marked on it!"

He stared at me. "Well, I'll be durned!" he said.

Ruthie was lookin' at me, her eyes all bright and happy. "Man," I was sayin', "I figgered you fer the bandit, first off.

I was figgerin' on gittin' you fer the reward, needin' that money like I was fer a ranch."

"An' I was tryin' to decide if I should take y' in or let y' go!" Sonora shook his head.

Ruthie smiled at me and then at him. "I'm going to try and fix it, Sonora," she said, "so he'll stay here. I think he'd be a good man around a ranch—someplace where he could take a personal interest in things!"

There was a tint o' color in her skin.

"Just what I think, ma'am." Sonora shoved back his chair. I got up and handed him the money belt. "And Ruthie," he continued, "if I was to ride by, y' reckon it'd be all right to stop in?"

She smiled as she filled my cup. "Of course, Sonora, and we'll be mighty glad to see you!"

SQUATTERS ON THE LONETREE

TANNER WAS FASTENING the tailgate when Wiley Dunn saw him and started across the street. Algosa held its collective breath, for this was the first meeting between the owner of Hat and the nester who had squatted on Lonetree.

For fifteen years Wiley Dunn and his hard-bitten Hat riders had ruled unchallenged over two hundred thousand acres of range, growing in wealth and power. Occasionally, ill-advised nesters had moved on Hat range, but the only nesters still there were buried. The others had departed hurriedly for parts as far away as possible. Tanner was the exception. He had squatted on a small, rugged corner with a lovely green meadow where there was plenty of both timber and water.

Dunn was a square, powerful man who walked with quick, knee-jerking strides. That Tanner defied his power nettled him. He could see no sense in the man starting a fight he had no chance of winning.

Tanner straightened as Dunn approached, and Dunn was startled to find his eyes piercingly black, although the nester's hair was a faded rust color. Tanner had a lean body, slightly stooped.

"Howdy, Dunn. Been aimin' to see you. Some of your critters been watering down around Sandy Point and getting caught in quicksand. You ought to have your hands throw up a fence."

"Thanks." Dunn was brusque. "Tanner, you have forty-eight hours to get off my range."

Tanner took a slow drag on his cigarette. "Now, Mr. Dunn, you know better than to tell me that. If I was fixin' to leave at all I'd have been long gone. That place appeals to me, so we're just a-stayin' on."

"Don't be a fool!" Dunn said impatiently. "You haven't a chance! My cattle have been grazing that range for years, and we're not about to give it up to some two-by-twice nester who comes driftin' into the country. I've got forty tough cowhands, and if you persist, I'll—"

"You'll get some of them hurt. Now, look here, Mr. Dunn. You've got a sight of range out there, and it's all government land. I'm not takin' much of it, so you just leave me alone."

"Be reasonable!" Dunn was not anxious to fight. He had done his share of fighting. "You can't make a living on that piece of ground."

"I aim to raise some shoats," Tanner said, squinting against the sun. "Put me in a few acres of corn." He indicated the sacks in the wagon. "Got my seed already."

"Hogs? This is beef country!"

"So I figure to raise hogs. Folks like a mite of side meat, time to time."

"You get off that land in forty-eight hours." Dunn was growing impatient. He was used to issuing ultimatums that were instantly obeyed, not to discussing them. He was also aware the whole town was watching.

"Look, Mr. Dunn, my folks and I like that little place. We can be right neighborly, but we can also be a mite mean, if pressed.

"We've got little to lose. You've got plenty. I don't want a fight, but if you start it I won't set and wait. I'll come after you, Mr. Dunn. I'll bring the fight to you."

Enraged, Dunn turned away, yet it was disappointment as much as anger. He had hoped there would be no fight, but if this man stayed, others would move in. None of them would make it. And when they started to go hungry they would start killing his cattle. He had seen it happen before. Moreover, the man baffled him. Tanner should have been frightened or worried. He was neither.

"Boss," Ollie Herndon suggested, "let me take him? He's askin' for it."

"No, no!" Dunn protested. "I won't have a man killed with his wife and children looking on."

"That's his wife's brother," Turner said, "they've only been married a couple of years."

"You let me have him," Herndon said. "He's too durned sure of hisself."

"Funny thing," Turner commented, "this is the third time I've seen that wagon in town, but I've yet to see tracks comin' from his place."

"What's that mean?" Dunn demanded.

"You figure it out, boss. I surely can't."

Despite his determination to rid himself of the nester, Dunn knew the man would be a hard nut to crack, and it would be apt to create quite a stir if there was a killing. And there could be.

Tanner had built his house of stone right against the face of a limestone cliff in the small valley of the Lonetree, a place approachable only from the front. Tanner was reputed to be a dead shot. Yet there was a way—catch him in an open field.

Hat made its try the following day.

Eight riders slipped close under protection of the willows, then charged. Tanner was in plain sight in the open pasture, nothing near him for shelter but a few scattered rock piles, bushes, and trees.

"Got him!" Ollie yelled triumphantly. "Now we'll show him!"

They rushed first to cut him off from the house, then swept down upon him. Only he was no longer there.

Tanner had vanished like a puff of smoke, and then a rifle boomed. A horse went down, spilling his rider; another boom, and the hat was knocked from Ollie's head. As the riders swirled past where they had seen Tanner they found nothing, absolutely nothing! It was unbelievable.

The angry riders circled. "Shots came from those rocks," one maintained.

"No, it was from that clump of brush."

A rifle boomed from the house, and one of the horses

started pitching wickedly. When the horse ceased bucking, a scattering of shots caused them to scatter in flight. Hastily, they hunted cover.

"It ain't possible!" Ollie protested. "We all seen him! Right out there in plain sight!"

At daybreak the following morning, irritated by the report of the previous day's events, Wiley Dunn was up pacing the floor. He walked out on the wide veranda, and something caught his attention.

Three large watermelons lay on the edge of the porch, beside them a sack of roasting ears. Pinned to the sack was a note:

Figured these would go well with beef. Better keep
your outfit to home. They git kind of carried away with
theirselves.

Wiley Dunn swore bitterly, glaring at the melons. Sobering a little, he decided they did look mighty tasty.

Ollie Herndon's report worried him. Dropped from sight, Ollie said. Obviously the mountain man had been concealed in the brush, but why hadn't they found him? Ollie was no pilgrim. He should have been able to smoke him out.

Three days went by before they attacked again. Ollie led this one, too, and he had seven men. They rode to within a few hundred yards, then concealed their horses and approached on foot. They did not talk, and they had waited until it was good and dark before they began their approach. They could see the lights in the cabin, and they started across the field through the grass, walking carefully. They were halfway across when Ollie suddenly tripped, staggered, and fell. Instantly a gun boomed.

Flat on their faces in the grass, they lay cursing. That shot had been close, and it sounded like a shotgun.

Ollie ran his fingers through the grass. "Wire!" he said with disgust. "A durned trip wire!" He glanced up. The lights were gone.

Ollie was furious. To be tricked by a damned nester! He

got to his feet and the others arose with him. Red moved closer to Ollie. "No use goin' up there now. That ol' catamount's ready for us."

It was a fact understood by all. There was literally nothing else they could do. The stone house was situated in such a position that one had to cross the meadows to approach it, and the corrals, stock, and hay were all in a box canyon entered from beside the house. To get nearer without being heard was no longer possible, and shooting at the stone house would simply be a waste, as well as dangerous. It was a thousand to one against their scoring a hit, and their gun flashes would reveal their positions, making them good targets in the open meadow.

Disgusted, they trooped, grumbling, back to their horses and rode back to the ranch.

Wiley Dunn was irritated. The continued resistance of Tanner was not only annoying and disconcerting, but was winning friends for Tanner. Even his own lawyer made a sly comment on it, but to Dunn it was not amusing. He had hoped that Tanner could be pushed off without any real bloodshed, but it appeared that the only way to be rid of him was to kill him. Ten years ago he would not have hesitated, but the times had changed, and people were looking askance at big outfits running roughshod over people.

He was tempted to turn Ollie Herndon loose, but hesitated. There should be some other way. If he could only catch Tanner on the road and destroy his place while he was gone.

Somehow the story had gotten around that Dunn's hands had failed in an attack on the Lonetree nester and he had repaid them with watermelons. The next time Dunn appeared in town Ed Wallis asked, "How were the melons, Wiley? Didn't upset your stomach, did they?"

Dunn's smile faded. "That nester's askin' for it. He's been warned to get off my place!"

"It ain't like it was, Wiley. Why don't you let him be? A man like that might prove to be a good neighbor. He seems a decent sort."

"Look, Ed, if I allowed Tanner to stay on that place my

range would be overrun by squatters. Besides, in a bad year I'd need that water."

Wallis shrugged. "It's none of my affair, although folks are saying that with two hundred thousand acres you should let a man have enough to live on. As for water, you'd have plenty of water, and grass, too, if you didn't overgraze. You've got more cattle on that grass than it can carry."

"You tellin' me my business? I've been in the cow business twenty-five years, and no small potatoes storekeeper is going to tell me how to do it."

Ed Wallis turned abruptly. "Sorry I spoke to you, Dunn. It is none of my business. You handle your own affairs." He returned to his store.

Wiley Dunn stared after him, angry at Wallis but even more angry at himself. What was he getting mad at Ed for? They had been friends for fifteen years. But that talk about carrying too much stock was stupid, although, in a year like this when he was going to be in a tight spot for feed, it might make sense. It was that damned nester's fault, he decided. If Tanner hadn't moved onto that range he would have been all right.

He started along the street to the post office, and was just turning in at the door when Tanner and his wife came out.

Tanner was no more than thirty at best, his wife a good ten years younger, a quietly pretty girl whose eyes widened when she saw him. That she was frightened angered Dunn even more. What kind of a person was he supposed to be, that a young woman should be afraid of him? What had Tanner been telling her?

"Tanner," he said abruptly, "have you moved yet?"

Tanner smiled. "Why, howdy, Mr. Dunn! No, we haven't moved and we don't plan to. That's government land, Mr. Tanner, and you've no rightful claim to it. On the other hand, I've filed on it for a homestead. All we want is to make a livin', so leave us alone, Mr. Dunn."

People were listening, and Wiley Dunn was aware of it. There was such a thing as prestige, and by simply telling the Tanners they might stay on undisturbed he could have established a reputation of another kind; on the other hand, he had lived so long with the psychology of the feudal baron it was not in him to change quickly. This Tanner had to be put in his place.

"Now, you see here, Tanner. I am not going to fool around any longer. You're on my water and I want you off. You get off now, or you'll answer to me. I'll send my men around to take care of you."

"What's the matter, Mr. Dunn?" Tanner's voice was suddenly soft, but something in it brought Wiley Dunn up short. "Can't you fight your own battles? Have you been hidin' behind Ollie Herndon so long you don't remember what it means to get a bloody nose?"

Wiley Dunn stared at Tanner. Not for years had anyone dared challenge him. Not for years had he had a fight of any kind. He was a burly, husky man who had won many a rough-and-tumble fight in years gone by, but there was something about Tanner that warned Dunn he would be hard to handle. Yet Dunn had had the reputation of being a fighter, and he had won it the hard way.

"I don't mix in dirty brawls, Tanner. It won't be a matter of fists if I come after you."

Tanner was no longer smiling. "Mr. Dunn, I have never hunted trouble with any man, although here and there trouble has come to me. I've not hunted trouble with you, but your boys have attacked my home twice.

"Now, Mr. Dunn, I've always hoped I'd never have to kill another man, but if it is guns you want it is guns you can have. Right now, right here at this minute, if you want it that way. I'm carrying a gun, Mr. Dunn. Are you?"

Wiley Dunn felt butterflies in his stomach. Maybe he was getting old. "No," he said honestly, "I am not carrying a gun, but—"

Sheriff Collins had been watching and now he stepped in. "All right, break it up! There will be no talk of guns while I'm sheriff of this county." Collins looked at Tanner, his expression harsh. The sheriff was a cattleman himself. "Do you hear that, Tanner?"

"I hear it," Tanner replied calmly, "but while you're at it, you tell Dunn to keep his men away from my place. They've attacked me twice, with guns."

"I know nothing about that," Collins replied stiffly. "If you want to file a complaint, I will act upon it."

"I've always fought my own battles, Sheriff, but I would like to call your attention to something. You were standing here listening when he threatened me and ordered me off land on which I have legally filed. If there is a court case I'll certainly have you called as a witness."

He turned to his wife. "Sorry, honey; I didn't mean to keep you waitin'."

Slowly the crowd dispersed. Only Collins and Dunn remained.

For a few moments nothing was said, then Dunn spoke. "I wish the damned fool would move off that place! I don't want trouble, Jim, but I need that water."

"You've got water elsewhere. You've a lot of land, Wiley. Maybe you should pull in your horns."

"And let him whip me?"

"Can't you see, Wiley? Tanner ain't tryin' to whip you. He wants to stay. Why don't you slap him on the back and tell him if he gives you a piece of side meat from time to time he can stay."

There was good sense in what Collins advised, and Collins was a good man. "But I can't let him get away with this, Jim. He called me a coward to my face. Nobody has done that since the Powell boys."

Wiley Dunn had killed the Powell boys, all three of them. He had been fourteen years younger then, but he was still, he told himself, a tough man.

"You're asking for it, Wiley, but let me give you a word of advice from a friend. Don't get the idea that Tanner is easy. He ain't."

On his way back to the ranch, Wiley Dunn mulled that over, and he had to admit his impression was the same. There was something in Tanner's manner that warned Dunn that the man was no pilgrim. And what was that Tanner had said? That he did not want to kill *another* man?

Suddenly, he remembered what Rowdy or somebody had

said about there being no tracks leaving Tanner's place. What could that mean?

His curiosity aroused, Dunn turned the bay off the trail to the ranch and cut across the hill to the county road. It took him only a few minutes to find the tracks of Tanner's returning buckboard, his saddle horse tied behind. For three miles he followed the tracks and then, suddenly, they were gone.

Puzzled, he reined the bay around and rode back. Crushed grass told him where Tanner had turned off, and he followed the tracks over a low hill and alongside a dry wash. He was now not more than five miles from Tanner's cabin, but separated from it by the bulk of Wildhorse Mesa, a huge block of basaltic rock some four hundred feet high by eight miles long, and at least two miles wide. If this was the route Tanner took to his home, it was far out of the way.

Turning back, Dunn reached the trail and started for the ranch. Frowning, he considered what he had learned. It seemed stupid for a man to go so far out of his way to avoid trouble on the trail, yet going over the mesa was an impossibility. It was true, he had never skirted the mesa on the north, but he had been within a quarter of a mile many times on the south side, and the steep talus slides ended in an abrupt cliff, at least a hundred feet of sheer rock.

Maybe he was being a damned fool. After all, Lonetree lay far from the home ranch and they had rarely watered there, holding it rather for emergencies than otherwise. He could let it go and never miss it. Irritably, he shook off the thought. The land was his, and he was going to keep it.

Had he persisted in trailing Tanner he would have had a further surprise. In such broken, rugged country, even a man who has lived and ridden there for years sometimes misses things. Had he been skirting the mesa on foot, something no cowhand would dream of doing, he would have discovered it was not, as it seemed, a continuous wall.

A few days after Tanner had completed the building of the stone house in Lonetree Canyon, he had taken his rifle and ridden out to hunt for a deer. Picketing his horse on a patch of grass, he had taken his rifle and walked up a tiny creek toward its beginning at the mesa's base.

He drank from the spring, then straightened up and turned west. He was wiping his mouth with the back of his hand when he realized he was looking at a break in the wall of the mesa. Moreover, there was a dim game trail leading from the spring back into the notch.

The trail entering the opening went in parallel with the mesa's wall, which was fractured, leaving one point of rock extended along the face of the mesa so that from a short distance away it appeared to be one unbroken wall.

Following the dim trail through talus and broken rock and pushing through brush, he found that it turned sharply south, and he was standing in a gap where the mesa was actually separated into two. Lying before him was a meadow at least a hundred yards wide. Following it, he discovered that at one place it became almost a half-mile wide, then narrowed again as it neared the north side. At the lowest point there was a small lake, almost an acre in extent. The opening on the far side emerged in a thick stand of aspen, and in the distance, he could see the smoke from Algosa. Not only had he discovered a private trail out of his ranch, but added grazing and a much shorter route to town.

From the Bar 7, a ranch several miles to the west, he bought twenty young heifers, and turned them into the grassy basin. Then he prepared a pole gate and fence at the far end, and another at his own end of the opening.

Each time he used the route through the mesa he took care to cover his tracks, wiping them out near a shelf of rock so the tracks seemed to vanish on the rock itself. Over the way into the aspen he placed a dead tree, still attached to its base by a few shreds of wood. This he could swing back and forth, making the route seem impassable to a buckboard.

When Morgan Tanner returned to the stone house, he helped Ann from the buckboard. For a moment she stood close to him. "Will they ever leave us alone, Morgan?"

"I believe they will. There will be trouble first, I think. Ollie Herndon is hunting trouble, with or without orders from Dunn. We've got to be careful."

During subsequent days he explored the rift in the mesa, finding several ice caves, and in one of them a stone hammer.

He prowled the canyon, often alone, but sometimes with either Johnny Ryan or Ann. He did a lot of thinking about what he had discovered.

Algosa was no longer just a cow town. Mines were being opened in the backcountry, and although not very rich they had large ore bodies and gave evidence they might last, turning Algosa into a market town.

Morgan Tanner had come from mountain country where cattle were more valued for milk, butter, and cheese than for beef, but so far as he was aware the only milk cow in Algosa was owned by the postmaster.

What Dunn might be planning he could not guess, but the raids ceased. Tanner rarely went to town, and the place was never empty. When he did go into town he met people, and he asked a few questions, listened a lot.

Johnny Ryan, his wife's brother, was a hardworking youngster of thirteen. With Johnny helping, Morgan Tanner handled the cattle and strove to improve the place. When he did go to town he wore a gun, but avoided places where there might be trouble. Several people made a point of telling him what Dunn had done to the Powell boys, and he knew they all expected a showdown between Dunn and himself.

Yet none of the Dunn riders appeared, and as long as he was left alone, Tanner was satisfied. The sun came out hotter each day, and the sky was cloudless. Wiley Dunn rode his sorrel out on the range beside his worried foreman. "What do you think, Ollie? Is the range all as bad as this?"

"There's places that are better. Back up in the breaks and in the deepest canyons. The water holes haven't slacked off too much yet, except that one down to Spur. That's gone dry."

There was silence, and Herndon asked cautiously, "Boss? D' you reckon we might sell a few head? Ease up on the grass a mite?"

Wiley Dunn stiffened. "No. Anyway, the price is off. We'd lose money to sell now."

Ollie Herndon said nothing. Gunman he might be, but he was also a cattleman. It was hard to sell when prices were down, yet better to sell now while they had beef on their bones than to let them lose weight. But he knew better than to make suggestions. Wiley Dunn had always had a fixation on numbers.

"If we had that Lonetree place it would help," he suggested. "You give me the word and I'll tackle Tanner."

Dunn waited while a man might have counted ten, staring out over the long brown miles of his range. He was wishing this affair had never come up. The expression in the eyes of Tanner's pretty wife had hurt him more than he would have admitted to anyone. He had grown more sensitive, he reflected, as he grew older. And if he faced Tanner now there would be no telling the outcome. If he died, what good would all these vast acres be? And if Tanner died, what would become of that lovely girl?

"No," he said finally, "not yet."

He saw nothing of Tanner. Twice he rode up the valley, keeping well out of sight, and another time he rode along a ridge overlooking the place from a distance.

Lonetree was more lovely than he remembered it. There had always been water there, but now there were long, perfectly lined rows of planted crops, and over against the far side there was a field of alfalfa, or what seemed to be alfalfa.

Tanner was no fool. He had a good thing there. He stared at the hay. Yet that was a lot of feed for the stock he had. . . . Suspicion leaped into his mind. Had Tanner turned to rustling? Had he, like other nesters in the past, started stealing cattle?

Suppose he had a small herd of Hat cattle that he was secretly fattening? With sudden decision, Dunn turned away. This was the explanation. There could be no other.

IN THE STONE house against the cliff Morgan Tanner looked across the table at his wife. "Honey, I've been thinking. If we had us a Jersey bull now, a right fine Jersey from good milk stock, we might crossbreed those heifers into better milkers in a few seasons."

Ann Tanner looked at him thoughtfully. "You want to use that money Uncle Fred left us? Is that it?"

"It's your decision. It's up to you and Johnny. He was your uncle."

"But he left it to all of us! What do you think, Johnny?"

"I've been thinking about it, Sis. Morg never spoke of it before, but it's been in my mind. There's a market for milk and butter down at Algosa. This country has plenty of beef."

"All right," Ann agreed. "Buy a bull whenever you can find one you want."

"I'll go into town tomorrow," he said.

Morgan Tanner reached town at ten the following morning, and a few minutes earlier Wiley Dunn, Ollie Herndon, and twelve Hat hands swept down on the Lonetree ranch. It had been shrewdly planned, for Ollie had been watching the ranch with glasses and had seen the boy ride off on some mission. Instantly he was down off the ridge and they were riding.

There was no one about when they rode into the yard. Dunn shouted and, white-faced, Ann Tanner came to the door. "Just what is it you want, Mr. Dunn? Have you taken to fighting women now?"

His face flushed but his jaw was set. "I'm fighting no one, but we've come to search the range! That damn no-good husband of yours has taken to rustling cows. We seen some of them."

"We have no cattle but our own! Now I am ordering you to get off this place at once!"

She turned quickly to grasp the shotgun, but Herndon leaped from his horse and caught the barrel as she was swinging it up. He wrenched it roughly from her hands. "Right purty, ain't you? Maybe you could do with a good man after we string up that husband of yours!"

She slapped him across the mouth and Herndon struck her. She had stepped back, but the blow caught her on the forehead and knocked her down.

"Ollie!" Dunn was white-faced with anger. "For God's sake, man! Get into your saddle now, and be damned quick about it. I'll have no man strike a woman in my presence!" He pointed. "Get into your saddle, do you hear?"

Turning to Ann he said, "Sorry, ma'am, but you shouldn't have reached for that gun."

"And let you steal our cattle. You're asking for trouble, Mr. Dunn. You don't know Morgan as I do. Morgan Tanner's mother was a Lowry, from the Nueces country. You may remember what happened to the Fullers."

Wiley Dunn stared at her, shocked. Every detail of the twenty-five-year feud was known to everybody in cattle country. The Fullers, or some people who called themselves that, had killed a Lowry boy in an argument over horses, and every Fuller had died.

Suddenly, with startling clarity, he remembered the scene from years before. He himself had witnessed the final shoot-out. He had been visiting in Texas, planning to buy cattle, and four of the Fuller outfit had cornered two Lowrys, Bill Lowry and some youngster of sixteen or seventeen. They had shot Bill Lowry in the back, and then the kid turned on them.

The boy had drawn as he turned, a flashing, beautifully timed draw. Ed Fuller caught the first bullet in his midsection as the boy fired. Thirty seconds later the youngster was in the saddle, riding out of town, leaving three Fullers dead and another dying. Now, suddenly, the face of that boy merged with that of Morgan Tanner. Of course! That was why there had always been something disturbingly familiar about the man.

There was no turning back now. "I'll stay here, Pete. The rest of you scatter out and find the cattle. When you find them, drive them out here."

"Those are not your cattle. We bought and paid for them."

Ollie Herndon did not leave. "Boss, let me go get him. I want him."

"Don't be a fool!" Dunn was worried and his temper was short. "That's the sheriff's job."

He paused. "Anyway, you're not in his class. Morgan Tanner is the one they used to call the Lowry kid."

"Aw, I don't believe it! Why, that—!"

"Mr. Dunn is right," Ann Tanner replied, "and when he learns what you have done, he will kill you. I wish you would ride now. I wish you would leave the country before he finds you."

Herndon laughed. "Since when have you started carin' about me?"

"I don't care about you. You're a cheap, loud-mouthed braggart, and a coyote at heart. You've gotten away with a lot because you ride in Mr. Dunn's shadow. I just do not want my husband to have to kill another man."

As they drove the cattle away, Ann looked after them, heartsick with worry and fear. Johnny appeared from the trees. "I seen 'em, Sis, but I didn't know what to do. I figured I'd better ride to town after Morg."

"No," she was suddenly thinking clearly, "you stay here and don't let them burn us out. I'll ride into town and see Sheriff Collins."

While Johnny was saddling her horse she hastily changed, fixed her hair, and got some papers from the strongbox.

————

COLLINS WAS SHOCKED. "Ma'am, you can't do this! You can't arrest Dunn for stealin'! Why, he's the biggest cattleman in these parts!"

"Nevertheless, I have sworn out a warrant for his arrest, and I want you to come with me." She showed him the bill of sale for the cattle. "He has driven these cattle from my place, taking them by force, and Ollie Herndon struck me." She indicated the bruise on her brow.

"Sheriff, my husband is a Lowry. I want Wiley Dunn behind bars before my husband finds him."

"Just what happened out there, ma'am?" Reluctantly, he got to his feet. "Is that right? Is Morg the one they called the Lowry kid?"

At her assent, he started for the door. "You come along, ma'am, if you will. I don't want any killing here if it can be helped."

The Lowry kid was credited with nine men in all, but locally Morgan Tanner had been a quiet, reserved man, well-liked in the area, and always peaceful. Yet Collins knew the type. The West was full of them. Leave them alone and they were solid, quiet men who worked hard, morning until night; push them the wrong way and all hell would break loose.

Suddenly Tanner was in the door. "Ann? What's wrong? I thought I saw you come in here." Then, "What's happened to your head?"

He listened, his face without expression, but as he turned to the door, Collins said, "Morg? Leave this to the law."

"All right. Except for Ollie. I'll take care of him."

"You're well-liked around here, Morg. You want to spoil that by killing a man?"

"I won't kill him unless I have to. I'll just make him wish he was dead."

Wiley Dunn was talking with Ollie Herndon on the porch when Sheriff Collins, Morgan Tanner, and Ann rode into the ranch yard. By then there was a livid bruise where she had been struck.

"Dunn," Collins spoke apologetically, "I've got a warrant for your arrest. You and Ollie there. For rustlin'."

Ollie was watching Tanner. The expression in his eyes was almost one of hunger. "You huntin' me?"

"Pull in your neck," Tanner said calmly, "you'll have your turn."

Dunn's face was flushed with anger. "You'd arrest *me*? For *rustling*?"

"That's right," Collins said. "Mrs. Tanner has a bill of sale for those cattle you drove off. She bought 'em from the Bar Seven. Paid cash for 'em."

Dunn was appalled. "Look, this is a mistake. I thought—!"

"The trouble is that you didn't think at all," Tanner cut him off. "You've let yourself get so fatheaded and self-centered you didn't think at all.

"Dunn, all I've ever wanted from you is peace. You've no legal right to any of that range you hold. You've used it and misused it. Right now you're destroying the range with five thousand more cattle than the grass will carry.

"If you want to know the truth, Dunn, I've given serious thought to sending word back to Texas for two dozen friends of mine to come in and settle on your range. They'd file on it legally, and they are fighters. You'd be lucky to keep the house you live in."

"Tanner, maybe I've been some kind of a blind fool, but you wouldn't want to press those charges, would you? I might be able to beat your case, but I'd look the fool. You name the damages, and I'll pay. That all right with you, Sheriff?"

Collins waved a hand. "If Tanner drops his charges I'll say no more."

Morgan Tanner looked at Dunn and could find no malice in his heart. All that had been washed away back on the Nueces. He wanted only peace now, and Ann.

"No more trouble about Lonetree?"

"No more trouble. That's decent of you, Tanner. You had me over a barrel."

Herndon swore. "Boss? What's come over you? Knucklin' under to this plow-jockey? I'd see myself in—!"

His voice broke off and he started to draw as Tanner turned.

Tanner's draw was smooth and much faster. His first shot broke Ollie's arm at the elbow, spinning him half around. A second shot notched his ear, and as Ollie's other hand grabbed at the bloody ear, another bullet cut the lobe on the remaining ear.

Herndon turned and began to run clumsily. Tanner walked after him, gun poised. "You start riding, Herndon, and if you ever show up in this country again, I'll kill you.

"You aren't a tough man. You wouldn't make a pimple on a tough man's neck. You're a woman-beater. Now hit your saddle and get out of here."

Deliberately, he turned his back and walked to his own horse. He mounted, then glanced at the sheriff. "Thanks, Collins."

As Ann rode to him he looked around. "Have your boys drive those heifers back, Dunn. And drop around yourself sometime, for supper."

Farther along the road he said, "You know, that man Dunn might make a good neighbor. He's pigheaded, but in his place I might have been just as bad. Anyway, what a man needs in this country is good neighbors."

Then he added, "We'd better hurry. Johnny's apt to be worried, holdin' the fort there by himself."

When they rode into the yard Johnny came out from the house, a rifle in the hollow of his arm. At last it was sundown on the Lonetree.

THAT SLASH SEVEN KID

JOHNNY LYLE RODE up to the bog camp at Seep Spring just before noon. Bert Ramsey, foreman of the Slash Seven outfit, glanced up and nodded briefly. Ramsey had troubles enough without having this brash youngster around.

"Say!" Johnny hooked a leg around the saddle horn. "Who's this Hook Lacey?"

Ramsey stopped walking. "Hook Lacey," he said, "is just about the toughest hombre around here, that's all. He's a rustler and a horse thief, and the fastest hand with a gun in this part of the country since Garrett shot Billy the Kid."

"Ride alone?"

"Naw. He's got him a gang nigh as mean as he is. Nobody wants any part of them."

"You mean you let 'em get away with rustling? We'd never cotton to that back on the Nueces."

Ramsey turned away irritably. "This ain't the Nueces. If you want to be useful why don't you go help Gar Mullins? The heel flies are driving cows into that quicksand faster'n he can drag 'em out."

"Sure." Johnny Lyle swung his leg back over the saddle. "Only I'd rather go after Lacey and his outfit."

"*What?*" Ramsey turned on him. "Are you crazy? Those hombres, any one of 'em, would eat three like you for breakfast! If that bunch tackles us, we'll fight, but we'll not go huntin' 'em!"

"You mean you don't want me to."

Ramsey was disgusted. What did this kid think he was doing, anyway? Like a fool kid, to make a big play in front of the hands, who were listening, to impress them how tough he was. Well, there was a way to stop *that*!

"Why, no," he said dryly. "If you want to go after those outlaws after you help Gar get the cattle out of the quicksand, go ahead."

Sundown was an hour past when Gar Mullins rode up to the corral at the Slash Seven. He stripped the saddle from his bronc, and after a quick splash and a wipe, he went in and dropped on a bench at the table.

Old Tom West, the owner, looked up.

"Where's the kid?" he asked. "Where's my nephew? Didn't he come in?"

Gar was surprised. He glanced around the table.

"Shucks, ain't he here? He left me about three o'clock or so. Said Bert told him he could get Hook Lacey if he finished in time."

"What!" Tom West's voice was a bull bellow. His under jaw shot out. "Bert, did you tell him that?"

Ramsey's face grew red, then pale. "Now, look, boss," he protested, "I figured he was talking to hear hisself make a big noise. I told him when he helped Gar get all them cows out, he could go after Lacey. I never thought he'd be fool enough to do it."

"Aw!" Chuck Allen grinned. "He's probably just rode into town! Where would he look for that outfit? And how could he find 'em when we ain't been able to?"

"We ain't looked any too hard," Mullins said. "I know I ain't."

Tom West was silent. At last he spoke. "Nope, could never find 'em. But if anything happens to that boy, I'd never dare look my sister in the face again." He glared at Bert Ramsey. "If anything does happen to him you'd better be halfway to the border before I hear it."

Johnny Lyle was a cheerful, easygoing, free-talking young-ster. He was pushing eighteen, almost a man by western stan-dards, and as old as Billy the Kid when Billy was leading one of the forces in the Lincoln County War.

But Johnny was more than a brash, devil-may-care young-ster. He had been born and raised on the Nueces, and had cut his riding teeth in the black chaparral between the Nueces

and the Rio Grande. When his father died he had been fourteen, and his mother had moved East. Johnny had continued
to hunt and wander in the woods of the Virginia mountains,
but he had gone to New York several times each month.

In New York he had spent a lot of time in shooting galleries. In the woods he had hunted, tracked, and enjoyed fistic
battles with rugged mountaineers. He had practiced drawing
in front of a mirror until he was greased lightning with a gun.
The shooting galleries gave him the marksmanship, and in
the woods he had learned to become even more of a tracker
than he had learned to be in the brush country of his father,
to which he returned for his summer vacations.

Moreover, he had been listening as well as talking. Since
he had been here on the Slash Seven, Gar Mullins had several times mentioned the rough country of Tierra Blanca
Canyon as a likely hangout for the rustlers. It was believed
they disposed of many stolen cattle in the mining camps to
the north, having a steady market for beef at Victorio and in
the vicinity.

Tom West loved his sister and had a deep affection for his
friendly, likable nephew, but Johnny was well aware that Tom
also considered him a guest, and not a hand. Mullins could
have told him the kid was both a roper and a rider, and had a
lot of cow savvy, but Mullins rarely talked and never volun-
teered anything.

Johnny naturally liked to be accepted as an equal of the
others, and it irritated him that his uncle treated him like a
visiting tenderfoot. And because he was irked, Johnny decided to show them, once and for all.

Bert Ramsey's irritable toleration of him angered him.

Once he left Mullins, when the cattle were out of the
quicksand, he headed across the country through Sibley Gap.
He passed through the gap at sundown and made camp at a
spring a few miles beyond. It could be no more than seven or
eight miles farther to the canyon of which Mullins had
talked, for he was already on the Tierra Blanca.

At daybreak he was riding. On a sudden inspiration, he
swung north and cut over into the trail for Victorio.

The mining town had the reputation of being a rugged spot, and intended to keep it. The town was named after the Apache chieftain who had several times taken a bad whipping trying to capture the place. Several thousand miners, gamblers, gunmen, and outlaws made the place a good one to steer clear of. But Johnny Lyle had not forgotten the talk about Slash Seven beefs being sold there by rustlers.

———

JOHNNY SWUNG DOWN from his horse in front of the Gold Pan Restaurant and walked back to a corral where he saw several beef hides hanging. The brand was Seven Seventy-seven, but when he turned the hide over he could see it had been changed from a Slash Seven.

"Hey!" A bellow from the door brought his head up. "Git away from those hides!"

The man was big. He had shoulders like the top of an upright piano and a seamed and battered face.

Johnny walked to the next hide and the next while the man watched. Of the five fresh hides, three of them were Slash Sevens. He turned just in time to meet the rushing butcher.

Butch Jensen was big, but he was no mean rough-and-tumble scrapper. This cowhand was going to learn a thing or two.

"I told you to get away!" he shouted angrily, and drew back his fist.

That was his first mistake, for Johnny had learned a little about fighting while in New York. One thing was to hit from where your fist was. Johnny's fist was rubbing his chin when Jensen drew his fist back, and Johnny punched straight and hard, stepping in with the left.

The punch was short, wicked, and explosive. Jensen's lips mashed under hard knuckles and his hands came up. As they lifted, Johnny turned on the ball of his left foot and the toe of his right, and whipped a wicked right uppercut into Jensen's huge stomach.

Butch gasped, and then Johnny hit him with both hands and he went down. Coolly, Johnny waited for him to get up. And he got up, which made his second mistake. He got up and lunged, head down. A straight left took him over the eyebrow, ripping a gash, and a right uppercut broke his nose. And then Johnny Lyle went to work. What followed was short, interesting, and bloody. When it was over Johnny stood back.

"Now," he said, "get up and pay me sixty dollars for three Slash Seven steers."

"Sixty!" Butch Jensen spluttered. "Steers are going for twelve, fifteen dollars!"

"The steers you butchered are going at twenty dollars," Johnny replied calmly. "If I ever find another hide around here, the price will be thirty dollars."

He turned away, but when he had taken three steps, he stopped. There was a good crowd around, and Johnny was young. This chance was too good to miss.

"You tell Hook Lacey," he said, "that if he ever rustles another head of Slash Seven stock I'll personally come after him!"

Johnny Lyle swaggered just a little as he walked into the Gold Pan and ordered a meal.

Yet as he was eating he began to get red around the ears. It had been a foolish thing to do, talking like that. Folks would think he was full of hot air.

Then he looked up into a pair of wide blue eyes. "Your order, sir?"

Two days later Chuck Allen rode up to the ranch house and swung down. Bert Ramsey got up hastily from his chair.

"Chuck," he asked eagerly, "you see him?"

Chuck shook his head. "No," he said, "I ain't seen him, but I seen his trail. You better grab yourself a bronc, Bert, and start fogging it for the border. That kid's really started something."

The door opened and Tom West came out. "What's up?" he demanded. His face was gray with worry. "Confound it, what's the matter with these hands? Two days now I've had you all ridin' to find that kid, and you can't turn up a clue! Can't you blind bats even find a tenderfoot kid?"

Chuck grew a little red around the ears, but his eyes twinkled as he looked at Bert out of the corner of his eyes. "I crossed his trail, boss, and she's some trail, believe you me!"

West shoved Bert aside. "Don't stand there like a slab-sided jackass! What happened? Where is he?"

———

CHUCK WAS TAKING his time. "Well," he said, "he *was* in Victorio. He rode in there the morning after he left the ranch. He found a couple of Slash Seven hides hanging on Butch Jensen's fence. They'd been burned over into Seven Seventy-sevens, but he found 'em, and then Butch Jensen found him."

"Oh, Lord!" West paled. "If that big brute hurt that kid, I'll kill him!"

"You won't need no war paint," Chuck said, aggravatingly slow, "because the kid took Butch to a swell three-sided whipping. Folks say Johnny just lit all over him, swinging in every direction. He whipped Butch to a frazzle!"

"Chuck," Bert burst out, "you're crazy! Why, that kid couldn't whip one side of—"

"But he did," Chuck interrupted. "He not only beat Butch up, but he made him pay for three head at twenty dollars a head. He further told him that the next hide he found on Butch's fence would cost him thirty dollars."

West swallowed. "And Butch took it?"

"Boss, if you'd seen Butch you'd not ask that question. Butch took everything the kid could throw, which was plenty. Butch looks like he'd crawled face-first into a den of wild-cats. But that ain't all."

They waited, staring at Chuck. He rolled a smoke, taking his time.

"He told everybody who was listening," he finally said, "and probably three or four of 'em was friends of Lacey, that if Hook rustled one more head of our stock, he was going to attend to him personal."

West groaned and Bert Ramsey swallowed. But Chuck was not through.

"Then the kid goes into the Gold Pan. He ain't there more'n thirty minutes before he has that little blond peacherino crazy about him. Mary, she's so crazy about that kid she can't even get her orders straight."

"Chuck," West demanded, "where's Johnny now? If you know, tell me!"

Chuck Allen grew sober. "That's the trouble, boss. I don't know. But when he left Victorio he headed back into the mountains. And that was yesterday afternoon."

Bert Ramsey's face was pale. He liked his job on the Slash Seven and knew West was quite capable of firing him as he had promised. Moreover, he was genuinely worried. That he had considered the boss's nephew a nuisance was true, but anybody who could whip Butch Jensen, and who could collect for stolen cattle, was no tenderfoot, but a man to ride the river with. But to ride into the hills after Hook Lacey, after whipping Jensen, threatening Hook, and then walking off with the girl Hook wanted—that was insanity.

Whipping Jensen was something, but Hook Lacey wouldn't use his fists. He would use a gun, and he had killed seven men, at least. And he would have plenty of help.

West straightened. "Bert," he said harshly, "you get Gar Mullins, Monty Reagan, and Bucky McCann and ride after that kid. And don't come back without him!"

Ramsey nodded. "Yes, sir," he said. "I sure will get him."

"How about me?" Chuck asked. "Can I go, too?"

At the very hour the little cavalcade was leaving the ranch, Johnny Lyle was lying on a ridge looking down into the upper part of the Tierra Blanca Canyon. A thin trail of smoke was lifting from the canyon, and he could see approximately where the camp was. He lay high on the rugged side of Seven Brothers Mountain, with the camp almost fifteen hundred feet below.

"All right, boy," he told himself, "you've made your brags. Now what are you going to do?"

North of the camp the canyon ran due north and south, but just below it took a sharp bend to the west, although a minor canyon trailed off south for a short distance in less rugged country. Their hideout, Johnny could see, was well chosen. There was obviously a spring, judging from the way their camp was located and the looks of the trees and brush, and there was a way out up the canyon to the north.

On the south, they could swing west around the bend. Johnny could see that this trail branched, and the branch beyond also branched. In taking any route they were well covered, with plenty of chance of a getaway unseen, or for defense if they so desired.

———

YET IF THEY had to ride north up the canyon there was no way out for several miles. With a posse closing in from the south, one man could stop their escape to the north. Their camp at the spring, however, was so situated that it was nearly impossible for them to be stopped from going south by anything less than a large posse. It was fairly obvious, though, that if they were attacked they would ride south.

The idea that came to him was the wildest kind of a gamble, but he decided to take the chance, for there was a possibility that it might work. To plan ahead was impossible. All he could do was start the ball rolling and take advantage of what opportunity offered.

Mounting his horse, he rode along a bench of Seven Brothers and descended the mountain on the southwest. In the canyon to the west he hastily gathered sticks and built a fire, laying a foundation of crossed dry sticks of some size, gathered from canyon driftwood and arranged in such a way as to burn for some time. The fire was built among rocks and on dry sand so there was no way for it to spread, and no way for it to be seen, though the rising smoke would be visible.

Circling farther south and east, he built three more fires. His hope was that the smoke from all of them would be seen by the outlaws, who would deduce that a posse, having approached during the night, now was preparing breakfast, with every way out blocked. If they decided this, and without a careful scouting expedition, which would consume time, the outlaws would surely retreat up the canyon to the north.

Johnny Lyle worked fast and he worked hard, adding a few sticks of green wood to increase the smoke. When his last fire had been built, he mounted again and rode north on the

east side of Stoner Mountain. Now the mountain was between him and the outlaws and he had no idea of what they
would do. His gamble was that by riding north, he could hit
the canyon of the Tierra Blanca after it swung east, and intercept the escaping outlaws.

He rode swiftly, aware that he could travel faster than they,
but with no idea whether or not they had seen his fires and
were moving. His first idea was to ride into the bottom of the
canyon and meet them face-to-face, but Hook Lacey was a
rugged character, as were his men, and the chances were they
would elect to fight. He chose the safer way and crawled
down among some rocks.

An hour had passed before they appeared. He knew none
of them, but rightly guessed the swarthy man with the hook
nose was Lacey. He let them get within thirty yards, then
yelled:

"All right, boys! Drop your guns and get your hands up!
We've got you bottled!"

There was an instant of frozen silence, then Lacey's gun
leaped to his hand. He let out a wild yell and the riders
charged right up the slope and at Johnny Lyle.

Suddenly panic-stricken, Johnny got off a quick shot that
burned the hindquarters of Lacey's plunging horse and hit
the pommel of the rider following him. Glancing off, it
ripped the following man's arm. Then the riders were right at
him.

Johnny sprang aside, working the lever of his Winchester,
but they were too close. Wildly he grabbed iron, and then
took a wicked blow on the skull from a clubbed six-shooter.
He went down, stunned but not out, and managed a quick
shot with his six-gun that dropped a man. And then he was
up and running. He had only time to grab his Winchester and
dive into the rocks.

Cut off from his horse, he was in desperate straits.
It would be a matter of minutes, or even seconds, before they
would realize only one man had been shooting. Then
they would come back.

Scrambling into the rocks, he worked himself higher,

striving for a vantage point. They had seen him, though, and a rifle bullet ricocheted off the rocks and whined nastily past his ear. He levered three fast shots from his rifle at the scattering riders. Then the area before him was deserted, the morning warm and still, and the air was empty.

―――――

HIS HEAD THROBBED, and when he put a hand to his skull he found that despite his protecting hat, his scalp had been split. Only the fact that the rider had been going away when he fired, and that the felt hat he was wearing was heavy, had saved him from a broken skull.

A sudden move brought a twinge. Looking down, he saw blood on the side of his shirt. Opening it, he saw that a bullet—from where he had no idea—had broken the skin along his side.

Hunkered down behind some rocks, he looked around. His position was fairly secure, though they could approach him from in front and on the right. His field of fire to the front was good, but if they ever got on the cliff across the canyon, he was finished.

What lay behind him he did not know, but the path he had taken along a ledge seemed to dwindle out on the cliff face. He had ammunition, but no water, and no food.

Tentatively he edged along, as if to move forward. A rifle shot splashed splinters in his face and he jerked back, stung.

"Boy," he said to himself, "you've played hob!"

Suddenly he saw a man race across the open in front of him and he fired a belated shot that did nothing but hurry the man. Obviously that man was heading for the cliff across the canyon. Johnny Lyle reloaded his Winchester and checked his pistol. With both loaded he was all set, and he looked behind him at the path. Then he crawled back. As he had suspected, the path dwindled out and there was no escape.

The only way out was among the boulders to his right, from where without doubt the outlaws were also approaching. His rifle ready, he crouched, waiting. Then he came up with a lunge and darted for the nearest boulders. A bullet whipped by his ear, another ricocheted from a rock behind him. Then he hit the sand sliding and scrambled at once to a second boulder.

Someone moved ahead of him, and raising himself to his knees, Johnny shucked his pistol and snapped a quick shot.

There was a brief silence, then a sudden yell and a sound of horses. Instantly there was another shout and a sound of running. Warily Johnny looked out. A stream of riders was rushing up the canyon and the outlaws were riding back down the canyon at breakneck speed.

Carefully, he got to his feet. Gar Mullins was first to see him and he yelled. The others slid to a halt. Limping a little on a bruised leg, Johnny walked toward the horsemen.

"Man," he said, "am I ever glad to see you fellers!"

Ramsey stared at him, sick with relief. "What got into you?" he demanded gruffly. "Trying to tackle that bunch by your lonesome?"

Johnny Lyle explained his fires and the idea he'd had. "Only trouble was," he said ruefully, "they rushed me instead of dropping their guns, but it might've worked!"

Gar Mullins bit off a chew and glanced at Chuck with twinkling eyes. "Had it been me, it would've worked, kid." He glanced at Bert. "Reckon we should finish it now they're on the run?"

"We better let well enough alone," Ramsey said. "If they think there's a posse down canyon, they'll hole up and make a scrap of it. We'd have to dig 'em out one by one."

"I'd rather wait and get 'em in the open," Monty Reagan said honestly. "That Lacey's no bargain." He looked with real respect at Lyle. "Johnny, I take my hat off to you. You got more nerve than me, to tackle that crowd single-handed."

Bucky McCann came up. "He got one, too," he said, gloating. "Pete Gabor's over there with a shot through the head."

"That was luck," Johnny said. "They come right at me and I just cut loose."

"Get any others?"

"Winged one, but it was a ricochet."

Gar spat. "They count," he said, chuckling a little. "We better get out of here."

CONSIDERABLY CHASTENED, JOHNNY Lyle fell in alongside of Gar and they started back. Several miles farther along, when they were riding through Sibley Gap, Gar said:

"Old Tom was fit to be tied, kid. You shouldn't ought to go off like that."

"Aw," Johnny protested, "everybody was treating me like a goose-headed tenderfoot! I got tired of it."

The week moved along slowly. Johnny Lyle's head stopped aching and his side began to heal. He rode out to the bog camp every day and worked hard. He was, Ramsey admitted, "a hand." Nothing more was said about his brush with the Lacey gang except for a brief comment by Bucky McCann.

There was talk of a large band of Mexican bandits raiding over the border.

"Shucks," Bucky said carelessly, "nothing to worry about! If they get too rambunctious we'll sic Johnny at 'em! That'll learn 'em!"

But Johnny Lyle was no longer merely the boss's nephew. He was a hand, and he was treated with respect, and given rough friendship.

Nothing more was heard of Lacey. The story had gone around, losing nothing in the telling. The hands of the Slash Seven cow crowd found the story too good to keep. A kid from the Slash Seven, they said, had run Lacey all over the rocks, Lacey and all of his outfit.

Hook Lacey heard the story and flushed with anger. When he thought of the flight of his gang up the canyon from a lot of untended fires, and then their meeting with the Lyle kid, who single-handed not only had stood them off but had killed one man and wounded another, his face burned. If there was one thing he vowed to do, it was to get Johnny Lyle.

Nobody had any actual evidence on Lacey. He was a known rustler, but it had not been proved. Consequently, Lacey showed up around Victorio whenever he was in the mood. And he seemed to be in the mood a great deal after the scrap in Tierra Blanca Canyon. The payoff came suddenly and unexpectedly.

Gar Mullins had orders to ride to Victorio and check to see if a shipment of ammunition and equipment intended for the Slash Seven had arrived. Monty Reagan was to go along, but Monty didn't return from the bog camp in time, so Lyle asked his uncle if he could go.

Reluctantly, Tom West told him to go ahead. "But don't you go asking for trouble!" he said irritably. But in his voice was an underlying note of pride, too. After all, he admitted, the kid came of fighting stock. "If anybody braces you, that's different!"

Victorio was basking in a warm morning sun when the two cowhands rode into the street. Tying up at the Gold Pan, Johnny left Gar to check on the supplies while he went to get a piece of apple pie. Not that he was fooling Gar, or even himself. It was that blonde behind the counter that he wanted to see.

Hook Lacey was drinking coffee when Johnny entered. Lacey looked up, then set his cup down hard, almost spilling the coffee.

Mary smiled quickly at Johnny, then threw a frightened look at Lacey.

"Hello, Johnny," she said, her voice almost failing her. "I—I didn't expect you."

Johnny was wary. He had recognized Lacey at once, but his uncle had said he wasn't to look for trouble.

"Got any apple pie?" he asked.

She placed a thick piece before him, then filled a cup with coffee. Johnny grinned at her and began to eat. "Mmm!" he said, liking the pie. "You make this?"

"No, my mother did."

"She sure makes good pie!" Johnny was enthusiastic. "I've got to get over here more often!"

"Surprised they let you get away from home," Lacey said, "but I see you brought a nursemaid with you."

Now, Tom West had advised Johnny to keep out of trouble, and Johnny, an engaging and easygoing fellow, intended to do just that, up to a point. This was the point.

"I didn't need a nursemaid over on the Tierra Blanca," he

said cheerfully. "From the way you hightailed over them rocks, I figured it was you needed one!"

Lacey's face flamed. He came off the bench, his face dark with anger. "Why, you—"

Johnny looked around at him. "Better not start anything," he said. "You ain't got a gang with you."

Lacey was in a quandary. Obviously the girl was more friendly to Johnny than to him. That meant that he could expect no help from her should she be called on to give testimony following a killing. If he drew first he was a gone gosling, for he knew enough about old Tom West to know the Slash Seven outfit would never stop hunting if this kid was killed in anything but a fair fight. And the kid wasn't even on his feet.

"Listen!" he said harshly. "You get out of town! If you're in this town one hour from now, I'll kill you!"

Slamming down a coin on the counter, he strode from the restaurant.

"Oh, Johnny!" Mary's face was white and frightened. "Don't stay here! Go now! I'll tell Gar where you are. Please go!"

"Go?" Johnny was feeling a fluttering in his stomach, but it angered him that Mary should feel he had to leave. "I will not go! I'll run *him* out of town!"

Despite her pleading, he turned to the door and walked outside. Gar Mullins was nowhere in sight. Neither was Lacey. But a tall, stooped man with his arm in a sling stood across the street, and Johnny Lyle guessed at once that he was a lookout, that here was the man he had winged in the canyon fight. And winged though the man was, it was his left arm, and his gun hung under his right hand.

Johnny Lyle hesitated. Cool common sense told him that it would be better to leave. Actually, Uncle Tom and the boys all knew he had nerve enough, and it was no cowardice to dodge a shoot-out with a killer like Hook Lacey. The boys had agreed they wouldn't want to tangle with him.

Just the same, Johnny doubted that any one of them would dodge a scrap if it came to that. And all his Texas blood and training rebelled against the idea of being run out of town.

Besides, there was Mary. It would look like he was a pure D coward to run out now.

Yet what was the alternative? Within an hour, Hook Lacey would come hunting him. Hook would choose the ground, place, and time of meeting. And Hook was no fool. He knew all the tricks.

What, then, to do?

The only thing, Johnny Lyle decided, was to meet Lacey first. To hunt the outlaw down and force him into a fight before he was ready. There was nothing wrong with using strategy, with using a trick. Many gunfighters had done it. Billy the Kid had done it against the would-be killer Joe Grant. Wes Hardin had used many a device.

Yet what to do? And where? Johnny Lyle turned toward the corral with a sudden idea in mind. Suppose he could appear to have left town? Wouldn't that lookout go to Hook with the news? Then he could come back, ease up to Lacey suddenly, and call him, then draw.

Gar Mullins saw Johnny walking toward the corral, then he spotted the lookout. Mullins intercepted Johnny just as he stepped into the saddle.

"What's up, kid? You in trouble?"

Briefly Johnny explained. Gar listened and, much to Johnny's relief, registered no protest. "All right, kid. You got it to do if you stay in this country, and your idea's a good one. You ever been in a shoot-out before?"

"No, I sure haven't."

"Now, look. You draw natural, see? Don't pay no mind to being faster'n he is. Chances are you ain't anywheres close to that. You figure on getting that first shot right where it matters, you hear? Shoot him in the body, right in the middle. No matter what happens, hit him with the first shot, you hear me?"

"Yeah."

———

JOHNNY FELT SICK at his stomach and his mouth was dry, his heart pounding.

"I'll handle that lookout, so don't pay him no mind." Gar looked up. "You a good shot, Johnny?"

"On a target I can put five shots in a playing card."

"That's all right, but this card'll be shooting back. But don't you worry. You choose your own spot for it."

"Wait!" Johnny had an idea. "Listen, you have somebody get word to him that Butch Jensen wants to see him. I'll be across the street at the wagon yard. When he comes up, I'll step out."

He rode swiftly out of town. Glancing back, he saw the lookout watching. Gar Mullins put a pack behind his own saddle and apparently readied his horse for the trail. Then he walked back down the street.

He was just opposite the wagon yard when he saw the lookout stop on a street corner, looking at him. At the same instant, Hook Lacey stepped from behind a wagon. Across the street was Webb Foster, another of the Lacey crowd. There was no mistaking their purpose, and they had him boxed!

Gar Mullins was thirty-eight, accounted an old man on the frontier, and he had seen and taken part in some wicked gun battles. Yet now he saw his position clearly. This was it, and he wasn't going to get out of this one. If Johnny had been with him—but Johnny wouldn't be in position for another ten minutes.

Hook Lacey was smiling. "You were in the canyon the other day, Gar," he said triumphantly. "Now you'll see what it's like. We're going to kill you, Gar. Then we'll follow that kid and get him. You ain't got a chance, Gar."

Mullins knew it, yet with a little time, even a minute, he might have.

"Plannin' on wiping out the Slash Seven, Hook?" he drawled. "That's what you'll have to do if you kill that kid. He's the old man's nephew."

"Ain't you worried about yourself, Gar?" Lacey sneered. "Or are you just wet-nursing that kid?"

Gar's seamed and hard face was set. His eyes flickered to the lookout, whose hand hovered only an inch above his gun. And to Webb, with his thumb hooked in his belt. There was no use waiting. It would be minutes before the kid would be set.

And then the kid's voice sounded, sharp and clear.

"I'll take Lacey, Gar! *Get that lookout!*"

Hook Lacey whipped around, drawing as he turned. Johnny Lyle, who had left his horse and hurried right back, grabbed for his gun. He saw the big, hard-faced man before him, saw him clear and sharp. Saw his hand flashing down, saw the broken button on his shirtfront, saw the Bull Durham tag from his pocket, saw the big gun come up. But his own gun was rising, too.

The sudden voice, the turn, all conspired to throw Lacey off, yet he had drawn fast and it was with shock that he saw the kid's gun was only a breath slower. It was that which got him, for he saw that gun rising and he shot too quick. The bullet tugged at Johnny's shirt collar, and then Johnny, with that broken button before his eyes, fired.

Two shots, with a tiny but definite space between them, and then Johnny looked past Lacey at the gun exploding in Webb Foster's hands. He fired just as Gar Mullins swung his gun to Webb. Foster's shot glanced off the iron rim of a wagon wheel just as Gar's bullet crossed Johnny's in Webb Foster's body.

The outlaw crumpled slowly, grabbed at the porch awning, then fell off into the street.

———

JOHNNY STOOD VERY still. His eyes went to the lookout, who was on his hands and knees on the ground, blood dripping in great splashes from his body. Then they went to Hook Lacey. The broken button was gone, and there was an edge cut from the tobacco tag. Hook Lacey was through, his chips all cashed. He had stolen his last horse.

Gar Mullins looked at Johnny Lyle and grinned weakly. "Kid," he said softly, walking toward him, hand outstretched, "we make a team. Here on out, it's saddle partners, hey?"

"Sure, Gar." Johnny did not look again at Lacey. He looked into the once bleak blue eyes of Mullins. "I ride better with a partner. You got that stuff for the ranch?"

"Yeah."

"Then if you'll pick up my horse in the willows, yonder, I'll say good-bye to Mary. We'd best be getting back. Uncle Tom'll be worried."

Gar Mullins chuckled, walking across the street, arm in arm with Johnny.

"Well, he needn't be," Gar said. "He needn't be."

HOME IN THE VALLEY

S TEVE MEHAN PLACED the folded newspaper beside
his plate and watched the waiter pour his coffee. He was
filled with that warm, expansive glow that comes only from
a job well done, and he felt he had just cause to feel it.

Jake Hitson, the moneylending rancher from down at the
end of Pahute Valley, had sneered when he heard of the attempt, and the ranchers had shaken their heads doubtfully
when Steve first told them of his plan. They had agreed only
because there was no alternative. He had proposed to drive a
herd of cattle from the Nevada range to California in the
dead of winter!

To the north the passes were blocked with snow, and to the
south lay miles of trackless and almost waterless desert. Yet
they had been obligated to repay the money Hitson had
loaned them by the first day of March or lose their ranches to
him. It had been a pitifully small amount when all was considered, yet Hitson had held their notes, and he had intended
to have their range.

Months before, returning to Nevada, Steve Mehan had
scouted the route. The gold rush was in full swing, people
were crowding into California, and there was a demand for
beef. As a boy he had packed and freighted over most of
the trails and knew them well, so finally the ranchers had
given in.

The drive had been a success. With surprisingly few losses
he had driven the herd into central California and had sold
out, a few head here and a few there, and the prices had been
good.

The five ranchers of Pahute Valley who had trusted their
cattle to him were safe. Twenty thousand dollars in fifty-

dollar gold slugs had been placed on deposit in Dake & Company's bank here in Sacramento City.

With a smile, he lifted his coffee cup. Then, as a shadow darkened his table, he glanced up to see Jake Hitson.

The man dropped into a chair opposite him, and there was a triumphant light in his eyes that made Steve suddenly wary. Yet with the gold in the bank there was nothing to make him apprehensive.

"Well, yuh think yuh've done it, don't yuh?" Hitson's voice was malicious. "Yuh think yuh've stopped me? Yuh've played the hero in front of Betty Bruce, and the ranchers will welcome yuh back with open arms. Yuh think when everything was lost you stepped in and saved the day?"

Mehan shrugged. "We've got the money to pay yuh, Jake. The five brands of the Pahute will go on. This year looks like a good one, and we can drive more cattle over the route I took this time, so they'll make it now. And that in spite of all the bad years and the rustlin' of yore friends."

HITSON CHUCKLED. HE was a big man with straw-colored brows and a flat red face. From one small spread down there at the end of the Pahute he had expanded to take in a fair portion of the valley. The methods he had used would not bear examination, and strange cattle had continued to flow into the valley, enlarging his herds. Many of the brands were open to question. The hard years and losses due to cold or drouth did not affect him, because he kept adding to his herds from other sources.

During the bad years he had loaned money, and his money had been the only help available. The fact that he was a man disliked for his arrogant manner and his crooked connections made the matter only the more serious.

Hitson grinned with malice. "Read yore paper yet, Mehan? If yuh want to spoil yore breakfast, turn to page three."

Steve Mehan's dark eyes held the small blue ones of Hitson, and he felt something sick and empty in his stomach. Only bad news for him could give Hitson the satisfaction he was so obviously feeling.

Yet even as Steve opened the paper, a man bent over the table next to him.

"Heard the news?" he asked excitedly. "Latch and Evans banking house has failed. That means that Dake and Company are gone, too. They'll close the doors. There's already a line out there a hundred yards long and still growin'!"

Steve opened his paper slowly. The news was there for all to read. Latch & Evans had failed. The managing director had flown the coop, and only one interpretation could be put upon that. Dake & Company, always closely associated with Latch & Evans, would be caught in the collapse. February of 1855 would see the end of the five brands of Pahute Valley. It would be the end of everything he had planned, everything he wanted for Betty.

"See?" Hitson sneered, heaving himself to his feet. "Try and play hero now! I've got you and them highfalutin friends of yores where I want 'em now! I'll kick every cussed one of 'em into the trail on March first, and with pleasure! And that goes for you, Steve Mehan!"

Steve scarcely heard him. He was remembering that awful drive. The hard winds, the bitter cold, the bawling cattle. And then the desert, the Indians, the struggle to get through with the herd intact—and all to end in this. Collapse and failure. Yes, and the lives of two men had been sacrificed, the two who had been killed on the way over the trail.

Mehan remembered Chuck Farthing's words. He had gone down with a Mohave Indian's bullet in his chest.

"Get 'em through, boy. Save the old man's ranch for him. That's all I ask!"

It had been little enough for two lives. And now they were gone, for nothing.

The realization hit Steve Mehan like a blow and brought him to his feet fighting mad, his eyes blazing, his jaw set.

"I'll be eternally blasted if they have!" he exploded, though only he knew what he meant.

He started for the door, leaving his breakfast unfinished behind him, his mind working like lightning. The whole California picture lay open for him now. The news of the failure would have reached the Dake & Company branches in

Marysville and Grass Valley. And in Placerville. There was no hope there.

Portland? He stopped short, his eyes narrowed with thought. Didn't they have a branch in Portland? Of course! He remembered it well, now that he thought of it. The steamer from San Francisco would leave the next morning, and it would be carrying the news. But what if he could beat that steamer to Portland?

Going by steamer himself would be futile, for he would arrive at the same time the news did, and there would be no chance for him to get his money. Hurrying down the street, his eyes scanning the crowds for Pink Egan and Jerry Smith, punchers who had made the drive with him, he searched out every possible chance, and all that remained was that seven hundred miles of trail between Sacramento and Portland, rough, and part of it harassed by warring Modocs.

He paused, glancing around. He was a tall young man with rusty brown hair and a narrow, rather scholarly face. To the casual observer he looked like a roughly dressed frontier doctor or lawyer. Actually, he was a man bred to the saddle and the wild country.

———

OVER THE ROOFS of the buildings he could see the smoke of a steamboat. It was the stern-wheeler *Belle,* just about to leave for Knights Landing, forty-two miles upstream.

He started for the gangway, walking fast, and just as he reached it a hand caught his sleeve. He wheeled to see Pink and Jerry at his elbow.

"Hey!" Smith demanded. "Where yuh goin' so fast? We run two blocks to catch up with yuh."

Quickly, Steve explained. The riverboat tooted its whistle, and the crew started for the gangway to haul it aboard. "It's our only chance!" Steve Mehan exclaimed. "I've got to beat that steamboat from Frisco to Portland and draw my money before they get the news! Don't tell anybody where I've gone, and keep yore eyes on Hitson!"

He lunged for the gangway and raced aboard. It was foolish, it was wild, it was impossible, but it was their only chance. Grimly, he recalled what he had told Betty Bruce when he left the valley.

"I'll get them cattle over, honey, or I'll die tryin'!"

"You come back, Steve!" she had begged. "That's all I ask. We can always go somewhere and start over. We always have each other."

"I know, honey, but how about yore father? How about Pete Farthing? They're too old to start over, and the ranches are all they have. They worked like slaves, fought Indians, gave a lot in sweat and blood for their ranches. I'll not see 'em turned out now. Whatever comes, I'll make it."

As the riverboat pushed away from the dock, he glanced back. Jake Hitson was staring after him, his brow furrowed. Jake had seen him, and that was bad.

Mehan put such thoughts behind him. The boat would not take long to get to Knights Landing, and he could depend upon Knight to help him. The man had migrated from New Mexico fifteen years before, but he had known Steve's father, and they had come over the Santa Fe Trail together. From a mud-and-wattle hut on an Indian mound at the landing, he had built a land grant he got from his Mexican wife into a fine estate, and the town had been named for him.

Would Jake Hitson guess what he was attempting? If so, what could he do? The man had money, and with money one can do many things. Hitson would not stop at killing. Steve had more than a hunch that Hitson had urged the Mohaves into the attack on the cattle drive that had resulted in the death of Chuck Farthing. He had more than a hunch that the landslide that had killed Dixie Rollins had been due to more than purely natural causes. But he could prove nothing.

His only chance was to reach Portland before the news did. He was not worried about their willingness to pay him the money. The banks made a charge of one-half of one percent for all withdrawals over a thousand dollars, and it would look like easy profit to the agent at the banking and express house.

Nor was it all unfamiliar country, for Steve had spent two years punching cows on ranches, prospecting and hunting through the northern valleys, almost as far as the Oregon line.

When the *Belle* shouldered her comfortable bulk against the landing at Knights, Mehan did not wait for the gangway. He grabbed the bulwark and vaulted ashore, landing on his hands and knees.

He found Knight standing on the steps of his home, looking down toward the river.

"A hoss, Steve?" Knight repeated. "Shorest thing yuh know. What's up?"

While Steve threw a saddle on a tall chestnut, he explained briefly.

"Yuh'll never make it, boy!" Knight protested. "It's a hard drive, and the Modocs are raidin' again." He chewed on his mustache as Steve swung into the saddle. "Boy," he said, "when yuh get to the head of Grand Island, see the judge. He's an old friend of mine, and he'll let yuh have a hoss. Good luck!"

Steve wheeled the chestnut into the street and started north at a spanking trot. He kept the horse moving, and the long-legged chestnut had a liking for the trail. He moved out eagerly, seeming to catch some of the anxiety to get over the trail that filled his rider.

At the head of Grand Island, Steve swapped horses and started north again, holding grimly to the trail. There was going to be little time for rest and less time to eat. He would have to keep moving if he was going to make it. The trail over much of the country was bad, and the farther north he got toward the line, the worse it would be.

His friends on the ranches remembered him, and he repeatedly swapped horses and kept moving. The sun was setting in a rose of glory when he made his fourth change of mount near the Marysville Buttes. The purple haze of evening was gathering when he turned up the trail and lined out.

He had money with him, and he paid a bonus plus a blown horse when necessary. But the stockmen were natural allies, as were the freighters along the route, and they were always willing to help. After leaving Knights Landing he told no one his true mission, his only explanation being that he was after a thief. In a certain sense, that was exactly true.

At ten o'clock, ten hours out of Sacramento, he galloped

into the dark streets of Red Bluff. No more than five minutes later, clutching a sandwich in his hand and with a fresh horse under him, he was off again.

Darkness closed around him, and the air was cool. He had no rifle with him, only the pistol he habitually wore and plenty of ammunition.

The air was so cold that he drew his coat around him, tucking it under and around his legs. He spoke softly to the horse, and its ears twitched. It was funny about a horse—how much they would give for gentleness. There was no animal which responded so readily to good treatment, and no other animal would run itself to death for a man—except, occasionally, a dog.

The hoofs of the horse beat a pounding rhythm upon the trail, and Steve leaned forward in the saddle, hunching himself against the damp chill and to cut wind resistance. His eyes were alert, although weariness began to dull his muscles and take the drive and snap from them.

Twenty miles out of Red Bluff he glimpsed a fire shining through the trees. He slowed the horse, putting a hand on its damp neck. It was a campfire. He could see the light reflecting from the front of a covered wagon, and he heard voices speaking. He rode nearer and saw the faces of the men come around toward him.

"Who's there?" A tall man stepped around the fire with a rifle in his hand.

"Mehan, a cattleman. I'm after a thief and need a fresh hoss."

"Well, 'light and talk. Yuh won't catch him on that hoss. Damn fine animal," he added, "but yuh've shore put him over the road."

"He's got heart, that one!" Steve said, slapping the horse. "Plenty of it! Is that coffee I smell?"

The bearded man picked up the pot. "It shore is, pardner. Have some!" He poured a cupful, handed it to Steve, and then strolled over to the horse. "Shucks, with a rubdown and a blanket he'll be all right. Tell yuh what I'll do. I've got a buckskin here that'll run 'til he drops. Give me twenty to boot and he's yores."

Mehan looked up. "Done, but you throw in a couple of sandwiches."

The bearded man chuckled. "Shore will." He glanced at the saddle as Steve began stripping it from the horse. "Yuh've got no rifle?"

"No, only a pistol. I'll take my chances."

"Haven't got a rifle to spare, but I'll make yuh a deal on this." He handed Steve a four-barreled Braendlin repeating pistol. "Frankly, mister, I need money. Got my family down to Red Bluff, and I don't want to come in broke."

"How much?"

"Another twenty?"

"Shore, if yuh've got ammunition for it."

"I've got a hundred rounds. And it goes with the gun." The man dug out the ammunition. "Joe, wrap up a couple of them sandwiches for the man. Got smokin'?"

"Shore thing." Steve swung into the saddle and pocketed the extra pistol. He put the ammunition in his saddlebags. "Good luck."

"Hope yuh catch him!" the man called.

Steve touched a spur lightly to the big buckskin and was gone in a clatter of hoofs. Behind him the fire twinkled lonesomely among the dark columns of the trees, and then as he went down beyond a rise, the light faded and he was alone in the darkness, hitting the road at a fast trot.

Later, he saw the white radiance that preceded the moon, and something else—the white, gleaming peak of Mount Shasta, one of the most beautiful mountains in the world. Lifting its fourteen-thousand-foot peak above the surrounding country, it was like a throne for the Great Spirit of the Indians.

In darkness and moving fast, Steve Mehan rode down the trail into Shasta and then on to Whiskeytown.

————

A DRUNKEN MINER lurched from the side of a building and flagged him down. "No use hurryin'," he said. "It ain't true!"

"What ain't true?" Steve stared at him. "What yuh talkin' about?"

"That Whiskey Creek. Shucks, it's got water in it just like any creek!" He spat with disgust. "I come all the way down here from Yreka huntin' it!"

"You came from Yreka?" Steve grabbed his shoulder. "How's the trail? Any Indians out?"

"Trail?" The miner spat. "There ain't no trail! A loose-minded mule walked through the brush a couple of times, that's all! Indians? Modocs? Man, the woods is full of 'em! Behind ever' bush! Scalp-huntin' bucks, young and old. If yuh're headin' that way, you won't get through. Yore hair will be in a tepee 'fore two suns go down!"

He staggered off into the darkness, trying a song that dribbled away and lost itself in the noise of the creek.

Mehan walked the horse down to the creek and let him drink.

"No whiskey, but we'll settle for water, won't we, Buck?"

The creek had its name, he remembered, from an ornery mule who lost the barrel from its pack. It broke in Whiskey Creek, which promptly drew a name upon itself.

Steve Mehan started the horse again, heading for the stage station at Tower House, some ten miles up the road. The buckskin was weary but game. Ahead of him and on his right still loomed the peak of Mount Shasta, seeming large in the occasional glimpses, even at the distance that still separated them.

He almost fell from his horse at Tower House, with dawn bright in the eastern sky beyond the ragged mountains. The stage tender blinked sleepy eyes at him and then at the horse.

"Yuh've been givin' him blazes," he said. "In a mite of hurry?"

"After a thief," mumbled Steve.

The man scratched his grizzled chin. "He must be a goin' son of a gun," he commented whimsically. "Want anything?"

"Breakfast and a fresh hoss."

"Easy done. Yuh ain't figurin' on ridin' north, are yuh? Better change yore plans if yuh are, because the Modocs are out and they're in a killin' mood. No trail north of here, yuh know."

With a quick breakfast and what must have been a gallon of coffee under his belt, Steve Mehan swung into the saddle and started once more. The new horse was a gray and built for the trail. Steve was sodden with weariness, and at every moment his lids fluttered and started to close. But now, for a while at least, he dared not close them.

Across Clear Creek he rode into the uplands where no wagon road had ever been started. It was a rugged country, but one he remembered from the past, and he wove around among the trees, following the thread of what might have been a trail. Into a labyrinth of canyons he rode, following the vague trail up the bottom of a gorge, now in the water, then out of it. Then he climbed a steep trail out of the gorge and headed out across the long rolling swell of a grass-covered mountainside.

The air was much colder now, and there was an occasional flurry of snow. At times he clung to the saddle horn, letting the horse find his own trail, just so that trail was north. He rode into the heavily forested sides of the Trinity Mountains, losing the trail once in the dimness under the tall firs and tamaracks, but keeping on his northern route. Eventually he again hit what must have been the trail.

His body ached, and he fought to keep his eyelids open. Once he dismounted and walked for several miles to keep himself awake and to give the horse a slight rest. Then he was back in the saddle and riding once more.

Behind him somewhere was Jake Hitson. Jake, he knew well, would not give up easily. If he guessed what Mehan was attempting he would stop at nothing to prevent it. And yet there was no way of preventing it unless he came north with the boat and reached Portland before him. And that would do no good, for if the boat got to Portland before him, the news would be there, and nothing Hitson could do would be any worse than the arrival of that news.

Egan and Smith would have their eyes on Jake Hitson, but he might find some means of getting away. Certainly, Steve thought grimly, nothing on horseback was going to catch him now.

The wind grew still colder and howled mournfully under the dark, needled trees. He shivered and hunched his shoulders against the wind. Once, half asleep, he almost fell from the horse when the gray shied at a fleeing rabbit.

As yet there were no Indians. He peered ahead across the bleak and forbidding countryside, but it was empty. And then, not long later, he turned down a well-marked trail to Trinity Creek.

———

HE SWUNG DOWN in front of a log bunkhouse. A miner was at the door.

"A hoss?" The miner chuckled. "Stranger, yuh're shore out of luck! There ain't a hoss hereabouts yuh could get for love or money!"

Steve Mehan sagged against the building. "Mister," he mumbled, "I've just got to get a hoss. I've got to!"

"Sorry, son. There just ain't none. Nobody in town would give up his hoss right now, and they are mighty scarce at that! Yuh'd better come in and have some coffee."

Steve stripped his saddle and bridle from his horse and walked into the house. He almost fell into a chair. Several miners playing cards looked up. "Amigo," one of them said, "yuh'd better lay off that stuff."

Mehan's head came up heavily, and he peered at the speaker, a blond giant in a red-checked shirt.

"I haven't slept since I left Sacramento," he said. "Been in the saddle ever since."

"Sacramento?" The young man stared. "You must be crazy!"

"He's chasin a thief," said the miner Steve had first seen. He was bringing Steve a cup of coffee. "I'd want a man awful bad before I rode like that."

"I got to beat the steamer to Portland," Steve said. It was a lie in a way, but actually the truth. "If I don't the fellow will get away with fifteen thousand dollars!"

"Fifteen thou—" The young man laid down his hand. "Brother," he said emphatically, "I'd ride, too!"

Steve gulped the coffee and lurched to his feet.

"Got to find a hoss," he said and lunged outside.

It took him less than a half hour to prove to himself that it was an impossibility. Nobody would even consider selling a horse, and his own was in bad shape.

"Not a chance!" they told him. "A man without a hoss in this country is through! No way in or out but on a hoss, and not an extry in town!"

He walked back to the stable. One look at his own horse told him the animal was through. There was no chance to go farther with it. No matter what he might do, the poor creature could stagger no more than a few miles. It would be killing a good horse to no purpose. Disgusted and discouraged, numbed with weariness, he stood in the cold wind, rubbing his grizzled chin with a fumbling hand.

So this was the end. After all his effort, the drive over the mountains and desert, the long struggle to sell out, and then this ride, and all for nothing. Back there in the Pahute the people he had left behind would be trusting him, keeping their faith. For no matter how much they were sure he would fail, their hopes must go with him. And now he had failed.

Wearily he staggered into the bunkhouse and dropped into his chair. He fumbled with the coffeepot and succeeded in pouring out a cupful. His legs and feet felt numb, and he had never realized a man could be so utterly, completely tired.

The young man in the checkered shirt looked around from his poker game.

"No luck, eh? Yuh've come a long way to lose now."

Steve nodded bitterly. "That money belongs to my friends as well as me," he said. "That's the worst of it."

The blond young fellow laid down his hand and pulled in the chips. Then he picked up his pipe.

"My sorrel out there in the barn," he said, "is the best hoss on the Trinity. You take it and go, but man, yuh'd better get yoreself some rest at Scott Valley. Yuh'll die."

Mehan lunged to his feet, hope flooding the weariness from his body.

"How much?" he demanded, reaching for his pocket.

"Nothin'," the fellow said. "Only if yuh catch that thief, bring him back on my hoss, and I'll help yuh hang him. I promise yuh."

Steve hesitated. "What about the hoss?"

"Bring him back when yuh come south," the fellow said, "and take care of him. He'll never let yuh down."

Steve Mehan rode out of Trinity Creek ten minutes later, and the sorrel took to the trail as if he knew all that was at stake, and pressed on eagerly for Scott Valley.

The cold was increasing as Steve Mehan rode farther north and the wind was raw, spitting with rain that seemed to be changing to snow. Head hunched behind the collar of his buffalo coat, Steve pushed on, talking low to the horse, whose ears twitched a response and who kept going, alternating between a fast walk and a swinging, space-eating trot.

Six hours out of Trinity Creek, Steve Mehan rode into Scott Valley.

The stage tender took one look at him and waved him to a bunk.

"Hit it, stranger," he said. "I'll care for yore hoss!"

Stumbling through a fog of exhaustion, Steve made the bunk and dropped into its softness. . . .

STEVE MEHAN OPENED his eyes suddenly, with the bright sunlight in his face. He glanced at his watch. It was noon.

Lunging to his feet, he pulled on his boots, which somebody had removed without awakening him, and reached for his coat. The heavyset red-haired stage tender walked in and glanced at him.

"See yuh've got Joe Chalmers's hoss," he remarked, his thumbs in his belt. "How come?"

Steve looked up. "Chasin' a thief. He let me have it."

"I know Chalmers. He wouldn't let Moses have this hoss to lead the Israelites out of Egypt. Not him. Yuh've got some explainin' to do, stranger."

"I said he loaned me the hoss," Steve said grimly. "I'm

leavin' him with you and I want to buy another to go on with. What have yuh got?"

Red was dubious. "Don't reckon I should sell yuh one. Looks mighty funny to me, you havin' Joe's hoss. Is Joe all right?"

"Well," Steve said wearily, "he was just collecting a pot levied by three treys when I talked to him, so I reckon he'll make out."

Red chuckled. "He's a poker-playin' man, that one! Good man, too." He hesitated and then shrugged. "All right. There's a blaze-faced black in the stable yuh can have for fifty dollars. Good horse, too. Better eat somethin'."

He put food on the table, and Steve ate too rapidly. He gulped some coffee, and then Red came out with a pint of whiskey.

"Stick this in yore pocket, stranger. Might come in handy."

"Thanks." Mehan wiped his mouth and got to his feet. He felt better, and he walked to the door.

"Yuh ain't got a rifle?" Red was frankly incredulous. "The Modocs will get yuh shore."

"Haven't seen hide nor hair of one yet!" Steve said, smiling. "I'm beginnin' to think they've all gone east for the winter."

"Don't you think it!" Red slipped a bridle on the black while Steve cinched up the saddle. "They are out, and things up Oregon way are bad off. They shore raised ructions up around Grave Creek, and all the country around the Klamath and the Rogue is harassed by 'em."

Somewhere out at sea the steamer would be plowing over the gray sea toward Astoria and the mouth of the Columbia. The trip from there up to the Willamette and Portland would not take long.

The black left town at a fast lope and held it. The horse was good, no question about it. Beyond Callahan's, Steve hit the old Applegate wagon trail and found the going somewhat better and pushed on. Just seventy hours out from Knights Landing he rode into Yreka.

After a quick meal, a drink, and a fresh horse, he mounted and headed out of town for the Oregon line. He rode through

Humbug City and Hawkinsville without a stop and followed a winding trail up the gorge of the Shasta.

Once, after climbing the long slope north of the Klamath, he glimpsed a party of Indians some distance away. They sighted him, for they turned their horses his way, but he rode on, holding his pace, and crossed Hungry Creek and left behind him the cairn that marked the boundary line of Oregon. He turned away from the trail then and headed into the back-country, trying a cutoff for Bear Creek and the village of Jacksonville. Somewhere, he lost the Indians.

He pushed on, and now the rain that had been falling intermittently turned to snow. It began to fall thick and fast. He was riding out of the trees when on the white-flecked earth before him he saw a moccasin track with earth just tumbling into it from the edge.

Instantly he whipped his horse around and touched spurs to its flanks. The startled animal gave a great bound, and at the same instant a shot whipped by where he had been only a moment before. Then he was charging through brush, and the horse was dodging among the trees.

An Indian sprang from behind a rock and lifted a rifle. Steve drew and fired. The Indian threw his rifle away and rolled over on the ground, moaning.

Wild yells chorused behind him, and a shot cut the branches overhead. He fired again and then again.

Stowing the Smith & Wesson away, he whipped out the four-barreled Braendlin. Holding it ready, he charged out of the brush and headed across the open country. Behind him the Modocs were coming fast. His horse was quick and alert, and he swung it around a grove of trees and down into a gully. Racing along the bottom, he hit a small stream and began walking the horse carefully upstream. After making a half mile, he rode out again and took to the timber, reloading his other pistol.

Swapping horses at every chance, he pushed on. One hundred and forty-three hours out of Knights Landing, he rode into Portland. He had covered six hundred and fifty-five miles. He swung down and turned to the stable hand.

"That steamer in from Frisco?"

"Heard her whistle," said the man. "She's comin' up the river now."

But Steve had turned and was running fast.

———

THE AGENT FOR the banking express company looked up and blinked when Steve Mehan lurched through the door.

"I'm buying cattle," Steve told him, "and need some money. Can you honor a certificate of deposit for me?"

"Let's see her."

Steve handed him the order and shifted restlessly. The man eyed the order for a long time and then turned it over and studied the back. Finally, when Steve was almost beside himself with impatience, the agent looked up over his glasses at the bearded, hollow-eyed young man. "Reckon I can," he said. "Of course there's the deduction of one-half of one percent for all amounts over a thousand dollars."

"Pay me," Steve said.

He leaned over the desk, and suddenly the deep-toned blast of the steamer's whistle rang through the room. The agent was putting stacks of gold on the table. He looked up.

"Well, what do you know? That's the steamer in from Portland. I reckon I better see about—"

Whatever he was going to see about, Steve never discovered, for as the agent turned away, Steve reached out and collared him. "Pay me!" he said sharply. "Pay me now!"

The agent shrugged. "Well, all right! No need to get all fussed about it. Plenty of time."

He put out stacks of gold. Mentally, Steve calculated the amount. When it was all there, he swept it into a sack—almost fifty pounds of gold. He slung the sack over his shoulder and turned toward the door.

A gun boomed, announcing the arrival of the steamer, as he stepped out into the street. Four men were racing up the street from the dock, and the man in the lead was Jake Hitson!

Hitson skidded to a halt when he saw Steve Mehan, and his face went dark with angry blood. The blue eyes frosted and he stood wide legged, staring at the man who had beaten him to Portland.

"So!" His voice was a roar that turned the startled townspeople around. "Beat me here, did yuh? Got yore money, have yuh?" He seemed unable to absorb the fact that he was beaten, that Mehan had made it through.

"Just so yuh won't kick anybody out of his home, Jake," Steve said quietly, "and I hope that don't hurt too much!"

The small man in the black suit had gone around them and into the express company office. The other men were Pink Egan and a swarthy-faced man who was obviously a friend of Hitson's.

Hitson lowered his head. The fury seemed to go out of him as he stood there in the street with a soft rain falling over them.

"Yuh won't get back there," he said in a dead, flat voice. "Yuh done it, all right, but yuh'll never play the hero in Pahute, because I'm goin' to kill yuh!"

"Like yuh killed Dixie and Chuck?" challenged Steve. "Yuh did, yuh know. Yuh started that landslide and the Mohaves."

Hitson made no reply. He merely stood there, a huge bull of a man, his frosty eyes bright and hard under the corn-silk eyebrows.

Suddenly his hand swept down.

When Steve had first sighted the man, he had lowered the sack of gold to the street. Now he swept his coat back and grabbed for his own gun. He was no gunfighter, and the glimpse of flashing speed from Hitson made something go sick within him, but his gun came up and he fired.

Hitson's gun was already flaming, and even as Steve pulled the trigger on his own gun, a bullet from Hitson's pistol knocked the Smith & Wesson spinning into the dust! Steve sprang back and heard the hard, dry laugh of triumph from Jake Hitson's throat.

"Now I'll kill yuh!" Hitson yelled.

The killer's eyes were cold as he lifted the pistol, but even as it came level, Steve hurled himself to his knees and jerked out the four-barreled Braendlin.

Hitson swung the gun down on him, but startled by Steve's movement, he swung too fast and shot too fast. The bullet ripped through the top of Mehan's shoulder, tugging hard at the heavy coat. Then Steve fired. He fired once, twice, three times, and then heaved himself erect and stepped to one side, holding his last shot ready, his eyes careful.

———

HITSON STOOD STOCK-STILL, his eyes puzzled. Blood was trickling from his throat, and there was a slowly spreading blot of blood on his white shirt. He tried to speak, but when he opened his mouth, blood frothed there and he started to back up, frowning.

He stumbled and fell. Slowly he rolled over on his face in the street. Blood turned the gravel crimson, and rain darkened the coat on his back.

Only then did Steve Mehan look up. Pink Egan, his face cold, had a gun leveled at Hitson's companion. "You beat it," Pink said. "You get goin'!"

"Shore!" The man backed away, staring at Hitson's body. "Shore, I'm gone! I don't want no trouble! I just come along, I—"

The small man in black came out of the express office.

"Got here just in time," he said. "I'm the purser from the steamer. Got nearly a thousand out of that bank, the last anybody will get." He smiled at Mehan. "Won another thousand on your ride. I bet on you and got two to one." He chuckled. "Of course, I knew we had soldiers to put ashore at two places coming north, and that helped. I'm a sporting man, myself."

He clinked the gold in his sack and smiled, twitching his mustache with a white finger.

"Up to a point," he added, smiling again. "Only up to a point!"

RED BUTTE SHOWDOWN

GUNTHORP WAS WALKING up from the spring with two wooden buckets filled with water when he saw the boy. He was no more than thirteen, and he was running as fast as he could, his breath coming in gasps. "Hold it, son," Gunthorp called out. "What's wrong?"

The boy skidded to a halt, his eyes wide and staring, shrinking back in such fear that it chilled Gunthorp.

"They're after me!" he panted. "Kelman's men."

"What do they want?"

"They caught me and beat me—" He twisted his arm to show Gunthorp an ugly black bruise. The boy's shirt was torn and his back lacerated. Gunthorp's eyes narrowed and he felt his scalp tighten.

"Come on up to the house," he said. "We'll fix that back."

"I can't." The boy was almost beside himself with terror. "They'll catch me! Kelman's with them."

"Forget them. You come with me. No use you running off. Where would you go?" Gunthorp waved a hand at the burnt red ridges. "Nothing out there but desert. No water, nothing. You stay with me, let me handle Kelman."

He led the way to the log house and pushed open the door. A fire was burning brightly on the hearth, and the smell of coffee was in the air. "Basin's over there, son. You better get that shirt off and wash a little. I'll wash that back of yours myself, then I'll fix it up."

There was the hard pound of hoofs and the boy started as if stung. Tears of sheer terror started to his eyes, and Gunthorp looked at him with a sort of horror. He had never seen anything human so frightened.

He picked up a double-barreled shotgun and placed it beside the door. Then he opened the door and stood there, his hand on the shotgun.

———

THE RIDERS REINED in abruptly when they saw him. The nearest was a big, powerfully built man with a clean-shaven face, and as he spoke he swung his horse broadside to the house.

"Did you see a boy running by? Just a kid?"

"He didn't run by. He's here."

"Good! You've saved us some trouble, man. We've had a time running down the little thief. Joe, you go in and bring him out."

"Joe can stay right where he is," Gunthorp said. "The kid came here, and here he stays."

Kelman's eyes were level and cold. It was not yet too dark for Gunthorp to see that expression and read it. This man was cruel. He was also a killer, and he was not used to being stopped in anything he did.

"You'd better give me that boy without trouble, my man. You're new here. When you've been around longer, you'll understand better."

"I've been around long enough. You swing your horses around and get out of here."

Kelman's temper flared. "Joe! Get that kid!"

"Joe stays where he is unless he wants a skinful of buck-shot." Gunthorp lifted the shotgun with a smooth, flowing movement. "If he moves, I'll kill him with the first shot and you with the second."

Kelman's face was like a fiend's. His nostrils flared, his jaw jutted, and the anger that danced in his eyes was wicked. "You—you—fool! I'll kill you for this! I'll burn this shack over your head! I'll—"

"Get out."

Gunthorp did not raise his voice. His bleak eyes shifted from face to face. "Get out! You come around here again and I'll do my own killing. Your blood runs as free as this boy's. Maybe a good whipping is what you need."

Joe's face was white. "He means it, boss. We'd better haul our freight."

"That's good advice. You ride out, Kelman, or those men of yours can take you back lashed over a saddle. I'm not particular which. Any man who'll beat a kid like that doesn't deserve to live!"

Joe was stirred by none of Kelman's rage, and he was sure that Gunthorp would shoot. He turned his horse toward the gate, and the others moved after him. For an instant longer, Kelman stared at Gunthorp. Then, suddenly, the fury seemed to leave him.

"For you, my friend, I'll make some special plans!" he promised.

With a wicked jerk, he whipped his horse's head around and drove in the spurs. The horse literally sprang from a standing start into a dead run and charged by the other three riders at breakneck speed.

Gunthorp watched for a moment longer, then spat. Calmly, he put the gun down and closed the door. Then he looked over at the boy. "You'd better take your shirt off, son. We'll see if we can't fix that back up."

He was not a tall man, reaching just a hair over five feet nine inches, but Gunthorp was massively muscled and heavy. He walked with a rolling gait that oddly suited his build. His face was a square-jawed, mahogany-tinted combination of strength and humor atop a thick neck that descended into his powerful shoulders. As he bathed the boy's back he said, "He called you a thief. Did you steal anything, boy?"

"No, sir. Not anything of his. It was somethin' that belonged to Pop. A pocketbook."

"Money in it?"

"Only a little. I wanted some papers."

"Your father's wallet, eh?" Gunthorp dipped the cloth in the warm water again, squeezed part of the water out, and started on another cut. "Where's your father, boy?"

"He's dead—killed in a mine."

"Sorry. Was it a cave-in?"

"Yes, sir. Kelman came and said he was my guardian, and

that I must do as he said. He had Pop's wallet, which he got from the drawer where Pop always left it when he went to work in the tunnel."

"Why'd he beat you?" Gunthorp looked searchingly at the boy, who was slipping into a clean shirt that belonged to Gunthorp and looked about a dozen sizes too big.

"He wanted me to tell him where Pop hid some papers he couldn't find, and he wanted me to ask the judge to have him left in charge of my father's place."

"And you wouldn't tell?"

"No, sir."

Gunthorp nodded, admiration in his eyes. "You've got grit, boy. You've a lot of grit. Don't tell anybody else about those papers for now. Do you know what's in them? What's the value?"

"I—I don't know. Only, Pop told me they were very important and I must keep them. He said that somebody might try to get them from me, but they were all he could leave to my sister and me if anything happened."

"So you have a sister? Where is she?"

"Out in California. She's going to school but I think she's coming back soon. I wrote her when Father was killed, and she said she was coming home."

"That's good." Gunthorp started putting dishes and food on the table.

While they were eating, he looked across the table at the boy. His nose was flat, and there was a scar on his upper lip. "Kelman's after something your father owned? You don't know what it could be?"

"No, sir. Unless it's the mine. It was a good mine, I think, but Pop never got much out of it. He owned a lot of land in the valley."

"That desert land? What did he want with that?"

"I don't know, sir. I think Kelman knows, though."

Gunthorp nodded. "What makes you believe so?"

"He told Pop once that he knew. I heard him say something like 'Pretty smart, aren't you, Stevens? But I've got it figured out. Are you taking me in?' It was something like that . . . pretty close, anyway."

"Hm. Interesting. It gives me a clue, boy. Stevens your name then? And the first one?"

"Lane, sir. My name is Lane Stevens."

"It's a good name. You've been well brought up, too, I can see that." Gunthorp looked up over his coffee cup. "Where's your mother, son?"

"She's dead, sir. A long time ago. I don't remember her very well."

"More credit to your father, then. Have you been to school?"

"A little, and my father taught me some, too. He taught me to read, sign, and to know the different minerals, and how to shoot a rifle and use a single jack."

"A wise man, your father." Gunthorp was listening as he spoke. "A man who knows how to teach a boy practical things. Still, they are of little account unless one knows what lies behind them. The thoughts behind things, and the reasons for them . . . that's important, too."

He got up. "Finish your supper, boy. The sheriff will be here in a few minutes for you."

Lane started up. "The sheriff?"

"Sit still. There's no reason for excitement. Let the man come. He's an unlikely man, not sure of himself, and he will come because Kelman will urge him. Tonight we can, I hope, talk him out of it. Tomorrow may be another thing."

The sound of horses on the hard-packed earth of the yard made him nod. "Of course. Now put the light out, boy, and stand away from the door. I've no trust for the look in that Kelman's eye."

"Hallo, the house!"

Gunthorp opened the door. "How are you, Sheriff Eagan. Ah, I see you've brought Kelman with you. Are you taking him under arrest then? Do you want me for a witness?"

"Arrest?" Eagan was confused. "Why should I arrest him?"

"For beating the lad, for beating him until there's cuts a finger deep on his back. If you want, I'll come to town and swear out a warrant for him myself."

"Forget that and get on with it, Eagan!" Kelman snapped roughly.

Gunthorp stood in the door, his big hands on his hips, his enormous shoulders and chest seeming to fill the door. He smiled.

"Now, now, Kelman," he said mildly. "Let's not be ordering the sheriff around. Mr. Eagan knows his duties, and it isn't any citizen's place to order him about. You don't take orders from Kelman, do you, Sheriff?"

"Certainly not!" Eagan blustered. "Now, enough of that. I've come for the boy. He's a thief, and I'm arresting him."

"A thief? What did he steal? A wallet, wasn't it? And the wallet belonged to his father. He is his father's heir, or one of them. You can't arrest this boy for stealing. I'm sure it wouldn't hold up."

Eagan turned toward Kelman, uneasily. "You didn't tell me the wallet belonged to Stevens," he protested.

"That's neither here nor there!" Kelman's rage was mastering him again. "Take the boy and let's go. If that blundering fool wants to try to stop us, I'll handle him!"

"Stop you?" Gunthorp smiled. "I'd never think of it, Sheriff. I've a great respect for the law and officers of the law. The boy was taken to Kelman's ranch, where he was beaten to make him tell where some papers were. The boy escaped, and in escaping took his father's wallet, to which he certainly had more right than Kelman. No, Sheriff, the boy is better off here." He smiled again. "When he is needed for any court appearance, I shall gladly answer for him."

"We want him, and we want him now," Kelman flared.

Gunthorp nodded. "I'm afraid you are mistaking yourself for some sort of official, Kelman. Mr. Eagan is his own man and he can do his own thinking. If he can't . . . well, we'll see who gets the votes in the next election."

Eagan shifted uncomfortably in his saddle. Secretly, he was afraid of Kelman, but he resented the man's arrogant manner and the ordering about he constantly took from him. The way Gunthorp was putting it, Eagan would practically prove he was crawling to Kelman's orders if he took the boy.

Gunthorp comprehended something of what was in the

sheriff's mind, so he offered him an easy way out. "Anyway," he added, "Sheriff Eagan is a man who knows the law. I'm not saying the boy is here, but he can't search my house without a warrant."

Eagan clutched at the opportunity. "That's right, Kelman," he said, "I'd have to have a warrant for the boy to go into that house and search for him."

"Warrant, blazes!" Kelman exploded with rage.

He flung himself toward the house. "Get away from the door!" he roared at Gunthorp.

Gunthorp did not move, but with his eyes on Kelman, he said to the sheriff, "Eagan, if he comes at me, I'll defend myself."

Before Eagan could speak, Kelman's hand swept back for a gun, and at the same instant, Gunthorp moved. His left hand shot out and gripped Kelman's wrist. His right hand dropped to Kelman's left bicep.

Kelman was a big man, and a skillful boxer, but here he had no chance. Gunthorp's big brown hands shut down hard, the right fingers digging into the muscles of Kelman's arm, the fingers of the left hand shutting down like a powerful vise on the wrist of the gun hand.

Kelman might have been stricken with paralysis. Gunthorp's hands gripped with crushing power, and Kelman's face went white. The gun had come clear of the holster, but Kelman cried out with pain, and the gun dropped from his hand. Then, still gripping him by the wrist and upper arm, Gunthorp lifted the man clear off his feet and hurled him bodily into the yard.

His face had not changed. "I'm sorry, Sheriff, but he attacked me. You saw it. I refuse to allow any search without a warrant. Go to Judge McClees and get one, if you wish."

Eagan knew just as well as Gunthorp did that Judge Jim McClees was not going to grant any warrant without making a thorough study of the case; and that would be the last thing Kelman would want.

Kelman, his right hand almost useless from the crushing grip, caught the pommel of the saddle with his left and hauled himself up. Gunthorp retrieved the gun and handed it to Eagan.

"Return this to him when you think it's appropriate," he said, smiling.

———

WHEN DAYLIGHT BEGAN lifting the shadows from the sun-blasted ridges, Gunthorp ate a hurried breakfast, and then he took the boy to the door.

"You see that cottonwood with the dead limb? Right opposite the end of that limb, in the wall of the cliff, is a cave. You go up there with this grub I packed and this canteen, and don't you stir out of there until I come for you . . . or 'til three days have gone by. If you don't hear from me in three days, somebody got me.

"In that cave there's more water. You can also see this place, but you keep still up there or somebody might see you moving."

With that, Gunthorp swung into the saddle and started for the hills. He knew where the Stevens mine was and he was taking a chance that no one would be around. He rode swiftly, and when he found himself among the piñons on the slope above the canyon where the mine lay, he ground-hitched the gelding and slid farther down the hill to where he looked over the mine and a shack nearby. A half hour's careful watch showed no movement.

He went down the hill with long strides, sliding gravel around him, his weight carrying him almost at a run. When he reached the bottom of the steep slope, he surveyed the buildings once more. No movement. Swiftly, he crossed to the mine, took one quick, last look around, then disappeared into the tunnel.

As he walked along the drift, he remembered what he had seen in that quick glance. The mine was in the face of the rock at the end of a deep notch in the mountain, a notch that widened out until it opened upon the desert valley below. Stevens had purchased this canyon and considerable land in the valley, although the extent of his buying was unknown. He had told those who were curious that he did not wish to be crowded, but they had laughed and said there was no chance of anyone ever moving near him, for the land he bought was the driest and worst around.

This much Gunthorp knew, for he was a man who listened well, and there were men enough who talked freely. He carried a candle with him, and after a while he stopped to study the wall of the tunnel. There was very little mineral here, but the big vein might be farther inside.

He walked swiftly, counting his paces as he went. Suddenly, he rounded a turn in the drift and was brought up short, finding himself staring at the end where the drift had collapsed. He had walked almost a quarter of a mile from the entrance.

Thoughtfully, he studied the rock around him, and particularly that in the face. Then he turned and with the same swift strides hurried back. A quick look around showed no one in sight, so he stepped out and started for the wash.

"Hey!" The shout stopped him in his tracks, and he turned to see a man rushing toward him. "Who are you? What do you mean by going into that mine without permission?"

Gunthorp faced the unshaven, burly watchman.

"Permission from who?"

"From Kelman, that's who!" The man faced Gunthorp, glaring at him. "You come back up here and wait until he comes. I ain't sure he'd like you being in there!"

Gunthorp's bleak eyes showed humor. "I'm quite sure he wouldn't, my friend. However, if I were you, I'd pick up and leave just as quickly as I could. Kelman's through in this country."

The man laughed harshly. "That's likely! He's the boss around here. You coming with me, or do I take you?"

Gunthorp chuckled. "Why, I guess you take me," he said simply. He waited, his hands down, smiling at the other man.

"Come on," the watchman blustered, "I don't want no trouble!"

"Then go on back to your shack and keep your mouth shut. If you don't tell Kelman, he'll never know I was here. Then you won't get in trouble at all."

The watchman was disturbed. A second look told him that although this man might not be as tall as he, he was a solid mass of bone and muscle. Moving him wouldn't be easy. Staring into those bleak eyes made him doubt the advisability of trying the pistol in his holster.

A rattle of hoofs on the trail decided the man. "Get out of here, quick!" he said. "If Kelman found you here, he'd have my scalp!"

In three fast steps, Gunthorp was in among the piñons. He glanced back to see three horsemen riding up to the mine. The man in the lead was Joe, but Kelman himself was not among them.

When he reached his horse, he mounted and cut back across the mountain. There was no regular trail, but he wove in and out among the trees until he could see into a narrow canyon beyond. When he was in position, he stopped his horse and studied this new area with thoughtful eyes.

This canyon was green, deeply green, thick with cotton-woods and tamarisk and a small stream flowing along the bottom. At one point the stream disappeared into a wide area of marshy sand and reeds. Gunthorp glanced at the sun, and seeing there was yet time, turned his horse down the trail and rode down through to the cottonwoods.

The small river flowed out of the rock, described a wide half circle through a meadow, and then vanished into the sand on the same side from which it emerged. It was no more than four or five feet across, but the water was clear and cold and ran swiftly.

As his horse drank, Gunthorp turned in his saddle and surveyed the valley. Mining operations had begun here, too. Across from him he could see the mouth of a drift and the pile of waste outside it. The tunnel mouth was low down against the valley floor. Gunthorp turned his horse and started for town, his face serious.

———

RED BUTTE'S RESIDENTIAL section was composed of some forty or fifty buildings, built haphazardly down the slope from the mesa. Beyond the buildings and corrals, the land sloped away for two miles and disappeared under the unsightly waters of an alkali lake.

Gunthorp tied his horse at the hitching rail and stepped up on the boardwalk, heading for the office of Judge Jim McClees. At that moment, the door of the restaurant thrust open and Kelman stepped out, accompanied by an uncommonly pretty girl. They saw him at the same instant.

"That's the man!" Kelman pointed at him with a stiff arm. "That's him."

The girl walked right up to Gunthorp, her heels clicking on the walk. "Where is my brother?" she demanded, her eyes sparking. "I want you to take me to him at once. And you must return the papers you took from him."

She was young, and very pretty, and he liked the determined set of her chin. "Miss Stevens," he said quietly, "your brother is safe, and no thanks due to Mr. Kelman. If there are any papers, he alone knows where they are."

"Look here!" Kelman thrust himself forward. "Madge Stevens has returned to settle her father's estate, and to do that, she must have those papers. Your little scheme has failed, so you can bring the boy in and turn the papers over to me."

Gunthorp glanced at the girl. "Is that what you want?"

"It is." Her chin lifted. "You have no right to interfere in this matter, none at all. Mr. Kelman was doing all that could be done."

Gunthorp smiled. "No doubt. But is he doing what is best for your interests and the boy's, or his own?"

"That doesn't matter," she flared. "It certainly is none of your business."

"No doubt Kelman has made you an offer for the land your father owned? Was he going to take all that wasteland off your hands as a favor?"

From the puzzled look in her eyes, he knew that he was right. "What did he offer you for it?"

"That's neither here nor there." Kelman's anger was growing. "All you have to do is take us to the boy."

Gunthorp ignored Kelman. "Miss Stevens," he said, "I don't know what he has offered you for the land, but whatever it is, I'll double it."

Her eyes widened. "For that worthless land? Why, that's absurd! That would be ten dollars an acre for—"

"Ten?" Gunthorp's eyes brightened. "Miss Stevens, I'll give you more. If you say ten dollars, he must have offered you only five. I'll give you twenty dollars an acre and a twenty percent share in any profit I make."

"But I don't understand," she protested.

"The man's trying to pull the wool over your eyes," Kelman interrupted. His tone was desperate, and anger was growing in him. "Anyway, it doesn't matter now. You've sold the land to me for five dollars an acre, and you've been paid for it." He turned back to Gunthorp. "See, my friend? You are too late. Now will you turn the boy over to us and get out of here?"

Gunthorp stood flat-footed, shaken by the statement the girl did not deny. If she had sold the land . . . Suddenly, he smiled.

"Miss Stevens," he asked politely, "I know it is always wrong to ask a woman's age, but how old are you?"

"Why, I'm eighteen, almost nineteen, but how does that matter?"

Kelman's face changed. "You mean you're not of age?"

Gunthorp looked up at him. "It really wouldn't matter, Kelman," he said softly. "You see, Lane is an heir, too, and she would have no right to sign away his rights. Miss Stevens has no right to dispose of the property without the authority of his legal guardian."

"But she's his older sister," Kelman protested furiously. "She's his guardian."

"Not unless the court appoints her so, and as she's under-age, that isn't likely. I suggest we talk with Judge McClees."

Madge Stevens stared from one to the other, frightened and confused. In each of the three letters that had come to her from Kelman, he had assured her of his friendship for her father and herself, and had offered to dispose of the land her father had, he suggested, foolishly bought. Now this man whom Kelman had said was forcibly holding her brother was suddenly making everything seem very different.

Kelman noticed the indecision in her face. "Come over here," he said to Gunthorp. "I want to talk to you!"

Gunthorp followed him to one side, his calm eyes on Kelman's excited face. "Listen," Kelman protested when they were out of hearing. "Let's not fight over this! That land is worth a fortune! You know that as well as I do! Let's make a deal on this! If you insist, we can cut the girl in, but there's no reason why we should! You and I can handle this by ourselves! To blazes with that girl and her kid brother."

Gunthorp smiled. "Kelman," he said loudly, "I've heard a lot about you. You have already labeled yourself as a liar and a skunk, but now you hit a new low. Asking me to cheat youngsters is about as bad as a man can get!"

"You double-damned—!" Kelman's hand dropped to his gun.

Gunthorp's left fist whipped up, crashing into the pit of Kelman's stomach, and then a bone-shattering wallop to the chin. Stricken, the big man toppled back off the boardwalk and fell into the street. For an instant, he lay stunned, and then he grabbed again for his pistol.

Gunthorp tried to reach him at the same instant, but Kelman had fallen a step or two away. Kelman's gun whipped up, flame stabbed from the muzzle, and Gunthorp felt his hat lift from his head. Then Kelman's gun roared again and something struck Gunthorp solidly. His mouth widened, then closed as his body twisted under the bullet's impact.

Suddenly, things grew hazy and Gunthorp started to turn around, but seemed to trip. Hands grabbed him and eased him to the boardwalk. A man in a wide white hat with a mustache and goatee was bending over him.

"Judge—" His voice had no more focus than his eyes, and he had to fight to arrange the words properly. "Judge, you . . . care for this girl. Brother . . . her brother's in a cave at my place."

———

FOUR DAYS LATER Gunthorp was lying on the bed in the spare bedroom of Judge McClees's home. The door opened and Madge Stevens came in, with Lane beside her. Her eyes widened at the sight of him lying there.

"You—you're better now?"

"Sure. Doc says I'll be up and around before long. I guess I'll carry a couple of slugs, though."

"I'm so sorry . . . that I ever doubted you. Judge McClees arrested Mr. Kelman, you know. They took him away yesterday."

"That's good." He was still very weak.

"About the land?" she said. "Men have been out to look at the mine. They say it's worthless, and the land is worse."

Gunthorp smiled. "Don't you believe them. Your father knew what he was up to. That isn't a mine at all. It's a tunnel to bring water from a canyon back there. There is a great volume of water, easily enough to irrigate five hundred acres of good hay land, and the level of the land your father bought is below that of the canyon, so irrigation for growing hay will be simple."

"But hay? Is it valuable?"

"Well," he said with a grin, "last year it sold for sixty dollars a ton, and fairly good meadow land will run a ton to the acre. This land you've got, irrigated, will do a whole lot better than many mines."

"The judge said that given all that has happened he should appoint a legal guardian for my brother and me until I turn twenty-one. He thought that it should be you."

"Well, one way or another, I guess I already got started a couple of days ago," Gunthorp said.

"But Lane and I thought it should be more of a partnership. If you'll help us finish Father's tunnel, we'll split whatever we make on the hay three ways."

"With an offer as good as that there is no chance I could turn it down . . . I always was a sucker for kids in trouble."

"Kids!" She arched one eyebrow. "I hope you are only talking about Lane." They turned and left the room, but not before she had paused to fluff his pillow and pull up the covers.

"I wonder," Gunthorp mused, "what I've gotten myself into now. . . ."

JACKSON OF HORNTOWN

HORNTOWN BELONGED TO the desert. Whatever claim man had once had upon it had yielded to the sun, the wind, and the blown sand. A double row of false-fronted buildings faced a dusty street into which the bunch-grass and sagebrush ventured. It had become a byway for an occasional rabbit or coyote, or the rattlers that had taken refuge in the foundations of The Waterhole, a saloon in which water had rarely been served.

A solitary burro wandered like a gray ghost among the weather-beaten, abandoned buildings.

To the east and west, craggy ridges of ugly red rock exposed their jagged crests to the sky. To the north, the narrow valley tapered away to a mere gully down which a dim trail led the unwary to that sink of desolation that was Horntown. To the south the valley widened into the Black Rock Desert. There were few trees and less water.

Had there been a watcher in the ghastly emptiness of the lifeless ridges he might have seen a lone horseman riding up the trail from the desert.

He rode a long-legged buckskin, which shambled wearily through the sagebrush, and even the sight of the ghost town failed to awaken any spark in either man or horse.

The watcher, had there been one, could have determined from the way the man rode that he was riding to a known destination. All the way across the waterless waste he had ridden as to a goal, and that in itself meant something.

For Horntown was a forgotten place, slowly giving itself back to the desert from which it had come. It had lived wildly, desperately, and it had died hard in a red-laced flurry of gunshots and powder smoke. The bodies of those who fell had been left where they had fallen, and the survivors had simply gone away and no one among them had looked back. Horntown was finished, and they knew it well.

Yet the sun-browned man with the bloody bandage on his head had kept his trail to Horntown; through all that broken country he had deviated by no more than a few feet from the direction he had chosen.

The red-rimmed gray eyes that occasionally stared back over the trail behind held no hint of mercy or kindness. They were the eyes of a man who had looked at life over a gun barrel, a man who had lived the hard, lawless way, and expected to die as he had lived.

It was fitting that he rode to Horntown, for the place had bred many such men. It had begun over a hundred years earlier, when a westbound gold-seeker decided he had gone far enough. It died its first death two years later because the founder owned a horse, and a passing stranger needed a horse.

Jack Horn died with a gun in his hand. Seven months later a Mexican named Montez moved into the abandoned buildings and opened a saloon. He combined selling bad whiskey with robbing casual travelers until he chose the wrong man and died on his doorstep. It was after that the first Jackson came to town.

Enoch Jackson was from Tennessee. Tall, leather-tough, and rawboned, he stopped in Horntown with his six sons, and the heyday of the town came into being.

It is a curious thing that no matter how sparse the vegetation or how remote the place, how difficult the problem of materials, a man who wants a drink will make one. The Jacksons had always had whiskey, and they had always made their own. They drank their own product, but drank it sparingly. Once set up in Horntown they drank even more sparingly for, of course, they alone knew the ingredients.

No one ever guessed and few asked what the whiskey was made from, but it fed fire into the veins of a hardy brood who turned the country to the south into a whirlwind of evil with their gunfighting, rustling, and holdups.

For fifty years the small hell that was Horntown was ruled by Enoch and his powerful son, Matt Ben Jackson. A roving gunman, sore and hunting trouble, sent Enoch to his final payoff with a bullet in his skull, and then died with Matt Ben's bullet just two hours later. He died where Matt Ben caught up with him, right where the valley of Horntown opened into the Black Rock Desert.

After that Matt Ben ran the show at Horntown with his brother, FireHat Jackson, as his lieutenant.

Several months later Sheriff Star Redman rode to Horntown with a posse of thirty men. They never reached their destination, but when the survivors rode home there were four empty saddles, and five men carried Jackson lead, to be removed later.

Redman was not of a yielding breed, and he had been elected to do a job. He returned, and on the fourth attempt the final bloody battle was fought. Star Redman had sworn he'd bring an end to Horntown or never return. There were twenty-six men in that last posse, and only seven of them returned unscathed. Several were buried in Horntown, and two died on the way back.

Behind them only one man remained alive, Matt Ben himself. Forty, tough, and badly wounded, he watched the last of the attackers ride away. Then, like a cornered rattler, he crawled back to The Waterhole and poured himself a drink.

A month later a wandering prospector found him dead on the floor, his gun in his hand. Matt Ben had amputated his own foot and shot himself when apparently dying of blood poisoning.

Searching the town, the prospector, who knew Horntown well, found the bodies of all the Horntown bunch but one. That one was FireHat. Or rather, all but two, for with FireHat had vanished Matt Ben the Younger.

"They'll come back," Sheriff Star Redman said bitterly, yet half in admiration. "He's a Horntown Jackson, and he'll be back. What I can't understand is why he ran away in the first place."

"Them Jacksons are feuders, Sheriff," the prospector reminded. "When FireHat left he took young Matt Ben with him, and he was only six and too young to fight."

"Maybe so," Redman admitted. "It could be he wanted to save him for seed."

FireHat Jackson died alone, ten years later, down in Sonora. The word drifted back to Webb City, sixty miles south of Horntown. Star Redman took the news with a strange light in his eyes. "Sonora, eh? How did he die?"

"Rurales surrounded him. He took eight of them along for company."

Redman spat. "You just know it! Them Jacksons never die alone. If one of 'em has a gun he'll take somebody along!"

"Well," somebody commented, "that ends the Horntown bunch. Now we can rest easy."

"Don't be too sure," Redman warned. "Matt Ben the Younger is somewhere around."

"But he wasn't one of the old bunch, Sheriff. He was too young to have it matter much. He won't even remember Horntown."

Star Redman shifted his tobacco in his jaws, chewed, then spat. "He was a Horntown Jackson!" He spat again. "You'll see. He'll be back."

"Sometimes, Star," the old storekeeper commented, "I think you almost wish he'd come back."

Redman had started toward the door, and now he turned. "He was one of the old breed. I'd rather he rode for the law, but say what you like about them Horntown Jacksons, they were *men*!"

The lone horseman slowed the yellow horse to a shambling trot, then to a walk. The buildings of Horntown were just ahead. He slid the Winchester from its boot. With his rifle across the saddle in front of him, he rode slowly up the one street of Horntown.

There were no more than twenty buildings still standing. The nearest was a gray, wind-battered house, and beyond were several shacks and corrals. Then the great, rambling old structure with its faded sign: The Waterhole.

The rider of the yellow horse with the black tail and mane rode up the empty street. Here and there tumbleweeds had lodged. Sand had drifted like drifts of snow, doors hung on sagging hinges, creaking dismally in the wind. At one side of

The Waterhole the runoff from the roof had worn a deep gully.

A spot of white at the corner of a building caught his eyes. It was a human skull, white and bleached. Grimly, he studied it. "More than likely he was one of my uncles," he said aloud.

He swung down in front of The Waterhole and tied the buckskin to the old hitching rail. His boots had a hollow, lonesome sound on the boardwalk. He opened the door and walked in.

Dust and cobwebs hung over everything. The chairs and tables remained much as they must have been when the fight ended. A few poker chips were scattered about, an empty bottle stood on a table, another on the bar beside a tipped-over shot glass. Propped against the bar was a skeleton, rifle beside it, gun belt still hanging to the lank white bones. One foot was missing.

Slowly the man uncovered his head. "Well, Pa, you died hard, but you died game."

Outside he went to where the spring was, the reason why old Jack Horn had stopped in the first place. Crystal-clear water still ran from the rocks and trickled into a natural basin, then trickled off down through the rocks and into the wash, where it lost itself in a small cluster of cottonwoods and willows.

He filled his canteen first, as any sensible man would, then he drank, and, removing the bloody bandage, carefully bathed his head where a bullet had cut a furrow. Then, still more carefully, he washed his hair.

He led the buckskin to water, then picketed him on a small patch of grass he remembered from the days when he had played there as a youngster.

Inside the saloon he found dishes, washed them, and, working at the fireplace, prepared a rough meal.

He was digging a grave for his father's bones when he heard a faint sound, then another. His gun slid easily into his hand and he waited, listening to the slow steps, shambling, hesitant. Then a long gray head appeared around the corner.

Matt Ben holstered his gun, then he climbed out of the

grave and held out his hand to the burro. "Hi, Zeke! Come here!"

At the sound of the familiar name the burro's head lifted, and the scent of this man apparently touched a chord of memory, but still he hesitated. Matt Ben called again and again, and slowly the old burro walked toward him.

"It's all right, Zeke. It's just a Jackson, come home at last. I'm glad you waited."

Three days later Pierce Bowman walked into the sheriff's office in Webb City. "Wire for you, Star. Looks like you were right. Matt Ben's on his way home."

"He's already here," Redman commented dryly. "Tim Beagin came by there day before yesterday. Saw smoke in The Waterhole's chimney.

"I didn't plan to bother him. Seems sort of natural, havin' a Jackson out there, but this here wire changes matters. I got to go get him."

"You takin' a posse?"

"No. Just me. If he's a Jackson we'd never get nigh him. Them Jacksons always could smell a posse ten mile off."

"What do they want him for?"

"Sheriff over at Carson tried to take him and he wouldn't go, said he was just ridin' through. The sheriff made a mistake then. He reached for his gun, and Matt Ben put him out of commission."

"Jacksons always could shoot. How d' you figure to take him, Star?"

"Darned if I know. I think I'll just go talk to him." He paused. "You know something, Bowman? Nobody ever did try just talkin' to a Jackson. They always went for them with guns and ropes. Maybe somebody should have tried talkin' a long time ago."

Star Redman took the trail to Horntown carrying no pleasant thoughts. He had no desire, at his age, to shoot it out with a Horntown Jackson. Once, when he was younger, he might have felt otherwise, but time had tempered his courage with wisdom. The Jacksons, like himself, had been products of their times, but not really bad men. They never killed except when firing at an equal in open combat.

There had been, he remembered, a certain something on their side. His job was to arrest young Matt Ben, and of course that was what he must do. This young Jackson might be different, but again he might not. The Jackson blood was strong.

He remembered very well the time the shooting ended at Horntown. "I think he's dead," somebody commented. "Shouldn't we go in and find out?"

An old-timer in the posse looked around. "You want to go in, you go. Me, I wouldn't go in if you offered me your ranch!"

Star Redman knew the hills. He believed he knew them better than young Matt Ben, and in his knowledge he saw his chance—to get close without arousing suspicion. He glanced skyward. "Smells like snow," he said to himself. "Time for it, too."

Young Matt Ben was thinking the same thing. He began gathering wood and scrap lumber, which he piled alongside The Waterhole. He began making repairs in the room he expected to use, and also in the stable where he could keep the buckskin.

In the lower meadow, just beyond the willows, he found a fine stand of hay, and began mowing it with a scythe he sharpened in the blacksmith shop. It was time for snow to fall, and if he expected to winter at Horntown he had best be ready for it.

He enjoyed working with his hands. He repaired the door, making it a tight fit. He found the old livery stable had almost fallen in, and rescued some good-sized timbers for burning. His father's house was down the street, and there was a good stack of wood there, enough for a winter.

He avoided the thought of food. He had enough for three or four days, with care. He worked from dawn until dark mowing hay, and the sun would cure it. Yet he would have to get it in before snow fell.

Here and there he found where passersby had camped. Prospectors or sheepmen, perhaps some drifting cowhand.

Old Zeke hung around, wary, but liking the company. Several times he tried to entice the old burro to come into the stable, but he was too wary, and would have none of it. Finally, by dropping bunches of grass, he got him to go inside. He left the door open but Zeke was liking the buckskin's company.

"The last of the Jacksons!" he said aloud. "Me and a jackass!"

He studied the sky grimly. It was surely going to snow.

Twenty miles north and east was the hideout of Stony Budd. The Budd gang had looted two banks, run off a bunch of fine saddle stock, and holed up over there.

"Come along, Matt," Budd suggested, "that's old Jackson country. We could use you up there."

"Not me. I'm through with the outlaw trail. From here out I'm ridin' a straight trail. If they'll let me," he added.

He meant it, too. There was food, warmth, and security up there with Stony Budd. All he needed to do was to saddle the buckskin and head for the hills.

To stay here might mean to invite trouble. People would learn a Jackson had returned, and he would have to live down a hard name. Well, it was high time a Jackson did live it down. Old Enoch would have agreed with that. Times had changed. Even old FireHat had told him so.

He would have had no trouble but for that sheriff in Carson. The man had tried to arrest him without reason. The sheriff, wanting to build a reputation, figured arresting a Horntown Jackson would convince the voters. Matt Ben had been about to go along with it until something in the man's snaky eyes changed his mind.

"Tell me what you want me for, and I'll go. Otherwise I am settin' right here."

"I'm arresting you on suspicion," the sheriff had said. "Now, cut the palaver and come along."

"Suspicion of what?"

"It don't make no matter. You come along."

Matt Ben hesitated, then surrendered his belt gun. "Now, damn you," the sheriff said. "Here's where I kill me a Jackson!"

He had failed to notice the open button on the front of

Matt Ben's shirt, and when he dropped his hand for his gun, Matt Ben shot him. Then he retrieved his own six-shooter, mounted his buckskin, and rode out of town.

Matt Ben was frying bacon over the fire when he heard a light step. The frying pan was in his left hand, a fork in his right. For an instant, he froze.

"Don't try it, son," Star Redman said. "I don't want to kill you."

"Then you're different from that sheriff back in Carson," Matt Ben said. "That was just what he planned to do."

He glanced at the tall man standing inside the door. He was a lean, rangy man with quizzical gray-blue eyes and a white, drooping mustache.

"I suppose you're Star Redman," he said. "Come up to the fire. The coffee's hot."

Redman, holding his gun steady, stepped over and slid the guns from Jackson's holsters.

"Sorry, Jackson. I knew you were here and didn't plan on botherin' you until I got word from Carson."

"Sit down and we'll eat. I'm runnin' shy on grub, but we'll manage." He looked up. "FireHat said you were a fair man, Sheriff, and that you were a fighter."

Redman sat down opposite Jackson and studied him as he prepared the meal. He was a well-built man, obviously strong, with all the marks of a rider. A glance at his hands showed evidence of hard work.

"Morning is soon enough to start, isn't it, Redman?" Matt Ben asked. "This has been a long day."

"We'll start tonight," Redman said. "I don't want to spend the night here." He smiled. "No, I'm not worried about ghosts. It's snow. There's a feel of it in the air."

"FireHat told me about this country," Matt Ben said, "and he said Horntown was rightly mine. Is that true?"

"It is," Redman admitted. "Enoch proved up on a claim and so did seven of the others. Actually, you own all the water for miles around, and what range you don't own lies between pieces you do own. I've seen it all on a map. Old Enoch was no damn fool."

Matt Ben served the bacon and the sourdough bread and refilled their cups. So this was the end of the dream! He had thought to return here, to whip the place into some kind of shape and by hard work to establish himself as a peaceful rancher. If it had not been for that sheriff in Carson—

There was always Stony Budd.

A fire quickened within him. Well, why not? He had the name, so he might as well take the game. It was a long way to Webb City, and many things might happen, particularly if it began to snow.

The old sheriff might be a fighter, but with all his posses he couldn't crack the Jacksons, and he would not crack this one now.

He would need a gun.

Well, he had planned for this, knowing it might happen, although it was trouble with Stony and his crowd that he expected.

He was not fooling himself about Budd. The outlaw leader wanted him because he was good with a gun, but even more because he was afraid Matt Ben might start operations of his own. Stony Budd had his own reputation. He was rumored to have killed five men in gun battles.

Matt Ben, expecting trouble, had two guns hidden out. Two on which he could depend. There was a six-shooter hidden under a canvas in the manger where he stabled the buckskin. There was another in the folds of his slicker.

Outside the wind was picking up. They could hear it growing stronger. It would be a bad night.

"We'd better get movin'," Redman said, pushing back his plate.

Matt Ben got up and began tossing things into his warbag, then turned to pick up his slicker. As he stooped for it Redman spoke.

"If'n I was to have a hideout gun," he spoke casually, "I'd be likely to have it hidden in my slicker."

Matt Ben straightened, the folded slicker in his hands. After all, Star Redman had killed several of his relatives, and if right now he were to leap to one side and shoot from the slicker he'd have no worse than an even break. Then he realized he did not want to kill the old man. He did not even want to hurt him. And on the trail he would have his chance. A chance to slip away in the storm.

"Seems you've outguessed me, Mr. Redman," he said, "because I surely do have a gun here."

Star took the gun from the open folds of the slicker. His eyes were thoughtful. "You could've taken a chance, son. You might have nailed me."

He smiled. "Of course, I was ready, but you can never tell. It's a chancy game, son."

Watched by the sheriff, he went into the stable to get the buckskin. When in the stall and momentarily beyond view of Redman, Matt Ben slipped the manger gun into the front of his shirt. He had already donned the slicker as protection from the cold wind, and the gun made no bulge that could be seen through its looseness.

Straddling the yellow horse he spoke to Zeke. "You stay inside where it's warm," he whispered. "I'll be back or send the sheriff to open up for you when the storm's gone. I'm still planning to stay here in Horntown with you."

At the last minute, worried that the burro might be forgotten and starve, he left the door ajar. He rode out of town, Star Redman following. Once, he looked back. The old gray burro was walking after them into the desert, and into the storm.

Star Redman stared at the sky, obviously worried. Yet they had been riding for an hour when the first snowflake fell. Then there was another, and suddenly the air was white with them.

"We'll keep goin'," Redman said, "maybe it won't be so bad."

They both knew what it might mean to be caught out in the wastes of the Black Rock in a blizzard, and the snow was falling thickly now. There was little wind, and that was a blessing. They rode on, Matt Ben watching for his chance. If he could get even fifty yards away he could not be seen.

The horses moved more slowly. Matt Ben glanced back. Their tracks were covered almost as soon as they stepped out of them. The wind was rising. It blew a sudden gust, almost sucking the air from his lungs.

"Gettin' mighty bad!" Redman shouted.

Matt Ben was almost imperceptibly widening the gap between them. Just a little more and he would be completely obscured by falling snow.

He let the yellow horse find his way into a deep gully. Here the snow had drifted, and he let the buckskin pick his way with care down the steep side of the ravine. A misstep here and a horse could break a leg.

Glancing around, he instantly went into action. The sheriff was still out of sight beyond the lip of the ravine. Turning the yellow horse, he touched spurs to him and raced away up the ravine. After a momentary spurt he let the yellow horse take his own speed. Behind him he heard a shout, then another.

Matt Ben Jackson rode on. He reined the buckskin to a stop, listening. There was no sound but the wind, and his trail was already blotting out. He was free again.

When he had ridden another mile he found a place where he could climb the horse out of the ravine. The minute his head cleared the top he felt a blast of icy wind which struck him like a blow. They had been drifting ahead of the wind when going toward Webb City; now he must face it.

Horntown was the safest place now. There was fuel and there was shelter from the wind and snow. He could last out the storm, then head for Stony Budd's and then up to Wyoming.

The snow was falling heavier now, the wind rising. It was to be a bad storm. He turned the yellow horse toward the trail down which they had come; some of the route had been sheltered from the worst of the wind. He doubted the old sheriff would attempt a return in this storm. He would wait until it was over, and then come with a posse. Matt Ben knew his escape had been the merest fluke.

He cut their trail near a rocky shoulder which offered some protection from the wind, and dismounted to rest the buckskin. Then he saw their tracks. Here, sheltered from the wind, they had neither filled with snow nor blown away. And there, over the tracks of his horse and that of the sheriff, were the unmistakable hoofprints of the old gray burro. It was strange the storm had not turned it back.

Matt Ben stared at the tracks, swearing under his breath. From where he now stood it was at least forty-five miles to Webb City, and that old gray burro, the last survivor of Horntown, would never make it.

He would die out here on the snow-covered desert. The tracks indicated the old burro was lagging far behind, as the horse tracks had begun to fill before the sharper burro tracks were made.

"Matt Ben," he told himself disgustedly, "you're a fool for what you're thinking." Yet even as he said it he knew he was going back after the old burro. He was going to get Zeke and take him back to Horntown. It wouldn't be right to let the old fellow die out there alone. Around the town, with shelter, he might live several years.

He mounted again and turned the buckskin back on the trail. It was somewhat sheltered in places, and occasional tracks remained. Several times he had to stop, judging the wind. He hoped it was holding to the north. It was a full hour later when he found the ravine where he had lost the sheriff.

Reining in, he took his six-gun from his shirt and thrust it behind his belt under the slicker. Then he felt his way down the steep trail.

When he reached the bottom Zeke was standing not a half dozen yards away. Nearby, propped against the rock wall was Star Redman. His head was slumped on his chest and near him was a small pile of sticks beginning to be covered with snow. His horse stood a few feet to one side.

"What the devil?" Matt Ben scowled. For a moment he stood in the slowly falling snow and simply stared, filled with a great exasperation.

Zeke saw him first and lifted his head, ears canted forward. "It's all right, Zeke. Everything's all right."

Bending over the sheriff, he put a hand on his shoulder. Redman stirred, wincing sharply. Matt Ben looked down. Even under the snow he could see an odd twist to Redman's leg.

"What happened?"

"Hoss slipped comin' into the ravine. Fell with me, an' busted my leg. Guess I must've passed out as I was tryin' to build a fire." He looked up. "I yelled at you, but I guess you didn't hear."

Matt Ben straightened up, swearing mentally. He walked over to the sheriff's horse. The horse was sound. He led it over to Redman.

"I can't leave you here. I'll take you back to Horntown. It's closer."

Rousting around in the frozen brush, he found a couple of sticks and made a crude splint for the leg. Then he lifted the old man into the saddle. For a man of his frame he was surprisingly light. Matt Ben steadied him in the saddle. "Can you stick it? Damn it, Redman, you're too old a man to be livin' this kind of life."

The sheriff looked down at him. "I know, son, but what else can I do? I kept the peace in the country while all the others got rich in the cattle or sheep business. All of a sudden I was an old man who had nothing but a star and a reputation for doin' my job."

Matt Ben climbed into his own saddle after leading Redman's horse up the bank. "Come on, Zeke," he said, "you got to show Redman you're tough as he is. Let's go home."

It was slow going. The wind was an icy blast which stung their faces with frozen snow. The sheriff bowed his head into the wind and clung to the saddle horn. He made no sound, but Matt Ben knew he was suffering.

A long time later Matt Ben dismounted and stamped his almost-frozen feet. He was cold all the way through. He swung his arms in a teamster's warming and walked around, rubbing the legs of the horses and of old Zeke, who stood patiently, as though he had lived all his life with men, when in fact he had run wild for years.

Mounting, he pushed on, followed by the others. From time to time he looked over his shoulder to see if they were still behind him.

They were riding right into the wind, and that should be right, but suppose the wind had shifted? Even if it shifted but little, it still might cause him to miss the canyon mouth and ride on into the endless wastes of the desert.

The horses were of little help, as neither was from Horntown. Their inclination was to turn their tails to the wind and drift but in that direction there was at least fifty miles of empty, windswept desert.

He looked around at Zeke. The old gray burro stood a few yards away, almost at right angle to their route, staring back at him. On a hunch, he turned the buckskin toward the burro and, as if waiting for that very thing, Zeke walked off, quartering into the wind.

"Hope you know where you're goin', old fellow," Matt Ben muttered, "because I surely don't."

Zeke was obviously going somewhere. He walked steadily ahead, as though completely sure of his ground. What if the burro thought he was being herded in that direction? It was a risk he must take, but the old burro was desert-wise, and it stood to reason he would head for shelter.

Hours later, it seemed, half frozen and numb with cold, the buckskin stumbled. Matt Ben, jerked from a half doze, looked up to see the gray burro walking straight at a jumble of unfamiliar rocks. Above the rocks, barely visible through the snow, towered a mountain. It might be one of the mountains behind Horntown!

Yet nothing was familiar. He swung down and, leading his horse, he plodded ahead. Suddenly the wind was gone. Looking up, he found the burro had led them into a rock-walled canyon. Plodding after the burro, his feet clumsy with cold, he found himself back in the wind again. He stopped, not believing what he saw.

There before him was a cluster of buildings covered with snow!

Zeke was walking straight ahead, for Zeke knew where he was going. He was returning to Horntown!

Two hours later, a fire roaring in the fireplace, Matt Ben handed another cup of scalding coffee to the sheriff. "Hadn't been for that old burro we'd have froze to death."

"Yes," Redman agreed, "and if you hadn't been good-hearted enough to worry about that burro, I'd be dead by now. You could have left me there, anyway."

"Huh?" Matt Ben stared at him sourly. "Now, why the devil would I do that? There wouldn't be anybody to fight with, then." He added a snowy log to the fire. "But you'd better get some help. You're too old for this sort of thing."

"How'd you happen to shoot that man in Carson?"

Matt explained. "He was fixin' to kill me. He wanted the name of killin' the last of the Jacksons of Horntown.

"The law has nothing against me but that. I've done a few things I shouldn't have done but there's nothing anybody can prove, and nothing they've got me tied to. I was through with all that. Being on the dodge all the time is no life for a man."

"We might find witnesses," Redman said thoughtfully. "Maybe somebody saw it. Seems to me that somebody always sees things, even when we think nobody is around. If we could prove that was a fair shooting we could get you off. That officer had a bad reputation among us who knew him. He had the instincts of a bully, and used his badge for protection."

He tugged at his mustache. "Anyway, I'd say a man who would come back and help an officer who'd just taken him prisoner couldn't be all bad.

"Another thing. You're right about me gettin' on in years. I need help. I need a deputy who can use a gun when needed but isn't anxious to go around shooting folks."

Matt Ben went out into the storm and crossed to the stable. The two horses and the old burro were chewing methodically on the grass in their mangers, and they rolled their eyes at him when he came in.

The sheriff had carried a little grub and a lot of coffee, and with what Matt Ben had they could live out the storm.

Matt Ben walked over to Zeke and rubbed the old burro's back. "Zeke, you old gray devil. I think we Jacksons have come back to Horntown to stay."

He stood a moment, his hand resting on the burro. Outside, the wind moaned around the eaves. It was cold out there, but the stable was snug and warm.

He went outside, closing the door carefully behind him,

then, turning the top of his head into the wind, he crossed the street to The Waterhole.

At the door, half sheltered from the wind, he looked back. Old Enoch had built well. The barn was old but it was strong against the wind.

Enoch had meant to sink roots here, to found a family. Well, it was up to him now, to Matt Ben Jackson the Younger.

RIDE OR START SHOOTIN'

Chapter 1

THE BET

TOLLEFSON SAW THE horses grazing in the creek bottom and pulled up sharply. "Harry," his voice was harsh and demanding as always, "whose horses are those?"

"Some drifter name of Tandy Meadows. He's got some fine-lookin' stock there."

"He's passin' through?"

"Well," Harry Fulton's reluctance sprang from his knowledge of Art Tollefson's temper, "he says he aims to run a horse in the quarter races."

Surprisingly, Tollefson smiled. "Oh, he does, does he? Too bad he hasn't money. I'd like to take it away from him if he had anything to run against Lady Luck."

Passman had his hat shoved back on his head. It was one of those wide-across-the-cheekbones faces with small eyes, a blunt jaw, and hollow cheeks. Everybody west of Cimarron knew Tom Passman for a gunfighter, and knew that Passman had carried the banner of Art Tollefson's legions into the high-grass country.

Ranching men had resented their coming with the big Flying T outfit and thirty thousand head of stock. Passman accepted their resentment and told them what they could do. Two, being plainsmen, elected to try it. Harry Fulton had helped to dig their graves.

It was Passman who spoke now. "He's got some real horses, boss."

Tollefson's coveting eyes had been appreciating that. It

was obvious that whoever this drifter was, he knew horse-flesh. In the twenty-odd head there were some splendid animals. For an instant a shadow of doubt touched him. Such a string might carry a quarter horse faster than Lady Luck. But the doubt was momentary, for his knowledge of the Lady and his pride of possession would not leave room for that. Lady Luck had bloodlines. She was more than range stock.

"Let's go talk to him," he said, and reined his bay around the start down the slope toward the creek.

Within view there was a covered wagon and there were two saddled horses. As they rode down the slope, a man stepped from behind the wagon to meet them. He was a short, powerfully set up Negro with one ear missing and the other carrying a small gold ring in the lobe. His boots were down at heel and his jeans worn.

"Howdy!" Tollefson glanced around. "Who is the owner here?" The tone was suited to an emperor, and behind the wall of his armed riders, Tollefson was almost that. Yet there is something about ruling that fades the perspective, denying clarity to the mind.

"I'm the owner."

The voice came from behind them and Tollefson felt sudden anger. Fulton, who was not a ruler and hence had an unblunted perspective, turned his head with the thought that whoever this man was, he was cautious, and no fool.

As they came down the hill the Negro emerged just at the right time to focus all their eyes, and then the other man appeared from behind them. It was the trick of a magician, of a man who understands indirection.

Tollefson turned in his saddle, and Fulton saw the quick shadow on Tom Passman's face, for Passman was not a man who could afford to be surprised.

A tall man stood at the edge of the willows. A man whose face was shadowed by the brim of a flat-crowned gray hat, worn and battered. A bullet, Fulton noticed, had creased the crown, neatly notching the edge, and idly he wondered what had become of the man who fired that shot.

The newcomer wore a buckskin vest but had no gun in sight. His spurs were large-roweled, California style, and in his hand he carried a rawhide riata. This was grass-rope country, and forty-five feet was a good length, yet from the look of this rope it was sixty or more.

"You the owner?" Tollefson was abrupt as always. "I hear you're plannin' to race a quarter horse against my Lady Luck."

"Aim to." The man came forward, moving with the step of a woodsman rather than a rider.

"I'm Tollefson. If you have any money and want to bet, I'm your man. If you don't have money, maybe we could bet some stock."

Tandy Meadows pushed back his hat from his strong bronzed face, calm with that assurance that springs from inner strength. Not flamboyant strength, nor pugnacious, but that of a man who goes his own way and blazes his own trails.

"Yeah," Tandy said slowly, digging out the makings, "I've two or three quarter horses. I figured to run one of them. It isn't much point which of them." He scratched a match on his trouser leg. "What made you figure I had no money? I got a mite of change I aimed to bet."

Tollefson's smile was patronizing. "I'm talking about *money,* man! I like to bet! I was thinking," he paused for effect and he deliberately made his voice casual, "five thousand dollars."

"Five?" Meadows lifted an eyebrow. "Well, all right. I guess I can pick up a few more small bets around to make it interesting."

Tollefson's skin tightened over his cheekbones. He was no gambling man, but it built his ego to see men back up and hesitate at the thought of five thousand dollars in one bet. "What do you mean? You want to bet *more* than five thousand dollars?"

"Sort of figured it." Meadows drew deeply on his cigarette. "I heard there was a gambling man down here who liked to bet enough to make it interesting."

Tollefson was deeply affronted. Not many men could afford to bet that kind of money, and he liked to flaunt big bets and show them who they were dealing with. Yet here was a man who calmly accepted his bet and hinted that it was pretty small potatoes. Somewhere in the group behind him he thought he detected a subdued snicker, and the casual indifference of this man Meadows irritated him.

"Whatever you want to put up," he snapped, "I'll cover! Name your price! I'll cover all you can get at two to one odds!"

"Now you're talkin'," Tandy said, sliding his thumbs behind his belt. "Aren't you the Tollefson from the Flying T? How about bettin' your ranch?"

Art Tollefson was shocked. He was profoundly shocked. This down-at-heels stranger offering to cover a bet against his *ranch*! Against the Flying T, sixty thousand head of stock and miles of rolling grassland, water holes, and buildings!

Lady Luck was his pride, a symbol of his power and money. She was the fastest thing he had ever seen on legs, and he liked to see her win. Yet his bets were merely for the sake of showing his large-handed way with money, of making him envied. At heart he was not a gambler and only put his money up reluctantly, but he was rarely called. Yet now he had been, and he knew that if he backed down now he would become the laughingstock of the range. It was a humiliation he neither wanted nor intended to endure.

"That's a rather large bet, my man," he said, for suddenly he realized the man must be bluffing. "Have you any idea what you're saying? You'd have to show a lot of money to cover it."

Meadows smiled. It was the first flicker of expression that had come to his face, but the smile was pleasant. Yet there was a shadow beneath it that might have been faintly ironic. "What's the matter, Tollefson?" he taunted gently. "Gettin' chilly around the arches? Or were you bluffin' with that big money talk? Back down, if you like, and don't waste my time. I'll cover your little spread and more if need be, so put up or shut up."

Tollefson's fury broke. "Why, you impudent chump!" He stopped, his jaw setting hard. "All right, get on your horse and come to the bank with me! John Clevenger knows my ranch, and he knows horses! If you've got the collateral, you can put it up, and you've made a bet!"

Tandy swung astride one of the saddled horses. Tollefson's quick eyes saw the build of the animal. Arab, with a strain of Morgan by the look of it. If this horse was any evidence . . . He shook off a momentary twinge of doubt.

Meadows turned his horse, then hesitated. "Don't you even want to see my horses? I've not decided which to run, but you're welcome to look 'em over."

"It's no matter!" Tollefson's fury was still riding him. He was bitter at the trap he had laid for himself. If this fool didn't have the money, why, he would . . . Just what he would do he wasn't sure but his face was flushed with angry blood.

Art Tollefson was not the only one who was feeling doubt. To Harry Fulton, who rode behind him, this seemed too pat to be an accident, and to Tom Passman it seemed the same way but with an added worry. Gifted at judging men, he knew Tandy Meadows should have been carrying a gun; yet there was none in sight, and it worried him.

Tandy Meadows looked straight down the road, aware that the crossroads of all his planning had been reached, and now everything depended on John Clevenger. He knew little about the banker except that the man was known and respected on the frontier, and that he was one of the original breeders of quarter horses. He was hardheaded, yet western man to the very heels of his boots, and a man with the courage of his convictions. It was rumored of him that he had once accepted four aces in a poker game as collateral for a bank loan.

The bank at El Poleo was a low, gray stone building that looked like the fort it had to be to survive. Situated as it was, across the street from the Poleo Saloon, half the town saw Art Tollefson and the stranger draw up before the bank. It was in the nature of things that in a matter of minutes everyone in town knew what they had come for. The town was aghast.

Chapter 2

A Trap Closes

JOHN CLEVENGER SAW them coming with no idea of what they wanted. He had opened his bank against great odds and against even greater odds had kept it going. He had faith in his fellow man and his judgment of them, and was accustomed to the amazing ways of western men. More than once he had loaned money on sheer courage and character. So far he had not lost by it.

Tollefson was a shrewd, hardheaded businessman, yet one of overbearing manner who carried things with a high hand. Tollefson dealt in force and money power, Clevenger in character and self-respect. That Tollefson should make such a wager was beyond belief, yet Clevenger heard them out in silence.

"You have collateral for such a bet?" Clevenger asked. He studied Meadows thoughtfully and approved of what he saw.

Tandy drew a black leather case from his hip pocket and extracted a letter and some legal-appearing papers. Clevenger accepted them, started as if struck, then looked again and became very thoughtful. Twice he glanced up at Meadows. At last he got to his feet and pulled off his glasses. There was the ghost of a twinkle in his eyes as he studied Meadows. "I hardly know what to say, Mr. Meadows. I—" His voice faltered, then stopped.

"That's my collateral," Tandy said quietly. "I think you're the best judge. Tollefson seems to want a big bet on this race. I've called him. We came to see if you would accept this as collateral and put up the money to cover the bet." He glanced toward the flushed face of the rancher. "Of course, if he wants to welsh on the bet, now's his last chance."

"I'll be double-slathered if I do!" Tollefson's fury was increased by his panic. He wanted nothing so much as to be safely out of this, but could see no escape without losing prestige, as important to him as life itself.

Clevenger stared thoughtfully at the papers. "Yes," he said at last, "I'll put up the money. Your bet's covered, Tollefson."

"Here—let me see that!" Tollefson's hand shot out, grabbing for the letter, but steely fingers caught his wrist.

Tandy Meadows jerked Tollefson's hand back and their eyes clashed. Half blind with fury, Tollefson stared at the younger man. "Take your hands off me!" he shouted.

"Willingly," Meadows replied shortly, "only you have neither the need nor the right to touch those papers. The contents are confidential. All you need is Clevenger's word that he will put up the money."

Stiffly, Tollefson drew back his hand, rubbing his wrist. He stared hard at Meadows, genuinely worried now. Who was this man? Where did he get such money? What had so astonished Clevenger about the papers? And that grip! Why, his fingers were like a steel trap!

Abruptly, he turned and walked from the bank followed by Fulton and Tom Passman. Together they entered the saloon. Fulton rubbed his jaw nervously, wanting to talk to Tollefson. This was a crazy bet! The equivalent of a quarter of a million dollars on a quarter-horse race against an unknown horse!

Of course, Lady Luck had consistently beaten all the horses that west Texas, New Mexico, and southern Colorado had found to race against the filly. There was no escaping the fact that she was fast. She was very fast.

"Boss," Fulton began hesitantly, "this bet ain't good sense. If I were you, I'd reconsider."

"You aren't me, so shut up!" Nobody needed to tell Tollefson that he had made a foolish bet. That was what pride could do for a man! The thought of withdrawing had rankled. He might have done it had Meadows not appeared so contemptuously sure he would. And in front of John Clevenger? The one man he had always failed to impress? Never!

He could just hear the laughter of the small ranchers whom he had forced back off their range. There was one thing he could not stand, and that was ridicule.

Outside the bank, Tandy Meadows stood and stared thoughtfully up the street. Now he had done what he had started out to do, and it remained only to win. Tollefson had deliberately forced Jim Whitten from his water hole, giving him only the choice of giving up his ranch or dying. And Gene Bates was now slowly recovering from a bullet wound from Passman's gun. That had been the only time Tom Passman had drawn a gun at El Poleo that he failed to kill. His shot had been high, but he had walked away from Bates believing him dead.

Suddenly, Tandy saw a girl come from a store, then turn and start toward him. It was Janet Bates!

At the same moment, within the saloon, Art Tollefson saw Janet, and saw her walk up to Tandy holding out her hand! He downed his drink with a gulp. Who was this Tandy Meadows?

Tom Passman was leaning on the bar alongside of him and he turned his head slightly. It rankled Passman that Tandy Meadows had gotten behind him. He had always said that no man could without him knowing it. He lifted his glass and his cold eyes studied the liquor. "Boss," he whispered, "let me handle it."

Relief broke over Tollefson. Yes, that was the way. It was the best way, but not yet. Only as a last resort. It would be too obvious, altogether too obvious.

Anger hit him then. What was he worrying about? When had Lady Luck failed him? Why should he be afraid that she might now? After all, suppose she did win? The idea came to him that if she did, he would have twice as much money, and it gave him a sudden lift. And so easy, for Lady Luck was fast. She had never been beaten. She had never even had a hard fight to win. Her last quarter had been in twenty-three, and she had done equally well on at least two other occasions.

Janet Bates was staring up into Tandy's eyes. "Oh, Tandy! I was never so glad to see anyone in my life! But is it true? That you are going to race against Lady Luck?"

"Sure, I'm going to run Cholo Baby."

"Tandy, you mustn't! Dad says there isn't a horse in the country can touch Lady Luck."

"Your dad's a good cattleman, Janet, but he's never seen

Cholo Baby. She's fast—fast enough to beat—" He stopped, then shrugged. "She's a runnin' little horse, honey. She really is."

"I hope Tollefson doesn't think so!" Janet said gravely. "If he did, he would stop at nothing. He's not a man who can stand losing, Tandy! He forced Dad off his range and then had him shot when he made trouble. He has a gunman who rides wherever he goes."

"I saw him." Meadows was serious. "Tom Passman's no bluffer. I know that. He doesn't remember me because I was just a kid when he last saw me, but I've seen him sling a gun, and he's fast."

"Are you having dinner with us? Dad will want to see you even though it isn't like it used to be on the ranch."

He hesitated, searching her eyes. "I might come, Janet." His eyes wandered up the street toward where Passman was loitering. "Are—are you married?"

"Married?" She was startled, but then her eyes crinkled with laughter. "Whatever gave you that idea?"

"Seems to be a fairly common practice"—he was grinning his relief—"when a girl gets to be your age. I figured I'd come back and see if you're still as dead set against a man who tramps around the country racing horses."

"Tandy," she said seriously, "you'll have to admit it wouldn't be much of a life for a girl, even though," she added reluctantly, "it might be exciting."

"It isn't so important where folks are," he commented, "as long as they are happy together."

"I've thought of that." She studied him. "Tandy, are you ever going to settle down? Haven't you had enough of it yet?"

"Maybe. We'll see. I figured when I left I would never come back at all. Then I heard what happened to Jim Whitten and to your dad. Why, your father took me in when I was all shot up, and if you two hadn't cared for me, I would sure enough have passed in my checks. As for Whitten, he never made trouble for anybody. So I had to come back."

There was quick fear in her eyes now. "Don't think about it, Tandy. Please don't. Nothing is worth what they could do to you. Tollefson's too strong, Tandy; nobody has a chance with him, and there's that awful Tom Passman."

"Sure. But why is he strong? Only because he has money, that's all. Suppose he lost it?"

"But how could he?"

"He could." Meadows squeezed her arm gently. "Believe me, honey, he could!"

Turning, he started down the street, aware that Tom Passman was watching him. He knew one reason for the man's curiosity. He was wondering if Meadows carried a gun, and if so, where it was. And if not, why not?

Snap was sitting on the wagon tongue when Tandy rode up to the camp in the creek bottom. Snap got to his feet and strolled out to meet Meadows, the shotgun in the crook of his arm. He was grinning expectantly. "You got a bet?" he asked softly.

Meadows nodded, smiling. "We sure have, Snap! And a lively hunch Tollefson would like nothing so much as to be safely out of it! We're going to have to be careful!" Meadows paused, then added:

"The man's no gambler. He's got a good horse, we know that. A mighty fast horse. We've got to hope ours is faster."

Snap nodded gravely. "You know I've seen that Lady Luck run, Mistuh Tandy. She's a mighty quick filly."

"Think she can beat Cholo Baby?"

Snap smiled. "Well, now. I reckon I'm some prejudiced about that! I never seen the horse I figured could beat our baby. But it will be a race, Mistuh Tandy! It sure will!"

The race was scheduled for the following Wednesday, three days away. By the time Meadows rode again to El Poleo, the town was buzzing with news of the bet. Tandy had done much to see the story got around, for the more who knew of it the less chance of Tollefson backing out. Yet the town was buzzing with more than that, for there was much speculation about Tandy Meadows, where he came from and where he got the money to make such a bet.

Nobody in town knew him but several had seen Janet Bates greet him like an old friend, and that in itself was puzzling. Art Tollefson was curious about that, and being the man he was, he went directly to the source, to Bates's small ranch forty miles north of El Poleo. Johnny Herndon, a Bates hand, was hazing a half dozen cattle out of the brush, and his eyes narrowed when he saw Tollefson.

"You off your home range, Tollefson?" he said abruptly. "Or are you figurin' on pushin' us off this piece, too?"

Tollefson waved a hand. Yet his eyes had noted the grass and that some of it was subirrigated. It was an idea, at that. "Nothing like that," he replied shortly. "Just ridin' around a little. Saw a puncher down to El Poleo with some fine horses, a man named Meadows."

"Tandy Meadows?" Herndon had heard nothing of the bet, and he was instantly curious. "So he came back, did he? I sort of reckoned he would. Does he have some racin' stock with him?"

"Some, I reckon. Is he from around here?"

"Meadows? He's from nowhere. He rode in here one night over a year ago, shot to doll rags and barely hangin' to his horse. That was the first any of us ever saw of him. Gene Bates took him off his horse and they spent two months nursin' him back to health. Then he loafed around another month, sort of recuperatin'.

"Personally, I never figured he'd leave, for Janet sort of took to him, and the way they acted, it was mutual, but he finally pulled out."

"You said he'd been shot up? How did that happen? He doesn't even carry a gun now."

"No? Now, that's funny. They tell me he was some slick. I heard of him after he left here, but it was the story of some shootin' scrape down to Santa Fe before he drifted this way. Good two years ago. He never did say who shot him up, but some of us done some figurin' an' we reckoned it was the Alvarez gang. Story was they stole a bunch of horses off him, and that must be so. He got me to help him ride north and haze a bunch out of a canyon up there, and mighty fine stock.

"He'd evidently left them there when he was shot up, but he just had to close the gate as they were in a box canyon hideout with plenty of grass and water. They were somewhat wild but in fine shape."

"You mean the Alvarez gang had taken the horses there? Did you see any of them?"

Herndon shrugged, rolling a smoke. It was a bright, sunny morning and he had talked to nobody in three days. "Didn't figure I would. Meadows told me there wouldn't be any trouble, and he's the sort of man who would know.

"No, we saw hide nor hair of nobody. At the up end of that canyon there was an adobe, and Tandy advised me to stay away from it. But once I did get sort of close and there was somethin' white lyin' there that I'd swear was a skeleton."

"Has he got any money?"

"Who, Tandy?" Herndon chuckled. "I doubt it. He's a saddle tramp. Thinks of nothin' but what's the other side of the hill and racin' his horses. If he ever had more than a thousand dollars in his life it would surprise me."

Chapter 3

TRICKERY

ART TOLLEFSON WAS a cautious man, and he had been very lacking in caution when he had allowed his pride to trap him into the bet with Meadows, but now he was doing a lot of serious thinking. The following morning he mounted up, and saying nothing to anyone, he rode north, avoiding the Bateses' range and heading for the area in which the box canyon had been.

From Herndon's comments it was not too hard to find, although had he not been expecting it, a man could have ridden by within a dozen yards and never guessed its existence. The bars were up, but he took them down and rode into a pleasant little canyon, grass covered and shady with probably two hundred acres of rich land in the bottom, and a good spring at the head of it.

Nearing the adobe he rode more cautiously, and when several yards away, he drew up. Obviously, no one had been this close to the cabin for a long time, and Herndon's surmise had been correct. It was a skeleton.

Buzzards had stripped the bones bare since, but the chaps and gun belts remained, their leather stiff as board from weathering. Not far from the bones lay a rusted six-shooter.

Tollefson trailed his reins and walked up to the door. He stopped there, his mouth suddenly dry. Here three men had died, and they had died hard. The table was turned on its side and nearby lay another skeleton, facedown on the dirt floor. Another slumped in the corner with a round hole over the eye, and the third was sprawled under some fallen slickers in a corner.

The scene was not hard to reconstruct. They had been surprised here by a man who had walked in through the doorway. The fourth man had evidently been drawn by the gunfire or had come up later. It was a very thoughtful man who turned his horse toward El Poleo somewhat later. If Tandy Meadows had walked away from that cabin alive, he was nobody with whom to play games. The sooner Passman knew, the better.

At four o'clock on the afternoon of the day before the race, Tandy Meadows watched Snap prepare an early supper. He was as good a hand with food as with horses, and he worked swiftly and surely, yet his eyes were restless and he was obviously on edge. "You reckon he'll make trouble, boss?"

"I'd almost bet on it," Meadows replied, "but you can't tell. His pride might keep him from it. He figures Lady Luck will win, I know, but he's not a gambling man, and he'd like to be sure."

"You'd better watch that Passman," Snap advised. "He's a bad man."

Tandy nodded. He was the last man in the world to take Tom Passman lightly, for he had seen him throw a gun, and the man was deadly. Moreover, he was a tough man with a lot of pride in his skill, no braggart, and no four-flusher. Only death itself would stop his guns.

Cholo Baby, a beautiful sorrel, lifted her head and whinnied softly as he approached. She was fifteen hands high, with wide-spaced and intelligent eyes. She stretched her velvety nose toward his hand and he touched her lightly. "How's it, girl? You ready to run for me tomorrow?"

Baby nudged him with her nose and Tandy grinned. "I doubt if you ever lived a day when you didn't feel like running, Cholo. And I hope there never is!"

He strolled back to the wagon, his eyes alert and searching the mountainside, the willows and the trail. He ate without talking, restless and disturbed despite himself. So far everything had been too quiet. Much too quiet.

He could neither rest nor relax. A hint of impending danger hung over the camp and he roved restlessly about. Snap seemed to feel it, too, and even the horses were alert as if they sensed something in the air. Of course, Tandy reflected, if anything happened to Cholo Baby, he could ride Khari, the half-Morgan, half-Arabian horse he usually rode. Not so fast as Cholo Baby over the quarter, but still a fast horse for one with so much staying power.

He still carried his rawhide riata. He was a California rider, and like them he valued the use of the riata, and was amazingly proficient with it. The California riders always used rawhide riatas of great length, and used them with such skill they were almost part of them. Suddenly, Tandy Meadows stopped. Hard upon the trail he heard the pounding hoofs of a hard-ridden horse!

Snap was on his feet, leaning against the off wheel of the wagon, his shotgun resting over the corner of the wagon box to cover the trail. Tandy fell back near the wagon where his Winchester stood, and waited, his lips tight, his eyes cool. Yet when the rider drew nearer he saw it was Janet Bates.

She drew up sharply and dropped to the ground. "Oh, Tandy!" Her face was pale. "What have you *done*? I just heard today you'd made a bet with Tollefson for his whole ranch! Tandy, you know you haven't that kind of money! If you lose, what will you do? One man did fail to pay off Tollefson once and he had been lashed to a tree and whipped by Tom Passman! He'd kill you, Tandy!"

Meadows smiled at her anxiety. "So you do worry about me? You do like me a little, then?"

"Be serious." Her eyes flashed. In the dusk she seemed even more lovely than ever. "You're in trouble, and you don't even know it. Lady Luck always wins, Tandy. He'll kill you!"

"He must have figured my bet was all right," Meadows replied. "Clevenger backed me."

"Oh, I know, Tandy! But you fooled him somehow. I just know you fooled him! If you don't win, what will you do?"

"I'll win," he replied simply. "I've got to win. I've got to win for you, Janet, and for your father and Jim Whitten. I came back here to force Tollefson out of the country, and I'll not rest until I do! Your dad was mighty kind to me when I was all shot up and dyin'. Without you two I'd not be here, so when I heard of what had happened, I figured this out. I'd heard of Lady Luck, and I knew Tollefson was a mighty big-headed and stubborn man, so I deliberately worked on his pride."

"That isn't all I heard," Janet persisted quickly. "Tollefson was up near our ranch twice. He talked to Johnny about you, asking all sorts of questions. He seemed very curious about how you'd been wounded that time, and the next day Johnny Herndon saw him riding north toward the box canyon where you left your horses that time."

Meadows scowled. What did that mean, anyway? The Alvarez gang had been notorious outlaws, and the killing of them would be considered a public service. Or would have been at the time. Yet with such information a man of his influence might find some way to do him harm.

"Boss," Snap's voice was urgent, "somebody comin'."

Tandy Meadows turned and watched the horsemen. There were four in the group and one of them he recognized instantly as Tom Passman. When they drew nearer he saw that another was Fulton, while the two riding with them were Sheriff George Lynn and his deputy Rube Hatley.

"Meadows," Lynn said, "we rode out here after you. You've got to come back to town and answer a few questions."

"Always glad to answer questions, Sheriff. Can't I answer them here?"

"No." Lynn's voice was testy. "You can answer them in my office. There's a place for such things and this isn't it!"

"All right, Sheriff," Meadows agreed. "But how about lettin' Hatley stay here to guard my horses?"

Lynn hesitated, disturbed by the request. It was reasonable enough, but when Art Tollefson had told him what to do, George Lynn had been reasonably certain what lay behind it. If he left Hatley he would be defeating the purpose of the trip. "Sorry," he replied abruptly, "I need Hatley with me!"

"Then of course you'll be responsible for my horses?" Meadows persisted. "I don't think they should be left alone."

"They'll be safe enough." Lynn was growing angry. "The responsibility is your own. Are you coming," he asked sharply, "or do we take you?"

"Why, I'm coming, Sheriff. I've never suggested anything to the contrary." He put his foot into the stirrup, then swung aboard Khari. "Snap," he said loudly, "if any varmints come around, don't take chances. Shoot to kill." Then he added, "You'll be perfectly safe because nobody would be fool enough to come near racin' stock on the night before a race. So don't forget, shoot to kill!"

"Sure thing, boss. I got me a shotgun loaded for bear!"

Nothing more was said as they rode back to town. Several times Tandy saw Passman watching him, but when they reached town only a few loafers noticed them ride down the street to the sheriff's office.

Inside, Lynn came to the point at once. "I've brought you in to ask you questions about a shootin' scrape, sometime back."

"Why, sure!" Meadows dropped into a chair. "I didn't figure Tollefson rode all the way up to that canyon for nothing. He must be really worried if he's tryin' this hard to find a way out of his bet. But aren't you and Passman buckin' a stacked deck? Who will you work for if I win?"

"I work for the county!" Lynn said sharply. "That horse race has nothing to do with this inquiry!"

"Of course not! That's why Fulton and Passman were with you, Sheriff! Because the race has nothing to do with it! That's why you waited to bring me in until the night before the race! I hope somebody tries to bother those horses tonight! Snap's a whiz with a shotgun!"

He turned his head. "Passman came along hopin' I'd make some wrong play so he could plug me."

Passman's eyes were flat and gray. "You talk a lot," he said shortly, "but can you shoot?"

Lynn waved an irritated hand. "Who were those hombres you shot up north?"

"I shot?" Meadows looked mildly astonished. "Why, Sheriff, I didn't say I shot anybody. I did hear something about the Alvarez gang catching some lead over some horses they stole, but beyond that I'm afraid I don't remember much about it."

"You deny you shot them? You deny the fight?"

"I don't deny anything, and I don't admit anything."

Tandy's voice was cool. "If you're planning to arrest me, by all means do it. Also, get me a lawyer down here, then either file charges against me or turn me loose. This whole proceeding, Sheriff, is highly irregular. All you have is Tollefson's word that he saw some skeletons somewhere. Or some dead men, or some bullet holes, or something. You know that I was wounded about the same time, but even if they were not horse thieves, you'd have a tough time proving any connection."

Lynn was uneasy. This was the truth and he knew it, but this was what Tollefson wanted, and what he wanted he got. Yet for almost three hours he persisted in asking questions, badgering Meadows with first one and then another, and trying to trap him. Yet he got nowhere. Finally, he got to his feet. "All right, you can go. If I want any more questions answered, I'll send for you."

Meadows got to his feet and let his eyes, suddenly grown cold, go over the four men. "All right, Sheriff, I'm always glad to answer questions, but get this: if anything has happened to my horses while I was in here, I'm coming back, and I'll be looking for each and every one of you.

"And that, Lynn," his eyes turned to the sheriff, "goes for you, sheriff or no sheriff! I'm a law-abiding man, and have always been, but if you've conspired with that fatheaded Tollefson to keep my horse out of that race, and through it harm comes to my horses, you'd better start packing a gun for me! Get that?"

George Lynn's face whitened and he involuntarily drew back. Worriedly, he glanced at Fulton and Passman for support. Fulton was pale as himself, and Passman leaned against the wall, nonchalantly rolling a cigarette. Rube Hatley stood near the door, his position unchanged. Meadows turned and walked past him, scarcely hearing the whispered, "Luck!" from Rube.

After he was gone, Lynn stared at Fulton. "Harry, what will we do?"

Rube Hatley chuckled. "Only one thing you can do, Sheriff. You can light a shuck out of the country or you can die. Either way, I don't care. I wanted no part of this yellow-bellied stunt, and if they were my horses I'd shoot you on sight."

"Passman?" Lynn was almost pleading. "You're the gunslinger."

Passman shrugged. "When I get my orders. Until then I don't make a move." He turned on his heel and walked out into the night.

Lynn stared at Fulton. "Harry," he begged, "you know. What did they do?"

"Do?" Fulton's hand shook as he lighted his smoke. "Tollefson's too smart to pull anything too raw. He just had some of the boys take those horses out and run them over the desert for three hours, that's all! By daylight those horses will be so stiff and stove up they wouldn't be able to walk that quarter, let alone run it!"

"What about the black boy?"

Fulton shrugged. "That's another story. Who cares about him?"

"Meadows might."

"Yeah." Fulton was thoughtful. "He might at that. But you can be sure of one thing, after the runnin' his horses got this night, through cactus, brush, and rocks, they'll do no running tomorrow. I can promise you that! You leave the rest to Passman!"

"Did Tollefson actually *see* those skeletons?"

"He sure did." Fulton's voice was dry, emotionless. "And from what he said, if that was Tandy Meadows who walked into that shack after the Alvarez boys, he's got nerve enough to crawl down a hole after a nest full of rattlers, believe me!"

Chapter 4

GILT-EDGED COLLATERAL

MORNING DAWNED BRIGHT and still, and for the better part of two hours it remained bright and still, and then the boys from the ranches began to show up in El Poleo. Hard-riding youngsters, most of them, with here and there older men whose eyes were careful and wary with the sense of trouble.

Buckboards, a fringed surrey, a Conestoga wagon, and many horseback riders, all coming in for the races, and all curious about what would happen. Some had heard there had been trouble the night before, but what or when, they did not know.

Art Tollefson came in about noon. The covered wagon stood in the creek bottom disconsolate and alone. No horses were in sight, nor movement of any kind. His lips thinned with cruelty and his eyes were bright with triumph and satisfaction. Try to buck Art Tollefson, would they!

He was walking into the saloon when he saw a buckboard draw up between two buildings, and Gene Bates and Jim Whitten got down. His lips tightened and he walked on into the saloon.

The usual jovial laughter stilled as he entered. With a wave of the hand he invited all and sundry to join him at the bar. Each year this was his custom at this time, but now there was no concerted rush for the bar.

This time, not a man moved.

Impatiently, he stared around the room but all eyes avoided his. Then Fulton stepped to the bar followed by several of his own Flying T riders. His face and neck crimson, Tollefson stared down at his drink, his jaw set hard.

Gene Bates and Jim Whitten walked into the saloon and to the bar. "Tollefson's buyin'," the bartender explained hurriedly.

"Not our drinks!" Bates's voice was flat. "I'll drink with no man who hires his killin' done and hires other men to ruin a man's horses so he loses a race!"

Tollefson whirled. The truth was hard to take, he found. "Who said that?" he demanded. "That's a lie!"

Bates faced him. The white-haired old man's blue eyes were fierce. "Better back up on that, Tollefson," he advised coldly. "Passman's not here to do your shootin' for you this time!"

Tollefson's fingers stiffened, and for an instant he seemed about to draw, but at Fulton's low-voiced warning, he turned back to the bar.

Sheriff George Lynn pushed through the doors and walked to the bar. He spoke under his breath to Tollefson. "They did it all right! They ran those horses half to death! I passed 'em out on the flat not thirty minutes ago, and a worse-lookin' bunch you never did see! I couldn't get close, but it was close enough!"

"What will Meadows do now?" Fulton asked, low voiced.

Rube Hatley had come in. He overheard Fulton's remark and leaned both elbows on the bar. "Do?" Rube chuckled without humor. "If I were you hombres I'd do one of two things. I'd start ridin' or start shootin'!"

The course was the same straightaway course they had used for this race for several years. There were several two-twenty and three-thirty races to be run off before the quarter races began.

Tollefson watched nervously, his eyes roving the crowd. He saw neither Tandy Meadows nor Snap. Janet Bates rode in with Johnny Herndon, and they joined her father and Jim Whitten.

Fulton sat with Tollefson and Sheriff Lynn, and the last to arrive was Tom Passman. He dismounted but kept free of the crowd. Tollefson noted with relief that he was wearing two guns, something he rarely did. When he walked to the edge of the track, people moved away from him.

The quarter-horse race was announced, and Tollefson touched his lips uneasily with his tongue as he watched Lady Luck walking into place in the line. Three other horses were entered in this race and they all showed up. All but one had been beaten by the Lady in previous races, and Tollefson began to breathe easier.

What a fool he had been to take such a chance! Well, it was over now, and he was safe. But where was Meadows?

Fulton grabbed his arm. *"Look!"* he gasped. "Look there!"

Another horse had moved into line, a sorrel, and beautifully made. The rider on the last horse was Snap, Meadows's Negro rider.

Tollefson's face flushed, then went white. He started forward, but stopped suddenly. Gene Bates was standing in front of him with a shotgun. "Let's let 'em run," Bates suggested. "You keep your place!"

Tollefson drew back, glancing around desperately. Sheriff Lynn had disappeared, but Rube Hatley loafed nearby. "Do something, man!" Tollefson insisted.

"For what?" Hatley grinned at him, his eyes hard. "Nobody's busted any law that I can see. That shotgun's in the hollow of his arm. Nobody says he can't carry it there."

Now the horses were moving together toward the far end of the course. As in a trance, Art Tollefson watched them go, watched most of all that sorrel with the squat black rider. Suddenly, he felt sick. If that horse won, he was through, *through*! It was unthinkable.

He turned sharply. "Tom!" he said. Passman looked around, his eyes level and gray. "When you see him! And there's a bonus in it for you!"

Passman nodded but made no other reply. Fulton felt a constriction in his chest. He had heard Tollefson order men beaten, cattle driven off, homes burned, but this was the first time he had actually heard him order a man killed. Yet nowhere was there any sign of Tandy Meadows.

Tollefson sat his horse where he could see the race, the full length of the course. His eyes went now to the far end where the horses were lining up, and his heart began to pound. His fingers on the saddle horn were relaxed and powerless. Suddenly, the full impact of his bet came home to him, and he realized, almost for the first time, what losing would mean.

How had he ever been such a fool? Such an utter and complete fool? How had he been trapped into such a situation?

His thoughts were cut sharply off by the crack of a pistol, and his heart gave a tremendous leap as he saw the horses lunge into a dead run. Lady Luck had seemed almost to squat as the pistol cracked, and then bounded forward and was down the track running like a scared rabbit.

Tollefson, his breath coming hoarsely, stood in his stirrups, his agonized stare on the charging horses, and suddenly he realized he was shouting his triumph, for the Lady was well off and running beautifully. Then, even as he cheered, a sorrel shot from the group behind the Lady and swooped down upon her!

His pulse pounding, his eyes bulging with fear and horror, he saw that rusty streak of horse come up behind the Lady, saw its head draw abreast, then the nose was at the Lady's shoulder, and the Lady was running like something possessed, as if she knew what great change rode with her. Tollefson was shouting madly now, almost in a frenzy, for out there with those running horses was everything he owned, everything he had fought for, burned for, killed for. And now that sorrel with its crouching black rider was neck and neck with the Lady, and then with the finish line only a length away the sorrel seemed to give a great leap and shot over the finish line, winner by half a length!

Tollefson sagged back in his saddle, staring blindly down the hill. Tricked—tricked and beaten. Lady Luck was beaten. He was beaten. He was through, finished!

Then he remembered Tom Passman, and saw him standing down by the finish line, away from him. *Passman!* Tollefson's eyes suddenly sharpened. He could still win! Passman could kill them! He could kill Meadows, Whitten, Bates! Anyone who fought or resisted him! He would turn his riders loose on the town, he would—

Then a voice behind him turned him cold and still inside. "Well, you lost, Tollefson. You've got until sundown to get out of the country. You can load your personal belongings, no more. You can take a team and a buckboard. Get moving!"

Passman seemed to have heard. He turned slowly, and he was looking at them now from forty yards away. In a daze, Tollefson saw Tandy Meadows step out toward the gunman, holding in his hands nothing but the rawhide riata.

Tom Passman crouched a little, his eyes riveted on Meadows, his mind doing a quick study. If he drew and killed an unarmed man, there was a chance not even Tollefson could save him. Yet was Meadows unarmed? At what point might he not suddenly flash a gun from his shirt front or waistband?

Meadows took another step, switching the rope in his hands with seeming carelessness. Again Passman's eyes searched Meadows's clothing for a suspicious bulge, and saw none. Surely, the man would not come down here without a weapon? It was beyond belief. "What's the matter, Tom?" Meadows taunted. "Yellow?"

As he spoke, his hands flipped, and as Passman's hands swept down for his guns he saw something leap at him like a streak of light. He threw up a hand, tried to spring aside, but that rawhide riata loop snapped over his shoulders and whipped taut even as his hands started to lift the guns, and he was jerked off balance.

He staggered, trying desperately to draw a gun, but his arms were pinned to his sides. Meadows took two running steps toward him, throwing another loop of the rope over his shoulders that fell to his ankles. He jerked hard and the gunman fell, hitting hard in the dust. He struggled to get up, and Tandy jerked him from his feet again. Tandy stood off, smiling grimly.

Then, stepping in quickly, he jerked the guns from Passman's holsters and tossed them aside. Springing back, he let Passman fight his way free of the noose. As the loop dropped from the gunman, he wheeled on Meadows, and Tandy struck him across the mouth with the back of his hand.

It was deliberate, infuriating. Passman went blind with rage and rushed. A left smeared his lips and a roundhouse right caught him on the ear. He staggered sideways, his ears ringing. Meadows walked into him then and slugged two wicked underhand punches into the gunman's body. Passman sagged and went down, landing on his knees.

Tandy jerked him erect, struck him again in the stomach, and ignoring the futile punches the man threw, stepped back and smashed him full in the mouth with a right. Passman went down again.

Bloody and battered, he lay gasping on the ground. Meadows stood over him. "Tom," he said coldly, "I could have killed you. You never saw the day you were as fast as I am. But I don't want to kill men, Tom. Not even you. Now get out of the country! If you ever come north of the river again, I'll hunt you down and kill you! Start *moving*!"

Tandy stepped back, coiling his rope. He glanced around. Tollefson was gone, and so was Fulton.

Rube Hatley gestured toward Passman. "He means it, Tom," he said, "and so do I. I'd have run you out of here months ago if it hadn't been for Tollefson and Lynn. Take his advice and don't come back, because I may not be any faster than you, Tom, but if you ever ride this way again, you've got me to kill, and I sort of think we'd go together!"

Hatley glanced at Tandy. "You had me fooled. What happened to your horses?"

"Janet and Snap figured something would happen, so they drove them back into the hills a mile or so, and then they moved in a bunch of half-broke Flying T broomtails down on that meadow. In the dark they never guessed they were drivin' some of their own remuda!"

Janet came up to Tandy, smiling gravely, her eyes lighted with something half affection and half humor. "I was glad to help. I thought if you won this race you might settle down."

Meadows shrugged, grinning. "I don't see any way out of it with a ranch to manage and a wife to support."

Janet stared suspiciously from Meadows to Clevenger. "Now tell me," she insisted. "What would you have done if Cholo Baby had lost? How could you have paid up?"

The banker looked sheepish. "Well, ma'am, I reckon I'd have had to pay off. That was my money backing him."

"Yours?" she was incredulous. "Without collateral?"

"No, ma'am!" Clevenger shook his head decisively. "He had collateral! In the banking business a man's got to know what's good security and what isn't! What he showed me was plumb good enough for any old horseman like myself. It was Cholo Baby's pedigree!

"Why, ma'am, that Cholo Baby was sired by old Dan Tucker, one of the finest quarter-horse stallions of them all! He was a half brother to Peter McCue, who ran the quarter in twenty-one seconds!

"Like I say, ma'am, a banker has to know what's good collateral and what ain't! Why, a man what knows horses could no more fail to back that strain than he could bet against his own mother!

"And look," he said grinning shrewdly. "Was it good collateral, or wasn't it? Who *won*?"

REGAN OF THE SLASH B

DAN REGAN CAME up to the stage station at sundown and glanced quickly toward the window to see if the girl was there. She was. He stripped the saddle from his horse and rubbed the animal down with a handful of hay. Lew Meadows came down from the house and watched him silently.

"You don't often get over this way," Meadows said, pointedly.

Dan Regan paused from his work and straightened, resting a hand on the sorrel's withers. "Not often," he said. "I keep busy in the hills."

Meadows was curious and a little worried. Dan Regan was a lion hunter for the big Slash B outfit, but he was a newcomer to the country, and nothing much was known about him. There were too many men around the country now, too many that were new. Tough men, with hard jaws and careful eyes. He knew the look of them, and did not like what that look implied.

"Seen any riders up your way?"

Regan had gone back to working on the sorrel. He accepted the question and thought about it. "Not many," he said, at last. "A few strangers."

"They've been coming here, too. There's a couple of them inside now. Burr Fulton and Bill Hefferman."

Dan Regan slapped the sorrel on the hip and wiped his hands. "I've heard of them. They used to waste around down to Weaver."

"Having a daughter like mine is a bad thing out here," Meadows told him, the worry plain in his voice. "These men worry me."

"She looks fit to hold her own," Dan commented mildly.

Meadows looked at him. "You don't know Fulton. He's a lawless man; so are they all. They know what's happening. The word's gone out."

"What word?" Dan asked sharply.

Meadows shrugged. "Can't you see? The Slash B runs this country, always has. The Slash B was the law. Before Billings's time this was outlaw country, wild and rough, and the outlaws did what they wanted. Then Cash Billings came in and made law where there was none. He had an outfit of hardcase riders and when anybody overstepped what Billings thought was proper, the man was shot, or ordered out of the country. They made a few mistakes, but they had order. It was safe."

"The country's building up now. There's a sheriff."

Meadows spat his disgust. "Bah! Colmer's afraid of his shadow. Fulton ordered him out of the saloon over at the Crossing the other night and he went like a whipped dog."

"What about the Slash B? Has it lost its authority?"

"You don't hear much, up there in the hills. The Slash B is through, finished. Cash is a sick man, and that nephew of his is a weakling. The foreman is drunk half the time, and the old crowd is drifting away. That's why the wolves are coming. They know there's no bull moose for this herd. They want to start cutting it for their own profit."

Meadows nodded toward the house. "Where do Fulton and Hefferman get their money? They spend it free enough, but never do a pat of work. They sell Slash B cows, that's how. I wish somebody could talk to Cash. He doesn't know. He lives alone in that big house, and he hears nothing but what they tell him."

————

MEADOWS WALKED OFF toward the house and Dan Regan stood there in the darkening barn and brushed off his clothes. This was not quite new to him. He had known some of it, but not that it had grown so bad. Maybe if he went to Cash Billings . . . No, that would never do. Cash knew he had a lion hunter, but he didn't know he was Dan Regan, which was just as well.

Regan was a lean young man, as accustomed to walking as riding. He understood the woods and trails, knew cattle and lions. He was killing a lot of the latter. He walked on up to the house and into the big dining room where they fed the stage passengers and any chance travelers following the route. The table was empty except for a fat-faced drummer with a wing collar, and the two riders Lew Meadows had mentioned.

Burr Fulton was a lean whip of a man, as tall as Regan but not so broad. Hefferman was beefy, a heavy-shouldered man with thick-lidded eyes and a wide, almost flat, red face. He looked as tough and brutal as Regan knew him to be. Neither of them looked up to see who had entered. They did not care. They were men riding a good thing, and they knew it.

Dan Regan had seen this thing happen before. He had seen big outfits lose their power. He had seen the wolves cut in and rip the herds to bits, taunting the impotent outfit that had once wielded power, and rustling its herds without retaliation. It was always the big herds, the strong outfits, that went down the hardest.

He seated himself on the bench some distance away from the others, and after a minute Jenny Meadows came in and brought his dinner. He glanced up and their eyes met quickly, and Jenny looked hastily away, a little color coming into her cheeks.

It had been a month since she had seen this man, but she hadn't forgotten a thing about him, remembering the lean strength of his face, the way his dark hair curled behind his ears, and the way his broad shoulders swelled the flannel of his shirt.

She put his food down, then hesitated. "Coffee?"

"Milk, if you've got it. I never get any up in the mountains."

Hefferman heard the word and glanced over at him.

"Milk," he said to Fulton. "He drinks milk."

Burr laughed. "He's from the Slash B. I think they all drink milk these days!"

Regan felt his ears burning and some dark, uneasy warmth stirring in his chest. He did not look up, but continued to eat.

Meadows was standing in the door and overheard Fulton's comment. Now he sat down across the table from Regan and poured a cup of coffee.

"Meadows," Fulton said, looking up, "do you use Slash B beef? Best around here, and I hear it can be had cheap."

"I have my own cows," Meadows replied stiffly. He was a somber man, gray-haired and thin. Never a fighter, he had a stern, unyielding sense of justice and a willingness to battle if pushed. He had lived safely here, in the shadow of the Slash B.

"Might as well buy some of their beef," Hefferman boomed. "Everybody else is!"

Jenny returned and put a glass of milk in front of Regan. Her own face was burning, for the remarks had been audible in the kitchen, and she knew they were deliberately trying to make trouble. It irritated her that Regan took no offense and she was ashamed for him.

Moreover, she was sure that Dan Regan had come to the stage station to see her. Remembering the impression he had made the first time, she also remembered his eyes on her, and how they had made her feel. He was, she knew, the first man who had awakened within her the sense of being female, of being a woman. It was a new sensation, and an exciting one.

The supplies he had bought on his last trip were enough for another month at least, yet he had come back now. Knowing he came to see her, and remembering the excitement he had roused in her on his last trip, she regarded him somewhat as her own. It displeased her to see him sit quietly before the taunts of the two badlands riders.

Meadows was thinking similar thoughts. Jenny worried him. It was bad enough to have a daughter to rear on the frontier, worse when she had no mother. He hated to think of her leaving him, yet he knew when she married it would be a distinct relief. His ideas on women were strict, dogmatic, and old-fashioned, yet he was aware that nature takes little note of the rules of men. Still, the malpais country offered little in the way of eligible males.

He was aware of the dark good looks of Burr Fulton, and that such a man might appear dashing and exciting to a girl like Jenny. Dan Regan's first visit to the stage station had arrested his notice as it had Jenny's, for here was a tall, fine-looking man with a steady way about him and a good job, even if it was with the declining Slash B.

Meadows wanted no trouble around his place, and yet, like Jenny, he was irritated that Regan took no offense at the ragging Fulton and Hefferman were giving him.

BURR LOOKED UP suddenly at Jenny.

"Dance over to Rock Springs next week. Want to ride over with me?"

"No," Jenny replied, "I don't want to ride anywhere with a man who makes a living by stealing other men's beef!"

Fulton's face flushed with angry blood and he half rose to his feet. "If you were a man," he said, "I'd kill you for that!" He remained hard. "Might as well come," he said. "You'll at least be going with a man who could protect you. I don't drink milk!"

"It might be better if you did!" she retorted.

After a few minutes, with a few more sarcastic remarks, the two got up and went outside, mounted, and rode away. After they were gone the silence was thick in the room. Dan Regan stared gloomily at his milk, aware of Meadows's irritation and Jenny's obvious displeasure.

He looked up, finally. "That was what I came down for, Jenny. I want to take you to that dance."

She turned on him, and her face was stiff. Her chin lifted. "I'd not want to go with you," she said bitterly. "You'd be afraid to stand up for a girl! You won't even stand up for your own rights! I thought you were a *man*!"

The moment the angry words were out, she would have given anything not to have said them. She hesitated, instantly contrite. Dan Regan took one more swallow of milk and got up. Coolly, but with his face pale and his eyes grim, he picked up his hat.

"I reckon that settles that," he said quietly, "and I'll be riding on."

Jenny took an impulsive step toward him, not finding the

words to stop him, but his back was turned. Only at the door did he turn.

"What did you want?" he asked coldly. "A killing? For so little? Is a man's life so small a thing to you?"

She stared at the door, appalled. Then her eyes went to her father's.

"But, Dad! He—it wouldn't have meant a killing!"

Meadows looked up, realization in his eyes. "It might, Jenny. It might, at that."

It was young Tom Newton who took her to the dance. A handsome boy he was, a year younger than she, and a rider for the Slash B. Yet the moment she walked through the door of the Rock Springs school she sensed the subtle difference in the atmosphere. The same people were there, but now a queer restraint seemed to sit upon them. The reason was not hard to see. Burr Fulton was there, with Bill Hefferman and some dozen other hardcase riders, all outside men, all tough, and all drinking.

Yet the affair started well, and it was not until after three dances that she glanced toward the door and saw Dan Regan. There was a subtle difference about him, too, and for a moment she could not place it, and then she saw. He was wearing two guns. It was the first time she had ever seen him with anything but a rifle, yet he wore the guns naturally, easily.

He wore a dark broadcloth suit that somehow suited him better than she would have believed. He did not wear it with the stiff, dressed-up manner of most western men, but with the ease of one long accustomed to such clothes. The change was good, she decided, for he managed to look not only perfectly at ease, but completely the gentleman.

As the evening wore on, the Fulton riders grew more boisterous. Hefferman walked out on the floor and took a girl from another man by the simple procedure of shoving the man away. White-faced, the girl danced with him, and when the dance was over, she and her friend left. Others began to drift away, and somberly, Dan Regan watched them go.

Jenny Meadows was perfectly aware it was time she left, but Dan had made no effort to come to her, nor to request a dance. Disappointed, and more than a little angry, she delayed even after Tom Newton began to urge her to leave with him.

Once, early in the evening, she had danced with Burr Fulton. He had teased her a little, but his behavior had been all she could have asked. Now he came to her again, his face flushed with drinking.

"Let's dance!" he said, grinning at her.

She was frightened at the lurking deviltry in his eyes, and she could see the temper riding him. Fulton was a reckless man, a man known to be ugly when drinking—and dangerous. She hesitated, and Newton spoke up quietly. "She has this dance with me, Burr."

———

FULTON STARED INSOLENTLY at Newton, and Jenny felt a rising sense of panic.

"You mean she did!" he said. "She has this dance with me, now!"

Newton's face paled, but he stood his ground. "I'm sorry, Burr. She dances with me this time. Another time, perhaps."

"This time." Burr Fulton's attention was centered on Newton now. "This time she dances with me. You take a walk or get your horse and ride home. I'll take care of her!"

She turned quickly to Newton. "We'd better go, Tom. We should have gone long ago."

Fulton's eyes turned to her then, and the taunting violence in them shocked her. "You stay until I get through with you!" he said. "Maybe I'll take you home tomorrow!"

Tom Newton's fist swung. It was a nice try, but Burr had been looking for it, hoping for it. He knocked the punch down and kicked Newton in the stomach. With a grunt, the boy fell to the floor, his face twisted with pain.

Suddenly Dan Regan had stepped between Jenny and Fulton. "That was a dirty trick, Burr," said Regan. "You didn't have to kick him. Now you and your boys had better go home, you're spoiling a good dance, and insulting women."

Fulton's face tightened. "Why, you lily-livered skunk, I'll kill—!"

The words stopped, for he was looking into a six-gun, and then he realized that the gun had been in Dan Regan's hands.

"So? A sure-thing operator, aren't you?" he sneered. "Walk up to a man with a gun in your hand! Don't take no chances, do you? Holster that gun and give me a fair shake! I'll kill you then! I'll shoot you like a dog!"

"You talk too much!" Regan said, disgust in his voice. "Take your coyote pack and trail out of here. Move now!"

His eyes ugly, Fulton turned his back on Dan and walked away. The dance broke up quietly. Regan stood alone and watched them go. Nobody came near him, nobody spoke to him, not even Jenny Meadows. Bitterly, he watched them go, knowing in his heart how they felt. He was afraid to give a man an even break, he came up with the drop on Fulton . . . he wouldn't take a chance.

All of them were glad that Fulton had been stopped before something more ugly happened, but this was not the way of the West. You faced a man, and you gave him an even break.

Dan Regan did not stop at the stage station on his way back to the hills. He just kept going until the high timber closed around him and his sorrel was soft-footing it over thick pine needles toward the cabin on the bench above Hidden Lake.

"We'd better forget her, Red," he told the sorrel. "She thinks we're yellow. And so do the rest of them."

Rumors came to him by occasional passing prospectors or hunters. Rustlers were harrying the Slash B by day and by night. The herds were decimated. Two of the Slash B riders had been shot. When the foreman had threatened reprisals, Burr Fulton had ridden right up to the Slash B bunkhouse, dragged the man from his bunk, and whipped him soundly. When the punchers had wanted to round up the gang, their frightened foreman had refused permission. What had begun as a series of raids on the Slash B had grown until almost a reign of terror existed in the malpais.

Three of the hands quit. Drifting out of the country, they stopped at Regan's cabin.

"Had enough!" Curly Bowne said with disgust. "I never worked for a white-feathered outfit, and I never will! If they'd turned us loose we could have cleaned out that bunch, but young Bud Billings is afraid of his shadow. The old man is sick, and Anse Wiley, the foreman, is plenty buffaloed now."

"Stick around," Regan told them. "No use you boys riding out of the country. There's plenty of grub here, and you can hole up and help me hunt lions for a few days. I've been sort of thinking about going down to talk to old Cash, myself."

Webb looked at him cynically. "Heard you had a run-in with Burr," he suggested.

Curly Bowne and Jim Webb studied their boot toes. Dan knew they were awaiting his reply. These men had always liked him, but nobody in the malpais knew much about Regan. He was just the Slash B lion hunter. The story they had heard about the dance did not show him up too well.

"I had a few words with him," Regan said calmly. "He dared me to holster my gun, said he'd kill me if I gave him an even break."

"You didn't do it?"

"No." Regan's voice was flat. "I've no use for killing unless forced to it, and there were women and old folks around. Anyway it wouldn't have been an even break for Burr. He never saw the day he could throw a gun with me."

He said it so calmly, in such a completely matter-of-fact tone that it didn't sound like boasting. Curly looked at him thoughtfully.

"Why don't you go down and see the old man?" he suggested then. "We'll hold on here for you."

DAN REGAN RODE by way of the stage station trail and arrived there at sundown once more. Jenny was putting food on the table when he went in, and her father glanced up at him.

"Howdy, Dan," Meadows said grimly. "Reckon you can say good-bye to us now. We're leaving!"

Regan twisted his hat in his fingers, avoiding Jenny's eyes. "Scared out?" he asked.

Jenny's old irritation with him surfaced once more.

"If I were you I'd not talk about being scared!" she said scornfully.

He glanced at her without expression. "All right," he said quietly.

"Or anything else!" she flashed.

"Did I say I was?" he asked gently.

Her face flamed and she whipped around and walked from the room, her chin high.

"Jenny's sort of upset lately," Meadows commented. "Don't seem like herself."

"Burr been around?"

"Every night. That Bill Hefferman, too. He's a mean one, he is."

"I'll be ridin' on, I reckon," Dan said. "Got to go over to the Slash B."

"Drawin' your time? They all quittin'?"

"No," Dan Regan said quietly. "I'm applying for a job. I want Anse Wiley's job—ramroddin' the Slash B."

Meadows stared. "You're crazy!" he said. "Plumb crazy! That outfit would run you out of the country or kill you! Burr Fulton has Wiley so buffaloed he doesn't know which end is up!"

The door slammed open and Bill Hefferman came in. "Coffee!" he roared. "Give me some coffee!" He grabbed Meadows by the collar and shoved him toward the kitchen just as Jenny appeared in the door, her eyes wide and startled. "Get me some coffee!"

"You make too much noise," Regan said, looking up at him. He sat on a seat against the wall, his arms folded.

Hefferman turned his big head and stared. He was a giant of a man. When he saw who it was he sneered.

"You? Don't even open your yap at me, cat hunter! I don't like you, and I'd like nothing better than to smash your face in!"

"Get out," Regan said, unmoving. "Get out and don't come back until tomorrow afternoon. I'll meet you here then, and if you want trouble, I'll whip you—bare-handed!"

"What?" Hefferman spoke in a hoarse whisper. "You'd fight me with your hands?"

"Yes, and beat your head to jelly! Now get out of here!"

"Get out, is it?" Hefferman started for Regan. "I'll throw you out!"

He was walking fast, and Dan reached out with a toe of his boot and hooked a chair with it, kicking it into the bigger man's ankles. Hefferman ran into the chair in midstride and came down with a stunning crash. He drew back to his knees, clumsily kicking the ruins of the chair loose from his ankles. When he lifted his dazed eyes he was looking into Dan Regan's six-shooter.

"Beat it!" Dan said quietly. "You light a shuck!"

Slowly, his eyes clearing, Hefferman got to his feet. "I'll kill you for this!" he said viciously.

"All right. Tomorrow. With your fists," Regan said. "Don't be late. Three is the hour!"

When he was gone, Meadows shook his head. "You sure do beat all!" he said. "You get out of fixes better than any man I ever saw! But now you've got a chance to get away, and you better do it!"

"Leave?" Regan smiled. "And miss all the fun? Don't worry, I'll be here tomorrow! And while I think of it, you'd best not sell out if you haven't, nor plan on leaving. There's going to be a change around here!"

He walked out, leaving Jenny staring after him with puzzled eyes. "Dad, what's the matter with him? Is he afraid, or is he a fool?"

Meadows lit his pipe. "I don't know, Jenny darling," he said, "but I've a feeling he's neither!"

———

IT WAS SPITTING snow when Dan Regan rode into the ranch yard of the Slash B. He walked his horse across the yard to the rail by the house, dismounted, and tied him. Then he started up the steps.

"Wait a minute!" It was Anse Wiley. "You can't go in there!"

"Who says I can't?"

"I do!"

"Then it doesn't mean a thing. Go on back to the bunk-house out of this snow. I want to see Cash."

"Cash?" Wiley's face was angry. "He's a sick man. No-body sees him!"

"That gag worked too long and too well for you and Bud," Regan said. "I know all about you. You've been stealing the place blind, both of you. Now the fun is over. Get out of town or get thrown in jail!"

The foreman stared at him, aghast.

"I'm not talking through my hat," Regan added. "I have facts and figures. You tell Bud, and you can have twenty-four hours' start. No more."

DELIBERATELY, HE TURNED on his heel and walked in. Bud Billings came out of his chair with a startled excla-mation. Dan moved by him toward Cash's room. "Stop!" Bud demanded. "What do you mean breaking in here?"

Regan looked at him. "Bud Billings, you're a cheap little thief! Now get out and join Wiley and get going or I'll throw you out!"

Bud stared, swallowed, and stepped out of the way. Dan Regan walked by him and threw open the door where old Cash lay propped up on some pillows.

The fierce old eyes blazed at him. "Who in tarnation are you?"

"Not one of the thieves you have around you!" Regan flashed back. "While you lie there in that bed, your nephew, Bud, has been stealing you blind and Wiley helping him! Now the rustlers have started in and they are cuttin' your herds day and night!"

"What's that?" Billings roared. "Who the devil are you?"

"I'm Dan Regan, Pat Regan's son!" Dan said calmly. "I've been working for you as a lion hunter and watching them steal you out of house and home until I got sick and tired of it!

"You lying there in that bed! You aren't sick, you old cata-mount! You just ate too much and laid around too much! After a man's been in the saddle as long as you he's got to die in the saddle! You figured you were rich and let Bud and Wiley talk you into taking it easy!"

Coolly then, Regan recited the events of the past few months, the whipping of Wiley, the laughing at the Slash B, the stealing without even attempting cover. "Bud didn't dare raise hob about it because he was stealin' himself!" he added.

Cash stared at him, chewing the ends of his mustache. "What right have you got to be here?" he demanded. "Your pa and I never did get along!"

"No, you sure didn't, you pigheaded old fraud!" Dan told him. "Pat Regan spent a lifetime pulling you out of holes, and he told me to keep an eye on you, and that's what I've done. Now make me your foreman so I can get things going around here!"

Cash Billings stared at him angrily, and then suddenly his eyes began to twinkle.

"Be dehorned if you ain't the spittin' image of Pat!" he said. "Only bigger! You're some bigger! All right! You're the new foreman! Now go ahead and run the show until I get on my feet!"

"You," Dan pointed his finger, "be on your feet in the morning, understand?"

He turned to go, and Cash stopped him. "Dan? Is that your name? You ever handled cows? What you been doin'?" Billings stared at him suspiciously.

Dan Regan smiled. "Why, I punched cows awhile, took three herds up the trail to Dodge and then Ogallala. After that I was a Texas Ranger for about four years."

He walked down to the bunkhouse and opened the door. Tom Newton sat disconsolately before the fire. He glanced up.

"Oh? It's you? Did you run Wiley off?"

"Uh-huh. I'm the new foreman. Tom, you straddle your bronc and hightail it for my cabin. Curly Bowne, Jim Webb, and Jones are holed up there. Get them back down here but fast. Tell them I want them at the stage station, and you, too, tomorrow not later than three."

"What happens then?" Tom asked, staring at this new Regan.

Dan smiled. "Why, first I'm going to lick the stuffing out of Bill Hefferman. Then I'm going to run Burr Fulton out of the country afoot and without pants! After that," he added grimly, "you and the rest of the boys are going to come with me. We're going to comb these brakes like they were never combed, and any man we find who doesn't start running when we see him will wear a hemp necktie or swallow lead! We're going to have this country fit to live in again!"

BILL HEFFERMAN WAS sore. Moreover, he was boastful. He was a big man and a fighter, and there was no cowardly bone in all his huge body. Victor in many barroom and rangeland brawls, he feared no man and was confident he could whip anyone. Dan Regan he regarded as small potatoes. In fact, the entire Fulton crowd regarded it as a huge lark—if Dan showed up, and the betting was five to one he wouldn't.

One bettor was Jenny Meadows.

The Fulton crowd arrived early. Bottles had been passed around freely. Burr swaggered into the long dining room and dropped at the table to drink coffee and eat doughnuts, always available at the stage station.

"He'll be here!" Jenny said. Suddenly, though she could not have said why, she was very sure. "You wait and see!"

"Him?" Burr was incredulous. "He won't show up! Aside from Bill, I've got my own little score to pay off with him, and if he shows up, I aim to pay off!"

"He'll show up!" Jenny said firmly.

Burr grinned insolently. "Want to bet? I'll bet you a dollar he doesn't show!"

"Are you a piker?" Jenny flashed. "A dollar!" Scorn was thick in her voice. "What do you think I am, a child? I'll bet you one hundred dollars to five hundred! Those are the odds they are offering that he shows up. I'll bet you another hundred dollars to five hundred that when he shows up he will whip Bill Hefferman!"

Fulton stared, then laughed. "Are you crazy?" he demanded. "He hasn't a chance! If he had nerve enough he couldn't do it, and he's yellow as buttercups! Never gave anybody an even break!"

"I made my offer!" Jenny's face was pale, her eyes flashing. "Are you a piker? You've talked so big about the money you have! Put it up!"

He laughed, a little uneasily. He was unused to betting with a woman, and while he had no doubt he would win, still . . .

"He's yellow!" Burr persisted. "If he should whip Bill, which he won't, I'd run him out of the country!"

Thoroughly angry, Jenny said, "All right, then! If I win I'll bet all I win on the first two bets that *he* runs *you* out of the country!"

Burr Fulton sprang to his feet, white with anger.

"Me?" he roared. "Run *me* out? Why, you lit—!" He broke off, staring at her. "All right," he said, "it's a bet!"

"Then let's put up our money!" Jenny said flatly. "If he runs you out of the country I'll have a hard time collecting! Here comes Dad and Colmer. We'll give the money to Dad to hold for us while Colmer is a witness!"

Burr slowly counted out the money, his face dark with anger and resentment. He felt that he had never been so insulted in his life. Secretly, he fancied himself another Billy the Kid, and this talk of running *him* out! He snorted.

As the hour hand straightened up to three o'clock, four riders came down the hill to the stage station and dismounted. Everyone there knew them—Tom Newton, Jim Webb, Curly Bowne, and Jack Jones. All were top hands, tough riders who had fought Indians and rustlers with the Slash B when Cash Billings was on his feet and ramrodding the spread himself. Lew Meadows eyed them thoughtfully, then stole a look at Burr. Fulton's face was a study in doubt and irritation.

Bill Hefferman peeled off his shirt and stepped out beyond the hitching rail. "Well, where is he?" he roared.

"Right here!" The reply was a ringing shout, and all heads turned. Dan Regan stood in the stable door. How he had gotten there or how long he had been there, nobody knew.

Jenny felt her heart give a great leap. He had come, then! He wasn't afraid!

Stripped to the waist, he looked a bigger man, and certainly a more rugged one, and powerfully muscled. He walked out and handed his shirt to Meadows. He wore two guns, tied low.

He stepped up to the mark Hefferman had drawn with a toe, and grinned at the big man.

"All right," he said cheerfully, "you asked for it!"

Both hands were carried chest high, rubbing the palms together, and as he spoke he smashed a straight left to Bill's mustache that staggered the big man and started a thin trickle of blood from his broken lips. Hefferman grunted and looped a roundhouse swing that missed. Dan Regan's left lanced that mustache three times, flashing like a striking snake. Then a right uppercut jerked the big man's head back, and the crowd roared.

Hefferman rushed, swinging. Regan parried one swing, ducked another, and caught the third on the chin going away, but went down hard. Bill rushed to get close and Dan rolled over and came to his feet. He stabbed another left to the mouth, took a smashing blow on the chin that rang bells in his head, and then he bored in, ripping wicked, short-arm punches to the body with all the drive of his powerful shoulders.

Bill pushed him away and swung with everything he had. The punch caught Regan on the chin, and he went down, turned a complete somersault, and lay stretched out on his face in the dust!

———

A SHOUT WENT up from the Fulton men, and they began dancing around, slapping each other on the back. Then Regan got up.

They stared. Hefferman, astonished beyond reason, rushed. He met that same stiff left hand in the teeth, and it stopped him flat-footed. Before he could get untracked, Regan knocked him down with a right.

Lunging to his feet, Hefferman charged. The two began slugging like madmen. Bill grabbed Dan by the belt and shirt and heaved him high, but Dan jerked up with his knee and smashed Bill's nose to crumpled bone and flesh. Hefferman staggered and Regan broke loose. Dropping to his feet he set himself and threw two powerful swings to Bill's chin.

Like a lightning-shivered oak, the big man staggered and his knees buckled. Dan Regan walked in, threw a left, and then let go with a right to the belly that drove every bit of wind Hefferman had into one explosive grunt. The big man doubled, and Regan brought a right from his knees that lifted him from his feet and dropped him on his back in the dust!

He lay perfectly still.

Dan Regan stepped back quickly, working his fingers. His work-hardened hands felt good. Skinned on the knuckles, but still supple and quick.

"All right, Fulton!" he said.

Burr wheeled. The gunman dropped into a half crouch, his eyes suddenly aware. Triumph lit his eyes, and with a sneer, he dropped his hands.

Then he froze, still clutching the butts. He blinked and swallowed. He was looking into a pair of twin six-guns that had appeared in Dan Regan's hands as if by magic.

"It was a trick!" he roared. "A sneaking trick!"

Dan smiled. "Why, you tinhorn, try it again!"

He dropped his guns into his holsters and lifted his hands free. Before Burr Fulton could so much as tighten his grip on his own guns, Regan's had leaped from his holsters.

"Burr," Regan said quietly, "I told you you wouldn't have a chance with me! You're not a bad man, you're just a wild-haired cowhand who got an idea he was fast! Back up and go to punching cows before you try to draw on the wrong man and get killed! You're no gunslinger! You couldn't even carry a gunslinger's saddle!"

Burr Fulton swallowed. It was hard to take, but he was remembering the speed of those guns, noting the steadiness of them. "Try it again!" he screamed. "And come up shootin'! I'd rather be killed than made a fool of!" He was trembling with fury, his face white and strained.

"Burr," Dan replied patiently, "you're strictly small-time, and I'm not a scalp hunter. You draw on me and I'll shoot holes in your ears!"

Burr Fulton froze. Perhaps nothing else would have done it. *Holes in his ears!* The brand of a coward! Why, he would be ruined! He would . . . !

He stepped back and straightened up. "All right," he choked. "You win!"

"Now," Regan said. "I'm ramrodding the Slash B from here on! Anyone caught rustling our stock will be strung up right on the ranch and left hanging until he dries up and blows away! You've all got just until daylight to leave the country. Tomorrow my boys start combing the brakes, hunting for strangers. I hope we don't find any!"

Webb, Newton, Bowne, and Jones suddenly stepped out in a solid rank. All four held double-barreled shotguns which Curly had taken from their horses under cover of the fight.

"All right, boys! Start moving!" Dan said quietly. They moved.

Dan Regan walked up on the porch and looked at Jenny.

"Well, I'm back," he said, "and there's another dance at Rock Springs on Saturday. Want to go with your husband?"

"That's the only way I'll ever go to another dance there!" she replied tartly. "Anyway, we can buy furniture with the money."

"What money?" he asked suspiciously.

"The money I won from Burr Fulton, betting on you at five to one!" she said, smiling a little, her eyes very bright.

LONIGAN

HEAT LAY LIKE the devil's curse upon the slow-moving herd, and dust clouded above and around them. The eyes of the cattle were glazed, and the grass beneath their feet was brown and without vigor or life-giving nourishment.

The sun was lost in a brassy sky, and when Calkins knelt and put his palm to the ground the earth was almost too hot to touch. He got slowly to his feet, his face unnaturally old with the gray film of dust and the stubble of beard on his jaws.

"You ask for the truth." His voice was harsher than normal, and Ruth Gurney recognized it at once, and looked at him quickly, for as a child, she had known this man and had loved him like an uncle. "All right, you'll get the truth. There's no chance of you making money on this herd. Half your cows will die this side of Dodge. They'll die of thirst and heat, and the rest won't be worth the drive. You're broke, ma'am."

Her lips tightened and as the truth penetrated she was filled with desperation coupled with a feminine desire for tears. All along she had guessed as much, but, one and all, the hands had avoided telling her.

"But what's the matter, Lon? The Circle G always made its drives before, and always made money. We've the same men, and the trail's the same."

"No." He spoke flatly. "Nothin's the same. The trail's bad. It's been a strikin' dry year, and we got a late start. The other herds got the good grass, and trampled the rest into the dust. She's hotter'n usual, too. And," he added grimly, "we ain't got the same men."

"But we have, Lon!" Ruth protested.

"No." He was old and stubborn. "We ain't. We got one new one too many, and the one we should have ain't here."

Her lips tightened and her chin lifted. "You mean Hoey Ives. You don't like him."

"You should spit in the river, I don't! Nor do the others. He's plumb bad, ma'am, whether you believe it or not. He's no-account. I'll allow, he's educated and slick talkin', but he's still an Ives, and a bigger pack of coyotes never drew breath."

"And you think this—this Lonigan would make a difference? What can one man do against heat and dust and distance? What could he do to prevent storms and rustler raids?"

"I ain't for knowing. If'n I did, mebbe this herd would get through in shape. But Lonigan would know, and Lonigan would take her through. Nor would he take any guff from Hoey Ives. I'll tell you, ma'am, Hoey ain't along for fun. He comes of a pack of outlaws, and education ain't changed his breed none."

"We won't talk about Mr. Ives any further, Lon. Not one word. I have utmost confidence in him. When the drive is over I . . . I may marry him."

Lon Calkins stared at her. "I'll kill him first, or die shooting. Your pappy was a friend of mine. I'll not see a daughter of his marry into that outfit." Then he added, more calmly, "If'n that's what you figure, Ruth, you better plan on hirin' new hands when you get back to Texas."

"Very well, then, that's what I'll do, Lon." Her voice was even, but inside her words frightened her. "That's just what I'll do. I own the Circle G, and I'll run it my way."

———

CALKINS SAID NOTHING for a long minute, and then he mused, "I wonder sometimes if'n anybody does *own* a brand. The Circle G, ma'am, ain't just a brand on some cows. It ain't just some range in Texas. It's more . . . much, much more.

"I ain't much hand to talkin' of things like that, but you remember when your pappy and us come west? The Comanches killed O'Brien and Kid Leslie on the Brazos. I reckon both of them were part of the Circle G, ma'am. And Tony, that lousy Italian grub hustler, the one who rolled under a chuck wagon down on the cowhouse. He was part of the Circle G, too.

"A brand ain't just a sign on a critter; it's the lives, and guts, and blood of all the men that went to build it, ma'am. You can't get away from that, no way. The Circle G is your pappy standin' over your mother when she died givin' birth to you. The Circle G is all of that.

"Nobody owns a brand, ma'am, like I say; nobody. It's a thing that hangs in the air over a ranch, over its cows, and over its men. You know why that kid Wilkeson got killed in Uvalde? An hombre there said this was a lousy outfit, and the kid reached for his gun. He died for the brand, ma'am, like a hundred good and bad men done afore this. And you want to wipe it out, destroy it, just because you got your mind set on a no-account coyote. I wish Lonigan was back."

"Lonigan!" she burst out furiously. "All you talk about is Lonigan! *Who* is he? *What* is he? What difference can one man make?"

"Well," Calkins said grimly, "your pappy made a sight of difference! If'n he was with this drive now, your fancy Hoey Ives would pack out of here so fast his dust would be bigger'n that raised by the herd! Or if Lonigan was. Fact is," he added grimly, "there ain't nary a cowhand down there wouldn't draw on Hoey tomorrow if'n he figured he had a chance. Hoey's killed ten men, all better'n him except with a gun."

"And yet you think Lonigan could beat him?" she asked wryly.

"Mebbe. I ain't sure, but I am sure of one thing. If Lonigan died you can bet your boots Hoey Ives would die with him! You say," he continued, "what difference can one man make? Well, he can make a sight of difference. Lonigan doesn't talk so much; he's a good worker, but he's got something in him, something more'n most men. He ain't so big, rightly he's not, but he *seems* big, and he rode for the brand, Lonigan did. He loved the Circle G. Loved it like it was his own."

"Then where is he now when we need him?" Ruth demanded bitterly. "This . . . this superman of yours. Where is he now? You say he never missed a trail drive, that he would drift off, but somehow like he knew the day and hour, he would show up and take his place with the herd. Where is he now?"

"Mebbe he's dead." Calkins was grim. "Wherever he is, he's with the Circle G, and we're with him."

They looked up at the sound of hoofs, and Lon Calkins's face tightened grimly. Abruptly, he reined his horse around. "I'll be ridin'," he said.

"You meant what you said about quitting?" she asked.

"If he stays," Calkins insisted, "I go."

"I'll be sorry to lose you, Lon. The Circle G won't be the same without you."

His old eyes met hers and he stared at her. "Believe me, it won't. Your father should have had a son."

He rode away then, and she stared after him, her body feeling empty as an old sack. The approaching hoofs drew nearer and slowed, and her eyes turned with relief toward those of Hoey Ives.

————

HE WAS A big young man with hard black eyes in which she had never seen the cruelty or calculation that lay in their depths. He rode magnificently and was a top hand. On this trip he had been her mainstay, ramrodding it through, talking to lift her spirits, advising her and helping her in countless ways. It was he who had selected the trail they took, he who had ridden out alone to meet the rustlers that would have stopped them, and who talked them out of trouble.

"What's the matter with the old man?" he asked. "What's he growling about now?"

"Oh, he was talking about the old days on the Circle G," she said, "and about Lonigan."

"Lonigan?" Hoey's gaze sharpened, and for an instant she seemed to read apprehension in his eyes. "He hasn't heard from him?"

"Nobody has. Yet he always made the drive."

"He's dead," Ives replied. "He must be. I knew he always made the drive, and that was why I waited before offering my services. We never got along, you see."

"What's he like?" she asked curiously.

"Lonigan?" Ives hesitated, while his bay stamped its foot restlessly. "He's a killer. Utterly vicious."

"But the boys liked him," Ruth protested.

"Sure. He was their pride and joy," Ives said bitterly. "He led the Circle G parade. No man, not even your father, had as much influence with the hands. He was loudmouthed and a braggart, but he appealed to them, and they found excuses for his killings."

"Yet he must have something . . . ?"

"Yes," Hoey Ives nodded reluctantly. "He had that. There was something about him, something that frightened men who didn't even know him. . . ."

Ives rejoined the herd, and Ruth Gurney rode on, lingering along the hillcrests away from the dust, watching the herd that meant everything to her. The sale of that herd could mean the ranch was out of debt, that it was hers, all hers. Yet she knew that what Calkins had said was true, bitterly true. Not half the herd would live to see Dodge, and she would be broke then, broke and finished.

She turned her horse and put him on up the slope to the very top of the long, low hill that ran beside the trail. On top there might be more breeze. And there was, although but little more. Yet she sat her horse there, looking over the brown, trampled-down grass that stretched on beyond it. There, too, the herds had been. The earlier herds that had started sooner.

The failure of Lonigan to appear had caused most of that delay. All along she had realized why Calkins was waiting, why the hands kept looking toward the trail, why they found excuses to ride into town, why they intercepted every drifting horseman to ask about him, but for the first time he had not appeared.

She pushed on across the ridge, riding due west. The sun was already far down toward the horizon but it was still unbearably hot. Heat waves danced and rippled against the sky along the ridges, and she slowed her horse to a walk and pushed on alone, lost now from the herd, with only the rising dust to mark its presence.

Half asleep, lulled by the heat and the even rhythm of the

walking horse, she dozed in the saddle, and then the horse stopped and coolness touched her face. She was atop another ridge, and far toward the west she seemed to see a thin edge of green, and then her eyes dropped and she saw the tracks of a horse. The horse was shod and the tracks were fresh.

Without doubt the tracks were no more than an hour old, two hours at most. In that time the herd had moved less than three miles, so its dust cloud would have been within sight. Why had the strange rider avoided them?

His horse had stopped here on this ridge, and from the tracks he must have watched the dust cloud. It was unusual for a rider to be so close and not to approach the herd. Unless—she frowned and bit her lip—unless he was an outlaw.

She realized instantly that she should ride to the herd and let Calkins know. Rather, let Hoey Ives know. It might be another raid, and rustlers had already hit them for over three hundred head of stock. Nevertheless, her curiosity aroused, she turned her horse and started backtracking the man.

———

FROM TIME TO time she paused to rise in her stirrups and look carefully around the prairie, yet nowhere could she see anything, not a sign of a rider beyond the tracks she followed. Aware that it was time to turn back, she pushed on, aware that the terrain was changing and that she was riding into a broken country of exposed ledges and sharp upthrusts of rock. Topping a rise, she drew up, frowning.

Before her lay a long green valley, several miles wide and grassy and well watered. This was the green, some of the grass showing from the hilltops, that she had seen from some distance east. What a waste to think their herd was passing over that miserable brown and dusty plain when all this was going to waste! It was too bad Hoey did not know of this.

She pushed on to the bottom of the valley and toward a water hole, the tracks for the moment forgotten. And then at the water hole she saw them again. Here the rider had stopped, a tall man with run-down boot heels and Mexican spurs, judging by the tracks in the sand.

She was lying on her stomach drinking when her eyes lifted in response to the sudden falling of a shadow. She saw shabby boots and the Mexican spurs, dark leather chaps, and then a slim-waisted man wearing a faded red shirt and a black kerchief around his throat. His hat was gray, dusty, and battered.

"Hello," he said, smiling at her. "You've got water on your chin."

She sprang to her feet irritably and dashed a quick hand across her mouth and chin. "Suppose I have? What business is it of yours?"

His face was browned from sun and wind, his eyes faintly whimsical. He wore, she noticed suddenly, two guns. He was rolling a cigarette, and now he placed it carefully in the corner of his mouth and struck a match left-handed. For some idiotic reason she suddenly wished the wind would blow it out. It didn't.

His eyes slanted from her to her horse and the brand. "Circle G," he murmured thoughtfully, "I reckon that's a Texas outfit."

"If you were from Texas," she replied with asperity, "you would know. There wasn't a better-known cattleman in Texas than Tom Gurney!"

"Relative of his?"

"His daughter. And my herd is just a few miles east of here."

"Yeah," his voice was suddenly sarcastic, "that's what comes of a woman ramroddin' a herd. You got your stock on dry grass with this valley offerin' shelter, graze, and plenty of water."

"For your information," she said coldly, "I'm not ramrodding the herd. My trail boss is. He evidently did not know of this valley."

"And evidently he didn't try very hard to find out about it. You got a lousy trail boss, ma'am."

"I didn't ask you! Mr. Ives is—" She was startled by the way his head came up.

"Did you say . . . *Ives*? You don't mean Hoey Ives?"

"I do. You . . . you know him?"

"I should smile. Your dad must be dead, then . . . for he'd never let an Ives ramrod a trail herd of his, else."

"Who are you?" she demanded. "You talk like you knew my father."

He shrugged. "You know this country. Folks pass stories along from camp to camp. A man can know a lot about a country without ever bein' there. I'm just from Wyoming."

Suddenly, he glanced up. "Cloudin' up for sure. You'll never make it back to the herd now before the rain comes. Mount up and we'll go down to the cabin."

She looked at him coldly, then cast an apprehensive glance at the sky. "I'll race the storm to the herd," she said coolly. "Thanks just the same."

"No," he said, "you'd never make it. I know these prairie thunderstorms. There may be hail, and sometimes the stones are big enough to beat your brains out. The cabin is closer."

EVEN AS HE spoke there was a rumble of thunder and a few spattering drops landed near them. Worriedly, she glanced at the sky. It was dark and lowering. She had been so preoccupied by the tracks and then by the valley that she had not noticed the rising clouds. Now she saw that there was indeed a bad storm coming, and recalling some of the gullies she had traversed she knew that the trail back would be fraught with danger. She glanced once at the strange rider, hesitated, then said swiftly, "All right, we'll go."

"We'd better make a run for it!" he said, swinging into the saddle. "She'll drop the bottom out of the bucket in a minute!"

Following his lead, she dashed off downstream at breakneck, reckless speed. Yet when they swept around the corner near the cabin his hand went up, and he turned toward her, his face dark and hard. With a gesture, he indicated several horses in the corral, and smoke rising from the ancient chimney. "This could be trouble!" he said grimly. "There was nobody here an hour ago, and nobody rides loose in this country right now who's honest!"

"Including yourself?" she asked quickly.

His grin was lopsided but not without humor. "Maybe even me," he agreed, "but you back me in whatever I say. Good or bad men, we need shelter!"

Swiftly they unsaddled their horses and led them to the stable. There was still room for two or three horses, indicating that some of the riders were less than particular about their mounts. Then the strange rider led the way toward the cabin. Out of the corner of his mouth, he said, "Call me Danny!"

He pushed the door open and stepped inside, the girl right behind him. He had known they would be observed and that the men within the cabin would have worked out some sort of plan if they were not honest men, and his first glance told him they were not. "How's for some grub?" he asked coolly. "We got caught in the rain!"

A big man standing with his back to the fireplace grinned. "Got caught in good company, I see! Ain't often a feller gets hisself caught out with a girl in these parts!"

"Especially," Danny said quietly, "when she's his boss!"

"Boss?" The big man's eyes sharpened. "Never heard tell of no woman cow boss!"

"You heard of one now." There were four men in the room, and two of them Danny recognized at once. Neither Olin Short nor Elmo Shain were names unknown to the law of half a dozen states and territories. The big man he did not know, nor the lean saturnine man with the scarred face. "This is Ruth Gurney, boss of the Circle G."

The big man stiffened and peered hard at her, then at Danny. "You don't look familiar to me," he said. "I figured I knowed the G riders."

"Then if you don't know me," Danny said quietly, "you ain't known 'em long."

Olin Short, who was neither short nor fat, glanced up. "Here's coffee for the lady," he said quietly. "You pick up a cup and rinse her under the rainspout . . . if'n you're particular."

Danny took the cup and without hesitation stepped to the door and rinsed the cup. When he stepped back inside his eyes sought Olin's face. The man was about thirty, not a bad-looking man with blue eyes and a stubble of beard. If there was one among them upon whom he might place some trust, it was Short.

"How far off's the G?" It was the scarred man who spoke.

Danny glanced at him. "Maybe six miles," he lied, "not over ten."

"Know where you are?"

Danny nodded. "Why not? Miss Gurney was riding an' when the storm started they sent me after her. I told 'em if we couldn't make it back we'd hole up here."

"How'd you know about this shack?" Now it was the big man who spoke, and his voice was suddenly hard.

DANNY FILLED HIS cup before replying. "I stopped here a week once, last winter," he said, "helped some boys drive some horses into New Mexico."

"Horses? Into New Mexico?" Shain laughed. "I thought Billy the Kid and his outfit had that sewed up."

"It was Billy's outfit." Danny spoke quietly and without seeming to notice the sudden shock on their faces. When they spoke again, however, there was new respect on their faces.

"Billy's outfit, huh? Who was with him?"

"Jesse Evans, Hendry Brown, and a couple of other hombres. They had the horses, and I was drifting toward Cimarron, but joined up with them and drove down to the Ruidoso instead."

The reply seemed to satisfy the men, for no more questions were asked. Ruth sipped her coffee slowly, soaking up the warmth of the room. She was sufficiently aware of the situation in west Texas to know these were hard, dangerous men. They were outlaws. And this man with her might be another of the same breed. She had heard of Billy the Kid, the soft-voiced boy of not yet eighteen who already had won a name for deadly gun skill, and of his friend, the man who in time would be on the opposite side, Jesse Evans.

Danny had taken his cup and moved back near the wall. He placed it on the floor and rolled a smoke deftly.

"What happens," the scar-faced man said suddenly, "if you don't show up with the lady come daylight?"

"Why, I reckon there'd be eight or ten of the toughest hands in Texas riding thisaway to find out why," Danny said quietly. Then his eyes lifted, and they seemed to blaze with sudden fire. The quiet was gone from them, and from his voice, which carried an edge that was sharp and clean. "But don't worry . . . we'll ride into that camp come mornin'. Nobody," he said, more quietly, "or nothing, will keep us from it."

Shain stared at him, sitting up from the wooden bunk where he had been reclining. "You talk plumb salty, stranger. Who are you? Maybe you are the Kid?" he sneered.

Danny smiled, suddenly. "Why, you boys been around here before, I take it," he said coolly. "If you were, maybe you'll recall the calling cards I left here. You see, I came back this way after that trip to Lincoln and the Ruidoso . . . and had occasion to leave some reminders."

Elmo Shain's sneer was wiped from his face as if by magic, and he shot a quick, horrified glance toward the big man by the fireplace. For some reason that comment electrified the group in the room. Ruth had the feeling that Short alone was pleased.

Conversation died again in the room, and Danny finished his coffee, then refilled both their cups. "Shain," he said suddenly, "when the lady finishes her coffee, how's for lettin' her have that bunk? She's some tired."

At the use of his name, Shain had glanced up sharply. For a slow minute he said nothing, and then he nodded. "Yeah," he said, "all right."

Danny finished his smoke and rubbed it out. His message had ruined whatever plans they had made, or had at least made them doubt their use. Now they knew either who he was or that he was somebody to be reckoned with. He would have small cause for worry until two of them excused themselves and went outside to talk things over. When they returned he would have to be even more watchful.

ALTHOUGH RELUCTANT TO lie down, Ruth suddenly found herself so exhausted that she began to doze almost as soon as she touched the bunk. Danny drew a blanket over her and squatted at the foot of the bunk, his back against the wall.

A slow hour paraded past. The scarred man got up and muttering something about wood for the fire, went out. Shain was asleep, sitting against the wall. The big man followed the scarred man after the wood, and Olin Short threw the last stick on the fire and leaning close to Danny, said quietly, "Watch yourself. The big hombre is Casselman. The mean one is the devil of the lot . . . he's Papago Brown."

"Where do you stand?"

Short's face hardened. "Only to help that girl. I'll see no woman wronged. Least of all, any girl of Gurney's."

"Good."

The door opened and the two men came in and dropped two armfuls of wood near the fireplace. Casselman looked down at her. "Looks mighty purty, lyin' there."

Danny got slowly to his feet. A new cigarette was in the corner of his mouth. "Stay away from her," he said.

Casselman's big head turned to look over his shoulder. He chuckled, a slow, sneering chuckle. "You'd stop me?"

Papago was still near the door. Danny nodded coolly, "I sure would, Casselman. You make a move toward her, and I'll kill you. I'll shoot low down, Casselman, and I couldn't miss.

"As for Papago," he added, "if he doesn't get his hand off that gun butt, I'll kill him now."

Casselman laughed and Brown stared at Danny, smiling. "That stuff about those three skeletons didn't faze us," Papago said. "We're goin' to call your bluff."

"All right," Danny said, "but did you ever hear of Lonigan missing?"

"Lonigan?"

At the name, Ruth Gurney was suddenly wide-awake. Who had said it? To whom? Papago Brown's face was white and Casselman moved slowly away from the fire.

"Can't be!" Shain was awake. "We heard—"

"Shut up!" Casselman turned on him in a fury.

"I know what you heard," Danny said quietly. "You heard I wouldn't be with them this trip. Ever figure you might be double-crossed? That your partner might figure on warning the G of you to put himself in solid?"

Nobody said anything, and after a minute Casselman picked up a couple of sticks and tossed them on the fire. Shain stared at him, then at Papago Brown. "I'm going to sleep," he said, and added significantly, "and I mean *sleep*!"

"I reckon," Short said quietly, "that's a good idea. For all of us."

Nobody said anything for several minutes, while the girl lay breathless, feeling the tension in the room. The fire crackled and a stick fell, sending up a thin column of sparks. A wrong move could turn this room into a red-laced hell from which none of them might emerge alive. Both Brown and Casselman knew that, for it would be point-blank shooting here.

Casselman sat down abruptly and began to pull off his boots. "I reckon," he said, "rest is the first thing."

Twice during the night Danny dozed lightly, but he was back in the shadows, and a watcher could not have told whether he dozed or whether the eyes were watchful from under his hat's low brim.

It was scarcely gray in the east when he touched her boot. Like a wraith he moved beside the bunk. "Come!" he whispered, and she followed him.

———

AFTER THE STUFFY air of the tightly closed room the morning was like wine in her lungs. The rain had broken, and there were scattered clouds with fire along their edges in the east. Swiftly, he saddled their horses and they took the trail.

Several times she glanced at him. "Did somebody speak of Lonigan last night? I thought I heard the name."

"Could be," he said, with the flush of the rising sun on his face. "I've heard the name, and I reckon," he smiled a little, "they had heard it, too!"

The drum of hoofs on the turf warned them and they looked up to see Calkins and Laredo Lee riding toward them. They drew up sharply when they saw she was not alone, and she had the feeling that Danny made some sharp signal from behind her back. "You all right?" Calkins demanded abruptly. "We was some worried."

"All right," she said. "This is Danny. He knows the Circle G."

"Yeah, I remember him," Calkins said. "Laredo, you ride on ahead with the boss. I want to make talk with Danny."

When they were well ahead, Calkins turned on him. "You son of a gun! Where you been? We need you the worst way."

"Not so bad as you will," Danny replied, and then went on to tell of the riders in the cabin. "And there'd been others there before them. When we came up I saw the tracks of maybe six or eight riders."

"She know who you are?"

Danny shook his head. "Doubt it. My name was mentioned last night, but I don't believe she quite got it. Not that it matters. Hoey will know me."

"He might not. You've changed, Lonigan. Changed a sight since he saw you. He was gone East, you know, an' you filled out a good bit, and you are some taller, too. Then . . . well, there's a different look about you. He might not be sure."

The herd came in sight and they drew up on the brow of the hill, looking down at them. "Reckon he knowed about that grass and water?" Calkins asked.

"He knew. He scouted it a couple of days ago. I spotted the herd quite a ways back, and when I saw what trail they were takin' I hung back, curious. Then I saw the old man wasn't with you and a girl was. So I waited, sizing up the layout."

"You figure he aims to steal the herd?"

"No . . . to buy it cheap. To get her scared of goin' broke, then making her an offer. He won't steal it unless all else fails. But chances are he'd steal the money back if he did buy it. He's deliberately kept this herd on the used-up trails to wear 'em down and scare her into a quick sale."

The herd pushed on into the brightening day, and Lonigan kept always on the far side of the herd from Hoey Ives. Calkins, riding near Ruth, warned her to say nothing of the new rider to Hoey. She glanced at him, and her chin lifted resentfully. Then she pulled on ahead.

Still, she was worried. What had the strange riders been doing in that cabin? Wasn't what she had heard true? That riders loitering in this area without herds were suspect? And that bunch! She was well aware that only the presence of the mysterious Danny had prevented trouble, and some curious understanding there was between Danny and those men. Could they be working together? Could all of that have been an elaborate pretense to get him with the herd?

<hr />

HOEY CANTERED HIS horse up to her and glanced at her sharply. "You all right? I was off looking in the other direction and just got back. We were all worried."

"I'm all right. Hoey," she asked suddenly, "why are we following this route? Why don't we go west to that valley? There's grass there."

He seemed astonished. "Grass? There is? I can't believe it! The last time I came over this trail it was a canyon of dust." He paused, then said, "If there's grass, of course we'll go. I'll turn the herd."

"Wait." She hesitated, then shook away her doubts. "Hoey, we've a new rider."

"What?" He drew up, his face stiff. "Where'd you get him?"

"I met him last night. There were some men in the cabin where we took shelter. He seemed to know them. A man named Casselman and one called Papago Brown."

"This rider knew them?" He seemed relieved, and Ruth watched him, puzzled and doubtful. "He's probably a good hand. I'll talk to him later. We can use the help."

The clouds did not leave, but hung low, bulging and ominous. Yet it was not cool, but sultry with heat. Ruth kept again to the crests, yet was glad when the first of the herd spilled over into the canyon and headed for the thin trickle of the stream. They waded into it, scattering along the stream for three-quarters of a mile, drinking, then moving out to crop the green grass.

Calkins rode up to her. "Why not bed down here?" he asked. "Let 'em get their fill? They'll drive easier tomorrow."

She moved back toward the chuck wagon and saw Laredo Lee already there, watching the cook make coffee. He looked up at her, a thin, sandy man with large freckles and cool blue eyes. He had been riding for the Circle G for three years and made the last drive with her father. "I hear you aim to make Ives foreman," he said, glancing at her. "If you do, why, figure to hire a man to take my place."

"I'd be sorry to lose you, Laredo," she said sincerely. Then she turned on him. "Well, who would you want for foreman?"

He grinned. "Why, this new man. Danny would do. The boys like him."

"Oh, no! Not him!" She accepted a cup of coffee and watched Hoey come riding up to the fire. He looked angry and he swung down from the saddle; then he walked over to her.

"Look," he said, "finding this grass an' water is a break, but I happen to know there isn't much of it. You are only halfway to Dodge and have rough country and trouble ahead. There's no need to make this drive. I'll buy your herd."

"You?" She was startled. "Why?" She looked up at him, puzzled. "For how much?"

"Four dollars a head. Right here and now. In cash."

"Four dollars?" She shook her head. "That's ridiculous! They will bring five times that in Dodge."

"If they are fat. If they get there. But what if you lose three or four hundred head?"

Laredo Lee stood silent, watching Ruth with keen eyes. He wanted to speak, but was wise enough to know it was not the time. This was Ruth Gurney's problem. A moment later Lee was stifling his grin in the coffee cup.

"No, Hoey," she replied calmly, "I'll not quit now. These cattle started for Dodge and they will go to Dodge. My father never quit a trail drive in his life, and I won't."

IVES'S FACE HARDENED and grew impatient. "Ruth, you don't know what you're gettin' into! Why, we haven't hit the hard part yet! There's Kiowas and Comanches up ahead, and that's to say nothin' of the rustlers."

"Boss," Lee spoke softly, "Mr. Ives ain't been over a trail with the G afore. He don't know how we are." The blue eyes were deceptively mild now as they looked at Hoey. "The G," he explained, "figures it's plumb salty. Why, we welcome a little brush with Indians. As for rustlers, we eat 'em up! The old man," he added affectionately, "liked a good fight. Last couple of drives he put most of that on Lonigan's shoulders."

"Well," Ives snapped, "Lonigan ain't here now! If he was," he sneered so openly that Ruth looked at him in surprise, "he couldn't do much!"

"Maybe," a new voice said, "you're right. Again, maybe you're not."

All turned. Calkins had come up, and several of the other hands, but it was Danny Lonigan who spoke. He stood alone in the middle of a little open space near the wagon, a tall young man, narrow in the hips and wide in the shoulder. He stood with his boots together, one knee slightly bent, his hands busied with rolling a cigarette.

Hoey Ives stared. Slowly, doubt, dismay, and uncertainty colored his features. "Who're you?" he demanded.

"Why, you remember me, Hoey," Lonigan said quietly, "I whupped the socks off you one time at a dance. That was afore you went away. You were trailin' with that big Casselman then, an' figured it made you some tough. You'll recall it didn't help you none."

Ives's lips tightened and his eyes grew cold. "So you came back, did you? Well, I'm the boss here now. You work for the G, you work for me."

"No," Lonigan said quietly, "I work for the lady boss. She's the Circle G, Ives, and from the way she stopped you on that offer to buy her out, I reckon she'll do to ride the river with. The old man," he said, "evidently bred true. I'll ride for her, Ives. Not for you."

"I reckon that speaks my piece," Laredo Lee interposed quietly.

"And mine," Calkins said.

Hoey Ives's face flushed. Then he laughed. "Well, that's fine! I wanted to be rid of you! I've got a bunch of boys ready to take over, and I'll have them in here by sundown. You boys can pack your duffle and hit the trail."

"No."

Ruth Gurney spoke in a clear, definite voice. All eyes turned to her. "Calkins told me something the other day that I've been thinking of. He said it was the hands that made the brand, the men who fought for it, worked for it, bled for it. They had a stake in the brand, and it was something above and beyond ownership. I believe that.

"Hoey, I'm sorry. You'll have to step out of your job. I want you with us, but not in charge of the work. I've made my decision and I'll abide by it." She turned her head. "Calkins, you take over. You're the foreman for the rest of the drive."

"But . . . ?" Calkins started to protest when Lonigan cut him short.

"Take it," he said briefly. "Let's move!"

"All right," Calkins said, pointing, "roll the wagon into that hollow under the cliff. We'll bed down here and roll 'em up the trail tomorrow."

Hoey Ives turned abruptly and stalked angrily away. Ruth took a step as though to follow, then turned back to the wagon. Her eyes met those of Lonigan. "Why didn't you tell me who you were?" she demanded impatiently. "I'd heard of you."

"What could I have said?" He shrugged. "Anyway, I'm with the drive again, and workin' with the G." He glanced at her quizzically. "Or, am I?"

"Ask Calkins," she returned sharply. "He does the hiring!"

———

THROUGHOUT THE DAY she saw no more of Ives, although she knew he was about. The hands rested when they were not riding herd, all but Danny Lonigan. He cleaned his guns carefully, then his rifle. After that he went to work and repaired a wooden bucket that had been broken the day before, and mended a halter. Several times he mounted and rode up to the rim of the canyon and sat there, studying the country.

Calkins stopped by her seat just before sundown. "What do you think, Calkins? Will we get the herd through?"

He hesitated, then nodded slowly. "I wouldn't want to get your hopes up, but I think so. Maybe this grass won't hold, but we'll chance it, although come rain we'd have to get to high ground. If there's much of this grass, we'll make it, all right. But it will be a tough squeeze and you won't make much money."

Lonigan walked slowly over to them, and as he drew near, he removed his sombrero. "Ma'am," he said, "I couldn't but overhear what was said. If . . . if you'll let me make a suggestion . . ."

"I hope," Ruth said with dignity, "that I am always open to suggestions. Yes, you may. What is it?"

"Why, just don't sell your herd atall!" he said calmly. "Hang onto it. You're gettin' to Dodge at the bad end of the season; prices will be down and your herd in plumb bad shape. I'd say, hold your cows until next spring, hold 'em on Nebraska grass, then fetch 'em back to market, fat as ticks."

Ruth Gurney shook her head. "It is a good suggestion," she admitted, "but I can't. Until I sell this herd I can't pay any of you. And I owe mortgage on the ranch."

Lonigan shook his head. "Nuh-uh. Ma'am, I know an hombre in Dodge who knows a good deal when he sees it. He'll advance the money and take a mortgage on your herd. You can pay up when you sell out. You'll have fat stock and the first market in the spring. Believe me, you'll get twice what you could get with a good herd now, let alone this scrawny lot. And you'll have calves," he added.

"Excellent idea," Hoey Ives said quietly. He had come up unobserved. "In fact, that was what I planned to do . . . and what I'll still do."

Four men were ranged behind him, four men with rifles. Two more stood by the wagon, facing toward the herd. While the riders had watched for horsemen they had slipped up on foot, working their way through the brush like Indians.

Lonigan's eyes went to the rifles, then the riflemen. "You're tryin' to get yourself killed, Hoey. Now take your boys and light a shuck."

Ives chuckled. "Oh, no! We've got our herd. When your boys hear us call, they'll come in. They'll never know what hit 'em!"

"You mean," Danny Lonigan's voice was casual, "like this?" His hands flashed for his guns, and for one startled instant, every man froze. Then as one person, Ruth dropped to the ground and Ives, Calkins, and Lee grabbed iron.

It was Lonigan's sudden move that decided it. His first two shots knocked Casselman staggering and his third dropped Shain dead in his tracks. "Drop it, Short!" Lonigan yelled, and switched both guns to Papago Brown.

Then, suddenly, it was all over and where the cannonade of guns had sounded there was stillness, and somewhere down the valley, a quail called plaintively in the late dusk. Gunpowder left an acrid smell that mingled with the woodsmoke of the freshly built fire.

———

DANNY LONIGAN LOOKED down at Hoey Ives. Caught in the crossfire of Calkins's and Lee's guns, he had been riddled with bullets before he could more than fire his first shot.

Ruth, lying on her face, had a rifle on the two startled men near the wagon. The cook held an old muzzle-loading Civil War rifle on them, too.

Calkins swore softly. "You oughta give a man warnin', Lonigan," he objected. "That was too sudden. They might have got us all!"

"Nuh-uh," Lonigan said quietly. "You see, I noticed that they were depending on the warning of the rifles. They didn't really expect anybody to take a chance. You see," he grinned grimly, "I noticed that none of their rifles were cocked! I knew I could get off several shots before they could cock and aim again."

"Yeah," Laredo said, "and what about Ives? What did you think he'd be doin'?"

"What he is doin'," Lonigan said quietly. "You see, I've rode the trail with you hombres before. Nobody needed to tell me what would happen. I knew."

He turned his head and looked at Olin Short. "You," he said, "would have sided me to help Miss Gurney in the cabin that night. I didn't want to kill you. Get your horse and slope. Take those others with you. And don't let 'em cross the trail again. As for you, Short, at heart you're too good a man for an outlaw. If you're down in Texas, stop by the G."

When he was gone, Lonigan turned to Ruth, who had got shakily to her feet, keeping her eyes averted from the fallen men. Taking her arm, he led her away from them, and away from the fire.

"We'll do what you said," Ruth said finally. "We'll drive to Nebraska and feed the stock there. Would you," she hesitated, "would you consider the foreman's job? I mean, in Calkins's place?"

"Why, no, I wouldn't." She turned toward him, half in surprise, half in regret. "No, I like Calkins, and he'll make a good foreman. The men like him, too. Besides, I've other plans."

"Oh." The word sounded empty and alone. "I . . . I hoped we'd see more of each other. You see, Dad . . ."

"We'll see more of each other, a lot more. When you put Hoey out as foreman and Calkins in, and again when you hit ground and grabbed that rifle, you showed what I said was right, that the old man bred true. You got what he had. You've nerve; you've iron in you. It's a line that should be carried on, so I'm not goin' to be your foreman. *I'm goin' to marry you.*"

She blinked.

"*Just like that?* Without any . . ."

"Courtin'?" He grinned. "Ma'am, there's no preacher this side of Dodge. Believe me, by the time you get there you'll be well courted, or my name ain't Lonigan!"

"Don't I get a chance to say yes or no?" she protested.

"You can say yes," he said, "if you say it fast, but for the next thirty minutes you're goin' to be busy." He put her chin up and his arm around her. "*Mighty* busy," he said softly.

Somewhere down the valley a quail called plaintively into the darkness, and the stream chuckled over the stones. It probably had considerable to chuckle about.

LIT A SHUCK FOR TEXAS

THE SANDY KID slid the roan down the steep bank into the draw and fast walked it over to where Jasper Wald sat his big iron-gray stallion. The Kid, who was nineteen and new to this range, pulled up a short distance from his boss. That gray stallion was mighty near as mean as Wald himself.

"Howdy, boss! Look what I found back over in that rough country east of here."

Wald scowled at the rock the rider held out. "I ain't payin' yuh to hunt rocks," he declared. "You get back there in the breaks roundin' up strays like I'm payin yuh for."

"I figgered yuh'd be interested. I reckon this here's gold."

"Gold?" Wald's laugh was sardonic, and he threw a contemptuous glance at the cowhand. "In this country? Yuh're a fool!"

The Sandy Kid shoved the rock back in his chaps pocket and swung his horse back toward the brush, considerably deflated. Maybe it was silly to think of finding gold here, but that rock sure enough looked it, and it was heavy. He reckoned he'd heard somewhere that gold was a mighty heavy metal.

When he was almost at the edge of the badlands, he saw a steer heading toward the thick brush, so he gave the roan a taste of the diggers and spiked his horse's tail after the steer. That old ladino could run like a deer, and it headed out for those high rocks like a tramp after a chuck wagon, but when it neared the rocks, the mossyhorn ducked and, head down, cut off at right angles, raging for the willows.

Beyond the willows was a thicket of brush, rock, and cactus that made riding precarious and roping almost suicidal, and once that steer got into the tangle beyond he was gone.

The Kid shook out a loop and hightailed it after the steer, but it was a shade far for good roping when he made his cast. Even at that, he'd have made it, but just as his rope snagged the steer the roan's hoof went into a gopher hole, and the Sandy Kid sailed right off over the roan's ears.

———

As HE HIT the ground all in a lump, he caught a glimpse of the ladino. Wheeling around, head down with about four or five feet of horn, it started for him.

With a yelp, the Kid grabbed for his gun, but it was gone, so he made a frantic leap for a cleft in the ground. Even as he rolled into it he felt the hot breath of the steer, or thought he did.

The steer went over the cleft, scuffling dust down on the cowboy. When the Kid looked around, he saw he was lying in a crack that was about three feet wide and at least thirty feet deep. He had landed on a ledge that all but closed off the crack for several feet.

Warily he eased his head over the edge and then jerked back with a gasp, for the steer was standing, red-eyed and mean, not over ten feet away and staring right at him.

Digging out the makings, the Kid rolled a cigarette. After all, why get cut up about it? The steer would go away after a while, and then it would be safe to come out. In the meantime it was mighty cool here and pleasant enough, what with the sound of falling water and all.

The thought of water reminded the Kid that he was thirsty. He studied the situation and decided that with care he could climb to the bottom without any danger. Once down where the water was, he could get a drink. He was not worried, for when he had looked about he had seen his horse, bridle reins trailing, standing not far away. The roan would stand forever that way.

His six-gun, which had been thrown from his holster when he fell, also lay up there on the grass. It was not over twenty feet from the rim of the crevice, and once it was in his hand, it would be a simple thing to knock off that steer. Getting the pistol was quite another thing. With that steer on the prod, it would be suicide to try.

When he reached the bottom of the crevice he peered around in the vague light. At noon, or close to that, it would be bright down here, but at any other time it would be thick with shadows. Kneeling by the thin trickle of water, the Kid drank his fill. Lifting his face from the water, he looked downstream and almost jumped out of his skin when he saw a grinning skull.

The Sandy Kid was no pilgrim. He had fought Apaches and Comanches, and twice he had been over the trail to Dodge. But seeing a skull grinning at him from a distance of only a few feet did nothing to make him feel comfortable and at ease.

"By grab, looks like I ain't the first to tumble into this place," he said. "That hombre must have broken a leg and starved to death."

Yet when he walked over and examined the skeleton, he could see he was wrong. The man had been shot through the head.

Gingerly, the Kid moved the skull. There was a hole on the other side, too, and a bullet flattened against the rock.

He was astonished.

"Well, now! Somebody shot this hombre while he laid here," the Kid decided.

Squatting on his haunches, the Sandy Kid puffed his cigarette and studied the situation. Long experience in reading sign had made it easy for his eyes to see what should be seen. A few things he noticed now. This man, already wounded, had fallen or been pushed into the crack, and then a man with a gun had leaned over the edge above and shot him through the head!

There was a notch in his belt that must have been cut by a bullet, and one knee had been broken by a bullet, for the slug was still there, embedded in the joint.

The Kid was guessing about the notch, but from the look of things and the way the man was doubled up, it looked like he had been hurt pretty bad aside from the knee.

The shirt was gone except for a few shreds, and among the rocky debris there were a few buttons, an old pocketknife, and some coins. The boots, dried and stiff, were not a horseman's boots, but the high-topped, flat-heeled type that miners wear. A rusted six-shooter lay a bit farther downstream, and the Kid retrieved it. After a few minutes he determined that the gun was still fully loaded.

"Prob'ly never got a shot at the skunk," the Sandy Kid said thoughtfully. "Well, now! Ain't this a purty mess?"

When he studied the skeleton further, he noticed something under the ribs that he had passed over, thinking it a rock. Now he saw it was a small leather sack which the dead man had evidently carried inside his shirt. The leather was dry and stiff, and it ripped when he tried to open it. Within were several fragments of the same ore the Kid had himself found!

Tucking the samples and the remnants of the sack under a rocky ledge, the Kid stuck the rusty six-shooter in his belt and climbed back to the ledge, where a cautious look showed that the ladino was gone.

The roan pricked up his ears and whinnied, not at all astonished that this peculiar master of his should come crawling out of the ground. The Kid had lost his rope, which was probably still trailing from the steer's horns, but he was not thinking of that. He was thinking of the murdered man.

WHEN HE AWAKENED the next morning he rolled over on his side and stared around the bunkhouse. Everyone was still asleep, and then he realized that it was Sunday.

Wald was nowhere around when the Kid headed for the cookshack. Smoke was rising slowly, for Cholly Cooper, the best cook on that range, was conscientious. When you wanted breakfast you got it, early or late. The Sandy Kid was glad that Wald was not around, for he had no love for his morose, quick-to-anger boss.

It was not a pleasant outfit to ride for, Cooper being the only friendly one in the bunch. Jasper Wald never spoke, except to give an order or to criticize in a dry, sarcastic voice.

He was about forty, tough and hard-bitten. Rumor had it that he had killed more than one man. His two permanent hands were Jack Swarr, a burly Kansas man, always unshaven, and Dutch Schweitzer, a lean German who drank heavily.

"Hi, Sandy." Cholly waved a fork at him. "Set yoreself down and I'll get some coffee. Up early, ain't you?"

"Uh-huh." The Kid pulled the thick cup toward him. "Sort of reckoned I'd ride up to the Forks. Few things I need. Shirts and stuff."

Cholly dished out a couple of thick slabs of beef and four eggs. "Better eat," he said. "I wouldn't want yuh pourin' them shirts onto an empty stomach."

While Cholly refilled the Kid's cup, he said in a low voice, "What did you-all do to the boss? He was shore riled up when he came in and saw yuh hadn't showed up with the rest of the hands."

"Reckon he was just sore. I tied in with an old mossyhorn up in the breaks and lost my rope. Durned steer had one horn, looked long enough for two steers, and a stub on the other end."

Cooper chuckled. "You ain't the first who lost a rope on Ol' Stob! You were lucky not to get killed."

"Rough country, over thataway," the Sandy Kid suggested. "Ever been over there?"

"No farther'n the creek, and I don't aim to. Only one man ever knowed that country, unless it was the Apaches, and that was Jim Kurland. He always claimed there was gold over there, but most folks just laughed at him."

"Rancher?"

"No, sort of a prospector. He mined some, I guess, afore he came here. Dead now, I reckon. He headed off into that country about a year ago and nobody ever saw hide nor hair of him again. His wife, she died about three, four months ago, and his daughter works down to Wright's Store. She handles the post office in there, mostly."

Jim Kurland. It was a name to remember. The Sandy Kid knew he was walking on dangerous ground. The killer of Kurland, if it was his skeleton the Kid had found, was probably still around, and any mention of Kurland's name might lead to trouble. It would be wise to proceed with caution.

The Sandy Kid was no hero. He had never toted a badge, and like most cowhands of his day, he looked upon the law as a nuisance originated mainly to keep riders from having a good time. He went his own way, and if someone made trouble for him, he figured to handle it himself. He would be ashamed to ask for help and figured all sheriffs were the same.

He was interested in gold. If there was a mine as rich as that ore seemed to indicate, he wanted it. Why, with a little gold a man could buy a spread of his own and stock it with those new whiteface cattle that carried so much more beef than a longhorn. A man could do right well with a little money to go on. . . .

When he rode into the Forks he headed right for the store. He was not planning on doing any drinking this day. It was Sunday, but Sim Wright kept his store open seven days a week the year 'round. The Sandy Kid, who was a lean six feet and with a shock of sandy hair and mild gray eyes, swung down from the roan and crossed the boardwalk to the store.

At first he thought it was empty. Then he saw the girl who stood behind the counter, her eyes on him.

He jerked his hat from his head and went toward her. "Ma'am," he said, "I better get me a couple of shirts. Yuh got anything with checks in it?"

"Big checks?" She smiled at him.

"Uh-huh, that's right."

She showed him the shirts, one of them with black and white checks as big as those on a checkerboard.

He fingered them thoughtfully. Then he said, "Ma'am, is yore name Kurland?"

"That's my last name. My first name is Betty."

"Mine's Sandy," he told her. "They call me the Sandy Kid."

He hesitated and then slid a hand into his pocket and took out the pocketknife and laid it on the shirts.

Her face went white as she caught it up. She looked at the Kid. "Where did you get this?"

Slowly, carefully, he told her. As he talked, she stared at him with wide eyes. "You think," she asked when he had finished, "that he was murdered? But why?"

"He had gold samples, ma'am. Folks will do a powerful lot for gold. I would, myself. I sort of figgered I'd keep quiet about this, and sort of hunt that claim myself, and when I found it, I'd stake her out. Then I heard about you, an' I figgered yuh'd like to know about yore pappy and have him buried proper."

"Who killed him?"

"That I don't know. I reckon if a body was to try, he could find out, but you'd have to keep still about findin' him for a while."

"If I keep still, will you find the murderer? If you do, I'll give you that claim."

"No, ma'am, I couldn't take yore claim. Menfolks in my family wasn't raised no such way. But I don't have a particle of use for a coyote that would murder a man like that, so if yuh want, I'll have a look around in my spare time."

Her eyes were large and dark. It was nice looking into them. The Sandy Kid reckoned he had never looked into eyes that were like hers. And her lips—she had right nice lips. Not too full and not thin, either. He liked that. Her neck was sure white—She was smiling at him, amused.

He flushed a deep red. "Reckon yuh must think I never saw a girl before," he said. "Well, I reckon mebbe I never did really look at one. Somehow, they never sort of called themselves to mind."

"Thank you, Sandy."

———

ALL THE WAY back to the ranch he was thinking how nice that name sounded from her lips.

The Bar W lay like an ugly sore in the bottom of the flat. There were three adjoining pole corrals, an unpainted frame bunkhouse, and a ranch house of adobe. The cookshack was also adobe, and there was smoke coming from the chimney when he rode in with his shirts.

It was still quite early, for the ranch was only a short piece from town. He unsaddled the roan and walked back toward the cookshack for coffee. They were all there. Nobody said anything when he came in, but Cholly threw him a warning glance. The Kid got a cup and filled it with coffee. Then he sat down.

"What happened to yuh last night?" Wald demanded, glaring at him across the table.

"Me? I had me a run-in with that old stub-horned ladino. Lost my rope."

"You still got that rock?"

"That?" The Sandy Kid shrugged carelessly. "No. I throwed it away. Reckon it was just iron pyrites or some-thin'."

Nothing more was said, but he felt uncomfortable. He had found Jasper Wald an unpleasant man to work for, and the sooner he got himself another job the better off he would be. There was something in Wald's baleful glance that disturbed him.

"In the mornin'," Wald said after a few minutes, "you work that Thumb Butte country."

The Kid nodded, but made no comment. The Thumb Butte area was six miles across the valley from the badlands where he'd had the run-in with Old Stob, that red-eyed mossyhorn. Was it accident or design that had caused Wald to send him to the other side of the ranch?

Yet the next day he realized that his new working ground had advantages of its own. He worked hard all morning and rounded up and turned into a mountain corral forty head of cattle that he had combed out of the piñons.

Switching his saddle to a bay pony, he took off into the draws that led south and west, away from the ranch. An hour's riding brought him to the Argo trail, and he cantered along to the little town at Argo Springs. Here was the only land office within two hundred miles or more where a mining claim could be registered.

A quick check of the books, offered him by an obliging justice of the peace who also served in five or six other capacities, showed him that no mining claim had been located in the vicinity of the badlands. Hence, if the killer of Jim

Kurland had found the claim, he was working it on the sly. He did some further checking, but the discovery he made was by accident. It came out of a blue sky when Pete Mallinger, at the Wells Fargo office, noticed his brand.

"Bar W, eh? You bring one of them boxes over here? The ones Wald's been shippin' to El Paso?"

"Me? No, I just rode over to get myself some smokin'." He grinned confidentially. "The boss doesn't even know I'm gone."

"I wouldn't let him ketch yuh. He's a tough one, that Jasper Wald is. Throw a gun on a man soon's look at him. Got money, too, he has. He's buyin' up most of that Agua Dulce Canyon country."

The Sandy Kid rolled a smoke and listened, his eyes sweeping the narrow street with its hitching rails and clapboarded buildings. Jasper Wald was not making enough on the Bar W to buy any land, not even with all his free-and-easy branding operations. Nothing you could really complain about, but nevertheless the Bar W brand was showing up on almost everything on the range that came within sight of a Bar W hand.

Before he left, the Kid managed to get his hands on the address in El Paso. The boxes were being shipped to Henry Wald, a brother of Jasper, and they were notably heavy.

The Sandy Kid strolled thoughtfully away from the door of the Wells Fargo office and crossed the dusty street to the saloon. He might as well have a drink while he was here. He pushed through the swinging doors into the bare, untidy barroom. Dutch Schweitzer was leaning an elbow on the bar, staring at him.

"Howdy." The Sandy Kid strolled up to the bar and ordered a drink. "Looks like we've both strayed on the same mornin'."

Dutch looked at him with sullen eyes. "No, I'm on the job. The boss sent me over here. He didn't send you."

"Shore he didn't. I rounded up enough stock for a full day in that country where I'm workin'. It's dry work, so I ambled over for a drink."

"At the Wells Fargo office?"

The Kid shrugged. He picked up his glass and tossed off his drink. "I'm on my way back," he said and turned to go. Schweitzer's voice halted him.

"Wait."

The Sandy Kid turned. Suddenly, he felt cold. He had never met a man in a gun battle, but there was cold deadliness in the big German's eyes. The Kid stood with his feet apart a little, and his mouth felt dry. He felt sure Dutch meant to kill him.

Schweitzer had been drinking but was not drunk. The man had an enormous capacity for liquor, yet he rarely drank to the point where he was unsteady or loose-talking. Only, when he drank he grew mean and cruel.

"You're a smart kid. Too blamed smart," he said meaningly.

Two men in the back of the room got up and eased out through the rear door. The Sandy Kid could see that the bartender was obviously frightened.

Curiously, the Kid was not. He watched Dutch carefully, aware that the man was spoiling for trouble, that he had a fierce, driving urge for brutality. Some inner canker gnawed at him, some bitter hatred that he seemed to nurse for everything and everybody. The Sandy Kid knew it was not personal animosity. It was simply that in these moods Dutch Schweitzer was a killer, and only the tiniest spark was needed to touch him off.

In that mental clarity that comes in moments of great stress, the Kid found himself aware of many things—a wet ring on the bar where his glass had stood, the half empty bottle near Schweitzer, the two empty tables in the back of the room. He saw the sickly pallor on the bartender's flabby face and the yellow hairs on the backs of Schweitzer's hands.

"You stick your nose into trouble." Schweitzer lifted the bottle with his left hand to pour a drink. Then his face suddenly twisted with blind, bitter fury, and he jerked the bottle up to throw it at the Kid.

Afterward, the Kid could never remember any impulse or feeling. He simply drew and fired without any thought or plan, and he fired at the bottle.

It exploded in a shower of glass and drenched Schweitzer with whiskey. He sprang back, amazed, and when he looked up at the Kid he was cold sober.

Slowly, his eyes wide and his face pale, Schweitzer lifted his hands in a gesture of surrender. "I ain't drawin'," he said, astonishment making his voice thick. "I ain't makin' a move."

"See that yuh don't!" the Sandy Kid said flatly. He glared at the bartender and then backed through the swinging doors and holstered his gun. With a wary eye on the saloon, he crossed to his horse, mounted, and rode out of town.

He moved in a sort of daze. He was no gunfighter and had never fancied himself as such. He was only a drifting cowhand who dreamed of someday owning his own spread. He had never found any occasion for split-second drawing, although he had practiced, of course.

He had been wearing a six-gun for years, and he practiced throwing it hour after hour, but more to ease the monotony of long nights on night guard than from any desire for skill. It had been something to do, like riffling cards, playing solitaire, or juggling stones.

———

LIKE ALL TEXAS men of his time he had done his share of fighting and he had done a lot of shooting. He knew he was a good shot and that he nearly always got what he went after, but shooting as quickly and accurately as he had done in the saloon had never been considered.

Out of town, he did not ride away. When Dutch Schweitzer returned he would tell Jasper Wald what had happened. There would be trouble then, the Kid knew, and the least he could expect would be to be fired. Yet there was something he would do before he left town. Riding around the town in the juniper-clad hills, he dismounted and seated himself for a long wait.

He saw Dutch ride out a short time later. He saw the streets become less peopled, and he saw the sun go down. When it was dark, he moved down to the Wells Fargo office. When

Dutch left he had been driving a buckboard, and that meant something to the Kid.

Using his knife, he cut away the putty around a pane of glass and then reached through and unfastened the window. Raising it, he crawled in.

For an instant he stood still, listening. There was no sound, so he struck a match and shielding it in his hands, looked around for the box. He identified it quickly enough by the address. It was not large but was strongly built. With a hammer he found lying on a shelf, he pried up one of the top boards. He struck another match and peered into the box. Inside, wrapped in sacking, was a lot of the same ore he had found in the leather bag under the skeleton of Jim Kurland!

He blew out the match and then pushed the board back in place, hitting it a couple of light taps with the hammer. Then he went out, closed the window, and replaced the pane of glass, using some slivers of wood to hold the pane in place.

Jasper Wald, then, had killed Jim Kurland and found the claim. Or perhaps he had found the claim first. The ore was extremely rich, and he was shipping it, a very little at a time, to El Paso, where his brother was probably having it milled.

A slow process, certainly, but it was high-grade ore, and no doubt Wald had made plans to file on the claim when there would be no danger of Kurland's disappearance being linked with the proceedings. Everyone from the Forks to the Stone Tree Desert and Agua Dulce Canyon knew Kurland was the only mining man around and also that he regularly penetrated the badlands of the Stone Tree.

THE SANDY KID took to the trail and put the bay to a fast trot. He was foolish, he told himself, to be mixing into something that was no concern of his. It would have been wiser to forget what he had seen after he came out of that crack in the mountain. Even now, he reflected, it was not too late to travel to some far-off place like the Blue Mountains or maybe that Grand Canyon country of Arizona, which he had never seen but had heard cowhands lying about.

Little as he knew about gold, he could tell that the ore he

had seen was fabulously rich, for the rock had been lined and threaded with it, and being so heavy, it had to be rich ore. Such a boxful as he had seen in the express office might be worth two or three thousand dollars.

Now that he thought about it, he had an idea where that claim was located. Not more than a half mile from where he had jumped into the crack to escape the steer, the plateau broke sharply off in a sheer cliff, some fifty or sixty feet high, that overhung the waterless, treeless waste of Stone Tree Desert and could even open upon the desert itself. That rupture, obviously the result of volcanic disturbance, could have exposed the vein from which the ore had come.

Pure speculation, of course, but the Sandy Kid had an idea he was nosing along the right trail. Also, he was aware that his interest did not arise from chivalry. He was not going into this to help a lady in distress. Trouble with Jasper Wald and his two hard-bitten henchmen was not lightly to be invited, and if he did go into it knowing what he was facing, it was only partly because of the way Betty Kurland had looked at him that he was following through.

It was a fool thing, he told himself. He had no particular urge to get money. Much as he'd like a ranch, he didn't want to have his head shot off getting it. He admitted to himself that if it had not been for Betty, he would never have gone all the way into this fight.

"The devil with it!" he said viciously. "I'll go back to the Bar W an' roll my soogan an' hit the trail!"

But when he came to the last forks, he kept on toward the mountains. He circled when he hit the willows and let the pony take its own gait. He was just edging out toward the cliff edge where he could see over into the Stone Tree when a rifle bullet hit the fork of his saddle with a wicked thwack, and then the bullet whined off ahead of him. It was a wonder it hadn't glanced back into his stomach or hit the pony's head.

The echo of the report drifted over him as he hit the ground running, and he grabbed the bridle and swung the bay pony back into the brush. Then he slid his Winchester .44 out of the saddle scabbard and Injun-crawled toward the cliff edge.

That shot meant that somebody wasn't fooling, so the Kid wasn't planning on fun himself. He was some shakes with a Winchester, and when he got to cover where he could see out, he looked around, trying to locate the spot the varmint had shot from. There was nobody in sight.

The Sandy Kid was not a trusting soul. His past dealings with Comanches had not been calculated to inspire any confidence in the serene and untrammeled appearance of woods or mountains. So after a long look, he left the bay pony tethered to a bush and crawled to the very lip of the cliff. When he glanced over, he could see something that looked like a pile of waste and rock taken from a mine tunnel, but he wasn't looking for that. All in good time he could have an interest in the gold.

Then, in the rocks farther along the rim of the cliff, he detected a slight movement. He looked again, widening and then squinting his eyes. It looked like a boot heel. Not much of a mark at that distance, and not much damage could be done if he hit it.

"We'll scare the daylights out of yuh, anyway!" he said, and lifting the Winchester, he nestled his cheek affectionately against the stock and squeezed off a shot.

———

DUST OBSCURED THE spot for a moment, but no dust could blot out the startled yell he heard. Somebody lunged into view then, and the Sandy Kid's jaw dropped. It was Betty Kurland! She was wearing a man's trousers and a man's shirt and limping with one boot heel gone, but that hair could belong to nobody else!

He got up, waving his arms, and ran out to meet her. She turned on him, and her own rifle was coming hip high when she got a better look and recognized him. She came on a couple of steps and then stopped, her eyes flashing with indignation.

"I thought you were my friend!" she flared at him. "Then you shoot at me!"

"You shot at me!" he declared. "How was I to know?"

"That's different!"

Such feminine logic was so amazing that he gulped and swallowed. "Yuh shouldn't have come out here," he protested. "It isn't safe!"

"I wanted to find my father," she said. "Where is he?"

He led her to the lip of the cliff, and they found a way down. The Kid wanted a look at that desert, first. They came around in full sight of the mine tunnel and were just in time to see a man climbing out of a hole.

"I'll go get what's left of Kurland," they heard the man say. "They'll never find him here!"

The Sandy Kid was cursing softly, for he had been so preoccupied with the girl that he had walked around unthinking and now found himself looking into a gun held by Jasper Wald. The rancher had seen him, even if Jack Swarr, climbing from the freshly dug grave, had not.

"Well, now!" Wald said. "If this ain't nice! You and that girl walkin' right up on us!"

"Don't you try nothin'," the Kid said. "This girl is known to be here. If she doesn't show up you'll have the law around."

Wald chuckled, "No, we won't. Not for long, anyway. I'll just tell them this Kurland girl showed up to meet you, and you two took off to get married, over to Lordsburg or somewheres. They'll figger yuh eloped and never even think of lookin' for yuh!"

Swarr grinned. "Hey, that's a good idea, boss! An' we can pile 'em in the same hole with her pa!"

"If I were you," the Sandy Kid said, "I'd guess again. I just come from Argo Springs. I know all about that gold ore you've been shippin' to El Paso, and I ain't the only one."

Jasper Wald hesitated. His idea for getting rid of the two had been a sudden inspiration and a good one, but the thought that the Kid might have mentioned the gold to someone in Argo Springs disturbed him. It would mean he would have to move slowly, or worse, that he was already suspected.

Suddenly there was a clatter of stones, and they looked up. Only Wald, who held the gun on the Kid, did not shift his eyes. The newcomer was Dutch Schweitzer.

"Watch that hombre, boss!" the German said hoarsely. "He's gun slick!"

"Him?" Swarr was incredulous. "That kid?"

"How old was Bill Bonney?" Dutch asked sarcastically. "He flashed a gun on me today so fast I never even saw his hand move!"

Angered and worried, Jasper Wald stared at the Kid. Quickly, Swarr explained.

"Aw, boss," Dutch said, "he's lyin'. I nosed around town after he left. After he left me, I mean. He never talked to nobody."

"How did I find out about the gold in that box yuh brought in? Addressed to Henry Wald, in El Paso?" the Kid asked him.

"He must have seen the box," Dutch protested.

The Sandy Kid's mind was running desperately ahead, trying to find a way out. "Also," he added, "I checked on this claim. You never filed on it, so I did."

"What?" Wald's shout was a bellow of fury. His face went dark with blood. "You filed on this claim? Why, you—" Rage drove all caution from his mind. "I'll shoot yuh, blast yuh, and let yuh die right out in the sun! You—"

"Boss!" Swarr shouted. "Hold it! Mebbe he's lyin'! Mebbe he didn't file! Anyway," he added craftily, "why kill him until he signs the claim over to us?"

Wald's rage died. He glanced at Swarr. "You're right," he said. "We can get possession that way."

The Sandy Kid chuckled. "You'll have no cinch gettin' me to sign anything."

"It'll be easy," Wald said sharply. "We'll just start by tyin' up that girl and takin' her boots off. By the time she gets a little fire on her feet, yuh'll sign!"

Dutch Schweitzer glanced at his chief. Then he helped Jack Swarr tie the girl. Swarr knelt and pulled off her boots. He drew deeply on his cigarette and thrust it toward her foot.

Dutch stared at them, his eyes suddenly hardening. "None of that!" he said. "I thought yuh were bluffin'! Cut it out!"

"Bluffin'?" Swarr looked up. "I'll show yuh if I'm bluffin'!" He jammed the cigarette forward, and Betty screamed.

Dutch Schweitzer's face went pale, and with an oath, he grabbed for a gun. At the same time, Jasper Wald swung his gun toward the German. That was all the break the Sandy Kid needed. His right hand streaked for his gun butt, and he was shooting with the first roar from Wald's gun.

The Kid's first shot took Jack Swarr in the stomach as the big man lunged upward, clawing for his pistol. Dutch had a gun out and was firing. The Kid saw his body jerk with the impact of Wald's bullet, and he swung his own gun. Wald faced him at the same instant.

———

FOR ONE UNBELIEVING instant, the Sandy Kid looked over the stabbing flame of his own Colt into the flaring muzzle of Wald's six-shooter. He triggered his gun fast at almost point-blank range.

He swayed on his feet, his legs spread wide, and saw Jasper Wald's cruel face turn white before his eyes. The rancher's knees sagged, and he went to the ground, glaring bitterly at the Sandy Kid. He tried then to lift his gun, but the Kid sprang forward and knocked it from his grasp. Wald slumped over on the sand, his face contorted.

Swarr, the Kid saw at a glance, was dead. Yet it had not been only his bullet, for the German must have got in at least one shot. Swarr's face and head were bloody.

Schweitzer lay on his back, his face upturned to the sun. The Sandy Kid knelt beside him, but a glance told him there was nothing he or anyone could do.

Dutch stared at him. "Never was no hand to abuse women," he said, "never—no hand."

The Sandy Kid turned to Betty Kurland, who stood staring down at Dutch. "He was a strange man," she said.

"Let's get out of here," the Kid said. Taking her by the hand, he led her toward the path down which Schweitzer had come.

On the cliff top, they stood for a moment together.

Betty's face was white now, and her eyes seemed unusually large and dark. He noticed then that she hadn't limped.

"Was yore foot burned badly?" he asked. "I didn't think to help yuh."

"It wasn't burned at all!" she told him. "I jerked my foot back as he thrust the cigarette at it."

"But you screamed?" he protested.

"Yes, I know," she said, looking at him. "You had to have your chance to draw, and they hadn't taken away your guns. And I knew about Dutch Schweitzer."

"Knew about him? What?"

"The Apaches killed his wife. They burned her. I thought, maybe—That was why he drank so much, I guess."

When they were on the trail toward the Forks, he looked at her and then glanced quickly away. "Well, yuh've got yore claim," he said. "All yuh've got to do is stake it out and file on it. I never did. Yuh found yore pa, too. Looks like yuh're all set. I reckon I'll hug the rawhide and head out of the country. A loose horse is always huntin' new pastures!"

"I'll need a good man to ramrod that mine for me!" she protested. "Wouldn't you do that? I promised you half, too!"

"Ma'am"—the Sandy Kid was growing red around the gills and desperate, for she was sure enough a pretty girl—"I reckon I never was made to stay no place. I'm packin' my duffle and takin' the trail out of here. If anybody comes around askin' for the Sandy Kid, you tell 'em he lit a shuck and went to Texas!"

He turned his horse at the fork of the road and headed for the Bar W. His own horse was there, and since Wald wouldn't be needing this bay pony, he might need him out west there, Arizona way. He sure did aim to see that Grand Canyon down which flowed the Colorado. A mile deep, they said. Of course, that was a durned lie, but she might be pretty deep, at that.

Once, he glanced back over his shoulder. The girl was only a dim figure on the skyline.

"First thing we know," he said to the bay pony, "she'd have me a-settin' in church a-wearin' a fried shirt. I'd shore be halter broke."

The bay pony switched his tail and picked up its feet in an Injun trot, and the Sandy Kid broke into song, a gritty baritone that made the bay lay back its ears.

Oh, there was a young cowhand who used to go riding,
There was a young cowhand named Johnny
Go-day!
He rode a black pony an' never was lonely,
For a girl never said to him, "Johnny, go 'way!"

WEST OF DRY CREEK

O N A LATE afternoon of a bitterly cold day he returned to the hotel and to his room. There was a narrow bed, a straw mattress, an old bureau, a white bowl and pitcher, and on the floor a small section of rag rug. The only other article of furniture was a drinking glass.

Beaure, short for Beauregard, took off his boots with their run-down heels and stretched out on the bed with a sigh. He was dog-tired and lonely, with nothing to do but wait for the storm to blow itself out. Then he would ride a freight out of town to somewhere and hunt himself a job.

Two days ago he had been laid off by the Seventy-seven. After a summer of hard work he had but sixty-three dollars coming to him, and nobody was taking on hands in cold weather. It was head south or starve.

Beaure Hatch was twenty-two, an orphan since fourteen, and most of the time during those eight years he had been punching cows. Brute hard work and nothing to show for it but his saddle, bridle, an old Colt, and a .44-40 Winchester. Riding company stock all the time, he did not even own a horse.

The Spencer House was the town's second-best hotel. It occupied a place midway between the Metropole, a place of frontier luxury, and the hay mow of the livery barn, where a man could sleep if he stabled his horse there.

When a man had time to kill in Carson Crossing he did it at the Metropole, but to hang out there a man was expected to buy drinks or gamble, and a few such days would leave Beaure broke and facing a tough winter. He crumpled the pillow under his head and pulled the extra blanket over him. It was cold even in the room.

It was late afternoon when he went to sleep with the wind

moaning under the eaves, and when he awakened it was dark. Out-of-doors sounds told him it was early evening, and his stomach told him it was suppertime, yet he hesitated to leave the warmth of the bed for the chill of the room.

For several minutes he had been conscious of a low mumble of voices from beyond the thin wall, and then the sound broke into understandable words and he found himself listening.

"It ain't so far to Dry Creek," a man was saying, "otherwise I wouldn't suggest it in weather like this. We'll be in a rig and bundled warm."

"Couldn't we wait until the weather changes?" It was a girl's voice. "I don't understand why we should hurry."

Irritation was obvious in the man's reply. "This hotel ain't no place for a decent girl, and you'll be more comfortable out at the Dry Creek place. Big house out there, mighty well furnished."

Beaure Hatch sat up in bed and began to build a smoke. It was twenty miles to Dry Creek through a howling blizzard . . . and when that man said there was a comfortable house on Dry Creek he was telling a bald-faced lie.

Beaure had punched cows along Dry Creek and in its vicinity all summer long, and in thirty miles there were two buildings. One was the Seventy-seven line shack where he had bunked with two other hands, and the other was the old Pollock place.

The Pollock ranch had been deserted for six or seven years, the windows boarded up. A man could see inside, all right, and it was still furnished, left the way it had been when old man Pollock went East to die. Everything was covered with dust, and it would be icy cold inside that big old place.

The well was working—he had stopped to water his horse not three days ago—but there was no fuel around, and no neighbors within fifteen miles.

It was no place to take a girl in midwinter after telling her what he just had . . . unless, and the thought jolted him, she was not expected to return.

"But why should we go now?" she was protesting, "and

why don't you want to talk to anyone? When I sell the place people will certainly know it."

"I explained all that!" The man's voice was rough with anger. "There's folks want that range, and it's best to get it settled before they can start a court action to prevent it. If you get tied up in a lawsuit it may be years before the estate is settled. And you say you need the money."

"I should think so. It is all I have, and no relatives."

"Then get ready. I'll be back in half an hour."

The door closed and after a long silence he could hear the girl moving around, probably getting dressed for the drive.

Beaure finished his cigarette and rubbed it out. It was not his business, but anybody driving to the old Pollock place on a night like this was a fool. It was nigh to zero now, with the wind blowing and snow in the air. A man with a good team and a cutter could make it all right . . . but for what reason?

Beaure got to his feet and combed his hair. He was a lean, broad-shouldered young man with a rider's narrow body. He pulled on his shabby boots and shrugged into his sheepskin. Picking up his hat, he also made up his mind.

He hesitated at her door, then knocked. There was a sudden silence. "Is that you, Cousin Hugh?"

"No, ma'am, this here is Beauregard Hatch, ma'am, an' I'd like a word with you."

The door opened and revealed a slender young girl with large gray eyes in a heart-shaped face. Her dark auburn hair was lovely in the reflected lamplight.

"Ma'am, I'm in the next room to you, and I couldn't help hearing talk about the old Pollock place. Ma'am, don't you go out there, especially in weather like this. There ain't been nobody on the ranch in years, and she's dusty as all get-out. Nor is there any fuel got up. Why, ma'am, you couldn't heat that ol' house up in a week."

She smiled as she might smile at a child. "You must be mistaken. Cousin Hugh says it is just as it was left, and of course, there is the housekeeper and the hands. Thank you very much, but we will have everything we need."

"Ma'am," he persisted, "that surely ain't true. Why, I stopped by there only a few days ago, and peeked in through the boarded-up windows. There's dust over everything, and pack rats have been in there. It ain't none of my business, ma'am, but was I you, I'd sure enough ask around a mite, or wait until the weather breaks. Don't you go out there."

Her smile vanished and she seemed to be waiting impatiently for him to finish what he was saying. "I am sure you mean well, Mr. Hatch, but you must be mistaken. If that is all, I have things to do."

She closed the door in his face and he stood there, feeling like a fool.

Gloomily, he walked down the hall, then down the steps into the lobby. The fire on the hearth did nothing to take the chill from the room. What the Spencer needed was one of those potbellied stoves like at the Metropole, one with fancy nickel all over it. Sure made a place look up—and warmer, too.

It was bitter cold in the street and the snow crunched under his boots. Frost nipped at his cheeks and he ducked his face behind the sheepskin collar. When he glimpsed Abram Tebbets's sign, he knew what he was going to do.

Abram was tilted back in his swivel chair reading Thucydides. He glanced at Beauregard over his steel-rimmed spectacles, and lowered his feet to the floor. "Don't tell me, young man, that you've run afoul of the law?"

"No, sir." Beaure turned his hat in his hand. "I reckoned I might get some information from you. I been savin' a mite and figured I might buy myself a place, sometime."

"Laudable." Abram Tebbets picked a pipe from a dusty tray and began to stoke it carefully with a threatening mixture. "Ambition is a good thing in a young man."

"Figured you might know something about the old Pollock place."

Abram Tebbets continued to load his pipe without replying. Twice he glanced at Beaure over his glasses, and when he leaned back in his chair there was a subtle difference in his manner. Beaure, who could read sign like an Apache, noticed it. He had known Tebbets for more than a year, and it had been the lawyer who started him reading.

"Settin' your sights mighty high, Beaure. That Pollock

place could be sold right off, just anytime, for twenty thousand dollars. The Seventy-seven would like to own it, and so would a lot of others."

"Who owns it now?"

"Heirs to old Jim Pollock. His granddaughter was named in the will, but she dropped out of sight a few years back, and it's believed she died back East somewhere. If she doesn't show up in a few weeks it goes to Len Mason, and after that to Hugo Naley."

Beaure knew them both by sight, and Naley a little better than that. Mason lived in a small shack over on the Clearwater. He had been a prospecting partner of Jim Pollock's when the latter first came west. Hugo Naley was foreman of the Slash Five. The granddaughter's name, Tebbets informed him, was Nora Rand.

If he explained to Tebbets what he had overheard, Tebbets would advise him, and rightly, that it was none of his business and to stay out of it. Still, the old man might be able to help.

That girl had no business going out there alone, and he was not going to stand by and see her do it. He remembered Hugo Naley from the roundup. He was a burly, deep-voiced man with an arrogant, hard-heeled way about him, and the punchers had him down as a bad man to cross.

There was a jingle of bells in the street and Beaure turned quickly to look from the window, a fact not lost on Abram Tebbets. In the lights that fell from windows to the snow, Beaure saw it was a cutter containing two people. Beaure went down the stairs two steps at a time.

Abram Tebbets stepped past his chair into the living room of his apartment, and glanced from the window in time to see the cutter and its two passengers disappearing into the snow along the river road. At the distance and in the vague light there was no possibility of making them out. The horses and rig looked like one belonging to the livery barn.

The wind moaned under the eaves and snow swirled in the now-empty street. It was a bad night to be out. . . . Beaure Hatch was going into the livery stable.

Sighing, Tebbets put aside his pipe and shouldered into his

buffalo coat. That Beaure was thinking of buying a place was logical—it was a thought that came to many cowhands, and Beaure was more canny than the average. That he had saved any money at his wages was ridiculous.

Crossing to the Metropole, Tebbets ordered a drink. "Has Len Mason been in?"

"Len? Ain't seen him in a week or more. And not likely in this storm."

Beaure Hatch was a quiet young cowpuncher and not inclined to go off on tangents. Tebbets tossed off half his whiskey and scowled at the glass.

"Suppose everybody will be staying out of town, and don't know as I blame them."

"Naley was in from the Five. He didn't stay long."

Hugo Naley . . . Scowling, Tebbets crossed to watch the checkers game. Dickerson was the station agent, and he had played checkers in the Metropole every night for years.

"Quiet," he replied to Tebbets's question. "No passengers today, and only three last night. A couple of hands returning from Denver and some girl . . . a pretty little thing."

The big red horse Beaure rented from the livery stable had no liking for the storm, yet he forged ahead into the snow, evidently hopeful of a good bait of corn and a warm barn at the end of the trip.

The wind was stronger once clear of the town. Here and there it had swept the road free of snow, but there were drifts. The cutter had a good start and was making time. Beaure took out his muffler and tied it around his hat and under his chin, and with his collar around his ears, he could keep fairly warm.

After a while he dismounted and led the horse. His feet tingled with the cold that was in them. Only where the cutter went through a large drift were there visible tracks. Suppose they didn't go to the Pollock place at all? Try as he might, Beaure could not think of an alternative along this road.

Beaure wiped the red horse's eyes free of the snow that had gathered on its lids. It was bitter cold, and night had turned to solid blackness through which the wind howled and the blown snow snapped at the skin like tiny needles.

If Hugo Naley was planning to do away with the girl—and Beaure could think of no other reason for his lies—then he had chosen a perfect time. The girl would have been seen at the station and at the hotel, but it was unlikely anybody would think of her again.

She had taken her belongings, and nobody would have seen them leave town in this storm. If the girl never came back, who would there be to know?

But how could Naley hope to profit? Len Mason was due to inherit before Naley. Unless something happened to Mason, too. Living alone as he did, it might be weeks before anyone knew. Mason was nearly eighty, and he lived far out of town on a lonely part of the range. A number of times his friends had tried to get him to move to town. The girl was supposedly dead, and Mason's death would surprise no one.

There was no question of seeing anymore. The snow was swirling all around, and all sense of direction was lost. He must have been traveling a couple of hours, and during the first hour he had made good time. He could be no more than ten miles from Carson Crossing now, which would put him in the midst of a broad plain. Roughly a mile ahead would be the first of the timber. If he could get into that timber, the trail would be well defined by the trees themselves.

He put the wind on his left side and pointed the horse straight ahead, keeping the wind against the left side of his face. Suddenly they were floundering among the drifts at the edge of the woods, and Beaure recognized a huge old lightning-struck cottonwood, and knew he was less than a mile from the Pollock house. Turning into the wind, he rode along the edge of the timber. He had not kept to the trail, but despite the storm had made good time. Through a break in the storm he glimpsed a dark bulk ahead, and turned his horse into the trees.

Here the blowing snow was less, the fury of the wind was cut down, and there were places where he found relatively little snow.

Beaure drew up, snuggling his cheek against the sheepskin collar. Now that he was here he had no idea what he meant to do or could do. Had they arrived? He saw no light.

Thrusting his hand inside the coat he felt for his six-gun, touching the butt lightly. He also had his Winchester in the scabbard with an old bandanna tied around it to keep the snow out. He had no desire to go up against Hugo Naley, yet he surely couldn't allow anything to happen to that girl.

He sat in his saddle looking toward the Pollock house, and suddenly he began to feel foolish. Suppose he was wrong? Suppose Hugo had fixed the house up? Even had a fire going?

He peered through the snow. There was no smell of smoke, but in this wind it would be hard to tell.

There was a large stone stable, but that would be the very place Naley would head for. However, there was an old adobe out back where cowhands occasionally kept their horses and slept themselves when in the vicinity. It was back from the house, but it was tight, and there might even be a little hay.

Keeping under cover of the trees, Beaure Hatch rode north until he could cut across to the adobe. He opened the door and led his horse inside.

Suddenly, it was very still. He struck a match and looked around. The small building was dark and still. There was hay heaped in a corner, and there were four stalls in the small building. He led his horse into a stall, loosened the cinch, and put hay into the manger.

He took a handful of hay and rubbed his horse dry, and then peered out toward the house. No light was visible.

Suppose they had not even come here? Suppose Naley had taken her to his own place? He was owner of a small spread over at the head of Brush Canyon. No sooner had the idea occurred to Beaure than it was dismissed, for in this weather such a trip was not be considered.

He had been aware of a peculiar smell for several minutes, and now he struck another match and looked slowly around. He walked to the next stall and peered in. Nothing. Nor was there anything in any of the other stalls. Nevertheless, he did smell something, and suddenly he knew what it was—it was fresh earth.

He went quickly to the corner of the old barn where a door

opened into the old lean-to behind it. This was the only place he had not looked.

Opening the door, he stepped in, and struck a match. Before him gaped a hole. It was six feet long, and all of six feet deep, and it was freshly dug. The top layers of frozen earth had been hacked away with a mattock, which stood nearby, alongside the shovel. And Beaure needed no second glance to recognize them. They were the tools he had often seen on Len Mason's place. In fact, he had borrowed that shovel several times to help dig steers out of bogs, scooping mud away from their legs before pulling them out with a rope. He knew the scarred handle, the red spot on the end that Mason put on his tools to mark them against theft.

The match burned down to his fingers and he dropped it into the grave, for grave it was . . . or was intended to be.

He walked back through the darkness to the window and peered out at the snow-blanketed house. While he waited here, murder could be done.

But what about Len Mason? Was he in on it, too?

He shucked his gun and checked it, wetting his cold lips with his tongue. No getting around it, he was scared. He had never faced any man with a gun. He had never used a gun for anything but potshots at rabbits, and once he had killed a rabid coyote.

Thrusting the pistol back into its holster, he buttoned his coat and went out into the storm, closing the door behind him.

The wind tore at his coat, lashed his face with hard-driven particles. The snow was more than knee deep in the ranch yard as he plodded across it to the wall of the house. He had never been inside and had no idea whether it was advisable . . . or even how to get in.

He started around the house, then stopped. Dimly he could see the big barn, and a darker square showed through the white. The big door had been opened! Closed now, but the snow that had been blown against the boards had fallen off as it was moved.

A stir of sound came from within the old house. Turning swiftly, Beaure ran around to the back. The old slanting cellar door was partly broken, and he lifted it against the weight of snow and went down the steep steps into the cellar.

Above him the floor creaked. Feeling his way in the unfamiliar darkness, he found the steps and crept up them. Carefully, he tried the door that led into the house. It was unlocked, but stuck tight by dampness.

"I was warned not to come here."

"You're a liar—who could warn you?"

"A cowboy . . . he overheard us through the partition. He had the room next to mine, and he told me this place had been closed for years."

"Do you take me for a fool? In the first place, cowhands don't stay in hotels. When in town they sleep in the livery stable."

Beaure could hear sticks breaking. Hugo Naley was making a fire. If he was going to kill her, why was he waiting? And why build a fire at all?

He shivered, answering his question with his own bitter chill. His fingers were stiff and his face raw from the cold outside. He tried to warm his face in his hands, then realized he would need warm, pliable fingers to handle a gun, and thrust both hands inside his coat.

"Nobody knows you are alive, Nora, and they haven't kept a guest register at that hotel for years. Now, if you had stopped at the Metropole, I'd have been in trouble."

The breaking of sticks continued. He was stomping on heavier sticks to break them, and Beaure thought he might time his pushing of the door with one of these attempts, but there was no rhythm to them and he was afraid to try.

"If you got outside you'd just die in the snow," Naley was saying, "so you'd better be satisfied. You ain't been treated rough, and I don't aim to treat you so. Once I get this place all to myself I can have women, all the women I want. . . . Anyway, you're too skinny for my taste."

Beaure was angered. She was not skinny! Fact was, she was a mighty shapely little filly—willowy, maybe, but not skinny.

He heard a scrape of a boot and the snap of a clasp knife

opening. Nora screamed, and Beaure lunged against the door.

It gave suddenly under his weight, and he stumbled into the room and fell to his knees. He grabbed at the fastenings of his coat, and hearing the click of a gun hammer he looked up into the round muzzle of Hugo Naley's pistol.

"Well . . . you're Hatch, ain't you? What are you doing here?" Without taking his gun off Beaure, Hugo Naley folded his knife closed and stowed it in his pocket.

Beaure got to his feet very carefully. Nora was unwinding a freshly cut rope that had bound her wrists, her eyes were wide and frightened. He must look almighty foolish, falling into a room that way, and he wasn't cutting much figure as a rescuer. "Waiting for the Dutchman," he said. "I was hunting up some wood, figured to build me a fire and warm up until he got here. Reilly sent the Dutchman and me to work cattle out of Smoky Draw before they get buried."

Beaure was amazed at himself. The lie made more sense than anything he had done so far, and it had come to his lips very naturally. It was just plausible enough to be true.

Naley's pistol was steady. "Reilly told me he was letting most of the Seventy-seven hands go," he said.

Beaure had no idea what to do. Saying he had a chance, what was there he could do unless he could get his gun out?

He would have no chance in a fight with Hugo. Around the Seventy-seven chuck wagon they said Hugo Naley was a mean man in a fight, and Beaure had not fought since that scrap with the mule skinner in Gillette, Wyoming, three years ago. Naley would outweigh him by forty pounds.

"I'm finishing out the week." He had expected to do just that, but Reilly let them all go without saying aye, yes, or no. "The Dutchman said he would meet me here."

Naming the Dutchman—that was a good thing, too. Dutch Spooner was a tough man, just about the toughest on the Seventy-seven, and no nonsense about him. Beaure had no idea that the Dutchman would side him against anyone, but they had worked together.

"All right," Naley said, "we'll wait for him. I think you're lying."

Nora watched him cautiously from across the room. Obviously, she was thinking about his warning in town and was wondering just what he was up to. That was a question to which Beaure wished he had a better answer.

"Say," he asked innocently, "what are you-all doing here, and what was that yelling about?" He casually unbuttoned his jacket as he moved toward the fire, wanting his hands warm. Only Naley outguessed him and sidestepped suddenly, bringing the barrel of his six-shooter down on Beaure's head. He saw it coming and tried to duck, catching a glancing blow that dropped him to his knees. Before he knew what was happening, Naley put a foot between his shoulders and held him down while he slid his six-shooter out of its holster.

"That was the meanest thing I ever saw!" Nora Rand's face was white with anger. "You—you dirty coward!"

"Shut up," Hugo Naley said impatiently. "Shut up, Nora, I've got thinking to do."

Beaure had slumped down by the fire, and feeling the warmth soaking the chill from him, he remained there. He needed to get the stiffness of cold out of his muscles, and he needed time to think. So far he had acted the blundering fool. Through the throbbing pain in his skull, that fact stood out with pitiless clarity.

"He's going to kill us," Nora whispered. "He wants to inherit this ranch from my grandfather, and you're in it, too."

She was right, and the worst of it was there just wasn't anything anybody could do about it. Nobody knew the girl was here, nobody knew Beaure was. He had been paid off and had told everybody he was leaving, so nobody would be looking for either the girl or himself, and they could drop from sight and nobody the wiser.

Out of the slit of his eyes he looked up at Hugo Naley and was awed by the man's size. His face might have been carved from oak.

Naley was trying to think it out. Beaure knew that Naley placed little faith in the lie about the Dutchman, but it was a likely story because all the range knew the Seventy-seven had lost cattle by their bunching up in narrow draws which filled up with many feet of snow. There was a better chance for them in the wider valleys and canyons where the snow drifted less deep.

The Dutchman was a notoriously difficult, taciturn man. Hardheaded, opinionated, and obstinately honest, he was a man without humor and without fear. Moreover, it had been rumored that the Dutchman did not like Hugo Naley.

Beaure wished there was something he could do. Naley was so all-fired big and mean—and he had both guns.

The wind moaned under the eaves, and Beaure thought of that icy grave in the lean-to. Naley could bury them together, fill in that grave, and scatter straw over it, and come spring nobody would know the difference. Nobody ever went into that old lean-to, anyway.

The fire was warming him. Beaure thought of that. They were fairly trapped, but so was Naley. No man would be fool enough to try to cut across country in weather like this, and if he stopped by any of the ranches they would be curious as to why he was out. No passersby were likely in this weather, but somehow Naley had to be rid of them both.

"Suppose you do get rid of me?" Nora asked. "What about Len Mason?"

Naley shot her a glance out of his ice-blue eyes, but he did not comment. Beaure had a feeling that Naley had his own reasons for not worrying about Mason.

That livery stable man . . . He wouldn't worry about his horse for a day or two, and if the horse showed up without a rider, if Naley simply tied the stirrups up and let it loose, the hostler might curse Beaure out for leaving the horse to find his way back alone, but he probably wouldn't suspect any foul play.

Beaure sat up. "I want to see you try that on the Dutchman," he said. "I just want to see you try."

Naley walked to the window and peered out into the blinding snowstorm. Beaure looked at the broad back and studied the idea of jumping him, but realized the floor would creak and Naley would turn and let him have it.

Yet Naley was worried. Was it the storm? Or was he buying that story about the Dutchman?

"You'd better call this off, Naley. You kill us and you'll hang. I saw you and the girl in town today, and others did, too."

Naley ignored him, walking restlessly from window to window. Obviously he thought little of any attempt Beaure might make against him. It was the storm that worried him, for the wind was increasing. The cold was also increasing.

Beaure thought about the fuel situation and understood why Naley was worried. If the storm lasted three days, they would be burning the house itself. There were some deadfalls at the edge of the woods, but finding and cutting them up in this weather would be impossible, even if there was an ax available.

Beaure studied the situation and liked it none at all. Of course, Naley could break up the old stable out there. Not that there was much wood, except in the lean-to.

He leaned over and tossed a couple of pieces of broken board on the fire.

"Looks like the Dutchman should be here," Beaure commented thoughtfully. "This is the only shelter anywhere around."

Naley turned angrily. "Shut your mouth!" He laid a hand on his gun. For an instant Beaure felt a cold that was not from the winter storm. Naley was on a hair trigger in that instant, and prepared to kill him.

Nora got up.

The movement distracted Naley and he glanced at her, then swung his eyes quickly back to Beaure, who had remained where he was.

"It's going to be a cold night," Beaure said. "We'd all better be thinking about that."

It was at least ten degrees below zero. He thought of the horse out there in the stable. It would be warmer than they were, for it was a tight, well-built old building of adobe, and heavily thatched. Now it was covered with snow and snow had drifted against the walls. The horse would be warm enough.

The big old house was too high in the ceiling, and the rooms were big and hard to heat.

The noise was faint . . . but they all heard it. A faint call in the momentary lull of the wind.

Naley swore and turned swiftly to the window, peering out into the storm. When he turned from the window, he said, "Somebody's out there. If it's that damn Dutchman, I'll—!"

Beaure felt a sudden panic. Who could it be? Whoever it was would walk in out of the cold right into Naley's gun, and Beaure knew suddenly that Naley was through debating; he was primed and ready. A passerby stopping in for shelter might have been the salvation that they were hoping for— after all, how many people did Naley think he was going to kill?—but now Beaure had set him up to think that the toughest hombre in the county was about to come through the door. Whoever it was, really, was about to be shot down without ceremony.

Unwittingly, Beaure had put the newcomer in a trap. Expecting only shelter, he would walk right into a bullet.

Naley was facing the door and waiting.

Beaure felt sick. He should have known that his argument that the Dutchman would work Smoky Draw was a good one. He was just the man who would be given the job; he was that dependable. He glanced at Nora and she was looking at him. He turned his eyes back to Naley. He was going to have to try. He might get killed, but it was the only chance for all of them.

Naley moved a step toward the door, squaring himself a little for it. Suddenly there was a stamping on the porch outside, as somebody knocked the snow from his boots.

Naley eared back the gun hammer, and the click was loud in the room. At the same instant, the knob started to turn and Beaure threw himself at Naley.

The big man turned like a cat, firing as he turned. The hammer was back and the slightest pressure fired the gun—an instant before it was lined up on Beaure Hatch. And then Beaure hit him.

He hit him in a long dive, his hands grabbing for a hold. Naley clubbed with the gun, and fell back, off balance. Before he could bring the gun down in a line with Beaure, the young cowpuncher jumped, grasping the wrist with both hands and smashing it hard against the wall.

The gun fell, and both men got up. Naley circled toward the gun and Beaure went into him, taking a smashing blow over the eye. Surprisingly, the blow did not hurt as much as he expected. Beaure swung his own fist and caught Naley at the angle of the jaw. The big man bobbed his head, and Beaure spread his legs wide and cut loose with two round-house swings.

Naley staggered, and then Beaure closed in, taking another punch but landing both fists.

"All right, Beaure. Let him alone."

It was Abram Tebbets, and he was holding a six-shooter on Hugo Naley.

Beaure backed off, breathing hard and sucking a bloody knuckle.

Tebbets stepped forward and scooped Naley's gun from the floor.

"He's got my gun under his coat," Beaure said. Tebbets stepped in, whipped open the coat with his left hand, and took the gun. He was deft, sure, capable.

"You sure handle that gun like you know how," Beaure said. Abram Tebbets glanced at him. "I studied law while I was marshal of a cow town," he said, "and I was six years in the Army, fighting Indians."

Beaure walked over to Nora. "Are you all right?"

"I'm sorry I didn't listen to you." She put her hand on his sleeve. "Will you forgive me for all the trouble I've caused?"

"Yes, ma'am. I'm just glad this all worked out. I was afraid my talking about the Dutchman nearly got Mr. Tebbets killed," Beaure said. "I was just a-yarning, hoping to worry him."

"You did all right," Nora said.

"You know, it's funny you mentioned him," Tebbets commented. "He broke a leg early this morning and will be laid up for the winter. The Seventy-seven foreman was in town looking for you. If you want it, you have a job."

Beaure knelt and added fuel to the fire. It looked like they were going to have to tear down that lean-to, after all.

"I'll stay," he said, glancing around at Nora. "Seems like I'm just getting acquainted."

Beaure felt gingerly of his face, where it was puffed from a blow. "Thing that surprises me," he commented, "Naley didn't punch near so hard as that mule skinner up in Gillette."

THERE'S ALWAYS A TRAIL

H E SAT ON a bale of hay against the wall of the livery
stable and listened to them talk. He was a lean,
leather-skinned man with bleak eyes and a stubble of beard
on his jaw. He was a stranger in Pagosa, and showed no desire to get acquainted.

"It's an even bet he's already dead," Hardin said, "there
would be no reason to keep him alive once they had the
money."

"Dead or alive, it means we're finished! That was all the
money we could beg, borrow, or steal."

"Leeds was killed?" Hardin asked. He was a burly man
with a hard red face. Now his blue eyes showed worry. "Then
he can't tell us a thing!"

"That's just the trouble!" Caughey said. "We haven't a
clue! Salter starts to town from our ranch with our fifteen
thousand dollars and Bill Leeds along as bodyguard. Leeds
is dead, two shots fired from his gun, and Salter is gone."

"It's a cinch Salter didn't take our money," Hardin said,
"because he would have shot Leeds down from behind.
Salter knew Leeds was good with a gun, and he'd never have
taken a chance."

"Jake Salter isn't that sort of man," Bailey protested. "He's
a good man. Dependable."

The stranger in the dusty black hat crossed one knee over
the other. "Anybody trailin' them?" His voice had a harsh,
unused sound.

Hardin glanced around, noticing him for the first time.
"There isn't any trail. Whoever done it just dropped off the
edge of the earth. We hunted for a trail. The body of Bill
Leeds was lyin' on the road to town, and that was all there
was!"

"There's always a trail, but you aren't going to get your money back if you stand around talkin' about it. Why not scout around? There's always some sign left."

"Hunt where?" Hunt asked irritably. "A man's got to have a place to start. There's no trail, I said!"

The stranger's eyes were bored but patient. Slowly, he got to his feet. "If I'd lost that money, I'd go after it." He turned on his heel and started along the street toward the Star Saloon.

"Wait a minute! Hold on there!" Cass Bailey said. "Hey! Come back here!"

The man turned and walked slowly back. The others were looking at Bailey, surprised. "What's your name, friend?" Bailey asked.

"There's places they've said I was right handy, so just call me that, Handy."

"All right, Handy. You've done some talking. You said if that was your money you'd go after it. Well, four thousand of that money happens to be mine, and it represents every head of beef that was fit to sell on the CB range. As of now, half that money is yours, if you can get it. You lost two thousand dollars in the holdup, so now we'll see whether you're going to find a trail or not."

Handy stuck his thumbs behind his belt. "You said if you lost that money you were through, finished. Is that right?"

"It ain't only me," Bailey said. "We're all through if we don't get our money back."

"All right, Bailey, I like the way you talk. I'll accept that two thousand on one consideration. If I get it back it buys me a full partnership in your CB range."

Hardin jumped up. "Well, of all the—!"

Cass Bailey stood, feet apart, hands on his hips, staring at Handy. Obviously, the man was a rider. There was something about his hard assurance that Bailey liked.

"If you can get that money back, you've got yourself a deal."

"Find me a place to sleep," Handy said. "I'll be along in a few days."

Handy turned away and walked along to the Star Saloon and ordered a beer. He took a swallow of the beer, then put the glass back on the bar.

"Too bad about Leeds," the bartender suggested. He was a lean, loose-mouthed man with straw-colored hair and watery eyes.

"Too bad about Salter, too. Probably they'll kill him. That will be hard on his family."

"Salter? He's got no family. At least none that anybody knows of."

"What about his woman?"

"You know about her, huh? From all I hear, Maria won't do any frettin'. That Maria, she's a case, Maria is. She sure had ol' Jake danglin'. He was all worked up over her. Every time he saw her he acted like he'd been kicked in the head."

"Maria? Is she over at Cherry Hill?"

"Cherry Hill? You must be thinkin' of somebody else. There's nobody like Maria! They tell me those Spanish are somethin' special. Never knew one, m'self."

Handy finished his beer and strolled outside. Cass Bailey was nowhere in sight, but Handy had no sooner appeared on the boardwalk than a storm descended upon him.

It was five feet, three inches of storm, and shaped to make disaster inviting. Ann Bailey. Her hair was red, and there was a sprinkling of freckles across her nose, and what were probably very lovely lips were drawn into a thin line as her boot heels clackity-clacked down the walk toward him.

"Listen, you! If you're the one who sold my dad a bill of goods and got him to give up half his ranch—! Why, you no-good fish-eatin' crow-bait, I've a notion to knock your eyes out!"

"You've already done that, ma'am. But what's the trouble? Don't you want your money back?"

"Want it back? Of course I want it back! But you've no right to talk my old man into any such deal as that! Besides, what makes you think you can get it back? Unless you're one of the outlaws who stole it!"

"Do you live on the ranch?" he asked mildly.

"Where else would I live? In a gopher hole?"

"Ain't no tellin', ma'am, although if you did, that gopher would feel mighty crowded. Still an' all, I can see where makin' my home on the CB might be right nice."

He stepped into the street and tightened the cinch on the evil-eyed buckskin who stood at the rail looking unpleasant.

"Ma'am, I like my eggs over, my bacon not quite crisp, and my coffee black and strong. You just be expectin' me now!"

Handy reined the buckskin around and loped away down the street, followed by some language that, while not profane, certainly made profanity unnecessary.

"Spirit," he told the buckskin, "that's what I like!" The buckskin laid back his ears and told himself, "You just wait until the next frosty morning, cowhand, and I'll show you spirit!"

Hondo could have doubled for Pagosa, except that the Star Saloon was two doors farther along the street and was called the Remuda, probably because they played so much stud.

The bartender was fat, round, and pink-cheeked. He was also, by looks and sound, very definitely an Irishman. "I'm not one of the fighting Irish," he said, "I'm one of the loving Irish, and I like the girls when they're fair, fat, and forty."

"You wouldn't like Maria, then," Handy commented. "I hear she's slim, dark, and twenty."

"Don't you get any ideas, cowboy. Maria's spoken for. Her time's taken. Anyway, from a mere sideline observer I'd guess that twenty was a shade closer to thirty. But she's spoken for."

"I heard about Salter," Handy said.

The bartender's smile was tolerant, the smile of one who knows. "That's what Salter thinks! Maria is Buck Rodd's girl. She lets Salter hang around because he buys her things, and that's all it amounts to.

"Believe me," the bartender took a quick glance around the empty room and lowered his voice, "if she's smart she won't try any funny business with Buck Rodd!"

"Heard of him," said Handy, who hadn't, "and that crowd he runs with."

"You'll be liable to hear more before the day's over, if you stay in town. Buck rode in last night with that whole crowd, Shorty Hazel, Wing Mathy, Gan Carrero, and some other gent."

"That's enough for me," Handy said, finishing his beer. "I never heard of Maria. I'll stick to blondes when I'm in Hondo."

The bartender chuckled agreement and Handy went outside, where he found a chair and settled down to doze away what remained of the afternoon.

"The trouble with folks," Handy mused, "is they make it hard for themselves. A man leaves more than one kind of a trail. If you can't find the tracks that shows where he went you can nearly always backtrack him to where he came from. Then it usually comes down to one of them 'searches la fammy' deals like that tenderfoot was explainin' down at El Paso. If you're huntin' a man, he said, look for the woman. It makes sense, it surely does."

Three horsemen fast-walked their horses to the hitch rail near his own, and swung down. The slim, dark one would probably be Carrero, the one with the short leg would be Wing Mathy, and the one with the hard face and sand-colored hair would be Shorty Hazel.

Handy built himself a cigarette, innocently unaware of the three. The two guns he wore took their attention, but he did not look around when one of them muttered something to the others.

Wing Mathy stepped up on the boardwalk. "Hey? Ain't you from the Live Oak country?"

"I might be," Handy said, "but I could be from Powder River or Ruby Hills. So might you, but I ain't askin'."

Mathy smiled. "I ain't askin', friend. It's just that you looked familiar."

The three went inside and as the door swung to, Handy heard Wing say, "I've seen that gent somewhere. I know I have!"

Handy looked down at the cigarette. He rarely smoked, and didn't really want this one. It had been something to keep his fingers busy. He dropped it to the boardwalk, careful it did not go through to the debris below, and rubbed it out with his boot toe.

He was on the trail of something, but just what he was not sure. Right about now Buck Rodd was probably seeing Maria. At least, he might be.

Most people, when they went to chasing outlaws, spent too much time wearing horses out. He found it much more simple to follow the trails from a chair, even though he'd spent the largest part of his life in a saddle.

What had become of Jake Salter? That was the next problem, and just where was the money?

Jake Salter was out of his skull over Maria, and Maria was Buck Rodd's girl. Jake Salter, trying to impress her with how big a man he was, might have mentioned carrying all that money. She would surely have told Buck Rodd. There is very little, after all, that is strange about human behavior. All the trails were blazed long, long ago.

Handy led his horse to the livery stable. Livery stables, he had discovered, were like barber shops. There was always a lot of talk around, and if a man listened he could pick up a good deal. He led the buckskin inside, bought it a night's keep for two bits, and began giving the surprised horse a rubdown.

The buckskin was a little uncertain as to the proper reaction to such a procedure. Upon those past occasions when he had been rubbed down it was after a particularly grueling time on the trail, but on this day he had done practically nothing. He was gratified by the rubdown, but felt it would only be in character to bite, kick, or act up somehow. However, even when preoccupied, as he was now, Handy rarely gave him opportunities. The buckskin relaxed, but the idea stayed with him.

For two days Handy had idled about the livery stable in Pagosa before coming here, so he knew that Salter owned a little spread over on the Seco. The brand was the Lazy S. A few minutes now sufficed to show there was no Lazy S horse in the stable, but he waited, and he listened.

As night settled down he saddled the buckskin again and strolled outside. The night was softly dark, the stars hanging so low it seemed a tall man might knock them down with a stick. Handy sat down on a bench against the stable wall. A lazy-fingered player plucked a haphazard tune from a piano in the saloon up the street. Occasionally the player sang a few bars, a plaintive cow country song born some centuries ago on the plains of Andalusia, in far-off Spain. Nothing stirred. Once there was a burst of laughter from the saloon, and occasionally he could hear the click of poker chips.

Down the street a door opened, letting a shaft of lamplight into the darkness. A big man swaggered out. The door closed, and Handy could hear the jingle of spurs and boot heels on the boardwalk, and then, in the light from over the swinging doors of the Remuda, Handy saw a big man enter. He wore a black hat and a black shirt, and his handlebar mustache was sweeping and black. Buck Rodd.

Handy arose and rubbed a finger along the stubble of beard. It was no way in which to call on a lady. Still . . . he walked down the opposite side of the street from the saloon and turned in at the gate from which Rodd had emerged.

Hesitating to step up on the porch, he walked around to the side, past the rosebushes that grew near the window. He could see the woman inside; no longer a girl, but all woman, Maria looked like someone who knew what she wanted and how to get it.

Handy Indian-toed it to the back door and tried the canvas-covered outer door. It opened under his hand. It was warmer inside, and the air was close. There was a smell of food, and over it, of coffee.

He moved toward the lighted door and stopped as Maria framed herself there. Her breath caught, but she made no other sound. "Who are you?" she demanded. Maria, Handy saw, was not easily flustered.

"A driftin' cowhand who smelled fresh coffee and thought we might talk a little."

"We've nothing to talk about. Now rattle your hocks out of here before my man comes back."

"You mean Buck . . . or Salter?"

The beautiful eyes became less beautiful, but very cold and wary. "You'd better leave while you're able. If Buck should come back—"

"Maria," he said, "you're a beautiful woman. You're also a very smart one. By the time they've split that money so many ways there won't be enough left for your trouble. It won't hardly be enough for a woman like you."

"I don't know what you're talking about."

"Suppose only two of us was splitting it, and one of us wasn't greedy? I'm the kind of man who makes big money fast, so I'd not need half. I'd be happy with a third. Then I could ride on alone, or if you were so inclined—?"

There was cold calculation in her eyes now. Beautiful she might be, but Maria was dangerous as a rattler in the blind. Handy felt a little shiver go over him, and knew he could not relax for an instant when with this woman. Did Buck Rodd realize what dynamite he was playing with?

"How about that coffee, Maria?"

"I'll get it," she said.

She filled both cups and he watched, while seeming unconcerned.

"You're new around here." Her voice was low, almost friendly. He felt as a wild horse must feel at the soothing voice of a cowhand before he slipped the bit in his mouth.

"I've been new in a lot of places."

"Have I heard of you?"

"Wing Mathy thought he knew me."

"Then he will remember. Wing never forgets anybody, or anything."

"Maybe we won't be around then. That's a lot of money, Maria, and Frisco is a lot of town."

"What money are you talking about?"

"The money I got rooked out of. A few days ago over in Pagosa there was talk of a lot of cattle being sold. Damned poor prices, but these ranchers are all broke, anyway. I heard some talk, so I picked my spot and waited. The trouble was I waited too far up the road."

"What happened?" She was feeling him out now, trying him.

"How should I know? I didn't see it. However, I had heard about you and Salter. I also knew about you and Buck Rodd, which Salter didn't know. Fifteen thousand is a lot of money."

"You think I'd double-cross Buck Rodd for you?"

"Not for me, although the difference between what you'd get from Buck and what you'd get from me might make me a lot better-looking."

Maria studied him. "If you were shaved you'd be quite a handsome man. Fixed up, you'd look better than Buck Rodd."

"See what money does? I'm already looking better. Of course, you don't need it. I never saw so much woman in one package before. Finding somebody like you in a town like this makes me believe in miracles."

"You'd need the miracle if Buck found you here. Or any of his boys. They don't ask questions, believe me."

He smiled. "I know Buck Rodd."

"You don't seem buffaloed by him. Who are you, anyway?"

"Around here they call me Handy. In some other places they called me Sonora Hack."

"Sonora Hack!" She caught her breath. "But you—you were in prison!"

"Uh-huh. My horse stepped in a badger hole that time. They got me. But as you can see, I'm not in prison now. I served my time."

She was silent, refilling his cup. Obviously she was weighing possibilities.

"Where's the money, Maria? Whatever we do has to be done now. You tell me where that money is, and within a week we'll be in Los Angeles on our way to Frisco."

"There's only one way you could do it. You'd have to kill Buck Rodd, and the rest of them, too."

"That's quite a job."

He looked down into his cup. Not a half hour ago she had been in Buck's arms; now she was telling him how to kill him. Or was this a trap?

She put her hand over his. "Sonora! That's it! We could

split the reward, too! Nobody would guess that I have the money, and if they were gone the case would be closed! They would think the money was buried somewhere in the desert!"

"Where's the money, Maria? You tell me where it is and give me that shotgun."

She laughed, her eyes dancing. She moved around the table toward him. "Oh, no! You take the shotgun and do your part. When you come back both the money and I will be waiting for you."

He swore inwardly. Of course, he had been sure that was the way she would be. He had no intention of using any kind of a gun unless it was forced on him. The money meant a lot to Bailey, to say nothing of the others, and he meant to get it back if he could. As for a piece of Bailey's ranch, that was a dream and no more than a dream. When Bailey discovered he was Sonora Hack he would have no further use for him. He certainly would not want him as a partner. Yet one thing he had established: Maria either had the money or knew where it was.

He looked down at her. "Maria, you don't think I'd trust you, do you? You an' me, we ride the same trail. We both want money, and a lot of it. You don't trust me, and I don't trust you, but if we work together we both stand to win."

"What do you want me to do?"

"Get the money now. Split in two halves. I'll take mine, and then you call Buck Rodd and tell him there's a man in your house. When he comes I'll be waiting."

He could almost feel her thoughts. How could she lose? If she stayed with them her part of the split would be a thousand dollars or less. Go his way and she could keep half, and she could find a way to get his half also.

If the worst happened, and Hack was killed, there was every chance Buck or some of his men would also be killed. Either way, her share would be larger.

Suddenly a new thought came to him. "What about Salter? Does he cut into this?"

She shrugged. "He was a fool! He agreed to run off with the money if somebody took care of Leeds. Wing Mathy and

Carrero did that. When Salter got to where he was to meet me, Buck was waiting for him. It was a smooth job."

He stared at her from the shadows. Smooth, all right, and deadly, as ruthless and deadly as she herself.

"Good! Let's split the money now."

An instant she hesitated, then crossing the room she slipped back a portion of the base panel and got out a sack. "There it is, all of it."

A hinge creaked behind them and a cool young voice said, "I'll take that!"

Ann Bailey!

Sonora felt a shock of cold go through him. This was the end. Nobody would ever believe he intended to get the money and return it.

She stepped into the room, her gun held steady. "Oh, you're contemptible! You promise to get our money back, and then you're here with this, this awful woman! You were planning to kill all those men! I heard it! I heard every word!"

Maria's eyes flashed at him. "I'll live to see you die, Sonora Hack!"

"Hack?" Ann's eyes flashed at him. "You?"

"That's right, and, although you'll never believe it, I intended to get that money back to you. I had first to find out where it was."

He could almost feel Maria's hatred. He saw Ann's left hand grasp the sack, saw her start backing toward the door. At that instant there was a heavy step on the front porch and a loud voice boomed out, "Maria? Where are you? The boys are comin' over!"

Ann stepped out the back door as the voice sounded, and in the startled instant of surprise at the voice, Maria grabbed for the shotgun.

Sonora hit the back door running; the shotgun bellowed, but he was outside and to the left, wheeling around the house with but one thought, to get out of range of the shotgun. Ann had vanished as if she were a ghost. He vaulted the front fence just as three men stepped down off the boardwalk in front of the saloon. His horse was a block away in the livery stable, saddled, fortunately.

Once he was on the buckskin . . . but Ann? What of Ann?

Behind him Rodd was shouting, and he saw the three outlaws start to run down the street toward him. He dove for an opening between two houses, heard a gun bark behind him, charged around the end of the house, and ran full-tilt into a woodpile and sprawled over it to the ground!

Scrambling to his feet, his hands stinging with pain from the gravel beyond the woodpile, he grabbed for his guns. He still had them.

A running man rounded a corner and he snapped a shot from the hip. It was a near miss, and the man yelped with surprise and fired in return. Sonora ducked into a crouch and ran, running from one building to another.

At least he was keeping them occupied, and he hoped Ann was getting away with the money. Where had she gotten to so quickly? And how had she gotten there in the first place? She must have followed him! Then she had never trusted him at all; but then, why should she?

His breath coming in racking gasps, he made the last building and rounded the corner. Behind him there was running and yelling. He flattened against the building at the corner. A man was standing in front of the livery stable, staring up the street to see what was happening.

A half block up the street Gan Carrero, gun in hand, was surveying the street.

"Hsst!" Hack hissed.

The livery man turned his head sharply toward the sound. "Get that saddled buckskin out, pronto! Just turn him loose!"

The man ducked inside, and Sonora heard somebody blundering through the brush behind the building where he stood. Stepping into the street, he whistled shrilly for his horse.

Carrero wheeled and his gun came up, and Sonora fired. The outlaw stepped back. Sonora fired again, and Carrero fell to his face as the buckskin lunged from the stable, stirrups flopping.

Sonora hit the saddle on the fly, and the buckskin left town on a dead run. A bullet whistled by; another smacked viciously into some obstruction on his right. The buckskin was off and running now, and how that buckskin loved it!

Yet this was but the beginning; swinging into an opening under some cottonwoods, he began to circle back. What had become of Ann? They would want their money back, and they would want Ann dead, for she now knew of their guilt.

He walked the horse through the cottonwoods and up the slope toward a cut into the country beyond. The chaparral was thick, but there were plenty of openings, and he wove his way through. When he reached the cut he looked back. The lights of the town were plain, but he could see nothing else. Pursuit would be out there in the darkness, three deadly men and a woman, armed and prepared to kill.

Where was Ann? Scowling into the night, he tried to imagine what she would do, and how she would return to Pagosa. She knew the country much better than he for this was her home. Certainly, she would not keep to the trail, and if she had been shrewd enough to follow him she would be shrewd enough to think out an escape.

Yet behind her would be Buck Rodd, Shorty Hazel, and Wing Mathy. They would follow her, not him. She not only had the money, but her word could hang them.

Skirting a bluff, Hack rode down through a clump of Joshua trees where the cut was narrow. Due to the dip in the ground he would probably be unseen, so, dismounting, he knelt close to the earth and struck a match. He found no recent tracks.

Mounting, he started on through the cut. She should have a good start. His gunfight had delayed pursuit enough to give her a couple of miles' start, which she could use to advantage. Her horse was probably a good one, and she would keep moving. Yet, her horse had been ridden the twenty miles from Pagosa, and perhaps the distance from her ranch to town.

Her pursuers would be on fresh horses, and would know the country as well as she.

The trail dipped and followed the bank of a small stream,

which must be the same that flowed near Pagosa, and if so might offer an easy approach to the town. He again checked the trail for tracks.

Hoofprints! A horse had passed this way, perhaps within the last few minutes, for even as the match flared he saw a tiny bit of sand fall into one of the tracks.

A red-hot iron seemed to slash across his arm and, dropping the match, he dove off the trail, hearing a hard *spang* of a high-powered rifle.

He swung into the saddle, feeling the warm wetness of blood on his arm; yet he did not seem to have been badly hit, because his fingers were still working. Turning off the trail, he wove through the brush, keeping under cover. Pulling up for a moment, he felt carefully with the fingers of his other hand. The skin was only broken. With his bandanna he made a crude bandage to stop the flow of blood, which was slight in any case.

He was through in this country. Ann would escape now, and would return to tell them what she had heard. She would also tell them he was Sonora Hack, and they would discover he had only recently been freed from prison. His chance of settling down in Pagosa and making a place for himself would be finished. Well, it had been a wild idea at best.

Remembering the conversation, he felt himself flushing to think that she would believe he was that kind of man. That he would plot with such a woman the cold-blooded murder of her confederates.

In sullen despair he told himself to keep on riding. He was finished here.

As if impelled by the thought, the buckskin started walking up the long roll of the piñon-tufted mountainside, and Sonora let him go. The buckskin quickened his pace and Hack, from old habit, slid his gun from its holster and removed the shells fired back at Hondo, then reloaded the pistol.

The buckskin, he realized, had found a trail, and now, of his own volition, was traveling at an easy canter.

Buck Rodd would not give up easily. That was more

money than he was apt to see in a long time, and even if he had so wished, Maria would not permit it. He would follow Ann back to her ranch or to Pagosa.

Who in Pagosa could stand against him? Or the three together?

At this hour, there would be no one. Alerted, they might get men together to greet them, but now there would be no time for that. All three were men with notches on their guns, men willing and ready to kill.

That was their problem. He had made his bid and messed up. He should never have tried to get the money from Maria, yet he had been so close!

Killing had been no part of his plan. He had hoped to get the money back, leave Maria tied up, and return to Pagosa.

Remembering Ann's flashing eyes and vitriolic tongue, he grinned despite himself. She was a terror, that one. The man who got her would have his work cut out for him.

The thought of her belonging to some other man was a burr under the saddle blanket of his thoughts. And he did not like to ride away leaving her with the opinion of him she now had. It would be an ugly picture.

With neither conscience nor the memories of a red-haired girl to afflict him, the buckskin cantered briskly along the trail, making good time. Hack rode along with the unconscious ease of a man long accustomed to the saddle, deep in his own thoughts. It was not until there was a sudden flash of light in the corner of his eyes that he came to with a start.

He was on the edge of Pagosa! The buckskin had very naturally headed for the stable where he had been taking it easy these past few days.

Realization hit him with a rush of horses' hoofs, and he saw three horsemen come charging up to a fourth. A girl screamed and a man opened the door of a house. A rifle shot rang out, and a harsh voice ordered, "Get back in there or I'll kill you! This is none of your affair!"

Another voice said, "Get the sack, Shorty."

"What about the girl? Do we take her along?"

"Hell, no! She'd be nothing but trouble. We'll find plenty

of women below the border! We'll just leave her lay, to teach them a lesson!"

The buckskin felt the unexpected stab of the spurs and hit the trail running.

"Hey!" a voice yelled. "Look *out*!"

A gun roared almost in his face, a black body loomed before him, and he fired. A lance of flame leaped at him and he was in the midst of a wild tangle of plunging horses and shouting, swearing men. He caught a glimpse of Ann, hat gone, hair flying in the wind, breaking from the crowd and leaping her horse for the shelter of the buildings.

A head loomed near him and he slashed at it with his six-gun, seeing the man fall; then his horse swung around, and he was knocked from his horse but hit the ground staggering.

A big man rushed at him and he had just time to steady himself. He threw a hard punch into a corded belly, ripped up an uppercut, and then, from behind him as the man staggered, he heard somebody yell, "Look out, Rodd! Let me have him!"

Hack let go everything and hit the dirt just as a gun roared behind him.

Rodd grunted, gasped and then yelled, "You fool! You bloody fool! You've hit me! You've killed—!"

Shorty Hazel's voice shouted, "To hell with it, Wing! Grab the bag and let's go!"

Hack rolled over and came to his knee shooting. Something hit him below the knee and he rolled over, coming up against the body of a man, who might be alive or dead. Something grated on gravel and the man lunged to his feet, sack in hand, and sprang for the nearest horse.

He steadied himself, leaning on one elbow, and fired. The man dropped the sack and turned.

Fire stabbed the darkness, and the body of the man beside him jerked slightly. Sonora Hack was holding his left-hand gun and he fired in return. The other man turned, fell against his horse, then swung into the saddle.

Hack lifted his gun, then saw the sack lying in the road. "The devil with it! Let him go!"

He tried to get to his feet, but one leg wouldn't function

right. He crawled to the sack, felt the rustle of bills and the chink of gold coins. He got a grip on the sack and whistled.

The buckskin trotted to him and stood patiently while he caught hold of a stirrup and pulled himself up, then climbed into the saddle. He started the horse to the nearest house, gripping the sack in his right hand.

He shouted and the door opened, then other doors began to open, lamps were lighted, and people emerged. One of them was Ann. He thrust the sack at her. "Tryin' all the time. I was try—"

He felt himself falling, felt her hands catch him, then somebody else's hands. "He's passed out," somebody was saying. "He's—"

Something smelled like rain, rain and roses and coffee and other smells he could not place. Then he opened his eyes and he could hear the rain falling, and he stared out a curtained window at a piñon-clad hill beyond. Turning his head he saw his boots, wiped cleaner than they had been in months, and his gun belt hanging near them, over the back of a chair. His clothes were folded neatly on the chair, and there was another chair, a rocking chair with a book lying facedown on the seat.

The door opened and Ann Bailey came in. She was wearing an apron, and when her eyes met his, she smiled. "You're actually awake! You're not delirious!"

"What do you mean . . . delirious? Where am I? What's happened?"

"You're at home, on our ranch, and you were delirious. You talked," she blushed faintly, "an awful lot. You killed all those men."

"Not Rodd nor Hazel. Mathy killed Rodd by mistake. Hazel got away."

"He didn't get far. He fell off his horse about a mile down the road, and died before anyone found him."

"You got your money?"

"Of course." She looked down at him. "Half of this ranch is yours now."

"I won't take it. That isn't right."

"It is right. That was the deal, and we intend to stand by it.

Anyway, Dad needs help. He's needed somebody who can handle cattle. He can't do it all himself. You get some rest now, and we can talk of that later."

"What's that I smell?"

"I'm making some doughnuts. Why?"

"All right. I'll stay. I always did like doughnuts!"

WE SHAPED THE LAND
WITH OUR GUNS

WE MOVED INTO the place on South Fork just before the snow went off. We had a hundred head of cattle gathered from the canyons along the Goodnight Trail, stray stuff from cattle outfits moving north. Most of these cattle had been back in the breaks for a couple of years and rounding them up was man-killing labor, but we slapped our iron on them and headed west.

Grass was showing green through the snow when we got there and the cattle made themselves right at home. Mountains to the east and north formed the base of a triangle of which the sides were shaped by creeks and the apex by the junction of those creeks. It was a good four miles from that apex to the spot we chose for our home place, so we had all natural boundaries with good grass and water. There were trees enough for fuel and shade.

The first two weeks we worked fourteen hours a day building a cabin, cleaning out springs and throwing up a stable, pole corrals, and a smokehouse. We had brought supplies with us and we pieced them out with what game we could shoot. By the time we had our building done, our stock had decided they were home and were fattening up in fine shape.

We had been riding together for more than six months, which isn't long to know a man you go partners with. Tap Henry was a shade over thirty while I had just turned twenty-two when we hit the South Fork. We had met working for the Gadsen outfit, which took me on just west of Mobeetie while Tap joined up a ways farther north. Both of us were a mite touchy but we hit it off right from the start.

TAP HENRY SHOWED me the kind of man he was before we had been together three days. Some no-account riders had braced us to cut the herd, and their papers didn't look good to me nor to Tap. We were riding point when these fellers came up, and Tap didn't wait for the boss. He just told them it was tough, but they weren't cutting this herd. That led to words and one of these guys reached. Tap downed him and that was that.

He was a pusher, Tap was. When trouble showed up he didn't sidestep or wait for it. He walked right into the middle and kept crowding until the trouble either backed down or came through. Tall and straight-standing, he was a fine, upright sort of man except for maybe a mite of hardness around the eyes and mouth.

My home country was the Big Bend of Texas but most of my life had been lived south of the border. After I was sixteen the climate sort of agreed with me better. Tap drifted toward me one night when we were riding herd up in Wyoming.

"Rye," he said, that being a nickname for Ryan Tyler, "an hombre could go down in those breaks along the Goodnight Trail and sweep together a nice herd. Every outfit that ever come over this trail has lost stock, and lots of it is still back there."

"Uh-huh," I said, "and I know just the right spot for a ranch. Good grass, plenty of water and game." Then I told him about this place under the Pelado and he liked the sound of it. Whether he had any reason for liking an out-of-the-way place, I don't know. Me, I had plenty of reason, but I knew going back there might lead to trouble.

Two men can work together a long time without really knowing much about one another, and that was the way with me and Tap. We'd been in a couple of Comanche fights together and one with a Sioux war party. We worked together, both of us top hands and neither of us a shirker, and after a while we got a sort of mutual respect, although nobody could say we really liked each other.

Our first month was just ending when Jim Lucas showed

up. We had been expecting him because we had seen a lot of Bar L cattle, and had run a couple of hundred head off our triangle of range when we first settled. He was not hunting us this day because his daughter was with him, and only one hand. Red, the puncher, had a lean face and a lantern jaw with cold gray eyes and two low, tied-down guns.

Lucas was a medium-built man who carried himself like he weighed a ton. He sat square and solid in the saddle, and you could see at a glance that he figured he was some shakes. Betty was eighteen that summer, slim but rounded, tan but lovely, with hair a golden web that tangled the sunlight. She had lips quick to laugh and the kind that looked easy to kiss. That morning she was wearing homespun jeans and a shirt like a boy, but no boy ever filled it out like she did.

Right off I spotted Red for a cold ticket to trouble. He stopped his horse off to one side, ready for disturbances.

"Howdy!" I straightened up from a dam I was building across a beginning wash. "Riding far?"

"That's my question." Lucas looked me over mighty cool. Maybe I looked like a sprout to him. While I'm nigh six feet tall I'm built slim and my curly hair makes me look younger than I am. "My outfit's the Bar L, and this is my graze."

Tap Henry had turned away from the corral and walked down toward us. His eyes went from Lucas to the redhead and back. Me, I was off to one side. Tap wore his gun tied down but I carried mine shoved into my waistband.

"We're not riding," Tap replied, "we're staying. We're claiming all the range from the creeks to the Pelado."

"Sorry, boys"—Lucas was still friendly although his voice had taken on a chill—"that's all my range and I wasn't planning on giving any of it up. Besides"—he never took his eyes off Tap Henry—"I notice a lot of vented brands on your cattle. All I saw, in fact."

"See any of yours?" Tap was quiet. Knowing how touchy he could be, I was worried and surprised at the same time. This was one fight he wasn't pushing and I was sure glad of it.

"No, I didn't," Lucas admitted, "but that's neither here nor there. We don't like outfits that stock vented brands."

"Meaning anything in particular?" Tap asked.

Quiet as he was, there was a veiled threat in his tone now and Jim Lucas seemed suddenly to realize that his daughter sat beside him. Also, for the first time he seemed to understand that he was dealing with a different kind of man than he had believed.

"Meaning only," he said carefully, "that we don't like careless brands on this range or small outfits that start that way."

Tap was reasonable. More so than I had expected. "We rounded those cattle up," he explained, "from the canyons along the Goodnight. They are abandoned trail herd stock, and we got letters from three of the biggest outfits giving us title to all of their stuff we can find. Most of the other brands are closed out or in Montana. We aim to run this stock and its increase."

"Maybe. But run it somewheres else. This is my range. Get off it."

"Maybe you take in too much territory?" Tap suggested. "My partner and I aren't hunting trouble, but I don't reckon you hold any deed to this land from the government, the people, or God. You just laid claim to it. We figure you got your hands full, and we lay claim to the triangle of range described."

"Boss," Red interrupted, "I've seen this hombre somewhere before."

Tap did not change expression but it seemed to me that his face went a shade whiter under the tan. Betty was looking worried and several times she had started as if to interrupt.

"We can be neighbors," Tap persisted. "We wanted our own outfit. Now we've got it and we intend to keep it."

LUCAS WAS ABOUT to make a hot reply when Betty interrupted. She had been looking at me. Everybody else seemed to have forgotten me and that pleased me just as well. My old gray hat was ragged on the crown and my hair hung down to my shirt collar. My buckskin pullover shirt was unlaced at the neck, my jeans were patched, and my boots were weather-worn and scarred by horns.

Betty said quietly, "Why don't you and your friend come to the dance at Ventana Saturday night? We would all enjoy having you."

Jim Lucas scowled and started impatiently as if to speak, but then he seemed to see me for the first time. His mouth opened, but he swallowed whatever it was he was going to say. What held him I do not know but he stared hard at me.

"Sure," I replied to Betty, "we would be glad to come. We want to be neighborly like my partner said. You can expect us."

Lucas wheeled his horse. "We'll talk about this again. You've been warned." He looked at Tap when he said it, and then started off with Betty beside him.

Red lingered, staring at Tap. "Where was it," he said, "that we met before?"

"We never met." Tap's voice was flat and hard. "And let's hope you don't remember."

That was more of a warning than I ever heard Tap give anybody. Usually, if you asked for it he just hauled iron and then planted you.

We started for the cabin together and Tap glanced around at me.

"Ever sling a six-gun, Rye? If war comes we'll have to scrap to hold our land."

"If it comes"—I pulled off my shirt to wash—"don't you worry. I'll hold up my end."

"That gal . . ." he commented suddenly, "really something, wasn't she?"

Now, why should that have made me sore?

Saturday morning we shaved early and dressed for the dance. It was a long ride ahead of us and we wanted to get started. When I got my stuff out of my warbag I looked down at those worn and scuffed gun belts and the two six-shooters. Just for a minute there, I hesitated, then I stuffed a pair of old jeans in atop them.

Then I slicked up. My hair was long, all right, but my black broadcloth suit was almost new and tailored to fit. My clothes have to be tailored because my shoulders are so broad and my waist so slim I can never buy me a hand-me-down. With it I wore a gray wool shirt and a black necker-chief, and topped it off with my best hat, which was black and flat-crowned.

Tap was duded up some, too. When he looked at me I could see the surprise in his eyes, and he grinned. "You're a handsome lad, Rye! A right handsome lad!" But when he'd said it his face chilled as if he had thought of something un-pleasant. He added only one thing. "You wearing a gun? You better."

My hand slapped my waistband and flipped back my coat. The butt of my .44 Russian was there, ready to hand. That draw from the waistband is one of the fastest. There was no reason why I should tell him about the other gun in the shoulder holster. That was a newfangled outfit that some said had been designed by Ben Thompson, and if it was good enough for Ben, it was good enough for me.

It was a twenty-five-mile ride but we made good time. At the livery stable I ordered a bait of corn for the horses. Tap glanced at me.

"Costs money," he said tersely.

"Uh-huh, but a horse can run and stay with it on corn. We ain't in no position to ride slow horses."

Betty was wearing a blue gown the color of her eyes, and while there were a half dozen right pretty girls there, none of them could stand with her. The nearest was a dark-eyed se-ñorita who was all flash and fire. She glanced at me once from those big dark eyes, then paused for another look.

Tap wasted no time. He had crossed the room to Betty and was talking to her. Her eyes met mine across the room, but Tap was there first and I wasn't going to crowd him. The Mex girl was lingering, so I asked for the dance and got it. Light as a feather she was, and slick and easy on her feet. We danced that one and another, and then an Irish girl with freckles on her nose showed up, and after her I danced again with Margita Lopez. Several times I brushed past Betty and we exchanged glances. Hers were very cool.

The evening was almost over when suddenly we found ourselves side by side. "Forgotten me?" There was a thin edge on her voice. "If you remember, I invited you."

"You also invited my partner, and you seemed mighty busy, so I—"

"I saw you," she retorted. "Dancing with Margita."

"She's a good dancer, and mighty pretty."

"Oh? You think so?" Her chin came up and battle flashed in her eyes. "Maybe you think—!" The music started right then so I grabbed her and moved into the dance and she had no chance to finish whatever she planned to say.

There are girls and girls. About Betty there was something that hit me hard. Somehow we wound up out on the porch of this old ranch house turned school, and we started looking for stars. Not that we needed any.

"I hope you stay," she said suddenly.

"Your father doesn't," I replied, "but we will."

She was worried. "Father's set in his ways, Rye, but it isn't only he. The one you may have trouble with is Chet Bayless. He and Jerito."

"Who?" Even as I asked the question the answer was in my mind.

"Jerito Juarez. He's a gunman who works for Bayless. A very fine vaquero, but he's utterly vicious and a killer. As far as that goes, Bayless is just as bad. Red Corram, who works for Dad, runs with them some."

———

JERITO JUAREZ WAS a name I was not likely to forget, and inside me something turned cold. Just then the door opened and Tap Henry came out. When he saw us standing close together on the dark porch his face, in the light of the door, was not pleasant to see.

"I was hunting you, Betty. Our dance is 'most over."

"Oh! I'm sorry! I didn't realize . . . !"

Tap looked over her head at me. "We've trouble coming," he said, "watch your step."

Walking to the end of the porch, I stepped down and started toward the horses. Under the trees and in the deep shadows I heard voices.

"Right now," a man was saying, "ride over there and go

through their gear. I want to know who they are. Be mighty careful, because if that Tap is who I think he is, he'll shoot mighty fast and straight."

Another voice muttered and then there was a chink of coins. In an open place under the trees I could vaguely distinguish three men.

The first voice added, "An' when you leave, set fire to the place."

That was the man I wanted, but they separated and I knew if I followed the two that went back toward the dance, then the man who was to burn us out would get away. Swiftly, I turned after the latter, and when he reached his horse he was in the lights from the dance. The man was a half-breed, a suspected rustler known as Kiowa Johnny.

Stepping into the open, I said to him, "You ain't going noplace to burn anybody out. If you want to live, unbuckle those gun belts and let 'em fall. And be mighty careful!"

Kiowa stood there, trying to make me out. The outline of me was plain to him, but my face must have been in shadow. He could see both hands at my sides and they held no gun, nor was there a gun in sight. Maybe he figured it was a good gamble that I was unarmed. He grabbed for his gun.

My .44 Russian spoke once, a sharp, emphatic remark, and then acrid powder smoke drifted and above the sound of the music within I heard excited voices. Kiowa Johnny lay sprawled on the hard-packed earth.

Wanting no gunfights or questions, I ducked around the corner of the dance hall and back to the porch where I had been standing with Betty. The door that opened to the porch was blocked by people, but all were looking toward the dance floor. One of them was Margita. Moving among them, I touched her arm and we moved out on the floor together.

Right away she knew something was wrong. She was quick, that girl. And then the music stopped and Jim Lucas was standing in the middle of the floor with Sheriff Fred Tetley.

"Kiowa Johnny's been killed," Tetley said. "Looks like he had a fair shake. Who done it?"

Tap was right in the middle of things with Betty and I saw Red frown as his eyes located him. Almost automatically, those eyes searched me out. He was puzzled when he looked away.

"Had it comin' for years!" A gray-haired man near me was speaking. "Maybe we won't lose so many cows now."

"Who killed him?" Tetley demanded irritably. "Speak up, whoever it was. It's just a formality."

My reasons for not speaking were the best ones, so I waited. Lucas put a hand on the sheriff's shoulder.

"Best forget it, Fred. His gun was half drawn, so he made a try for it. Whoever shot him was fast and could really shoot. That bullet was dead center through the heart despite the bad light!"

His eyes went to Tap Henry, and then momentarily, they rested on me. Margita had me by the arm and I felt her fingers tighten. When she looked up at me she said quietly, "You saw it?"

Somehow, something about her was warm, understanding. "I did it." My voice was low and we were a little apart from the others. "There are good reasons why nobody must know now. It was quite fair." Simply, then, but without mentioning Red, I told her what I had heard.

She accepted my story without question. All of them at the dance knew every effort would be made to run us off South Fork, so my story was no surprise. Some women could keep a secret and I was sure she was one of them.

That we were on very shaky ground here both Tap and I knew. It was not only Lucas. As the biggest of the ranchers, and the one whose actual range had been usurped, he had the most right to complain, but Bayless of the Slash B was doing the most talking, and from what I had heard, he had a way of taking the law into his own hands.

Tap joined me. "You see that shooting?" he asked. Then without awaiting a reply, he continued, "Guess he had it coming, but I wonder who did it? That's the kind of shooting Wes Hardin does or the Laredo Kid. Heard anything?"

"Only that Johnny had it coming. He was the kind who might be hired to dry-gulch a man or burn him out."

Tap glanced at me quickly, but before he could speak, Betty hurried up to us.

"You two had better go," she whispered. "There's some talk around and some of the men are hunting trouble."

She spoke to both of us, but she looked at me. Tap shifted his feet. "What do you expect us to do?" he demanded. "Run?"

"Of course not!" she protested. "But why not avoid trouble until I can talk some sense into Dad?"

"That's reasonable, Tap. Let's go."

"If you want to back down"—his voice was irritable and he spoke more sharply than he ever had to me—"go ahead and go! I say face 'em and show 'em they've got a fight on their hands!"

The contempt in his voice got to me but I took a couple of deep breaths before I answered him. "Don't talk like that, Tap. When a fight comes, I'll be ready for it, only why not give Betty a chance? Once the shooting starts there'll be no more chance."

———

TWO MEN SHOVED through the door followed by a half dozen others. My pulse jumped and I grabbed Tap's arm. "Let's get out of here! There's Chet Bayless and Jerito Juarez!"

How could I miss that lithe, wiry figure? Betty Lucas gave me a swift, measuring look of surprise. Tap shook my hand from his arm and shot me a glance like he'd give to a yellow dog. "All right," he said, "let's go! I can't face them alone!"

What they must be thinking of me I could guess, but all I could think of was facing Bayless and Jerito in that crowded room. And I knew Jerito and what would happen when he saw me. The crowd would make no difference, nor the fact that innocent people might be killed.

Betty avoided my eyes and moved away from my hand when I turned to say good-bye, so I merely followed Tap Henry out the door. All the way home he never said a word, nor the next morning until almost noon.

"You stay away from Betty," he said then, "she's my girl."

"Betty's wearing no brand that I can see," I told him quietly, "and until somebody slaps an iron on her, I'm declaring myself in the running.

"I don't," I continued, "want trouble between us. We've rode a lot of rivers together, and we've got trouble started here. We can hold this place and build a nice spread."

"What about last night?" His voice was cold. "You took water."

"Did you want to start throwing lead in a room full of kids and women? Besides, fightin' ain't enough. Anybody with guts and a gun can fight. It's winning that pays off."

His eyes were measuring me. "What does that mean?" That I'd fallen in his estimation, I knew. Maybe I'd never stood very high.

"That we choose the time to fight," I said. "Together we can whip them, but just showing how tough we are won't help. We've got to get the odds against us as low as we can."

"Maybe you're right." He was reluctant to agree. "I seen a man lynched once because he shot a kid accidental in a gunfight." He sized me up carefully. "You seemed scared of those three."

We looked at each other over the coffee cups and inside I felt a slow hot resentment rising, but I kept it down. "I'm not," I told him, "only Chet Bayless is known for eight square killings. Down Sonora way Jerito is figured to have killed twice that many. That Jerito is poison mean, and we can figure on getting hurt even if we win."

"Never figured them as tough as all that," Tap muttered. Then he shot me a straight, hard glance. "How come you know so much about 'em?"

"Bayless," I said carefully, "is a Missourian. Used to run with the James boys, but settled in Eagle Pass. Jerito—everybody in Sonora knows about him."

The next few days followed pleasant and easy, and we worked hard without any words between us beyond those necessary to work and live. It irritated me that Tap doubted me.

On the fourth afternoon I was stripping the saddle off my

steeldust when I heard them coming. A man who lives like I do has good ears and eyes or he don't live at all. "Tap!" I called to him low but sharp. "Riders coming!"

He straightened up, then shot a look at me. "Sure?"

"Yeah." I threw my saddle over a log we used for that and slicked my rifle out of the scabbard and leaned it by the shed door. "Just let 'em come."

They rode into the yard in a compact bunch and Tap Henry walked out to meet them. Bayless was there, riding with Jim Lucas, but Jerito was not. The minute I saw that I felt better. When they first showed I had stepped back into the shed out of sight. There were a dozen of them in the bunch and they drew up. Bayless took the play before Lucas could get his mouth open.

"Henry!" He said it hard and short. "You been warned. Get your stuff. We're burning you out!"

Tap waited while you could count three before he spoke. "Like hell," he said.

"We want no nesters around here! Once one starts they all come! And we want nobody with your record!"

"My record?" Tap had guts, I'll give him that. He stepped once toward Bayless. "Who says I—!"

"I do!" It was Red Corram. "You rode with that Roost outfit in the Panhandle."

"Sure did." Tap smiled. "I reckon not a man here but ain't misbranded a few head. I ain't doing it now."

"That's no matter!" Bayless was hard. "Get out or be buried here!"

Lucas cleared his throat and started to speak.

Tap looked at him. "You feel that way, Lucas?"

"I'm not for killing," he said, "but—!"

"I am!" Bayless was tough about it. "I say they get out or shoot it out!"

Tap Henry had taken one quick glance toward the shed when they rode up, and when he saw me gone he never looked again. I knew he figured he was all alone. Well, he wasn't. Not by a long shot. Now it was my turn.

Stepping out into the open, I said, "That go for me, too, Chet?"

HE TURNED SHARP around at the voice and stared at me. My hat was pulled low and the only gun I wore was that .44 Russian in my waistband. I took another step out and a little bit toward the trail, which put Bayless in a bad spot. If he turned to face me his side was to Tap. "Who are you?" Bayless demanded. He was a big blue-jowled man, but right now the face under those whiskers looked pale.

"The name is Tyler, Chet. Ryan Tyler. Don't reckon you ever heard *that* name before, did you now?" Without turning my head, I said to Tap, but loud enough so they could all hear me, "Tap, if they want to open this ball, I want Bayless."

They were flabbergasted, you could see it. Here I was, an unknown kid, stepping out to call a rancher known as a gunman. It had them stopped, and nobody quite knew what to say.

"Lucas," I said, "you ain't a fool. You got a daughter and a nice ranch. You got some good boys. If this shooting starts we can't miss Bayless or you."

It was hot, that afternoon, with the clouds fixing up to rain. Most of the snow was gone now, and there was the smell of spring in the air.

"Me, I ain't riding nowhere until I've a mind to. I'm fixing to stay right here, and if it's killing you want, then you got a chance to start it. But for every one of us you bury, you'll bury three of you."

Tap Henry was as surprised as they were, I could see that, and it was surprise that had them stopped, not anything else. That surprise wasn't going to last, I knew. Walking right up to them, I stopped again, letting my eyes sweep over them, then returning to Bayless.

"Why don't you get down, Chet? If you go for that gun you better have solid footing. You don't want to miss that first shot, Chet. If you miss it you'll never get another.

"You aimed to do some burning, Chet. Why don't you get down and start your fire? Start it with a gun like your coyote friend did?" Without shifting his eyes, Bayless stared, and then slowly he kicked one foot out of a stirrup. "That's right, Chet. Get down. I want you on the ground, where you don't have so far to fall. This hombre"—I said it slow—"paid Kiowa Johnny to burn us out. I heard 'em. I gave Johnny a chance to drop his guns and would have made him talk, but he wanted to take a chance. He took it."

"You killed Johnny?" Lucas demanded, staring at me. "He was supposed to be a fast man with a gun."

"Him?" The contempt was thick in my voice. "Not even middling fast." My eyes had never left Bayless. "You want to start burning, Chet, you better get down."

Chet Bayless was bothered. It had been nigh two years since he had seen me and I'd grown over an inch in height and some in breadth of shoulder since then. My face was part shaded by that hat and he could just see my mouth and chin. But he didn't like it. There was enough of me there to jar his memory and Chet Bayless, while fast with a gun, was no gambler. With Jerito or Red there, he would have gambled, but he knew Red was out of it because of Tap.

"Lucas," I said, "you could be riding in better company. Bayless ain't getting off that horse. He's got no mind to. He figures to live awhile longer. You fellers better figure it this way. Tap and me, we like this place. We aim to keep it. We also figure to run our own cows, but to be fair about it, anytime you want to come over here and cut a herd of ours, come ahead. That goes for you—not for Bayless or any of his gun-handy outfit."

Chet Bayless was sweating. Very careful, he had put his toe back in the stirrup. Jim Lucas shot one glance at him, and then his old jaw set.

"Let's go!" He wheeled his horse and without another word they rode away.

Only Red looked back. He looked at Tap, not me. "See you in town!" he said.

Henry called after him, "Anytime, Red! Just anytime at all!"

When the last of them had gone he turned and looked at me. "That was a tough play, kid. S'pose Bayless had drawed on you?"

"Reckon he'd of died," I said simply enough, "but I didn't

figure he would. Chet's a cinch player. Not that he ain't good with that Colt. He is—plenty!"

Walking back, I got my rifle. "Gosh amighty, I'm sure hungry!" I said, and that was all. What Tap thought of it, I had no idea. Only a couple of times I caught him sizing me up. And then the following night he rode off and I knew where he was riding. He was gone a-courting of Betty Lucas.

That made me sore but there was nothing I could do about it. He sort of hinted that Margita was my dish, but that wasn't so. She was all wrapped up in some vaquero who worked for her old man, although not backward about a little flirtation.

One thing I knew. Chet Bayless was going to talk to Jerito and then they were going to come for me. Jerito Juarez had good reason to hate me, and he would know me for the Laredo Kid.

Me, I'd never figured nor wanted the name of a gunfighter, but it was sort of natural-like for me to use a gun easy and fast. At sixteen a kid can be mighty touchy about not being growed up. I was doing a man's job on the NOB outfit when Ed Keener rawhided me into swinging on him. He went down, and when he came up he hauled iron. Next thing I knew Keener was on the ground drilled dead center and I had a smoking gun in my hand with all the hands staring at me like a calf had suddenly growed into a mountain lion right before them.

Keener had three brothers, so I took out and two of them cornered me in Laredo. One of them never got away from that corner, and the other lived after three months in bed. Meanwhile, I drifted into Mexico and worked cows down there. In El Paso I shot it out with Jerito's brother and downed him, and by that time they were talking me up as another Billy the Kid. They called me Laredo for the town I hailed from, but when I went back thataway I went into the Nueces country, where the third Keener braced me and fitted himself into the slot of boot hill alongside his brothers.

AFTER THAT I'D gone kind of hog-wild, only not killing anybody but some ornery Comanches. Howsoever, I did back down a sheriff at Fort Griffin, shot a gun out of another's hand in Mobeetie, and backed down three tough hands at Doan's Crossing. By that time everybody was talking about me, so I drifted where folks didn't know Ryan Tyler was the Laredo gunfighter.

Only Chet Bayless knew because Chet had been around when I downed the Keeners. And Jerito knew.

After that I quit wearing guns in sight and avoided trouble all I could. That was one reason this out-of-the-way ranch under the Pelado appealed to me.

It must have been midnight and I'd been asleep a couple of hours when a horse came hell-a-whoppin' down the trail and I heard a voice holler the house. Unloading from my bunk, I grabbed my rifle and gave a call from the door. Then I got a shock, for it was Betty Lucas.

"Rye! Come quick! Tap killed Lon Beatty and a mob's got him! They'll hang him!"

No man ever got inside of his clothes faster than me, but this time I dumped my warbag and grabbed those belted guns. Swinging the belts around me, I stuck my .44 Russian into my waistband for good measure and ran for my horse. Betty had him caught and a saddle on him, so all I had to do was cinch up and climb aboard.

"They are at Cebolla!" she called to me. "Hurry!"

Believe me, I lit a shuck. That steeldust I was on was a runner and chock-full of corn. He stretched his legs and ran like a singed cat, so it wasn't long until the lights of Cebolla showed. Then I was slowing down with a dark blob in the road ahead of me with some torches around it. They had Tap, all right, had him backward on his horse with a rope around his neck. He looked mighty gray around the gills but was cussing them up one side and down the other. Then I came up, walking my horse.

"All right, boys!" I let it out loud. "Fun's over! No hanging tonight!"

"Who says so?" They were all peering my way, so I gave it to them.

"Why, this here's Rye Tyler," I said, "but down Sonora way they call me Laredo, or the Laredo Kid. I've got a Winchester here and three loaded pistols, and I ain't the kind to die quick, so if some of you hombres figure you'd like to make widows and orphans of your wives and kids, just start reaching.

"I ain't," I said, "a mite particular about who I shoot. I ain't honing to kill anybody, but knowing Tap, I figure if he shot anybody it was a fair shooting. Now back off, and back off easy-like. My hands both work fast, so I can use both guns at once. That figures twelve shots if you stop me then, but I got a Winchester and another gun. Me, I ain't missed a shot since I was eleven years old, so anybody fixin' to die sure don't need to go to no trouble tonight!"

Nobody moved, but out of the tail of my eye I could see some change of expression on Tap's face.

"He reached first," Tap said.

"But he was just a kid!" Who that was, I don't know. It sounded like Gravel Brown, who bummed drinks around Ventana.

"His gun was as big as a man's," Tap said, "and he's seventeen, which makes him old as I was when I was segundo for a fighting outfit driving to Ogallala."

Brown was no fighter. "Gravel," I said, "you move up easy-like and take that noose off Tap's neck, and if you so much as nudge him or that horse they'll be pattin' over your face with a spade come daybreak."

Gravel Brown took that noose off mighty gentle. I'd walked my horse up a few steps while Gravel untied Tap's hands, and then restored his guns.

"You may get away with this now, Tyler," somebody said, "but you and Tap better take your luck and make tracks. You're through here. We want no gunslingers in this country."

"No?" That made me chuckle. "All right, amigo, you tell that to Chet Bayless, Red Corram, and most of all, Jerito Juarez. If they go, we will. Until then, our address is the Pelado, and if you come a-visiting, the coffee's always on. If you come hunting trouble, why, I reckon we can stir you up a mess of that." I backed my horse a couple of feet. "Come on, Tap. These boys need their sleep. Let 'em go home."

We sat there side by each and watched them go. They didn't like it, but none of them wanted to be a dead hero. When they had gone, Tap turned to me.

"Saved my bacon, kid." He started riding, and after a ways he turned to me. "That straight about you being the Laredo gunfighter?"

"Uh-huh. No reason to broadcast it."

"And I was wondering if you'd fight! How foolish can a man be?"

———

IT SET LIKE that for a week, and nobody showed up around South Fork and nobody bothered us. Tap, he went away at night occasional, but he never said anything and I didn't ask any questions. Me, I stayed away. This was Tap's play, and I figured if she wanted Tap she did not want me. Her riding all that way sure looked like she did want him, though. Then came Saturday and I saddled up and took a packhorse. Tap studied me, and said finally, "I reckon I better side you."

"Don't reckon you better, Tap," I said, "things been too quiet. I figure they think we'll do just that, come to town together and leave this place empty. When we got back we'd either be burned out or find them sitting in the cabin with Winchesters. You hold it down here."

Tap got up. His face was sharp and hard as ever, but he looked worried. "But they might gang you, kid. No man can buck a stacked deck."

"Leave it to me," I said, "and we've got no choice anyway. We need grub."

Ventana was dozing in the sun when I walked the steeldust down the main alley of the town. A couple of sleepy old codgers dozed against the sun-baked front of a building, a few horses stood three-legged at the tie rail. Down the street a girl sat in a buckboard, all stiff and starched in a gingham gown, seeing city life and getting broken into it.

Nobody was in the store but the owner himself and he was right pert getting my stuff ready. As before, I was wearing three guns in sight and a fourth in that shoulder holster under my jacket. If they wanted war they could have it.

When my stuff was ready I stashed it near the back door and started out the front. The storekeeper looked at me, then said, "You want to live you better hightail it. They been waiting for you."

I shoved my hat back on my head and grinned at him. "Thanks, mister, but that sure wouldn't be neighborly of me, would it? Folks wait for me shouldn't miss their appointment. I reckon I'll go see what they have to say."

"They'll say it with lead." He glowered at me, but I could see he was friendly.

"Then I guess I can speak their language," I said. "Was a time I was a pretty fluent conversationalist in that language. Maybe I still am."

"They'll be in the Ventana Saloon," he said, "and a couple across the street. There'll be at least four."

When I stepped out on the boardwalk about twenty hombres stepped off it. I mean that street got as empty as a panhandler's pocket, so I started for the Ventana, watching mighty careful and keeping close to the buildings along the right-hand side of the street. That store across the street where two of them might be was easy to watch.

An hombre showed in the window of the store and I waited. Then Chet Bayless stepped out of the saloon. Red Corram came from the store. And Jerito Juarez suddenly walked into the center of the street. Another hombre stood in an alleyway and they had me fairly boxed. "Come in at last, huh?" Bayless chuckled. "Now we see who's nestin' on this range!"

"Hello, Jerito," I called, "nobody hung you yet? I been expecting it."

"Not unteel I keel you!" Jerito stopped and spread his slim legs wide.

Mister, I never seen anything look as mean and ornery as that hombre did then! He had a thin face with long narrow black eyes and high cheekbones. It wasn't the rest of that outfit I was watching, it was him. That boy was double-eyed dynamite, all charged with hate for me and my kind.

"You never seen the day," I said, "when you could tear down my meathouse, Jerito." Right then I felt cocky. There was a devil in me, all right, a devil I was plumb scared of. That was why I ducked and kept out of sight, because when trouble came to me I could feel that old lust to kill getting up in my throat and no smart man wants to give rein to that sort of thing. Me, I rode herd on it, mostly, but right now it was in me and it was surging high. Right then if somebody had told me for certain sure that I was due to die in that street, I couldn't have left it.

My pulse was pounding and my breath coming short and I stood there shaking and all filled with wicked eagerness, just longing for them to open the ball.

And then Betty Lucas stepped into the street.

She must have timed it. She must have figured she could stop that killing right there. She didn't know Chet Bayless, Corram, and those others. They would fire on a woman. And most Mexicans wouldn't, but she didn't know Jerito Juarez. He would have shot through his mother to kill me, I do believe.

Easy-like, and gay, she walked out there in that dusty street, swinging a sunbonnet on her arm, just as easy as you'd ever see. Somebody yelled at her and somebody swore, but she kept coming, right up to me.

"Let's go, Rye," she said gently. "You'll be killed. Come with me."

Lord knows, I wanted to look at her, but my eyes never wavered. "Get out of the street, Betty. I made my play. I got to back it up. You go along now."

"They won't shoot if you're with me," she said, "and you must come, *now*!" There was awful anxiety in her eyes, and I knew what it must have taken for her to come out into that street after me. And my eyes must have flickered because I saw Jerito's hand flash.

Me? I never moved so fast in my life! I tripped up Betty and sprawled her in the dust at my feet and almost as she hit dust my right-hand gun was making war talk across her body, lying there so slim and lovely, angry and scared.

Jerito's gun and mine blasted fire at the same second, me losing time with getting Betty down. Something ripped at my sleeve and then I stepped over her and had both guns going, and from somewhere another gun started and Jerito was standing there with blood running down his face and it all twisted with a kind of wild horror above the flame-stabbing .44 that pounded death at me.

Bayless I took out with my left-hand gun, turning him with a bullet through his right elbow, a bullet that was making a different man of him, although I didn't know it then.

He never again was able to flash a fast gun!

Jerito suddenly broke and lunged toward me. He was blood all over the side of his head and face and shoulder, but he was still alive and in a killing mood. He came closer and we both let go at point-blank range, but I was maybe a split second faster and that bullet hit bone.

When a bullet hits bone a man goes down, and he went down and hard. He rolled over and stared up at me.

"You *fast*! You . . . *diablo*!" His face twisted and he died right there, and when I looked up, Tap Henry was standing alongside the Ventana Saloon with a smoking gun in his hand, and that was a Christian town.

That's what I mean. We made believers out of them that day in the dusty street on a warm, still afternoon. Tap and me, we made them see what it meant to tackle us and the town followed the ranchers and they followed Jim Lucas when he came down to shake hands and call it a truce.

Betty was alongside me, her face dusty, but not so pale anymore, and Tap walked over, holstering his gun. He held out his hand, and I shook it. We'd been riding partners for months, but from that day on we were *friends*.

"You and me, kid," he said, "we can whip the world! Or we can make it plumb peaceful! I reckon our troubles are over."

"No hard feelings?" One of my arms was around Betty.

"Not one!" He grinned at me. "You was always head man with her. And us? Well, I never knowed a man I'd rather ride the river with!"

THERE'S MORE CATTLE on the Pelado now, and the great bald dome of the mountain stands above the long green fields where the cattle graze, and where the horses' coats grow shining and beautiful, and there are two houses there now, and Tap has one of them with a girl from El Paso, and I have the other with Betty.

We came when the country was young and wild, and it took men to curry the roughness out of it, and we knew the smell of gunsmoke, the buffalo-chip fires, and the long swell of the prairie out there where the cattle rolled north to feed a nation on short-grass beef.

We helped to shape that land, hard and beautiful as it was, and the sons we reared, Tap and me, they ride where we rode, and when the day comes, they can carry their guns, too, to fight for what we fought for, the long, beautiful smell of the wind with the grass under it, and the purple skies with the slow smoke of home fires burning.

All that took a lot of building, took blood, lead, death, and cattle, but we built it, and there she stands, boys. How does she look now?

TO HANG ME HIGH

H E WAS A fine-looking man of fifty or so, uncommonly handsome on that tall bay horse. He turned in his saddle like a commanding general, and said, "We will bivouac here, gentlemen. Our man cannot be far and there is no use killing our horses."

It wasn't the first time I had seen Colonel Andrew Metcalf, who was easily the most talked-about man in Willow Springs. He alone did not have to worry about his mount—he had brung one of his hands along, leading a beautiful Tennessee Walker, and twice a day, he switched off from one t'other, so as not to tire either of them out. Those horses, I thought, had a better life than some people. Them with a master given to allowin' his horses rest, even on a posse.

My name is Ryan Tyler, a stranger in this country, and by the look of things not apt to live long enough to get acquainted. The colonel had nine men with him and they had just one idea in mind: to ride me down and hang me high.

Only two of them fretted me much. The colonel was a hard-minded man, folks said, with his own notions about right and wrong. The other one who worried me was Shiloh Johnson.

Three weeks ago Shiloh and me had us a run-in out to Wild Horse Camp. He was used to doin' just about whatever he pleased, for the reason that most everyone was scared of him. Only me bein' a stranger an' all, he tackled more than he figured on.

Johnny Mex Palmer seen it, and he said I done wrong. "You should have killed him, Rye. He'll never let it rest now until you're buried deep."

He had seen me beat Shiloh 'til he couldn't stand up, and me never get any more than some skinned knuckles. Well, folks had the saying around that Shiloh was the toughest man in a fight, the fastest on the draw, and the best man on a trail from Willow Springs to the Mesquite Hills.

He set some store by that reputation, Shiloh did, and now he had been beaten by a youngster, and easy-like to boot.

The colonel was a hard-minded man and a driver. Once started after a man, he wouldn't be likely to stop. Shiloh was an Injun on a trail, with his meanness to keep him at it. Up there in those rocks, cold as it was, it didn't look good for me.

The colonel, he swung down like on a parade ground, his fine dark hair almost to his shoulders, those shoulders so square under that blue cavalry overcoat.

They went to building a fire, all but Shiloh. He commenced to hunger around, tryin' to make out my trail. Shiloh smelled coon, he did. He had it in mind that I was close by, and he was like an old hound on the hunt.

Colonel Metcalf, he watched Shiloh, and finally, sort of irritable-like, he said, "Let it go, Johnson. Time enough at daybreak."

"He's close by, Colonel," Shiloh said. "I know he is. That horse of his was about done up."

The colonel's tone was edged a mite. "Let it wait!" He turned then, abruptly, and walking to the fire he put his hands out to the blaze. Shiloh Johnson, he stood there, not liking it much. But Colonel Metcalf ran the biggest brand in the Willow Springs country and when he spoke, you listened. He was no man to cross.

Shiloh was right about my horse. That Injun pony had plenty of heart but not much else. He did all he could for me, and died right up in the rocks not far off the trail. They would find him in the morning, and then they would know how close they had been.

They would know they had come within a few minutes of takin' the man who walked up to Tate Lipman and shot him dead on his own ranch. Shot him dead with half his ranch hands a-standin' by.

Only they never heard what I said to him in that one particular instant before I did it. Only Tate Lipman heard me, which was the way it had to be. It was only that I wanted him to know why he was dyin' that I spoke at all.

In that partic'lar instant, I said to him, "Rosa Killeen is a good girl, Tate. She ain't the kind you called her. An' you ain't going to worry her no more." Then he died there on the hard-packed clay, his blood covering his shirt and the ground. Before his men knew what was happenin' I threw down on them. Then I locked the passel o' them in the bunkhouse and throwed my leg over a saddle.

Me, I ain't much account, I reckon. I'm a driftin' man, a top hand on any man's outfit, but too gun-handy for comfort. Twenty-two years old and six men dead behind me, not any home to my name, nor place to go.

But Rosa Killeen was a good woman, and nobody knowed it better than me, who was in love with her.

She lived alone in that old red stone house back of the cottonwoods, and she had her a few chickens, a cow or two, and she lived mighty nice.

Once I fetched her cow for her, and she gave me eggs a couple of times, and now or again I'd set my saddle and talk to her, tellin' her about my family back in Texas and the place they had. I come of good stock, but my line played out of both money and folks just when I was passin' ten. Whatever I might have been had my pa lived, I don't know, but I became a lonesome boy who was gun-handed and salty before I stretched sixteen.

Rosa was the best thing in my life, and soon it seemed she set some store by me. Only she had education, and even if she was alone, she lived like a lady.

Folks said she had night visitors . . . an' folks ought to be left to their opinions, but once a subject's been raised a couple of times it goes to bein' a rumor, and when the rumor is about a good girl like Rosa and it's bein' spread intentional-like—well, that tries my temper. That time with Shiloh, he saw that it riled me and so he kept it up. I told him to stop and I told him what kind of yellow dog I thought he was, and he grinned that mean grin of his and put his hand on the butt of that Navy Colt, so I hit him. He was set for a gunfight and it took him by surprise. He went down and I snatched his pistol away and tossed it out where the horses were picketed.

He got up and we fought. I knocked him down 'til he didn't have the wind nor the will to get up. Then I told him there, and the rest of them, too. "She's a lady, an' nobody talks one word agin' her. If he does, he better come a-smokin'. You understand that, Shiloh?"

It went against him, standin' there like that with four men lookin' on, four who saw me beat him down, an' him fighting dirty, too. Johnny Mex Palmer was right, I knew he was right. . . . I should have got at him with a gun and killed him then and there, but Shiloh was still alive, and now it was his turn.

Not only Shiloh knew Rosa had a night visitor. Me, I knew it, too. One night I had stopped my horse to watch her window light and wish . . . well, things I shouldn't be wishin'. I saw that horse ride up and saw a man with a wide hat go in. He stayed more than two hours and rode away . . . oh, I saw that, all right. But Rosa was a good girl, and nobody could make me feel different.

I asked her about it. Maybe I shouldn't have, it bein' none of my business, but there was a certain way that I felt about her an' I knew if I didn't ask I'd be worryin' and goin' crazy. So I asked but she didn't tell me, least not straight up like I wanted.

"I can't tell you, Rye," she said. "I'm sorry. I promise you it's not . . . a romance." She blushed, an' wouldn't look me in the eye. "You've got to believe me, but that's all I can say." Well, I can't say I was satisfied, but I was surprised how much better I felt. I believed her and I loved her and that's all that mattered.

Only I wasn't the only one who saw. Tate Lipman had seen him, too, and from all I heard, Tate knew who it was. I didn't know, nor did I want to. Me, I was trying to be a trustin' man.

Yet I'll not soon forget the mornin' Johnny rode up to camp and swung down. "Rye," he said, "Rosa asked me to see if you'd come over. She told me to say she was in trouble, and would you come."

That Injun pony was the freshest horse in camp, for we'd

been runnin' the wild ones. When I was in the leather, I looked back at them, but mostly at Shiloh.

"See you," I said, but there was a promise in it, too, and I didn't think any of them would make any remarks when I was gone.

She was by the gate when I came riding, and she was pale and scared. "I shouldn't have called you, Rye, but I didn't know what to do, and you told me—"

"Ma'am," I said, "I'm right proud you called. Proud it was me you thought of."

There was nothing but honesty in her eyes when she looked up at me, those dark and lovely eyes that did such things to the inside of me that I couldn't find words to tell. "I think of you a lot, Rye, I really do.

"Rye, Tate Lipman saw the . . . man who comes to see me. Oh, Rye, you know it's not what people think. I can't make them believe, but I hope you do. I'm a good woman, but I'm a good woman with secrets that I have to keep. It would hurt some good folks if I didn't. The man who visits me is a fine man, and I can't let harm come to him."

"All right," I said. Lookin' into her clear blue eyes I could do nothing but believe her.

"Tate Lipman saw him, Rye. And he's heard bad things people are saying about me. Tate rode over today. He . . . he said that no girl like me had a right to choose her man. If one man could have me, then he could, too. If I hadn't had the shotgun he might have—" She put her hand on my sleeve to hold me back. "No, wait, Rye. Let me tell."

"I'll see Tate," I told her. "He won't bother you no more."

"I want to tell you, Rye," she said. "Tate had seen this other man. He said if I refused him he would tell everyone what I was up to and who with. He laughed at me when I tried to tell him it wasn't what he thought, that I hadn't done anything people wouldn't approve of.

"Rye, believe me, if he does it would ruin the reputation of a man and a woman, and I would have to move away from the only people I love. . . . It would hurt me, Rye, and it would ruin a man who has been kind to me."

"I'll talk to Tate."

"Will he listen?" She seemed frightened then. "Rye, I don't want anything to happen to you. Please, I—"

That Injun pony put more miles behind him, and then I was ridin' up to Tate Lipman's place and saw him there before the house. The hands were settin' around by the bunkhouse and they could hear no word.

He was a big, red-faced man, Tate was. He figured he was a big wheel in this country, with a wide spread and ten tough hands to ride it. I'd never liked his kind, and I had heard him say there lived no woman who couldn't be had for a price, and mostly the price was mighty cheap.

What he seen when he seen me wasn't much. I'm a tall man and was a tall boy, mostly on the narrow side with a kind of quiet face. Not much beard yet, although I'm a full twenty-two, two years older than Rosa. My hair was light brown but curly because of the Irish in me, and I was wearin' some old Levi's and a buckskin jacket, much wore.

Well, I spoke my piece quiet and easy, tellin' him what it was I'd come for. His face just turned flat and ugly, and his hand dropped for his gun, and in that minute he was sure he was goin' to shoot me down.

My Colt came up slick an' smooth-like, and there was one stark, clean-cut moment when I saw the shock in his eyes, and when he knew he was goin' to die. And then my bullet dusted him on both sides and he took a short step to his toes and went down on his face, and I turned on them by the bunkhouse.

So that was how it was, and now Rosa Killeen was behind me, and I believed in what little she'd told me with no thought that it might be otherwise. She'd hoped I could reason with Tate, but he was too bigheaded, and that I knew. It was a grave on a windy hill for him and a fast horse for me.

Only the horse wasn't fast. Just a game, tough little pony with twenty miles under him when they first gave chase . . .

The night was cold and the wind bitter. . . . I made myself small among the boulders, with my hands under my arms. I watched the wind bend the fire over, the fire that made coffee for those men down below.

They bedded down, finally, Shiloh mighty reluctant. Hate

402 / Louis L'Amour

grows hot and strong in his breed of man, and I knew that
Shiloh and me would see each other across a gun barrel, one
day.

Night made all things black, and it was like a great tunnel
filled with roaring wind, a long wind that bent the trees down
and skittered the dry leaves along the hard ground.

They had a rope stretched for my neck down there, a rope
they figured to use. Tall Colonel Metcalf and Shiloh. The
colonel would order it done like a man orders executions in
the Army, and he would stand by slapping his leg with his
quirt when they set the knot, and Shiloh would look on, smiling that old secret smile of his, knowing the only man who
ever beat him was on the end of that hemp.

It took me most of an hour to work my way around to
where the horses were picketed, ten of them close together
for warmth, but the colonel's blood bay off to one side, like
the aristocrat he was.

Crouched down in the brush, I put my fingers back in my
armpits to warm them before moving out to untie that rope.
The wind moaned in the long canyon, the rushing leaves
swept by, and the dry branches brushed their cold arms together like some skeleton things, hanging up there between
me and the black night sky.

Then, when I was inching to the edge of the clearing, a
man came out of the trees. It was Colonel Metcalf.

He crossed to the big bay and stroked his neck, feeding
him a carrot or something that crunched in the night. I could
hear the faint sound below the rush of the wind, so close was
I. And then I saw the colonel hang something across the
bay's withers, and after a minute he turned and walked back
to camp.

Scarcely had he gone when Shiloh moved like an Indian
out of the brush, and stood there, looking around. It was too
dark to see very well, yet I could picture him in my mind's
eye, clear and sharp. Shiloh was a big man with stooped and
heavy shoulders and a long face, strong-boned and with eyes
deep set. You looked at him, then looked again. You thought
something was wrong with his face. The second look showed

nothing, but it left you the impression. He was a narrow, mean man, this Shiloh Johnson.

After a minute he followed the colonel, not going to the bay horse at all.

Waiting there in the blackness, I could see faintly the movements of Shiloh as he eased into his bed in the shelter of a log. When the movement under the blankets ceased, I straightened up.

There was a piece of carrot lying where it had fallen and I picked it up. After a minute, the bay took it from me, and then I untied the picket rope and walked him across the pine needles and down into the sand beyond. When I got him to where my saddle was cached, I saddled up, then put the bit between his teeth.

For the first time, I examined the sack that Colonel Metcalf had placed across the bay's shoulders. It was a sack of oats—maybe for a half dozen feedings. A strange thing to leave on a horse's back in the middle of the night.

It was a good horse I rode now, and I treated him like the gentleman he was, let him take his own pace, but held him away into the dark country, toward the high meadows and the long bare ridges. It was a strange land to me, and this worried me some, for Shiloh knew it well, and the colonel almost as well. Along the piñon slopes and into the aspen I rode, down grassy bottoms where the long wind moaned and into the dark pines, and through canyons among the rocks, and stopping at lonely creeks for a drink and then on.

When I had four hours of riding behind me I stopped and walked ahead of my horse, spelling him a mite. I made coffee then, from the little a cowhand always has with him, and let the bay crop the rich green grass.

Moving on, I turned at right angles and, climbing ahead of the horse, went right up a steep gravelly ridge. On top, just short of the skyline, I walked him along for half a mile, then picking a saddle, crossed the ridge and went down into the trees.

Sighting a dozen steers feeding, I started them off and drove them ahead of me for a ways, and then turned and started them back. They bunched for thirty or forty yards, enough to wipe out my horse tracks, and then I turned and rode downstream, keeping to the water until it became knee deep, when I scrambled out. So it went for two days.

Mine was a tough trail, hard to follow even for such a tracker as Shiloh, but he worried me, nonetheless. He knew the country, and when a man doesn't, he may lose a lot of time and distance.

Twice I'd killed rabbits, once a sage hen . . . at dusk I killed another, and in a tiny hollow among the trees and rocks I built a masked fire, built it in a hole and screened it so there'd be no glow on the trees overhead.

Along the way I'd seen some Indian breadroot, and dug a dozen of them. While fixing the sage hen I let these roots roast on the hot stones near the fire. Then I made some desert tea from the ephedra.

When I'd eaten I looked to the bay, moved him to better grass, scouted around, and then returned to my camp. Uneasy as I was, I was dead for sleep, and figured it was safe enough. . . .

———

WHEN I OPENED my eyes, Colonel Metcalf was sitting on a rock with a gun in his hand. "You're Tyler?" he said it, rather than asked, and he seemed to be measuring me, judging me.

Taking it careful, I sat up. There was a gun near my saddle, easy to hand.

"Do you know who I am?"

"Colonel Metcalf," I said. "I reckon ever'body knows you."

He kept his eyes on me. "Do you know who else I am?"

Some puzzled, I shook my head. And then he said sort of quiet-like, "Tyler, I'm the man who should have killed Tate Lipman."

It took a while for it to sink in, but even then I was not sure. "What does that mean?" I asked him.

"It has been said that the evil that men do lives after them—sometimes, Tyler, it lives with them. You deserve to know what I shall tell you. But only one other person knows. No one else must ever learn of it."

None of this made sense to me, so I sat still. Believe me, I was some worried. If he was here, then Shiloh wouldn't be far behind. And the rest of them, with the rope they carried for me.

He was freshly shaved. His clothes had been brushed. He looked like he always had, like Colonel Andrew Metcalf with his wide ranch and his position in town. His word was law . . . and mostly it was a good law. He was a hard man, but just—or so they said.

My fingers opened, and when his attention shifted an instant, they inched a little toward my gun.

"Tyler," he spoke quietly, "I'm Rosa Killeen's father."

That stopped me . . . it stopped me cold. I sat with my mouth half open, just looking at him.

"Her mother was a good woman . . . a fine woman. We crossed the plains together before the war, and her husband died on the way out. I was a young lieutenant then, riding with the escort, and she was a beautiful woman. . . . She had never loved her husband. He'd been . . . not a bad man but an unthinking one. After his death we were much together. Too much, and we both were young.

"She came of a fine old family, a very proud family. They were Spanish Californians mixed with Irish.

"The Army had orders waiting for me in Santa Fe, and they took me into the East and then to the Confederate War. It was a long time later that I got a letter she had written me. She was dying and there had been a baby girl . . . it was mine.

"I had married during the war. There was nothing I could do but provide for the child in every way I could. But I had to do so secretly . . . to have publicly accepted Rosa as mine would have been disastrous to my marriage, and would have all too plainly pointed the finger of scorn at her mother's family.

"I paid for Rosa's education and, when she grew old enough, kept her near me. It was all I could do, and Rosa understood the situation and accepted it. We did not, neither of us, foresee Tate Lipman."

Why was he telling this to me? If Shiloh and the others came up, not even Metcalf could keep them from putting a rope around my neck. Lipman had two riders in that crowd, two mighty tough men, and Shiloh would never give up this chance to get me where he wanted me.

But I sat still, waiting him out . . . all I knew was that I wanted to live, and to live I had to have that gun. No man at twenty-two is ready to die, and I sure wasn't. Especially for killin' a no-good like Tate Lipman.

"That ain't no business of mine," I told him. "I killed Tate Lipman because he had it comin'. No matter who her father was, Rosa is a fine girl."

"You love her?"

He looked at me sharply when he said that, those cold blue eyes of his direct and clear.

"Yes," I said, and meant it.

He got up. "Then pick up that gun you've been wanting to get your hand on," he said quietly, "and—"

Shiloh stepped out of the trees. "No, you don't," he said. "You touch that gun and I'll cut you down."

There it was . . . the one thing I'd been afraid of—Shiloh gettin' the drop on me, like he had now.

"Shiloh, there's reasons for all of this—" The colonel started to speak, but Johnson shook his head.

"No, you don't," he said again. "I heard all that talk. It don't make no difference to me." I could see the satisfaction in his eyes, the pleasure at having me under his gun. "Tyler murdered Lipman. It was seen. He'll hang for it."

It was there, plain and cold. Nothing the colonel could say was going to stop it now.

"I been suspicious o' you, Metcalf." There was no title used this time, and I could see the colonel heard the change in Johnson's attitude. "I seen you go to your horse that night, seen you leave that bag. Right then I couldn't figure why. . . . Come daylight, your horse gone, I figured some of it."

He had never once taken his eyes from me, and his gun was rock steady. With some men there might have been a chance. Shiloh was nobody to fool with.

"Only thing," he said it slow, like it tasted good to him, "I can't decide whether to shoot you now or see you hang."

There was silence in the clearing. Far off, I heard the wind in the pine tops, far off and away. It was a lonesome sound.

"I'm holding a gun, too, Shiloh," Metcalf said quietly. "If you shoot, I'll kill you."

No man ever spoke so matter-of-fact. And the colonel's gun covered Shiloh now, not me.

Shiloh was quiet for a long minute, and then he smiled. "You won't shoot me, Metcalf. You wouldn't dare chance it. Some of that crowd is mighty suspicious already, the way you held us back from catchin' him the other night. If I was to die now, along with him, they'd hang you."

Colonel Andrew Metcalf sat very still. Shiloh was smiling, and me, I sat there, wishin' I dared grab for that gun. But first I had to get my hand on it, make the first grab sure without lookin' toward it, then swing it into line. Time enough for a fast man to fire two, maybe three shots.

Then the colonel stood up. He was smiling a little. "Shiloh," he said quietly, "situations like this have always appealed to me. I've always been curious about what people do when the chips were down . . . well, the chips are down now."

Shiloh Johnson's face was a study. He didn't dare take his eyes from me, and the colonel was to his right and out of his line of vision. He stood there, his boots wide apart, his cruel little eyes locked on mine, his long jaw covered with beard. He wanted to look, but he didn't dare chance it.

"Tyler shouldered my responsibility when he killed Lipman. I'm not going to see him suffer for it. So I'm going to kill you."

Shiloh had it up in him now. He was cornered and he didn't like it. Not even a little.

"You shoot me in the back," he started to say, "and—"

"It won't be in the back," Metcalf said quietly. "I'm going to move right over in front of you. You may get one or even both of us—but one thing is dead certain. We'll get you."

Now I could see what the colonel meant about liking situations, and this was one. I wouldn't want to play poker with him . . . and Shiloh stood there with his face working, his eyes all squinched up, and ready to kill as he was, he wasn't no way ready to die.

It took a lot of cold nerve to do what the colonel said he would do—step over in front of a man ready to kill—but nobody would ever be able to say which of us had killed Shiloh, then.

"Now, look here . . ." Shiloh said. "I—"

"You have one other choice." Colonel Metcalf's voice was hard now, like a commanding general's. "Drop your gun belts, get on your horse, and ride clear on out of the country. Otherwise, you die right here."

As he spoke, the colonel began to shift around to get in front of Shiloh. There was panic in Johnson's voice. "All right! All right . . ."

He holstered his gun, then unbuckled his belts. There was plain, ugly hatred in his face when he looked at me. "But this ain't the end."

He stepped away from his belts and started toward his horse, which had walked up through the trees from where he had left it ground-hitched when he heard our voices.

Colonel Metcalf watched him go, then turned to me. He held out his hand. I ignored it.

His voice went cold. "Tyler, what's—"

Shiloh Johnson had reached his horse. He put a hand to the pommel, then wheeled, whipping a gun from the saddlebag. It was fast and it was smooth, but I was on my feet with a gun in my hand, and as he turned I shot him through the body. He fired . . . and then I triggered my gun for two quick shots and he folded, his horse springing away as he fell.

"At Wild Horse Camp," I said, "he always carried a spare."

The colonel stood there, very white and stiff. "My boy," his voice was strange and sort of old, like I'd never heard it sound, "I've sent her to Fort Worth. Go to her."

"But—"

"Ride, boy!" The old crack came back into his voice. "They'll have heard the shots!"

He stood there, not moving, and when I was in the saddle he said, "Fort Worth, son. She'll be waiting. Rosa loves you."

As he said it I'll swear there were tears in his eyes, but the bay was running all out and away before I recalled something else. There had been a dark splotch on his shirt front. That one shot—that wild shot Shiloh got off—it had hit him.

He carried it well that day, afraid I'd not leave him if I knew . . . but he carried it well for ten years, and was carrying it on our Texas ranch, when he held his grandchild on his knee.

WEST OF DODGE

LANCE KILKENNY LOOKED across the counter at the man with the narrow face and the scar on his jaw. "Watch yourself," Hillman said. "This is Tom Stroud's town. He's marshal here, and he's poison for gunfighters."

"I'll be all right." Kilkenny paid for his shells and walked to the door, a tall, spare man looking much less than his two hundred pounds. His was a narrow, Hamlet-like face with high cheekbones and green eyes.

His walk was that of a woodsman rather than a rider, but Hillman had known at once that he wore the two Colts for use rather than for show.

It disturbed Kilkenny to find himself known here, as a gunfighter if not by name. Here he had planned to rest, to hunt a job, to stay out of trouble.

Of Marshal Tom Stroud he knew nothing beyond the bare fact that some two months before, Stroud had killed Jim Denton in a Main Street gun battle.

Yet Kilkenny needed no introduction to reputation-hunting marshals. There had been Old John Selman and others who fattened their records on killing gunfighters—and were rarely particular about an even break.

At the hitch rail Kilkenny studied his gaunt, long-legged buckskin. The horse needed the rest, and badly. Torn between dislike for trouble and consideration for his horse, the needs of the horse won.

He headed for the livery. Glancing back at the store, he saw a slope-shouldered man with dark hair and eyes step awkwardly into the doorway to watch him ride away. Something about the way the man stood, one hand braced against the wall, made Kilkenny think that he was a cripple.

Hillman had not guessed his name. That was fortunate. A

man of his sort might guess if given time . . . of his sort . . . now where had that thought come from? Rubbing down the buckskin, Kilkenny gave consideration to the idea. What was Hillman's sort?

Something about the storekeeper had marked him in Kilkenny's mind, and it left him uneasy that he could not make a proper estimate of his instinct about the man, yet something disturbed him, left him wary and uncertain.

Hillman was a man in his thirties, as tall as Kilkenny, and only a little bulkier, but probably no heavier. He had a careful, measuring eye.

From the door of the livery stable Kilkenny studied the street, still thinking of Hillman and Stroud. Usually, a storekeeper would want to avoid trouble in a town. Maybe he believed a warning would cause Kilkenny to move on. Building a smoke, he considered that.

Like many western towns, this one was divided into two sections. One was a rough collection of saloons, shanties, and bawdy houses along the railroad and backed by a maze of corrals and feed sheds where cattlemen put up their herds while waiting for shipment east. This was the old town, the town that had been built by the hard-drinking track crews and cattle buyers in the wild days before the town had ever thought to build a church or a schoolhouse.

Running at right angles to the tracks was the newer Main Street. Away from the smell and the flies of the holding pens, it had been built by the merchants who came as the town grew. There were carefully built buildings made of white-washed planks or brick, with boardwalks connecting one to the next so that the shopper or businessman only occasionally had to brave the rutted mud of the street. There was only one saloon in this part of town, and it was a pretentious affair situated on the ground floor of the new two-story hotel. Behind the stores of the street were grids of one- to five-acre lots where the townspeople lived. Most of the houses had vegetable gardens growing corn and tomatoes, and each had a carriage house, stable, or barn. At the bottom of Main Street was the livery, where Kilkenny now stood, and opposite him, the marshal's office . . . a bridge, or a barrier, separating one world from the other.

Kilkenny crushed out his cigarette. He wore black chaps and a black, flat-crowned, flat-brimmed hat. Under his black Spanish-style jacket he wore a gray flannel shirt. They were colors that lost themselves in any shadow.

He was weary now, every muscle heavy with the fatigue of long hours of riding. His throat was dry, his stomach empty. His mind was sluggish because of the weariness of his body, and he felt short-tempered and irritable because of it.

Normally, he was a quiet, tolerant man with a dry humor and a liking for people, but in his present mood he was wary of himself, knowing the sudden angers that could spring up within him at such times.

Darkness gathered in the hollows of the hills and crept down into the silent alleys, crouching there to wait its hour for creeping into the empty streets. Kilkenny rolled another smoke, trying to relax. He was hungry, but he wanted to calm himself before walking into the company of strangers.

A stray dog trotted up the street . . . a door slammed. The town was settling down after supper, and he had not yet eaten. He dropped his cigarette, pushing it into the dust.

There was a grate of boot soles on gravel. A low sentence reached his ears from the bench outside the door. "Reckon Stroud knows?"

"Who can tell what he knows? But he was hired to keep the peace, an' he's done it."

"In his own way."

"Maybe there ain't no other."

"There was once. Stroud shut down the gambling and thievin', but he stopped the Vigilance Committee, too. They'd have strung the worst of them and burnt the old town to the ground. There's some say we'd be better off."

As he crossed the street Kilkenny did not turn to look at the men who had spoken behind him. He could feel the rising tensions. Something here was still poised for trouble. Alive to such things, currents that could mean death if unwatched, he was uneasy at remaining, yet he disliked the idea of going on. Towns were scarce in this country.

It was no common frontier-style boardinghouse he entered, but a large, well-appointed dining room, a place suited to a larger city, a place that would have a reputation in any city.

There was linen on the tables and there was silver and glass, not the usual rough wood and crockery. A young woman came toward him with a menu in her hand. She had a quiet face and dark, lovely eyes.

He noticed the way her eyes had seemed to gather in his dusty clothes and rest momentarily on the low-hung guns. She led him to a corner table and placed the menu before a place where he could sit with his back in the corner, facing the room.

His eyes crinkled at the corners and he smiled a little. "Does it show that much?"

Her own eyes were frank, not unfriendly. "I'm afraid it does."

"This," he indicated the room, "is a surprise."

"It is a way of making a living."

"A gracious way." She looked at him more directly as he spoke. "It is a way one misses."

A small frown gathered between her eyes. "I wonder— why is it that most gunfighters are gentlemen?"

"Some were born to it," he said, "and some grow into it. Men are rude only when they are insecure."

He was eating his dessert when the door opened and a man came in. It was, Kilkenny guessed at once, Tom Stroud.

He was a square-faced man with the wide shoulders and deep chest of mountain ancestry. He was plainly dressed and walked without swagger, yet there was something solid and indomitable about him. His eyes were blue, a darker blue than that usually seen, and his mustache was shading from brown to gray.

Stroud seated himself, glanced at the menu, and then his eyes lifted and met those of Kilkenny. Instant recognition was there . . . not of him as a name, but as a gunfighter. There was also something else, a narrow, measuring gaze.

The slope-shouldered, limping man that he had seen at Hillman's earlier entered the room and crossed to Stroud's table. Stroud's face indicated no welcome, but the man sat down and leaned confidentially across the table. The man talked, low-voiced. Once, Stroud's eyes flickered to Kilkenny. Deliberately, Kilkenny prolonged his coffee.

The woman, Laurie Archer, walked over to him. "Will you be with us long?"

"A day . . . perhaps two."

"You would be wise to move on—tonight."

"No."

"Perhaps you would take a job outside of town? I have cattle, and I need a foreman."

"How many hands?"

"Two . . . now."

In reply to his unspoken question she added quietly, "I had a foreman—Jim Denton."

Neither spoke for several minutes and then, knowing he needed the job, he said, "I would only hire to handle cows. Denton was none of my affair."

"I want it no other way."

"My name's Lance. By the way, what about him?" He indicated Stroud. "What will he think about you hiring me?"

She shrugged. "I have no idea."

———

At THE RANCH two men awaited him, a capable, tough-looking man of past fifty named Pike Taylor, and a gawky youngster of seventeen, Corey Hatch. There was a small cabin where Laurie Archer stayed when on the ranch, a bunkhouse, a stable, and corrals. There was a good bit of stacked hay, and several thousand acres of unrestricted grazing, much of it bottom land.

For a solid week, Kilkenny worked hard. He rode the fence, repaired broken stretches, put in new posts. He fenced off some loco weed, cleaned several water holes, dug out a fresh one where the green grass indicated water near the surface. He found some fifty head of mavericks and branded them, moving all the cattle to lower ground for the best grass. And he thought about Laurie Archer.

Corey Hatch liked to talk. "Some folks don't take much to

Stroud," he said. "Hillman an' them, they hired him to clean up the town, but some figure he done too good a job. The gamblers an' them, they'd like to get a shot at him."

When he rode into town he stabled his horse and then dropped in at the store. Hillman filled his order, then said, low-voiced, "Watch yourself. There's been talk."

"Talk?"

"That you're takin' up for Denton. Stroud will be watchin' his chance."

The warning made him angry. Why couldn't people let well enough alone? No doubt Stroud was getting the same sort of talk . . . was it planned that way? Deliberately, to build it into trouble?

But Hillman had been the man who hired Stroud, so that made no sense. He himself did not want trouble. He had a good job on the ranch, and was earning sorely needed money. He wanted no trouble. He considered going to Tom Stroud, having it out.

Yet that might precipitate that very trouble he was attempting to avoid. He crossed to the restaurant and was scarcely seated before Stroud came in. Two men at an intervening table got up and left without finishing their meals.

After dinner he walked down the street and across the tracks to a saloon. He sat at a table, apparently lost in thought but keeping an ear on the conversations around him. "Used to be a live town," a man said, "before they hired Stroud."

"Whyn't they fire him?"

"Them across the way hired him. Hillman, an' them shopkeepers. They want to keep him."

Restless, and disturbed by the feeling in town, he walked outside. From up the street there was a sudden shot, then a wild yell and pounding hoofs. A rider came down the street and slid from his horse. He was swaying and drunk, waving a drawn pistol. It was Pike Taylor, from the ranch.

"Where's that murderin' son? I'll kill—!"

Tom Stroud materialized from a dark alley beside the saloon. Pike's side was toward the marshal. Pike had fired a gun, still held it gripped in his fist, had threatened to kill. Stroud had only to speak and shoot.

It would be murder, cold-blooded, ruthless, efficient. Kilkenny stepped out on the street, waiting. His mouth was dry, his hands loose and ready.

Stroud did not see him, yet he knew that if Stroud moved to kill the old man, he would kill Stroud.

Stroud had hesitated an instant only, then he walked through the soft dust toward Pike. Taylor started to turn but the marshal was swift, incredibly so. His left hand dropped to the old man's wrist with a grasp of iron, while his right hand came up under the barrel and broke the gun back against Pike Taylor's thumb.

Death had stalked the street, and then Pike stood disarmed and helpless. Seizing the old man's arm, Stroud started him toward the jail. And as he turned he saw Kilkenny.

Thirty yards apart their eyes met. Stroud's gun hand gripped the old man's arm.

Kilkenny heard a sharp intake of breath, then from the shadows a voice. "Now's your chance—*take him*!"

Kilkenny walked slowly forward. "Havin' trouble, Marshal?"

Stroud's eyes, wary but faintly curious, met his in the light from the windows. "Careless shootin'. Are you going to take him back to the ranch, or does he sleep it off in jail?"

"In jail—it will keep him out of trouble."

Stroud nodded, started to turn away. Kilkenny said, "You could have killed him, Marshal."

Stroud turned sharply. "I never kill men," his voice was utterly cold, "unless it has to be done."

Kilkenny walked back to the saloon and ordered a drink. The bartender came leisurely down the bar and slammed a glass before Kilkenny. He slopped whiskey into it. His eyes were insolent when he looked up.

Kilkenny did not change expression. "Drink that yourself. Then get a fresh glass and pour it without spilling."

The bartender hesitated, not liking it, but not liking what might follow. Suddenly, he tossed off the whiskey and followed instructions.

The man with the sloping shoulders and the limp edged

along the bar, faint contempt in his eyes. "Had him dead to rights. He got you buffaloed?"

"Why should I shoot him? He means nothing to me."

"He's gunnin' for you."

"Is he?"

"Everybody knows that. Sure he is."

"I've seen no signs of it." Kilkenny lifted his eyes. "And I can read sign. If you ask me there's a lot of skunk tracks around here."

Kilkenny gave him time to reply, but the man stood silent, his face tight and worried. Events had taken a turn the limping man did not like. After a moment he shrugged, then shuffled back across the room and sat down at a table covered with papers. He took up a pencil and began adding what looked like a column of figures. Again, Kilkenny had that strange feeling that he'd met this man before, and that the man had just done something that by all rights should have told Kilkenny where that memory came from.

"I never knew Jim Denton," Kilkenny said then. "His troubles were his own. Anybody who hopes to promote a battle is wastin' time. I fight my own wars . . . this one ain't mine."

Irritably, Kilkenny walked to the hotel, got a room, and turned in. He had slept scarcely an hour when, restless, he awakened. He sat on the edge of the bed and lit a cigarette.

Obviously, he had been elected to kill Tom Stroud, but who had done the electing? Whoever, they would not cease planning because of his statement in the saloon. What they seemed to need was a scapegoat, for evidently the powers in town were evenly balanced, and the Hillman crowd—What was it about him that never ceased to worry Kilkenny?

What about Laurie? Where did she stand? Despite her comment that he was not to take up Denton's quarrel, Kilkenny was not at all sure. She was poised, intelligent. Her interests would seem to be aligned with those of the storekeepers, but was she not a little ruthless? Yet, he had seemed to detect something in her manner to Stroud that was different.

Was he becoming too suspicious? Maybe, but if he killed Stroud or they killed each other, it could be set down as a gunman's quarrel. Perhaps a certain group would then find a marshal more susceptible to corruption.

What would they do now? Still considering that, he fell asleep.

He awakened for the second time with a faint scratching outside his window. He swung his feet to the floor and moved swiftly to where he could see. The alley was empty.

The moon was behind a cloud, but as he flattened against the wall he suddenly caught a faint flicker of movement. Somebody was at the end of the alley, standing in the shadows. It was a woman. It was Laurie Archer. He could see the arm of her gray coat . . . she gestured to him.

He held his watch to the faint light—it was past three o'clock. What would she be doing up and around at this hour?

Hurriedly, he dressed. Belting on his guns, he stepped from the window into the alley. Swiftly and silently he moved to the end of the alley where Laurie had disappeared, and then he saw her, some distance off. He hurried after her, and then she vanished.

He crouched at the base of a huge old cottonwood, debating this. Suddenly, he heard a horse stamp. Turning his head, he beheld the animal standing not a dozen yards away, bridle reins trailing . . . and that meant the horse had been ridden lately and would be ridden soon again. He went to the horse . . . its flanks were damp. He touched the brand—a Lazy A, Laurie Archer's brand!

There had been no time for her to get to the ranch and return. Therefore, Corey Hatch must be in town.

Why?

A kid . . . proud, defiant, loyal . . . a kid riding for the brand, and Pike Taylor arrested. Remembering his own youthful feelings, Kilkenny knew how Corey must feel. He would believe Pike must be freed—but how had he known about Pike?

Somehow, someone had gotten word to him. That meant the man behind the scenes was setting up a situation that could only lead to violence, and somehow, in the confusion, Stroud would be killed.

Only Stroud?

Very likely he, Kilkenny, was to be killed, too. That meant they had to get him on the scene of the fight, and that meant Laurie was part of it somehow. But she had led him nowhere, she—he stared around him, suddenly.

A half dozen cottonwoods and some willows behind a building . . . a blacksmith shop. And next door? Suddenly he came to his feet, tense and ready.

They had succeeded, they had led him into a trap. They had gotten him close to Stroud, and when they killed both it could be signed off as a gun battle. Didn't everybody know they were hunting each other?

For the building next door to the blacksmith shop was the jail—and Tom Stroud lived in the front of the jail.

Time was short, only seconds must remain, for they could not hope to keep him here long. . . .

A crash from the jail started him running. He ducked around the blacksmith shop, and was just in time to see the marshal step into the door. The moon had come from under a cloud and he caught a fleeting glimpse of Stroud in the doorway. At the corner of the building was Corey Hatch, gun in hand!

Kilkenny opened his mouth to shout a warning, and then the night was ripped apart by a crashing volley. Tom Stroud took one step forward and then fell headlong, sprawled across the steps.

Kilkenny triggered his gun into the darkness from which the shots had come, then ducked and ran to the fallen man. Corey stood where he had been, his mouth opened wide, then, the surprise wearing off, he dropped to the ground.

Stroud was hit several times, but alive. Kilkenny looked up. "Corey! Over here!"

Startled, yet knowing the voice, the boy slipped onto the porch. Together they got the marshal inside and stretched on a bed. Taking a sawed-off shotgun from the wall, Kilkenny handed it to the boy. "Take that and guard the door. Let nobody in! Understand? *Nobody!*"

Kilkenny stripped the shirt from Stroud's body. He had been hit once high in the chest, once in the leg. His side had been grazed by another bullet, his shirt torn in several other places.

Swiftly, Kilkenny went to work. From of old, he knew bullet wounds and what to do about them. A half hour later, he joined the boy near the front of the jail.

"Nobody stirrin'," Corey said. "What happened, boss? I don't get it."

"I'll explain later. Let's get Pike."

Taylor was on his feet and at the door of his cell. He had, he explained, received a note. When he read the note he got loaded and started for town.

The note? He took it from his shirt pocket. It was printed on a coarse bit of wrapping paper:

> Jim Denton was bringing this bottle to you when he was murdered by Stroud. Figured you should have it. He's going to get your new boss the same way.
>
> A Friend

The very simplicity of it angered Kilkenny. The writer must have known the old man would have a drink, and then another, and he would think about Denton dead, and this new boss, Lance, about to be killed. So he got a gun and started for town.

"How about you?" Kilkenny asked Corey.

Corey took a note from his jeans. It was the same coarse paper, the same pencil style:

> Stroud's got Pike in jail. Pull the bars off the window while I handle Stroud.
>
> Lance

Kilkenny explained the situation. Obviously, whoever led the element opposed to Stroud hoped to get him killed, and to kill Kilkenny or one of the men from the ranch in the fight. That tied it to a grudge battle over Denton, and would arouse no controversy with the townspeople, nor would they be likely to suspect a plot.

Kilkenny walked back to the door. The blinds were drawn

and tightened down. Nobody outside could see what happened inside. They might know Kilkenny was there, and if they did they would act, and soon.

Stroud was awake and breathing heavily when Kilkenny stepped to the bed. The marshal looked up at him. Kneeling beside the bed, Kilkenny began to talk. He told what had happened as he saw it clearly, concisely.

"Now," he said, "you make me your deputy."

Stroud's brow puckered. "What—?"

"Don't worry. I'll carry on while you're down. Just make me your deputy."

Speaking in a hoarse whisper, Stroud swore him in before Pike Taylor and Corey Hatch.

Leaving the two to guard the wounded man, Kilkenny let himself out the back door. It would soon be daylight. He had little hope of finding anything that would lead him to the ambushers, but it was a chance.

From somewhere, they might be watching. On the other hand, as it was nearing day, they might return home and stay quiet, waiting for the news of the morning. For whatever had happened would be known to everyone shortly after daybreak.

Circling around, Kilkenny examined the ground where the ambushers had been concealed. They had hidden behind a water trough that stood near the mouth of an alley. No brass shells remained. The tracks were confusion.

Kilkenny went down the street and crossed, in the first graying of the eastern sky, to the house where Laurie Archer slept. He was starting up the walk when he stopped, frowning.

The yard had been watered the evening before with a hand sprinkler, and water had run across the sand path to the doorway. So much water had been used that the sand had been left quite damp, and it was smooth, unbroken by any tracks!

Circling the house, he found there was no back door. The windows were high, too high to be used with comfort. He was standing, staring around, when she spoke to him from the window.

"Just what exactly are you looking for?"

He walked toward the window. "I'd like to talk to you. It's important."

She wore a wrapper, and her hair was rumpled, but she looked even more lovely and exciting. "All right. I'll open the door."

When he was inside, he looked around. It was a pleasant sitting room, not so cluttered with bric-a-brac as most such rooms of the period, but done in the Spanish style, with Indian blankets and only a couple of pictures. It was somehow like her; it had charm and simplicity.

"Where's your gray jacket?" he asked abruptly. "And that gray hat?"

She waited an instant, studying him. "Why . . . why, I left them at the restaurant. Is it important?"

"Yes . . . Did you leave this house last night? Or very early this morning?"

She shook her head. "I had a headache. I came home early and went to bed. I had just gotten up when you came."

He glanced around him again. Everything was neat, perfect. Had it been someone else wearing her clothes last night, one of the girls from down on the tracks, perhaps?

She noticed the star on his chest, and she frowned. "Where did you get that?" Her voice was a little sharp. "Where's Tom Stroud?"

Briefly, he explained. He was startled to see her face turn deathly pale. She put a hand on the table at her side. "He . . . he'll live? I mean . . . ?"

"I think so."

"I must go to him."

"No."

The harshness of his reply startled her. She looked up quickly, but before she could speak he said abruptly, almost brutally, "Nobody will see him but myself and my two men until this is cleared up. He's being cared for."

"But—"

"No," he said firmly and definitely. "Too many people want him dead."

Leaving her house, he walked swiftly down the street. The

limping man . . . Pike had said his name was Turner, and told him where to find him. He went up the walk to the house and, without knocking, shoved the door open and stepped in.

Two men were sitting at a table cleaning rifles. They took one look, glimpsed the badge, and the nearest one grabbed for his gun. Kilkenny shot him in the throat, his Colt swinging to cover the other man who slowly lifted his hands, gray-faced.

"Fast," the man said. "You're fast, Lance."

"I've had to be." Lance looked at him and said, "The other name is Kilkenny."

The man jumped as if stabbed. "Kilkenny," he said, "the Nueces gunfighter!"

"Who hired you?" Kilkenny's voice was low. "Just tell me that, and you can ride out of here."

"Nobody." He started to continue, but Kilkenny's gun muzzle tilted and he stopped. "Look, I—"

"You've got one minute," Kilkenny said, "then you get a hole in your ear. I don't reckon I'll miss. Howsoever, I might notch it a little close."

The man swallowed. "All right. It was Turner."

He saw the man into a saddle, and then walked back to the house and sat down. The body of the dead man had been removed to the barn. He looked around the bare room and saw on the wall a picture. It was a faded tintype of the main street of Dodge.

Kilkenny stood up for a closer look, and suddenly, it hit him like a flash. He started to turn, and then stopped. The limping man stood in the open door, and he held a gun in his hand. "Howdy, Lance." His eyes were faintly amused, yet wary. "Like that picture?"

Kilkenny lifted a hand slowly to his cigarette and dusted the ash from it, then returned it to his lips. "I went up the trail a couple of times," he drawled conversationally. "She was quite a town, wasn't she?"

Obviously, the two men he had surprised in the cabin had been two of those who ambushed Stroud. Turner would be another. The three could have done it, but there had probably been at least one more.

"Where's the boys?" Turner moved into the room, keeping Kilkenny covered.

"One's lyin' out in the barn." Kilkenny's voice did not change. "He's pretty dead. The other one got a chance to take out, and he pulled his freight."

Turner studied him. He was puzzled. Kilkenny was so obviously in complete possession of himself. This man who called himself Lance was a mystery in many ways. He—

"When you were in Dodge," Kilkenny said, "did you ever hang out at the Kansas House?"

Turner's face seemed to tighten and his eyes went blank. "Remember the place," he said.

"So do I."

Kilkenny drew deep on his cigarette. "Better put that gun down, Turner. You're through here. Stroud isn't dead. I'm the deputy marshal." He jerked his head toward the town. "The folks over there know it. You try anything now, and they'll all come down here and burn you out. I might say they've been considerin' it."

Turner hesitated, not liking it. He hitched around, looking quickly out the door. Kilkenny made no attempt to grab for his gun. He just waited. "You're through, Turner." Kilkenny's words repeatedly went through his head. He had a deep-seated fear of the people across the tracks. He knew many of them disliked the saloons and gambling houses, and lived only for the day when the town could be cleaned up.

"You fellows should know when you're well off," Kilkenny continued. He was remembering bloody Kansas and a cold rage was settling over him. "If you'd only known, Stroud was keepin' you alive. With him down, there ain't a thing to prevent them comin' across here and makin' a cleanup. As long as he kept the peace, they kept their hands off. But you were greedy. Those trail-town days are over. You can't turn the clock back."

Turner suddenly looked up. "All right," he said, "give me a chance and I'll ride."

"No," Kilkenny said, and drew. His Colt came out fast and Kilkenny stepped in close to Turner and had the muzzle pressed against his ear before the crippled man could bring his gun to bear. He snatched Turner's pistol away with his left hand and pushed Turner back into one of the chairs.

"That picture got me thinking. I remember you from Kansas . . . a long time ago. You were using the name Barney Houseman back then. You and your family skinned a lot of good people out of their money. Killed a few, too." Kilkenny moved to one side and gestured with his free hand. "Get up."

"Lance." The man turned in the chair. "You let me ride out of here. I know I can make it worth your while."

"You're wrong. Stroud made me take an oath when I pinned on this badge. If I hadn't, you'd be dead right now." Barney Houseman looked at him blankly. "We've never met, but I've heard of you. I'm Kilkenny."

Houseman's eyes narrowed, and his knuckles stood out white where he gripped the chair. "All right," he croaked. He struggled to get his lame foot under him as he stood. Awkwardly, he reached down to steady himself against the chair—and pulled a short-barreled Colt Lightning from a hideout holster!

Kilkenny stepped back and Houseman's gun roared, the slug catching him across the front of the shoulder. He shot, but he was already falling and the bullet went wild. Houseman frantically pulled the trigger three more times as Kilkenny scrambled for cover behind the table, hot lead catching him again, this time in the thigh. His gun was gone, the room full of powder smoke.

Houseman slammed out the door and half fell into the road. He headed for Main Street, reloading. Kilkenny was wounded, maybe dying. They had to move quickly but, he consoled himself, they had done it before and it was time. This had been a good bet, but he knew when his time was up. He had always known. The others had stayed behind at Bannock and at Dodge and other places. He pulled stakes before the Vigilance Committees and United States marshals got wind of him. He had always moved when the time was ripe. It was ripe now.

Hillman had just opened his store when Houseman limped across Main Street and followed him inside. "Open the safe,

Hill," Turner said, "we're getting out. I've just had a shoot-up with Kilkenny."

Hillman looked incredulous, and the limping man shrugged. "I'm not crazy. That gunfighter Lance—he was Kilkenny. I should have remembered. He's used the name before.

"We've got to move! Get the safe. He's in no shape, but people heard the shots and he'll get help."

The look in Hillman's eyes stopped him. Hillman was looking in back of him, over his shoulder.

Houseman turned and stared, his hands hanging. Kilkenny stood in the doorway, his chest covered with blood from the still-oozing cut across collarbone and shoulder. Standing silent in the doorway he was a grim, dangerous figure, a looming figure of vengeance.

Hillman drew back. "Not me, Kilkenny. I'm out of it. He's made life hell for all of us, Barney has. He's made us all do his dirty jobs. And I won't move on to rob another town."

Kilkenny did not speak. He was squinting his eyes against the pain. He could feel the blood trickling down his stomach. He was losing a lot of blood, and he had little time.

Barney Houseman was a murderer many times over. He was a thief and a card cheat, but always he had let his brother and uncle carry the burden of suspicion while he handled the reins. In Dodge they had believed it was he who left Kilkenny's saddle partner dead in an alley with a knife in his back.

Kilkenny had long given up the chase, but his memory was good.

The limping man . . . Barney Houseman.

"I beat you just now," Barney said, "I'll do it again." His hand went down for the gun and grasped the butt, and then Kilkenny took a step forward, his gun sprang to his fist, and something slapped at Barney's pocket. He was angry that anything should disturb him now. He started to lift his gun, and something else slapped him and he suddenly felt very weak and he went down, sinking away, and saw the edge of the table go by his eyes. Then he was on his back, and all he could see was a crack in the ceiling, and then the crack was gone and he was dead.

Hillman twisted his big-knuckled hands. "He was my nephew," he said, "but he was a devil. I was bad, but he was worse."

Kilkenny asked him then, "Who is Laurie Archer?"

"My daughter."

Kilkenny walked back through the street and people stared at him, turned when he passed, and stared after. He walked up to the jail, and Laurie stood on the steps. Her face was drawn and pale. "Can I see him now?"

"Yes," he said. Then he added, "Barney's dead."

She turned fiercely, her eyes blazing. "I'm glad! *Glad!*"

"All right." He was tired and his head ached. He wanted to go back to the hotel and wash up and then sleep for a week, and then get a horse, and—

He indicated the man on the bed inside. "You're in love with Stroud?"

"Yes."

"Then go to him. He's a good man."

Kilkenny turned around and started back up the street, and the morning sun was hot on his shoulder blades and there were chickens coming out into the street, and from a meadow near the creek, a smell of new-mown hay. He was tired, very tired . . . rest . . . and then a horse.

MONUMENT ROCK

Chapter 1

L ONA WAS AFRAID of him. She was afraid of Frank
Mailer, the man whom she was to marry. She realized
that it was not size alone that made her afraid of him, but
something else, something she saw in his blue, slightly
glassy eyes, and the harshness of his thin-lipped mouth.

He was big, the biggest man she had ever seen, and she
knew his contempt for smaller men, men of lesser strength
and lesser will. He was five inches over six feet and weighed
two hundred and fifty pounds. Whenever he stood near her,
the sheer mass of him frightened her and the way he looked
at her made her uneasy.

Her father looked up at him as he came in. "Did you get
that north herd moved before the rain set in?"

"Yeah." Mailer did not look up, helping himself to two
huge slabs of beef, a mound of mashed potatoes, and liberal
helpings of everything else. He commenced his supper by
slapping butter on a thick slice of home-made bread and taking an enormous bite, then holding the rest of it in his left
hand, he began to shovel food into his mouth with his right.

Between bites he looked up at Poke Markham. "I saw the
Black Rider."

"On our range?"

"Uh-huh; just like they were sayin' in town, he was ridin'
the high country, alone. Over toward Chimney Rock."

"Did you get close to him? See what he looks like?"

"Not a chance. Just caught a glimpse of him over against
the rocks, and then he was gone, like a shadow. That horse of
his is fast." Mailer looked up and Lona was puzzled by the
slyness in his eyes as he looked at her father. "You know

what the Mexican boys say? That he's the ghost of a murdered man."

The comment angered Markham. "That's foolishness! He's real enough, all right! What I want to know is who he is and what he thinks he's doin'."

"Maybe the Mex boys are right. You ever see any tracks? I never did, an' nobody else that I ever heard of. Nobody ever sees him unless it is almost dark or rainin', an' then never more than a glimpse."

"He's real enough!" Markham glared from under his shaggy brows, his craggy face set in angry lines. "Some outlaw on the dodge, that's who he is, hangin' out in the high peaks so he won't be seen. Who's he ever bothered?"

Mailer shrugged. "That's the point. He ain't bothered anybody yet, but maybe he wants one certain man." Mailer looked up at Poke, in his malicious way. "Maybe he's the ghost of a murdered man, like they say, an' maybe he's tryin' to lure his murderer back into the hills."

"That's nonsense!" Markham repeated irritably. "You'll have Lona scared out of her wits, ridin' all over like she does."

Frank Mailer looked at her, his eyes meeting hers, then running down over her breasts. He always made her uncomfortable. How had she ever agreed to marry him? She knew that when he drank he became fiercely belligerent. Nobody wanted to cross him when he was drinking. Only one man ever had tried to stop him when he was like that. Bert Hayek had tried it, and Bert had died for his pains.

His fighting had wrecked several of the saloons in town. All, in fact, except for the Fandango. Was it true, what they said? That Frank was interested in that Spanish woman who ran the place? Nita Howard was her name. Lona Markham had seen her once, a tall young woman with a voluptuous figure and beautiful eyes. She had thought her one of the most beautiful women she had ever seen. Lona's intended was often seen visiting with a beautiful woman who ran a saloon and gambling hall and Lona found she didn't care . . . not at all.

When supper was over Lona left hurriedly. More and more

she was avoiding Frank. She did not like to have him near her, did not want to talk to him. He frightened her, but he puzzled her, too. For more and more he seemed to be exerting authority here on the Blue Hill ranch, and more and more her father was fading into the background. People said that Poke Markham was afraid of no man, but of late she'd begun to wonder, for several times he had allowed Mailer to overrule him.

She crossed the patio through a light spatter of rain to her own quarters in the far wing of the rambling old house. Once there, she hung up her coat and crossed to the window, looking off over the magnificent sweep of land that carried her eyes away to the distant wall of the mountains in the southwest. It was over there the strange rider had been seen.

Suddenly, as if in response to her thoughts, a horseman materialized from the rain. He was out there, no more than a hundred yards from the back of the house, and scarcely visible through the now driving rain. As she looked she saw him draw up, and sitting tall in the saddle, he surveyed the ranch. Under his black flat-brimmed hat nothing of his face was visible and at that distance she could not make out his features. He was only a tall horseman, sitting in the rain, staring at the ranch house.

Why she did it, she never knew, but suddenly she caught up her coat, and running out into the rain, she lifted her hand.

For a moment they stared at each other and then suddenly the horse started to walk, but as he moved, the Black Rider raised a hand and waved!

Then he was gone. One instant he was there, and then he had vanished like a puff of smoke . . . but he had waved to her! Recalling the stories, she knew it was something that had never happened before. She returned to her room, her heart pounding with excitement. She must tell Gordon about that. He would be as surprised as she was. In fact, she paused, staring out at the knoll where the Rider had stopped, Gordon Flynn was the only one who seemed to care much what she thought or how she felt. Gordon, and of course, Dave Betts, the broken-down cowhand who was their cook.

MAILER DROPPED INTO a big chair made of cowhide. He rolled a smoke and looked across at Markham. The old man was nodding a little, and it made Frank smile. Markham, if that's what he wanted to be called, had changed. He had aged.

To think how they all had feared him! All but he himself. All but Frank Mailer. Markham had been boss here for a long time, and to be the boss of men like Kane Geslin and Sam Starr was something, you had to admit. Moreover, he had kept them safe, kept them away from the law, and if he had taken his share for all that, at least he'd held up his end of the bargain. He was getting older now, and he had relinquished more and more of the hard work to Mailer. Frank was tired of the work without the big rewards; he was ambitious. Sure, they had a good thing going, but if one knew the trails, there were easy ways out to the towns and ranches, and a man could do a good job on a few banks, along about roundup time. It beat working for money, and this ranch was as good as his, anyway, when he married Lona.

Looking over at the old man, he began to think of that. Why wait for it? He could shoot the old man right now and take over. Still, it would be better to marry the girl first, but he was not ready for that. Not yet. He wanted to move in on that Spanish woman at the Fandango, first.

There was that bodyguard of hers to be taken care of. He did not like the big, dark man who wore two guns and always sat near her door, faithful as a watchdog. Yet it would pay to be careful. Webb Case had been a fairly handy man with a gun, and he had tried to push this Brigo into a gunfight, planning to kill him. From all accounts, it had taken mightily little of a push, but Webb's plans backfired and he took a couple of slugs and got planted out on Boot Hill.

He began to think of that bank at the Crossing. Four . . . no, five men. Geslin and Starr, of course, among them. Geslin was a lean, wiry man with a pale, hatchet face and white eyes. There was no doubt that he ranked among the fastest gunmen of them all, with Wes Hardin, Clay Allison, Bill Hickok, or Kilkenny.

The bank would keep the boys happy, for however much Poke Markham was satisfied with the ranch, his boys were not. Poke made money, but most of the men at Blue Hill ranch were not punchers. They were wanted, one place or another, and when they'd tired of cooling their heels, they'd leave. Frank Mailer wanted to take advantage of the situation before that happened. The bank should go for eight or nine thousand, and they could make a nice split of that. Four men and himself. That would be enough. Nobody would tackle a gang made up of Geslin, Starr, and himself, let alone the other two he would pick.

Thoughtfully, Frank Mailer considered Geslin. How would he stack up with Geslin? Or Starr? He considered it a moment, then shrugged. It would never happen. They were his men, and they had accepted him as boss. He knew how to handle them, and he knew there was a rivalry between Starr and Geslin. If necessary, he could play them off against one another. As for Poke, he intended to kill Markham himself when the time came.

He heaved himself out of his chair and stretched, enjoying the feeling of his powerful muscles. He would ride into town and have a talk with that Howard woman at the Fandango. He thought again of Jaime Brigo, and the thought bothered him. There was something about the big, silent man that disturbed him. He did not think of Lona. The girl was here when he wanted her, and he did want her, but only casually. His desire for Nita Howard was a sharp, burning thing.

———

THE FANDANGO WAS easily the most impressive place in Salt Creek, and finer than anything in Bloomington. In fact, finer than anything this side of Santa Fe. Nita Howard watched the crowd, well pleased. Her hazel eyes with tiny flecks of darker color were large and her lashes were long. Her skin was the color of old ivory, her hair a deep, beautiful black, gathered in a loose knot at the nape of her neck. Although her lips were full, slightly sensual, there was a certain wistful, elusive charm about them, and a quick, fleeting humor that made her doubly beautiful. She was a tall woman, somewhere just beyond thirty, but her body was strong, and graceful.

Standing in the door, she said, without looking down at the man in the tipped-back chair, "Any message, Jaime?"

The Yaqui gunman glanced up. "No, señorita, there is none. He has been seen this day near Monument Rock. You have seen the map."

Nita Howard relaxed. "Yes, I know. As long as he is well, we had best leave him alone."

"He is loyal. A long time ago Markham, he befriended the señor when he was wounded and in danger. The señor does not forget. So he comes here. And you come here; so this means I do, too." Brigo shrugged. "We are all loyal to one another, but for now you must trust that our friend knows what he is doing."

The door opened suddenly and Frank Mailer stepped into the room; behind him were Kane Geslin and Sam Starr with another man known as Socorro. Mailer's eyes brightened with satisfaction when he saw Nita and he turned abruptly and walked toward her.

How huge he was! Could anything ever stop this man if he became angered? Nita watched him come, her mind coolly accepting the danger but not disturbed by it. Her father had died long ago and left her the doubtful legacy of a tough saloon on the Rio Grande border. She had directed its fortunes herself, with Brigo at her side, he who loved her like his own sister, and all because of her father's friendship to him.

Mailer stopped before her, his hard eyes surveying Nita with appreciation. "You're all woman, Nita!" he said. "All woman! Just the kind I've been lookin' for!"

She did not smile. "It is said around town that you are to marry Lona Markham."

Mailer was irritated; there was no reason to think of Lona now and he disliked the subject being brought up. "Come on!" he said impatiently. "I'll buy a drink!"

"Good!" she said smoothly. Lifting her eyes, she glanced over at the bartender. "Cain"—the big bartender glanced up sharply—"the gentleman is buying a drink." Her eyes turned to Mailer. "You meant you were buying for the house, did you not?"

Crimson started to go up Mailer's neck. He had meant nothing of the kind, yet he'd been neatly trapped and he had the feeling that he would appear cheap if he backed out. "Sure," he said grudgingly, "for the house! Now come on." He reached for her arm. "You drink with me."

"Sorry, I do not drink. Cain will serve you." She turned and stepped through the door, closing it behind her.

Frank Mailer's eyes grew ugly. He lunged toward the door at the end of the bar.

"Señor." Brigo was on his feet. "The señorita is ver' tired tonight. You understand?"

Mailer glared at Brigo, but the Yaqui's flat dark face was expressionless. Mailer turned on his heel and walked to the bar in baffled fury.

The big bartender finished pouring the drinks, then looked over at Mailer. "That'll be thirty bucks," he said flatly.

His jaws set, Mailer paid for the drinks. Geslin was in a game with several others. One of them was a red-haired puncher, stocky and tough-looking. Mailer dropped into an empty chair and bought chips.

At the end of the third hand the redheaded puncher looked up at him. "Mailer, don't you ramrod that Blue Hill spread? I'm huntin' for work."

Frank Mailer's eyes slanted to the redhead. He was a tough, capable-looking man with hard, steady eyes. He packed his gun low. "You been anywhere I might've heard about?"

"I rode for Pierce an' for Goodnight."

"Then I can use you, all right." With the riding he planned to do with Geslin and the others, he would need a few good hands. Also, unless his guess was altogether wrong, this man had ridden the owl hoot himself. "Texas man, hey?"

"Big Bend."

"Know Wes Hardin?" Mailer asked. "I hear he's fast."

"Plenty, an' with both hands. Maybe as fast as Kilkenny."

"Kilkenny?" Geslin turned his white eyes toward the redhead. "You say he's faster than Hardin? Did you ever see Hardin?"

"Uh-huh." Rusty Gates picked up his cards. "I seen Kilkenny, too."

All eyes were on him now. Men who had seen Kilkenny to know him were few and far between. The strange drifting gunfighter had a habit of appearing under various names and nobody ever really knew who he was until suddenly there was a blaze of guns and then he was riding out of town. "What's he like?" Mailer asked.

"Fast."

"I mean, what's he look like?"

"Tall, black hair, green eyes that look right through you when he's riled up. Quiet feller, friendly enough mostly."

"Is it true what they say? That he's killed forty or fifty men?"

Gates shrugged. "Doubt it. A friend of his told me it was no more than eighteen. An' he might have been exaggeratin'."

Hours later, when the game had broken up, Rusty Gates crossed to the bar for one last drink. The others had started back to the ranch and he was to come out the following day. He accepted his drink, and Cain grinned at him and shoved his money back. "I got the job," Gates said.

"Good!" Cain nodded emphatically. "I'll tell the boss."

BRIGHT SUNLIGHT LAY across the Blue Hill when Lona left the house the following morning. Frank Mailer had gone out early, and her father was fussing over some accounts in his office. Yet the night had neither lessened her curiosity nor changed her mood, and she started for the corral to catch up a horse, believing the hands were all gone.

The ranch lay between two peaks with its back to the low bench where Lona had seen the Black Rider on the previous night. These peaks lifted five hundred feet or so above the ranch house, and it was from one of them that the ranch had taken its name. The ranch house faced northwest, and off to the right, also running toward the northwest, lay the Old

Mormon Trail to Utah. Beyond the trail the cliffs lifted high, and at one point a crown of rock reached out to need no more than a half mile to join the twin peaks at Blue Hill.

She had reached the corral when she heard a boot scuff stones and turned to face a strange, redheaded puncher who grinned at her in a friendly fashion. "Can I help, ma'am? I'm Rusty Gates, a new hand."

"Oh, would you? I was going to saddle my horse. The black mare."

Gates nodded. "I been studyin' that mare, ma'am. She's sure all horse."

He shook out a loop and caught the black. As the rope settled, the mare stood still, and when she saw Lona she even walked toward the gate. Rusty led the horse outside and glanced at Lona. She was very young, very pretty, and had a trim, neat figure, auburn hair, and gray eyes. She caught his glance and he grinned. "Your hair's 'most as red as mine, ma'am," he said. "I reckon that makes us partners."

There was something so friendly in his manner that she warmed to him instantly. On impulse, she confided in him. "Rusty," she said, "don't you tell a soul what I'm going to tell you, but I'm going to see the Black Rider!"

Rusty gave her a sidelong, cautious glance. "To see him? How do you figure to do that?"

"I'm going to ride out and look along the ridges for him, then if I see him, I'll leave it up to Zusa to do the rest. She'll run him down if anything can."

Gates was silent. After a while he asked, "You ever see the Rider?"

"I saw him last night, right back on the bench in the rain. I waved to him, and he waved back! Isn't it exciting?"

She expected him to disapprove or to caution her, but strangely, he did not. He merely nodded, then said, "Ma'am, if I wanted to see that Black Rider, you know what I'd do? I'd head across the valley for Monument Rock, an' then if I saw him, I wouldn't take after him none at all. I'd just sit still an' wait."

"Wait?" Lona's eyes widened doubtfully. "You mean he might come up to me?"

Rusty chuckled. "Ma'am, they do say that the Rider's a ghost, but flesh and blood or ghost, if anything that *is* male or *was* male saw you settin' a horse waitin' for him, he'd sure come a-runnin'!"

She laughed. "Rusty, you're just like all the cowhands! Full of the old blarney!"

"Sure I am. But, ma'am"—his voice dropped a note lower and the look in his eyes was not a teasing look—"you do what I say an' see if it don't work. But," he added, "don't you ever tell anybody on this ranch I suggested it. Don't you tell."

"Thanks, Rusty. I won't." She turned to go and he caught her bridle rein.

"Ma'am," he said, "before you go . . . who's your best friend on this ranch? I mean, ma'am, somebody who really loves you."

Surprised, she looked down at him, but he was in dead earnest. The question brought her up short, too, for it made her wonder. Who were her friends? Did she have any?

Frank? She shuddered slightly. Her father? For a long time she hesitated. He had never been close to her, never since she returned from school. He had been strict and stern, had given her what she wanted, but allowed her little freedom. She realized suddenly that her father was almost a stranger to her.

"I . . . I guess I haven't many friends, Rusty," she said, in a small voice. "I guess . . . Dave, the cook, and Gordon."

Gates relaxed his grip. "Well, ma'am," he said, his voice thick, "I reckon you can count on another friend now. You can count on me. If ever you need a friend, I'd admire to have you call on me." He turned away, then stopped and turned, glancing up out of his bright blue eyes. "Maybe you've got more friends than you realize, ma'am."

Lona turned the mare up the trail to the bench, and drawing up, she looked carefully around. There were no tracks!

A curious little thrill of fear went through her. Was it possible the stories were true? Had it been a ghost who waved at her? The rain could have wiped them out, of course, and there was much rock. She rode on, cutting diagonally across toward the Old Mormon Trail, which would make for easier riding until she had to leave the trail and ride across the rough grass country toward the high cliffs at Monument Rock.

North and east of her, the cliffs made a solid barrier that seemed to cut off the world from this valley, cliffs from four hundred to nine hundred feet high, a dark barrier of dull red now, with the sun just showing above them. Yet that barrier was not as solid as it appeared, for there were a score of places where a horseman might find a way through, and there were, almost due east of the ranch, three canyons that branched like three spread fingers from a given point. The only one she knew was Salt Creek Wash, and only the first half mile of that. Her father had never liked her to ride up into those rugged mountains alone.

It was early spring, yet the air was warm and vibrant, clear as only desert air can be. The black mare felt good, and wanted to go, but Lona held her in, scanning the country ahead and around her, hoping to see the Black Rider.

She had been wrong to come in the morning, especially when it was clear, for he was never seen but at dusk or in the rain. Was there method in that? So that he would be impossible to follow for long? Dust arose from her horse's hoofs and she rode on until the cliffs began to rise above her and the sun was not yet high enough to show above their serrated rim. She reined in and looked up at their high battlement crest, then let her eye travel along it, but she saw no horseman, nothing but the rock itself.

What she had expected, she did not know. If she had expected her presence to bring the Black Rider suddenly springing from the solid rock, she was mistaken. It was still here, and lonely. She had stopped with Zusa headed north, so she started on, walking her along the low slope that ended in the cliffs.

Ahead of her she knew the cliffs took a bend eastward and through the gap flowed the occasional waters of Salt Creek, but there was, she knew, another wash beside Monument Rock, so she followed along and entered a narrow opening that had rock walls lifting six hundred feet and more on either side of her. It was shadowy and cool and so still as to be almost unbelievable. She rode on, the canyon echoing to her horse's hoofs.

She drew up in a sort of amphitheater, the dark piñons clustering against the wall, and climbing it wherever a faint ledge gave precarious root hold. It was still here, and she drew up, her eyes wide and every sense alert. Even Zusa was on edge, for the mare's sensitive nostrils expanded and her eyes were wide and curious.

No sound disturbed the still afternoon. From the stillness she might have been sitting in a mighty cathedral, yet there was no cathedral so splendid or so tall as this, no man-made temple as grand or magnificent. And then Zusa's muscles twitched, and turning her head, Lona Markham looked straight into the eyes of the Black Rider!

He was about fifty yards away, his horse standing on a tiny knoll, outlined sharply against the green of the piñons behind him. The horse was a buckskin, a long-legged, magnificent animal, and the rider was tall, broad in the shoulder, and clothed in black trousers, a dark gray shirt, and a black Mexican-style jacket.

For an instant she might have turned and fled, so frightened was she, so startled by the horseman's unexpected appearance, but she sat her mare, her eyes wide and expectant, and then the buckskin started to walk down the knoll toward her.

Under the low flat brim of his black hat, the Rider's face was scarcely visible, and as he drew near she noticed that he wore two guns, tied down. He drew up suddenly and, to her relief, lifted a gloved hand and brushed his hat back.

She saw first that he was handsome, with a strong, rugged face, brown from wind and sun, and green eyes that had the look of the desert at their corners. "You are Lona?" he asked.

His voice was strong, clear, friendly. "Yes," she said, "how did you know my name?"

"I have known it for a long time," he said. "Why did you come here today?"

"Why, I . . ." She hesitated. "I was curious!" she said. "Just plain curious."

He chuckled, and she liked the sound. There was droll

humor in his eyes. "Don't blame you! From what I hear, a lot of folks are curious. How about Frank Mailer an' Poke Markham? Are they curious?"

"A little. I think Father is more curious than Frank."

At her use of the word *father,* he looked at her again. "You call him Father?" he asked.

"Why, of course! He *is* my father. What else would I call him?"

"I could think of a number of things," he said grimly. "Want to talk awhile?" he suggested suddenly. "No use you coming clear out here to see the strange rider and not getting to talk with him."

She hesitated, but he swung down, and so she dismounted. He took the bridle of her horse and ground-hitched them both on a patch of grass in the lee of a cliff where subirrigation kept the grass green. Then he took off his hat and walked toward her. He had dark curly hair and a quizzical humor in his eyes.

"Don't worry about this," he said, smiling at her. "I know this is a mighty lonely place for a girl to be talkin' to a stranger, but later you'll understand."

"What will I understand?" she said evenly. She was frankly puzzled by him and by his attitude. He had known her name, and he seemed to know something about her, but certainly there was nothing in his manner that would in any way offer a cause for resentment.

"Lots of things." He dug out the makings and dropped to a rock facing her. He was, she noticed, also facing the opening up which she had ridden. "How'd you happen to come here?"

"I heard you had been seen on the rims, and that I should come here and wait. Rusty, he's our new hand, told me that. Very mysterious, if you ask me!"

He grinned. "He's quite a guy, Rusty is. You can trust him."

"Oh, you know him?" She was startled.

"Rusty? If you ever need a friend, he's your man."

He drew deep on the cigarette. "You were away to school quite a while, weren't you? How old were you when you left?"

She looked at him seriously. "Oh, I was only five then.

Father sent me away to the sisters' school, said a ranch was no place to raise a girl who had so far to go. I mean, so many years in which to grow up. I used to return for vacations after I was fifteen. Once in a while, that is."

"I don't remember a lot of things from when I was five," he said casually. "Do you? I mean, do you remember your father very well?"

"Some things about him, but it's all sort of funny and mixed up. He was awfully good to me, I remember that. He was sort of sweet, too. I remember riding in a wagon for ever so long, and how he used to tell me stories about my mother—she died a year before we started west—and about the ranch that was waiting for us out here. The place where he had hoped to take my mother. He said he had taken it in my name, and it would always be mine."

"Has your dad changed much?"

She nodded. "Quite a lot. But he's had trouble, I guess. He never says much anymore, not to me, at least, and sometimes he acts sort of strange. But he's all right," she added hurriedly. "I love him."

He turned his green eyes full upon her and there was something so searching in those eyes that she was disturbed. "Is that wrong?" she asked indignantly. "To love your father?"

"No, it isn't." He threw down his cigarette and rubbed it out with his toe. "In fact, that's the way it should be. On the other hand, maybe this particular gent doesn't deserve loving." He looked over at her. "Lona, we've got to have more than one talk, I can see that. Some things I might want to tell you, you wouldn't want to believe now. Later you might.

"But first off, I want to ask you to mention meeting me to no one. Rusty would be all right, if you could do it where nobody could hear. Remember this: I'm your friend and you've got to trust me. You're in a position right now where you'll need friends, and badly!"

"Why do you say that?" she demanded.

"Haven't they talked to you about marryin' Frank Mailer?"

She nodded. "Yes, of course. Father wants me to marry him."

"You want to marry him?"

Lona hesitated. Why was this stranger asking all these questions? Who was he?

"No," she said honestly. "I don't."

"Then," he said, "you mustn't. No matter what they say or what they do," he insisted, "don't marry him! Don't refuse right out, just evade the issue. Find excuses . . . clothes you have to have, plans for the wedding, just anything. You won't have to delay it long, because I think there will be a lot happening and soon. If the worse comes to the worst, see Rusty. You can trust him, like I said."

He walked to the horses. "And can you meet me here again? The day after tomorrow?"

Lona hesitated. "Why should I? I don't know what you are talking about! These are all riddles and I have no idea why you say I may need friends, or why I should trust this new puncher! Or why I should either trust or listen to you!"

The Rider took a breath. "I don't blame you for that, but you must listen. You don't know it yet, but you're in trouble. Your marriage to Frank Mailer was planned a long time ago, Lona, before you ever heard of him, and it's bad! Plumb bad!"

"Something else I want you to do," he added. "I want you to think about the times when you were a youngster, before you ever went away to school. Every minute from now on I want you to think about that wagon trip. The way it started, everything that happened. The more you try to remember, the more it will come back. It's very important to you." He hesitated. "You see, I knew your mother."

"What?" She turned on him, wide-eyed. "You knew . . . ? But why didn't you tell me?" Then suddenly she hesitated. Her eyes were suddenly frightened. "You . . . what did you know about her?"

"That she was a mighty fine woman, Lona. You look a lot like her, too. Yes, she was mighty fine. One of the sweetest, finest women I ever knew. I knew your father in those days, and he was a fine man."

"Why don't you come to see him, then?" she said, frowning at him.

He hesitated. "Lona, that man is not your father. He is no

relation to you at all. There never was a 'Poke' Markham! Isiah Markham was your father. That man down there is Poke Dunning, a onetime gunfighter and outlaw from the Big Bend country. I don't know what it is he's doing here, but I aim to find out! Your father was once a friend to me when I needed him. That's why I, now, am a friend to you."

Chapter 2

A T THE CORRAL bars she slid from the saddle as if stunned, then stood for a long time, staring at the far blue line of the cliffs from which she had just come.

Poke Markham was not her father!

The thought stood stark and clear in her mind, written across her consciousness in black, staring letters.

After the first minutes of stunned disbelief had come the uneasy memories which she had put aside and tried to forget. They came flooding into her mind. Little things and haunting details that had made her unhappy and puzzled.

The vague memories of her father before she went away to school had always been confused. Somehow she'd never been able to sort them out, to shape them into any plain picture. She knew now the reason for that confusion; it was that the memories of two individuals, two separate men, had mingled in her mind. This was why whenever she looked back to those years, the face of her father was always blurred, never sharp and clear.

The strange rider had said he was her real father's friend, that her mother had been a fine, sweet woman.

It was that last that flooded her mind with relief, for always when she had asked Poke Dunning about her mother, he had put her aside, evaded the issue, and so finally she had come to believe there was something shameful in her past, something in her story of which her father did not wish to be reminded. Lona had come to believe that her mother must have done something that had hurt and disgraced them both. Now she knew that was not true.

She knew?

Lona stopped at the thought, testing it, turning it over. Yes, she did know. The Rider was a stranger to her, and yet his voice had in it the ring of truth, and it was not only because she wanted so much to believe that her mother had been a fine, splendid woman, but simply because she knew it was the truth.

Now that the thought was there, a thousand minute details of the past came flooding back. Now she no longer had to fight the idea that she detested the man she had believed was her father. Always she had made excuses for him, avoided the question of his character and his little cruelties. Now she could face it, and she could wonder that she had ever believed him to be her father.

She remembered how few his letters had been, how she had never had from him any of the love or affection she wanted or that other girls had, how she had returned home on her first vacations with eagerness and then with increasing reluctance.

Stripping the saddle from the mare, Lona turned her into the corral. It was already past mealtime, and the hands were gone again. Rusty Gates was nowhere around, nor did she see Poke or Frank. She walked to the house and looked into the kitchen. Old Dave Betts looked up and his red face wrinkled in a smile. "You're late, ma'am, but come on in. I saved you something and kept it hot for you."

"Thanks, Dave."

He put out the food on the kitchen table. He was already preparing the evening meal, getting a few things ready in order to save time later. He glanced at Lona. "You aren't sick, are you?" he asked anxiously.

"No, Dave. Just thinking." She started to eat, but despite the long ride in the fresh, clear air, she was not hungry. "Dave," she asked suddenly, "how long have you worked for . . . Father?"

If he noticed her hesitation, he gave no sign or it made no impression. "Most of six years, ma'am. I come up to this country from Silver City. Went to Cimarron first, worked in a eatin' place there, then went back to punchin' cows for the XIT, then drifted back west an' come here. Poke Markham needed a cook, so I hired on. I was gettin' too stove up for ridin' much."

"Was Frank with him then?"

"Mailer?" Betts's face became cautious. "Well, no. No, ma'am, he wasn't. Frank didn't show up until shortly before you come home from school. He rode in here one day with Socorro an' they both hired on. Mailer, though, he'd knowed your dad somewhere else. That's why he hired him on as foreman."

"Is he really a gunman?" Lona looked up at Dave.

Betts swallowed uneasily and, stepping to the door, peered into the dining room, then outside. "I reckon there's no mystery about that. He sure is. Mighty bad . . . I mean, mighty good with a gun. So's Geslin." He looked at her quickly. "You better not ask many questions about him, ma'am. Mailer's right touchy about that. He don't like folks talkin' about him."

There was a sound of approaching horses and Lona glanced out the open door. Gordon Flynn and Rusty Gates had ridden into the yard and were swinging down. Flynn glanced toward the door, and when he saw her, he waved, then said something to Rusty and walked toward the house.

"Howdy, ma'am!" he said, his boyish face flushing a little. He had removed his hat and stood there, his wavy hair damp along his forehead where the hat had left a mark. The admiration in his eyes was obvious. "See you had been ridin' some. Why didn't you come over to the north range to see us?"

"Just riding," she said. "It was a pretty day for it and I wanted to think."

"I reckon there's no better way," he agreed. "It sort of just *makes* a body think, ridin' slow across the hills with lots of distance around you." He stepped into the room. "Dave, you got more of that coffee? Rusty an' me . . . ?"

"It ain't grub time," Dave said testily, "but you pull up a chair. I reckon I can do that for you, but I doubt if the boss would like either of you bein' here right now."

Rusty came into the room and took a quick, sharp look at Lona. He seemed satisfied with what he saw, and turned to

Dave. "We have to go down to Yellow Butte after some cows and this was on our way. Drink up, Gord, and don't sit there looking calf-eyed at Miss Lona."

Flynn blushed magnificently. "Who's lookin' calf-eyed?" he demanded, blustering. "Can't a man speak to a girl without folks sayin' things like that?"

Gates turned a chair back to the table and straddled it, grinning from one to the other. "Don't know's I blame you," he said. "She's a right pretty girl, and believe you me, if I was as good-looking as you are and not so durned bowlegged, I'd sure say my piece, too!"

Flynn's face was grim. "You're new around here," he said. "Miss Lona is engaged to the foreman."

Gates shrugged and looked pointedly at Lona. "When did a man ever let a thing like that stand between him and the girl he wanted? It sure wouldn't stop me!"

"Don't you be advisin' that sort of thing!" Betts turned irritably to Gates. "You don't know Frank Mailer! Anybody who steps on his toes or tries to move in on his girl had better be fast with a gun! He durned near killed one of the hands with his fists and boots just for talkin' to her!"

"Then I'll be careful," Gates said. Gulping his coffee, he shoved back from his chair and got up. "I just wouldn't let him catch me. But if I wanted a girl, I wouldn't stand by and see her go to another man, unless I was right sure she wanted that other man." He turned on his heel and walked out, letting the door slam behind him.

The kitchen was silent. Flynn was staring into his cup, and Lona's heart was pounding, why she could not have said. Glancing up, she could see the stubborn, angry look on Flynn's face and the sharp disapproval on the face of Dave Betts. After a minute Flynn swallowed his coffee and ducked out without saying another word.

Lona gathered the dishes and placed them on the drain board, stealing a glance at Betts's face from the corner of her eye. "You be careful," Dave said suddenly, without turning. "You don't know Frank Mailer like I do. Don't you let no fool puncher talk you into trouble."

Lona hesitated. "What's the matter, don't you think Gordon is a nice fellow?"

Dave Betts turned sharply. "I sure do, ma'am. Flynn's one of the finest boys I know, an' he's a top hand, too. He's worth any four like Geslin or Starr, but he's too nice a boy to see shot to doll rags, ma'am, or to see stomped to bloody ruin like I've seen men stomped right here on this ranch!"

———

THE CANYON WHERE Lona had come upon the Black Rider had several branches, all box canyons. There was, however, a trail to the rim if one knew the way and rode a good mountain horse. Not far up this steep trail there was a ledge that made a sharp turn around a jutting corner of rock. Here, in an almost hidden corner of rock, was a wide shelf, all of fifty yards across and something more in length. It was concealed from the canyon below by piñons, so that from below one would believe the cliff was unbroken. From above, due to a steep slide that broke off in the sheer drop, there was no way of approaching the ledge or looking down into the rocky niche.

Here, in this secret place, was good green grass and a thin trickle of water from a spring. At the back end of the niche was a deep undercut in which cliff dwellers had built several houses, walling part of the undercut with stone. In this hidden place the Rider had his retreat.

Dismounting, he stripped the saddle and bridle from the horse and let it go on a long picket rope. There was grass enough here, and water. From the look of the place, it had never been visited since the Indians had gone, yet one never knew. No better hiding place could be found, and here, he hoped, he was secure.

His rides over the country had given him a fair knowledge of the lay of the land, and he had been watching the Blue Hill ranch through his glasses and knew the daily procedure, yet despite the progress he had made that day in his talk with Lona Markham, he was restless, and he knew why. He wanted to see Nita.

She should never have come here, he knew. He had tried to

convince her that the job was his alone, but she would have none of it, and in the end he had given in. He was pleased now that he had, for his restlessness was in a sense appeased by knowing her nearness. Once it had been decided that she was to come, Brigo, of course, had come, too. Jaime Brigo had been asked by Nita's father to watch over her, and that was an oath he had never broken.

Cain Brockman, the bartender, doubled Nita's protection, and it had been simple enough for Rusty Gates to hire out to the ranch, which put one of their own men in the enemy's camp. Yet there was much to be done, even now.

That somehow Poke Dunning had taken Markham's place, taken his ranch and usurped his position as father was obvious. Yet what had become of Markham? And what had become of his wife, Lona's mother? Where did Poke fit in? Also, was there any evidence that the ranch actually belonged to Lona other than Markham's statement to her? It seemed that the mere fact that Dunning was carefully deceiving this young girl showed that he was convinced that the ranch he had been running all these years actually belonged to her. It also seemed that Poke Dunning had somehow gotten control of the ranch by posing as her father, an act made all the easier by the fact that no one in these parts had known the original Markham. For all anyone knew, Dunning was the man who had given her the property, but now he was planning on transferring legal control to Mailer by having the girl marry him. Once the wedding took place, Dunning would not have to worry about his charade, and if something happened to Lona, Mailer would inherit the ranch simply by being her husband.

Dunning would say nothing to Lona about her mother. Was that because he did not know? And Lona had said her father had told her that her mother had died before they came on west, but was that statement made by her real father, or by Dunning?

Before facing Dunning, it was necessary to learn how title to the ranch was placed, and to have something substantial to go on. In so many years Dunning had had time to shape stories and the papers that would give him title, yet why, if that was true, had he kept the girl?

Collecting dry sticks that would make no smoke, he built a fire, and squatting above it, the Rider prepared his evening meal. He was a tall man, and his eyes were green; a sharp, straight look came into them at times that disturbed those he looked at, and at times changed quickly to easy humor and a ready smile.

Shadows were long and his meal was finished when he heard a distant sound. He straightened swiftly and, hitching his guns into place, moved swiftly from the side of the cliff dwelling across the green sward of the ledge. His horse was standing with his head up and his nostrils wide. "Easy, Buck!" he said gently.

Through the junipers he could look down into the canyon, and as he looked he heard a tapping of metal on metal. He listened a moment, then grinned and spoke aloud, knowing his voice would carry in the still air. "Straight ahead and left around the boulder."

In a few minutes he heard the horse, and then Rusty Gates appeared. It was dusk, yet light enough to see, and the cowhand stared around him in astonishment. "Now, how in the ever-so-ever did you find this place?" he demanded. "A man would sure never guess it was here!"

"It's well hidden. Come on back, I've put more coffee on."

When they were squatted over the small fire, Gates grinned across the coals at him. "Kilkenny," he said, "you have the damnedest nose for hideouts of any hombre I ever knew!"

The tall rider shrugged. "Why not? Lots of times I need 'em. It gets to be an instinct."

"You talked to Lona?"

"Uh-huh. I didn't tell her much, only that Poke was not her father."

"I thought so. She was walkin' in a trance when she got back to the spread. By the way," he added, "there's a hand on that ranch that's so much in love with her he's turnin' in circles. Name of Gordon Flynn. Nice lad."

"Well, they can work that out by themselves. I'm goin' to see she gets justice, but I'll be durned if I'll play Cupid."

Rusty chuckled. "Leave that to me! I already put a bug in their ears." He pushed a couple of sticks on the fire. "Lance, something is building down there, but I don't know what. Mailer has been doin' a lot of talking, strictly on the private, with Geslin, Starr, and Socorro. I think they've got somethin' up their sleeves."

"Not Dunning?"

"No, the old man isn't in on it. They are very careful not to get bunched up when he's around."

"What do you think of Mailer, Rusty?"

"Damned if I know!" Gates looked up, scowling. "Good as Geslin is, he listens to him. So does Starr. I guess they knowed each other before comin' to Blue Hill, too. That Socorro came in with Mailer."

"How's Nita?" Kilkenny asked, looking up.

"I was wonderin' when you'd get around to that. She's fine. Man"—he chuckled—"that girl is good! She's got brains aplenty, but, Kilkenny, she's got troubles, too! Frank Mailer is makin' a strong play for her."

Lance Kilkenny got to his feet. "Mailer?" He was incredulous. "I thought he was due to marry Lona?"

Gates looked cynical. "How much difference would that make to a man like Mailer? He's mostly interested in that ranch, I'm thinking, as far as she's concerned, anyway. But he's red-eyed over Nita."

"Has there been trouble?"

"Not yet." Gates told what had happened at the Fandango and how Nita had handled it. "So he wound up spending thirty bucks he hadn't figured on. But that won't be the end of it."

"How do Dunning and Mailer stand?" Kilkenny asked thoughtfully.

"I've been thinkin' about that. From what I hear, they trusted each other at one time, but I think a break is due. One thing: when it comes down to it, the old man will be standing all alone. The boys are all with Mailer; that is, all but Flynn, the cook, an' me. We're on the outside of that fuss."

Gates got to his feet. "I'd better get out of here before the moon comes up." He turned to go, then hesitated. "Lance, you make no mistake, Frank Mailer is dangerous."

"Thanks. I'll remember that." He grinned over the fire at Rusty.

"Hope we beat this deal without a shootin'," Rusty said.

"Me, too," Kilkenny said, almost wistfully. "Especially with that girl around, that's a tough crowd down there."

Long after Rusty Gates was gone, Lance Kilkenny sat over his lonely fire. There had been too much of this, too much of hiding out in the wilderness, yet it was this or be recognized, and when he was recognized, there was always some wild-eyed puncher who wanted the reputation of killing Kilkenny.

He had never intended to gain a reputation, but his own choice of keeping himself anonymous had helped to begin the stories. He had become a strange, shadowy figure, a drifting gunfighter whom no man knew, until suddenly, in a blasting of gunfire, he wrote his name large across yet another page of western history.

Long ago he had taken to haunting the lonely places or to roaming the country alone under an assumed name. He would drift into a new country and for a time he would punch cows or wrangle horses or hire out as a varmint hunter, and then trouble would come, and Kilkenny, who had rarely drawn a gun in his own battle, would fight for a friend, as he was fighting now.

This time, for the first time, he was not fighting alone. He had friends with him, good friends, and he had Nita Riordan, now using the name Howard, for there were those who knew that Nita Riordan was connected with Kilkenny.

Alone over his fire, he studied the situation. What was in the mind of Frank Mailer? What did he plan? How much opposition could Poke Dunning offer, if it came to that? If it came to a fight over the ranch? Kilkenny was enough of a strategist to appreciate the fact that in a gunfight, Dunning and Mailer might eliminate each other and so save him the trouble. Once they were out of it, he could face the others or they would leave.

What he needed to know now was how Dunning had come into possession of the ranch. When Markham had started west so long ago, he was going to this ranch, which he had acquired sometime before. Hence, Dunning had to have come into the picture after Markham left Santa Fe. Also, he must learn whether Markham's statement to Lona that the ranch was now hers was merely an idle comment or whether he had actually given the girl the title.

Yet there was on him something else, a driving urge to see Nita. He got to his feet and walked the length of the ledge, speaking softly to the buckskin, and then he walked back. The fire was dying, the embers fading. Maybe now was the time, if he could slip into Salt Creek quietly and get to the Fandango without noise. He turned the idea over in his mind, contemplating every angle of it. At last he shook his head, and replenishing the fire, then banking the coals, he crawled into his blankets and was soon asleep.

———

OLD POKE DUNNING got restlessly to his feet. He was alone much of the time now. Lona had been keeping to her quarters and he missed her. Scowling, he thought of that, and his eyes narrowed as he remembered the time of her marriage was coming nearer. That marriage was a deal that he had cooked up with Frank Mailer. But since that time he had come to distrust the man. Soon after he made his offer to guarantee them clear title to Blue Hill, Frank had started acting like he owned the place. Suppose Mailer made up his mind to go it alone? He, Dunning, would have no status, nothing that would stand up legally. Of late, Mailer had been making decisions without consulting him.

If he had it out with Mailer, he decided, he would need an edge. Only a fool would take chances with Mailer. The man was too big, too tough. He looked as hard to stop as a bull elephant.

That Rider. The presence of the Rider might not bother Mailer, but it did bother him. He was suspicious and could find no reason for the man's continual evasion of contact with anyone.

The Black Rider must have provisions. How did he obtain them? The logical place was Salt Creek. Poke nodded; that was it. He would have a spy watching in Salt Creek, and then when someone resembling the Rider appeared, he would trail him. After that he would have a line on the man.

It was late, but he would ride into Salt Creek now and he knew just the man. The road was white in the moonlight, but Dunning rode swiftly on a powerful gray. He had not seen Mailer, and no doubt the man was again in town, and the boys with him.

Although well past fifty, Dunning was a strong and rugged man in the peak of condition. Age was no problem to him as yet, for his outdoor life and the rough, hearty food of the frontier had kept him in fine shape. He had made vast improvements on the ranch and it had provided a welcome cooling-off place for men on the dodge, as he once had been.

He had always insisted that the boys not pull any jobs while they "worked" for him, and while he paid all his men monthly, those on the run had handed back far more than their salaries in private. He also insisted that his hands not spend any of their ill-gotten gain in town or do anything that would indicate who and what they actually were. The kickbacks and free labor he had availed himself of over the years had helped make Blue Hill a profitable enterprise. Poke Dunning took great pride in the ranch. There was just Mailer and that matter of the girl and the confounded deed!

Salt Creek was a rough-looking town of some three-score buildings of which most were homes and barns. Along the one street of the town, a dozen or more buildings stared at each other, and the express office and Fandango were the biggest buildings in town. The Express, as it was known, was much more than its name implied. It was a general store as well as the post office and office of the justice of the peace, and had a small bar where drinks were sold, mostly to the older men in the community.

Up the street only two doors was another saloon, this one run by Al Starr, a brother of Sam, and beyond it another store and the livery stable, and beyond that the Fandango. It was ablaze with light when Poke Dunning rode the gray into town, but he stopped at the Express and shoved through the door.

Aside from Mr. Lisa, the Portuguese proprietor, only three men were in the Express. A couple of oldsters who were dry-farming near town, and the man Dunning sought, a hanger-on known about town as Kansas.

Kansas was more than a loafer, he was a man of unknown background and capacity. What his life had been in the years before he arrived in Salt Creek, nobody knew. He had a wife, and the two lived in a small cabin on the edge of town. It was nicer inside than most houses, for Kansas seemed to have a knack with tools, and he had even varnished the furniture and there were curtains in the windows and neatness every-where. Moreover, Kansas had a dozen books, more than the rest of the town combined.

Yet he was a loafer, a short, heavy man with a round face and somewhat staring eyes who did odd jobs for his money. He smoked a corncob pipe, blinked like an owl, and had a faculty for knowing things or knowing how to find out. He had been in the War Between the States, and someone said he had once worked on a newspaper in the East. His conver-sation was more varied than customary in Salt Creek, for he knew something more than cows and the range. In fact, he knew a little of everything, and was nearly as old as Dunning himself.

"Howdy, Kansas!" Dunning said affably. "Have a drink?"

"Right neighborly of you, Poke! B'lieve I will!" He let the dark-faced Lisa pour his drink, then looked over at Dunning. "We don't see you much anymore. I guess you leave the business mostly to Mailer."

"Some things," Dunning agreed. It was the truth, of course, that Mailer had been doing the business, yet it nettled him to hear it said. "Any strangers around town?" he asked casually.

To Kansas, the question was not casual. He could not re-call that Poke Markham had ever asked such a question be-fore, and he was aware that the conversation of people will usually follow certain definite patterns. Hence it followed that the remark was anything but casual and that Markham was interested in strangers, or some particular stranger.

"Not that I know of," Kansas replied honestly enough. "Not many strangers ever come to Salt Creek. Being off the stage route and miles from the railroad, it doesn't attract folks. Were you expecting somebody?"

"No," Dunning replied, "not exactly." He steered the conversation down another trail and let it ride along for a while before he opened up with another question. "I expect like ever'body else you've seen that Black Rider they talk about," he suggested.

"Can't say I have," Kansas replied. So old Markham was forking that bronc, was he? What was on his mind, anyway? There was a point behind these questions, but Kansas could not place it.

"I've got my own ideas about him," he added, "an' I'd bet a little money they are true."

"What sort of ideas? You know who he is? Why he's here?" Poke was a little too anxious and it showed in his voice. Kansas needed some extra money and this might be the way to get it.

"Oh, I've been studyin' on it."

The two oldsters had started for the door and Lisa was opening a barrel of flour. Poke Dunning leaned closer to Kansas. "You find out who he is and I'll make it worth your while."

"How much is my while worth?" Kansas asked.

Poke hesitated, then dug into his jeans. "Twenty dollars?"

It was a talking point, but Kansas decided he might get more. He never accepted a man's first offer. "Make it fifty," he said.

"Too much." Poke hesitated. "I'll give you thirty."

Kansas sighted through his glass. "All right," he said, "I'll find out for you."

"What was your hunch?" Dunning wanted to know.

Kansas hesitated. "You seen this Nita Howard over to the Fandango?"

"Not yet."

"You take a good look. I think she's Nita Riordan."

The name meant nothing to Dunning and he said as much. Kansas turned his head toward Dunning. "Well, Nita Riordan is associated with Kilkenny. He met her down on the border during that wire war in the Live Oak country. Then she was with him over to the Cedars in that ruckus."

"Kilkenny . . ." Dunning's eyes narrowed as he half spoke, half gasped the word. Now, there was a thought! Why, if he could hire Kilkenny . . . ! When the split came with Mailer, it would pay to have the mysterious gunman on his side.

He scowled suddenly. "Why would he be here? What would he be doin' here?"

Kansas shook his head. "What he's doing here, I don't know. But Kilkenny keeps to himself like this Rider does. Moreover, the Howard woman at the Fandango calls her bartender Cain, an' Cain Brockman was with Kilkenny in that last fuss."

Dunning peeled a couple of twenties from a buckskin-wrapped roll of them and slapped them in the man's hand. "If you can get word to him, I'll give you another thirty. I want to see him on the quiet, an' don't let it get around, you hear?"

Kansas nodded, and Poke Dunning walked out and stopped on the step.

Kilkenny! If it were only he! But maybe he wouldn't take the job; there were stories that Kilkenny's gun was not for hire. That was sure nonsense, of course; any man's gun could be hired for enough money, and he had the money. To be rid of Mailer it would be worth plenty.

———

LONA WAS UP at daybreak, having scarcely slept a wink. She had followed the Rider's instructions and tried to recall all she could of the ride on the wagon, but it was little enough. She recalled the town where the fat lady had been so nice to her and where she had given her maple sugar brought out from Michigan in a can. There had been Indians there, and a lot of people. She was sure that town was Santa Fe.

She waited until the hands were gone and then got a hurried breakfast from Dave Betts. "Rusty?" Betts asked. "Sure, I know where he went. He went south, down to Malpais Arroyo. Mailer sent him down there to roust some stock out of that rough country an' start it back thisaway."

Zusa was ready and eager to go, and Lona let the mare run.

She was curious to talk to Gates again, for she was sure now that he knew who the Rider was. Though he seemed young, the Rider had known her father. Maybe Rusty would know.

She found him by as fine a flow of profanity as she had ever heard. He was down in the brush fighting an old ladino who had Rusty's rope on his horns but who had plunged into the brush even as the rope snagged him, and at the moment it was a stalemate, with Gates venting his irritation in no uncertain terms.

"Hi!" she called. "Having trouble?"

He shoved his hat back on his sweaty forehead and grinned at her. "That goll-durned, ornery critter!" he said. "I got to get him out of here, and the durned fool wants to stay! You just wait, I'll show him!" Rusty eased his horse sideways and then loosened his rope from the saddle horn. Before the steer could back up any farther into the brush, he whipped the rope around the stub of an ancient tree and tied it off. "There!" he said. "We'll just let him sit for a while."

Rusty walked over to her, his eyes curious, but if he had a question, Lona beat him to the draw. "Rusty, who is the Black Rider?"

Gates wrinkled his nose at the fancy name. "He'll tell you, ma'am, when he's ready, and he's the one to do it."

"But how could he have known my father?"

Rusty looked up quickly. "Ma'am, how he knew your father, I don't exactly know, only it seems to be your pa helped him when he was a kid and havin' it tough. I guess your pa talked a good bit about his plans. He only found out a short time ago that your pa was dead an' that there might be trouble here. Naturally, bein' the man he is, he had to do somethin' about it."

The sound of a horse made them both look up, and Lona felt herself grow pale as she saw Frank Mailer!

"Lona!" His voice was hoarse with anger. "What's goin' on here? What are you doin', meetin' this puncher down here?"

"I'm talking to him!" she flared. "Why shouldn't I? He works for me! And it might be a good idea," she added with spirit, "for you to remember that you work for us, too!"

Frank Mailer's face stiffened and his eyes narrowed. "You seem to forget that you are the girl I'm to marry," he said, in a tone less harsh. "Naturally, I don't want you around like this."

"Well, until we are married," she said coldly, "it happens to be none of your business! If you'd like to change your mind, you may. In fact, I don't like your bullying tone and I think I've changed *my* mind!"

Frank Mailer was furious. He glared, struggling for speech. When he did speak it was to roar at Gates. "Get that steer out of that brush, you blamed farmer! Get it out an' you get them cows back to the ranch, pronto!"

Rusty Gates calmly went to work freeing the steer. Lona and Zusa started out of the arroyo. "Wait!" Mailer shouted. "I want to talk to you!"

She turned in her saddle. "Until you learn how to act like a gentleman, I haven't got a thing to say!"

Touching a spur to the mare, she was gone like a streak. Frank stared after her, then swearing bitterly, he reined his horse around and rode away, ignoring Gates.

Chapter 3

FRANK MAILER WAS in a murderous mood when he returned to Blue Hill. He left his saddled horse to Flynn and went up the steps to the house. Poke Dunning was standing in front of the fireplace when Mailer stormed into the room.

"Poke!" Frank said. "I've had about enough out of that girl! She threw her weight around too much today! Let's fix that marriage for next week!"

Dunning was lighting his pipe and he puffed thoughtfully, his eyes on the flame. Here it was, sooner than he wanted it. Well, there was more than one way to stall.

"What's the matter? What did she say?"

"I found her down at Malpais with that new puncher. I told her I didn't like it and she told me it didn't matter whether I did or not, that I worked for her! For her!"

Dunning chuckled. "Well, in a way she's right!" he said slyly. "This here is her ranch. And you're the foreman."

Mailer's eyes narrowed vindictively and he felt hot rage burning inside him. There were times when he hated Dunning. He glared at him. "I'm a damn sight more than any foreman!" he flared.

"Are you?" Dunning looked up under shaggy brows. His hands were on his hips, whether by accident or design, but his eyes were cool and steady.

Frank Mailer felt everything in him suddenly grow still. He turned on Dunning, and with a shock, he realized something he had been forgetting, that Poke Dunning was a gunman himself, and that he was not, by any means, too old. Right now he looked like a fairly dangerous proposition, and Mailer found that he did not like it, he did not like it one bit. He felt sure he could beat Poke, but he might get a slug in the process, and tomorrow they would be leaving on that job.

No fight . . . not now.

"What's the matter, Poke? You on the prod?"

Dunning recognized the change in Mailer's tone and it puzzled him. He knew the big man too well, yet here, with an even break between them, or almost an even break, for Dunning all but had the butts of his guns in his hands, Mailer was avoiding the issue. It puzzled Dunning, and worried him. He had known Mailer too long not to know the man was a schemer.

"No, Frank, I'm not," he said quietly. "Only here lately you've been taking in a little too much territory. We have our plans, but we can't ride into this roughshod. That girl has a mind of her own, and suppose she lights out of here to Salt Creek and raises hell about bein' forced to marry you? It might stir up some talk, an' we can't afford that.

"You've got to play it smart, Frank. You can't push Lona around; she's got too much fight in her. Take it easy, win her over. You can't handle a woman by shouting at her; they need soft talk."

There was truth in what Dunning said, and Mailer knew it. He was, he admitted, bullheaded. And he had been taking on a lot of weight around here. Anyway, first things come first, and there was that bank job to be handled. There would be time enough to take care of Dunning when that was off his hands. Geslin and Starr both wanted the money they would get from that job, and if he expected to keep them around, he must keep them busy, give them a chance to make a few dollars.

"Maybe you're right," he agreed. "It's a shame that Markham had to fix things that way."

"He did, though," Dunning said. "We don't dare take over until you marry her, then her property is legally yours an' we can do what we want."

"Sure, you've explained that," Mailer agreed grudgingly. He turned toward the door. "By the way, Poke," he said, in more affable tones, "I'm takin' some of the boys on a little trip tomorrow. I heard about some cattle and want to look them over. We'll be gone two days. Flynn and Gates will handle things on this end."

Dunning nodded absently. "All right. Good luck on the trip."

Outside on the porch, Frank Mailer stared angrily into the darkness. "We'll need it," he muttered. "And once I've married that girl, you'll need it!"

One thing he knew. The time was coming for a showdown. He would wait no longer. That Spanish woman, now . . . if he were owner of the Blue Hill, she would pay attention to him. She liked him, anyway, but was just stalling. That was always the woman's way, any woman. The fact that he would be married to Lona would matter but little. He would have things in his hands then, and he would know how to handle matters. Poke Dunning had to die.

———

LANCE KILKENNY WAS riding to Salt Creek. Despite his desire to remain unknown, he had missed Nita so much that he could no longer stay away. Also, with his instinct for trouble and his knowledge of the situation in Salt Creek and on the ranch, he knew the lid was about to blow off. It was high time that he appeared on the scene.

Yet reaching town, he did not ride immediately into the

street, but studied it carefully. He could see the lights of the Fandango, and nearer, the lights of Starr's Saloon and the Express. He rode the buckskin into the street and swung down in front of the Express.

He stepped up onto the boardwalk, feeling all that tightness he always knew when appearing for the first time in a strange town. His eyes slanted down the street, studying each building with strict attention. Every sense was alert for trouble, for a man who had used a gun as he had would have enemies, and in a strange town one never knew whom one would see.

The street was empty and still, its darkness alleviated only by the windows of the four or five lighted places in Salt Creek. He turned and opened the door to the Express and walked in.

Down the left-hand side was a row of boxes and sacks backed by a wall of shelves filled with various articles of cutlery and other tools. On his right were shelves of clothing, a few wide hats, and nearer the counter at the end was the ammunition, and beside it the bar. There were groceries and several opened barrels. Near a stove, now cold, sat two old men. At the bar Kansas was talking to Lisa.

Kilkenny walked down the right side of the long room whose middle was also stacked with boxes and barrels. As he approached the near end of the bar, Kansas looked up. In that instant the gunfighter knew he was recognized.

"Rye, if you would," Kilkenny said quietly. His eyes turned to Kansas, alert, probing. "What are you drinking, friend?"

Kansas's mouth was dry. He started to speak, swallowed, and then said, "Rye. Mine's rye, too, Lisa."

The Portuguese noticed nothing out of the ordinary, and put the glasses on the bar. His quick glance, however, noticed that the gray shirt was new and clean, the flat-brimmed hat was in good condition, and Kilkenny was clean-shaven. He left the bottle on the bar. He knew when a man could pay for his drinks.

Kansas recovered himself slightly. Here was his chance to do that job for Poke, dropped right in his lap. Luck seemed to be with him, but he reflected uneasily that Kilkenny did not have a reputation as the sort of man who would hire his gun. "Driftin' through?" he said.

"Maybe."

"Nice country around here."

"Seems so."

"There's jobs. Mailer, he's foreman out to the Blue Hill, he took on a hand the other day." He dropped his voice. "Poke Markham was talkin' to me. Seems he's huntin' a particular man for a very particular job. From the way you wear those guns, you might be just the man."

Kilkenny looked into his glass. Now, what was this? A trap? Or was Dunning looking for gunmen? "We might talk about it," he said. "I just might be interested."

Kansas was pleased and disappointed at the same time. He had heard much of Kilkenny, and while if he did this job for Poke, it might mean more money, which he could always use, he was sorry that Kilkenny would consider such a thing.

"Many folks in town?" Kilkenny asked quietly.

"A few. Mailer's here, if you're interested, but better not talk to him about this Markham job. I had the idea Markham was hiring someone confidential."

Kilkenny nodded. . . . So? Was there a break there? If so, it might work out very well for him. And Rusty had said Mailer was planning some move in which Dunning was not concerned. Maybe Poke knew more than Mailer realized.

"This Mailer," he said carelessly, "what sort of hombre is he?"

"Mighty big an' mighty bad," Kansas replied honestly. "He's hell on wheels with a gun an' ready to use one on the slightest provocation, but he would rather use his fists and boots. Sometimes I think he likes to beat a man." There was animosity in Kansas's voice, and Kilkenny noticed it at once.

"Where's he from?"

"You've got me," Kansas admitted. "Folks around here have done a lot of wondering about that. Where he came from or what he was, I don't know. Somebody did say they saw him talking to Port Stockton over to Bloomfield once."

Port Stockton was a name Kilkenny knew. Boss of the Stockton gang, marshal of Bloomfield, and formerly in the

Lincoln County War in the faction opposed to the Tunstall-McQueen outfit that had Billy the Kid. Stockton was no honest man, by all accounts, and a dangerous one. It was worth looking into, that angle.

He straightened. "You tell Markham I'll talk to him. I'll get in touch with him myself within the next couple of days." Turning, he walked to the door, scanned the street briefly, and then stepped out.

The Fandango was ablaze with lights, and Kilkenny did not hesitate; he walked at once to the doors and pushed them open. The place was crowded. Nita had a faculty for knowing the sort of place the range people liked, and she gave them lots of light and music. A half dozen card tables were going now, and the long bar was lined with booted and spurred men.

A few men in business suits mingled with the roughly dressed cowhands, but one and all they were wearing guns. The first person who saw him was Jaime Brigo, and the big Yaqui did not smile, merely reaching back with his knuckles and tapping a signal on the door.

Nita Riordan heard that signal. She was at her mirror, and for a minute she stared at her reflection. She had known Kilkenny now for more than three years, and had loved him every minute of them, but after one of these absences it never failed to leave her breathless when she heard his voice, his step, or heard the signal that signified his presence.

Kilkenny had walked to the end of the bar, and Cain Brockman moved at once to him and placed a glass and a bottle there. His head moved ever so slightly, and Kilkenny's eyes followed the movement. He saw Frank Mailer towering above the crowd, his face red and flushed from drinking, his glassy-blue and slightly protuberant eyes bold and domineering as they surveyed the crowd around him.

The slender hatchet-faced man would be Geslin, of course. Starr was there, and the sallow, dark-haired Socorro.

Mailer, Kilkenny observed, kept turning his head to glance toward the door where Brigo sat. Kilkenny studied him without seeming to, watching the man with the side of his glance. The fellow was a bull, but big as he was, there was no evidence of fat. Even his thick neck looked like a column of muscle; there was cruelty in the man's eyes and in his thin lips, and there was brutality showing all through him. Even without knowing who he was and why he was here, Kilkenny would have felt the same animal antagonism for the man.

Suddenly Nita was in the room. He knew it without turning his head. He would always know it, for there was that between them, that sharp, strong attachment, something physical and yet more than physical. He turned and their eyes met across the room and he felt something well up within him. She smiled, ever so slightly, and turned to the nearest card table, speaking to one of the players.

Frank Mailer had seen her, too, and he turned abruptly away from the bar. "So there you are!" he boomed. "Come and have a drink!"

"I don't drink. I believe I have told you that."

"Oh, come on!" he insisted, reaching for her arm. "Don't be foolish! Come on an' have a drink with me."

Suddenly Nita Riordan was frightened. Kilkenny had moved away from the bar; he was coming toward them.

"I'm sorry," she said coldly. "I'll not drink with you. Why don't you join your friends?"

Kilkenny was beside her now, but Mailer had eyes for nobody else. He had been waiting for this woman to come out, and he had been drinking, thinking of her, wanting her. He told himself she wanted him, and there had been enough of foolishness. "Come on!" he said roughly. "I want to talk to you!"

"But the lady does not want to talk to you!" Kilkenny said. Frank Mailer turned his big head sharp around. For the first time he saw Kilkenny. "Get lost!" he snarled. "Get . . . !"

What he was going to say never came out. He was seeing Kilkenny, really seeing him for the first time, looking into those hard green eyes, level and dangerous now, into the bronzed face of a man that he instinctively recognized as being something different, somebody new and perhaps dangerous. "Who the hell are you?" he demanded.

"The man who tells you the lady does not wish to talk to

you," Kilkenny said. He turned. "Miss Howard, do you wish to go to the bar?"

She turned instantly and started to go off with him. Mailer found himself left in the middle of the floor alone, and he had made his brags about this woman and himself. They had an understanding, he had hinted. In fact, he had convinced himself it was true. Somebody snickered, and Frank Mailer blew up.

Lunging, he grabbed at Nita's shoulder, but knowing his man, Kilkenny had been watching. He moved swiftly and thrust the hand aside. Instantly, Frank Mailer struck. He struck with his ponderous right fist that had already lifted with the violence of his grab at the girl, but Kilkenny rolled his head and smashed a left and right to the body.

Lance Kilkenny knew the manner of man he was facing and knew that if ever he had been in for a battle, he was in for one now. He struck fast and he struck hard, and the blows smashed Mailer back on his heels. Before he could catch his balance, Kilkenny hooked high and hard with a left and the blow knocked Mailer crashing to the floor.

He hit hard, in a sitting position, knocked back all of four feet, and as he hit he knew he had been struck with such force that all the other blows he had taken seemed mere child's play. He hit the floor drunk and raging, but he came up with a lunge, and cold sober.

Skilled in the rough-and-tumble style of barroom brawling, Lance Kilkenny knew what he was facing, yet he had more than that sort of skill on which to draw, for long ago in New Orleans he had studied the art of boxing and become quite proficient at it.

Mailer came up with a lunge and charged, swinging. Kilkenny nailed him on the mouth with a straight, hard left and then smashed another right to the ribs before the sheer weight of the rush smashed Kilkenny back against the bar. Mailer blazed with fury and confidence. Now he had him! Against the bar!

One hand grasped Kilkenny's throat, pushing his head back. Then he jerked up his knee for Kilkenny's groin. Yet Kilkenny's own knee had lifted an instant quicker and blocked the rise of Mailer's drive. At the same time Kilkenny struck Mailer's left hand away from his throat by knocking it to the right, and he lunged forward, smashing the top of his skull into Mailer's nose and mouth.

Blood streaming from his smashed lips, Mailer staggered, pawing at the air, and Kilkenny let him go, standing there, breathing easily, and waiting. The crowd had been shoved back, he saw, and Jaime Brigo was standing beside Nita with drawn gun. Over the bar behind him he heard Brockman speak, Brockman whom he had once fought in just such a battle, before they were friends. "Don't worry, boss. Nobody butts in!"

Mailer recovered his balance and stared at Kilkenny with malignant eyes. With the back of his hand he mopped the blood from his lips, staring at Kilkenny. "Now," he said, his voice low and dangerous, "I'm goin' to kill you!"

He moved in, his big fists ready, taking his time now. This man was not going to be smashed down in a couple of driving rushes. Mailer was not worried. He had always won, no man could stand against him.

Mailer moved in, feinted, then lunged. Kilkenny did not step away or retreat; he stepped inside and his legs were spread and he smashed wicked, hooking drives to the ribs that jolted and jarred Mailer. Frank shortened his own punches and caught Kilkenny with a mighty right that knocked him to the floor. With a roaring yell, Mailer sprang into the air and leaped to come down on Kilkenny's body, but Lance rolled over and sprang to his feet like a cat, and Mailer, missing, lunged past him against the bar. Kilkenny smashed a wicked right to the kidney, and as Mailer turned and grabbed for him he swung the man over his back with a flying mare.

Mailer came up fast and rushed and they stood toe to toe, swapping punches. Shifting his feet, Kilkenny was caught with a foot off the floor and he went back into the bar. The big man lunged and grabbed Kilkenny around the waist with both mighty arms.

Growling with fury, he tightened that grasp, but Kilkenny, caught with his hands down and inside that mighty hug, jerked both thumbs into the lower abdomen, low and hard. Mailer jerked back from the thumbs, and instantly Kilkenny turned his hips inside the hollow left between their bodies, and grasping Mailer's right sleeve with his left hand, he slid his right arm around his waist, and jerking down with the left, he swung Mailer across his hip and crashing to the floor with a thud that shook the building. He sprang back then, getting distance between them, and mopping the blood and sweat from his eyes. Frank Mailer got to his feet, throttling rage in his throat mingled with something else, something he had never felt before, the awful, dreadful fear that he might be beaten!

He lunged, and Kilkenny stepped into him. The gunfighter was utterly savage now. Watching, Cain Brockman cringed with the memory, for Kilkenny's fists cracked like ball bats on Mailer's face. It was a driving, utterly furious attack that smashed Mailer back with solid blow after solid blow. Mailer lunged, grabbed him again, and jerked him clear off the floor, hurling him down. Kilkenny hit hard, and one of his guns went scooting, but Nita stooped quickly and caught it up.

Kilkenny was on his back and Mailer lunged for him. Kilkenny swung a boot up and caught the oncoming man in the solar plexus, and the drive of the rush and the moving boot carried the big man over like a catapult and he hit the floor beyond, his fall broken by the crowd that could not move fast enough.

Kilkenny rolled over and was on his feet. Punch-drunk, Mailer came up, and Kilkenny let go with both hands. Mailer sagged and his knees buckled and Kilkenny threw an uppercut with all the power that was in him. It lifted the big man from his feet and turned him over, and Frank Mailer hit the floor on his shoulder blades, out cold!

Kilkenny drew back, feeling for his gun. The right gun was still with him and he faced the crowd, his eyes desperate, blazing with cold fire. He swept the crowd until he found Geslin and Starr. Their eyes met and he stood there, his chest heaving with the struggle for air, sweat streaming down his face, his shirt in rags about him. He stood there, and suddenly Nita spoke. "In your holster!" and he felt his left-hand gun slide home. For a minute he held their eyes, steady, waiting.

Nobody moved, nobody spoke. He straightened then and glanced down at the beaten and bloody man who sprawled on the floor. "Tell him all the roads are open, but they run one way . . . out of town!"

———

It WAS A silent, grim bunch of men who took the trail that night back to Blue Hill, but while they rode slowly, and Frank Mailer slumped heavily in his saddle, his great head thudding with a dull ache, there was a man ahead of them who rode very swiftly, indeed. It was Kansas, and he was riding to be the first to report to Dunning. This was something Poke would want to know, something he needed to know.

———

After KANSAS WAS gone, Poke Dunning paced the floor alone. Frank Mailer whipped! It was unbelievable! Had the earth opened and gulped down the Blue Hill, the ranch and its neighboring peak, he could have been no more shocked. That Mailer might be beaten with a gun, he knew. But with fists? In a rough-and-tumble fight? It was impossible!

But it had happened. Mailer was beaten. Despite his satisfaction, Dunning was worried. He turned in late, but he did not sleep, lying there and staring up into the darkness. He had worked a long time for this ranch, and he meant to keep it. He would kill anybody who endangered his possession of the ranch. Even Lona. Even Lona, the girl he had reared.

———

Kilkenny AWOKE EARLY the following morning. He had returned at once to his hideout, but now he was awake. His hands were swollen and battered, and in the mirror he carried, he could see one eye was swollen almost closed. There was a welt on the corner of his mouth and a blue swelling on his cheekbone. He heated water on the fire and soaked his hands; carefully he cleaned the cuts and scrapes on his head and arms.

He was still tending to his injuries at noon when Gates appeared. He swung down and crossed to Kilkenny with jingling spurs. "Man! Did you beat that big lug! He was still punch-drunk when they left this morning!"

Kilkenny looked up sharply. He didn't feel too good himself. "They left? How many of them?"

"Mailer himself and four hands. Geslin, Starr, Socorro, and a mean-faced hombre with a scar that I've not seen around much."

"Thin? Stoop-shouldered with yellowish eyeballs?"

"That's him, who is he?"

"That's Ethridge, one of the Stockton gang." Kilkenny got to his feet, drying his hands. "That gives me a hunch, now. I think I know who Mailer is. If I'm not wrong, he's one of a bunch that operated out of Durango. Used a flock of names. One of them was Lacey or something like that."

"Yeah, I've heard of him."

Kilkenny studied his swollen hands. "Look," he said presently, "we're going to wind this up. Lona should come to see me today, and I've got to go see Poke Dunning. He left word with Kansas down at Salt Creek. He's got a proposition for me."

"Watch yourself."

"I will. But I want to see him. The lid's set to blow off anyway, and we might as well start the ball rolling while Mailer is gone."

"He said he'd be gone two days."

"All right, that gives us some time. I'll talk to Lona, then I'll ride down and see Dunning. You be ready, and you talk to Flynn and that cook."

After Gates was gone, he thought it over again. Kilkenny had taken care to learn something about the extent of the Blue Hill holdings, and the ranch was vast in area and in stock. There were thousands of head of cattle, and in the breaks to the west there were sheep. It was a big stake, truly.

How had Mailer worked into the deal? He was sure that

Poke had started it alone . . . in fact, in his own mind he was sure that Dunning had killed Markham. But somehow Mailer had come into it.

He was thinking about that when he heard Lona ride into the amphitheater below, so he got to his feet and swung into the saddle.

She smiled brightly when she saw him, then gasped as she saw his face. "Oh, what happened to you? You're hurt!"

Kilkenny chuckled. "No, not really. I had a fight last night. Didn't you hear about it?"

"No . . . how would I hear?"

He took off his hat and swung down to a seat near her on a boulder. "It was your man Mailer I was fighting."

She came to her feet. "You . . . fought Frank Mailer?"

He smiled, painfully. "If you think I look bad, you should see him!"

"You . . . whipped him?" Lona was amazed. The more she looked at the tall young man on the rock, the more impossible it became that this man could have beaten Mailer.

Kilkenny grinned. He didn't like to brag, and yet . . . well, what man doesn't like to have a pretty girl think well of him? "Well, to tell you the truth, I did, and if you'll pardon my saying so, I did a bang-up job of it. Not that I didn't catch a few!" He felt with delicate fingers of the lump on his cheekbone.

"He'll kill you now." She was very positive. "He'll never let you get away alive."

"It's going to get to that point anyway," Kilkenny said. "I'm going to make sure that ranch is in your hands, all free and clear, with Poke Dunning and Mailer both out of the picture. Do you believe now that Dunning's not your father?"

She looked at him seriously. "I . . . I never really doubted that. He was always funny around me, and he would never tell me anything about my mother. I remember a lot of little things now."

"Anything about that wagon trip?" he asked quickly.

"Not much. I remember a town where there were Indians, and from all else I recall, it must have been Santa Fe. There was another man with us then. And we came west from there."

"You remember nothing after that?"

"Well . . . sort of. It's not very clear, not at all, but I have a memory of a place . . . of coming up a long canyon with a small stream in the bottom. We came up it for a long, long way, it seems to me. Once we climbed out of it I remember Father pointing at a great peak or mesa that was far away. He . . . I remember that because he said something about an orphan at the time, and I pestered him to tell me what an orphan was. I guess it wasn't long after that I became one."

Kilkenny nodded. "That helps. We're getting places now. I would bet fifty dollars that the long canyon was Canyon Largo. The Orphan makes sense. You see, that's the name of a mesa over in the desert near Largo. They call it El Huérfano . . . the Orphan, because it stands alone."

"Isn't that funny?" she said. "I never connected the mountain and the orphan, at all! Now, let's see, there was something else, too. Last night I was thinking about it and I dreamed something about a night when there was a fire and I woke up and I could see the light dancing on a rock wall. I've thought about that real often. You know how it is, you forget so much and then two or three things sort of stick in your mind? It was that way with this. . . . I remember waking up and being afraid because I could see that Father was not in his blankets, but when I called to him, he spoke to me from far off and told me to be quiet. I went back to sleep then."

Kilkenny squinted his eyes at her. "You remember anything else about that?"

She shook her head. "No, only I think it was the next day that we got here and the old Indian woman took care of me. I didn't see Father again for a long time."

"Probably you never saw him again, not actually." Kilkenny got to his feet. "You know, I've a hunch that night you woke up was the night your father was killed, and if you got to the ranch the next day, it could not have been far from here."

"Oh, but I can't be sure!" she objected. "It's been so long, and telling it this way makes it seem a lot more real than it actually was! It's pretty vague."

"Nevertheless, I think I'm right. Before I see Dunning today, I'm going to have a look."

"But how could you find it after all this time?" she asked.

"I'll have to be lucky," he admitted. "Mighty lucky. But there aren't many trails across this country from Santa Fe, and I don't believe he ever brought the wagons on much farther than that. He may have burned them, and if he did, they may still be there, or the rims may. I'll have a look, anyway."

"But why? What's to be gained?"

"I don't know," he confessed. "Maybe nothing. I'd like to get something on Dunning, though. Something definite. And there might be a clue."

She nodded, looking out past the screen of pines toward the distant hills.

Then suddenly, almost as she turned her head, he was gone from the rock! She stared, then started to her feet. Where in the world . . . ?

"Lona!" She whirled. It was Gordon Flynn. "What in the world are you doin' way back here?" he asked. He was sitting a dun pony that he often rode, and he looked around wonderingly. "An' how did you ever find this place? I'd never have guessed it was here."

"I found it."

Kilkenny stepped from behind a clump of piñon, and Flynn gulped. "You . . . you're Kilkenny?"

Lona's eyes flew open and she gasped, "Kilkenny!"

"Yes, ma'am," he replied, "that's my name."

Chapter 4

THE HAMLET OF Aztec Crossing was born of a broken axle and weaned and reared on Indian whiskey. For three weeks the town was a covered wagon and three barrels of whiskey, but by that time "Hungry" Hayes, onetime buffalo hunter and freighter, had built a dugout roofed with poles and earth.

With those three barrels of Indian whiskey to prime the pump of prosperity, and a Winchester to back the priming,

Hayes turned his broken axle and the river crossing into a comfortable fortune. Indian whiskey is a simple concoction of river water, not strained, straight alcohol (roughly two gallons to the barrel), three plugs of chewing tobacco, five or six bars of soap (very strong lye soap), one half pound of red pepper, and a liberal dose of sagebrush leaves. To this is added two ounces of strychnine, and the resulting brew is something to make a mummy rear on his hind legs and let out a regular Comanche yell. This recipe was not, of course, original with Hungry Hayes. He merely adopted the formula in use throughout the Indian country, the ingredients varying but little.

The first two settlers of Aztec Crossing halted because of proximity to the source of supply, yet neither proved as hardy as the durable Hayes. The first to pass on was helping Hayes mix the whiskey and decided that he preferred it straight, without the addition of the river water. The following morning Hayes planted him on the bank of the river with due ceremony. The second settler departed this world after a brief but emphatic altercation with four Apaches. His mistake was entirely due to a youthful disdain for mathematics, for having slain three Apaches, he straightened up from his protecting buffalo wallow to leave, and took an arrow through his chest. He was buried, after an interval of sunshine and buzzards, by Hayes, taking with him a surplus of arrows but considerably less hair.

Yet, as time passed, Aztec Crossing grew. Ranching began, and the town acquired a general store, four saloons, a livery stable, a bank, and various other odds and ends of business enterprise. Hungry Hayes, fat with money, departed for the East and settled down in a comfortable Kentucky homestead, where people forever after regarded him as a liar for telling what was actually less than the truth.

The latest institution, and from Frank Mailer's viewpoint, the most interesting, was the Aztec City Bank.

With a dozen ranches nearer to Aztec than any other town, the bank was at times fairly bulging with coin. This fact had not gone unnoticed, and the five hard-bitten gentlemen who drifted into Aztec on the bright and sunny morning in question had decided to give some attention to this money.

Aztec was drowsing in the sun. The weather-beaten boards of the walk in front of the Aztec Saloon supported the posteriors of four old settlers, talking of great deeds against the warlike Comanche. In front of the livery stable, half asleep, old Pete chewed tobacco in drowsy content. In the store, his glasses as far down on his nose as possible, Storekeeper Worth studied a month-old newspaper. A dun pony flicked a casual tail at a fly who buzzed in deep bass, and the morning was warm, pleasant, and sleepy.

Frank Mailer, mounted on a blood bay, walked his horse down the main street with the saturnine Socorro beside him. Reining in at the bank hitching rail, he swung down, and Socorro did likewise, and stayed between the horses, fussing with some saddle gear, his carbine close at hand.

Geslin and Starr came down from the opposite direction, and Geslin drew up, taking time to light a smoke while his slate-gray eyes studied the street with a cold, practiced gaze. Starr chewed tobacco, and sat his horse, his thick thighs bulging the cloth of his jeans. Ethridge walked up from behind the bank and stopped at the corner of the building. He carried a Henry rifle, and with Socorro faced one way and he another, they could cover the street with ease.

Mailer, his face swollen and ugly, jerked his head at Geslin. Starr followed. Geslin was worried, for he had never seen Mailer as he was today. Always brutal, the man was now in a vicious mood, his whole manner changed. The beating he had taken had aroused all the ferocity innate in his being. He pushed open the door and walked in and toward the office of the president. Geslin went to one window, and Starr to the other. Starr took the man who was standing there and spun him sharply, smashing a Colt down over the man's skull.

"All right," he said, "sack it up!"

The cashier looked, paled, gulped, and reached for a sack. Mailer had the president out, and with three men under their guns and the fourth on the floor out cold, they proceeded to strip the bank.

Across the street Johnny Mulhaven was coming out of the saloon, and Johnny Mulhaven had more nerve than brains. He saw the sudden collection of horses, he saw two men facing the street with rifles, and he let out a shrill Texas yell and went for his gun.

Ethridge dropped the rifle on him and fired . . . the shot was too quick and too high. It hit Johnny in the shoulder and he dropped his gun, but caught it in the air with his left hand and snapped a quick shot at Ethridge. His shot was quick but lucky. Ethridge caught the bullet where his ribs parted and dropped his rifle.

The old Comanche fighters dove for shelter, two of them under the walk, one behind a watering trough; another dashed for the saloon. Without doubt he was headed for a drink to ballast his shocked nerves, but he was doomed to die thirsty. He caught a slug from Socorro's rifle and went down on the very step of his goal, and in a matter of seconds the street was laced with gunfire, stabbing, darting flames.

Young Johnny Mulhaven was still on his feet, carrying enough lead for three men to die, and he was still firing left-handed. Scar Ethridge had made one attempt to get up, but Johnny made sure of him with a bullet through the skull. One of the horses sprang away, and then the bank door burst open and three men charged into the street.

Mulhaven took the full blast of their fire and went down hard, blood staining the gray boards of the walk. A rifle spoke from the livery stable, another from the store. Three men were unlimbering guns from within the saloon. Old Pete, at the first shot, had come erect with a lunge, swallowed his chewing tobacco, and methodically pulled his old pistol, aimed, shot, and put a slug into Kane Geslin.

And then, suddenly as it had begun, it was over. Five men had come into town, and four rode out. Two of them were wounded.

It was only then that the full story was known. Within the bank, the slugged man told it. He had come out of it just in time to see Mailer strike the banker down, then unlimber his pistol and kill all three of the men within the bank. Wisely, he lay still and lived.

Four men were dead, but Johnny Mulhaven, miraculously, was still alive, but with nine wounds.

Headed east and riding fast were the four remaining outlaws. Geslin had a flesh wound and Socorro had come out of it with a bloody but merely burned shoulder. All four were ugly, despite the success of their venture, and three of them were worried. They had known Mailer for a long time, but not the Mailer in the bank. They were all men who had killed and would kill again, yet those three killings were cold-blooded, unnecessary, and dangerous to their safety. Dangerous because while many a western town might overlook a bank robbery, they would never overlook a cold-blooded killing.

They swung north, leaving the trail for the rough country, and circled west, heading for a crossing above White Canyon. They had good horses, and doubted if a pursuit would immediately get under way. Silent, brooding, and bloody, the four men crossed the Rio Grande and headed up Pajarito Canyon, crossed to Valle de los Posos, and headed for the Rio Puerco.

Nobody talked. Geslin had lost blood and felt sick and sore. The movement of the horse hurt him. Sweat smarted the burn on Socorro's arm and his mood became vile. Steadily, they pushed on under a baking sun, their shirts stained with blood and sweat, their horses plodding more wearily. Behind them there might be pursuit, and they could easily be followed. There were Indian trackers at Aztec Crossing.

No clouds marred the faint blue of the sky where the sun hung brassy and broiling. Nothing moved but the sage, and there was no wind, only a heavy, stifling heat. Sam Starr alone seemed unaffected, but from time to time his eyes turned toward the huge sullen figure of Frank Mailer. Mentally, he told himself he was through. *When I get mine,* he told himself, *I'm pullin' stakes.*

Alkali dust lifted in soft clouds and dusted a film over their clothing. Socorro cursed monotonously and Geslin stared ahead with bleak, desperate eyes, his lips dry, his body aching for rest and water. Frank Mailer, indomitable and grim, rode on ahead. Starr stared phlegmatically before them, his eyes squinting against the intense white glare of the sun. He watched his horse carefully, keeping it to good ground whenever possible, knowing how much depended on it.

At last the night came and shadows reached out and touched them with coolness. In a tiny glade on the Rio Puerco, the men swung stiffly from their horses. Starr eyed the sacks thoughtfully, and Socorro with greedy, eager eyes, watchful eyes, too, for they shifted vaguely to the night, and then with more intentness on the men close by.

Bulking black against the starry sky, looming almost above them, were the rugged San Pedro Mountains. Starr got some food together, and nobody talked. Geslin bathed his wound and bandaged it; Socorro did likewise. Mailer stared into the flames, hulking and dangerous.

"Will we make it back tomorrow?" Socorro asked suddenly.

"No," Geslin replied, "there isn't a chance."

"Let's split the money now," Socorro suggested.

Starr wanted nothing more than that, but he was hesitant to agree. His eyes shifted to Mailer and they all waited for him to speak, but he said nothing. Starr had seen men like this before when killing was on them. There was only one end to it. Death. They killed and killed until they themselves were slain. He wanted no part of it. He wanted to get away. He also wanted his money.

Dawn found them pushing northeast, heading up Capulin Creek. With the San Pedros to the south and the bulk of Mesa Prieta to the north, there was no way to see if there was any pursuit or not. Geslin was willing to bet there was, and Starr agreed. They told each other as much during a moment when they had fallen behind.

It was dusk when they drew up at a spring and slid from their horses. "We'd better stop," Geslin said. "My arm's givin' me hell!"

Mailer turned on him. "What's the matter?" He sneered. "You turnin' into an old woman?"

Geslin's face whitened and for an instant they stared at each other. "Go ahead!" Mailer taunted. "Reach for it!"

Sam Starr stepped back, his eyes watchful. Geslin was in no shape for this. The man's nerves were shot, he was weakened from loss of blood, and beaten by the endless riding.

"What's the matter?" Mailer said. "You a quitter? You yellow?"

Geslin's hand flashed for his gun, and Frank Mailer swung his pistol up with incredible speed. An instant it held, then the shot bellowed, thundering between the cliffs. Geslin went down, his gun spouting fire into the dirt, shot through the heart.

Socorro touched his lips with his tongue, and Sam Starr stood very still, staring at Mailer. The man was fast; he was chained lightning.

Mailer's eyes went to Socorro, then sought Starr, but Sam had his back to darkness and shooting at him would have been a poor gamble. "Anybody sayin' anything?" Mailer demanded. He waited while one might have counted five, and neither man spoke. Then he turned away. "No time for loafin'. We're ridin' on."

———

THREE DAYS BEFORE, Lance Kilkenny had set out on the trail of what he suspected was a thirteen-year-old murder. Following Lona's vague memories of the journey to the Blue Hill ranch and his own knowledge of the best route to that area from Santa Fe, Kilkenny cut across country to a spot he hoped would intersect the path the Markham wagon had taken. By morning he was in Canyon Largo, headed west, with the sun at his back. Lona had told him that she had gone on only one more day after she'd been told that her father had traveled on ahead. That meant that the site of that last camp and possibly the site of the killing was relatively close to the ranch. By going a good sixty miles farther east than would seem necessary, Kilkenny hoped to follow the best path for a wagon and therefore have some hope that he might discover the exact way that Markham, Lona, and Poke Dunning had approached the ranch. He was covering ground faster than any wagon could have, not bothering to look for any true clues of the Markham family's passing, just getting a feel for the slope of the land, watching for deep arroyos and trying to think like a man would when driving with a heavy load.

By noon he had stopped at a place where the stream had eddied back on itself and made a good watering hole. From the growth of trees and brush, Kilkenny figured that it was a place that had remained unchanged for many years and was not the creation of some recent alteration in the flow of water.

He got down and, leaving Buck to graze on whatever grass he could find, scouted around on foot. In twenty minutes he had discovered nothing, so he mounted up and headed off again figuring that he'd cross and head on out north of Angel's Peak. He had not gone a score of yards when he saw it.

He drew up staring at a crude drawing scratched on the rock wall of Canyon Largo. It was scarcely three feet from the ground and was a crude, childish representation of a girl with stick legs and arms. An Indian drawing? he wondered. But no Indian had ever made a drawing like that!

He rode straight up now, his eyes searching the canyon walls and the sandy bed. Although he had found no campsite, and Lona had not mentioned making this drawing, he was sure that he had stumbled onto their route.

The following morning, scarcely ten miles from the ranch, he watered his horse and rested on the east side of Thieving Rock. Idly wandering about, Lance Kilkenny suddenly saw a charred wheel, then some bolts.

Near a sheltering overhang, half hidden by brush, were the old remains of a large fire. Here a few stones had been huddled together and blackened with soot. He dropped to his knees and dug in the sand, feeling around to see what he might turn up.

At the bottom of the inner wall, the water or wind of some bygone age had scoured out a small crevice in the stone. It was partly covered, but his eye caught a glimpse of something more than sand, and stopping, he prodded at it with a stick. It moved and he saw that it was an iron box!

Kneeling, he grabbed the corner, and brushing away the sand, he pulled out the box. It was ancient and badly rusted, so picking up a stone he struck at the lock.

Another blow and the box broke open. Within it were a

few silver pieces, black with age, and a handful of papers. Carefully, he picked them up. A birth certificate for Lona! Markham's marriage certificate! A last will and testament! And the deed to the ranch, placing it in Lona's name, along with the old original deed given him when he himself acquired the ranch!

Probably he had been afraid of Dunning and had concealed this box each night to prevent it being found by him if anything happened.

———

THAT EVENING KILKENNY had ridden down the Old Mormon Trail to Blue Hill. Rusty Gates was mending a bridle and he glanced up at him as he rode in. Gordon Flynn was working around the corral and Lona saw him coming and smiled nervously as he swung down. "I'm hunting Poke Markham," Kilkenny said loudly. "Is he around?"

Dunning appeared in the door. He was wearing two guns, Kilkenny noticed, whereas he had worn but one heretofore. "Come on in!" Poke said, and turned and walked back into the room.

Lance followed him across the porch, then stopped, closing his eyes for an instant so he would see better inside away from the sunlight. He took in the room with one quick glance. A glance that gauged the distance to all the doors and placed the main articles of furniture. A lot might happen before he left this room.

"You wanted to see me?"

Poke Dunning looked up from under shaggy gray brows. His eyes were hard, measuring. "You're Kilkenny?"

"That's right."

"You whipped Frank Mailer the other evening. You reckon he will take it lyin' down?"

"He can take it as he chooses."

"He'll meet you with a gun, Kilkenny, and he's fast as greased lightnin'."

Kilkenny waited, saying nothing. This old man wore his guns with the butts well forward. Some gunmen liked them that way.

"You can't get away from meeting him unless you run, an' you don't set up like a running man. I want you to meet him right away. Soon as he comes back."

"Where's he gone?"

"How'd I know? Don't care, neither. He's a bad hombre, that one, and he's got to be killed. You got to kill him, anyway, but if you hunt him down or kill him as soon as he gets back, any way you like, I'll give you five hundred dollars!"

The way he said it made the sum sound big . . . but was it big enough? What were the stakes to Poke Dunning?

"No. I'll meet him when I have to. I won't hunt him down." Kilkenny pulled out his tobacco and began to build a smoke. "Nice place you've got here. Had it long?"

Dunning tightened up inside. The old fear was always on him. "Quite a spell," he replied. "Been some changes made."

"I heard it belonged to your daughter, to Lona."

"Well, you're right. I gave it to her when she was just a child."

"You going to start another place someday?" Kilkenny touched the tip of his tongue to his cigarette, then placed it in his mouth. He dug out a match and lit up, glancing through the first smoke at Dunning. "Let her have her inheritance?"

"Maybe," Poke said flatly. "Someday." Poke Dunning stared at Kilkenny. What was this, anyway? He had the man out here to try to hire him, and now he was asking questions. Too many questions.

"I was wondering. . . . Why is it that they call you 'Poke,' Mr. Markham? What was your given name?"

He faced Kilkenny. "What's it to you?"

"Just curious."

"Too durned curious! You ain't takin' me up on Mailer?" Poke wanted to change the subject.

"No." Kilkenny moved a step toward the door. "But I'll be back to see you, 'Poke.' " He stopped at the door. "You see, Ike Markham was a friend of mine!" As he spoke he stepped quickly back into the shadows, dropped a hand to the porch rail, and vaulted it neatly. "Buck!" he called.

The horse came to him, holding his head high and to one side so as not to step on the trailing bridle reins. Catching them up, Lance Kilkenny wheeled the horse and vanished into the darkness.

He need not have hurried. In the big room of the old ranch house, Poke Dunning was standing where Kilkenny had left him, his face ashen, his cheeks sunken and old.

For all these years he had been afraid of just this. A dozen times he had thought of what he might do if ever faced with somebody who knew Markham, and now the moment had come and gone, and he had let the man get away. He should have killed him! But why, if someone had to come, did it have to be Kilkenny, of all people?

Alone in his room, he paced the floor. After all these years! Why, there had to be a way out! There had to be! There was no justice in it!

Mailer! If he could only steer Mailer into Kilkenny! They might kill each other off, or at least make it easy for him to kill the survivor. In that case, there might still be a chance.

He paced the floor, cursing Mailer's absence as once he had blessed it, eager for the man to return.

It was this fear that had caused him to keep the gunmen on the payroll even after he had given up banditry and rustling. This fear that someday, someone would come over the Old Mormon Trail who knew the truth. He had made a bold play, that long-ago night in the dark shadow of Thieving Rock. . . . Markham had been a friendly man when they met, and he had talked cheerfully of the ranch he had for his young daughter, and little by little Poke had worked the information out of him, that his wife was dead, that he had no near relatives but Lona. Poke Dunning could see his big chance, and in the following nights he sat across the fire from the man who was carrying him west, and waited for his chance. It came, finally, only a day's drive from the ranch itself. It came when he was growing desperate with anxiety, and he knew that Markham had begun to suspect him, that the man moved his bed at times, shifting it from one place to another after they had turned in.

Yet, in the accomplishment, it had been easy. He had tossed a stone into the darkness near the horses, and Markham, seeing him lying there, apparently asleep, had risen and walked out to the horses, fearful that a mountain lion might come down on them. Poke Dunning had slid out of his blankets and followed him in his sock feet. He had used a pick handle, and it was only after the third and last blow had fallen that little Lona called from her blankets and he had replied that everything was all right, keeping his voice low.

The next day he told the child her father had gone on ahead to make ready for them. Later he told her that he was off doing business for the ranch and made arrangements to send her to school. Once she was gone, he had gambled that she would not remember after the years. He had even gone so far as to change his own ways, to use gestures and mannerisms the father had used, and even grow a beard in the same style as her father. It had been a bad moment when she returned on her first holiday, but after eleven years the memory had dimmed, and although he saw doubt in her eyes, he soon managed to make her forget those doubts. When she finally came home after many years, the memories from when she was five or almost five had been erased but for a few moments. The rest was a shadowland where memory and fantasy mingled, where the face of her father was never quite distinct.

Poke Dunning had made his big gamble, and he had won. Now he might lose. He would lose if something was not done. For years he had built up the ranch. Though Lona was the actual owner, in his mind the ranch was his and his alone. And now he was threatened.

When she had first returned from school, Poke had been worried and he had started planning how to take back control without raising a lot of questions. Frank Mailer had been his first hope.

He had hoped that Frank Mailer, the outlaw that owed him for so much, would be a fitting partner in the ranch. But now he was increasingly sure that Frank had his own plans and that Poke Dunning did not figure in them. Mailer could be handled, but somehow he must stall him on marrying Lona until after Kilkenny was out of the way. Then he could take care of big Frank, and he would enjoy doing it. He was going to make sure that Mailer died. He was going to make sure that Kilkenny died. And now that his long-held plan to legally wrest ownership of the ranch from Lona had fallen apart, he would kill her, too. If she died, wouldn't he, as her only surviving relative, inherit the ranch? After all, wasn't he supposed to have given it to her?

Only *Lona's* death had to look like an accident. Gunmen like Kilkenny and outlaws like Mailer were always dying violently. He could shoot Mailer himself, and if he carefully revealed what he knew about the big man's outlaw past and various aliases, no one would think twice about it. But killing a woman, a girl, was another thing entirely.

As if his murderous fantasy was echoing in his mind, Dunning suddenly heard her voice. She was in the kitchen talking to old Betts, and something was said about coffee. At this hour on nearly every night Dave Betts made coffee for the two of them. Dunning suddenly heard a new voice, Flynn's, making some laughing comment.

Poke's eyes narrowed. What was going on here? What was Flynn doing in the house so late at night? The hands rarely came for coffee this late unless working cattle close by, and they were not now. He turned and started for the kitchen.

Voices suddenly stilled as he opened the door. He glanced at Lona, her face bright with laughter, the light catching in her auburn hair, and then at Flynn. Dave had drawn back near the big cooking range, his face drawn.

"What's goin' on here?" Dunning demanded. "Flynn, you should be in bed asleep. Ain't nothin' for you at the house this time of night."

"I was just palaverin'," Flynn replied.

"We was havin' coffee," Betts offered. "You want a cup?"

"Yes, won't you have some?" Lona looked up at him, and there was something level and hard in her eyes that he had never seen there before. "I like to talk to Gordon."

"So it's Gordon, is it?" He glared balefully at the puncher. "Get out!" he growled.

Flynn hesitated, and Dunning's gun flashed in his hand. He was thinking that something else had been going on behind his back, that this Flynn . . . "Get out!" he said quickly.

Gordon Flynn backed to the door. Never before had he seen the old man go for a gun, and on his best day he could not have come within twice the time to match that draw. He was no gunfighter. On the other hand, his eyes met Lona's. "Go, Gordon. I'm all right." She spoke softly and he opened the door and backed out, his face white.

Poke Dunning stood very still, first glaring at Dave, then at Lona. "You come in here!" he said. "I want to talk to you!"

"All right." Lona got to her feet. She felt a queer, frightened sensation inside her, yet in another sense she was perfectly calm, her thoughts working carefully.

Kilkenny had come to see Dunning. The man might know his secret, kept for so long, was now about to be exposed. What would he do? What would he try?

She stepped past him into the big room and walked past the long dining-room table in the huge old parlor of the ranch house. She crossed to the fireplace, and stood there straight and looking suddenly taller than she was as she awaited him.

Poke Dunning slammed the door behind him and crossed the room. He dug his pipe into a can of tobacco and tamped it home. Then he looked up, his eyes bitter and hard, like flecks of steel under his shaggy brows. "We've got to have a talk. Sorry I got sore out there. Don't like to think of you wastin' time on those cowhands. You're too good for them."

"But you approve of Frank Mailer?" she asked coolly.

He looked up then, measuring her with his glance. "No," he said flatly, "and you ain't goin' to marry him. That was a bad idea."

"I agree." Lona waited, wondering.

He rubbed his chin. "Lona," he said hesitantly, "I got a confession to make. When Mailer first come down here, I figured him a right upstandin' young feller. Lately, he ain't seemed so much what he should be; in fact I been hearin' some things from up Durango way."

"Things?" She looked at him, puzzled. "What do you mean?"

"Stories. Stories of robberies and such. When he comes back I may have to fire Frank Mailer."

At that moment they both heard a shout, then a sound of running horses, and Mailer's hard voice, talking to Socorro.

Dunning turned on the girl. "Get to your room!" he said. "An', Lona, you keep your mouth shut to what we've been talking about!"

Chapter 5

MILES BACK, ALONG the trails north and west of Aztec Crossing, there rode a small, grim-faced group of men. In the van were three men on gray horses, three men who answered to the names of Jim, Pat, and Terry Mulhaven, the brothers of Johnny, who was alive but badly shot up back in Aztec.

There were eight of these men in all, headed by an Apache tracker, and these were the men who had built the Crossing from nothing to a fairly stable little outpost. Storekeeper Worth, answering to the name of Bill, was among them, his old Sharps across his saddlebow.

The peace and contentment of their town had been violated and good citizens had been done to death, so the attitude of the posse, self-appointed, was harsh and determined. A dozen times they had lost the trail, and a dozen times they had found it again. Their progress had been slow, but it was relentless.

Most often, it was the distinctive tracks of the blood bay ridden by Mailer that they found. They knew this horse by sight, and they knew his tracks.

"I wonder how much farther?" Worth asked.

"We got all summer," Jim Mulhaven replied shortly. "This is one trail I ain't leavin' until those hombres stretch hemp."

A good day and a half behind the outlaws, they had come upon the body of Kane Geslin. The sign made evident what had happened here. "Killed by one of his own men," Worth commented.

"One less for us," Pat said grimly. "Let's be ridin'!"

They rode on, into the hot, still afternoon, their eyes grimly upon the trail.

AT BLUE HILL, Mailer had wasted no time in facing Poke Dunning. He went at once to the ranch house, opened the door, and closed it, looking at the older man across the big room. "Poke, let's get this over with. Come Saturday, I'm marrying Lona!"

He could see that something had happened—what, he did not know—but Mailer was a changed man, not suddenly insistent, demanding, but with some deeper, more deadly change.

"I don't think so, Frank. She doesn't want to marry you. And now I agree with her."

Frank Mailer looked at old Poke Dunning through narrowed eyes. "You double-crossin' me, Dunning?" he asked.

"It could be I'm protectin' myself from a double cross. An' don't think that I'm scared of you telling people who I really am. I've been here for years and most of those that haven't forgot who Poke Dunning was are dead."

"What if you died, mighty sudden," Mailer suggested, his eyes holding Poke's, "an' I married Lona?"

Dunning shrugged. "The trouble with that is"—he spoke carefully, knowing how slender was the thread along which their course was holding, a thread that might snap with a burst of gunfire at any moment—"that Kilkenny knows."

"Who?" Mailer started at the name. "Kilkenny? Is he here?"

"Who do you think whipped you, Frank?" Dunning asked. "That was him, all right. Kansas tipped me off."

"Kilkenny!" All thoughts were suddenly gone from Mailer's mind but the one. It was fantastic. He had heard of the gunfighter for years, but had never seen him. Remembering the description that Gates had given in the saloon the first night they met, he knew Poke was telling the truth. Despite himself, he was awed and worried.

Had anyone suggested that the name frightened him, he would have scoffed at it. He had never been frightened of anything, but one could not hear the countless stories surrounding that name without it taking on an almost magical quality. He felt a strange, deadly chill within him. Kilkenny!

And the man had beaten him with his fists, but perhaps with a gun . . . ?

"Look," Poke said softly, "we've had our troubles, Frank. We both have it in for each other, but it ain't necessary. We started in this deal an' we can do all right with it yet. I can't let you marry Lona yet . . . not until I can trust you. We can settle this; the only thing in the way is this Kilkenny. We've got to get rid of him."

"We?" Mailer looked at Dunning, trying to assemble his thoughts. The knowledge that Kilkenny was in this deal disturbed him.

"Sure! Look, alone neither of us can win. Together we can. As long as Kilkenny is in the picture, we stand to lose, so what we've got to do is get him out of it. Then we can settle this deal between us, or work partners on it. Our first job is to be rid of him."

"Maybe you're right," Mailer agreed grudgingly, "but that won't be so easy. Got any ideas?"

"Sure. I've been thinking about it. Look, he came over to the ranch once, so we can get him here again. He was a friend of Lona's father. All right, we send him a message from her. He'll come, an' when he does, we'll be waitin' for him. Geslin, Starr, Socorro, an' us."

"Not Geslin. He's dead."

"Dead?"

"Yeah." Mailer's cold eyes shifted to Dunning's. "We had some words an' he tried to draw on me. I killed him."

Poke Dunning absorbed that and didn't like it. He had known Mailer was good, but if he was good enough to get Geslin and not even collect a slug in the process, then he was even more dangerous than Poke had believed.

"Ethridge is dead, too." Mailer was rolling a smoke. "We took that bank at Aztec Crossing."

Rage boiled up inside of Poke Dunning. He had refused to allow anything of the kind. This was going directly against his orders. For an instant he was about to give vent to his fury, but he throttled his anger. "That's no matter. We can use Socorro an' Starr. It will be easy enough. You an' me an'

Starr will be out of sight. We can have Socorro mendin' a saddle or something. Kilkenny rides in, an' we take him in a cross fire. Four guns. He won't beat that."

"All right," Mailer agreed. "It's a good plan. Can you get word to him?"

"Sure. Through Kansas or that Spanish girl."

"You're right, there's something between them."

"Yeah"—Dunning nodded—"we should have guessed it. She's that Nita Riordan who was with him on the border and at the Cedars. Remember? We heard about her."

So that was it? Kilkenny's girl? But after Kilkenny died?

"Poke," Mailer said suddenly, "I think I'm goin' to like this. You get word to Kansas or the girl. Let's get started on this an' get it over with."

———

SAM STARR WALKED into the bunkhouse and pulled off his boots. Behind him Socorro followed, and Rusty Gates opened his eyes and looked at them in the darkness. He could see only vague outlines, but he heard Socorro's muttered curse, then Starr's low question. "How do you feel?"

"Bad," Socorro said. "My whole arm and shoulder are so stiff it hurts to move."

"You feel better than Geslin."

Socorro did not say anything for a minute. Then he said, "Frank should have buried him. If there's a posse, they are liable to stumble on the body."

Rusty Gates was wide-awake now. What went on here? To speak would cause them to clam up, and he wanted to hear more. He lay still and listened.

"There *will* be a posse," Starr said. "Aztec is a tough place. I knew that kid who opened up on us. He was one of the Mulhaven boys, an' there's four or five more."

"Gunfighters?"

"No, but tough hands, and clannish as all get-out. You can bet we've got a Mulhaven on us now, somewhere."

"What you plannin' to do?"

Sam Starr let that question slide. It was not that he did not know, but Socorro was pretty thick with Mailer. Starr planned to get his share of the loot and light a shuck for Texas. But fast.

A long time after, Gates saw Gordon Flynn come into the room, get something out of his bunk, and leave again. Mailer still had not come in. When he did he undressed and fell right into bed.

———

AFTER MAILER LEFT him, Dunning moved swiftly. He had to prepare for battle on two fronts. The trap had to be set for Kilkenny and he needed to be ready for Mailer's next move, whether they'd done in Kilkenny or not. He crossed the patio and rapped lightly on Lona's door. "Who's there?" she asked.

"It's me . . . Pa. Get your clothes an' come out of there. You sleep in the back room tonight. Beside Dave Betts."

Lona thought quickly. Why Dunning wanted her to move she could not guess, but being close to Dave would make her feel much safer. She knew the old man's affection for her, and his loyalty. "All right," she said after a minute.

"You'll be all right there. Mailer's back."

She said nothing but went to the room mentioned, barred the door, and climbed into bed. Poke Dunning walked into Lona's bedroom and sat down on the empty bed with his six-shooter in his hand.

His hunch might be wrong, but Lona was the pawn in the game now. Possession of her person was as important as possession of the ranch itself, even more important, as things stood. If Mailer came . . . it was almost daylight when he heard the soft rustle of grass, then heard a low voice. "Lona!"

He sat very still, and then a head and shoulders loomed at the open window. "Lona!" the voice called.

Poke Dunning fired.

———

MAILER, GATES, AND Starr came awake on the instant. Starr thought first of a posse, Gates and Mailer were thinking of Kilkenny. Gates kicked off the blankets and reached for his boots. Mailer stared at him, then leaned back in bed.

Going out into that yard was something he had no idea of doing right now. Firing a pistol and then waiting might be just the trick Poke Dunning would try. "See what it is," he said, and sagged back in his bunk.

Rusty Gates walked out into the yard, but there was no sound and no movement. He waited, then crossed the hard-packed earth of the ranch yard toward the house. He heard a faint stirring and turned toward the wing of the house. Someone had lighted a lantern, and he rounded the corner to see the dark figure of a man bending over another one on the ground.

Rusty had his gun out. "Who is it?" he demanded.

Dunning turned, saw Gates, and saw the gun. "It's Flynn," he said. "He tried to get into Lona's window and got shot."

"Shot? Lona shot Flynn?" Gates could not believe that.

He bent over the cowhand. "Dead?"

"No, he ain't, but he's bad hurt. Let's get him inside."

Poke was cursing his luck, for when he fired he was sure that it was Mailer he had under his gun. But why was Flynn here? Had Lona planned to escape?

When they put the boy down on Lona's bed, Gates worked over him, and Dunning watched. "Where do you stand in this, Gates?" Poke asked suddenly.

Rusty looked up. He had wondered if he would be asked. "Now, that's a good point, Dunning. I don't know where I stand. I don't know what the fuss is all about. However," he added, "this is a deal where I'd look to see where the money was."

"I've got it. You work for me an' you can make yourself a fast stake."

"That sounds good to me. What do I do?"

"Saddle a horse an' see that girl at the Fandango. Tell her Poke Dunning wants to see Kilkenny tomorrow at three. Then you get back here and stand ready to side me . . . against anybody."

"What does it get me?" Rusty knew the question was expected.

"Two-fifty for five days. Double if you have to fight."

Rusty SADDLED UP and rode out of the ranch but he did not ride more than a half mile before he swung off the road and headed for Monument Rock. He would ride directly to Kilkenny. Whatever this meant he did not know, but Kilkenny could make his own decision after he apprised him of the facts.

Kilkenny heard him out in silence. The return of three men to Blue Hill when five had gone out, the shooting of Gordon Flynn. "No," Gates said, when asked, "he's not dead. But he's got a bad wound and lost a lot of blood. When I left, Dave was takin' care of him, and old Betts is a good hand with a gunshot."

Kilkenny got to his feet and paced nervously beside the fire. It was daylight now, but the morning was still cool. They wanted him there at three o'clock, and between now and three many things could happen, and Gates was here. "You get back to the ranch," he said. "You watch your chance, and if there is one, get that girl out of there. If there isn't, watch her close. Maybe it's just best to do that."

"Are you comin' at three?"

"I think so."

"It may be a trap."

"Could be. Anyway, tell him I'll be there."

He watched Rusty go with misgiving. Dunning, Mailer, Starr, and Socorro would be there to meet him, yet there seemed to be no suspicion of Rusty, and it would be only a matter of hours until he would go himself.

Over his coffee, he considered the whole setup at Blue Hill, remembering every detail of the ranch and its layout.

This was to be a showdown, he knew that. Whether or not Poke Dunning wanted to talk business, Kilkenny knew very well that if he did not agree to whatever Dunning demanded, he would have to fight his way out. Knowing this, he made plans to stay in. Dunning was going to deal the cards, but he would play his own hand the way that suited him best.

The killing of Geslin interested him. Frank Mailer was fast, for Geslin had been very fast and an excellent shot. And Mailer had killed him.

From what Gates said, they had been in some sort of a gun battle, for Ethridge, too, was dead. They had brought back sacks stuffed with money, and that might mean a holdup at any one of a dozen places.

Shortly before noon Kilkenny mounted the buckskin and left his hideout, but he did not ride out into the flatlands toward Blue Hill; instead he crossed Salt Creek Wash and rode up the canyon that opened opposite Monument Rock and ran due north. Emerging from the canyon at a place just west of Popping Rock, he struck an old trail across the highlands back of the cliffs that formed the northern boundary of the Blue Hill range. It was a trail he had used before, and one he well knew. Within an hour of easy riding, he was on the point of rocks opposite Blue Hill, and here, after concealing his horse among the piñons, he found a place on the crest of the cliffs and began to make a systematic study of the ranch through his glasses.

His point of observation could scarcely have been better, for he was at an altitude of some six thousand feet, while the ranch itself was all of five hundred feet lower and scarcely a mile away. From his vantage point in the clear mountain air, he could easily see the figures and, knowing them, could distinguish one from the other, even though features would not be discernible. Yet after fifteen minutes of careful study, he saw no one.

Becoming increasingly anxious, Kilkenny moved down a little lower and somewhat closer to the edge of the cliff, and studied the terrain still more carefully. A few of the buildings were concealed by the bulk of the nearer peak, but the house and the bunkhouse he could plainly see, and there was still no movement.

He got up at last and rode west. He had a ride of at least two miles before there was a way down from the rim, and when he made it, he was on the Old Mormon Trail. Worried, he studied the trail, but there was no evidence of any recent travel. Turning off the trail, he chose a way that would keep him close against the cliffs, where he would have the partial cover of desert brush, piñon, and fallen boulders until he could reach a point that would put the bulk of the peak between himself and the ranch buildings.

From time to time he halted and studied the ranch anew through his glasses, and there was still no movement. The place might have been deserted for years; it lay silent and crystal clear in the bright noonday sun.

Far away across the desert the heat waves danced weirdly, and the towering shoulders of Monument Rock were purple against the sky, while between rolled the salmon, pink, and shadowed magenta of the desert, flecked with islands of cloud shadow. The air was so still that one felt as if a loud voice might shatter it to fragments, or dissolve the whole scene like something reflected in the rounded surface of a soap bubble.

Uneasily, Kilkenny pushed back his hat and mopped the perspiration from his brow and face. It was very hot. No breath of wind stirred the air. He dried his palms on his handkerchief and stared thoughtfully at the silent ranch, then let the buckskin pick his way forward another hundred yards. He hesitated again, every sense alert for danger, and he loosened the guns in their holsters and squinted his green eyes hard against the glare.

He studied the ranch again, near enough now to discern the slightest movement, but there was none. Removing the glasses from his eyes, he wiped them off, then studied the ranch again. If he went much farther, he would have to ride out in the open, and a marksman atop the peak would have him in easy shooting distance. For a long time he studied the rim of the nearer peak, then the buildings and corrals of Blue Hill, yet he saw nothing.

Something was radically wrong. Something had happened, and it must have happened since Rusty left the ranch . . . or after Rusty returned, for there was no sign of him, either.

If it were indeed a trap, it had been set much too soon, for he was not due for almost an hour. Furthermore, they would have left somebody in sight; they would have had some natural, familiar movement to lull his suspicions. Yet there was nothing; for all the movement, the scene might have been painted on glass.

Far away over the range a lonely steer moved, heading for water, miles away. Above, the heat-dancing air, where a buzzard swung on lazy, waiting wings. Kilkenny shoved his glasses back in the saddlebag and rode forward, clinging still to the cliff shadow and its slight obscurity. Now he slid his Winchester from the scabbard and, turning the buckskin away from the cliff, rode directly across to the shadow of the peak opposite.

When he could ride no closer without presenting too large a target, he swung down from the buckskin, and speaking to him softly, he moved forward. Always light on his feet, he moved now like a wraith, then halted, scarcely forty yards away from the ranch house, to look and listen. He waited there while a man might have counted a slow fifty. There was no sound, no movement. A flat, uneasy stillness hung over the place.

What had happened?

Kilkenny arose swiftly from behind the shrub and moved with swift, silent strides to the wall of the building and along the wall to Lona's window, from which he had seen the girl's shadow on that first day before she emerged to wave to him. The window was open, and the lace curtain hung limp and lifeless in the dead, still air.

Inside the room a mirror hung on the wall, and from the side he could see it, and it gave him a view of most of the inside of the room. There was nothing. He had left his Winchester with the horse, but now he slid a Colt into his hand and stepped quickly past the window to get the view from the opposite side. The room was empty. He stepped over the sill and stood inside.

There was some blood on the sill where Flynn had been shot the previous night. The door was open on the silent, sunlit patio. Kilkenny returned his gun to his holster and crossed to the door, studying the patio.

Under the eaves of the porch hung an *olla,* its sides dark with the contents of clear, cold water. Several strings of peppers hung from the eaves across the way and a spring bubbled from the ground into a tiny pool in the center of the patio, then trickled off through a stone pipe to empty into the water trough away at the corral.

Listening, he heard nothing. Yet within any one of the half dozen windows or two doors, a gun might wait. Back inside the window where he would be invisible, either Dunning or Mailer might stand, gun in hand. A gourd dipper hung near the *olla* and another at the spring. Kilkenny's mouth was dry and he longed for a drink. His ears straining with the effort to hear some sound, he waited a moment longer, then stepped out into the patio, and crossed it, to the door opposite. As he walked he glanced sharply right toward the open side from which he could see the corrals and the stable. All was bright and still.

The kitchen was empty. He placed a hand on the coffeepot, and it seemed to be vaguely warm. Lifting the lid of the stove, he saw a dull red glow among the few coals atop the gray of ashes and the grate. He stepped past the stove and walked into the dining room, and then he stopped.

In a doorway on his left a hand was visible, lying flat and lax, palm down on the floor. It was an old hand, worn and brown.

Stepping quickly around the table, Kilkenny saw the man who lay there, his bald head rimmed with a fringe of graying hair, his shirt dark with blood, and the floor beneath him stained with it.

A six-shooter lay near his hand and he still wore the apron that marked him for who and what he was. Dave Betts was dead. He had been shot twice through the chest.

Stepping quickly past him, Kilkenny looked into the room from which Betts had apparently emerged. It was definitely bachelor quarters. Turning to the room beside it, he found a mussed bed, and bending over, he sniffed the pillow, detecting a faint perfume. This, then, was where Lona had spent the night, but where was she?

And where were they all?

Stepping past the old man's body, Kilkenny moved the length of the long table and stepped through the open door into the large living room.

No one. This, too, was empty and still.

Somewhere, thunder rumbled distantly, mumbling in the far-off hills like a giant disturbed in his sleep. A faint breath of wind coming alive stirred out over the desert, and he heard the rustle of the peppers on their strings in the patio, and the curtain stirred faintly as though moved by a ghostly hand.

Kilkenny mopped his face of sweat and moved carefully across the room. The wind stirred again, and suddenly he heard another sound, a sound that sent a faint chill over him, making his shoulders twitch with the feeling of it. It was the sound of a strained rope, a rope that hung taut and hard, creaking a little, with a burden.

He stepped quickly to the door, his mouth dry. As though drawn by foreknowledge, his eyes went to the stable, whose wide-open door he could now see. From the cross beam over the high door, made high to admit racks of hay, he saw a long and heavy form suspended by a short rope.

Nearer, sprawled upon the ground in the open, lay an outstretched body. Gun in hand, Kilkenny stepped quickly outside, his eyes shooting right and left, then he ran across to the stable. One glance at the face, and he straightened, sorely puzzled. The man was a total stranger!

Crossing to the barn, he found where the rope was tied and unfastened it, lowering the man who had been hanged. His spurs jingled as the dead man's heels touched the ground. One glance at the blue face and he knew. It was Socorro.

Walking to the bunkhouse, he hesitated, for the steps were bloodstained. Then he moved inside. On the floor before him lay another stranger, his body fairly riddled with bullets, and against the end of the room sat Sam Starr, his head hanging on his chest, guns lax near his hands, and his shirt and trousers soaked in blood.

Crouching beside him, Kilkenny lifted Starr's chin, and miraculously, the man's lids stirred, and his lips worked to form words. "Shot . . . me," he whispered, his lips working at the words he could not shape, "Mulhavens."

Kilkenny motioned to the dead man inside the door. "Is that a Mulhaven?"

Starr indicated assent. "Tough," he said, "plenty . . . tough."

"Where's Dunning?"

Starr shook his head.

Kilkenny grasped the dying man's shoulder. "Tell me, man! Where's that girl! Where's Lona? Dammit, speak up!"

Starr's eyes forced themselves open and he struggled to speak. "D . . . d . . . don't know. Poke, he . . . away."

"Poke Dunning has her," Kilkenny said. "Is that it?"

Starr nodded. "Mailer's craz . . . y. Plumb gone bats . . ." Sam Starr's voice trailed away, and he fainted.

Carefully, Kilkenny eased the man to a prone position and grabbed a pillow for his head from the nearest bunk.

Swiftly, he worked over the dying man, doing what he could to ease his position and his pain. Then he hurried from the bunkhouse and made a quick survey of the ranch.

He found no one else. Four dead men and the dying Sam Starr. Dunning, Mailer, Lona, Rusty Gates, and Gordon Flynn were all gone.

Hurrying back with a bucket of cool water, he found Starr conscious. Holding a gourd dipper to the man's mouth, he helped him drink. Starr looked his gratitude. "Mailer's gone after . . . after your girl," he gasped. "He's crazy!"

"My girl?" Kilkenny was dumbfounded. "At Salt Creek?"

Starr nodded weakly. "An' . . . an' the Mulhavens are after G . . . G . . . Gates."

"What?" Kilkenny sprang to his feet. "But he wasn't an outlaw!"

"You try tellin' 'em that!" Starr's face was turning gray.

Kilkenny stood flat-footed and still above the dying man. Frank Mailer, kill-crazy and full of fury, was gone to Salt Creek after Nita. Somewhere, Poke Dunning was escaping with Lona, and his friend Rusty Gates, the man who had come into this only to help him, and probably with a wounded man for company, was riding to escape a blood-hungry posse whose reason had been lost in a lust for revenge for the killing of their own friends and brothers!

Kilkenny knew of the Mulhavens. A family of tough Irishmen, three of them veterans of the Indian wars. Hard, honest, capable men. He knew, too, the men of Aztec Crossing, and they were not men to take the bloodletting Mailer had visited upon them without retaliation. If they had trailed those men to this ranch, they would regard all upon it as tarred with the same brush and would make a clean sweep. Two of their group had died here, and that would make matters no easier.

Leaving Starr, he dashed outside and stopped in the sunlight. Where to go? Nita was in danger. Rusty was being pursued by a hanging mob, and Lona . . .

Kilkenny forced himself to coldness. Brigo was at Salt Creek with Nita, and so was Cain Brockman. He would have to gamble that they were protection enough. Lona, wherever she was, must wait, for it was not immediately apparent what danger she might be in. Rusty had evidently taken Flynn and somehow managed an escape, knowing that the wounded Flynn would certainly be taken as one of the outlaws. Rusty had come into this only to help him, and to have him hanged by mistake would be a horrible responsibility.

He took swift strides toward the corral, glancing over the remaining horses. Rusty's mount was not there.

Turning, he whistled shrilly, and in a moment saw Buck come trotting around the building toward him.

Again in the saddle, Kilkenny began a painstaking sweep of the ranch, yet his job was in a measure simplified by knowing that Gates must make his escape by some route that would take him from the rear of the buildings. Forcing himself to take his time, Lance Kilkenny soon found the tracks of Gates's horse and another. He studied the hoofprints of this other horse carefully, then mounted and worked the trail out of the brush and rocks to a shallow dip south and west of Blue Hill.

Apparently, Rusty was heading for the rough country of Malpais Arroyo, and walking his horses. Was that because of the wounded Flynn? Or to keep from attracting attention?

He was something over a mile south of the ranch when a bunch of tracks made by hard-running horses came in from the north. Lance felt his stomach turn over within him. The Aztec posse! They had seen them and were in pursuit. Touching a spur to the buckskin, he went into a lope, then a run. The tracks were easy to follow now. The wind whipped at his face, and thunder rumbled over the mountains beyond Monument Rock. The brim of his hat slapped back against his skull, but the buckskin, loving to run, ate into the distance with swiftly churning hoofs.

The trail dipped into the arroyo and led along it, and heedless of ambush, thinking only of his friend, Kilkenny rode on, his face grim and hard. He knew mobs and how relentless and unreasoning they could be. There would be no reasoning with this bunch. If he met them, it could well be a payoff in blood and bullets. He had never, to his knowledge, killed an honest man, but to save his friend he would do just that.

Suddenly he saw that the pace of the horses he followed had slowed, and he drew up himself, walking his horse, and listening. Then, carried by the echoing walls of the arroyo that had now deepened to a canyon, he heard a yell. Soon somebody called, "Boost him up here, durn it! Let's get this job over with!"

The voices were just around a bend in the rocks ahead. His stomach muscles tight and hard, his mouth dry, Kilkenny slid from his horse. His hands went to walnut-butted guns and loosened them in their holsters, then he moved around the bend and into sight.

There, beneath a huge old cottonwood, stood Rusty Gates, and beside him, Gordon Flynn. The wounded man was being held up by a man who stood directly in front of him. There were seven men here, seven hard, desperate men.

Flynn's eyes went past them and he saw Kilkenny.

"Kilkenny!" he yelled.

As one man, the posse turned to face the owner of that dread name.

He spoke, and his voice was clear and strong. "Step back from those men, damn you for a lot of brainless killers! Get away, or I'll take the lot of you!"

Chapter 6

SURPRISE HELD THE men of the posse immobile, and in the moment of stillness Kilkenny spoke again. His voice was sharp and clear. "You've got the wrong men there!

While you try to string up a couple of honest cowhands, the real killers are gettin' away!"

"Oh, yeah?" Terry Mulhaven's voice was sharp. He had suddenly decided he was not going to be bluffed, Kilkenny or no Kilkenny. "You keep out of this! Or maybe," he added, his voice lowering a note, "you're one of them?"

Kilkenny did not reply to him. Instead, he asked quickly, "Did any of you see the holdup? Actually see it?"

"I did," Worth said sharply. "I saw it."

"All right, then. Look again at these men. Were they among those you saw?"

Worth hesitated, glancing uneasily at Terry Mulhaven. "The redhead wasn't. I saw no redheaded man, but we wounded two of them, anyway, and this man is wounded." He gestured at Flynn. "That's enough for me."

"It's not enough!" Kilkenny returned crisply. "If all you want to do is kill, then kill each other or try killing me. But if you want justice, then try thinking rather than stringing up the first men you meet!"

"All right, mister. You tell us how we should be thinking. You talk quick, though."

"That man was shot by Poke Dunning when he tried to help a girl get away from that bunch of outlaws." Kilkenny spoke swiftly, for he had them listening now, and he knew western men. Quick to anger and quick to avenge an insult or a killing, they were also, given a chance, men of good heart and goodwill, and essentially reasonable men. They were also men of humor. Such men had been known to let a guilty man go free when he made some humorous remark with a noose around his neck, or under a gun. They respected courage, and given a chance to cool down, they would judge fairly.

He had them talking now, and he meant to keep them talking. "The men who rode to the Crossing were led by Frank Mailer, the worst of the lot," he continued rapidly, arresting and holding their attention by his crisp, sharp speech and the confidence of his knowledge. "With him rode Geslin, Sam Starr, Socorro, an' Scar Ethridge.

"Ethridge never came back. You hanged Socorro and

killed Starr at the ranch. You also killed an honest man, Dave Betts."

"We got Ethridge at the Crossin'," Mulhaven said, "but if that honest man was the hombre on the floor inside the house, we didn't kill him. He was dead when we got there!"

This was news to Kilkenny. Apparently Dave had given his life in trying to protect Lona Markham. Dunning had evidently carried her off.

"Mailer's still loose and I'm after him myself," Kilkenny added. "These two men were the only honest hands on the place aside from that old man you found dead."

Bill Worth walked over to Flynn and took the noose from his neck, then he removed the loop from Rusty's neck. "Glad you showed up," he said shortly. "I tried to tell these hombres that redhead wasn't among 'em!"

Kilkenny had no time for conversation. "Rusty," he said swiftly, "get Flynn back to the ranch. I'm ridin' to Salt Creek after Mailer. Then we'll have to hunt Poke Dunning."

Turning abruptly, he swung into his saddle, and with a wave at the posse and his friends, he was off at a dead run.

Terry Mulhaven stared after him, then mopped his brow. "Man!" he said. "When I turned around an' looked into them green eyes, I figured my number was up for sure!" He glanced at Rusty. "Is he as fast as they say?"

"Faster," Gates said wryly.

Bill Worth looked at the Mulhavens. "Let's pick up the bodies," he said gently, "and head for home. The folks will be worried."

"Yeah"—Terry nodded—"we better." He glanced sheepishly at Rusty and Flynn. "No hard feelin's?"

Gates stared at him, then his red face broke into a grin. "Not right now," he said, "but a few minutes ago I was some sore!"

In a tight knot, the posse headed north for the ranch, and later, with the bodies of the two fallen men across their saddles, they started toward home. They rode slowly and they talked but little, and as a result they were startled by a sudden grunt from their Apache tracker. "Look!" he said. "Big red hoss!"

They looked, and the tracks were there. Terry Mulhaven glanced at his brother, then at Worth. "Well," he said, "we know that track. We followed it all the way from Aztec. Let's see what we find this time!"

Grimly, they turned their horses down the trail made by Frank Mailer's horse. This time somebody would pay the cost of the heavy burden the two lead horses carried, the burden left upon them by the murdered men in the bank.

———

DUE EAST OF Monument Rock and the hideout used by Kilkenny was an old prospector's cabin. This adobe shelter had been used by drifting cowhands, by rustlers and sheepherders as a temporary shelter, but for some years now it had been passed by and forgotten. It was huddled in a tight little corner of rock far down one of the southern-reaching tentacles of Salt Creek Wash, and here Poke Dunning had taken Lona Markham.

She had not gone willingly. In the confusion of the Blue Hill ranch gun battle, Poke had made his move. His first thought had been to try to put a bullet in Frank Mailer, but as he moved to the window that faced the bunkhouse and the ongoing fracas, rifle in hand, he'd spotted big Frank sliding down the side of the wash that ran across one side of the ranch yard. He had a set of saddlebags over his shoulder and was out of sight before Dunning could shoot. Poke figured that the saddlebags probably held the loot from Mailer's robbery.

Realizing that no matter what happened during the shootout, he'd still have Mailer to deal with, Dunning headed for Dave Betts's room and Lona. Knowing that he had only moments before the posse turned its attention on the main house, he plunged into the room.

"Out the window, quick!" he snapped. "We're gettin' out of here."

"You go. I'm staying here." Lona had made the mistake of thinking that Kilkenny had come, and although she had been afraid because of all the shooting, she was now sure that if Poke was running, then Kilkenny must be winning.

"Dammit, girl!" He grabbed her by the arm and dragged her toward the window.

"You hold up there, Mr. Markham!" Dave Betts was frightened by the fear he saw in Lona's eyes . . . something was wrong here. He grabbed Poke's shoulder.

Turning, Poke drew his right-hand gun and shot Dave twice in the chest; then, as Lona opened her mouth to scream he knocked her unconscious with a diagonal swipe of the barrel. He shoved her out the window, and then dropping out after her, he headed for the corrals.

IN THE REMOTE cabin, never visited in these days by anyone, he left Lona tied securely.

He had not been able to escape the ranch on either his or Lona's personal mount. Her horse, Zusa, was essential to his new plan. He was tired of playing games with Mailer and Lona and everybody else. Lona was going to die. The two of them escaped the confusion back at the ranch. Frank Mailer would be revealed to be the vicious bank robber that he was, but in their escape there would be a tragic accident . . . a riding accident. His daughter would pass away and no one would ask any questions about his continuing to live on the ranch. There might eventually be some documents to be filed, but the right kind of lawyer could handle that.

He was headed now for Blue Hill, intending to arrive there just after dark. With this idea in mind, he cut an old trail south and rode on until he was in the tall shadow of Chimney Rock. He drew up and got stiffly from the saddle.

This place was lonely and secure. He would wait here until almost dark, then he was going to sneak in and get Lona's horse . . . once he'd done that, he could take her out, kill her with a blow to the neck, and fake the fall. Seating himself on the ground in the shadow of the Chimney, he filled his pipe and began to smoke.

It bothered him to contemplate the idea of murdering the girl that had lived as his daughter for so many years. She'd always been a tool, but he would admit that he was fond of her. For a few minutes he considered taking the money he'd hidden away and starting over somewhere else, but there wasn't quite as much as he'd have liked, and after all, he'd never been a quitter.

Nearby, a huge old cottonwood rustled its leaves and he leaned back, knocking out his pipe. There would be a couple of hours to kill, and he was in no hurry. He would sleep a little while. His lids became heavy, then closed, his big hands grew lax in his lap, and he leaned comfortably back among the rocks. It was a joke on Mailer that he had taken the big bay, Frank's favorite horse. The cottonwood had a huge limb that stretched toward him, and it rustled its leaves, gently lulling him to sleep.

He did not hear the slowly walking horses, even when a hoof clicked on stone. He was tired, and not as young as he once had been, but no thought of murdered men behind him, or of the girl, bound and helpless in a remote cabin, disturbed him. He slept on. He did not awaken even when the silent group of men faced him in a crescent of somber doom. Silent, hard-faced men who knew that blood bay, and carried with them the burden of their dead. It was the creak of saddle leather when Terry Mulhaven dismounted that awakened him.

Five men faced him on horseback, another on foot. Still another had thrown a rope over that big cottonwood limb, and Poke Dunning, who had lived most of his adult years with the knowledge that such a scene might be prepared for him at any moment, came awake suddenly and sharply, and his hand flashed for a gun.

He was lying on his side, his left gun beneath him, and somehow, in stirring around, his right gun had slipped from the holster. Not all the way, but so far back that when he grabbed it, he grabbed it around the cylinder, and not the butt.

The difference might seem infinitesimal. At this moment it was not. At this moment it was the difference between a fighting end and a hanging. Pat Mulhaven's rifle spoke, and the hand that held the gun was shattered and bloody.

Gripping his bloody hand, Poke Dunning stared up at

them. "What do you want me for?" he protested. "You've got the wrong man!"

"Yeah?" Pat Mulhaven sneered. "We heard that one before! We know that horse! We know you!"

"But listen!" he protested frantically. "Wait, now!" He got clumsily to his feet, his left hand gripping the bloody right. Great crimson drops welled from it and dripped slowly from his finger ends to the parched grass and sand beneath him.

He started to speak again, and then something came over him, something he had never experienced before. It was a sense of utter futility, and with it resignation. Roughly, they seized him.

"Give me a gun," he said harshly, "with my left hand! I'll kill the lot of you! Just my left hand!" he said, his fierce old eyes flaring at them.

"Set him on his hoss," Bill Worth said calmly, "behind the saddle."

———

SOMETIME LATER THEY rode on, turning their horses again toward home, and walking slowly, their task accomplished, with the feeling that their dead might ride on toward that dim cow-country Valhalla, attended by the men who had handled the guns.

Behind them, the shadow of Chimney Rock grew wider and longer, and the leaves of the cottonwood rustled gently, whispering one to the other as only cottonwood leaves will do, in just that way. And among them, his sightless eyes lifted skyward as if to see the last of the sunlit sky, and the last of the white clouds, looking through the cottonwood leaves, was Poke Dunning.

———

THE POINT SHADOWS of night had infiltrated the streets of Salt Creek when Lance Kilkenny came again to the town. The long-legged buckskin entered the dusty street with a swinging trot and did not stop until he reached the hitching rail of the Fandango. Yet already Kilkenny knew much. He knew that nothing had happened here tonight.

Before the Express, Lisa, the Portuguese, was sweeping the boardwalk, and he glanced up to see Kilkenny ride in; then, unaware of his identity, he returned to his sweeping. Before Starr's Saloon, Al Starr smoked his pipe, unaware that his brother was at this moment lying dead and chockfull of Aztec Crossing lead on the bunkhouse floor at Blue Hill. At the Fandango, Cain Brockman was arranging his stock for a big night.

All was sleepy, quiet, and peaceful. Although it was early, a lamp glowed here and there from a cabin window, and there was a light in the Express. The advancing skirmishers of darkness had halted here and there in the cover of buildings, gathering force for an invasion of the street. Lance swung down, spoke softly to the buckskin, and stepped up onto the boardwalk. There he turned again, and swept the street with a quick, sharp, all-encompassing glance. Then he pushed through the swinging doors into the almost empty saloon.

Brockman looked up quickly and jerked his head toward the door where Brigo sat, but Kilkenny walked directly to the bar, waving aside the bottle that Cain immediately lifted. "Has Mailer been in?"

Cain's eyes sparked. "No, ain't seen him. What's up?"

"Hell to pay!" Swiftly, Kilkenny sketched out what had happened. "He was headed for here," he added.

"Let him come!" Cain said harshly. "I've got an express gun loaded with buckshot."

Brigo was on his feet and coming over. Leaving Cain to tell him what had happened, Kilkenny went swiftly to Nita's door and rapped. At her reply, he opened the door and entered.

She stood across the room, tall, lovely, exciting. He went to her at once and took her hands, then stood and held them as he looked at her, his heart swelling within him, feeling now as no other woman had ever made him feel, as none ever could, none but this Spanish and Irish girl from the far borderlands. "Nita, I've got to find Lona and Frank Mailer . . . then I'm going to come back, and when I do, we're going to make this a deal. If you'll have me, we'll be married. We'll go on farther west, we'll go somewhere where nobody's ever heard of Kilkenny, and where we can have some peace, and be happy."

"You've got to go now?"

"Yes."

It was like her that she understood. She touched him lightly with her lips. "Then go . . . but hurry back."

He left it like that and walked back into the saloon. Brigo and Cain turned to look at him. With them was a tall, sandy-haired cowhand.

"This fellow says he saw Dunning and Lona riding east. He was some distance off, but he said it looked like she was tied. He lost them in the canyons of Salt Creek."

"All right. We'll have a look." Kilkenny took in the sandy-haired hand with a sharp, penetrating glance. This was a good man, a steady man. "You want to ride to Blue Hill and tell Rusty? Then if you want, have a look. That girl's in danger."

"I'll look," Sandy said. "I've heard about the fightin' this mornin'."

"You be careful," Kilkenny warned. "Poke Dunning is handy with a gun."

"I know him," Sandy said shortly. "We had trouble over some strays, once. He's right handy with a runnin' iron, too."

Where to look for Lona was the next thing. While he was looking for her he had to be cautious not to run afoul of Mailer. The man was dangerous, and he would be doubly so now.

"Night and day," Kilkenny told Cain and Brigo, "one of you be around. Never let up."

IN THE MORNING Kilkenny mounted the buckskin. He returned to the house at Blue Hill and scouted around, but the profusion of tracks told him nothing. Working the trail a bit farther out proved helpful in that he found the tracks of several riders. They seemed to be scouting around some and he figured they were out looking for the lost girl, same as he was. Their tracks had obliterated the original trail and so he followed them quickly, covering ground as fast as possible.

He had stopped at a well due west of Chimney Rock when he saw a rider approaching. It was Sandy. His face was drawn and gray. "Been ridin'," he said. "Rusty is out, too. An' that Flynn."

"How is he?"

"In no shape, but he won't quit. Head poundin' like a drum, I can tell. Pale around the gills. We tracked Poke as far as Monument Rock, then lost him. Other tracks wiped his out."

"The posse, maybe?"

"I reckon." Sandy wiped his chin after a long drink. "Maybe they got him."

"If they found him, somebody is dead." Kilkenny knew the men. "They didn't like it even when I stopped them hanging the wrong men. They wanted an eye for an eye."

"Dunning won't be taken easy," Sandy said. "Where you headin'?"

"Northeast. Look," he added, "why don't you swing back and follow the posse tracks? If they turn off the route back to Aztec, you've got a lead."

Sandy turned his bronc. "See you," he said, and cantered off.

Kilkenny wiped the back of his hand across his mouth. His eyes were dark with worry. Someplace in these bleak hills that girl was with Dunning. Someplace Mailer lurked. Neither was pleasant to think of. He swung into the saddle and glanced northeast. The tower of Chimney Rock loomed against the sky, beyond it the mountains, and there was a trail into them by that route. He turned the buckskin.

He rode with a Winchester across his saddle, his eyes searching every bit of cover, his ears and eyes alert. He saw nothing, heard nothing.

———

ON A POINT of rocks near Eagle Nest Arroyo, Frank Mailer, his face covered with a stubble of coarse black beard, watched Kilkenny riding north through his glasses, and he swore softly. Twice, the gunfighter had been close to him, and each time Mailer had held off rather than dare a confrontation. Being on the dodge had him worried, for too long he'd lived the easy life at Blue Hill, taking off to do jobs outside the territory but always with the safety of Dunning's ranch to return to if things got bad. He had learned of what had happened, knew of the end of Sam Starr and Socorro. He had found the body of Poke Dunning, lynched for the crimes that he, Mailer, had committed, but strangely he felt depressed. There was the man that he had wanted dead, and he was dead. He had the nine thousand dollars from the Aztec bank, a good horse, and a beltful of ammunition. But the good old days were gone. The hanging of Poke Dunning affected him as nothing else had; there was an inevitableness about it that frightened him.

Frank Mailer, six feet five in his socks and weighing over two hundred and fifty pounds, walked back to his gray horse. He stood with a hand on the pommel, and something was gone out of him. For the first time since he was a youngster, he was really on the dodge. He was running.

Poke had run, too, and it hadn't done him any good. Dunning had beat the game for years, and now look at him. Somehow it always caught up with you. Frank Mailer heaved himself into the saddle and turned his horse across country.

The sight of Dunning's body had even driven the lush beauty of Nita Riordan from his mind. He rode on, sullen and dazed; for the first time he had a feeling of being hemmed in, trapped.

Kilkenny was hunting something; was it him? Now there was something he could do. He could seek out a showdown with Kilkenny and beat him. There was a deep, burning resentment against the man. If he had stayed out of it, all would have been well.

A MERE HALF dozen miles north, Kilkenny rounded a sandstone promontory and saw just beyond a horseman picking his way over the rounded gray stones and gravel of a wash. The man looked up and waved. It was Sandy again.

"Found her," he said when they were closer. "Flynn found her. She was tied in a shack back in the hills. Dunning left her there with water and a little grub. Never saw nothin' like it. She was tied in the middle of the 'dobe with ropes running around her body an' off in all four directions. She couldn't move an inch one way or the other, an' couldn't get free, but she had her hands loose. Those ropes were made fast in the walls an' windows, knots so far away she couldn't reach 'em. She picked at one of the ropes until her fingers were all raw, tryin' to pull it apart."

"She's all right?"

"I reckon so. They took her to Blue Hill." Sandy eyed him thoughtfully. "Dunning left her the day before yesterday. You ain't seen him?"

"No. Nor Mailer."

"I'm headin' home." Sandy was regretful. "The boss will be raisin' hell. See you." He turned his horse, then glanced back. "Luck," he said.

Kilkenny sat his horse for a moment, then turned and started south again. Now he was hunting Mailer, not to kill him, unless he had to, but to make sure he was gone, out of the country, before he relaxed his guard.

"He will want to see," Kilkenny told Buck. "If he's on the dodge but hasn't left the country, he'll have headed for the ridgelines."

Shadows grew long and crawled up the opposite wall of the mountains, and Kilkenny turned aside, and in a hollow in the rocks, he bedded down. He built no fire, but ate a little jerked beef and some hardtack before crawling into his blankets.

He was out at dawn, and had gone only a few miles when he saw the tracks of a big horse cutting across his trail. A big horse . . . to carry a big man. Kilkenny turned the buckskin abruptly. He had no doubt that this was Frank Mailer's horse. It was rough terrain into which the trail was leading, country that offered shelter for an ambush. Yet he followed on, taking his time, following the sign that grew more and more difficult. A bruised branch of sage, a scratch on a rock, a small stone rolled from its place, leaving the earth slightly damp where it had rested but a short time before. Once he saw a scar atop a log lying across the trail where a trailing hoof had struck, knocking the loose bark free and leaving a scar upon the bark and the tiny webs in the cracks beneath the bark.

It was a walking trail. Whether Mailer knew he was tracked or not, once in the mountains he had been exceedingly careful, and it could not be followed at a faster pace than a walk. Sometimes Kilkenny had to halt, searching for the line of travel, but always there was something, and his keen eyes read sign where another might have seen nothing, and they pushed on.

Kilkenny drew up, and sitting his horse close against a clump of piñon, he rolled a smoke. His mouth tasted bad and his hair was uncombed. He squinted his eyes against the morning glare of the sun and studied the hills before him. He put the cigarette in his lips and touched a match to it, feeling the hard stubble of beard on his chin as he did so. His shirt felt hot and had the sour smell of stale sweat from much riding without time to change. He felt drawn and hard himself, and he worked his fingers to get the last of the morning damp out of them.

Then he rode out and he met the hard, flat sound of a rifle shot and felt the whip of it, barely ahead of his hat brim. He left the saddle, Winchester in hand, but there was no further shot. Staring up at the rocks, his eyes hard and narrow, he waited. There was no sound.

The warm morning sun lay lazily upon the sandstone and sage; a lizard came out from under a rock, and darted over another rock that was green with copper stain and paused there. Lying where he was, Kilkenny could see the beat of its tiny heart against its side. Then something flickered and he saw a vanishing leg and fired quickly, the .44 thundering in the depths of the canyon.

Chips flew from the rock where the leg had vanished and from the opposite side of the rock where his second shot had struck. Then he heard the sound of a running horse, and he came out and climbed into the saddle.

In a few minutes he had found the trail. A big horse carrying a heavy man and running swiftly. He moved after it, riding more warily now, knowing that Mailer knew he was on the trail, and that from now on it would be doubly hard.

He forded Coal Mine Creek, carrying little water now, and headed for the five-hundred-foot wall of the Hogback, a high, serrated ridge biting with its red saw teeth at the brassy sky. Then, suddenly, as though in a painting, horse and man were outlined sharp against the sky. An instant only, but Kilkenny's rifle leaped to his shoulder and the shot cracked out, echoing and reechoing from the wall of the Hogback. Kilkenny saw the horse stumble, then go down, and the man spring clear. He fired again, but knew he had missed.

Coming up through the brush, he dismounted near the fallen horse and returned his rifle to its boot. The Hogback reared above him in a brown and broken-toothed height that offered a thousand places of concealment. Kilkenny dug into his saddlebags and got out his moccasins. Leaving his boots slung on the pommel, he moved out after Mailer on foot.

There was no way of telling how he had gone, or where. Yet Kilkenny moved on, working his way in among the boulders. Then, at a momentary pause, he saw some birds fly up and directed his course that way, but working to get a little higher on the cliff. He was on a narrow ledge, some seventy feet above the jagged rocks below, when he heard a low call. Startled, he looked up, to see Mailer on a ledge some fifty yards higher ahead of him.

The man was smiling, and as he smiled he lifted his pistol. Kilkenny drew left-handed and snapped a shot. It was a fast draw and the shot was more to move Mailer than with the expectation of a hit. Mailer lunged sidewise and his own shot clipped the rocks above Kilkenny and spat dirt and gravel into his face.

A small landslide had scoured out a hollow in the mountain, and Kilkenny started up it. The climb was steep and a misstep might send him shooting all the way to the bottom, but the soft moccasins gave him a good toehold. When he reached the higher ledge he was panting and winded.

The sun was blazing hot here, and even the rocks were hot under his hands. The burned red sandstone was dotted with juniper and it broke off in a steep slope. Steep, but not a cliff.

He moved up behind a juniper and studied the mountain carefully. All was hot and still. Sweat smarted his eyes and he rubbed them out, then mopped the sweat from his brow and cheeks.

Overhead, an optimistic buzzard circled in widening sweeps. Far away over the valley that lay in the distance was Blue Hill. Almost due west was Salt Creek. A thin trail of smoke lifted near the town. Below, the terrain was broken into canyons and arroyos, and the color shaded from the deep green of the juniper to the gray-green of sage, and from the pale pinks and yellows of the faded sand to the deep burned reds and magentas of the rock.

Some thirty yards away a tree had died and the dry white bones of its skeleton lay scattered in a heap. Nearby a pack rat had built a mound of branches in a clump of manzanita. Kilkenny pulled his hat brim down to shade his eyes and moved out cautiously, walking on his cat feet across the mountainside.

Ahead of him a startled jackrabbit suddenly sprang from the ground and charged full tilt right at him. Kilkenny whirled aside and felt the blast of a bullet by his face. He started forward, running swiftly, and saw Frank Mailer spring up, gun in hand. Mailer fired and missed, and Kilkenny's shot blasted . . . too quick, but it cut through Mailer's shirt and then the man dove for him.

Kilkenny fired again, but whether he scored or not he had no idea, for he sprang forward and smashed a driving blow to Mailer's face. The punch was a wicked one and it caught the big man lunging in, caught the corner of his mouth and tore the flesh, so that Mailer screamed. Then he wheeled and grabbed Kilkenny's throat, wrenching him backward. Lance Kilkenny kicked his feet high and went over with Mailer, the sudden yielding carrying the big man off balance. Both went down and Mailer came up, clawing for his pistol, and Kilkenny drew his left-hand gun and fired. Mailer went to his knees, then grabbed wildly and caught Kilkenny's ankle. As Lance came down he lunged to his feet and dove for shelter in a nest of boulders. Flat on the ground, Kilkenny crawled to retrieve his gun, then loaded the empty chambers. Then he saw blood on the ground, two bright crimson stains, fresh blood!

A shot kicked dirt in his teeth and he spat it out and shot back, then lunged to his feet, his own position being too exposed, and sprang for the rocks and shelter.

He lit right into Mailer and the big man came up with a grunt and chopped for Kilkenny's skull with a pistol barrel. Bright lights exploded in his head and he felt his knees melting under him and slashed out with his own pistol, laying it across Mailer's face. He hit ground, heard an explosion, and Mailer fell on him.

Panting, bloody, and drunk with fury and pain, Frank Mailer leaped to his feet and stood swaying, a thin trickle of blood coming from a blue hole under his collarbone. He lunged at Kilkenny.

Exhausted, beaten, and punch-drunk himself, Kilkenny swung wildly and his fist connected with a sound like a rifle shot striking mud, and Mailer stopped, teetered, and fell.

Kilkenny backed up, his chest heaving, his lungs screaming for air, his skull humming with the blow he had recently taken. He caught up a gun and turned just as Mailer rolled on his back, a gun also in his hand. Both guns bellowed at once, and Kilkenny was knocked back on his heels, but as he staggered he pulled his gun down and fired again.

Where Mailer's ear had been there was blood, and the big man, seemingly indestructible, was getting up. With a wild, desperate kind of fury, Kilkenny flung himself on the rising man, and he heard guns bellowing, whether his own or Mailer's or both, he did not know, and then Mailer rolled free and fell away from the boulders. Slowly, ponderously, at each roll seemingly about to stop, the big man's body rolled over and over down the slope.

Fascinated, Kilkenny stared after him. Suddenly the man caught himself, and then, as if by magic, he got his hands under him. Something inside of Kilkenny screamed, *No! No!* and then he saw Mailer come to his feet, still gripping a gun.

Mailer swayed drunkenly and tried to fire, but the gun was empty. His huge body, powerful even when shot and battered, swayed but remained erect. Then, fumbling at his belt for cartridges, he began, like a drunken man trying to thread a needle, to load his gun. Kilkenny stared at him in astonishment, his own mind wandering in a sort of a sunlit, delirious world. Mailer faced him and the gun lifted, and Kilkenny felt the butt of his own gun jump and Mailer's hips jerked back grotesquely and he went up on his tiptoes. Then his gun spat into the gravel at his feet and he fell facedown on the slope.

———

WHEN KILKENNY OPENED his eyes again, it was dark and piercing cold. A long wind moaned over the mountaintop and he was chilled to the bone. He was very weak and his head hummed. How badly he was wounded he had no idea, but he knew he could stand little of this cold.

Near the pack rat's nest he found some leaves that crackled under his touch. And shivering with such violence that his teeth rattled and his fingers could scarcely find the matches, he struck and pushed the match into the leaves. The flames caught and in a moment the nest was crackling and blazing.

He knew he had been hit once, and perhaps twice. He had a feeling he was badly wounded, and how long he could survive on this mountaintop he did not know. He did know that it was in view of Salt Creek, if anyone happened to be outside. The flames caught the gray, dead wood and blazed high and he lay there, watching the inverted cone of flame climbing up toward the stars, filled with a blank cold and emptiness.

Finally, as the fire died and its little warmth dissipated, he turned and crawled back among the boulders and lay there, panting hoarsely and shivering again with cold.

When he got his eyes open again, the sky was faintly gray. He could distinguish a few things around him and there were here and there a few scattered sticks. He got them together with a handful of grass and put them on the coals of last night's fire, then cupped his hands above the small flame. He felt a raw, gnawing pain in his side and his face was stiff and his hands were clumsy. Overhead, a few stars paled and vanished like moths flying into smoke, and he added another small stick and felt for his gun. It was gone. He moved, scraping the fire along until he was beneath the dead tree. Slowly he built up the fire around its dried-out trunk, and as it caught he rolled backward, away from the flames. He lay there as the white branches went up in a rush of smoke and flame, and as he passed out he prayed for help.

His eyes flickered open again at a sun-brightened world and he saw a huge turkey buzzard hunched in a tree not fifty yards away. He yelled and waved an arm, but the buzzard did not move. It sat there, waiting, and then its head came up, and it launched itself on lazy wings and floated off over the desert.

Kilkenny lay still, staring up into the brassy vault of the sky, his mind floating in a half-world between delirium and death. Out of it floated a voice, saying, "Here's a hat!"

And then another voice. "They can't be up there! It ain't reasonable!"

There was a long silence, and suddenly his eyes flashed open. That was no delirium! Somebody was searching! Hunting for him! He tried to call out, but his voice would muster no strength, and then he gathered himself, and picking up a small stick from near the fire, he threw it.

"He's got to be here. You saw all that smoke an' that's Buck down there, an' where you find that horse he ain't far away!"

"Do you see him?" The voice was unfamiliar, sarcastic. "I don't."

Then the other. "I'm goin' on top!"

"You're crazy!"

A long time later a loud whoop and then running feet. "Here's Mailer! Hey, would you look at that? Man, what happened up here, anyway?"

He tried to call out again, and this time they came hurrying. Cain Brockman, Rusty Gates, Gordon Flynn, his head bandaged and his face thin, and with them several men from town. "You all right, Lance?" Gates pleaded, his face redder still with worry.

"What do you think?" Kilkenny muttered.

And when he opened his eyes again, he was lying in darkness between clean white sheets and he felt vastly relaxed and comfortable. And Nita came in, walking softly, and sat down beside him. "Everything all right?" she asked.

"Yes, ma'am," he whispered. "As long as when I'm well we're goin' to California to sit by the sea."

She smiled. "There's a little port town called San Pedro, and I expect the railroad workers and dock men will want a gambling hall as much as anyone." She kissed him gently. "When I see you're better, I'll have Cain start packing the wagons."

A GUN FOR KILKENNY

NOBODY HAD EVER said that Montana Croft was an honest man. To those who knew him best he was a gunman of considerable skill, a horse and cow thief of first rank, and an outlaw who missed greatness simply because he was lazy.

Montana Croft was a tall, young, and not unhandsome man. Although he had killed four men in gun battles, and at least one of them a known and dangerous gunman, he was no fool. Others might overrate his ability, but Montana's judgment was unaffected.

He had seen John Wesley Hardin, Clay Allison, and Wyatt Earp in action. This was sufficient to indicate to him that he rated a very poor hand indeed. Naturally, Montana Croft kept this fact to himself. Yet he knew a good thing when he saw it, and the good thing began with the killing of Johnny Wilder.

Now, Wilder himself was regarded as a handy youngster with a gun. He had killed a few men and had acquired the reputation of being dangerous. At nineteen he was beginning to sneer at Billy the Kid and to speak with a patronizing manner of Hardin. And then the stranger on the black horse rode into town, and Johnny took in too much territory.

Not that Johnny was slow—in fact, his gun was out and his first shot in the air before Croft's gun cleared leather. But Johnny was young, inexperienced, and impatient. He missed his first shot and his second. Montana Croft fired coolly and with care—and he fired only once.

Spectators closed in, looking down upon the remains. The bullet had clipped the corner of Johnny Wilder's breast pocket, and Johnny was very, very dead.

Even then, it might have ended there but for Fats Runyon.

Fats, who was inclined to view with alarm and accept with enthusiasm, looked up and said, "Only one man shoots like that! Only one, I tell you! *That's Kilkenny!*"

The words were magic, and all eyes turned toward Croft. And Montana, who might have disclaimed the name, did nothing of the kind. Suddenly he was basking in greater fame than he had ever known. He was Kilkenny, the mysterious gunfighter whose reputation was a campfire story wherever men gathered. He could have disclaimed the name, but he merely smiled and walked into the saloon.

Fats followed him, reassured by Croft's acceptance of the name. "Knowed you right off, Mr. Kilkenny! Only one man shoots like that! And then that there black hat, them black chaps—it couldn't be nobody else. Sam, set up a drink for Kilkenny!"

Other drinks followed . . . and the restaurant refused to accept his money. Girls looked at him with wide, admiring eyes. Montana Croft submitted gracefully, and instead of riding on through Boquilla, he remained.

In this alone he broke tradition, for it was Kilkenny's reputation that when he killed, he immediately left the country, which was the reason for his being unknown. Montana Croft found himself enjoying free meals, free drinks, and no bill at the livery stable, so he stayed on. If anyone noticed the break in tradition they said nothing. Civic pride made it understandable that a man would not quickly ride on.

Yet when a week had passed, Montana noticed that his welcome was visibly wearing thin. Free drinks ceased to come, and at the restaurant there had been a noticeable coolness when he walked out without paying. Montana considered riding on. He started for the stable, but then he stopped, rolling a cigarette.

Why leave? This was perfect, the most beautiful setup he had ever walked into. Kilkenny himself was far away; maybe he was dead. In any event, there wasn't one chance in a thousand he would show up in the border jumping-off place on the Rio Grande. So why not make the most of it?

Who could stop him? Wilder had been the town's toughest and fastest gun.

Abruptly, Croft turned on his heel and walked into the hardware store. Hammet was wrapping a package of shells for a rancher, and when the man was gone, Croft looked at the storekeeper. "Hammet," he said, and his voice was low and cold, "I need fifty dollars."

John Hammet started to speak, but something in the cool, hard-eyed man warned him to hold his tongue. This man was Kilkenny, and he himself had seen him down Johnny Wilder. Hammet swallowed. "Fifty dollars?" he said.

"That's right, Hammet."

Slowly, the older man turned to his cash drawer and took out the bill. "Never minded loaning a good man money," he said, his voice shaking a little.

Croft took the money and looked at Hammet. "Thanks, and between the two of us, I ain't anxious for folks to know I'm short. Nobody does know but you. So I'd know where to come if it was talked around. Get me?" With that, he walked out.

Montana Croft knew a good thing when he saw it. His first round of the town netted him four hundred dollars. A few ranchers here and there boosted the ante. Nobody challenged his claim. All assumed the demands were for loans. It was not until Croft made his second round, two weeks later, that it began to dawn on some of them that they had acquired a burden.

Yet Croft was quiet. He lived on the fat of the land, yet he drank but sparingly. He troubled no one. He minded his own affairs, and he proceeded to milk the town as a farmer milks a cow.

Nor would he permit any others to trespass upon his territory. Beak and Jesse Kennedy discovered that, to their sorrow. Two hard cases from the north, they drifted into town and after a drink or two, proceeded to hold up the bank.

Montana Croft, watching from the moment they rode in, was ready for them. As they emerged from the bank he stepped from the shadow of the hardware store with a shotgun. Beak never knew what hit him. He sprawled facedown in the dust, gold spilling out of his sack into the street. Jesse

Kennedy whirled and fired, and took Croft's second barrel in the chest.

Montana walked coolly over and gathered up the money. He carried the sacks inside and handed them back to Jim Street. He grinned a little and then shoved a hand down into one of the sacks and took out a fistful of gold. "Thanks," he said, and walked out.

Boquilla was of two minds about their uninvited guest. Some wished he would move on about his business, but didn't say it; others said it was a blessing he was there to protect the town. And somehow the news began to get around of what was happening.

And then Montana Croft saw Margery Furman.

Margery was the daughter of old Black Jack Furman, Indian fighter and rancher, and Margery was a thing of beauty and a joy forever—or so Montana thought.

He met her first on the occasion of his second decision to leave town. He had been sitting in the saloon drinking and felt an uneasy twinge of warning. It was time to go. It was time now to leave. This had been good, too good to be true, and it was much too good to last. Take them for all he could get, but leave before they began to get sore. And they were beginning to get sore now. It was time to go.

He strode to the door, turned right, and started for the livery stable. And then he saw Margery Furman getting out of a buckboard. He stared, slowed, stopped, shoved his hat back on his head—and became a man of indecision.

She came toward him, walking swiftly. He stepped before her. "Hi," he said, "I haven't seen you before."

Margery Furman knew all about the man called Kilkenny. She had known his name and fame for several years, and she had heard that he was in Boquilla. Now she saw him for the first time and confessed herself disappointed. Not that he was not a big and fine-looking man, but there was something, some vague thing she had expected to find, lacking.

"Look," he said, "I'd like to see you again. I'd like to see more of you."

"If you're still standing here when I come back," she told him, "you can see me leave town."

With that she walked on by and into the post office.

Croft stood still. He was shaken. He was smitten. He was worried. Leaving town was forgotten. The twinge of warning from the gods of the lawless had been forgotten. He waited.

On her return, Margery Furman brushed past him and refused to stop. Suddenly, he was angered. He got quickly to his feet. "Now, look here," he said, "you—!"

Whatever he had been about to say went unsaid. A rider was walking a horse down the street. The horse was a long-legged buckskin; the man was tall and wore a flat-brimmed, flat-crowned black hat. He wore two guns, hung low and tied down.

Suddenly, Montana Croft felt very sick. His mouth was dry. Margery Furman had walked onto her buckboard, but now she looked back. She saw him standing there, flat-footed, his face white. She followed his eyes.

The tall newcomer sat his buckskin negligently. He looked at Croft through cold green eyes from a face burned dark by the sun and wind. And he did not speak. For a long, full minute, the two stared. Then Croft's eyes dropped and he started toward the buckboard, but then turned toward the livery stable.

He heard a saddle creak as the stranger dismounted. He reached the stable door and then turned and looked back. Margery Furman was in her buckboard, but she was sitting there, holding the reins.

The stranger was fifty yards from Montana Croft now, but his voice carried. It was suddenly loud in the street. "Heard there was a gent in town who called himself Kilkenny. Are you the one?"

As if by magic, the doors and windows were filled with faces, the faces of the people he had robbed again and again. His lips tried to shape words of courage, but they would not come. He tried to swallow, but gulp as he would, he could not. Sweat trickled into his eyes and smarted, but he dared not move a hand to wipe it away.

"I always heard Kilkenny was an honest man, a man who set store by his reputation. Are you an honest man?"

Croft tried to speak but could not.

"Take your time," the stranger's voice was cold, "take your time, then tell these people you're not Kilkenny. Tell them you're a liar and a thief."

He should draw . . . he should go for his gun now . . . he should kill this stranger . . . kill him or die.

And that was the trouble. He was not ready to die, and die he would if he reached for a gun.

"Speak up! These folks are waitin'! Tell them!"

Miraculously, Croft found his voice. "I'm not Kilkenny," he said.

"The rest of it." There was no mercy in this man.

Montana Croft suddenly saw the truth staring him brutally in the face. A man could only die once if he died by the gun, but if he refused his chance now he would die many deaths. . . .

"All right, damn you!" he shouted the words. "I'm not Kilkenny! I'm a liar an' I'm a thief, but I'll be damned if I'm a yellow-bellied coward!"

His hands dropped, and suddenly, with a shock of pure realization, he knew he was making the fastest draw he had ever made. Triumph leaped within him and burst in his breast. He'd show them! His guns sprang up . . . and then he saw the blossoming rose of flame at the stranger's gun muzzle and he felt the thud of the bullet as it struck him.

His head spun queerly and he saw a fountain of earth spring from the ground before him, his own bullet kicking the dust. He went down, losing his gun, catching himself on one hand. Then that arm gave way and he rolled over, eyes to the sun.

The man stood over him. Montana Croft stared up. "You're Kilkenny?"

"I'm Kilkenny." The tall man's face was suddenly soft. "You made a nice try."

"Thanks . . ."

Montana Croft died there in the street of Boquilla, without a name that anyone knew.

Margery Furman's eyes were wide. "You . . . you're

Kilkenny?" For this time it was there, that something she had looked for in the face of the other man. It was there, the kindliness, the purpose, the strength.

"Yes," he said. And then he fulfilled the tradition. He rode out of town.

IN VICTORIO'S COUNTRY

T HE FOUR RIDERS, hard-bitten men bred to the desert and the gun, pushed steadily southward. Red Clanahan, a monstrous big man with a wide-jawed bulldog face and a thick neck descending into massive shoulders, held the lead. Behind him, usually in single file but occasionally bunching, trailed the others.

It was hot and still. The desert of southern Arizona's Apache country was rarely pleasant in the summer, and this day was no exception. Bronco Smith, who trailed just behind Red, mopped his lean face with a handkerchief and cursed fluently, if monotonously.

He had his nickname from the original meaning of the term *wild and unruly* and the Smith was a mere convenience, in respect to the custom that insists a man have two names. The Dutchman defied the rule by having none at all, or if he had once owned a name, it was probably recorded only upon some forgotten reward poster lining the bottom of some remote sheriff's desk drawer. To the southwestern desert country he was, simply and sufficiently, the Dutchman.

As for Yaqui Joe, he was called just that, or was referred to as the "breed" and everyone knew without question who was indicated. He was a wide-faced man with a square jaw, stolid and silent, a man of varied frontier skills, but destined to follow always where another led. A man who had known much hardship and no kindness, but whose commanding virtue was loyalty.

Smith was a lean whip of a man with slightly graying hair, stooped shoulders, and spidery legs. Dried and parched by desert winds, he was as tough as cowhide and iron. It was said that he had shot his way out of more places than most men had ever walked into, and he would have followed no man's leadership but that of Big Red Clanahan.

The Dutchman was a distinct contrast to the lean frame of Smith, for he was fat, and not in the stomach alone, but all over his square, thick-boned body. Yet the blue eyes that stared from his round cheeks were sleepy, wise, and wary.

There were those who said that Yaqui Joe's father had been an Irishman, but his name was taken from his mother in the mountains of Sonora. He had been an outlaw by nature and choice from the time he could crawl, and he was minus a finger on his left hand, and had a notch in the top of his ear. The bullet that had so narrowly missed his skull had been fired by a man who never missed again. He was buried in a hasty grave somewhere in the Mogollons.

———

OF THEM ALL, Joe was the only one who might have been considered a true outlaw. All had grown up in a land and time when the line was hard to draw.

Big Red had never examined his place in society. He did not look upon himself as a thief or as a criminal, and would have been indignant to the point of shooting had anybody suggested he was either of these. However, the fact was that Big Red had long since strayed over the border that divides the merely careless from the actually criminal. Like many another westerner he had branded unbranded cattle on the range, as in the years following the War Between the States the cattle were there for the first comer who possessed a rope and a hot iron.

It was a business that kept him reasonably well supplied with poker and whiskey money, but when all available cattle wore brands, it seemed to him the difference in branded and unbranded cattle was largely a matter of time. All the cattle had been mavericks after the war, and if a herd wore a brand it simply meant the cattleman had reached them before he did. Big Red accepted this as a mere detail, and a situation that could be speedily rectified with a cinch ring, and in this he was not alone.

If the cattleman who preceded him objected with lead, Clanahan accepted this as an occupational hazard.

However, from rustling cattle to taking the money itself was a short step, and halved the time consumed in branding and selling the cattle. Somewhere along this trail Big Red crossed, all unwittingly at the time, the shadow line that divides the merely careless from the actually dishonest, and at about the time he crossed this line, Big Red separated from the man who had ridden beside him for five long, hard frontier years.

The young hard case who had punched cows and ridden the trail herds to Kansas at his side was equally big and equally Irish, and his name was Bill Gleason.

When Clanahan took to the outlaw trail, Gleason turned to the law. Neither took the direction he followed with any intent. It was simply that Clanahan failed to draw a line that Gleason drew, and that Gleason, being a skillful man on a trail, and a fast hand with a gun, became the sheriff of the country that held his hometown of Cholla.

The trail of Big Red swung as wide as his loop, and he covered a lot of country. Being the man he was, he soon won to the top of his profession, if such it might be called. And this brought about a situation.

Cholla had a bank. As there were several big ranchers in the area, and two well-paying gold mines, the bank was solvent, extremely so. It was fairly, rumor said, bulging with gold. This situation naturally attracted attention.

Along the border that divides Mexico from Arizona, New Mexico, and Texas was an ambitious and overly bloodthirsty young outlaw known as Ramon Zappe. Cholla and its bank intrigued him, and as his success had been striking and even brilliant, he rode down upon the town of Cholla with confidence and seven riders.

Dismounting in front of the bank, four of the men went inside, one of them being Zappe himself. The other four, with rifles ready, waited for the town to react, but nothing happened. Zappe held this as due to his own reputation, and strutted accordingly.

The bank money was passed over by silent and efficient tellers, the bandits remounted, and in leisurely fashion began to depart. And then something happened that was not included in their plans. It was something that created an impression wherever bad men were wont to gather.

From behind a stone wall on the edge of town came a withering blast of fire, and in the space of no more than fifty yards, five of the bandits died. Two more were hung to a convenient cottonwood on the edge of town. Only one man, mounted upon an exceptionally fast horse, escaped.

Along the dim trails this was put down to chance, but one man dissented, and that man was Big Red Clanahan, for Big Red had not forgotten the hard-bitten young rider who had accompanied him upon so many long trails, and who had stood beside him to cow a Dodge City saloon full of gunfighters. Big Red remembered Bill Gleason, and smiled.

———

TWICE IN SUCCEEDING months the same thing happened, and they were attended by only one difference. On those two occasions not one man survived. Cholla was distinctly a place to stay away from.

Big Red was intrigued and tantalized. Although he would have been puzzled by the term, Big Red was in his own way an artist. He was also a tactician, and a man with a sense of humor. He met Yaqui Joe in a little town below the border, and over frequent glasses of tequila, he probed the half-breed's mind, searching for the gimmick that made Cholla foolproof against the outlaw raids.

There had to be something, some signal. If he could learn it, he would find it amusing and a good joke on Bill to drop in, rob Cholla's bank, and get away, thumbing his nose at his old pard.

The time was good. Victorio was on the warpath and had run off horses from the Army, killed some soldiers, and fought several pitched battles in which he had come off well, if not always the victor. The country was restless and frightened and pursuit would neither be easily organized nor long continued when every man was afraid to be long away from home.

"Think!" Red struck his hairy fist on the table between them. "Think, Joe! There has to be a signal! Those hombres didn't just pop out of the ground!"

Yaqui Joe shook his head, staring with bleary eyes into his glass. "I remember nothing—nothing. Except . . ."

His voice trailed off, but Big Red grabbed his shoulder and shook him.

"Except what, Joe? Somethin' that was different! *Think!*"

Yaqui Joe scowled in an effort to round up his thoughts and get a rope on the idea that had come to him. They had been over this so many times before.

"There was nothing!" he insisted. "Only, while we sat in front of the bank, there was a sort of light, like from a glass and the sun. It moved quickly across the street. Like so!" He gestured widely with his hand, knocking his glass to the floor.

Clanahan picked up the glass and filled it once more. He was scowling.

"And that was all? Yuh're shore?"

Waiting until he was sure Gleason was out of town, Big Red rode in. He did not like to do it, but preferred not to trust to anyone else. At the bank he changed some money, glancing casually around. Then his pulse jumped, and he grinned at the teller who handed him his money.

He walked from the bank, stowing away his money. So that was it! And of course, it could be nothing else.

The bank stood in such a position that the windows caught the full glare of the morning light, and that sunlight flowed through the windows and fell full upon the mirror that covered the upper half of the door that led behind the wickets where the money was kept.

If that door was opened suddenly, a flash of light would be thrown into the windows across the street! A flash that would run along the storefronts the length of the street, throwing the glare into the eyes of the bartender in the saloon, the grocer and the hardware man, and ending up on the faces of the loafers before the livery stable. One at least, and probably more, would see that flash, and the warning would have been given.

He gathered his men carefully, and he knew the men to get for the job. Yaqui Joe, because when sober he was one lump of cold nerve, then Bronco Smith and the Dutchman because they were new in the Cholla country, and skillful, able workmen. Then he waited until Victorio was raiding in the vicinity, and sent a startled Mexican into town with news of the Apache.

With Sheriff Bill Gleason in command, over half the able-bodied men rode out of town, and Big Red, with Yaqui Joe at his side, rode in. Bronco Smith and the Dutchman had come in a few minutes earlier, and it was Smith who blocked the opening of the mirrored door.

The job was swift and smooth. The three men in the bank, taken aback by the blocking of their signal, were tied hand and foot and the money loaded into canvas bags. The four were on their way out of town before a sitter in front of the livery stable recognized the half-breed.

———

UNDER A HOT, metallic sky the desert lay like a crumpled sheet of dusty copper, scattered with occasional boulders. Here and there it was tufted with cactuses or Joshua palm and slashed by the cancerous scars of dry washes. A lone ranch six miles south of Cholla fell behind them and they pushed on into the afternoon, riding not swiftly but steadily.

Clanahan turned in the saddle and glanced back. His big jaws moved easily over the cud of chewing tobacco, his gray-green eyes squinting against the hard bright glare of the sun.

"Anything in sight?" Bronco did not look around. "Mebbe we'll lose 'em quick."

"Gleason ain't easy lost."

"You got respect for that sheriff."

"I know him."

"Maybe Joe's idea goot one, no?" The Dutchman struck a match with his left hand, cupping it to his cigarette with his palm. "Maybe in Apache country they will not follow?"

"They'll follow. Only in Victorio's country they may not follow far. When we shift hosses we'll be all set."

"How far to the hosses?"

"Only a few miles." Red indicated a saw-toothed ridge on the horizon. "Yonder."

"We got plenty moneys, no?" The Dutchman slapped a thick palm on his saddlebags and was rewarded with the chink of gold coin. "Och! Mexico City! We go there and I show you how a gentlemans shall live! Mexico City with money to spend! There iss nothing better!"

Two ridges gaped at the sky when they reached the horses, two ridges that lay open like the jaws of a skull. Red Clanahan turned his horse from the dim trail he had followed and dipped down into the gap where lay a wide space of flat ground, partially shaded by two upthrust ledges that held a forty-degree angle above the ground. Four horses waited there, and two pack mules.

Smith nodded, satisfied. "Those mules will take the weight of the gold off our horses. Grub, too! Yuh think of everything, Red!"

"There's a spring under that corner rock. Better dump yore canteens and refill them. Don't waste any time."

"How about south of here?" Bronco stared off over the desert. "Is there more water?"

"Plenty water." Joe accepted the question. "Latigo Springs tomorrow night, and the day after Seepin' Springs."

"Good!" Smith bit off a chew of his own. "I was dry as a ten-year-old burro bone when I got here."

He needed nobody to tell him what that bleak waste to the south would be like without water, or how difficult to find water it would be unless you knew where to look.

"How much did we get?" Dutch inquired. "How much? You know, eh?"

"Fifty thousand, or about."

"I'd settle for half!" Smith spat.

"Yuh'll settle for a lot less." Red turned his hard green eyes on Smith. "I'm takin' the top off this one. Took me four weeks of playin' tag with Gleason to get the layout."

"What do yuh call the top?"

"Seventeen thousand, if she comes to fifty. You get eleven thousand apiece."

Bronco pondered the thought. It was enough. In seven years of outlawry he had never had more than five hundred dollars at one time. Anyway, he wouldn't have stayed that close to Gleason for twice the money. That sheriff had a nose for trouble.

When Big Red first suggested the raid on Cholla, Smith had thought him crazy, but he had to chuckle when he remembered the astonishment on the cashier's face when he stepped around and blocked the door with the mirror before it could be opened, and how Big Red had come in through the door on the other side that looked like it wasn't there.

The escape into Victorio's country was pure genius—if they avoided the Apaches. Yaqui Joe's idea had been a good one, but Red had already planned it in advance, as was proved by the waiting horses. Of necessity a pursuing force would have to go slow to avoid the Indians, and they would have no fresh horses awaiting them at the notch.

Under a hot and brassy sky they held steadily southward over a strange, wild land of tawny yellows and reds, bordered by serrated ridges that gnawed at the sky. Clanahan mopped the sweat from his brow and stared back over the trail, lost in dancing heat waves. As usual there was nothing in sight.

———

HOURS PASSED, AND the only movement aside from the walking of their horses was the wavering heat vibrations and, high under the sun-filled dome of the sky, the distant black circling of a buzzard. On the ground not even a horned frog or a Gila monster showed under the withering sun.

"How much farther to water, Joe?"

"One, maybe two mile."

"We'll drink and refill our canteens," Red told them, "but we stop no longer than that. We've got gold enough to do somethin' with and we'd better be gettin' on."

"No sign of 'Paches."

Red shrugged, then spat, wiping the sweat from the inside of his hatband.

"The time to look for Injuns is when there's no sign. Yuh

can bet the desert's alive with 'em, but if we're lucky they won't see us."

Latigo Springs was a round pool of milky-blue water supplied by a thin trickle from a crack in the sandrock that shaded it. The trickle waged a desperate war with the sun's heat and the thirsty earth. Occasionally, it held its own, but now in the late summer, the water was low.

They swung down and drank, then they held their canteens into the thin flow of the spring. They filled slowly. One by one they sponged out the nostrils and mouths of their horses and led the grateful animals to the water.

Bronco wandered out to where he could look back over their trail. He shaded his eyes against the sun, but then as he started to turn back, he hesitated, staring at the ground.

"Red." His voice was normal in tone, but it rang loudly in the clear, empty air.

Caught by some meaningful timbre in his tone, the others looked up. They were wary men, alert for danger and expecting it. They knew the chance they took, crossing Victorio's country at this time, and trouble could blossom from the most barren earth.

Big Red slouched over on the run-down heels of his worn boots. Mopping his face and neck with a bandanna, he stared at the tracks Bronco indicated.

Two horses had stood here. Two riders had dismounted, but not for long.

"Hey!" Clanahan squatted on his heels. "Those are kids' tracks!"

"Uh-huh." Bronco swore softly. "Kids! Runnin' loose in Apache country. Where yuh reckon they came from, Red?"

Red squinted off to the south and west. The direction of the tracks was but little west of their own route.

"What I'm wonderin' is where they are goin'," he said dubiously. "They shore ain't headed for nowhere, thataway, and right smack into the dead center of the worst Injun country!"

Smith stared off over the desert, shook his head wonderingly, then walked back to the spring and drank deeply once more. He was a typical man of the trail. He drank when there was water, ate whenever there was food, rested whenever there was a moment to relax, well knowing days might come when none of the three could be had. He straightened then, wiping the stubble of beard around his mouth with the back of his hand.

"Somet'ing iss wrong?" The Dutchman glanced at Red. "What iss, aboot a kid?"

"Couple of youngsters ridin' south. Boy, mebbe thirteen or fourteen, and a girl about the same age." He mopped his face again, and replaced his hat. "Mount up."

They swung into their saddles and Red shifted his bulk to an easy seat. The saddle had grown uncomfortably hot in the brief halt. They started on, walking their horses. It was easy to kill a good horse in this heat. Suddenly the trail the kids were taking veered sharply west. Clanahan reined in and stared at it.

"Childer!" the Dutchman exclaimed in a puzzled voice. "Und vhy here?"

"They are shore headin' into trouble," Smith said, staring at their trail. His eyes stole sheepishly toward Clanahan, and he started to speak, then held his peace.

The Dutchman sat stolidly in the saddle. "Mine sister," he said suddenly, absently, "has two childer. Goot poys."

―――――

YAQUI JOE LOOKED over his shoulder at their trail, but it was empty and still. Off on their far right a line of magenta-colored ridges seemed to be stretching long fingers of stone toward the trail the kids had taken, as though to intercept them. A tuft of cactus lifted from the crest of the nearest hill like the hackles on an angry dog.

Red's mouth was dry and he dug into his shirt pocket for his plug and bit off a sizable chunk. He rolled it in his big jaws and started his horse moving along the trail to the west, following the two weary horses the youngsters were riding.

Smith stared at the desert. "Glory, but it's hot!"

He suddenly knew he was relieved. He had been afraid Red would want to hold to their own route. Safety lay south, only danger and death could await them in the west, but he kept thinking of those kids, and remembering what Apaches could do to a person before that person was lucky enough to die. Thoughtfully, he slipped a shell from a belt loop and dropped it into his shirt pocket.

An hour had passed before Clanahan halted again, and then he lifted a hand.

"Joe," he said, "come up here."

The four gathered in a grim, sun-beaten line. Five unshod ponies had come in from the east and were following the trail the youngsters had left.

"'Paches," Joe said. "Five of them."

Red's horse seemed to start moving of its own volition, but as it walked forward Red dropped a hand to the stock of his Winchester and slid it out and laid it across his saddlebow. The others did likewise.

Suddenly, with the tracks of those unshod ponies, the desert became a place of stealthy menace. These men had fought Apaches before, and they knew the deadly desert warriors were men to be reckoned with. The horses walked a little faster now, and the eyes of the four men roved unceasingly over the mirage-haunted desert.

Then the faraway boom of a rifle jarred them from their drowsy watchfulness. Red's gelding stretched his long legs into a fast canter toward a long spine of rock that arched its broken vertebrae against the sky. Suddenly he slowed down. The rifle boomed again.

"That's a Henry," Bronco said. "The kid's got him a good rifle."

Red halted where the rocks ended and stood in his stirrups. A puff of smoke lifted from a tiny hillock in the basin beyond, and across the hillock he could see that two horses were down. Dead, or merely lying out of harm's way?

In the foreground he picked up a slight movement as a slim brown body wormed forward. The other men had dropped from their saddles and moved up. Still standing in his stirrups, Clanahan threw his Winchester to his shoulder, sighted briefly, then fired.

The Apache leaped, screamed piercingly, then plunged over into a tangle of cholla. Bronco and the Dutchman fired as one man, then Joe fired. An Indian scrambled to his feet and made a break for the shelter of some rocks. Three rifles boomed at once, and the Indian halted abruptly, took two erect, stilted steps, and plunged over on his face.

They rode forward warily, and Clanahan saw a boy, probably fifteen years old, rise from behind the hillock, relief strong in his handsome blue eyes.

"Shore glad to see yuh, mister." His voice steadied. "I reckon they was too many for me."

Red shoved his hat back and spat. "You was doin' all right, boy." His eyes shifted to the girl, a big-eyed, too-thin child of thirteen or so. "What in thunderation are yuh doin' in this country? This here's 'Pache country. Don't yuh know that?"

The lad's face reddened. "Reckon we was headed for Pete Kitchen's place, mister. I heerd he was goin' to stay on, Injuns or no, an' we reckoned he might need help."

Clanahan nodded. "Kitchen's stayin' on, all right, and he can use help. He's a good man, Pete is. Your sister work, too?"

"She cooks mighty good, washes dishes, mends." The boy looked up eagerly. "You fellers wouldn't be needin' no help, would yuh? We need work powerful bad. Pa, he got hisself killed over to Mobeetie, and we got our wagon stole."

"Jimmy stole the horses back!" the girl said proudly. "He's mighty brave, Jimmy is! He's my brother!"

Clanahan swallowed. "Reckon he is, little lady. I shore reckon."

"He got him an Injun out there," Smith offered. "Dead center."

"I did?" The boy was excited and proud. "I guess," he added a little self-consciously, "I get to put a notch on my rifle now!"

———

BRONCO STARTED AND stared at Red, and the big man hunkered down, the sunlight glinting on his rust-red hair.

"Son, don't yuh put no notch on yore rifle, nor ever on yore gun. That there's a tinhorn trick, and you ain't no tinhorn. Anyway," he added thoughtfully, "I guess killin' a man ain't nothin' to be proud of, not even an Injun. Even when it has to be did."

The Dutchman shifted uneasily, glancing at the back trail. Yaqui Joe, after the manner of his people, was not worried. He squatted on his heels and lighted a cigarette, drowsing in the hot, still afternoon.

"We better be gettin' on," Clanahan said, straightening. "Them shots will be callin' more Injuns. I reckon you two got to get to Kitchen's all right, and this is no country to be travelin' with no girl, no matter how good a shot yuh are. That Victorio's a he-wolf. We better get on."

"Won't do no good, Red," Smith said suddenly. "Here they come!"

"Gleason?"

"No. More 'Paches!"

A shot's flat sound dropped into the stillness and heat, and the ripples of its widening circle of sound echoed from the rocks. Joe hit the ground with his face twisted.

"Got me!" he grunted, staring at the torn flesh of his calf and the crimson of the blood staining his leg and the torn pants.

Clanahan rolled over on his stomach behind a thick clump of creosote bush and shifted his Winchester. The basin echoed with the flat, absentminded reports of the guns. Silence hung heavy in the heat waves for minutes at a time, and then a gun boomed and the stillness was spread apart by a sound that was almost a physical blow.

Sweat trickled into Red's eyes and they smarted bitterly. He dug into his belt loops and laid out a neat row of cartridges. Once, glancing around, Red saw that the little girl was bandaging Joe's leg while the Yaqui stared in puzzled astonishment at her agile, white fingers.

Out on the lip of the basin a brown leg showed briefly against the brown sand. Warned by the movement, Clanahan pointed a finger of lead and the Apache reared up, and the Dutchman's Henry boomed.

It was very hot. A bullet kicked sand into Red's eyes and mouth. His worn shirt smelled of the heat and of stale sweat.

He scratched his jaw where it itched and peered down across the little knoll.

Across the basin a rifle sounded, and Smith's body tensed sharply and he gave out a long "Aaahh!" of sound, drawn out and deep. Red turned his head toward his friend and the movement drew three quick shots that showered him with gravel. He rolled over, changing position.

Bronco Smith had taken a bullet through the top of the shoulder as he lay on his stomach in the sand, and it had buried itself deep within him, penetrating a lung, by the look of the froth on his lips.

Smith spat and turned his eyes toward Red. "Anyhow," he said hoarsely, "we put one over on Gleason."

"Yeah."

Red shifted his Winchester, and when an Apache slithered forward, he caught him in the side with a bullet, then shifted his fire again.

Then for a long time nothing seemed to happen. A dust devil danced in from the waste of the desert and beat out its heart in a clump of ironwood. Red turned his head cautiously and looked at the boy. "How's it, son? Hotter'n blazes, ain't it?"

Later, the afternoon seemed to catch a hint from the purple horizon and began to lower its sun more rapidly. The nearby rocks took on a pastel pink that faded, and in the fading light the Apaches gambled on a rush.

Guns from the hollow boomed, and two Indians dropped, and then another. The rest vanished as if by a strong wind, but they were out there waiting. Clanahan shifted his position cautiously, fed shells into his gun, and remembered a black-eyed girl in Juarez.

A lizard crawled from a rock, its tiny body quivering with heat and the excited beat of its little heart as it stared in mute astonishment at the rust-red head of the big man with the rifle.

———

SHERIFF BILL GLEASON drew up. When morning found the posse far into the desert, he decided he would ride forward until noon, and then turn back. The men who rode with him were nervous about their families and homes, and to go farther would lead to out-and-out mutiny. It was now mid-morning, and the tracks still held west.

"Clanahan's crazy!" Eckles, the storekeeper in Cholla, said. He was a talkative man, and had been the last to see and the first to mention that Big Red was on a trail. "What's he headin' west for? His only chance is south!"

Ollie Weedin, one of the Cholla townsmen, nudged Gleason. "Buzzards, Bill. Look!"

"Let's go," Gleason said, feeling something tighten up within him. The four they trailed were curly wolves who had cut their teeth on hot lead, but in the Apache country it was different.

"Serves 'em right if the Injuns got 'em!" Eckles said irritably. "Cussed thieves!"

Weedin glanced at him in distaste. "Better men than you'll ever be, Eckles!"

The storekeeper looked at Weedin, shocked. "Why, they are thieves!" he exclaimed indignantly.

"Shore," someone said, "but sometimes these days the line is hard to draw. They took a wrong turn, somewheres. That Clanahan was a good man with a rope."

In the hollow band of hills where the trail led, they saw a lone gray gelding, standing drowsily near a clump of mesquite. And then they saw the dark, still forms on the ground as their horses walked forward. No man among them but had seen this before, the payoff where Indian met white man and both trails were washed out in blood and gun smoke.

"They done some shootin'!" Weedin said. "Four Apaches on this side."

"Five," Gleason said. "There's one beyond that clump of greasewood."

A movement brought their guns up, and then they stopped. A slim boy with a shock of corn-colored hair stood silently awaiting them in sun-faded jeans and checkered shirt. Beside him was a knobby-kneed girl who clutched his sleeve.

"We're all that's left, mister," the boy said.

Gleason glanced around. The eyes of Yaqui Joe stared into the bright sun, still astonished at the white fingers that had bandaged his leg in probably the only kindness he had ever experienced. He had been shot twice in the chest, aside from the leg wound.

Bronco Smith lay where he had taken his bullet, the gravel at his mouth dark with stain.

The Dutchman, placid in death as in life, held a single shell in his stiff fingers and the breech of his rifle was open.

Gleason glanced around, but said nothing. He turned at the excited yell from Eckles. "Here's the bank's money! On these dead mules!"

Ollie Weedin stole a glance at the sheriff, but said nothing. Eckles looked around and started to speak, but at Weedin's hard glare he hesitated, and swallowed.

"It was one buster of a fight," somebody said.

"There's seventeen Injuns dead," the boy offered. "None got away."

"When did this fight end, boy?" Gleason asked.

"Last night, about dusk. They was six of 'em first. I got me one, and he got two or three with a six-shooter. Then they was more come, and a fight kind of close up. I couldn't see, as it was purty dark, but it didn't last long."

Gleason looked at him and chewed his mustache. "Where'd that last fight take place, son?" he asked.

"Yonder."

Silently the men trooped over. There was a lot of blood around and the ground badly ripped up. Both Indians there were dead, one killed with his own knife.

Weedin stole a cautious look around, but the other men looked uncomfortable and, after a moment of hesitation, began to troop back toward their horses. Gleason noticed the boy's eyes shoot a quick, frightened glance toward a clump of brush and rocks, but ignored it.

Ollie shifted his feet.

"Reckon we better get started, Bill? Wouldn't want no running fight with those kids with us."

"Yuh're right. Better mount up."

He hesitated, briefly. The scarred ground held his eyes and

he scowled, as if trying to read some message in the marks of the battle. Then he turned and walked toward his horse.

All of them avoided glancing toward the steeldust, and if anyone saw the sheriff's canteen slip from his hand and lie on the sand forgotten, they said nothing.

Eckles glanced once at the horse that dozed by the mesquite, but before he could speak his eyes met Ollie Weedin's and he gulped and looked hastily away. They moved off then, and no man turned to look back. Eckles forced a chuckle.

"Well, kid," he said to the boy, "yuh've killed yuh some Injuns, so I reckon yuh'll be carvin' a notch or two on your rifle now."

The boy shook his head stiffly. "Not me," he said scornfully. "That's a tinhorn's trick!"

Gleason looked over at Ollie and smiled. "Yuh got a chaw, Ollie?"

"Shore haven't, Bill. Reckon I must have lost mine, back yonder."

THAT PACKSADDLE AFFAIR

RED CLANAHAN, A massive man with huge shoulders and a wide-jawed face, was no longer in a hurry. The energetic posse which had clung so persistently to his trail had been left behind on the Pecos. Their horses had played out and two of them were carrying double.

Red had pushed on to Lincoln, where he'd swapped his sorrel for a long-legged, deep-chested black with three white stockings. Then with only time out for a quick meal and a changing of saddles, he'd headed west for the Rio Grande and beyond it, the forks of the Gila.

Packsaddle Stage Station was a long, low building of adobe, an equally long, low stable, and two pole corrals. There was a stack of last year's hay and a fenced-in pasture where several stage horses grazed, placid in the warm morning sun. Three saddled horses stood three-legged at the hitch rail, and a drowsy Mexican, already warming up for his siesta, sat in the shade alongside the building.

Slipping the thongs from his pistol butt, Clanahan rode down the last hundred yards to the station and dismounted at the trough. Keeping his horse between himself and the station, he loosened the cinch a little and then led the horse to a patch of grass in the shade alongside the trail. Only then did he start for the station.

A narrow-shouldered man with a thin wolf's face had come from the stage station and was watching him. He wore a gun butt forward in a right-side holster, which might be used for either the left or right hand.

"Come down the trail?" he asked, his narrow eyes taking in Clanahan with cool attention.

"Part way. Came down from the Forks and across the Flat."

"Stage is late." The tall man still watched him. "Wondered if you'd seen it?"

"No." Clanahan walked on by and opened the station door. It was cool and shadowed inside. There were several tables, chairs, and a twenty-foot bar at which two men lounged, talking to the barkeep. Another man sat at a table in the farthest corner. Both the men at the bar looked rough and trail wise.

Red Clanahan moved to the end of the bar and stopped there where he could watch all the men and the door as well. "Rye," he said, when the bartender glanced his way.

As he waited, he rested his big hands on the bar and managed a glance toward the silent man in the corner. The man just sat there with his hands clasped loosely on the table, unmoving. He wore a hat that left only his mouth and chin visible at this distance and in this light. He wore a string tie and a frock coat.

There was a situation here that Red could not fathom, but he realized he had walked into something happening or about to happen—probably connected with the arrival of the stage.

The man from outside came back in. His hips were wider than his shoulders and the holster gave him a peculiarly lop-sided appearance.

Red Clanahan had a shock of red hair and a red-brown face with cold green eyes above high, flat cheekbones. Once seen, he was not easily forgotten, for he was six feet three and weighed an easy two hundred and thirty pounds. And there were places where he was not only known, but wanted.

There was a matter of some cattle over in Texas. Red's father had died while he was away, and when he returned he found that the three thousand head his father had tallied, shortly before his death, had mysteriously been absorbed by two larger herds. With no legal channels of recovery open to him, Red had chosen illegal methods, and one thing had led to another. Red Clanahan was high on the list of men wanted in Texas.

He finished his drink and had another. Then he looked over at the bartender. "How about some grub?"

The bartender was a big man, too, with a round face and two chins but small, twinkling eyes and a bald head. He removed his cigar and nodded. "When the stage comes in—'most any time."

The two men turned to look at him. Then the tall man looked around at the bartender. "Feed him now, Tom. Maybe he wants to ride on."

Red glanced up, his cold green eyes on the speaker. "I can wait," he said coolly.

One of the other men turned. He was short and thickset, with a scar on his jaw. "Maybe we don't want you to wait," he said.

Red Clanahan looked into the smaller man's eyes for a long, slow minute. "I don't give a royal damn what you want," he said quietly. "Whatever you boys are cookin', don't get it in my way or I'll bust up your playhouse."

He reached for the bottle and drew it nearer as the short man started toward him. "Listen, you—"

He came one step too close and Red Clanahan hit him across the mouth with the back of his big hand. The blow seemed no more than a gesture but it knocked the shorter man sprawling across the room, his lips a bloody pulp.

Red met the gaze of the other men without moving or turning a hair. "Want in?" he said. "I'm not huntin' trouble but maybe you're askin' for it."

The tall man with the narrow shoulders looked ugly. "You swing a wide loop, stranger. Perhaps you're cuttin' into something too big for you."

"I doubt it."

His cool assurance worried Ebb Fallon. They had a job to do, and starting a fight with this stranger was no way to do it. Who was the man? Fallon stared at him, trying to remember. He was somebody, no doubt about that.

Shorty Taber got up slowly from the floor. Still dazed, he touched his fingers to his crushed lips and stared at the blood. Pure hatred was in his eyes as he looked up at Clanahan.

"I'll kill you for that," Taber said.

Red Clanahan reached for the bottle and filled his glass.

"Better stick to punchin' cows," he said. "Quit goin' around pickin' fights with strangers. You'll live longer."

Taber glared at him and his right hand dropped a fraction. Red was looking at him, still holding the bottle. "Don't try it," he warned. "I could take a drink and shoot both your ears off before you cleared leather."

Taber hesitated, then turned and walked to his friends. They whispered among themselves for a few minutes while the bartender polished a glass. Through it all, the man at the table had not moved. In the brief silence there was a distant pounding of hoofs and a rattle of wheels.

Instantly, two of the three turned to the door. The third stepped back and dropped into a chair near the wall, but facing the door. The bartender looked nervously at Red Clanahan. "We'll serve grub when the passengers arrive," he said. "They change teams here."

The stage drew up out front and then the door opened. Two men and a woman came in, and then a girl. She was slender and tall, with large violet eyes. She looked quickly toward the bar. Then her eyes touched fleetingly on Red's face, and she went on to the table and seated herself there. Obviously, she was disturbed.

Red Clanahan saw her eyes go to the third of the three riders, the fattish man who had remained indoors. Red happened to turn his head slightly and was shocked by the expression on the bartender's face. He was dead-white and his brow was beaded with sweat.

The passengers ate quietly. Finally the driver came in, had a drink, and turned. "Rolling!" he called. "Let's go!"

All got to their feet, and as they did, Ebb Fallon walked to the door, standing where the passengers had to brush him to get by. The girl was last to leave. As she turned to the door, the man at the nearby table got up.

"All right, Ebb," he said, "tell 'em to roll it."

He moved toward the girl. "My name's Porter, ma'am. You'd best sit down."

"But I've got to get on the stage!" she protested indignantly. "I can't stay."

She started past him and Porter caught her wrist. "Came to see your father, didn't you?" the man said. "Well, he's here."

That stopped her. Outside, the stage was in motion; then they heard it go down the trail. When the rumble of wheels had died away, the door of the station opened, and Taber stepped in. He looked at the bartender, then at Red. His eyes shifted on to the girl.

"Well, where is he?" she demanded.

Ebb Fallon lifted his hand and pointed to the man seated at the table in the corner. But before the girl could move, the bartender put one hand on the bar. "Ma'am," he said, his voice strangely gentle, "don't go to that man. They are tryin' to trick you. They want the claim."

"But, I—" She looked from one to the other. "I don't understand."

Fallon had turned on the bartender, and as he looked across the hardwood at him, his eyes were devilish. "I'll kill you for that, Sam."

"Not while I'm here," Red Clanahan said.

Fallon's face turned dark. "You keep out of this!" he flared. "Be glad you got off so easy before!"

Red continued to lean on the bar. "Ma'am," he said, "I've no idea what this is all about, but I'm your friend."

The girl turned sharply and went to the man in the corner. Yet as her hand touched him, he fell slowly forward, his hat rolling to the floor. He slumped on the table, his cheek against the tabletop. His eyes were wide and staring. Over one eye was a blue hole.

She stared back in horror. "Dan! That's Dan Moore, Daddy's friend!"

"That *was* Dan Moore," Fallon replied. "You come with us, ma'am."

Fallon started toward her and she shrank back. Shorty Taber and Porter turned suddenly on the bartender and Red. "Just stay where you are, you two. This girl goes with us. She'll be all right," he added. "We just want some information and then she can go on her way."

Red Clanahan straightened at the bar and reached for the bottle. Coolly, he poured a drink. "You're wastin' your time," he said patiently. "She doesn't know anything about it and never did."

Ebb Fallon turned sharply. "What's that? What did you say?"

"You heard me right. She knows nothing about the claim. Whoever hired you sure picked the dumbest help he could find. First you kill the one man who could help you; then you risk hell by kidnappin' this girl off that stage. And she not knowin' a thing!"

He looked from Fallon to Porter, his eyes cold with contempt. "Ever stop to think what'll happen when that stage reaches the end of the line and that driver finds she was taken off here? If you recall, western folks don't take to men troublin' women." He filled his glass. "I look to see you hang."

"Who are you?" Fallon persisted. "What do you know about this?"

"Who I am doesn't matter," Red replied, "except that I'm tougher than the three of you and would admire to prove it. But I'll tell you this: you did a blundering job of killing this girl's father. He wasn't dead when you left him."

"What?" Fallon's face was livid. "What's that?"

"I said he wasn't dead. He got into a saddle and rode all of ten miles before he passed out. He was a game man. I found him on the trail, cared for him—sat with him until he died. That was about daybreak this mornin'."

"I don't believe it!" Taber burst out. "You're lyin'!"

Clanahan glanced at Taber. "Do you want to get slapped around some more? I'd enjoy doin' it."

Taber stepped back, his gun barrel lifting. "You try it!" he snarled. "I'll kill you!"

Red ignored him. "Her pa told me about the claim. Told me where it was, all about it." He smiled. "Fact is, I was there this mornin', and if you want to talk business, get your boss down here with some cash."

"Cash?"

"I'm sellin' my information," Red replied, "for fifteen thousand dollars."

"But that claim belongs to the girl!" the bartender protested.

"Not if they get down there first and change the stakes and filin' notice." Red Clanahan shrugged, and gave Sam a half smile. "You get your boss down here with some money."

They hesitated, not liking it. Yet Red could see that they were worried. The blunders they had made were now obviously to them, and there was a good chance the girl did not know where the claim was. "Don't trust him," Taber said. "There's something fishy about this."

Clanahan chuckled. "You boys figure it out, but be fast. I don't have much time. If it wasn't for that, I'd stay and work the claim for a while, myself. As it is, I can't stay that long."

Fallon turned on him, suddenly aware. "You're on the dodge!"

"Maybe."

Through it all, the girl sat quiet, numbed by the shock of her father's death and only vaguely aware these men were bartering her future. Sam looked trapped. He was polishing the same glass for the third time, his face pale and perspiring. But what could he do? What could any one man do? His one possible ally had failed him.

"You hurry," Red told them. "My information is for sale."

At that the girl looked up. "And you said you were my friend!" she said bitterly. "You're as bad as they are!"

Red shrugged. "Worse, in some ways. Sure, I'm your friend. I won't see you hurt or abused, but, lady, fifteen thousand is a lot of money! Your father refused a million for that claim."

"Stay here," Fallon said suddenly. "I'll go."

"No, you stay here," Porter interrupted. "I'll talk to him." He turned and went out of the door.

Clanahan glanced at the bartender. "Have the cook pack me some grub." He tossed a couple of silver dollars on the bar, and as the bartender reached for them, Red spread out two of his fingers, indicating two lunches. Only Sam could see the signal. He picked up the money and went back to the kitchen.

Shorty Taber crossed to the bar. His lips were swollen. Although the bleeding had stopped, his shirt was spotted with blood and his mouth split and bruised. He took a drink and then swore as the liquor bit sharply at the raw cuts. He glared viciously at Clanahan, who studiously ignored him.

Red picked up his glass and walked to the girl's table, never turning his back to the room. He sat down abruptly and said under cover of the movement: "Everything's all right. Main thing is to get you out of here."

Her eyes were cold. "After you've all robbed me? And murdered my father?" Her lips trembled.

Hastily, he said, "He was all right at the end, ma'am. He really was. Passed away, calm and serene."

Silence hung in the room and Red felt his own weariness creeping up on him. It seemed a long time since he had slept. The chase had been long and he had spent endless hours in the saddle. His head nodded, then jerked and his eyes were open. Shorty Taber was staring at him, his eyes gleaming with malice.

Red Clanahan turned to the girl. "I'm dead from sleep. When you hear a horse, wake me. Don't let them come near me. If they start to edge nearer, push me."

Almost at once, his head was over on the table on his arms. Elaine McClary sat very still, her hands on the table before her. Carefully, she kept her mind from any thought of her father. She dared not give way to grief. For the first time she began to be aware of her situation.

She had used almost her last money to get here to meet her father after his letter about the rich strike. She had not worried, because he had told her he had become a rich man. There was no one to whom she could now turn. She was alone. She was stranded. The one thing of value her father had managed to acquire was the claim and she had no idea where it was. Apparently nobody knew but the big redheaded man beside her.

She glared at him, seeing the rusty-red curls around his ears, the great leonine head, the massive shoulders. She had never seen any man with so much sheer physical power and strength. The size of his biceps was enormous to her eyes, and she remembered, with a queer little start, those cold green-gray eyes. Yet, had they been so cold?

A board creaked and her head turned swiftly. Taber was

moving toward them. "Stay back," she said, "or I'll wake him."

Ebb Fallon looked up. "Shorty!" he snapped angrily. "Stay away from there! If anything happens to him, where do we stand?"

Taber turned with angry impatience and went back to the bar. "You weren't the one he hit," he said sullenly.

"Take your time," Fallon said. "This show ain't over yet."

Minutes went slowly by, and the big man beside her slept heavily. Several times he sighed and muttered in his sleep, and what she could see of his face was curiously relaxed and peaceful. His sun-faded shirt smelled of old sweat and dust, and now that she was closer to him, she could sense the utter and appalling weariness of the man. The dust of travel was on him, and he must have come far.

"Look, ma'am." Fallon seated himself at a nearby table and spoke softly, reasonably. "Maybe we've gone at this all wrong. I admit we want that claim, but maybe we can make a dicker, you and us. Maybe we can do business. Now the way things shape up, you'll get nothin' for that claim. You could use money, I bet. You make a deal with us, and you won't lose it. You sell us your interest and we'll give you five hundred dollars."

"That claim is worth a million or more," she answered. "Father refused that for it, he said."

"But you don't know where it is. Think of that. According to law, you have to do assessment work on a claim; so much every year to hold it. Well, if you don't do your work, the claim is lost anyway. How can you do it if you don't know where it is?"

Elaine shifted a little in her chair. All this was true, and it had already fled through her mind. She was so helpless. If there were only— If she could talk to Sam!

"I'll have to think about it," she said. "But what can I do?"

"Sign a bill of sale on that claim, and get the big hombre's gun. You're right beside it. All you have to do is take it. That hombre's an outlaw anyway, ma'am. He'll sell you out."

But they had murdered her father! She couldn't forget that. They had not even troubled to deny it.

Her eyes lifted and she saw Sam give her a faint negative shake of the head. "I'll think about it," she stalled.

If she took his gun, what then? They would kill this man as they had her father. Did that matter to her? Suddenly, she remembered! This big, lonely man beside her, this very tired big man, he had trusted her. He had asked her to help. Then, like a tired boy he had put down his head and slept among a bunch of murderers, trusting to her to warn him.

How soon would the mysterious boss be back? How far had Porter to go? How much time did she have?

Suppose *she* had the gun? Then she would be in a bargaining position herself! They would have to listen to her. But could she force the big man to talk? She knew that would be impossible for her. But not, she thought then, impossible for these other men. She read correctly the bitter hatred in Taber's eyes.

Frightened and alone, she sat in the lonely stage station and watched the hard, strange faces of these men she had never seen until scarcely an hour before. Now these strangers suddenly meant life and death to her.

She looked down at her hands, listening to the bartender put down a glass on the back bar and take up another. Then she heard a faint drumming of horses' hoofs, and suddenly— why she would never know—she sprang to her feet, drawing the big redheaded man's gun as she did so and stepping back quickly.

Almost as suddenly, and catlike, wide-awake where a second before he had been sleeping, the big man was back against the wall. He stared at her, then around the room. "Give me that gun!" he said hoarsely.

"No."

Shorty Taber laughed suddenly, triumphantly. "How do you like it this way, big boy? Now look who's in the saddle!"

"Let me have the gun, ma'am," Fallon said reasonably. "I'll take it now."

She stepped back again. "No. Don't any of you come near me."

Her eyes caught the shocked horror in the bartender's eyes

and doubt came to her. Had she done wrong? Should she have awakened the big man? She heard the horses draw up, heard two men dismount.

Porter entered, then another man—a big, wide-faced man with a tawny, drooping mustache and small, cunning blue eyes. He took in the tableau with a quick glance, then smiled.

His eyes went slowly to Clanahan. "Well, friend, looks like you weren't in such a good spot to bargain. Do you know where that claim is?"

"I sure do," Red snapped. Out of the corner of his mouth, he said to the girl: "Give me that gun, you little fool!"

"If she does, I'll shoot her," Taber said. "I never shot a woman yet, but so help me, I will. I'll shoot her, and then you."

"Shootin' a woman would be about your speed, Shorty." Red's tone was contemptuous. "Ever tackle a full-growed man?"

Shorty's nostrils flared and he swung his gun. "By the—"

"Taber!" The big man with the tawny mustache took a step forward. "You shoot and I'll kill you myself! Don't be a fool!"

There was a short, taut silence. "Now, Red," the big man said quietly, "we can do business. Looks to me like you're on the dodge. I saw your horse out there. A mighty fast horse, and it's come far and hard. I know that horse. It's from the Ruidoso, over in Lincoln County. Unless you knew that outfit well, you'd never have it. And if they let you have it, you're an outlaw."

"So?"

Red Clanahan stood very still, his big feet apart, his eyes wary and alert. Like a photograph, that room with every chair, table, and man was in his mind.

"So we can do business," the tawny-mustached man said. "Tell me where that claim is and I'll give you a thousand dollars."

Red chuckled. "You foolin'?"

"You better." The newcomer was casual. "If you don't, you'll never get out of here alive. Nor will the girl."

They faced Red and the girl, who were seven or eight feet

apart. Fallon was closest to her. Porter and the boys were nearest to Red.

"And you'd lose a million dollars." Red grinned tightly. "You make me smile. How many men are crawlin' over these hills now, lookin' for lost mines? How many will always be doin' it? Mister, you know and I know there's nothin' so lost as a lost mine. Gold once found is mighty shy about bein' found again. If you kill me, you haven't one chance in a million of findin' that gold."

"We could make him talk," Shorty suggested.

Red Clanahan laughed. "You think so? You little coyote, you couldn't make a ten-year-old kid talk. The Apaches worked on me for two days once, and I'm still here."

The boss eyed him. "Who are you, Red? Seems I ought to know you."

"You wouldn't, only by hearsay. I run with the lobos, not with coyotes."

The boss seemed to tighten and his eyes thinned down. "You use that word mighty free. Suppose we work on the girl? I wonder how fast you'd talk then?"

Red Clanahan shrugged. "How would that hurt me? She's a pretty kid, but I never saw her before she walked in here. She's nothing in my life. You torture her and all you'd get would be the trouble of it. You'd be surprised how I could bear up under other people's trouble."

"He ain't as tough as he looks," Taber said. "Let's work on the girl."

"No," the boss said, "I don't—" His voice broke off. Some of Red's relief must have shown in his eyes, for the boss suddenly changed his mind. "Why, yes, Shorty, I think we will. You take—"

The girl's gun seemed to waver, and Fallon grabbed for it. Instantly, the girl fired and Red Clanahan lunged.

He was cat-quick. With a bound he was half across the room. His shoulder struck Porter and knocked him careening into the boss, and both fell against the bar. Red's move had the immediate effect of turning all the fire away from the girl, shifting the center of battle. But his lunge carried him into a table and he fell over a chair. Yet as he hit the chair his big hand emerged from under his shirt with a second gun.

Fallon was struggling with the girl, and Red's first bullet caught Shorty in the midriff. Shorty took a step back, his eyes glazing. Guns exploded and flame stabbed. Red lunged to his feet, moving forward, swaying slightly, spotting his shots carefully, the acrid smell of gunpowder in his nostrils. Then suddenly the room was still.

Only the boss was on his feet and Fallon was stepping away from the girl, his hands lifted. The boss had blood trickling from his left shoulder. Shorty Taber was down, his eyes wide and empty.

Porter was slumped against the bar, a gun beside his hand, the front of his vest dark with blood, which was forming a pool under him.

Red moved swiftly and gathered up his second gun from where it had fallen. "Fifteen thousand, boss," he said quietly, "and I'll tell you what I know. I'll give you the map the girl's father drew for me." Red Clanahan holstered one gun. "Act fast," he said. "I haven't much time."

Sam looked at the boss. "You want me to get it out of the safe, Johnson?"

Johnson's voice was hoarse. He clutched his bloody shoulder. "Yeah." Then he begged, "Let me get my shoulder fixed. I'll bleed to death."

"Afterward." Clanahan watched Sam go to the safe. "Johnson own this place, Sam?"

"Uh-huh."

"Looks like you're through here, then."

"You're tellin' me?" Sam brought two sacks to the counter. "They'd kill me after this."

"Then go saddle two horses. One for yourself and one for the lady.

"Miss," Clanahan gestured to her, "write him out a bill of sale to the claim designated on that map."

"But—" Elaine started a protest, then stifled it at Red's sudden impatience.

"Hurry!" he said angrily. "Do what I tell you!"

Red Clanahan saw Sam come around the building with the saddled horses, and yelled at him: "Tie Fallon," he said. "But let Johnson alone. By the time he gets Fallon loose and that shoulder fixed, we'll be too far off. And if he follows, we'll kill him."

Johnson took the map and the bill of sale, smiling suddenly. "Maybe it was worth a bullet-shot shoulder," he said. "That's a rich claim."

Sam picked up the gold and sacked it into the saddlebags. Then he picked up the lunch he had packed earlier, and two hastily filled canteens.

In the saddle, Red said hoarsely, "Ride fast now! Get out of sight!"

Elaine glanced at him and was shocked by the sudden pallor of his face. "You! You're hurt!" she cried.

His wide face creased in a grin. "Sure! But I didn't dare let those hombres guess it. Keep goin' a few miles. I can stick it."

Beside a stream they paused and bandaged his wound. It was a deep gouge in the side, from which he had bled freely. He watched the girl work over it with quick, sure fingers.

"You'd do to take along, ma'am. You're sure handy."

"I worked for a doctor."

Back in the saddle, they switched off the trail and headed up through the timber.

Sam rode beside them, saying nothing. His round face was solemn.

"By the way," Red said, "I better tell you. I looked at your dad's claim. And he was wrong, ma'am. It wasn't worth a million. It wasn't worth scarcely anything."

Shocked, she looked around at him. "What do you mean?"

"Your dad struck a pocket of free gold. It was richer than all get-out, but your dad was no minin' man. There ain't a thousand dollars left in that pocket."

"Then—"

"Then if you'd kept it, you'd have had nothing but hard work and nothin' more. You got fifteen thousand."

"But I thought—"

Red chuckled. "Ma'am," he said, "I never stole from no woman. I just figured those hombres wanted that claim so bad, they should have it."

———

CRESTING THE DIVIDE, two days later, they saw the smoke of a far-off town. Red Clanahan drew up. "I leave you here. My trail," he pointed north, "goes that way. You take her to town, will you, Sam?"

The older man nodded. "Where are you headed, Red? The Roost?"

Clanahan glanced at him, wry humor in his eyes.

"Yeah. You know me?"

"Sure. I seen you once before, in Tascosa."

Clanahan glanced briefly at the girl. "Take it easy with that money, ma'am." He lifted a hand. "So long."

The flanks of the horse gleamed black a time or two among the trees.

Elaine stared after him, her eyes wide and tear-filled.

"He—he is a good man, isn't he?" she said softly.

"Yeah, a real good man," Sam answered.

"What did you mean? The Roost?"

Sam rode on in silence; then he said, "Robber's Roost, ma'am. It's a hangout for outlaws up in the Utah canyon country. The way he rode will take him there."

"You knew him?"

"By sight, ma'am. His name's Red Clanahan, and they say he's killed nineteen men. It's said that he is a real bad man."

"A good bad man," she said, and looked again at where the horse had vanished in the trees. Once, far on a blue-misted ridge she thought she saw movement, a rider outlined briefly on the horizon. And then it was gone.

She might have been mistaken.

About Louis L'Amour

"I think of myself in the oral tradition—as a troubadour, a village taleteller, the man in the shadows of the camp-fire. That's the way I'd like to be remembered—as a story-teller. A good storyteller."

IT IS DOUBTFUL that any author could be as at home in the world re-created in his novels as Louis Dearborn L'Amour. Not only could he physically fill the boots of the rugged characters he wrote about, but he literally "walked the land my characters walk." His personal experiences as well as his lifelong devotion to historical research combined to give Mr. L'Amour the unique knowledge and understanding of people, events, and the challenge of the American frontier that became the hallmarks of his popularity.

Of French-Irish descent, Mr. L'Amour could trace his own family in North America back to the early 1600s and follow their steady progression westward, "always on the frontier." As a boy growing up in Jamestown, North Dakota, he absorbed all he could about his family's frontier heritage, including the story of his great-grandfather who was scalped by Sioux warriors.

Spurred by an eager curiosity and desire to broaden his horizons, Mr. L'Amour left home at the age of fifteen and enjoyed a wide variety of jobs including seaman, lumberjack, elephant handler, skinner of dead cattle, miner, and an officer in the transportation corps during World War II. During his "yondering" days he also cir-cled the world on a freighter, sailed a dhow on the Red

Sea, was shipwrecked in the West Indies and stranded in the Mojave Desert. He won fifty-one of fifty-nine fights as a professional boxer and worked as a journalist and lecturer. He was a voracious reader and collector of rare books. His personal library contained 17,000 volumes.

Mr. L'Amour "wanted to write almost from the time I could talk." After developing a widespread following for his many frontier and adventure stories written for fiction magazines, Mr. L'Amour published his first full-length novel, *Hondo,* in the United States in 1953. Every one of his more than 100 books is in print; there are more than 300 million copies of his books in print worldwide, making him one of the bestselling authors in modern literary history. His books have been translated into twenty languages, and more than forty-five of his novels and stories have been made into feature films and television movies.

His hardcover bestsellers include *The Lonesome Gods, The Walking Drum* (his twelfth-century historical novel), *Jubal Sackett, Last of the Breed,* and *The Haunted Mesa.* His memoir, *Education of a Wandering Man,* was a leading bestseller in 1989. Audio dramatizations and adaptations of many L'Amour stories are available from Random House Audio publishing.

The recipient of many great honors and awards, in 1983 Mr. L'Amour became the first novelist ever to be awarded the Congressional Gold Medal by the United States Congress in honor of his life's work. In 1984 he was also awarded the Medal of Freedom by President Reagan.

Louis L'Amour died on June 10, 1988. His wife, Kathy, and their two children, Beau and Angelique, carry the L'Amour tradition forward with new books written by the author during his lifetime to be published by Bantam.

FORGET THE LAW OF THE JUNGLE...

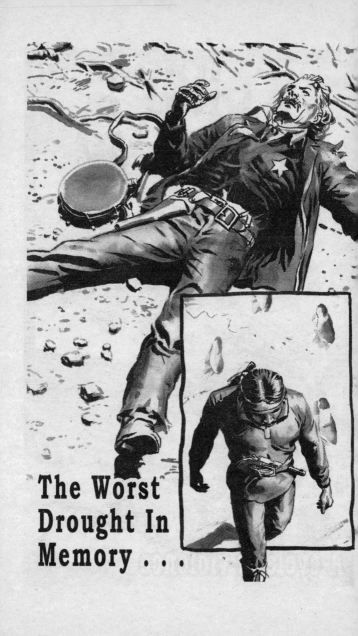

The Worst
Drought In
Memory . . .

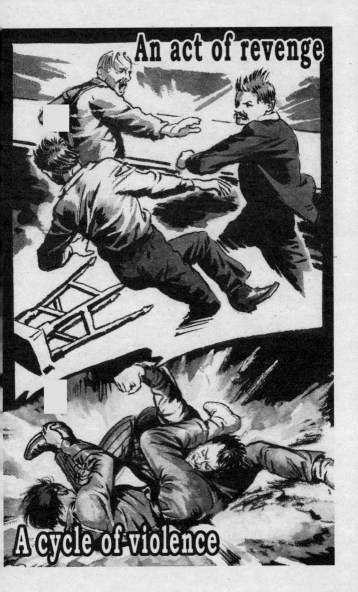

There Are
No Heroes

Only Survivors

LAW OF THE DESERT BORN

Praise for
Law of the Desert Born

"This actually may be the story's ideal form....
The result is **stunning and richly textured.**"
—*Publishers Weekly*

"Yeates' artwork is **incredible.**"
—GraphicNovelReporter.com

"*Law of the Desert Born* is a **fantastic**
example of how relevant the Western can be."
—Suvudu.com

"The **richer plot and characters** from
L'Amour's son Beau and collaborator Kathy
Nolan add appeal and value in addition to
the finely crafted visuals."
—*Library Journal*

"The novel's illustrations add a new
dimension to an already **gripping tale.**"
—*American Cowboy*

"An **amazing level of detail and ambience**
that breathes new life into Louis L'Amour's
already stunning story."
—*Cowboys & Indians*

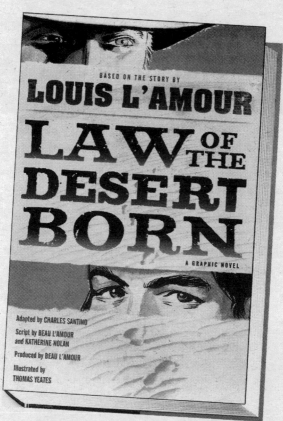